POSSESSED BY A PHANTOM

"It all started long, long ago. Don't ask me when, because I don't know. But it was long before my grandparents were born, or their grandparents before them. It's the story of the phantom horse. Now, I call it a horse, but it isn't really a horse—it's an evil spirit that takes over the body of a horse. It always chooses a horse that belongs to someone who loves it and trusts it. Once it has possessed the horse, the phantom is out for blood. To this day it's roaming the earth looking for its next victim . . ."

THE SADDLE CLUB

PHANTOM HORSE

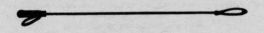

BONNIE BRYANT

A SKYLARK BOOK

NEW YORK · TORONTO · LONDON · SYDNEY · AUCKLAND

RL 5, 009–012

PHANTOM HORSE

A Bantam Skylark Book / October 1996

ISBN 0-553-48372-2

Published simultaneously in the United States and Canada.

Bantam Books are published by Bantam Books, a division of Bantam Doubleday Dell Publishing Group, Inc. Its trademark, consisting of the words "Bantam Books" and the portrayal of a rooster, is Registered in U.S. Patent and Trademark Office and in other countries. Marca Registrada. Bantam Books, 1540 Broadway, New York, New York 10036.

PRINTED IN THE UNITED STATES OF AMERICA

OPM   0 9 8 7 6 5 4 3 2 1

*I would like to express my special thanks
to Catherine Hapka for her help
in the writing of this book.*

"Boo!" shouted Stevie Lake.

Her boyfriend, Phil Marsten, turned around and grinned. "Eeek," he said calmly.

Stevie stuck out her tongue and plunked down next to him. He was sitting on a hay bale in the indoor ring at Pine Hollow Stables, where Stevie took riding lessons. It was Halloween, and the owner of Pine Hollow was throwing a party for his young riders. Max Regnery was a strict stable owner and an even stricter riding instructor, but he also believed in having a good time, and that was what this party was all about. Strings of festive red-orange lights were strung around the ceiling, cutouts of bats and black cats decorated the walls, and a large, well-stocked refreshment table stood

1

at one end of the ring. Best of all, the students were allowed to invite friends, so Stevie had invited Phil, who lived in another town and rode at a different stable.

"Where did Carole and Lisa go?" Stevie asked as she handed Phil the paper cup of punch she had brought him. Carole Hanson and Lisa Atwood, who also rode at Pine Hollow, were Stevie's two best friends.

Phil shrugged. "I don't know," he said. He took Stevie's hand and gazed into her eyes. "Who cares? Wouldn't you rather be alone with me anyway?"

Stevie looked back at him suspiciously. "All right, what do you three have planned? Ghosts and goblins? Shrieks in the night? Or just a good old-fashioned—" She whirled around just in time to catch Carole and Lisa sneaking up behind her.

"Boo!" all three girls yelled at once.

Carole and Lisa burst out laughing. "We should know better than to try to beat her at her own game," Lisa said.

"It was worth a try," Carole replied, sitting down cross-legged on the floor at Stevie's feet. "It wouldn't be Halloween without a few tricks to go with the treats." She took a big bite out of the pumpkin-shaped cookie she was holding.

"True," Stevie said. "Although it will be a cold day in July before you guys can out-trick me."

Carole and Lisa grinned. Stevie's mischievous nature was one of the things her friends loved best about her. The three girls were such good friends that they had started The Saddle Club. The group had only two rules: Members had to be horse-crazy, and they had to be willing to help one another whenever necessary. Stevie, Carole, and Lisa were the three main members of The Saddle Club, but there were also several out-of-town members, including Phil and his best friend, A.J.

Phil nudged Stevie with his elbow. "Hey, who's that guy?" he asked, staring at someone across the room.

Stevie followed Phil's gaze to a tall, thin young man dressed in black jeans and a leather motorcycle jacket. His brown hair was cropped almost as short as the stubble that dotted his jaw, and the overhead lights caught a flash of silver at his ear.

"That's Troy," Stevie said.

At Phil's confused look, Lisa explained. "His name's Troy Lasker. He's a college student who's taking the semester off to earn some money. Max just took him on as a temporary groom."

"That guy's a groom?" Phil asked in surprise.

"He doesn't exactly look like your typical groom, does he?" said Stevie. "If you get a chance, check out his ear. He's got three earrings in it, and one of them is shaped like a skull and crossbones."

"He may not look like a groom, but he is one," Carole reminded them. "Max wouldn't have hired him if he wasn't qualified. And he really seems to know what he's doing around the horses." That was such a Carole-like comment

3

that her friends couldn't help but smile. Of the three horse-crazy members of The Saddle Club, Carole was the horse-craziest. She already knew she wanted to spend her life working with horses, although she hadn't decided yet what her exact career would be. Trainer, rider, stable manager, veterinarian—they all sounded exciting to her. Luckily she still had plenty of time to make up her mind.

As Troy strolled across the ring, a raggedy-looking brown-and-white mutt trotted along behind him. Stevie pointed the dog out to Phil. "That's Princess," she said. "She worships Troy. She follows him everywhere he goes."

"When she's not sleeping, that is," Lisa said. "I almost tripped over her the other day in the tack room. She'd decided to take a nap right inside the door."

"Hey, don't look now," Carole said, "but we're not the only ones paying attention to Troy. Veronica must have decided she likes older men this week."

The others looked where Carole was pointing and saw Veronica diAngelo hurrying toward Troy. Veronica was their least favorite person at Pine Hollow. She was a good rider and she owned a gorgeous horse named Danny, but those were her only positive qualities as far as The Saddle Club could see. Veronica was a snobby, spoiled rich girl who always wore expensive clothes. Her family lived in a huge house with tennis courts and a swimming pool, and she loved to brag about all the servants they had. She often seemed to think that Max's head stable hand, Red

4

O'Malley, was on her personal payroll, and she usually made him take care of Danny for her.

"Disgusting," Stevie declared, watching as Veronica walked over to Troy, smiling and batting her eyelashes. "Now that all the boys at Pine Hollow—not to mention all the boys at school—have realized what a rat she is, she has to go searching for some fresh blood."

"Never mind," Lisa said. "It doesn't look like Troy is interested." As The Saddle Club watched, Troy gave Veronica a polite little smile, then turned and walked away without a backward glance. Princess slunk after him. Veronica watched Troy go with a pout on her face, then whirled and stomped off in the other direction.

Carole giggled. "It looks like Troy smelled a rat."

"I guess that makes him pretty normal after all," Phil said. "Even if he does look a little unusual."

"Speaking of looks, I just realized who Troy reminds me of," Lisa said. "It's this character in the book I'm reading."

"You mean that mystery novel you've been carrying around for the past three days?" Stevie asked.

Lisa nodded. "*Murder at Teatime* by Ernestine Collier. It's set in England, and it's really good. There's a character in it who looks just like Troy—I mean, that's how he's described. And he's really quiet and keeps to himself, just like Troy. The heroine, Camille, thinks he may be the murderer."

"Is he?" Stevie asked.

Lisa shrugged. "I don't know yet. I'm only a little over

halfway through. I haven't had much time to read this week, but I'm hoping to finish it later tonight. I can't wait—I stopped at a really exciting part."

"Well, Troy may dress oddly, but I think it's pretty safe to say he's probably not a murderer," Carole said. She leaned back against the hay bale and looked around at the people enjoying themselves. "This is a great party," she added.

"If you think this is a great party, just wait until you see what my parents have planned for next week," Phil said with a smile. "You're all still coming, aren't you?"

"Of course we are. We can't wait," Stevie answered for all of them. "None of us has ever been to a bar mitzvah before." Phil was Jewish. He had recently turned thirteen, and that meant it was time for the religious ceremony in which he would officially become an adult member of his synagogue and of the Jewish community.

"What kind of party will it be?" Carole asked curiously.

"Well, it won't be exactly like this one, although there will be lots to eat and drink and plenty of people having fun," Phil said. "There will be more older people—all my relatives, and my parents' friends, and people from my synagogue."

Lisa knew that a synagogue was where Jewish prayer services were held, but that was all she knew. "What about the service?" she asked, shifting to a more comfortable position on the sawdust-covered floor. "That comes first, right?"

"Right," said Phil. "It's actually just the usual Saturday-

6

morning service, but I'll get to read from the Torah and then chant the haftarah. Then I give a speech about what I've read—sort of like a preacher's sermon." The girls knew that although Phil's mother was Jewish, his father was Christian. That meant that even though Phil considered himself Jewish, he knew a lot about his father's religion, too.

Carole looked confused. "I understand the sermon part, but what's a hava—haffto—"

"Haftarah," Phil corrected with a smile. "It's a passage from the words of the Prophets in the Torah."

"The Torah is the Jewish Bible, right?" Lisa asked.

Phil took a sip of his punch and nodded. "It's what Christians call the Pentateuch. That's the first five books of the Old Testament."

"You mean you'll read Bible passages?" Stevie asked. "I mean, Torah passages?"

"Right," Phil said. "The Torah service is kind of complicated if you're not used to it, but I think it's pretty interesting, too. You see, it's an old tradition that seven different people have to read from the Torah in Hebrew for the service to be complete. A lot of synagogues these days have a professional reader do all the Torah reading: Even though members of the congregation are still called, the reader reads the verses for everyone. But the rabbi at my synagogue likes to do it the traditional way on days when someone is becoming a bar mitzvah. After the seven people have read, an eighth person goes up who's called the *maftir*. That means

7

'the one who will conclude.' At my bar mitzvah, I'll be the *maftir*."

Carole picked up a stray piece of straw and twirled it between her fingers. "Wow," she said. "That does sound kind of complicated. Is the reading hard?"

"Well, it's not exactly easy, but I've been getting lots of practice in Hebrew school," Phil said. The girls knew that Phil attended Jewish education classes several times a week after school and on weekends. "One of the hardest things to get used to is that the Torah is written without any vowels. And of course it's in Hebrew, and you have to sing it in the traditional chants and everything. I'm sure I'll be nervous when the day arrives, but right now I'm just excited. My parents are excited, too."

"Even your dad?" Lisa asked. Then she blushed. "Sorry, that doesn't sound very nice. But I mean, he isn't Jewish, so . . ."

"It's a fair question," Phil said, smiling at her to show he wasn't offended. "And the answer is that Dad is almost as excited as I am. When he and Mom got married they decided they would raise their kids to be Jewish—that was really important to Mom and her family. And since becoming bar mitzvahed—or bat mitzvahed for my sisters—is so important to the rest of the family, that means it's important to my dad, too. In fact, he picked out my tallith, with a little help from Grandfather Friedman. He was so excited about it

8

he couldn't even wait until my bar mitzvah to give it to me."

"That's great," Lisa asked. "But I have one question. What's a tallith?"

Phil laughed. "Sorry," he said. "I've been so wrapped up in all this stuff lately that I keep forgetting that my non-Jewish friends don't know all these words. The tallith is a prayer shawl worn by all Jewish men. A lot of kids get one from their parents as a bar mitzvah gift. Come on, I brought mine in to show it to you guys." He got up.

"I've already seen it," Stevie told her friends. "The tallith is really beautiful."

Lisa and Carole stood up and followed Phil and Stevie out of the indoor ring and down the hall toward the student locker room. One wall of the room was lined with cubbies where the young riders could store extra clothes and boots, schoolbooks, and the like.

As they entered the room they saw two students sitting close together on the long bench in front of the cubbies. The couple jumped up quickly when they heard the group enter, and The Saddle Club recognized Joe Novick and his new girlfriend, a quiet girl named Shannon Brice. Most of the girls at Pine Hollow agreed he was the best-looking boy in their riding class. Shannon didn't ride at Pine Hollow, but she went to Stevie's school, Fenton Hall. Stevie didn't know Shannon well, but she knew that the Brices were extremely wealthy and lived in a house even bigger than Veronica's.

"Oh, s-sorry," Joe stammered. "Er, I mean, we didn't know anyone would be coming in here." Shannon didn't say anything, but her face was turning red and she looked embarrassed. She stared down at her expensive-looking skirt and pretended to brush lint from it.

"No, we're sorry," Phil said. "We're the ones who didn't know anyone would be in here. But we'll only be a minute."

"That's okay," Shannon said softly. She turned to Joe. "I'm a little thirsty. Can we get some punch?"

"Sure thing," Joe said. He took her hand and led her toward the door. "Catch you guys later," he said, glancing back at The Saddle Club. Shannon didn't look around.

"Bye," Carole and Stevie said in one voice, and Lisa gave a little wave. As soon as Joe and Shannon had left the room, the three girls burst into giggles.

"Oops," Carole said. "I guess we ruined their plans to be alone."

"No kidding," said Phil with a grin. He headed for Stevie's cubby, but the three girls continued to stand by the door and talk.

Lisa nodded. "I feel bad. She looked awfully embarrassed."

"Don't worry about it," Stevie said. "She always looks that way at school, too. She's really shy."

"I wonder why," Carole said. "She's incredibly rich,

10

right?" Carole and Lisa went to the public school across town from Fenton Hall, so they knew even less about Shannon than Stevie did.

"That's for sure," Stevie said. "Her family makes the diAngelos look like paupers. But at least Shannon doesn't brag about her money all the time like Veronica does. I'm just surprised she and Joe are a couple. He's so nice and friendly, and she's so quiet and boring."

"Just because she's quiet doesn't mean she's boring," Lisa pointed out.

"True," Carole agreed with a smile. "She could have some wild, exciting secret life we don't know about."

"I hope so, for her sake," Stevie said with a shrug. "But somehow I doubt it. Going out with Joe is probably the most exciting thing she's done in her whole life."

Meanwhile Phil had pulled his backpack out of Stevie's cubby and set it on the bench. He called the girls over, and they came and watched as he carefully took out a black velvet bag with colorful embroidery along the edges.

"This is the bag I keep the tallith in when I'm not using it," he explained. He opened the top and pulled out a bundle of fabric. When he unfolded it the girls saw that it was a large square of white silk with blue stripes woven into it. Tassels hung from each of the four corners, and embroidery decorated the edges.

"It really is beautiful," Lisa said, reaching out to touch the soft fabric. Carole nodded in agreement.

11

Then Phil reached into his backpack again and took out a small black skullcap. When he held it up the girls could see that it was embroidered as well. In the center of the cap was a picture of a lion standing on its hind legs. Phil's name was embroidered along the edge in golden thread. "This was another gift," he explained. "My aunt and uncle sent it from Israel. They live there, but they're flying over for my bar mitzvah."

"That's a yarmulke, right?" Lisa asked.

"Right," Phil said. "It's also called a *kippah*. That's the Hebrew word; *yarmulke* is the Yiddish word."

"So what other presents did you get?" Stevie asked, peering into Phil's backpack.

"Mostly money," Phil said matter-of-factly. "All my relatives and my parents' friends have been sending checks. I'll probably get a lot more on the day of the bar mitzvah. My sisters will probably chip in together to get me something."

"Wow," Stevie said. "It sounds like you'll be rich when it's all over."

"Don't start hitting me up for loans yet, Stevie," Phil teased. "Most of the money I get will go straight into my college fund." He grinned. "Although I may have just enough left to take my three favorite Saddle Club members out for ice cream—my treat."

"It's a deal," Stevie said quickly, and her friends laughed.

Phil showed them how he put on the prayer shawl and let them each examine his yarmulke.

12

"Your bar mitzvah sounds like it will be great, Phil," Lisa said, watching Phil put the tallith away in its bag and tuck the yarmulke on top of it. "I'm glad you invited us."

"Me too," Stevie said. But as the four friends got up and headed back toward the party, she couldn't help feeling a little jealous. The bar mitzvah sounded to her like a bigger and better version of a birthday party. And afterward Phil was going to be practically as rich as Shannon Brice. Stevie usually got some birthday money from her relatives, but her parents always made her put most of it in the bank. The amount they let her spend was barely enough to cover a few weeks' worth of bills at TD's, The Saddle Club's favorite ice cream parlor. Even if Phil had to put most of his money away for college, too, it didn't seem fair that because he was Jewish he got a huge celebration just for turning thirteen.

At that moment Phil turned to her with a smile, then reached over and took her hand in his. Stevie smiled back, feeling a little guilty about her thoughts. Fair or not, she was glad Phil liked her enough to invite her and her friends to share his special day. She squeezed his hand and felt him squeeze back. She wouldn't miss this bar mitzvah for the world.

13

W<small>HEN</small> T<small>HE</small> S<small>ADDLE</small> C<small>LUB</small> and Phil returned to the party, they saw a group of people gathered around Max and Red O'Malley.

"I wonder what's going on?" Stevie said. Without waiting for a response from her friends, she hurried forward to find out.

Max looked up and saw her. "Ah, Stevie, you're just in time. Red and I were just saying that it wouldn't be Halloween without some good ghost stories. What do you say?"

"I say count me in," Stevie said as her friends joined the group. "Can I start? I have a good one."

Max nodded, and Stevie sat down and waited for the

partygoers to gather around her on the floor. When everyone was comfortable, Max lowered the overhead lights so that the strings of orange-reddish bulbs were the only illumination in the room.

When a silence fell over the group, Stevie began.

"It was a dark and stormy night," she intoned in a low, serious voice. "A night much like this one."

"It's not stormy tonight," a rider named Betsy Cavanaugh pointed out.

Stevie glared at her. "Quiet," she commanded. "The spirits don't like it when you interrupt me."

"Sorry," Betsy said with a giggle.

Stevie cleared her throat and continued. "As I was saying, it was a dark and stormy night—a night much like this one, at a stable much like this one. A rider was there taking care of her horse, and she was all alone in the night. Not another human was in the place. She had just finished cleaning the horse's water bucket when she suddenly heard it." Stevie paused for effect. "*Thump! Thump! Thump!* The noise was coming from the hayloft overhead."

"Rats?" Phil guessed with a grin.

"*Big* rats," Meg Durham added.

Stevie frowned at them but ignored their comments. "It sounded like something big, something . . . inhuman. She was scared, and she thought about running away. But she knew she couldn't leave the horses in danger. She had to

15

find out what it was. So she walked slowly toward the ladder leading up to the loft. She walked step . . . by step . . . by step . . . by step . . ."

Stevie glanced around at her audience to see if her story was having the intended effect. Everyone looked attentive, if not particularly scared.

"At last she reached the ladder," Stevie went on. "And now she knew she couldn't turn back. She had to climb it. So she did . . . step . . . by step . . . by step . . . by step . . . by step . . ."

"We get the picture, Stevie," Adam Levine called from the back of the group. "Step it up, okay?"

"All right, all right," Stevie said. "The girl was quivering with fear by the time she reached the top of the ladder. It was dark in the hayloft, so she had to wait until her eyes adjusted before she could see. And when she could, she saw a huge . . . black . . . shadowy shape in the corner of the loft. It wasn't moving. Quietly and slowly, she climbed up into the loft and started moving *verrry* slowly toward the shape. Step—"

"By step, by step, by step," chanted the audience.

Stevie couldn't help grinning. "That's right," she said. "By this time she was shaking and quivering and quaking. She tiptoed over to the big dark shape, and when she was only a couple of feet away she realized what it was. It was nothing more than a big stack of hay bales piled against the

16

wall. She heaved a sigh of relief and began to relax. But then, suddenly, a swarm of vampire bats flew out from behind the hay and attacked her. And from that day on she was never heard from again."

Phil snorted. "Is that it? I'm quaking in my boots," he said sarcastically. "I mean, I'm shaking and quivering and quaking."

"Yeah," Joe said. "I may never be able to go up in the loft again."

"So Stevie, if it was just bats up there, what were the thumps?" asked Betsy.

Carole grinned as she watched Stevie defend her story against its critics. Then she glanced around and noticed that a few people weren't paying much attention to the storytelling. One was Veronica, who had managed to slide over so that she was sitting next to Troy. She was leaning close to him, glancing at him adoringly as she whispered into his ear. He wasn't looking back; in fact, he was frowning and looking as though he would rather be anyplace else. Carole's grin widened. Then it faded as she noticed Shannon Brice. She was sitting beside Joe, but she didn't seem to be having much fun. Her face was pale, and she kept glancing around anxiously at the dark corners of the ring. If Carole hadn't known better, she would have sworn that Stevie's silly story had actually scared Shannon.

Finally Stevie held up her hands against her questioners.

17

"Fine," she said. "I guess you didn't like that one. I was hoping I wouldn't have to resort to this, but I'm going to have to tell you a *really* scary story."

"It's about time," Adam called out.

"You asked for it. But don't say I didn't warn you," Stevie said. "Okay, this one also takes place at a stable very much like this one. A new rider came to the owner of the stable and asked if she could board her horse there. The owner told her that the stable was almost full. In fact, there was only one empty stall left, and he didn't think she'd want that one. The girl asked why, and the owner told her the stall was haunted. The girl said that was silly—she didn't believe in ghosts. She wanted the stall. At first the stable owner argued, but finally he gave in and agreed to let her horse move in. After all, he knew she would only find out what many others had found out before her.

"The next morning the girl brought her horse in. She put fresh straw down and filled the water bucket. Then she went off to school, planning to come back that afternoon to take a ride."

"Boy, this is a scary one, all right," Joe said with a fake yawn.

"Quiet," Stevie commanded. "After school the girl came back, just the way she'd planned. Despite what she'd told the stable owner, she was a little worried. She didn't believe a stall could be haunted, but you never know. She was re-

18

lieved when she arrived and saw that her horse looked just fine. The only problem was that his stall was dirty—much dirtier than it usually was after just one day. Still, she figured it was because he was getting used to his new home or something. She cross-tied him and mucked out the stall, then tacked him up and went for a ride.

"It was a very pleasant ride, but when the girl got back, an unpleasant surprise was waiting for her. The stall, which she had just cleaned, was dirty again! And now the girl realized what the stable owner had been warning her about. It was every rider's worst nightmare come true—a stall that's always dirty, no matter how often it's mucked out! She jumped on her horse and rode screaming from the stable, and neither one of them was ever heard from again."

By the time Stevie finished, most of her listeners were roaring with laughter. Mucking out stalls was everyone's least favorite job around the stable. To a rider who'd already spent hours cleaning tack, grooming horses, and other work, it often seemed as if *all* the stalls at Pine Hollow were haunted, so everyone could appreciate Stevie's story. She grinned proudly.

"See? I knew that one would scare you," she said.

Max shook his head, smiling. "No argument there," he said. "In fact, I think it might be time for you to step down as storyteller and let someone else have a chance. We wouldn't want anyone to die of fright."

"Okay," Stevie said agreeably. "I guess my story about the saddle soap that makes tack dirtier instead of cleaner will have to wait until next Halloween."

"Right," Max said. "Now, does anyone else have any scary stories for us?" He glanced around, but nobody seemed eager to volunteer. "Red? How about you?"

The head groom shrugged. "Sorry, Max. I can't think of a single story that would scare this crowd."

Lisa glanced around, wondering where Mrs. Reg had gone. "Mrs. Reg" was what all the riders at Pine Hollow called Max's mother, who was also the stable manager. She was renowned for her stories, although they weren't usually scary and often took a while to figure out. But she was nowhere in sight.

Finally, after another moment of silence, Troy stood up. "I'll take a turn," he said in his low, even voice.

The students glanced at each other, surprised, as Troy walked to the center of the group. The new groom usually didn't have much to say to anyone. They couldn't believe he was volunteering to tell ghost stories.

Stevie took her place next to her friends. "Who would have guessed Troy is a storyteller?" she commented quietly.

"He probably just volunteered to keep you from telling any more of your crazy stories," Phil teased.

Before Stevie could retort, Troy began his first tale. It was about a stable in the mountains of West Virginia that was haunted by the ghost of a horse thief. It might have been the story itself, or Troy's low, flowing voice, or some combination of the two, but for whatever reason, the story was spooky. Stevie found herself huddling closer to Phil, and once or twice she caught Lisa scooting closer to Carole.

When Troy finished, there was a moment of silence. Then the students broke out into excited chatter. Troy waited for a minute, then launched into another story.

For the next half hour he kept them enthralled with tales of spooky forests, dark haylofts, treacherous trails, and an evil riding instructor. Finally he stood up and announced that he was finished. The students protested, begging for another story.

At last Troy relented. "All right," he said. "Just one more. But I'd better warn you, this is the scariest one I know. And that's because every word of it is true.

"It all started long, long ago. Don't ask me when, because I don't know. But it was long before my grandparents were born, or their grandparents before them. It's the story of the phantom horse. Now, I call it a horse, but it isn't really a horse—it's an evil spirit that takes over the body of a horse. It always chooses a horse that belongs to someone who loves it and trusts it. Once it has possessed the horse, the phantom is out for blood. To this day it's roaming the earth, looking for its next victim.

"I first heard about the phantom horse years ago when I was a few years younger than most of you are now, when it made an appearance at a barn I know down along the coast of North Carolina—not so far from where we are here in Virginia, come to think of it. It seems there was a young man there by the name of Dixon, Colin Dixon. This fellow was a born rider, had loved horses all his life, and was never happier than when he was with them. But his family was poor, so he had to be content to ride the stable horses when he could, scraping together what money he could to pay for the rides and working off the rest with stable chores. But young Colin swore that one day he'd get together enough money to buy his own horse if it was the last thing he did.

"Time passed, and Colin managed to save a little here and there from odd jobs and the like. By the time he was thirteen or so he had almost enough in his bank account to buy a horse—if he was content with an old bag of bones past its prime, that is. He decided he wouldn't settle for that and continued to save every penny he could. Then one autumn a hurricane hit the town where Colin and his family lived and just about swept the whole town out to sea. The Dixons considered themselves fortunate to have survived the storm without the loss of any family members, as many of their friends and neighbors hadn't been so lucky. But the fact remained that everything else they had was gone—house, car, Papa Dixon's tourist boat, everything. Most of it was covered by insurance, but not that boat, which was called the *Moonshine*. It was a clear loss, and that meant Colin's papa had no way to earn a living. Now Colin, being the upstanding boy that he was, knew what he had to do. He

22

went right on down to the bank—*that* was still standing, anyway—and withdrew all the money from his account. With all that Colin had saved, along with what his brothers and sisters could contribute, there was enough to buy their papa a new boat, which he named the *Moonshine II*.

"The rest of the Dixons were happy enough with that, but poor Colin was heartbroken. It seemed impossible that his dream of owning a fine horse would ever come true, and he resigned himself to riding borrowed nags for a long time to come. He figured it would take him years to save up enough money again. But one day less than a year later, the owner of the stable, whose name was Janssen, came to Colin and told him of a horse he'd heard of for sale in the next county. The horse's owner had to get rid of him quick and was willing to sell him to the first fellow to show up with some cash. Mr. Janssen didn't know why the horse was so cheap, but every vet who saw him swore he was in perfect condition, and he looked awfully fine, too. If Janssen hadn't been full up with his own horses at the time, he would surely have snatched the creature up himself; but as it was he figured nobody deserved that kind of bargain more than the hardworking Colin.

"Before Colin knew it, and with Mr. Janssen's help, the deal was done. The second he laid eyes on his new horse—a tall, good-looking bay with a sickle moon on his brow—Colin knew he'd found his perfect horse at last.

"For the first time in his life he had everything he wanted.

23

He named the horse Moonshine after his papa's new boat, and he spent every moment he could with him, training, grooming, and of course riding. And it appeared that the vets were right—there wasn't a thing wrong with Moonshine. As far as Colin and everyone who knew him were concerned, he had the perfect horse."

Troy's voice grew even quieter and slower, forcing his listeners to lean forward to hear. "I guess young Colin was lucky in that he was allowed a few years of happiness before the phantom made its appearance. One cold autumn night Colin was working late at the stable, cleaning up some stalls to help pay Mr. Janssen back for Moonshine's keep—the same way a lot of you do here at Pine Hollow. After he'd finished he ambled on back to Moonshine's stall to say good night. At least that's what others at the stable assumed later, because they knew it was the boy's habit. Nobody knows for sure, of course. What I'm telling you is the best guess at what happened next.

"When Colin got to the stall, it was empty. He must have panicked, thinking some horse thief had come along and taken his beloved Moonshine. But as he turned around to go for help, he saw his horse standing in the stable aisle behind him. For just a second poor Colin may have felt only relief, but once that second passed he surely realized something was wrong, terribly wrong. Colin had never been truly afraid of any horse in his life, but now he must have felt real fear as he looked at the horse he had loved and thought he knew.

24

Moonshine was still the tall, handsome horse he'd always been, but now there was something odd about him, something not quite right about the eyes and face. Moonshine started to snort and paw at the floor. And as he did, his eyes, which had always been beautiful and liquid brown, began to glow. Soon they were as red as the flames of hell, and Moonshine's red gaze was directed straight at young Colin. The creature bared its teeth like a mad dog, and its mane and tail danced in the air, although there wasn't a breath of wind in the stable that night. I'd wager that at this point the terrified Colin was frozen to the spot, not knowing what to do. Moonshine was blocking his exit from the building, and there was nobody around to help him. Finally Colin must have decided the only thing he could do was run into the empty stall that had been Moonshine's, barricade himself in, and try to climb out the tiny window. But he'd barely gotten himself turned around before the beast came at him. He heard the terrible shriek, like no real horse has ever made in this world, and he looked over his shoulder in time to see the flashing hooves coming at him. He threw up his arms to try to protect his face, but it was too late. The phantom horse had laid claim to yet another victim."

Troy paused for a moment, then went on. "The next day, Mr. Janssen was the one to find what was left of young Colin. When the stable owner told the story to some of the older folks around town, he learned something chilling. Thirteen years before, the same thing had happened in a stable in the Blue Ridge Mountains. And thirteen years before that, in one down toward New Orleans. One old-timer who'd lived out West in his younger days remembered hearing of the phantom horse showing up on a dude ranch thirteen years before *that*. Among them they managed to piece together what Colin's last moments must have been like as the phantom horse made its horrible appearance. Nobody knows where it comes from, or where it goes between bodies, but everybody who knows about it knows one thing: It always comes back, every thirteen years, to do its worst to unsuspecting horse people." Troy paused again. "Come to think of it, seems to me it's about time for it to come around again. So next time a horse you *think* you know starts acting a little odd, it could be the weather or a change in its feed. But then again, it could be possessed by a phantom that's biding its time . . . waiting to spill a river of blood."

Stevie was the first to speak. "Wow. Great story, Troy," she said admiringly. She grinned. "You almost had me convinced that it was true."

"Who says it isn't?" Troy said without smiling back. He stood up. "I've got to get going. Thanks for your attention, y'all. I'll be seeing you." And then he was gone.

Stevie turned to her friends. "Pretty awesome story, huh? Who would think someone could make a scary story out of getting your own horse?"

Lisa rolled her eyes. "I don't know," she said. "I think it was mostly the way he told it that made it scary. Did you notice how he lingered over the words, making you think something spooky was happening even when it wasn't? You know, like playing up the big storm, and the thing about the phantom coming back every thirteen years . . ."

"Tell me about it," Phil said with a chuckle. "I'm pretty sensitive to the number thirteen right now, but even my rabbi doesn't mention it as often as Troy did in that story. It *was* a good story, though."

Carole wrapped her arms tightly around herself as she listened to her friends talking about Troy's spooky tale. For some reason she didn't feel like joining in. The story had left her with a strange feeling, and she wasn't quite sure what it was. She glanced around at the dark corners of the room, seeming to catch things moving just beyond the range of her eyes. Then she shook her head and smiled at herself. The spooky Halloween atmosphere must be going to her head. After all, Lisa was right. The story they had heard was just a simple, rather silly tale told by an expert storyteller. There was no such thing as a phantom horse.

Carole stood up and stretched, vowing to forget all about phantom horses with glowing red eyes and unearthly screams. "I don't know about all of you," she said, "but these ghost stories have made me awfully hungry. Anyone for more of those yummy pumpkin cookies?"

NOT LONG AFTER the storytelling had ended, Carole left her friends eating the last of the cookies and headed to check on her horse, Starlight. She had bedded him down earlier in the evening, but she wanted to say good night before she left the stable. As soon as she turned the corner into the aisle leading to his stall, the tall, handsome bay stuck his head out over the half door and nickered a greeting.

"Hey there, boy," she said softly. She hurried up to the stall, and Starlight lowered his head to snuffle her hair. She stroked his forelock, pushing it aside so that the lopsided white star on his forehead was visible. The sounds of music and laughter were faintly audible, drifting down the quiet corridor from the indoor ring. "Have you been listening to the party? Don't feel left out. I brought you a special Halloween treat." She reached into her pocket and pulled out a bag containing a handful of carrot pieces. Holding them on her open palm, she allowed Starlight to lift each one with his soft lips.

Carole was concentrating so hard on her horse that she didn't hear the footsteps approaching behind her. When a voice at her shoulder spoke her name, she let out a startled yelp and jumped. At the same time her hand involuntarily swung up, smacking Starlight under the chin. The gelding threw up his head and snorted in surprise.

Carole whirled around and saw Troy standing behind her. "Oh!" she exclaimed. "You scared me!"

"Sorry about that," Troy said.

But Carole had already turned back to Starlight, who was backing away into the corner of his stall. The whites of his eyes were showing, and he was tossing his head. The orange party lights were reflected in his eyes, giving him an eerie look. She talked soothingly to him, trying to coax him forward again.

"Better to let him alone for a few minutes," Troy advised, stepping forward to peer into the stall. "Looks like you spooked him, whacking him in the jaw like that."

Carole bit her lip to keep from responding angrily. Troy made it sound as if Carole had hit Starlight intentionally when it was Troy's fault for sneaking up on her. "Don't worry," she said coldly. "I know my horse. He'll be okay."

"Whatever you say," Troy said. He glanced at the nameplate on the stall. "Starlight, hmm? He's a beauty."

Immediately Carole relaxed. If there was one thing she couldn't resist, it was praise of her horse. "I know," she said. "I'm lucky to have him. He's really terrific."

Troy glanced at her with a crooked smile. "You sound pretty sure about that," he said. "Weren't you listening to my story earlier? You never can tell about things, you know. For all you know, sweet Starlight could have a demon inside him."

Carole was pretty sure Troy was making a joke, but she didn't think it was funny. Remembering the spooky story about the phantom horse made her shiver.

"If you think about it," Troy continued thoughtfully, still smiling slightly, "it's an odd coincidence about his name. Starlight . . . Moonshine . . . they're pretty similar. And your horse is a bay with an unusual white patch on his fore-

30

head. Moonshine was a bay with a white sickle on his forehead. It kind of makes you wonder." He gestured at the gelding, who was standing in the corner of the stall eyeing them warily.

"I think I might have an easier time calming him down if I were alone," she said pointedly. She knew she wasn't being very polite, but she didn't care. She'd had enough of Troy and his scary tales for one evening.

Troy took the hint. "All right, I'm going home. It looks like the party's breaking up, anyway. See you around." He strode off down the aisle toward the tack room, whistling as he went.

By the time Lisa, Stevie, and Phil found Carole a short while later, Starlight's frightened mood had passed. He had allowed Carole to coax him to the front of the stall again, and he was crunching on the last of the carrot pieces.

"Hi, Carole," Lisa said. "Are you almost ready to go?"

"I'm ready," Carole said. After giving Starlight one last pat, she headed down the aisle with her friends. She had just started to tell them about her encounter with Troy when they heard a shriek from the direction of the student locker room.

"That sounded like Betsy," Lisa said. "Let's go see what happened."

When The Saddle Club reached the locker room, they saw Betsy Cavanaugh sitting on the floor in front of her cubby, her things spread out all around her.

"It's gone!" she was exclaiming, looking angry. "I can't believe it. Someone stole it!"

"What happened? What's gone?" Stevie asked, pushing her way to the front of the small crowd that had gathered around Betsy.

"My gold bangle bracelet," Betsy said. "It was in here before the party. I set it right on top of my jacket so it wouldn't fall down with the other stuff and get lost. But now it's gone."

"Are you sure it's not in your cubby somewhere?" Adam Levine asked.

"I'm sure," Betsy replied. "Somebody get Max."

A few minutes later Max was there, looking concerned. "Did you check your cubby carefully, Betsy?" he asked. "And behind it, too? Sometimes things fall back there."

"I checked," Betsy said impatiently. "It's gone."

"Well, maybe somebody who already left picked it up accidentally," Max said, rubbing his chin thoughtfully. "I'll make an announcement at the next lesson if it hasn't turned up by then. I'm not sure what else to do. I'm sorry, Betsy."

Betsy frowned but said nothing as she began putting things back into her cubby.

"In the meantime, it looks like the party is over," Max said to the group. "Why don't you all keep an eye out for Betsy's bracelet while you pack up?"

Lisa and Carole sat down together on the bench in front of their cubbies, leaving Stevie and Phil talking to Betsy, who

32

still looked annoyed. "Do you think someone really stole Betsy's bracelet?" Carole asked as she pulled on her jacket.

"I doubt it," Lisa said, leaning forward and reaching into her cubby. "This is Pine Hollow. Who here would steal . . . ?" Her voice trailed off.

Carole glanced at her friend. "What's the matter?"

"My book," Lisa said with a frown. "I left it sitting on top of my purse, but it's not there anymore."

Carole's eyes widened. "Really? Are you sure that's where you left it?"

"Positive," Lisa said. "I put it where I couldn't possibly forget it because I couldn't wait to get back to reading it. I didn't want to leave it here by accident and have to wait until tomorrow to find out what happens next."

Stevie and Phil walked over at that moment. "What's going on?" Stevie asked, noticing Lisa's puzzled expression.

"Lisa's book is missing," Carole said.

Stevie's eyes widened. "First Betsy's bracelet, now your book? It looks like we've got a thief at Pine Hollow!"

"Let's not jump to conclusions," Carole said. "Just because a couple of things are missing doesn't mean they were stolen."

Just then they heard an outraged shriek from the other end of the room. It was Veronica, and she was holding up one brown suede glove. "All right, what's the big idea?" she exclaimed to the room at large. "Who took my other glove?"

Stevie glanced over at Veronica, then raised one eyebrow

as she turned back to her friends. "What else could it mean?" she demanded. "Things don't just get up and walk away by themselves."

"Not even on Halloween," Phil put in with a smile.

"This isn't funny," Stevie told him. "We have to find out who took this stuff. Otherwise none of us is safe."

"Don't get carried away yet, Stevie," Lisa said. "Veronica loses things all the time. And I'm not one hundred percent sure yet that my book is really missing. Let me look around a little bit first."

"Maybe the book fell out of your cubby and someone picked it up," Carole suggested. "I'll go ask Max if anyone turned it in."

She found Max in his office. He smiled when he saw her. But as soon as she explained why she was there, his smile turned into a frown. "Are you sure the book is really missing?"

"Lisa's still looking for it," Carole said. "But it seems to be gone. Didn't anybody turn it in?"

"No," Max replied. "Come on, let's go see if it's turned up." Without another word he strode toward the locker room. Carole shrugged and followed.

As soon as Stevie saw Carole and Max come in, she hurried over to them, her face grim. "All right, this has gone too far," she announced. "There's a thief at Pine Hollow, all right. And whoever it is has no shame. Phil's yarmulke is missing!"

"I STILL CAN'T BELIEVE someone at Pine Hollow is a thief," Stevie said. It was the next day, and Stevie, Carole, and Lisa were getting ready to go on a trail ride.

"I still can't believe someone took my book," Lisa grumbled as she led Prancer, the pretty Thoroughbred mare she usually rode, toward the door. "Now I might never find out what happens."

Carole mounted Starlight. Then she paused to touch the good-luck horseshoe hanging on the stable wall. No rider had ever been seriously hurt after touching the horseshoe, so it was a stable tradition to do so before every ride. "It's a shame about your book, Lisa. But you have to admit, it's pretty terrible that Phil lost his special yarmulke."

35

"I know," Lisa said as she led Prancer toward the mounting block. "That's really much worse. It's hard to imagine what kind of person would steal an important religious object like that. Who do you think it could have been?"

"I don't know, but I'm going to find out," Stevie said. The three girls turned their horses and started across the broad fields behind Pine Hollow. They rode three abreast so that they could talk more easily.

"How are you planning to do that?" Lisa asked, sounding skeptical.

"You mean how are *we* planning to do that," Stevie corrected her. "And the answer is I'm not sure yet. But this sounds like a Saddle Club project. After all, you were one of the victims, and you're a Saddle Club member. Also, Phil's a member, remember?"

"Say that three times fast," Lisa said. At Stevie's blank look, she said, " 'Member, remember,' get it?"

"Never mind that," Stevie said crisply. "Let's get down to work. Who are our suspects? Carole?"

Carole shrugged. "I can't think of anybody."

Stevie frowned. "Lisa?"

"I don't know. It's hard to believe that anyone at Pine Hollow could be a thief," Lisa said, pulling up Prancer slightly to keep her from moving ahead of the other horses. As a former racehorse, the mare tended to be competitive, even on trail rides. "I mean, we know everyone pretty well."

Stevie raised an eyebrow. "We *think* we know them well.

36

But obviously there's at least one person we don't know as well as we thought."

Stevie's comment reminded Carole of the story of the phantom horse, as well as Troy's later comments. Was it really possible to *think* you knew someone when you actually didn't know him or her at all? Carole knew that people weren't always what they seemed. Could the same be true of horses? She didn't think so. Still, it was a frightening thought.

"We can't discount anyone as a suspect," Stevie went on. "We have to consider all the possibilities."

Lisa rolled her eyes. "Right. So what you're saying is, maybe Max is the thief. Or were you thinking of Mrs. Reg?"

"Don't be silly," Stevie said. "Come on, get serious and help me figure out who did it."

"I can't even figure out *why* someone would have done it," Lisa protested. "If you think about it, it's pretty strange. Why would someone steal my book, which is hardly worth anything, when my purse was sitting right under it? I had a ten-dollar bill in there that wasn't touched. And why would someone choose Phil's yarmulke over the tallith, which looks much more valuable?"

"Maybe the thief didn't have time to comparison shop," Stevie said. They had just reached the edge of a field, and she brought her horse, Belle, to a stop and leaned over to unlatch the gate. "Maybe he just took whatever was handy and ran for it."

"That still doesn't explain why anyone would take one of Veronica's gloves and not the other," Lisa pointed out. "Does that mean we're looking for a one-handed, cold-headed thief who reads murder mysteries?"

Stevie closed the gate behind them, and the girls started across the wide meadow that lay between them and the woods. "Well," Stevie said, looking thoughtful. "Now that you mention it, Veronica's gloves are awfully suspicious. And that means Veronica is starting to look awfully suspicious to me."

"You think Veronica is the thief?" Lisa asked with a laugh. "Come on. Why would she steal her own glove?"

"Attention," Stevie replied. "Think about it. What better way for her to—"

At that moment Stevie's words were interrupted by a sudden shrill shriek from Starlight. Without warning, the horse dropped one shoulder, spun around in a tight circle, and with one strong buck sent Carole flying into a nearby bush.

Lisa gasped. "What—" she began.

But Stevie interrupted her. "Go check on Carole," she said quickly. "I'll get Starlight." She urged Belle forward after the bay gelding, who was still bucking and kicking as he raced across the meadow toward the woods.

Lisa obeyed Stevie's command, sliding off Prancer and hurrying to where Carole was trying to clamber out of the bush.

"Are you okay? Did you break anything?" Lisa called anxiously. She dropped Prancer's reins in front of the mare, praying that all her careful lessons on ground-tying would pay off. Prancer cast a nervous eye across the field to where Belle was just catching up with Starlight, but she stood still, and Lisa breathed a sigh of relief as she hurried to Carole's side—or as close to Carole's side as she could get, since Carole was still entangled in the bush.

"I'm still in one piece," Carole said as Lisa reached out to help her to her feet. She straightened up and winced. "But I think I'm going to be one giant bruise in an hour or two. Not to mention the lovely scratches I'm going to have all over my body, thanks to that bush."

"It's probably lucky the bush was there to catch you," Lisa pointed out sensibly. "What happened, anyway?" Lisa reached forward to pull a branch out of her friend's hair. "One minute Starlight was acting perfectly normal, and the next he just went crazy."

Carole nodded, brushing leaves and dirt off her jeans as she glanced over at Starlight. Stevie had managed to catch him by the bridle and was now talking to him soothingly as she led him back toward the others. "I don't know. He's never done that before," she said, her voice a little shaky. "He caught me by surprise."

"As soon as he calms down enough we'd better check his hooves," Lisa said. "He might have stepped on a piece of glass or something."

"I guess it's possible something punctured his frog," Carole said doubtfully. The frog was the sensitive center part of a horse's foot. "But I've never seen that kind of reaction to an injury like that. Besides, he doesn't seem to be limping."

Lisa looked and saw that Carole was right. She shrugged. "Well, something must have gotten into him."

"I know," Carole said. She gulped, thinking of Troy's story. "It's—it's like he suddenly became a whole different horse." She immediately felt foolish for saying it out loud. The groom's ghost story had spooked her, but that was no reason to start acting crazy and superstitious.

Luckily Lisa hadn't heard. She was hurrying forward to help Stevie with Starlight. The gelding was still giving an occasional shudder and tossing his head, but he had calmed down considerably. "How is he?" Lisa asked, taking Starlight's bridle as Stevie slid down from Belle's back.

"Much better already," Stevie said. "In fact, he told me he's very sorry about the whole incident. Are you okay, Carole?"

"I'm fine," Carole said. She was gazing at her horse with a worried expression.

"Come on, let's check him over and see if we can figure out what set him off," Stevie said. She could tell that Carole was shaken by the fall, so it was up to her to take charge. "Lisa, if you'll hold his head I'll take a look at his hooves. Carole, why don't you check the saddle—maybe a thorn slipped under there or something."

Lisa was patting Starlight's sweaty neck soothingly a few

minutes later when she noticed a small bump a few inches in front of his withers. She ran her fingers over it, and Starlight flinched and tossed his head. "Hey, look at this," she said to her friends. "I think I may have found the problem."

Carole and Stevie looked at Starlight's neck.

"Insect bite?" Stevie asked.

Carole nodded. "Looks like it."

"Well, I guess that would explain the reaction," Stevie said. "But it must have been some bug. Ouch."

"Do you think it was a bee?" Lisa asked.

Stevie peered closely at the bump. "I don't see a stinger," she said. "It was probably a fly, or maybe one of those flying red ants. Those bites hurt. My brother Alex sat on a whole family of them once, and believe me, he screamed a lot louder than Starlight."

"We'd better get him back to the stable so Max can take a look," Carole said. "I'll ride behind one of you, and the other one can lead him, okay?"

"Hold on just a minute," Lisa said. "Starlight doesn't seem to be in any serious pain, right? So shouldn't you follow that advice you're always giving other people and get back in the saddle right away?"

"She's right, Carole," Stevie said. "You can ride him back. It won't hurt him, and it'll make both of you feel better."

Carole bit her lip, glancing up at Starlight. He gazed back at her calmly, as if nothing had happened. He was her horse, and she loved him. She had fallen off him before, and she would again. It was all just a part of riding. So why didn't she want to follow her friends' advice and climb back aboard? She didn't know the answer to that, but something inside her was resisting what her logical mind was telling her.

She decided the best thing to do was to ignore her nervousness. "Give me a leg up, will you, Stevie?"

Stevie stepped forward and cupped her hands. Taking a deep breath, Carole swung aboard Starlight's broad back.

"There you go," Stevie said. "Feel better?"

Carole nodded, then urged Starlight forward. She rode him in a circle, then a figure eight. Then she signaled for a trot. He responded immediately, shifting into the smooth, comfortable gait Carole had always loved. She automatically began posting, and Stevie and Lisa, obviously satisfied that all was well, turned back to their own horses. But for some reason Carole couldn't relax and enjoy the ride. Each time she had fallen before, her feelings of nervousness had gone away after a few seconds back in the saddle. But this time they seemed to have settled in a hard, cold lump in her stomach, and they weren't showing any sign of melting.

Stevie and Lisa remounted and trotted to join her. "Everything all right now?" Stevie asked.

"Sure," Carole said as the three friends turned their horses toward home. "No problem."

But deep down inside, she wasn't sure she meant it.

CAROLE TIGHTENED THE girth around Starlight's belly, then checked all his tack once again before mounting. She was heading out to the ring to work with him on jumping, and she wanted to be sure nothing went wrong. She patted his neck as she rode forward to touch the lucky horseshoe. But strangely, it wasn't in its usual place on the wall.

Carole frowned, wondering what had happened to it. She had never seen the doorway without the comforting shape of the horseshoe beside it, and the bare wall looked very odd to her. Still, there was nothing she could do about it now. The stable was deserted, so there was no one she could ask about it. Besides, she didn't want to waste any of her training time with Starlight. With a shrug, she touched the spot on the wall where the horseshoe normally hung and rode outside.

When she reached the outdoor ring she got to work right away. A small jump course was already set up, and after warming up with a few turns around the outside edge of the ring, she sent Starlight toward the first obstacle. He cleared it easily, and Carole smiled. She had the perfect horse; she'd always known it, and Starlight kept proving it to her over and over. He continued through the course, taking each jump with more room to spare between his hooves and the top rail. Before long it seemed almost as if he were flying.

Then they cantered toward the final obstacle, a bright red fence with shrubbery around it. Carole frowned a little when she saw it. For some reason she hadn't noticed it until this moment, and when she did it struck her as odd. First, she didn't remember seeing the red-railed jump before. Second, it seemed strange that anyone would take the time to set up such an elaborate jump for a training course.

The seconds seemed to pass very slowly as Starlight made his approach to the jump, and Carole's mind seemed to be working very slowly as well. One part of her wanted to pull up and avoid the red jump, but for some reason she didn't seem able to do it. Her hands felt numb and helpless on the reins, but Starlight wasn't paying any attention to his rider's distress. He was gaining speed, and for a moment Carole was afraid he was going to plow right through the fence. But at just the right moment the gelding's forefeet lifted off the

44

ground, and Carole felt his powerful hindquarters propelling them forward and upward, like an exploding cannon. When she glanced down, the jump seemed to be yards beneath them.

Starlight's landing was perfect, like the rest of the jump. Carole's hands relaxed and she started to smile, but her smile froze when the horse suddenly came to a complete stop and began shaking his head and snorting. Perplexed by his behavior, Carole signaled for a trot. But Starlight ignored her, standing stock-still except for his head, which was now rolling from side to side so far that Carole could see the whites of his eyes. Something was very wrong, but Carole wasn't sure what it was. She gave the signal again, more firmly this time.

Suddenly, with a quick, powerful movement, Starlight reared and bucked. Carole flew out of the saddle, landing with a loud thud against the jump behind them. She shook her head to clear the red haze out of her mind. The first thing she saw was the red posts of the jump. As she stared at them, trying to get her eyes to focus properly, she heard an unfamiliar noise behind her. When she turned she saw Starlight, except that he didn't look like the Starlight she knew. This was a wild, unknown Starlight, with eyes that were beginning to burn as if lit from within by a red fire. And those eyes were trained directly on her as he pawed the ground and leaped forward . . .

Carole awoke in a cold sweat and sat bolt upright, her

45

eyes staring wildly into the dark corners of her bedroom, looking for a ghost horse to spring out at her at any second. As soon as she realized what had happened—it had all been a dream, just a bad dream—her heart started to slow down to its normal rate. She took a deep breath to calm herself and glanced at the digital alarm clock beside her bed. It was four o'clock in the morning.

"It was just a nightmare, that's all," Carole whispered to herself, shifting her legs, which had become entangled in the sheets. She flipped her pillow over to the cool side, then leaned back and closed her eyes. As soon as she did, the red-eyed phantom Starlight reappeared. Carole's eyes flew open again, and she sat up with a groan. She had the sinking feeling she wouldn't be going back to sleep that night.

By THE TIME Carole dragged herself downstairs for breakfast, her father had already left for work. Carole had spent a long time in the shower, standing under the coldest water she could bear to try to wake herself up, and she hadn't heard him leave. She remembered that he had a big project going on at work that week, which meant he had been putting in long hours at the office. In fact, she'd spent the past few nights alone watching the scary old movies they usually enjoyed together at this time of year. She felt annoyed that he had rushed away without even saying good morning. She would have liked to talk her nightmare over with him.

46

Heaving an irritated sigh, she grabbed two slices of whole-wheat bread and stuck them in the toaster. She wasn't particularly hungry, but she knew she would be starving by lunchtime if she didn't eat something. She leaned on the counter as she waited for the toast to pop up, and her mind drifted back to her dream. It had seemed so real; she could still remember the feeling of flight as Starlight's hind legs propelled them over the jumps. But it hadn't been real. She had to keep reminding herself of that. Starlight was in his stall at Pine Hollow right now, and he didn't have glowing red eyes or a look of murderous rage or—

Carole jumped when the toast popped out of the toaster. Feeling annoyed with herself for being so nervous, she grabbed the toast, burning her fingers. She dropped the toast on the counter and stuck her fingers in her mouth, feeling more annoyed than ever. It was going to be a long day.

CAROLE WENT FROM class to class as usual, but her mind wasn't on her schoolwork. She had expected her memory of the nightmare to fade as the day wore on. That was what usually happened, whether the dream in question was good, bad, or indifferent. Once, years ago, she had had a wonderful dream about riding in the Grand National steeplechase race. She had wanted to remember and savor the dream for as long as possible. But by the time she had finished breakfast, she couldn't remember what she had been wearing, and by lunchtime she had forgotten her mount's name and what he looked like. By the next day all she had been able to retain was the wonderful feeling the dream had left her with.

This time it was different. Her nightmare was just as vividly imprinted on her mind now as it had been the second she woke up, and she had no idea why. The rational part of her mind knew that the dream didn't mean anything. Obviously her spill of the day before had combined with Troy's Halloween story to create the scary nightmare. But in the less rational part of her mind, Carole wondered: Was there such a thing as a phantom horse? Was it possible for an animal she thought she knew inside and out to change into another sort of creature entirely? Had Starlight's sudden outburst the day before *really* been the result of an insect bite?

Carole knew she was being silly. But she was tired, and as she dragged herself through the school day thoughts of her dream, Troy's phantom horse, and Starlight kept swirling through her head.

She had made plans to meet Stevie and Lisa at Pine Hollow after school for a trail ride, but by the end of the day she felt almost too tired to make it to the stable. Then another thought occurred to her. Her two best friends would be the perfect people to take her mind off her strange dream and even stranger thoughts. Lisa was so sensible that she would make things seem okay just by listening; and Stevie, despite her wild schemes and crazy sense of humor, was down-to-earth about the things that really mattered.

Carole felt relieved the moment she'd thought of this. School was almost over, and soon she'd be with her friends at the stable. All this nonsense would be behind her. Besides, just seeing Starlight himself would make her feel better—wouldn't it?

WHEN CAROLE ARRIVED at Pine Hollow, her friends were nowhere to be found, so she headed straight to Starlight's stall.
She ignored the slight fluttering in her stomach as she
turned the corner and headed down the aisle, and to her
relief the sight of his mahogany head peering out at her over
the half door of his stall brought an automatic smile to her
lips, just like always.

"Hi, boy," she said softly, reaching forward to stroke his
velvety muzzle. She let herself into the stall and ran her
hand down his neck, searching for the insect bite. It wasn't
difficult to find; in fact, it seemed to be larger than it had
been the day before. Carole frowned. It must have swollen
overnight.

"Carole? Are you in there?" called a voice from outside. It was Troy.

Carole let herself out of the stall. The groom was leaning against the wall, chewing on a piece of hay. Normally Carole might have found it an amusing sight—tough-looking Troy, in his leather jacket and earrings, chewing hay like a TV image of a country boy. But today she didn't feel much like laughing.

"There you are," Troy drawled. "I hope I didn't scare you this time."

Carole didn't bother to answer that. "I think Starlight's shoulder is swelling," she said. "He got a bug bite yesterday and it's bigger now than it was then."

"I know," Troy said calmly. "Max wanted me to come tell you he already had the vet in to look at it. She said it's nothing serious. You should just keep it clean and keep an eye on it, and call her if it doesn't start clearing up within a few days."

Carole glanced back at Starlight. "What about riding him? Did she say it would be okay?"

Troy shrugged. "She didn't say it wouldn't." He spit out the piece of hay and turned to go. "I guess it's your call. See you later."

"Bye. And thanks," Carole said. She watched him go, thinking about what he had said. The local equine veterinarian, Judy Barker, was one of Carole's heroes. Judy definitely knew what she was doing, and she was nothing if not cautious and thorough when it came to her patients' health. If she hadn't left orders that Starlight wasn't to be ridden, that meant it was okay for Carole to ride him.

Carole glanced at Starlight again. He looked back at her unblinkingly, his eyes large and dark. Carole bit her lip. Wasn't it possible that just this once Judy had forgotten to mention that Carole shouldn't ride Starlight? A swollen insect bite didn't seem very serious, but then again, neither did a cough, and that could lead to bronchitis, the flu, or pneumonia, which in turn could lead to broken wind.

Carole decided she'd better play it safe, and that meant no riding until the swelling went down. She felt relieved once she'd made the decision, but she wasn't entirely sure that her relief was because she knew she'd made the right choice. Was it possible that she didn't want to ride Starlight today anyway?

Instead of thinking about that, she went to look for Max. She found him in the grain shed helping Red mix the feed for the next week. The two men looked up as she entered.

"Hi, Red. Hi, Max," she said.

"Are you all right, Carole?" Red asked, an expression of concern on his freckled face. "Your eyes look a little red."

"Oh, it's nothing," Carole said, rubbing her eyes. "I didn't get enough sleep last night, that's all."

"I hope it wasn't because you were worrying about Starlight," Max said, measuring out a cupful of barley. "I noticed that bite was swelling, so I asked Judy to take a look. But she said there's nothing to worry about. It will be gone in a day or two."

Carole nodded. "Troy told me. But I think I'll let Starlight rest today, just to be on the safe side. I'm not going to ride him."

Max shrugged. "It's up to you," he said. "I really don't think there'd be any harm in riding him today, though. Anyway, I thought I saw your two co-conspirators arriving a few minutes ago. Won't they be disappointed if you have to cancel your trail ride, or whatever you three have planned?"

Carole shook her head, looking a little stubborn. "I'm not going to ride him today."

Max and Red exchanged glances. "Okay," Max said. "As I said, it's up to you. He's your horse. But I really would hate to see your friends disappointed. When Stevie gets disappointed, strange things have a way of happening. So why don't you take Barq out today, no charge? Actually you'd be doing me a favor. He hasn't been ridden for two days, and he's getting bored."

"Really?" Carole said. "Are you sure you wouldn't mind?"

"Of course not," Max replied with a smile. "Unless you'd rather stay here and help us mix this feed, that is."

"Thanks, Max," Carole said gratefully. She hurried out of the shed before Max could change his mind. She went to Belle's stall, arriving there as Stevie walked up carrying Belle's tack.

"There you are," Stevie said. "Lisa and I were wondering

where you'd gone. She looked for you after school, but you'd already disappeared."

"I came straight here," Carole said. "I guess I forgot to wait for her."

"Well, she *might* forgive you," Stevie teased. "Especially if you help her get Prancer tacked up. Is Starlight ready to go?"

"Um, I'm not riding Starlight today," Carole said. She was dying to tell Stevie all about her nightmare, but she decided to wait until Lisa was there, too. "That bite he got yesterday swelled up a little."

"Is he going to be all right?" Stevie asked, immediately concerned.

Carole nodded. "Judy said it's not serious. It'll be gone in a couple of days."

"But you can't ride him?" Stevie said. "What a pain in the neck. Get it? A pain in the neck?"

"Ha ha," Carole said. "Actually, Max said it would probably be okay to ride Starlight today. But I don't want to take any chances, and Max offered to let me ride Barq. I'd better go get his tack now."

"Oh. Okay," Stevie said. As she watched her friend walk down the aisle toward the tack room, her eyes narrowed curiously. Carole hadn't seemed very disappointed about missing a ride on Starlight. That wasn't like her at all. Usually she could hardly bear to be parted from her horse, even to eat, sleep, or go to school. Now she was switching to Barq with hardly a blink of the eye. After a moment Stevie shrugged and turned back to Belle. It was probably nothing. If something was wrong, Carole would tell her.

A FEW MINUTES later Carole, Stevie, and Lisa met up near the outdoor ring. Stevie was riding Belle, and Lisa was mounted on Prancer. Carole was aboard Barq, a lively Arabian with a white blaze down his nose, a favorite of many of the young riders at Pine Hollow. He was also the horse Carole had ridden regularly before she owned Starlight.

"Where should we go today?" Stevie asked as the threesome rode out of the stable yard and into the field beyond. The land around Pine Hollow was threaded with dozens of riding trails, and at one time or another The Saddle Club had explored nearly every one.

"Do you think it's too cold for our favorite spot?" Lisa asked. The other two knew immediately where she meant—a shady clearing in the woods overlooking the lazy little stream that had given the town of Willow Creek its name. On warm spring and summer days, the girls loved to sit on the banks of the creek and cool their feet in the clear water. It was one of their favorite places to hold Saddle Club meetings.

"It's never too cold," Stevie declared. "Even if we can't wade, that doesn't mean we can't just sit and watch the water go by."

"Good point," Lisa agreed. "Let's go."

Once they were under way, Carole decided it was time to

bring up the topic that was foremost in her mind. She cleared her throat. "I wanted to talk to you guys about something," she began. "I had this really weird dream last night."

"What kind of a dream?" Lisa asked.

"You didn't dream who the Pine Hollow Pilferer is, did you?" Stevie asked. "That's what I've decided to call our thief. What do you think?"

Lisa laughed. "I have to admit, that's pretty good," she said. "It sounds like the title of one of Ernestine Collier's novels: *The Mystery of the Pine Hollow Pilferer*."

"As I was saying," Carole said meaningfully, then paused.

"Oh, sorry, Carole. Go ahead," Lisa said contritely. "What was your dream about?"

"Well, I dreamed I was here at Pine Hollow," Carole began. As the threesome rode slowly across the fields, she described the entire nightmare, trying not to leave out any important details. ". . . and then I woke up," she finished.

"Wow. That's pretty spooky," Lisa said. "It reminds me of that story Troy told the other night at the party."

"Me too," Carole admitted. "Pretty silly, huh?"

"What's silly is to think you'd ever jump a course without walking it first," Stevie said. "As if an obstacle would ever catch *you* by surprise!"

Lisa laughed. "That's a good point," she said. "And how about this: Since when would Pine Hollow ever be deserted in the middle of the afternoon? It had to be a dream, Carole.

If it was real Max would have turned up, reminding you to clean your tack after you were finished."

"Or reminding you to keep your heels down and your elbows in," Stevie offered, sitting up a little straighter in her saddle to demonstrate.

"Or asking you to muck out some stalls when you had a free second," Lisa said. "Now *that's* what I call a nightmare!"

"Really?" Stevie asked. "Are you sure it's not a night*stallion*?"

"Actually, since Starlight was the star of the dream, I think technically it would have to be called a nightgelding," Lisa pointed out.

Carole sighed as she listened to her friends' joking. It was clear they hadn't understood how disturbed she had been by her dream. Otherwise they wouldn't be making silly jokes about it. On the other hand, it *was* pretty silly of her to be so upset by something that wasn't even real. The incident with Starlight the day before had been real enough, of course, but there was also a very real reason for his behavior. Troy's story and her dream hadn't been real at all. So why couldn't she just forget about them?

"Here's something to take your mind off nightmares, nightfoals, *and* nightponies," Stevie told Carole as the girls entered the woods and headed toward the creek. "The Pine Hollow Pilferer."

"I talked to Max about it today," Lisa said. "He's really mad that no one has turned in the missing stuff yet. But I got the impression he has no idea what to do about it."

"That's where we come in," Stevie said. "We'll have to track down the thief and retrieve the stolen goods. Especially Phil's yarmulke."

"What about my book?" Lisa asked, pretending to be hurt. "Don't you even care that I may die of suspense if I don't get it back soon?"

"Well, maybe a little," Stevie said with a grin. The path they were following through the woods had been wide enough for the girls to ride three abreast, but now it began to grow narrower. Carole pulled Barq up to let her friends ride ahead.

Lisa stuck out her tongue at Stevie, who was still beside her. "Very funny. So what's your plan to catch the thief? Sorry, I mean the pilferer."

"I'm not quite sure yet," Stevie admitted. "But I do know two things. One is that we have to do it before Phil's bar mitzvah on Saturday."

"That would be great," Lisa said. "It will be awful if Phil has to do without his special yarmulke on his big day, particularly since his relatives sent it all the way from Israel." She paused. "But if we're going to solve the mystery, we'll have to come up with some decent suspects. I mean, the detective in my book always says you should start with the most unlikely-seeming suspect and follow that lead first. But I

58

can't think of any likely unlikely-seeming suspects, if you know what I mean."

"I'm not so sure about that," Stevie said mysteriously, leaning forward to brush off a dead leaf that had fallen on Belle's neck. She twisted around in the saddle to make sure Carole could hear her. Carole just shrugged in response, and Stevie wondered if she was even paying attention to the conversation.

Lisa shrugged, too. "If you ask me, all the kids from our riding class are pretty unlikely." She pulled up Prancer a little as the frisky ex-racehorse tried to move ahead of Belle on the trail. "And we've known and trusted all the adults there for ages, except for Troy. That reminds me—"

"Aren't you going to ask me what the second thing is?" Stevie interrupted, looking impatient.

"Huh?" Lisa said. "What second thing?"

"I said I knew two things, and one was that we had to get the stuff back before Phil's bar mitzvah," Stevie reminded her.

"So what's the second thing?" Lisa asked.

Stevie paused, glancing back at Carole again to make sure she was close enough to hear. "The second thing is, I already know who the thief is. All we have to do is catch her."

"Her?" Lisa repeated. "You're not accusing Veronica again, are you? I know she's always a possible suspect for just about anything bad or sneaky, but in this case—"

"It's not Veronica," Stevie interrupted. "It's another suspect, one even more unlikely than Veronica. Only this one has already given away her guilt." She paused, looking like a cat that had just swallowed a particularly large and tasty canary.

"Who is it?" Lisa asked impatiently. "Are you going to tell us or make us guess?"

"I won't make you guess, because you'll never be able to," Stevie said. "The Pine Hollow Pilferer is . . . Shannon Brice."

"SHANNON BRICE? YOU mean Joe's girlfriend?" Lisa said in disbelief. "What on earth would make you think she's the thief?"

"I told you," Stevie said smugly. "She gave herself away. It happened today at school." The girls had reached the clearing by the creek, and there was a pause in the conversation while they dismounted, made sure their horses were comfortably settled, and walked down to the creek.

Lisa perched on a big rock and looked at Stevie. "All right. Let's hear it."

"Okay," Stevie said, stretching out on her side on the bank and resting her head on one hand. Carole sat down next to her and stared at the water tumbling by in the wide, shallow creek. "As you know, Shannon goes to my school," Stevie began. "In fact, she's in my math class. So today during math I was staring into sp—um, I mean, I was looking at the teacher, and I happened to notice something very strange about Shannon. Namely, that she was wearing Betsy's missing bracelet!"

Lisa gasped. "Are you sure?" she demanded.

"Well . . ." Stevie paused. "Ninety percent sure, anyway. It was a gold bangle bracelet, just like the one Betsy lost. And I'd never seen Shannon wear it before. I'm positive about that, because she usually wears this silver bracelet with little bells on it that jingle whenever she raises her hand or something."

Lisa tapped her fingers on the rock restlessly. She was thinking hard. "But you're really not sure it was Betsy's bracelet," she said slowly. "Even if Shannon never wore a gold bangle before, it's still not really evidence. Lots of people have bracelets like that. I have one myself, and so does Lorraine Olsen, and I've seen Veronica walking around with three of them on one arm. You have one, too, don't you, Carole?"

Carole nodded absently. "My dad gave it to me for my birthday."

"But that's not all," Stevie said, sitting up and brushing the leaves off her elbow. "I talked to Shannon about the bracelet after class, and she acted *very* suspicious."

"What do you mean?" Lisa asked. "What did you say to her? You didn't come right out and accuse her of stealing it, did you?" Even for Stevie, that would have been awfully impulsive, not to mention rude.

"Of course not," Stevie said, sounding slightly insulted. "I was very subtle about it. I just told her I liked the bracelet and asked her where she got it."

Lisa rolled her eyes. "Oh yeah," she said. "Real subtle. What did she say?"

"She didn't really answer," Stevie said. "In fact, she looked as though she didn't even want to talk about the bracelet at all. She just thanked me very politely for the compliment, then stuck her arm behind her back and said she had to go or she'd be late for her next class."

"Hmmm," Lisa said. "What do you think, Carole?"

"I don't know," Carole said, still staring at the water. "I guess that sounds sort of suspicious."

"You're telling me," Stevie said firmly. "Once I got to thinking about it, I realized we should have paid more attention to Shannon right from the beginning. She's always been kind of odd. She hardly ever talks to anybody, and in the past month or two it seems like she's been absent from school more than she's been there. I hadn't really thought about it before, but now it's clear that she's been acting suspicious for a long time. I wouldn't be surprised if the things from Pine Hollow aren't the first things she's stolen."

"Don't get carried away," Lisa said. "Besides, I have another idea about who may have done it. I started to tell you before."

"Another suspect?" Stevie said. "Who is it?"

"This afternoon when I got to the stable, I went to the student locker room to drop off my school stuff," Lisa said. "And guess who was coming out of the locker room just then?"

Stevie shrugged, not looking very interested. "I don't know. Max? Mrs. Reg? Veronica?"

Lisa shook her head. "Nope. It was Troy."

Stevie looked confused for a second; then her expression cleared. "Oh, I get it. You think Troy is the thief?"

"I don't know," Lisa said, tapping her fingers thoughtfully on the rock again. "It's certainly not evidence or anything, but it did make me think. There's no reason Troy shouldn't have been in the locker room, but there's no good reason he *should* have been there, either. Normally I wouldn't even have thought about it—"

"But now there's a mystery to solve, and anything could be a clue," Stevie finished for her, nodding. "And we don't know much about Troy, and he never talks about himself." She leaned back again on the dry, brown late-autumn grass. "Well, I guess it's possible that he could have done it. But I still think Shannon is a more likely suspect."

"But you've known Shannon for years, right?" Lisa said. "Even if she is a little shy and withdrawn, she's never done

64

anything before this to make you think she's a thief. Besides that, she's rich. What motive could she have to steal things?"

"Who knows what drives a criminal mind?" Stevie said mischievously. "But seriously, she could have the same motive we thought Veronica might have—wanting attention. Or maybe she's sick. You know, she could have that mental illness, the one that makes you steal things. What is it, kelpo—kleppa—"

"Kleptomania," Lisa supplied. "Come on. Isn't that a little farfetched, even for you, Stevie? The bottom line is, Shannon doesn't have any clear motive. Troy does. He's at Pine Hollow because he needs money, right?"

"True," Stevie said, watching as a fat horsefly flew lazily above her. "But if he's trying to make a living as a thief, he's not doing a very good job. How much money could he get selling black-market yarmulkes and paperback books? Not to mention a partnerless glove."

"Well, I guess you have a point," Lisa admitted. "But maybe it's like you said before—he didn't have time to be picky. He just grabbed what he could and ran."

Suddenly Stevie smiled. "Are you sure you're not suspicious of Troy because he looks like that character in your mystery book?" she joked. "You know, the leather jacket, the earrings, the dark stubble . . ."

"Of course not," Lisa answered quickly. She picked up a small pebble and tossed it into the creek, trying to make it skip. "Just because Troy looks like that character doesn't automatically mean he's a thief. That's patently absurd."

"Patently absurd?" Stevie repeated. She and Carole liked to tease Lisa about the fifty-cent words she sometimes used. "Couldn't you just say that's dumb, or, like, *duh*?"

Lisa stuck out her tongue at Stevie. "You know what I mean," she said.

Stevie giggled. "But that's beside the point," she said. "I have to admit, you may be on to something. He has the motive, he had the opportunity—as much as anyone else at the party, anyway—and we really don't know him at all. He hasn't given us any real reason to suspect him, but he hasn't given us any reason to trust him, either."

"So you think he's the thief?" Lisa asked.

"I didn't say that," Stevie said. "I still think it's Shannon. But we'll put him on the suspect list." She glanced at her watch and stood up. "I guess we should head back. Ready to go?"

"I'm ready," Lisa said, tossing one last pebble into the water before standing up herself. She shivered a little. "It's getting a little cold to keep sitting here. Ready, Carole?"

Carole nodded and followed her friends toward the horses. Lisa realized that Carole hadn't said much during their conversation, but she figured her friend was just tired. She'd mentioned that her nightmare had kept her up half the night. She was sure to snap out of it after a good night's sleep.

As The Saddle Club rode back toward Pine Hollow, Stevie and Lisa continued to talk about the mystery for a while, then eventually shifted to the topic of what they were going to wear to Phil's bar mitzvah. Stevie's parents were picking them up right after Horse Wise to take them to the synagogue, so they would have to shower and change clothes at the stable.

Carole responded when she was spoken to, but that was all. Most of her attention was not on the conversation but on her own thoughts. She knew that a bad fall could make even an experienced rider a little nervous for a while, but she didn't feel a bit nervous riding Barq today. It was only the thought of riding Starlight that made her stomach clench up in knots, and she didn't like what that seemed to mean.

Could Carole possibly be afraid of her own horse?

THE NEXT DAY, as soon as Stevie rode Belle into the outdoor ring for riding lessons, her eyes lit up. Shannon was there! She was leaning on the fence outside the ring with her eyes trained on Joe, who was clearly showing off for her as he rode his mount, a dark chestnut gelding named Rusty, around the ring at a trot.

"Check it out!" Stevie whispered to Lisa, who was right behind her on Prancer. "Joe must have invited her to watch the lesson."

"Hmmm," Lisa said.

"This will be the perfect chance to scope her out," Stevie said excitedly. "Not that I haven't been keeping an eye on her in school, of course. But this is much better. She's returned to the scene of the crime. Aren't all criminals supposed to do that?"

"I guess so," Lisa said. She glanced around. "By the way, where's Carole? Is she going to be able to ride today, or is Starlight's neck still bothering him?"

"I saw her inside," Stevie said. "She was carrying his tack, so I guess she's decided to ride him. If you ask me, she was being a little overcautious yesterday anyway."

In the barn, Carole was thinking the same thing as she carefully tacked up Starlight. She was also thinking that for once in her life she didn't feel like riding. She'd had another scary dream the night before in which Starlight became the phantom horse, and she couldn't stop thinking about it. She frowned at herself and did her best to put it out of her mind. If she was nervous and uncomfortable, her horse would pick up on it and become nervous and uncomfortable himself.

She tightened the gelding's girth and led him toward the stable entrance. It was time for the lesson to start, and Max hated it when his students were late. Carole wasn't looking forward to the coming hour, but she had to get through it somehow. She'd just have to concentrate on what she was doing and hope for the best.

As THE LESSON began, Stevie vowed to keep a close eye on Shannon. But Max had other ideas. Every time Stevie snuck a peek at Shannon, who was sitting in the bleachers between the ring and the stable building, Max noticed and yelled at her. That didn't stop Stevie from doing it, but it stopped her from doing it as often as she would have liked. And it kept her from being a hundred percent certain that Shannon hadn't moved from her seat.

When the lesson ended Stevie was the first one out of the ring. She led Belle over to where Shannon was sitting.

"Hi, Shannon," Stevie said, smiling sweetly. "Did you enjoy the lesson?"

Shannon seemed a little surprised that Stevie had come over to speak to her. "Yes, it was very interesting," she said in her soft voice. She lifted one arm to push back a stray lock of her long, wavy hair, and as she did so Stevie heard a soft jingle of bells. She looked at Shannon's arm and almost gasped aloud. At school that day Stevie had checked to see if Shannon was wearing the gold bracelet, and she was. But now she was wearing the silver bell bracelet instead!

Stevie had to tell Lisa and Carole. "Well, if you have any questions about anything, feel free," she said, backing away and almost bumping into Belle in the process. She turned and led the mare off, giving Shannon one last glance over her shoulder. But the other girl had already turned away and was smiling brightly at Joe, who was approaching with Rusty in tow.

Stevie untacked Belle in record time and left her munching a mouthful of hay in her stall, with a promise to return soon to give her a full grooming. Then Stevie raced to Starlight's stall. The big bay was there, but Carole was nowhere in sight. Stevie shrugged and went to Prancer's stall, where Lisa was busy combing the mare's mane.

"Guess what," Stevie said breathlessly. "I just noticed something important. Shannon isn't wearing the bracelet."

Lisa tugged gently at a stubborn knot in Prancer's mane. "So? Who says she has to wear the same jewelry every day?"

"But she *was* wearing it today," Stevie said. "In school. Now she's wearing that other one. She must have switched before she came to Pine Hollow. Now, why would she bother to do that unless she had a guilty conscience? Or, more to the point, unless she didn't want Betsy to notice her wearing her stolen property?"

"Interesting theory," Lisa said. "But still not proof."

"I know," Stevie said. "But Shannon's guilty. I can just feel it." She looked up and saw Mrs. Reg walking down the aisle in their direction. All the riders at Pine Hollow knew there was nothing Mrs. Reg hated as much as seeing people standing around chatting when there was work to be done. "Oops. I'd better get back to Belle. I owe her a grooming," Stevie said. "But I'm going to keep an eye on Shannon for as long as she hangs around here today, and you should do the same. Tell Carole, too, if you see her."

"Okay," Lisa said agreeably, turning her attention back to Prancer's mane as Stevie hurried away.

As she did her stable chores, Stevie tried to stay close to Shannon. But much to her disappointment, Shannon didn't do anything all afternoon that anyone, even Stevie, could call suspicious. That made Stevie start to wonder if Shannon really was the Pine Hollow Pilferer. Maybe she should have paid more attention to Lisa's theory about Troy after all.

Once her work was finished, Stevie walked slowly down the aisle toward the locker room, thinking hard. She was still convinced that the bracelet switch was a valuable clue, but maybe it wasn't wise to put all her eggs in one basket. Lisa had made some interesting points about Troy. It might not be a bad idea to start keeping an eye on him, too.

Just then Stevie heard excited chatter coming from the locker room. She hurried forward and entered the room. Half a dozen students were there—Lisa, Adam Levine, and several others. Max was there, too, and he was leaning over to peer into Adam's cubby. When he straightened up and turned around, Stevie saw that he looked worried.

"Are you sure it was here, Adam?" Max asked.

Adam nodded. "Definitely. I'm sure," he said. "It was in my jacket pocket." He pointed to a green nylon jacket that was lying on the floor in front of his cubby. "When I came in to get my stuff, my jacket was there on the floor and the pen was gone."

Stevie hurried over to Lisa. "What happened?"

"It looks like Adam's fancy gold-plated fountain pen has disappeared," Lisa said grimly. "He just got it today—it was a prize for a writing contest he won in school."

Stevie let out a low whistle. "It looks like our pilferer is

72

developing better taste," she said. "Or more expensive taste, anyway."

"It looks that way," Lisa agreed.

"You know what else this means, don't you?" Stevie said, glancing around to make sure she wouldn't be overheard. The other students were all clustered around Adam and Max or checking their own cubbies for missing items.

"What?" Lisa asked.

"It means Shannon is still our number one suspect," Stevie whispered.

"What makes you say that?" Lisa whispered back. "I still think Troy is just as likely a suspect, and he was here today, too. Not to mention Veronica, of course; although, as obnoxious as she is, I seriously doubt that she's the thief."

"But think about it," Stevie said. "Things have only disappeared when Shannon is around. Isn't that just a little too coincidental?"

"It's a bit strange," Lisa said. She went to the bench in front of her cubby and sat down to take off her riding boots. "But then again, things have only disappeared so far when the whole riding class is around, too. It could be a coincidence that Shannon has been here both times. If Troy is the thief, wouldn't it make sense for him to wait to take things until there are a lot of people around? Besides, we don't know for sure that nothing has disappeared at other times. Max wouldn't necessarily mention it if anyone in his adult riding classes has had things stolen, or his private students, or even the younger kids' class." She tossed the boots into her cubby and started lacing up her shoes.

"Well, maybe," Stevie said. She didn't look convinced. "But you have to admit it makes Shannon look awfully guilty."

"I'm not saying you're wrong," Lisa said tactfully. She knew that once her friend got an idea in her head it was usually hard to dislodge it. "I'm just saying we should keep our options open. For all we know, the thief could be someone we haven't even thought of yet."

"Like who? Max?" Stevie demanded impatiently.

Lisa rolled her eyes, feeling a little impatient herself. "I don't know, Stevie. But no matter what we think, we can't accuse anyone without some real evidence."

"Hmm," Stevie said thoughtfully. She watched as Max walked out of the room with Adam. Once they had convinced themselves that none of their things had been stolen, the other students began putting on their jackets and leaving. "I guess you're right about that. So there's only one thing to do. We have to lay a trap so we can catch Shannon red-handed."

"How are we going to do that?" Lisa asked.

"Just leave it to me," Stevie said. "I'll think of something. In fact, I think something is starting to come to me already. I'll be right back," she said suddenly. She turned abruptly and hurried out of the room.

Lisa shrugged and turned back to her cubby to get her

74

jacket and backpack. A moment later Carole entered and sat down on the bench next to her. "Oh, there you are," Lisa said, glancing up quickly and then continuing to dig through her backpack. She had just remembered that her science teacher had given the class homework, and she wasn't sure she'd brought home her science textbook. "You missed all the excitement." Not noticing the worried look in Carole's eyes, she began to fill her in on what had happened.

Meanwhile Stevie had found Joe and Shannon in the driveway, waiting for Shannon's mother to pick them up. They were standing close together and talking quietly, but that didn't stop Stevie. She walked over and came to a stop right in front of them.

"Hi there," she said with a big smile.

Joe looked up in surprise. "Oh, um, hi there, Stevie," he said. "What's up?" Shannon didn't say anything, but she smiled shyly at Stevie and took a step away from Joe.

"Not much," Stevie replied. "I just wanted to ask Shannon how she's liking spending time at Pine Hollow."

"Oh, she loves it," Joe assured Stevie, stepping a little closer to Shannon.

Stevie noticed Shannon edging away from Joe again. Stevie turned to her. "Is that right, Shannon?" she asked. "I mean, of course all of us love Pine Hollow or we wouldn't spend so much time here. But it's always interesting to see how newcomers react to it, especially people who don't ride."

75

"Shannon does ride," Joe said. "Her family has a small stable on their property, and she takes private lessons."

Stevie turned to Shannon, surprised. "Really? Then why don't you ride when you're here? Even if you don't want to join the lesson, I'm sure Max would let you take one of his horses out for a trail ride or something. His prices are very reasonable."

"I know," Shannon said. "I just like riding at home, that's all. But I like to watch Joe ride. And it's interesting to watch Max. My riding instructor is very good, but it's helpful to observe someone else's teaching style." Stevie noticed that the other girl was blushing furiously. She couldn't imagine what she had said that would embarrass her so much—unless, of course, Shannon had a guilty conscience.

Stevie smiled. She'd just had a great idea. "Well, in that case, I'm sure Joe has already invited you to our Horse Wise meeting on Saturday morning."

Joe's face lit up. "Actually, I hadn't, but that's a great idea, Stevie." He turned to Shannon. "Horse Wise is our Pony Club. Remember? I told you about it." Shannon nodded, and Joe went on. "Every other week we have unmounted meetings, and we're allowed to bring guests. And this week's meeting should be interesting. The farrier will be here to reshoe some of the horses, and we're going to watch."

"Is that why the meeting is earlier than usual?" Stevie asked, forgetting about her plan for a second. Two weeks

before, Max had told the students that the next unmounted
Horse Wise meeting would begin a couple of hours earlier
than usual. At the time Stevie hadn't bothered to wonder
why. The only thing she cared about was that it meant The
Saddle Club wouldn't have to miss the meeting because of
Phil's bar mitzvah.

Joe nodded. "The farrier, Alec McAllister, is pretty busy.
He has a lot of other stables to visit on Saturday, so Max
had to fit our meeting around Alec's schedule." He turned
back to Shannon again. "So how about it? Do you want to
come?"

Stevie held her breath. When the other girl nodded at Joe
and said she'd love to come, Stevie let out the breath in a
loud whoosh. When Joe and Shannon looked at her curiously, Stevie did her best to turn the sigh of relief into a
cough. Then she smiled at them innocently. "Great. See
you both on Saturday, then," she said. With a cheerful
wave, she left them and raced back inside to find her friends.

CAROLE FELT TEARS welling up in her eyes as she walked home
from the bus stop after the lesson. Starlight had fussed and
fidgeted throughout the class, and at one point he'd even
reached over and tried to nip Patch as they trotted by the
friendly old school horse. Carole knew that all horses have
off days when they feel cranky, and Patch *had* trotted into
Starlight's way. But it was out of character for her horse to
behave in such a bad-tempered manner.

77

To make matters worse, as she was untacking Starlight, Troy had wandered over and stood silently watching for a minute.

"Can I help you?" Carole had finally asked.

"Nope," said Troy. "Looks like you're the one who needs help. I was watching the lesson and I noticed that your horse was acting a little frisky. Just like a little demon."

"So?" Carole said, a sick feeling settling into the pit of her stomach.

"So I just thought he seemed better-natured when I first started working here. I wondered why the sudden personality transformation, that's all."

"He's just having a bad day," Carole said too loudly. As if to confirm her words, Starlight flung his head in the air and snorted.

"Yeah, right," Troy had said. "I guess all horses have bad spells." He had walked off before Carole could say anything else.

Carole stabbed at the lock with her key and let herself into the house. Her father was still at work . . .

". . . SO THEN STEVIE decided we should all have a sleepover at the stable on Friday night," Carole explained to her father that evening as they stood together making dinner. "Stevie already checked with Max and he said he didn't mind. We'll bring our clothes for Horse Wise and for the bar mitzvah, and Stevie's parents will drop me off here afterward. Is that okay?" Carole glanced at her father, for once wishing he was less reasonable. But she knew what he was going to say before he said it.

"That sounds fine to me," Colonel Hanson said. "I'll probably be working late Friday night anyway."

Carole nodded, but her heart sank. There was no way she could explain to her father that she wasn't looking forward to this sleepover one bit. He wouldn't understand, any more than her friends would, that the last thing Carole felt like doing was spending more time at the stable. As much as she hated to admit it, her dreams had changed everything. That was why she hadn't mentioned them to her father, even though she could usually discuss anything with him.

As she and her father sat down to eat a few minutes later, Carole was still thinking about her latest nightmare. This one had begun with her and Starlight trotting down the trail toward the creek. Aside from the different setting, the rest of the dream had followed the pattern of the first one. Everything had seemed normal at first; then suddenly Starlight had changed, tossing her off his back and moving in for the attack.

The dream had stayed in Carole's mind all day, especially when she was with Starlight. The big gelding had seemed a little jittery in class, probably in response to Carole's own nervousness. But she couldn't help feeling that something wasn't quite right between them. Part of her knew that the feeling was caused by Troy's ghost story combined with her frightening dreams, not to mention a lack of sleep. But Carole had spent her whole life around stables, and she wasn't used to feeling uncomfortable around any horse, let alone her own beloved Starlight. Usually when it came to any sort of problem having to do with horses, Carole had a pretty good idea of how to fix it. But this time she couldn't think of a single way to make things better.

STEVIE SPENT THE evening thinking just as hard as Carole, but on a completely different subject: her plan to catch the Pine Hollow Pilferer. After the disappearance of Adam's pen, she was once more convinced that Shannon was the thief, and now she knew how she was going to prove it. Finding some of the equipment would be a bit of a challenge. Fortunately she already knew exactly where to get the main prop she would need. She was quiet during dinner, going over the details of her plan in her head to make sure everything would work.

After a while her brother Chad noticed Stevie's uncharacteristic silence.

"What's the matter, Stevie?" he asked. "Horse got your tongue?" He let out a poor but loud imitation of a neigh, bringing annoyed frowns from both his parents.

Stevie rolled her eyes. "That's so funny I forgot to laugh."

"I know what her problem is," volunteered Stevie's twin brother, Alex. "Phil's bar mitzvah is only a few days away. Stevie's probably wondering how many baths she'll have to take between now and then to get the smell of manure out of her hair."

Chad, Alex, and their youngest brother, Michael, burst into laughter.

"Boys—" Mrs. Lake began.

Stevie waved her hand. "Never mind, Mom," she interrupted. "Let them have their little jokes if they want. It doesn't bother me."

Mr. and Mrs. Lake exchanged surprised glances.

"That's very mature of you, Stevie," Mr. Lake commented.

Stevie just shrugged and lapsed into silence again. She had more important things to think about than her stupid brothers if she wanted to get Phil's yarmulke back for him.

It was Stevie's turn to clear the table, and after quickly stacking the dishes in a precarious pile, carrying them into the kitchen, and dumping them, unrinsed, into the dishwasher, she hurried upstairs to make a phone call.

"Phil?" she said when his familiar voice answered. "Listen. I wanted to tell you my latest brilliant plan."

"Hello to you, too, Stevie," Phil teased.

"Never mind all that," Stevie said impatiently. "This is important. I think I can get your yarmulke back in time for the bar mitzvah. I have a foolproof plan."

"Great," Phil said. "Speaking of the bar mitzvah, I've been meaning to ask you if your parents need directions to get to the synagogue."

81

"No, I'm sure they know where it is," Stevie said. "But listen, about this plan—"

"You know, I can't believe Saturday is almost here," Phil said dreamily. Stevie had the funniest feeling he wasn't listening to a word she was saying. "It seems like just yesterday I started planning for it."

Stevie rolled her eyes. What was Phil talking about? Saturday was still days away, and it seemed like even longer to her. She couldn't wait to put her plan into action. She just wished Phil seemed more interested in hearing about it. After all, it was mostly for his benefit. "Okay," she said. "But don't you want to hear about how I'm going to get your yarmulke back for you?"

"How about later, okay?" Phil said. "Actually, I've got to get off the phone. My aunt and uncle are flying in from Israel late tonight and I'm supposed to help get the guest room ready for them. But that reminds me. I was going to call you and see if you can come for dinner on Thursday and meet them."

Stevie brightened immediately. "Sounds great," she said. "I'm sure my parents will let me. I'll check with them and call you back tomorrow, okay?"

"Good," Phil said. "I think it will be fun. I'll talk to you tomorrow."

Stevie said good-bye and hung up the phone, feeling happier. She was certain Phil would be more eager to discuss her plan in person on Thursday. Maybe he wanted his whole family to hear how much she was helping him, and that was why he hadn't wanted to talk about it now. She stood up and headed downstairs to find her parents.

Her mother heard her and came to the kitchen doorway, hands on her hips. "Come here a minute, Stevie," she said. "I need to explain something to you." She led Stevie to the dishwasher, which was standing open just as Stevie had left it. Mrs. Lake pointed inside. "The concept of the dishwasher is not to wash the leftover food. It's to wash the dishes. Got it?"

"Got it," Stevie replied humbly. Without waiting for her mother's command, she began unloading the caked and coated dishes and taking them to the sink to rinse. As much as she hated this chore, she wasn't going to complain about it tonight. Between the dinner at Phil's on Thursday night and the stable sleepover on Friday, the last thing she wanted to risk right now was a grounding.

9

By Thursday afternoon Carole was so exhausted from lack of sleep that she felt as though she were sleepwalking through the day. Her father was still going into his office early every morning and returning late every evening, looking almost as tired as Carole felt. He hadn't noticed that anything was wrong, and she didn't want to bother him, even though she'd had the phantom horse dream every night. She felt like bursting into tears every time she so much as thought about Starlight, although she hadn't seen him at all on Wednesday because of an after-school meeting. That meant she hadn't seen her friends at all, either, so she still hadn't told them about her problem. But she had decided to talk to somebody about it. Stevie and Lisa hadn't paid much attention the last time she'd told them about her dreams, but this time she would make them understand how frightened and confused she was. Then they would be sure to come up with a way to help her. The Saddle Club had never let her down before.

When she arrived at Pine Hollow after school, Carole almost collided with Stevie, who was racing out of the locker room as Carole was walking in.

"Whoa!" Stevie exclaimed, pulling up short just in time. "Sorry about that. Good thing it was you coming in and not Max." All the riders knew that one of Max's strictest rules was no running in the stable.

"I'm glad you're here," Carole said. "Where's Lisa?"

"She's at a ballet lesson, I think," Stevie said. "Or is it a flute lesson? I can't remember." Lisa's mother wanted her daughter to be well-rounded, which meant she made her take all sorts of lessons and classes after school. Stevie glanced at her watch. "Uh-oh, I'd better get going if I don't want to be late. See you later."

"What? Wait," Carole said. "Where are you going? I was hoping I could talk to you about something . . ."

"Can it wait until tomorrow's sleepover?" Stevie asked, glancing at her watch again. "Tonight's my dinner, remember?"

"Dinner?" Carole repeated blankly.

Stevie looked slightly annoyed. "At Phil's house," she said. "I told you all about it on the phone Tuesday night."

85

"Oh, right," Carole said. She vaguely remembered the conversation. Stevie had made a three-way call to her and Lisa to tell them about the dinner invitation, but Carole had been too tired to pay much attention.

"Anyway, I really have to run now," Stevie said. "I still have to change before my mom drives me over, and I don't want to be late. I mean, how would it look if the guests who came all the way from Israel are there on time and the one who's just coming from ten miles down the road keeps everyone waiting?" Without waiting for a reply, she gave Carole a little wave and dashed away.

Carole sighed and walked to her cubby to get her riding boots. As she pulled them out, they dislodged a pair of sunglasses, which clattered to the floor. As Carole bent to pick them up, she recognized them as her father's favorite pair. She had borrowed them from him a couple of weeks before and must have forgotten to return them. Setting the sunglasses on the bench so that she'd remember to take them home, she began pulling on her boots, already dreading the afternoon ahead.

FEELING COWARDLY, CAROLE decided she would work Starlight on the longe line that day instead of riding him. She told herself he was overdue for a review session of longeing over cavalletti. Horses needed a lot of repetition of every lesson if they were to learn it well, and Starlight was still relatively young. But in her heart she knew that was only an excuse because she didn't want to ride him.

Still, she felt a little better about her decision when she realized it wouldn't do Starlight one bit of good to ride him when she was this upset. There was no sense communicating any more of her tension to her horse than was absolutely necessary.

But the plan didn't work out as well as Carole had hoped. Even though she wasn't on his back, Starlight obviously sensed that something was wrong, and it affected his performance. He seemed confused about the simplest commands, acted restless and skittish, and generally didn't perform at his usual calm, competent level. Carole knew it was her fault for working with him when she was so tired and upset, but Starlight's erratic behavior certainly wasn't helping her mood. She finally gave up and led him inside, glad that nobody had been around to see their embarrassing performance, except for Troy's old dog. Princess had been lounging near the stable entrance for the past half hour.

After Carole had untacked and groomed Starlight and left him resting comfortably in his stall, she wandered to the locker room to collect her things. She pulled her schoolbag out of her cubby and looked around for the sunglasses. But they weren't where she'd left them.

Frowning, she bent down to look under the bench. The sunglasses weren't there, either.

"It figures," she muttered to herself. "The way this week is going, I'm not surprised I can't even keep track of a pair of sunglasses." Still, she *knew* she'd left them on the bench. Was it possible that the Pine Hollow Pilferer had struck again? If so, it seemed Stevie's theory was wrong. Shannon Brice hadn't been anywhere near Pine Hollow that day. Carole made a mental note to mention the disappearing sunglasses to her friends the next time she spoke to them. She packed up the rest of her things and got ready to go.

As she walked past Mrs. Reg's open office door, Carole glanced inside and gave the woman a listless wave. Mrs. Reg looked up, frowned, then called her inside.

"Carole, you don't look well," she said without preamble. "What's the matter?"

Suddenly the long days and longer nights of the past week were too much for Carole. She couldn't hold back any longer. She collapsed into the creaky old guest chair in front of Mrs. Reg's desk and poured out the whole story.

Mrs. Reg listened silently. When Carole had finished, the older woman nodded slowly.

"That reminds me of a story," she said.

Carole got ready to listen. She knew that Mrs. Reg's stories often contained helpful advice, although it could sometimes be difficult to figure out exactly what it was. But she was desperate, and willing to take help wherever she could find it.

"It has to do with a young fellow who used to ride here

many years ago," Mrs. Reg began, folding her hands on the desk in front of her. "He was a fine rider, but very, very superstitious."

Carole smiled a little at that. She knew that most horse people tended to seem a little superstitious to non-horse people. The lucky horseshoe was just one example of the many old stable superstitions at Pine Hollow.

Mrs. Reg noticed the smile and chuckled. "There are superstitions and there are superstitions," she said. "Some are harmless, funny, helpful, or lovely. But others can be stupid, troublesome, or even dangerous. This young man definitely had one of the latter kind."

"You mean dangerous?" Carole asked.

"No," Mrs. Reg replied. "I mean stupid. You see, he refused—absolutely refused—to ride any horse that had even a speck of black on it."

Carole laughed. "But that's so silly!" she exclaimed.

Mrs. Reg ignored the comment. Carole remembered that Mrs. Reg disliked interruptions and did her best to keep quiet.

"As you can imagine," Mrs. Reg went on, "the young man's choices were pretty limited when it came to which horses he could ride. Obviously he couldn't ride black horses or bays, since their points, manes, and tails are black. And most of the chestnuts we had at the time had at least a few black hairs on their muzzles or somewhere else on them. So all this fellow was left with were a chestnut roan gelding that was almost twenty years old and a brown-and-white Appaloosa mare that was so passive and gentle, we normally used her only for the very youngest and least experienced riders.

"Obviously Max did his best to talk some sense into this young man," Mrs. Reg said. "That's my Max, not your Max." Carole knew that Mrs. Reg was referring to her late husband, the current Max's father. "He tried everything he knew to convince him that the problem was in his mind rather than with the horses, but the young man refused to hear reason. As far as he was concerned, what he thought was what he thought, and that was that. He had no interest in facing up to it. All he was willing to do was work around it."

Mrs. Reg stopped talking, and Carole leaned forward in her chair. "What happened? Did the rider ever come around?"

Mrs. Reg shook her head and stood up. "Nope," she said. "And eventually the gelding died and we sold the mare, so the young fellow stopped riding at all. As far as I know, he never did get over that odd superstition of his." Mrs. Reg sat back and sighed, and Carole knew the story was over. Feeling more confused than ever, she got up and said good-bye to Mrs. Reg, then left the office.

As she walked slowly toward her bus stop at the shopping center near the stable, Carole thought about Mrs. Reg's story. Was she implying that Carole's fears were all in her mind? If so, maybe it was just as well that Carole hadn't had a chance to tell her friends or her father about the dreams. There was nothing they could do if the problem was all in her head. By the time she reached the bus stop and collapsed on the bench to wait, she had decided that the best thing to do was to ignore the nightmares and hope they went away.

STEVIE SIGHED IRRITABLY and fiddled with her fork. She was sitting at the Marstens' dinner table, wearing her best corduroy pants and a soft blue silk shirt she'd borrowed from her mother. The horseshoe pendant Phil had given her at Christmas was around her neck. The food was wonderful, and Phil's aunt and uncle were friendly and charming. But so far the dinner was not going the way Stevie had hoped. All anyone could talk about was Phil's bar mitzvah. And nobody, least of all Phil himself, had shown the slightest interest in hearing about Stevie's detective work. Every time she tried to bring up the missing yarmulke, somebody changed the subject back to Saturday's event.

At the moment Phil's uncle Paul, a large, jolly man with curly black hair, was telling a funny story about his own bar mitzvah. It had something to do with a snowstorm and an escaped cow, but Stevie wasn't really listening.

". . . and the first thing I mentioned in my *Dvar Torah* speech was the cow," Uncle Paul finished with a broad smile.

Stevie smiled weakly as all the Marstens roared with laughter. She had no idea what a *Dvar Torah* speech was, and at this point she didn't really care. Phil's ten-year-old sister, Rachel, poked Stevie in the ribs. "That sounds like something that would happen to you!" She turned to her aunt and uncle. "Stevie's always getting into all kinds of trouble," she announced. "And usually she ends up getting all her friends in trouble, too, including Phil."

"That's not true," Phil protested, with a grin that gave him away. "Stevie never finds trouble. It finds her!"

Aunt Karen smiled at Stevie, then turned to her nephew. "Well, you'd better watch out that she doesn't drag you into *too* much trouble from now on," she said teasingly. "After your bar mitzvah you can be held accountable, you know."

Phil laughed, then turned to Stevie to explain. "That's part of what a bar mitzvah is," he said. "Once you're a full member of your community, you're responsible for your actions."

Phil's mother nodded. "That's right. It's Jewish law. If a child does something wrong, large or small, the parents are responsible. But once that child becomes an adult"—she paused to smile at her son—"then that person is responsible for himself."

"Or herself," Rachel piped up, and Mrs. Marsten nodded.

"Uh-oh," Stevie said. "You'd better not tell my parents about that. Otherwise, the next thing I know, I'll be having a bar mitzvah of my own!"

Everyone laughed. Then Phil's older sister, Barbara, spoke up. "Actually, for girls the ceremony is called a bat mitzvah," she told Stevie. "It's a newer tradition than the bar mitzvah—it's been around for less than a hundred years. But I'm glad we have it now." She smiled at her family. "My bat mitzvah was one of the best days of my life. I really never expected it to be so special, but it was. I'd never paid much attention to being Jewish before. But once I had to sit down and really think about it, I realized how important it is to feel like a member of a community. I hope Phil's experience is as wonderful as mine."

Stevie raised an eyebrow in amazement, wondering if there was something wrong with her hearing. Usually Phil and his sisters fought and argued and teased each other like—well, like Stevie and her brothers. Now Phil and Barbara were smiling at each other like best friends. What was going on?

But Mr. Marsten didn't seem surprised at all. "Well said, Barbara," he told his daughter. He took his wife's hand and held it tightly as he spoke. "That sentiment holds true whether that community is the Jewish community, or your country, or your hometown, or even your own family."

"Especially your own family," Mrs. Marsten added, looking at her husband lovingly.

That made sense to Stevie. It even helped to explain why Phil and his sisters weren't fighting tonight. She smiled, thinking of her own family, then of The Saddle Club. Both were definitely communities she was glad to be a part of, brothers or no brothers.

"I can't wait for my bat mitzvah," said Phil's sister Lauren, who was seven years old. "I can already speak some Hebrew."

Aunt Karen reached for a second helping of potatoes. "Good for you," she said. "Speaking Hebrew is important. It's our ancient language, and it unites Jewish people everywhere. And Paul and I were certainly glad we already spoke it when we decided to move to Israel. But there's more to becoming a bat or bar mitzvah than speaking Hebrew, right, Phil?"

"That's for sure," Phil said sincerely.

For the first time, Stevie thought she was beginning to understand what he meant. Phil's bar mitzvah wouldn't be just another birthday party. It was a special event, a life-changing event, like a wedding or a college graduation. And just as on those days, the gifts and party and all the other trappings weren't the point. The point was the celebration itself—in this case, the celebration of the beginning of adulthood. That was why Phil wasn't more upset about his missing yarmulke. It was beautiful and special, but he could use another one for his bar mitzvah. That couldn't change what was special about the day.

Stevie was also beginning to feel a little guilty about her earlier impatience. Now that she had figured out why everyone was so excited, all she wanted was to be a part of it all. But she still wanted to get Phil's yarmulke back. In fact, she was more determined than ever. She didn't want anything as stupid as a petty theft to cast even the slightest dark spot on Phil's big day.

THE NEXT DAY after school The Saddle Club met at the Willow Creek Mall to shop for a bar mitzvah gift for Phil. Their parents had already dropped off sleeping bags, sandwiches, and everything else they would need for their sleepover at Pine Hollow, and Mrs. Atwood was going to pick the girls up from the mall and drive them to the stable.

"I want to make sure we get something really special," Stevie told Lisa and Carole as they strolled down the long mall corridor, glancing in store windows. She had already told her friends about the dinner and what she'd learned.

"Do you have any ideas for the gift?" Lisa asked. The Saddle Club had decided to pool their money instead of buying separate presents.

Stevie shrugged. "Not a single one," she admitted. "I was hoping you guys would have something brilliant in mind."

"Not me," Lisa said. "What about you, Carole?"

"Hmmm?" When Carole looked up, her friends could tell she hadn't been listening. For the first time, they also noticed that she looked tired.

"Are you okay, Carole?" Lisa asked, concerned. "You don't look too good. Are you sick or something?"

"No," Carole said. "I'm just a little tired, that's all. I haven't been sleeping too well because, um, my shoulder has been bothering me. I think I bruised it the other day when I fell off Starlight."

"Have you been to the doctor?" Stevie asked. "If it's still bothering you after five days, maybe you sprained it."

Lisa nodded. "Especially if it hurts so much you can't sleep."

"No, no," Carole said quickly. The last thing she wanted was to get involved in a conversation about her sleeping habits. She wasn't used to keeping things from her friends, but she was determined to follow her vow of the day before and ignore her dreams. The problem was, her sleeping self hadn't gotten the message. She had had another terrible nightmare the night before. "It'll be all right. Really. Now what about this gift for Phil? We'd better start looking if we want to find something before Lisa's mom comes to get us."

The others glanced at their watches and agreed. But as they continued through the mall, chatting lightly about possible gifts for Phil, Lisa couldn't help sneaking a glance at Carole, wondering about what she'd said. Was Carole hiding something? It wasn't like her to keep her problems hidden from her friends. After all, that was what The Saddle Club was all about—helping one another. And all of them had learned long ago that that was one of the best things about having friends.

As the girls entered a candy store called Sweet Nothings, Lisa glanced at Carole again and caught Stevie doing the same thing. Stevie met her gaze and shrugged. Obviously she, too, had noticed that something wasn't right. But what could they do if Carole didn't want to talk about it?

"IT's PERFECT," STEVIE declared. "Phil will love it."

"Definitely," Lisa agreed. The Saddle Club was watching as a sales clerk wrapped their purchase. They had spent a lot of time debating the best kind of gift to buy. At first Stevie had been determined to find something with a Jewish theme, since the gift was for a bar mitzvah. Lisa had been inclined to look in boutiques for a nice paperweight or other traditional gift item. And Carole, of course, had wanted to head straight to the tack shop for a piece of riding equipment.

In the end they had compromised. As they were leaving a fancy decorating store, Lisa's sharp eyes had fallen on the perfect item. It was a silver picture frame with a running horse etched on the top. Best of all, it was within their price range. Lisa and Carole had both been thrilled. Stevie had been unconvinced at first. But then Lisa had pointed out that Phil could put his favorite picture from the bar mitzvah in the frame and treasure it for years to come. That was all Stevie had needed to hear.

"What a relief," Lisa said as Stevie took the bag the clerk handed her and the three girls left the store. "I can't believe we finally found something."

"And it's perfect," Stevie said. She glanced at her watch. "We have a few minutes before our ride gets here. How about a snack?"

The others agreed immediately. Within minutes they were seated in a booth at their favorite Italian restaurant, hot slices of gooey pizza in their hands.

Stevie wiped tomato sauce off her chin. "Now that the mystery of what to get Phil is solved, let's get back to our other mystery," she said. "Do you think my plan to catch Shannon will work?"

Lisa sighed. "If it doesn't, there's no way we'll get Phil's yarmulke back before the ceremony."

"I know. That's why it has to work," Stevie said.

Suddenly Carole looked up, her eyes wide. "Oh!" she said. "I forgot to tell you something."

Immediately Stevie and Lisa were all ears, wondering if Carole was going to tell them what was really wrong.

But that wasn't what Carole had in mind. "Something else disappeared yesterday while I was at Pine Hollow," she said. "My dad's favorite sunglasses. I left them on the bench in the locker room while I was, um, riding, and when I came back they were nowhere to be found."

Stevie frowned. "Yesterday, huh? Did you happen to see Shannon anywhere around?"

Carole shook her head. "She wasn't there. Neither was Joe," she said. "I'm sure of that, because I saw Rusty out in the paddock when I got there." All the girls knew that that meant Rusty probably hadn't been ridden that day. And that meant Joe hadn't been at Pine Hollow.

"What are you going to do?" Lisa asked Stevie. "There doesn't seem to be much point in going ahead with your plan now. Maybe we should just forget about it."

"No way," Stevie said, looking determined. "We've got to try it. Maybe someone borrowed the sunglasses and forgot to return them. Besides, even if Shannon didn't do it—and I still think she did—Troy or Veronica or someone else could just as easily fall into my trap. We'll catch the thief, whoever it is."

"Not Veronica," Lisa said. "She's not going to be around tomorrow, remember? She's on vacation with her parents. They left on Tuesday night right after our riding lesson. She couldn't stop bragging about their special overnight flight."

"I forgot about that," Stevie admitted. "I did my best to tune her out because I wanted to concentrate on Shannon." She shrugged. "I guess that means she couldn't have taken the sunglasses, either. So that leaves us just two suspects."

100

"Actually, it only leaves one suspect," Lisa pointed out logically. "We just decided Shannon couldn't have taken the sunglasses, either."

"*If* the sunglasses were taken by the same person who took the other stuff," Stevie said stubbornly. Then she relented. "But anyway, all we really need is one good suspect, and we have one: Troy."

THAT NIGHT IN the hayloft Carole stayed awake longer than either of her friends, listening to the soothing night sounds of the sleeping stable below. But when she finally fell asleep the dream she'd been dreading came almost immediately.

This time she found herself riding Starlight across a blazing-hot desert. She thought she recognized the landscape from several trips she and her friends had taken to a dude ranch out West, although this time she was riding alone. Sweat dripped down her forehead as she searched the horizon for some sign of life. But there wasn't a single living creature in view except her and her horse. As soon as she realized that, she started to get nervous. And as if on cue, Starlight suddenly stopped short and started to paw the ground, snorting fiercely. Carole clung to the pommel of the heavy Western saddle. With a wild scream that tore the still air, Starlight reared, again and again, until finally he toppled over backward. Carole, who had managed to keep her seat, closed her eyes and prepared to feel the huge weight of the horse crush the life out of her . . .

But instead she opened her eyes to the moonlit darkness of Pine Hollow's hayloft. Her heart still pounding with the memory of the dream, she sat up and glanced at her sleeping friends. This was getting ridiculous. Was she ever going to be able to sleep again, or was this dream going to haunt her forever?

Carole decided there was only one thing to do. She had to go and see Starlight. Maybe avoiding him as she'd been doing was the wrong thing to do. If she could convince herself that he was just a normal horse, not a red-eyed phantom, maybe the dreams would stop on their own.

Once her eyes had adjusted to the dark, she carefully peeled back her sleeping bag and stood up. Stevie moaned and rolled over, and Carole froze. But after a moment Stevie's breathing was once again deep and even. Carole silently let out a breath of relief and tiptoed toward the ladder.

Once down among the horses, Carole paused to listen. All around her were the familiar sounds and smells of horses at rest. Usually Carole found the stable at night a comforting and safe place. But tonight every corner seemed filled by dark shadows, and the black, square opening of every stall seemed ominous and forbidding. Taking a deep breath, Carole turned and entered the long corridor leading to Starlight's stall. Max had installed small night-lights every few yards throughout the stable as a safety precaution, and now

Carole found their light, dim though it was, reassuring. As she glanced forward, she saw that the light across from Starlight's stall was off. *The bulb must have burned out,* she thought. But her heart was beginning to pound. She walked forward and looked into Starlight's stall. It was empty. Suddenly twin flashes of red light pierced the darkness at the end of the aisle. With a wild neigh, Starlight plunged forward toward her, his hooves flashing and a look of evil in his red, red eyes . . .

Carole awoke with a start to see Stevie's anxious face peering down into her own.

"Carole! What is it?" Stevie exclaimed.

"Wh-What?" Carole murmured, trying to clear her head. Where was she? She knew she'd been asleep, but instead of feeling her warm, soft bed under her, she felt scratchy hay . . .

The hayloft. She and her friends were having a sleepover, and she'd had the nightmare again. Two of them, in fact.

"Are you all right?" Suddenly Lisa's face came into view beside Stevie's. "Your screaming woke us up. Were you having a bad dream?"

Carole sat up and looked around, reassuring herself that she was really awake this time. She could hear the gentle creaking of the floorboards below as horses shifted their weight, and the pungent scent of hay filled her nostrils. She knew it was no use hiding the truth from her friends anymore. Taking a deep breath, she started to tell them all about the nightmares.

When she was finished, Lisa put an arm around her shoulders. "I'm sorry I didn't listen when you told us about that first one," she said. "I didn't realize how scared you really were. I guess I was kind of insensitive."

"That goes double for me," Stevie added, joining in the hug. "I was so busy thinking about the mystery that I guess I didn't really pay much attention to what you were saying."

"Can you forgive us?" Lisa asked.

Carole nodded and hugged them back. "Of course," she said. "It's not totally your fault, anyway. After that first day I wasn't sure whether I really wanted to talk about the dreams. I thought I was being silly."

"Don't be silly," said Stevie, and that made them all laugh.

As the moon rose and flooded the hayloft with silvery light, the girls talked about the nightmares a little more. Stevie and Lisa racked their brains, but they had no more idea than Carole did about how to stop them. But at least Carole felt better for having shared the problem with her friends.

Finally Carole started to yawn. "Believe it or not, I think I want to go to sleep now," she said, stretching and then snuggling down into her sleeping bag. She closed her eyes and smiled as she heard one of the horses just below nickering to its neighbors. She wasn't sure, but she thought it might be Barq. "I hope I don't wake you up again. But for once I think I'm actually too tired to dream."

And she was right.

THE NEXT DAY the girls were up early. There was a lot to do before Horse Wise, even without Stevie's pilferer-catching plan to worry about.

Carole felt more cheerful than she had in a week as she walked toward Starlight's stall to check on him. She knew her almost full night's sleep probably had a lot to do with it, but she was sure that talking to her friends had helped, too. If The Saddle Club couldn't come up with a way to get rid of the nightmares, no one could.

But as soon as Carole saw her horse, most of her nervousness came rushing back. When he tossed his head in greeting, all she could see was the vision of him tossing his head in fury just before he came at her in the dream. That eager, happy feeling she had always had around horses, especially around Starlight, and which she had always taken for granted, was gone. Would she ever get it back?

As they worked, The Saddle Club girls were distracted. All three were worried about Carole's dreams and looking forward to Phil's bar mitzvah. Besides that, Stevie had laid her trap and was doing her best to lure someone into it. Every chance she got, she told anyone who would listen about the fabulously rare ancient coin from Israel that she was giving Phil as a bar mitzvah present. She was careful to mention every time that the coin was in her cubby, tucked under her spare boots for safekeeping. She told Max about it. She told Adam Levine about it. She told Alec McAllister, the farrier, about it. She told Shannon and Joe about it twice. And every time Troy was within earshot, she made sure to mention it to whoever happened to be standing by—even if it was only Lisa.

Somehow all the chores got done, and soon it was time for the Horse Wise meeting to begin. Alec McAllister showed them how to use a gauge to test the levelness of the walls of a horse's hoof. As he demonstrated, using the calm, easygoing stable horse Patch as a model, Stevie's attention wandered. So did her gaze. She couldn't help sneaking a look at Shannon every chance she got. But the only remotely unusual thing she caught the other girl doing was holding hands with Joe.

When the lecture was over and Max had dismissed the group, The Saddle Club hurried to the locker room. Mr. and Mrs. Lake were picking them up for the bar mitzvah in an hour, and they wanted to be ready on time.

The first thing Stevie did was check under her spare boots. The coin was still there. "Rats," she muttered.

Lisa shrugged. "Tough luck," she said, looking almost as disappointed as Stevie. She had noticed that Troy wasn't with the group at the end of the farrier's lecture, and she had begun to think he might have actually fallen for Stevie's trap. "Maybe Veronica was the thief after all."

Stevie picked up the coin very carefully between her thumb and forefinger, carried it over to the trash can near the door, and let it fall with a thunk. Then she held up her fingers, which were stained bright red at the tips. "I guess the only one who's red-handed around here is me," she said glumly.

"Too bad. It was a good idea," Carole said. "If anyone had snitched the coin, it would have been easy to spot them with that dye on their hands. Where did you get that fake coin, anyway?"

"My brother's history project," Stevie said. "Chad made it out of clay when he was studying ancient Rome last year. But the red dye was my special addition, of course."

"Of course," Lisa said. She sighed. "I wonder if we'll ever find out who—"

Her words were interrupted by an outraged shout. The Saddle Club turned and saw one of the younger riders, May Grover, standing beside her friend Jasmine James. Jasmine looked worried, and May looked mad.

"What's the matter?" Lisa asked, hurrying over to them.

"Someone stole Jasmine's favorite barrette," May announced loudly. "It's real silver, and it has horses on it. She got it for her birthday, and now it's gone!"

"Are you sure it's really gone?" Lisa asked.

Jasmine nodded, looking close to tears.

May stamped her foot. "Who would dare take someone's special barrette?" she demanded. "I don't think anyone should leave here until she gets it back."

Max heard the commotion and hurried in. "What seems to be the problem here?" Lisa drifted back to rejoin her friends as Max began questioning Jasmine and May.

"Weird, huh?" Lisa said quietly.

Stevie didn't answer. She watched the scene, feeling confused and annoyed. The pilferer had struck again, but not where Stevie had been expecting. Now what was she supposed to do?

Just then she heard a noise behind her. She turned and saw Troy. He had paused in the doorway of the locker room, a curious expression on his face.

"What's going on in there?" he asked Stevie.

"Jasmine's barrette is missing," Stevie replied. As she looked at the young groom, a flash of gold from the direction of his chest caught her eye, and she bit her lip to keep from gasping. Was that a fountain pen sticking out of his shirt pocket? A *gold* fountain pen—just like the one Adam had lost?

"A missing barrette?" Troy drawled. "Better call in the National Guard." With a short, abrupt laugh, he continued down the corridor.

The second he was out of sight, Stevie grabbed a startled Carole by the arm. "Did you see that?" she whispered.

"See what?" Carole asked.

108

"What was in Troy's pocket," Stevie replied. "It looked like Adam's pen! At least it was a pen and it was gold. I mean, I didn't actually see Adam's pen before it was stolen—"

"Did you see the top of it?" Lisa asked urgently.

Stevie nodded. "It had some kind of silver band around it."

"That's Adam's pen," Lisa said grimly. "I saw it after they gave it to him in school. I knew Troy was the pilferer!"

"But what do we do now?" Carole asked. "We can't just go up to him and accuse him of being a thief, can we?"

"Not unless we have to," Stevie said. "Come on. Let's follow him. Maybe we can catch him with some of the other stuff."

"Shouldn't we just tell Max what we saw?" Lisa asked, glancing over her shoulder at the stable owner.

"Not yet," Stevie said. Before Lisa or Carole could protest any further, she turned and raced out of the room. With a shrug, they followed.

As they left the locker room, the girls were just in time to see Troy stroll around the corner into one of the aisles of stalls.

Stevie held a finger to her lips as they neared the corner. "Shhh," she cautioned, turning to give her friends a warning look. "We don't want him to know we're— Oh!" she gasped as she rounded the corner and bumped into someone.

It was Troy. "What's going on?" he asked them, rubbing

his shoulder where Stevie had hit him. "Don't you girls watch where you're going?"

"Oh, sorry," Stevie said. "Um, I guess we, um, ah— Say! Nice pen!"

Lisa did her best not to groan, and she suspected Carole was doing the same. If there was one quality that didn't come easily to their friend Stevie, it was subtlety.

Troy looked confused for a second, then glanced down at his shirt pocket. "Oh. You mean this?" he asked, fingering the pen.

Stevie nodded. "Where'd you get it?" she asked, with an expression of what she hoped was complete innocence. "Oh, if you don't mind my asking, that is. You see, my father's birthday is coming up, and I'd love to get him something like that as a present, and—"

"I found it," Troy interrupted her.

"Wow, really?" Stevie said. "Where did you find it? Was it in the student locker room?"

Troy stared at her suspiciously. There was a long moment of silence, during which both Carole and Lisa wished they could sink into the floor and disappear. They had the feeling Troy knew exactly what Stevie was driving at. But was that because Stevie wasn't as subtle as she thought, or was it because Troy had a guilty conscience?

"I was just wondering," Stevie said, beginning to babble a bit. "Because one of the students here lost a pen that looked a lot like that one, and I was just wondering if maybe it fell on the floor and then you found it, and if so if maybe you noticed a few other things that are missing, or . . ." Her voice trailed off. Troy's suspicious expression had just turned to one of dismay. Stevie held her breath. Maybe her questioning had worked. Maybe Troy was about to confess!

But instead of confessing, Troy just shouted one word: "*Princess!*"

THE SADDLE CLUB exchanged confused glances. "Princess?" they repeated in one voice.

Troy was shaking his head grimly. "That darn dog," he muttered. He glanced at the girls. "Come on," he said, his voice completely neutral. "If you want to get your missing stuff back, I have a pretty good idea where it might be."

The girls followed as the groom headed outside. He led them to a row of bushes near the main stable entrance and knelt down. Plunging his hand into the foliage, Troy fished around for a moment and then dragged a sleepy, startled-looking Princess from under the largest bush.

"Now let's see what we find," he said. Reaching under the bush again, Troy began pulling things out and dumping them at the girls' feet. "Here's an old sock . . . and a curry-comb . . . and a silver barrette . . . and a riding crop . . . and a pair of sunglasses . . . and a gold brace-let . . . and a book . . . and a little hat—"

"Phil's yarmulke!" Stevie cried, pouncing on it. She brushed it off, happy to see that it seemed completely un-damaged.

"Thank goodness," Lisa said. "He'll be so happy to get it back."

Stevie nodded. "And just in the nick of time, too."

"Last and least, here's what looks like a glove," Troy said, dropping one more item on the pile before standing up. "Looks like that was Princess's favorite—it's a little chewed."

That was an understatement. Most of the other items seemed undamaged, but Veronica's elegant leather glove was hardly recognizable anymore. The Saddle Club grinned, try-ing not to giggle.

The girls stopped smiling when they turned and looked at Troy, who was scolding Princess gently. It was just dawning on them that they hadn't exactly been fair to the young groom.

Lisa spoke for all of them. "Thanks for helping us find this stuff, Troy," she said. "Um, we couldn't figure out where it was all disappearing to. It was starting to seem like we had a thief right here at Pine Hollow."

"And you thought it just might be me," Troy said, not

looking at any of the girls. He was stroking Princess's ears.

"Of course we didn't," Stevie protested. The words rang false even to her own ears.

"Don't worry about it," Troy replied with a shrug. "It's not the first time. Old Princess here is a born kleptomaniac. Or maybe *pack rat* is a better term. Every once in a while she decides she's in a collecting mood, and she starts picking up anything and everything she notices lying around and taking it home with her. You can imagine how many times that little habit has gotten both of us in hot water."

The girls could imagine it very well. If things started disappearing when Troy was around, they guessed that they wouldn't be the only ones who might jump to conclusions because of the strange way he sometimes acted.

"We're really sorry, Troy," Carole said sincerely. "I hope there are no hard feelings or anything."

"Don't worry about it," Troy said again. "You girls aren't the first to think the worst of me. A lot of people around here don't like the way I look, my clothes or the way I wear my hair. I'm used to it by now. And it doesn't bother me. I know who I am." He gave Princess one last pat and stood up. "Now if you'll excuse me, I have some horses to look after. Oh, but first, why don't you take this, too." He pulled Adam's pen out of his pocket and handed it to Lisa. "I was going to take it to Mrs. Reg's office so she could try to find the owner. But if you know whose it is you can just go ahead and return it." He frowned at his dog. "Come on, girl. You'd better stick with me. You've caused enough trouble for to-day." He whistled to Princess, who fell in at his heels. Man and dog walked off into the stable building without a backward glance at the girls.

Carole looked from the pile of things on the ground to her friends. "I guess we messed up this time, huh?" she said softly.

Lisa nodded, looking guilty. "Big-time."

"This must be what my parents mean about not judging by appearances," Stevie said. She sighed. "So the Pine Hollow Pilferer turned out to be a dog. At least we got everyone's stuff back." She knelt and started to gather the things.

"I wonder if there's anything we can do to make it up to Troy," Carole said, bending down to help.

Lisa thought about that for a moment. "It doesn't seem like it," she replied at last. "What's done is done. We can't take back our suspicions. But we can promise ourselves we won't be so quick to jump to conclusions next time. Or to assume someone's guilty until proven innocent rather than the other way around."

Stevie and Carole nodded. Then Stevie glanced at her watch. "Oops!" she said. "We'd better get inside and get changed. My parents will be here to pick us up in forty-five minutes. First dibs on the shower!"

* * *

EXACTLY FORTY-FIVE MINUTES later the three members of The Saddle Club were dressed in their best clothes and climbing into the Lakes' station wagon. During the short ride to the synagogue, the girls told Stevie's parents about unmasking the Pine Hollow Pilferer.

At the synagogue, all anyone could talk about was the bar mitzvah. There were lots of cars in the parking lot, and groups of people were milling around outside the building, which was long and low and made of whitewashed brick.

"It doesn't look the way I expected," Carole commented. "I guess I thought it would look more like a church."

Lisa nodded. "Me too. But Phil told me there aren't any rules at all about what Jewish synagogues should look like, the way there are about churches and mosques and things in other religions."

Stevie straightened the hem of her skirt as her father pulled the station wagon into one of the few remaining parking places. Suddenly she felt nervous. She was sure that part of the feeling was sympathetic nervousness on Phil's behalf. He had been preparing for this day for a long time, and he wanted to do well and make his family proud. But Stevie thought part of the nervousness might also be for herself. Now that Phil was about to become an adult, would he still feel the same way about things like horses, friends, fun—and her?

The Saddle Club and Stevie's parents headed inside,

pausing occasionally to greet someone they knew. As they reached the wide double doors, Stevie was surprised by one familiar face in particular.

"Isn't that Shannon Brice over there?" she whispered to her friends.

"It is," Lisa confirmed. "I wonder what she's doing here?"

"Let's go find out," Stevie said. Promising her parents that the girls would meet them inside, she led Carole and Lisa over to where Shannon was standing. Mr. and Mrs. Brice, whom Stevie recognized from school events, were nearby.

Shannon looked surprised to see them at first. But then her face relaxed into a smile. "Oh, you're here to see Phil, right?"

"That's right," Stevie said. "Do you know Phil?"

"Sure," Shannon replied. "We're in the same Hebrew class. And our families have both gone to this synagogue for ages."

Stevie was surprised. She hadn't even known that Shannon was Jewish, let alone that she and Phil knew each other. Just then she noticed that Shannon was wearing the gold bangle bracelet she had thought was Betsy's. This time it was Stevie's face that turned red.

Carole noticed her friend's discomfort and came to the rescue. "Maybe you could fill us in on what to do, Shannon," she suggested. "None of us has ever been to a Jewish synagogue before, let alone to a bar mitzvah."

"Okay," Shannon agreed. She glanced at the three girls

shyly, beginning to blush a little. "If you want, maybe we could even sit together."

"That would be great," Lisa said. She looked at Stevie. "I'm sure your parents won't mind, right?"

Stevie nodded. She scanned the people around them. "By the way, do you know if Phil is already inside?" she asked Shannon. "I have something I was hoping to give him before the ceremony."

"I saw him go in a while ago," Shannon said.

Stevie frowned, disappointed. The recovered yarmulke was tucked carefully inside her purse. But now it seemed she'd been too late in getting it back after all.

Shannon noticed her expression. "Don't worry," she said with a shrug. "You can give it to him inside."

"Is that allowed?" Carole asked, surprised.

"Sure. Come on," Shannon said. She led them through the doors and into the main part of the synagogue. The walls were hung with velvet curtains embroidered with silver thread. Dark wood shone everywhere, reflecting the sheen of polished brass and silver. The girls thought it looked as beautiful as the inside of a church, but in a slightly different way.

One way that it was different was the noise and activity. Instead of the hushed whispers of a church, the large room rang with happy voices and laughter. Many people were already seated, but others were moving around, greeting friends and relatives.

"There are the Marstens," Shannon said, pointing toward the front of the room.

Stevie looked and saw Phil, looking even more handsome than usual in his dark suit. She noticed that he was wearing a plain black yarmulke. She also noticed that Mr. Marsten was wearing one as well.

"Why is Phil's dad wearing a yarmulke?" she asked Shannon as the girls headed up the aisle toward the Marstens' seats. "He's not Jewish."

"It's a sign of respect for all the men to wear one inside the synagogue, whether they're Jewish or not," Shannon told them. "They hand them out at the door to anybody who doesn't have his own."

Phil and his family looked up and smiled when they saw the girls.

"You girls all look wonderful," Phil's mother said. "I'm so glad you could come. Shannon, please tell your mother I said hello."

"I'm glad you guys made it, too," Phil added. "But really, Stevie, couldn't you even manage to change out of your riding boots for the occasion?"

Stevie glanced down at her feet, panicked. In all the excitement of solving the mystery, had she actually forgotten . . . ? But when she saw her clean blue shoes, her look of panic turned to a look of relief.

"Gotcha," Phil said, with a grin and a wink. Everyone laughed, even Stevie.

Suddenly Stevie remembered what was in her purse. She pulled out the yarmulke and handed it to Phil.

His eyes widened in surprise. "How did you get it back?" Without waiting for an answer, he turned to his aunt and uncle, who were sitting farther down the same row. "Hey, look at this!" he exclaimed. Within moments he had replaced the plain black skullcap with the beautifully embroidered one.

"That looks much better," Stevie told him with satisfaction. "Just wait until you hear about how we got it back!"

"If I know The Saddle Club, I bet it's an amazing story," Phil said as a group of people came toward him, smiles on their faces. "I can't wait to hear all about it later."

Stevie took the hint. "I guess we'd better go sit down now," she said, stepping aside so that the newcomers could congratulate Phil.

"Are you going to sit with Shannon?" Phil's sister Barbara asked Stevie. "She's having her own bat mitzvah in a few months, so she can fill you in on anything you don't understand."

"We are," Carole said. "See you later." The girls waved to Barbara and the rest of the Marstens as they left in search of seats.

As the four girls headed back up the aisle, Lisa spotted a red-haired boy waving frantically at them from the other side of the room. "Look, it's A.J.," she told her friends.

120

"Let's go sit with him," Stevie said eagerly. The girls hurried over. On the way they passed both Stevie's parents and Shannon's and told them where they would be sitting. After The Saddle Club enthusiastically greeted Phil's friend, Stevie introduced Shannon. "She's going to tell us what's going on," she told A.J.

"Thank goodness," A.J. said, straightening his yarmulke, which kept threatening to slide off the back of his head. "As many times as Phil tries to tell me, I still can't tell a Torah from a haftarah." As he reached to shake Shannon's hand, her bracelet slid out from beneath her sleeve. "Hey, nice bracelet," A.J. commented politely. Unlike most boys, A.J. actually noticed what people wore.

"Thanks," Shannon said, blushing. "Um, my boyfriend gave it to me."

Stevie, Lisa, and Carole exchanged quick glances. They had the funniest feeling they had just figured out why Shannon was so mysterious about the bracelet. She was so shy that she probably didn't want anyone from Pine Hollow to know it had been a gift from Joe.

Having had one of her questions about Shannon answered, Stevie couldn't resist trying to find out the answer to the other. "So Shannon," she said, trying to sound casual, "I noticed you've missed a lot of school lately. Have you been sick?"

"No," Shannon said. She seemed to be getting a little less

nervous about talking to The Saddle Club. "I haven't really missed that much time. Just a few days for Rosh Hashanah and Yom Kippur in September, and then a week when my family took a trip to Israel last month. The trip was sort of an early bat mitzvah gift for me, since I'd never been there."

"Oh," Stevie said. She knew that Rosh Hashanah and Yom Kippur were important Jewish holidays. Phil always missed school for them, too. Now that she knew the reasons behind what she had thought was Shannon's suspicious behavior, Stevie felt a little bad about suspecting her of being a thief. But she didn't have much time to think about it, because the service was starting.

Shannon explained everything that was going on, whispering in Stevie's ear so that she could pass it down to the others. First the cantor stepped forward to lead the opening prayers. As the service continued, The Saddle Club rose, sat, and bowed according to Shannon's instructions.

Stevie kept an eye on Phil, who was still sitting between his parents. "When does his part start?" she whispered to Shannon.

"Soon," Shannon whispered back. "It's time for the beginning of the Torah service now."

The girls watched as the people at the front of the room pushed back a curtain that hid a large wooden cabinet. Opening the cabinet, they bent and took out a large scroll.

"That's the Torah scroll," Shannon whispered as the congregation began to sing. "Now they'll carry it around the room so that everyone can have the chance to kiss or touch it."

After making the rounds, the people carrying the Torah returned it to the front of the room, setting it on what Shannon told The Saddle Club was the reader's desk. She explained that the readers would chant the words of the Torah, using traditional melodies.

The first reader was called. It was Phil's uncle Paul. He read from the scroll in Hebrew, singing the words in his loud, booming voice.

"I have no idea what he's saying, but it sounds good, doesn't it?" Lisa whispered to Carole.

Carole smiled and nodded. She was enjoying the service, but she felt a little sleepy. The good night's rest the night before had made her feel better, but it hadn't made up for a week of restless nights.

Several more readers followed, including Phil's mother and a young man Shannon identified as their Hebrew-school teacher. Finally Phil's name was called.

He stepped forward, looking solemn but happy. Taking his place at the reader's desk, he began to chant, the simple melody carrying the Hebrew words over the congregation in a rich, flowing stream. Stevie was impressed. Suddenly Phil really did look very grown-up, standing there.

When Phil's reading was over, Shannon explained that it

was time for him to give his speech, the *Dvar Torah*. Sure enough, Phil pulled a piece of paper from his pocket, glanced down at it, and began to speak in English.

He talked about the passage he had just read and what it had meant to him. Then he talked about what being Jewish meant to him. Glancing at his family as he spoke, he explained how much it meant to him to come from a family where each member was free to be himself or herself. He mentioned his father, who supported his wife and children's religion while practicing his own. He talked about his aunt and uncle, who had decided to move to Israel to experience a different kind of Jewish culture but still kept in close touch with the rest of the family. He even described the ways in which his sisters had supported him all his life—although the entire congregation chuckled when he added that they often did so by helping him practice debating skills and the skills of being patient and forgiving. He ended by saying that his family—and the Jewish community, which was another kind of family—had always encouraged him to speak up, to be himself, to explore the things that were important to him, such as riding, and in general to take control of his own life and shape it in the ways he wanted and needed to.

Carole could see the people around her nodding at Phil's words. Suddenly something Phil had said made an awful lot of sense to her, too. After listening to what he was saying about taking control of his own life, Carole had finally figured out what Mrs. Reg's story had meant, and it wasn't what she'd thought. She had a pretty good idea now what she had to do to make sure the phantom horse nightmares stopped for good. And once she'd figured that out, she was able to forget all about it and enjoy the rest of Phil's celebration.

THIS TIME CAROLE was riding Starlight on a treacherous mountain trail. Snow was just beginning to fall, and she shivered slightly despite her heavy jacket and pants. The trail led down into a shadowy valley, and that was where Starlight stopped and began the now familiar routine. He snorted, shook his head, and then bucked, sending Carole flying out of the saddle.

She was on her feet immediately. Turning to face the horse, she saw that his eyes were glowing red and his sharp hooves were pawing the ground. The familiar feeling of panic washed over her, and for a second her instinct was to turn and run. But this time, for the first time since the dreams had started, she fought that feeling. This was her dream, and she was going to take control. Instead of fleeing, she put her hand into her jacket pocket. Her fingers closed around the carrot she knew she would find there.

She took a deep breath and stood her ground as the phantom horse began his charge. Even though part of her knew that this was a dream, another part experienced it as perfectly real, and it was hard not to panic as the huge beast thundered toward her. At just the right moment Carole pulled the carrot from her pocket and held it out. "Hello, Starlight," she said, her voice trembling just a little. "Good boy."

The horse skidded to a stop, and the red glow faded a little from his eyes. Carole concentrated, smiling and talking soothingly. She pictured Starlight the way she had always known and loved him, willing the creature before her to revert to that familiar shape.

Carole wasn't sure exactly when or how it happened, but after a few moments had passed the phantom horse turned back into plain, lovable Starlight. At the same time, the entire mood of the dream shifted from forbidding and frightening to normal, even pleasant. Carole heaved a deep sigh of relief. She had the funniest feeling her nightmare week was over. As her dream horse stepped forward to take the carrot from her hand with his soft lips, Carole reached forward to fling her arms around his neck for a long, well-deserved hug.

* * *

THE NEXT MORNING a well-rested Carole arrived at the stable early. Barely taking the time to dump her jacket and bag in the locker room, she hurried to Starlight's stall, her heart in her throat. She had solved the problem of the dream Starlight. Would that solve her problems with the real one?

As soon as she saw him she knew that it would. Instead of the feelings of dread and nervousness that had followed her to his stall for the past week, she felt joy and affection when she looked at his calm bay face. She knew everything was going to be all right.

When Stevie and Lisa got to Pine Hollow a half hour later, they found Carole giving Starlight an extralong grooming.

Lisa, trying to be tactful, decided not to mention the nightmares. But Stevie had no such qualms.

"So did you have another bad dream?" she asked Carole, not even bothering to say hello first.

Carole smiled. "Sort of," she said. "I mean, I had the beginning of the same kind of dream. But the ending was different. I made sure of that."

"What do you mean?" Lisa asked, leaning against the wall outside Starlight's stall.

"I finally figured out what Mrs. Reg's story really meant," Carole explained. "Something Phil said yesterday made me realize it. Remember when he was talking about being himself and shaping his life and everything?"

128

Her friends nodded.

"Well, that made me realize that that was exactly what I *wasn't* doing with those dreams," Carole said. "If I wanted them to turn out differently, I was the only one who could make that happen. So I did."

Stevie looked confused, but Lisa just looked surprised. "You mean you changed the dream while you were having it?" Lisa asked. "I've read about people doing that, but I wasn't convinced it would really work."

"I wasn't sure, either," Carole admitted. "That's why I didn't tell you guys yesterday. But I was pretty sure Mrs. Reg believed it would, so I figured it was worth a try. You see, I realized the guy in her story didn't give up riding because he had a superstition, but because he wasn't willing to work to change it. So I knew I had to work to change what the dreams were doing to me, and the only way I could think of to do that was to take control of them while I was having them. And it was actually pretty easy once I made up my mind to do it. Last night when Starlight changed into the phantom horse, I just concentrated until he changed right back into Starlight again. And after that, everything was fine."

"Wow," Stevie said, impressed. "Do you think you'll stop having the nightmares now?"

Carole shrugged. "I think I probably will. But even if I have one again, now I'll know what to do."

129

"And Phil's speech helped you figure it all out?" Stevie said. "I'm sure he'll be glad to hear that—oh, unless you don't want me to tell him, that is."

"No, it's okay. You can tell him," Carole said, dropping Starlight's grooming tools back in the bucket and giving him a pat. "After all, he is an out-of-town member of The Saddle Club."

"And now he's our only official adult member," Lisa added with a smile, as the girls headed for the tack room. They had already decided to go on a long trail ride to make up for not riding at all the day before because of the bar mitzvah.

"Yesterday was quite a day, wasn't it?" Stevie said, hoisting Belle's saddle off its rack.

Carole nodded. "Phil was right. It was a great party." After the ceremony at the synagogue, Phil and his family and friends had gathered at the Marstens' house for a big party, complete with music and dancing and lots of food.

"It was," Stevie agreed. "But that's not exactly what I was thinking about."

Lisa slung Prancer's bridle over her shoulder. "I know," she said. "The party and the presents were a lot of fun. But the best part happened at the synagogue. It'll be hard to see Phil quite the same way after this, won't it?"

"Yes. But in a good way," Stevie said, leading her friends out of the tack room. She stopped in the hallway, a thoughtful look on her face. "After all, the bar mitzvah didn't change who Phil is in any important ways. It really did just the opposite, by making him think about who he is. It made him more *him*, you know?"

It was a typical confusing Stevie comment, but this time her friends knew exactly what she meant, and they said so.

"Anyway," Stevie said with a grin, "Phil may be an adult now, but he hasn't changed that much."

"What are you talking about?" Carole asked.

"Well, I don't know if you noticed," Stevie said, "but toward the end of the party, Phil and I went for a walk—just the two of us."

Carole and Lisa exchanged glances and smiles. "We noticed," they said in one voice.

"We went out to the barn," Stevie went on. The Marstens had a small barn behind their house where Phil's horse, Teddy, lived. "Phil said he wanted to get some fresh air, and also to check on Teddy. What with all the excitement about the bar mitzvah, he was afraid Teddy might have been feeling neglected." She paused, blushing just a little. "Actually, he said he was afraid I might be feeling the same way."

"That's nice," Lisa said, leaning against the wall and shifting Prancer's bridle to her other arm. "So I guess knowing that he still cares about you just as much as ever must have made you feel a lot better about him becoming an adult and everything, right?"

"Well, sure, I guess so," Stevie said. "But that was only

part of it. You see, while we were talking to Teddy, Phil's sister Barbara came out to the barn with her new boyfriend." She grinned. "I guess they were looking for some fresh air too."

Carole smiled. "What happened?"

"Oh, just what you'd expect from a real adult like Phil," Stevie said. "We hid in Teddy's stall, and just when Barbara and her boyfriend were *really* starting to enjoy the fresh air, Phil starting talking in this really deep voice, pretending to be Teddy." She laughed at the memory. "Boy, you should have seen the look on Barbara's boyfriend's face when he heard Teddy scolding him for luring Barbara out to the barn."

Carole and Lisa laughed, too. "Adult or not, I guess Phil's still the same person he always was," Lisa said.

"Thank goodness for that," Carole added. "I like Phil just the way he is."

"Me too. But I never had any doubts," Stevie said airily.

Then Lisa frowned. "It's too bad we've had a few too many doubts about certain other people lately," she said.

"You mean like Troy Lasker, for instance?" Stevie asked.

"And Shannon," Lisa added. "She turned out to be really nice, even if she is a little shy. But just because we didn't know either of them that well we jumped to all kinds of conclusions."

"I know," Stevie said. "I've been feeling bad about that."

132

"It's not all our fault," Carole said. "Troy does act kind of different sometimes, and his sense of humor can be downright weird. And Shannon was pretty mysterious about that bracelet, right?"

"We still shouldn't have decided they were criminals just based on that stuff," Lisa insisted. "Would you assume a horse was no good just because he was a funny color or had big ears?"

"Of course not," Carole said immediately. "The most important thing about a horse isn't the way he looks. It's whether he's sound, has a good disposition, and is generally healthy."

"And you can't always tell those things at first glance, right?" Lisa said. "If you just went by appearances, you could end up with a beautiful horse with a terrible personality. Or you could pass up a wonderful horse just because he'd been rolling in the dirt and looked like a mess."

"I see what you mean," Carole admitted.

Stevie nodded. "Me too," she said. "If we just went by first impressions, we might actually think Veronica diAngelo was a good person just because she's always neatly dressed and pressed. And if we'd never gotten beyond our first impression of Shannon, we might never have realized what an interesting person she really is."

Carole glanced at Stevie, who as usual was wearing a pair of faded jeans, a shirt that had seen better days, and a battered pair of boots. "If everyone only went by appearances, you might not have any friends at all, Stevie," Carole teased.

"Very funny," Stevie said, sticking out her tongue. "But you're right. We weren't very nice to Troy or Shannon. And we certainly weren't very good detectives. A good detective would have gathered more evidence before deciding on a suspect."

"Speaking of detectives, I finally finished my book last night," Lisa said. "And guess what? Remember that character I said reminded me of Troy? He wasn't guilty after all. In fact, he saved the detective's life at the end and helped her solve the mystery. It turned out that the butler did it."

"See? At least we weren't the only ones who suspected someone without enough evidence," Stevie said.

"True," Lisa said. "But as my father would say, the important thing is to learn from your mistakes. The detective decided she would think twice before she made the same mistake again. Maybe that's some advice The Saddle Club should take, too."

And as the other two girls headed off in different directions to saddle their horses, they couldn't help agreeing with that.

ABOUT THE AUTHOR

BONNIE BRYANT is the author of many books for young readers, including novelizations of movie hits such as *Teenage Mutant Ninja Turtles* and *Honey, I Blew Up the Kid*, written under her married name, B. B. Hiller.

Ms. Bryant began writing The Saddle Club in 1986. Although she had done some riding before that, she intensified her studies then and found herself learning right along with her characters Stevie, Carole, and Lisa. She claims that they are all much better riders than she is.

Ms. Bryant was born and raised in New York City. She still lives there, in Greenwich Village, with her two sons.

Don't miss Bonnie Bryant's next exciting
Saddle Club adventure . . .

HOBBYHORSE
The Saddle Club #60

Lisa's horrid, bratty cousin Amelia is staying with the
Atwoods. The nine-year-old nightmare child is
charming around adults, but to other kids she's a men-
ace! First Amelia spooks old Patch into causing a
stampede of horses that almost gets Pine Hollow's
owner trampled. Then she breaks an expensive hob-
byhorse the Atwoods own and tells Mrs. Atwood that
Lisa did it. The Saddle Club plans to teach Amelia a
lesson she'll never forget!

Fodor's 07

W9-CPB-753

MAUI

WITH MOLOKA'I AND LĀNA'I

Where to Stay and Eat
for All Budgets

Must-See Sights
and Local Secrets

Ratings You Can Trust

Portions of this book appear in Fodor's Hawai'i
Fodor's Travel Publications   New York, Toronto, London, Sydney, Auckland
www.fodors.com

FODOR'S MAUI 2007
Editor: Amanda Theunissen

Editorial Production: David N. Downing
Editorial Contributors: Wanda Adams, Don Chapman, Elaine Gast, Jack Jeffrey, Cathy Sharpe, Cheryl Tsutsumi, Joana Varawa, Amy Westervelt, Shannon Wianecki
Maps & Illustrations: David Lindroth, *cartographer;* William Wu; with additional cartography provided by Henry Columb, Mark Stroud, and Ali Baird, Moon Street Cartography; Rebecca Baer and Bob Blake, *map editors*
Design: Fabrizio La Rocca, *creative director;* Siobhan O'Hare, Chie Ushio, Tim Malaney, Brian Panto, Moon Sun Kim
Photography: Melanie Marin, *senior picture editor*
Cover Photo (green sea turtle with snorkeler): Michael S. Nolan/age fotostock
Production/Manufacturing: Angela L. McLean

ISBN-10: 1–4000–1640–1

ISBN-13: 978–1–4000–1640–2

ISSN: 1559–0798

SPECIAL SALES
This book is available at special discounts for bulk purchases for sales promotions or premiums. Special editions, including personalized covers, excerpts of existing books, and corporate imprints, can be created in large quantities for special needs. For more information, write to Special Markets/Premium Sales, 1745 Broadway, MD 6-2, New York, New York 10019, or e-mail specialmarkets@randomhouse.com.

AN IMPORTANT TIP & AN INVITATION
Although all prices, opening times, and other details in this book are based on information supplied to us at press time, changes occur all the time in the travel world, and Fodor's cannot accept responsibility for facts that become outdated or for inadvertent errors or omissions. So **always confirm information when it matters,** especially if you're making a detour to visit a specific place. Your experiences—positive and negative—matter to us. If we have missed or misstated something, **please write to us.** We follow up on all suggestions. Contact the Maui editor at editors@fodors.com or c/o Fodor's at 1745 Broadway, New York, NY 10019.

Be a Fodor's Correspondent

Your opinion matters. It matters to us. It matters to your fellow Fodor's travelers, too. And we'd like to hear it. In fact, we *need* to hear it.

When you share your experiences and opinions, you become an active member of the Fodor's community. That means we'll not only use your feedback to make our books better, but we'll publish your names and comments whenever possible. Throughout our guides, look for "Word of Mouth," excerpts of your unvarnished feedback.

Here's how you can help improve Fodor's for all of us.

Tell us when we're right. We rely on local writers to give you an insider's perspective. But our writers and staff editors—who are the best in the business—depend on you. Your positive feedback is a vote to renew our recommendations for the next edition.

Tell us when we're wrong. We're proud that we update most of our guides every year. But we're not perfect. Things change. Hotels cut services. Museums change hours. Charming cafés lose charm. If our writer didn't quite capture the essence of a place, tell us how you'd do it differently. If any of our descriptions are inaccurate or inadequate, we'll incorporate your changes in the next edition and will correct factual errors at fodors.com *immediately.*

Tell us what to include. You probably have had fantastic travel experiences that aren't yet in Fodor's. Why not share them with a community of like-minded travelers? Maybe you chanced upon a beach or bistro or B&B that you don't want to keep to yourself. Tell us why we should include it. And share your discoveries and experiences with everyone directly at fodors.com. Your input may lead us to add a new listing or highlight a place we cover with a "Highly Recommended" star or with our highest rating, "Fodor's Choice."

Give us your opinion instantly at our feedback center at www.fodors.com/feedback. You may also e-mail editors@fodors.com with the subject line "Maui Editor." Or send your nominations, comments, and complaints by mail to Maui Editor, Fodor's, 1745 Broadway, New York, NY 10019.

You and travelers like you are the heart of the Fodor's community. Make our community richer by sharing your experiences. Be a Fodor's correspondent.

Aloha!

Tim Jarrell, Publisher

CONTENTS

UNDERSTANDING MAUI

CLOSE UPS

MAPS & CHARTS

MAUI IN FOCUS

ABOUT THIS BOOK

Our Ratings

Sometimes you find terrific travel experiences and sometimes they just find you. But usually the burden is on you to select the right combination of experiences. That's where our ratings come in.

As travelers we've all discovered a place so wonderful that its worthiness is obvious. And sometimes that place is so experiential that superlatives don't do it justice: you just have to be there to know. These sights, properties, and experiences get our highest rating, Fodor's Choice ★, indicated by orange stars throughout this book.

Black stars highlight sights and properties we deem Highly Recommended ★, places that our writers, editors, and readers praise again and again for consistency and excellence.

By default, there's another category: any place we include in this book is by definition worth your time, unless we say otherwise. And we will.

Disagree with any of our choices? Care to nominate a place or suggest that we rate one more highly? Visit our feedback center at www.fodors.com/feedback.

Budget Well

Hotel and restaurant price categories from ¢ to $$$$ are defined in the opening pages of each chapter. For attractions, we always give standard adult admission fees; reductions are usually available for children, students, and senior citizens. Want to pay with plastic? AE, D, DC, MC, V following restaurant and hotel listings indicate if American Express, Discover, Diners Club, MasterCard, and Visa are accepted.

Restaurants

Unless we state otherwise, restaurants are open for lunch and dinner daily. We mention dress only when there's a specific requirement and reservations only when they're essential or not accepted—it's always best to book ahead.

Hotels

Hotels have private bath, phone, TV, and air-conditioning unless we specify otherwise. We always list facilities but not whether you'll be charged an extra fee to use them, so when pricing accommodations, find out what's included.

Many Listings
- ★ Fodor's Choice
- ★ Highly recommended
- ⌧ Physical address
- ↔ Directions
- 🕮 Mailing address
- ☎ Telephone
- 🖶 Fax
- ⊕ On the Web
- ✑ E-mail
- 🎟 Admission fee
- ☉ Open/closed times
- ⚑ Start of walk/itinerary
- ▭ Credit cards

Hotels & Restaurants
- 🏨 Hotel
- ⌸ Number of rooms
- ⚲ Facilities
- ✕ Restaurant
- ⚑ Reservations
- 🏛 Dress code
- ⚲ Smoking
- 🄱 BYOB
- ✕🏨 Hotel with restaurant that warrants a visit

Outdoors
- ⚑ Golf
- ⛺ Camping

Other
- ☺ Family-friendly
- ⁉ Contact information
- ⇨ See also
- ⌧ Branch address
- ☞ Take note

Experience Maui

WORD OF MOUTH

"My best Maui experience . . . would have to be the horseback ride with Makena Stables on a misty, rainy afternoon over the lava fields. So quiet, so peaceful."

—stellaluna

"My favorite Maui memory—being in a 28-foot boat and having a 45-foot-long humpback whale surface three feet from our side of the boat, exhale, and create a rainbow in her spray."

—ms_go

Getting Oriented

Any description of Maui's beauty is a cliché by now—we've all seen the postcards and the movies and heard stories from friends. Still, when you experience Maui firsthand, it's hard not to gush about the long perfect beaches, dramatic cliffs, greener-than-green rainforests, and that unbelievable plumeria perfume that hangs over it all. Add to that the fresh pineapple, the amazing marine life, the fascinating culture and history of the Hawaiian people, and the location (at nearly 1,900 mi from the next continent, the Hawaiian islands are the most isolated in the world—talk about getting away from it all), and it's easy to see why it has been such a popular destination for so long.

■ TIP➔ Directions on the island are often given as *mauka* (toward the mountains) and *makai* (toward the ocean).

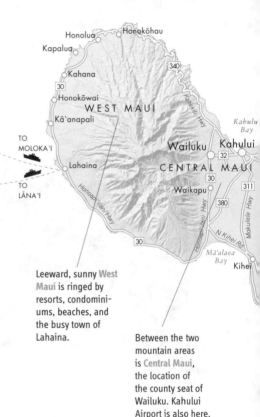

Leeward, sunny West Maui is ringed by resorts, condominiums, beaches, and the busy town of Lahaina.

Between the two mountain areas is Central Maui, the location of the county seat of Wailuku. Kahului Airport is also here.

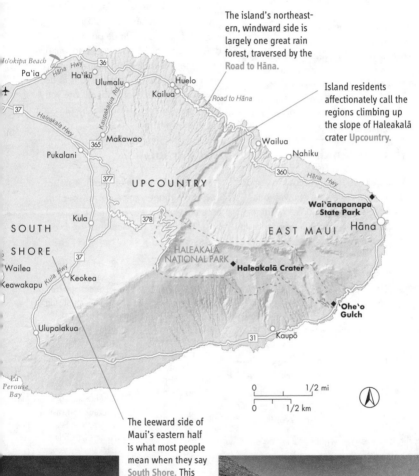

The island's northeastern, windward side is largely one great rain forest, traversed by the Road to Hāna.

Island residents affectionately call the regions climbing up the slope of Haleakalā crater Upcountry.

The leeward side of Maui's eastern half is what most people mean when they say South Shore. This popular area is sunny and warm year-round and is home to the beautiful resort area, Wailea.

MAUI PLANNER

When You Arrive

Most visitors arrive at Kahului Airport. The best way to get from the airport to your destination is in your own rental car. The major car-rental companies have desks at the airport and can provide a map and directions to your hotel. ■ TIP→→ Arriving flights in Maui tend to land around the same time. This can lead to extremely long lines at the car rental windows. If possible, send one member of your group to pick up the car while the others wait for the baggage.

Getting Around

If you need to ask for directions, try your best to pronounce the multi-vowel road names. Locals don't use (or know) highway route numbers and will respond with looks as lost as yours.

Tips for High Season Travelers

If you're coming during the peak season, be sure to book hotels and car rentals ahead of time. Advance booking of activities is also a good idea. This will ensure you get to do the activity you want and can often save you 10% or more if you book on individual outfitters' Web sites.

Traffic tends to overwhelm the island's simple infrastructure during these busy times. Try to avoid driving during typical commuter hours, and always allow extra travel time to reach your destination.

Where to Stay

Deciding where to stay is difficult, especially if you're a first-time visitor. To help narrow your choices, consider what type of property you'd like to stay at (big, flashy resort or private vacation rental) and what type of island climate you're looking for (beachfront strand or remote rain forest). If you're staying for more than a week, we recommend breaking your trip into two or even three parts. Moving around may sound daunting, and will rule out longer-stay discounts, but remember: each area of the island offers tons to do. If you stay in one spot, chances are you'll spend a lot of time driving to the sites and activities elsewhere.

Car Rentals

A rental car is a must on Maui. It's also one of the biggest expenses of your trip, especially when you add in the price of gasoline—higher on Maui than on O'ahu or the mainland.

■ TIPS→
■ Soft-top jeeps are a popular option, but they don't have much space for baggage and it's impossible to lock anything into them. Four-wheel-drive vehicles are the most expensive options and not really necessary.

■ Don't be surprised if there is an additional fee for parking at your hotel or resort, parking is not always included in your room rate or resort fee.

■ Booking a car-hotel or airfare package can save you money. Even some B&Bs offer packages—it never hurts to ask.

Island Hopping

If you have a week or more on Maui you may want to set aside a day or two for a trip to Moloka'i or Lāna'i. Tour operators such as Trilogy offer day-trip packages to Lāna'i which include snorkeling and a van tour of the island. Ferries are available to both islands. (The Moloka'i channel can be rough, so avoid ferry travel on a blustery day.)

Now that airport security checks and high prices have made island-hopping more of a challenge, your best bet for quick, scenic travel is a small air taxi. If you're not averse to flying on four- to 12-seaters, book with Pacific Wings or Hawai'i Air Taxi (*see* Smart Travel Tips). Pacific Wings flies to several small airports—Hāna,

Maui, and Kalaupapa, Moloka'i, for instance—in addition to the main airports. Hawai'i Air Taxi provides service only between Maui and Kailua-Kona on the Big Island.

■ **TIP➔** Most interisland flights on Hawai'i or Aloha are routed through O'ahu, even when it's out of the way.

Will It Rain?

Typically the weather on Maui is drier in summer (more guaranteed beach days) and rainier in winter (greener foliage, better waterfalls). Throughout the year, West Maui and the South Shore (the Leeward areas) are the driest, sunniest areas on the island—hence all the resorts here. East Maui and Hāna (the Windward areas) get the most rain, are densely forested, and abound with waterfalls and rainbows.

Timing Is Everything

Each season brings its own highlights to Maui. The humpback whales start arriving in November, are in full force by February, and are gone by April. The biggest North Shore waves also show up in winter, whereas kite boarders and windsurfers enjoy the windy, late summer months. Jacarandas shower Upcountry roads in lilac-color blossoms in spring, and the truly astounding silverswords burst forth their blooms in summer. Fall is the quietest time on the island, a good time for a getaway. And, of course, there's what's known as high season—June through August, Christmas, and spring break—when the island is jam-packed with visitors.

Guided Activities

In winter, Maui is *the* spot for whale-watching. Sure, you can see whales on other islands, but they're just passing through to get to their real hang-out. The same could be said for windsurfers and kite boarders, Maui's North Shore is their mecca. This chart lists rough prices for Maui's most popular guided activities.

ACTIVITY	COST
Deep Sea Fishing	$80–$180
Golf	$50–$300
Helicopter Tours	$125–$350
Lū'au	$50–$95
Parasailing	$48–$55
Kayaking Tours	$65–$140
Snorkel Cruises	$80–$180
Surfing Lessons	$55–$325
Windsurfing	$80–$120
Whale-Watching	$20–$40

TOP MAUI EXPERIENCES

Hike Haleakalā

(A) Be humbled as you trek down into Haleakalā National Park's massive bowl and see proof of how very powerful the earth's exhalations can be. You won't see landscape like this anywhere, outside of visiting the moon. The barren terrain is deceptive however—many of the world's rarest plants, birds, and insects live here. ⇨ *page 37.*

Kick back in Hāna

(B) "Kicking back," or relaxing, is an art perfected by Hāna residents. Try it: around town, wave to pedestrians, and "talk story" with locals in line at Hasegawa store. Watch offshore rainstorms roll in and turn to mist when they hit Hāna mountain. It's easy to forget what day it is while exploring the multi-colored beaches, waterfalls, and taro patches. ⇨ *page 47.*

Finding Nemo

(C) Snorkeling is a must. Wherever you duck under, you'll be inducted into a mesmerizing world underwater. Slow down and keep your eyes open: even fish dressed in camouflage can be spotted when they snatch at food passing by. ⇨ *page 79.*

Mākena (Big Beach)

(D) This is the sand dreams are made of: deep, golden and pillow-y. Don't be discouraged by the crammed parking lots, there's more than enough room. Big Beach is still wild. There are no hotels, mini-marts, or even public restrooms nearby—instead there's crystal clear water, the occasional pod of dolphins, and drop-dead gorgeous scenery (including the other sunbathers). ⇨ *page 64.*

Tropical fruit at a roadside stand

(E) Your first taste of ripe guava or mango is something to remember. Delicious lychees, mangos, starfruit, bananas, passion fruit, and papaya can be bought on the side of the road with the change in

your pocket. Go on, let the juice run down your chin. No one's looking!

Resorts, resorts, resorts

(F) Indulge your inner rock star at the posh resorts and spas around the island. Sip a "Tommy Girl" in the hot tub at the Four Seasons or get massaged poolside at the Grand Wailea. Even if you don't stay the night, you can enjoy the opulent gardens, restaurants, art collections, and perfectly cordial staff.

Escape to a B&B

(G) Being a shut-in isn't so bad at a secluded B&B. It's a sure way to get a taste of what it's really like to live in Paradise: ripe fruit trees outside your door, late night tropical rainstorms, a wild chicken or two. Rather than blasting the AC in a stuffy hotel room, relax with the windows open in a historic plantation house designed to capture sea breezes.

Whale Watch

(H) Maui is the cradle for hundreds of Humpback whales, who return every year to frolic in the warm waters and give birth. Watch a mama whale teach her one-ton calf how to tail-wave. You can eavesdrop on them, too; book a tour boat with a hydrophone or just plunk your head underwater to hear the strange squeaks, groans, and chortles of the cetaceans. ⇨ page 90.

Listen to Hawaiian music

(I) Before his untimely death, Israel Kamakawiwoole or "IZ" woke the world to the sound of modern Hawaiian music. Don't leave without hearing it live. The Ritz-Carlton's Slack Key Guitar Festival features guest performers who play Hawai'i's signature style. Willi K throws Irish ballads and Jimi Hendrix into the mix at Hapa's. The "Wailea Nights" show at Mulligan's might be the best—great dinner with unforgettable music by HAPA.

Surfing on the West Side

(J) The first thing your friends at home will ask is: did you learn to surf? Don't disappoint them. Feel the thrill of a wave rushing beneath your feet at any one of the beginner's breaks along Honoapi'ilani Highway. You can bring surf wax home as a souvenir. ⇨ *page 86.*

Old Lahaina Lū'au

(K) The Old Lahaina Lū'au performers won the hearts of TV viewers when they

danced hula at the Macy's Thanksgiving Day parade. This lūʻau has a warm heart—and seriously good poke (chopped, pickled raw tuna tossed with herbs and other seasonings). Tuck a flower behind your ear, mix a dab of poi with your lomi lomi salmon, and you'll be living like a local. ⇨ *page 183.*

Kayaking on the South Side
(L) Kayaking alone can be an unintended study in survival, but with a good tour company kayaking is just about the best introduction to Maui's marine world. ⇨ *page 72.*

Tour the Upcountry
(M) Diehard beach lovers might need some arm-twisting to head up the mountain for a day, but the 360-degree views are ample reward. On the roads winding through ranchlands, crisp, high-altitude air is scented with eucalyptus and lavender. Forget the spa! Just drive Upcountry and inhale! ⇨ *page 36.*

Ono-kine grinds
(N) "Ono-kine grinds" is local slang for the delicious food you'll find at a dozen restaurants island-wide. Maui chefs take their work seriously, and they have good material to start with: sun-ripened produce and seafood caught the very same morning. While munching on the freshest ʻahi you've ever had, you might find yourself inventing words to describe it. Sample as many types of fish as you can and don't be shy: try it raw.

Windsurfing at Kanaha or Hoʻokipa
(O) You might not be a watersports legend, but that doesn't mean you can't get out on the water and give it a try. In the early morning, some of windsurfing's big-wave spots are safe for beginners. Don't settle for the pond in front of your hotel—book a lesson on the North Shore and impress yourself by hanging tough where the action is. ⇨ *page 88.*

WHEN TO GO

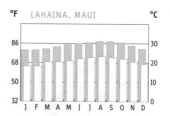

Long days of sunshine and fairly mild year-round temperatures make Hawai'i an all-season destination. Most resort areas are at sea level, with average afternoon temperatures of 75°F–80°F during the coldest months of December and January; during the hottest months of August and September the temperature often reaches 90°F. Higher "Upcountry" elevations typically have cooler and often misty conditions. Only at mountain summits does it reach freezing.

Moist trade winds drop their precipitation on the north and east sides of the islands, creating tropical climates, while the south and west sides remain hot and dry with desertlike conditions. Rainfall can be high in winter, particularly on those north and east shores.

Most travelers head to the Islands in winter, specifically from mid-December through mid-April. This high season means that fewer travel bargains are available; room rates average 10%–15% higher during this season than the rest of the year.

Climate

The preceding are average maximum and minimum temperatures for Honolulu; the temperatures throughout the Hawaiian Islands are similar.

🖪 Forecasts **Weather Channel Connection** ⊕ www.weather.com.

GREAT 1-DAY ITINERARIES

Maui's landscape is incredibly diverse, offering everything from underwater encounters with eagle rays to treks across moonlike terrain. Although daydreaming at the pool or on the beach may fulfill your initial island fantasy, Maui has much more to offer. The following one-day itineraries will take you to our favorite spots on the island.

Beach Day in West Maui

West Maui has some of the island's most beautiful beaches, though many of them are hidden by megaresorts. If you get an early start, you can begin your day snorkeling at Slaughterhouse Beach (in winter, D. T. Fleming Beach is a better option as it's less rough). Then spend the day beach-hopping through Kapalua, Napili, and Kāʻanapali as you make your way south. You'll want to get to Lahaina before dark so you can spend some time exploring the historic whaling town before choosing a restaurant for a sunset dinner.

Focus on Marine Life on the South Shore

Start your South Shore trip early in the morning, and head out past Mākena into the rough lava fields of rugged La Pérouse Bay. At the road's end, the ʻĀhihi-Kīnaʻu Marine Preserve has no beach, but it's a rich spot for snorkeling and getting to know Maui's spectacular underwater world. Head to Kīhei for lunch then enjoy the afternoon learning more about Maui's marine life at the Maui Ocean Center at Māʻalaea.

Haleakalā National Park, Upcountry & the North Shore

If you don't plan to spend an entire day hiking in the crater at Haleakalā National Park, this itinerary will at least allow you to take a peek at it. Get up early and head straight for the summit of Haleakalā (if you're jetlagged and waking up in the middle of the night, you may want to get there in time for sunrise). Bring water, sunscreen, and warm clothing (it's freezing at sunrise). Plan to spend a couple of hours exploring the various look-out points in the park. On your way down the mountain, turn right on Makawao Avenue, and head into the little town of Makawao. You can have lunch here, or make a left on Baldwin Avenue and head downhill to the town of Pāʻia where there are a number of great lunch spots and shops to explore. Spend the rest of your afternoon at Pāʻia's main strip of sand, Hoʻokipa Beach.

The Road to Hāna

This cliff-side driving tour through rainforest canopy reveals Maui's most lush and tropical terrain. It will take a full day, especially if you plan to make it all the way to ʻOheo Gulch. You'll pass through communities where old Hawaiʻi still thrives, and where the forest runs unchecked from the sea to the summit. You'll want to make frequent exploratory stops. To really soak in the magic of this place, consider staying overnight in Hāna town. That way you can spend a full day winding toward Hāna, hiking and exploring along the way, and the next day traveling leisurely back to civilization.

For more details on any of the destinations mentioned in these itineraries, see Chapter 2, Exploring Maui.

WEDDINGS & HONEYMOONS

With everything from turquoise bays surrounded by perfect white crescents to hidden waterfalls tucked into tropical rainforests, it's easy to see why Hawai'i is such a popular destination for all things romantic—weddings, honeymoons, anniversaries, you name it. The weather is perfect; the people are warm; the scenery is beautiful; there's an easy, laid back feel to everything; and, let's face it, everyone looks fantastic after a few days lounging on a beach. Planning a destination wedding, the perfect honeymoon, or an anniversary that brings back all the old magic can seem daunting at first, but Hawai'i has been in the love business for years, and there are many people and places just waiting to help celebrate yours.

Wedding Planning

The logistics. You must apply in person for a wedding license in Hawai'i, but you can download, fill in, and print the application from the State government's Web site: www.hawaii.gov/health/vital-records/vital-records/marriage/index.html. There is no waiting period and no blood test is required. The cost is $60, which must be paid in cash. The license is valid for 30 days. Your certificate of marriage will be mailed to you after the wedding; for $10 you can put a rush on the certificate, which can be very useful for brides intending to change their last names.

The ceremony. The idea of planning a wedding in a strange place, thousands of miles away, may be enough to cause night sweats for some, but fear not. Hawai'i is home to some of the world's best wedding planners, many of whom are employed by—go figure—the more popular destination wedding resorts. Narrow your locations down and contact a few planners for quotes. Many planners work in conjunction with caterers

and florists and offer packages; the resort-based planners have a variety of packages on offer. They're all used to people shopping around, so don't be afraid to haggle.

Those wishing to steer clear of the resort wedding and tap into old Hawai'i may also want to seek the help of a local planner, unless they have personal knowledge of their chosen destination or trustworthy friends or family in the area who can help taste food, scout locations, and meet potential officiants. There are certain things that are just too difficult to research from a distance, and having a wedding planner doesn't mean that your wedding will be expensive, nor does it mean that you'll end up with a Mainland wedding in Hawai'i or some sort of Hawaiian kitsch wedding (unless of course that's what you want!). These are people who know Hawai'i well and can help you find the perfect secluded beach, the local florist with the most beautiful orchids, a house on the water for you and your inner circle, and the best caterer to roast a pig for you in the backyard.

The traditions. Most people who wed on Hawai'i incorporate local traditions to some extent. These can include Hawaiian music, ancient Hawaiian chants and blessings, and traditional Hawaiian food at the reception. A simple lei exchange is customary for most couples—some exchanges include only the bride and groom. Others splurge and include leis for everyone. Typically green maile garlands are for grooms, and strands of pink and white pīkake flowers are for brides. In a traditional Hawaiian wedding ceremony, the officiant, called the kahuna pule in Hawaiian, binds the couple's hands together with a maile lei.

■ TIP→ Almost everything is less expensive in Hawai'i during the off-season (September to

mid-December), and weddings are no exception. Since the weather is perfect all year round, there's no reason to hold out for the more expensive summer months.

Honeymoon Planning

Hawai'i is a popular destination not only for everything it's got going for it, but for everything it's not as well—it's not all that far away; it's not outside the U.S. yet seems like another country; and it's not outrageously expensive if you plan well. The island tourism bureaus are excellent sources of information and a great place to find out about new promotions.

As for romance, yes, Hawai'i's romantic clichés—sunsets, beach strolls, moonlit walks—still work their magic, but there are also plenty of more unique ways to experience the romance of Hawai'i, whether you're looking to explore or just veg out together for awhile.

Almost as important as your choice of island is your accommodation choice. Although Maui is home to dozens of world-class resorts all waiting to anticipate your every need, there are also secluded B&Bs that are the perfect blend of luxury and total privacy. Many B&Bs have a honeymoon room or suite, and many of them offer stand-alone cottages. For even more privacy, there are private homes for rent throughout the island, many of which are in stunning locations and often rent for less per night than rooms at the big resorts. Maui's B&B association inspects properties and lists the best of them at www.bedbreakfastmaui.com.

■ TIP→ Hawai'i's tourism bureaus spend a lot of money every year to keep people coming back for all things related to romance. Part of that entails running regular promotions in bridal magazines and on websites, so be sure to take a look at the usual suspects for the latest offers before booking your trip (go to www.gohawaii.com, then click on the individual sites from there).

Top Spots for Romance on Maui

- **Sunrise from Haleakalā Crater.** The summit is the most beautiful place on Earth to greet a new day—just remember that that day has to start extra early. (⇨ *Chapter 2*, Exploring Maui.)

- **Skinny dipping at Little Beach in the Mākena Beach State Park.** The best outdoor place to be naked. Period. (⇨ *Chapter 3*, Beaches.)

- **Leisurely drives on the Road to Hāna.** One of the most scenic routes in the country. (⇨ *Chapter 2*, Exploring Maui.)

- **Hotel Hāna-Maui, Hāna.** The perfect blend of modern luxury and Hawaiian soul has no TVs, no phones, and best of all, no clocks. (⇨ *Chapter 7*, Where to Stay.)

- **Aloha Cottages, Makawao.** Outdoor Jacuzzis, custom-made beds, solitude, beautiful views, and the option to arrange a private, moonlit, organic dinner for two are all here, and all for far less than the average resort. (⇨ *Chapter 7*, Where to Stay.)

SNAPSHOT OF HAWAI'I

Know Your Islands

O'ahu. The state's capital, Honolulu, is on O'ahu; this is the center of Hawai'i's economy and by far the most populated island in the chain—875,000 residents adds up to 75% of the state's population. At 597 square mi, O'ahu is the third largest island in the chain; the majority of residents live in or around Honolulu, so the rest of the island still fits neatly into the tropical, untouched vision of Hawai'i. Situated southeast of Kaua'i and northwest of Maui, O'ahu is a central location for island hopping. Surfing contests on the legendary North Shore, Pearl Harbor, and iconic Waikīkī Beach are all here.

Maui. The second largest island in the chain, Maui's 727 square mi are home to only 118,000 people but host approximately 2 million tourists every year. Maui is northwest of the Big Island, and close enough to be visible from its beaches on a clear day. With its restaurants and lively nightlife, Maui is the only island that competes with O'ahu in terms of entertainment; its charm lies in the fact that while entertainment is available, Maui's towns still feel like island villages compared to the heaving modern city of Honolulu.

Hawai'i (The Big Island). The Big Island has the second largest population of the islands (159,000) but feels sparsely settled due to its size. It's 4,038 square mi and growing—all of the other islands could fit onto the Big Island and there would still be room left over. The southernmost island in the chain (slightly southeast of Maui), the Big Island is home to Kīleau, the most active volcano on the planet. It percolates within Volcanoes National Park, which draws 2.2 million visitors every year.

Kaua'i. The northernmost island in the chain (northwest of O'ahu), Kaua'i is, at approximately 540 square mi, the fourth largest of all the islands and the least populated of the larger islands, with just under 55,000 residents. Known as the Garden Isle, Kaua'i claims the title "wettest spot on Earth" with an annual average rainfall of 460 inches. Kaua'i is a favorite with honeymooners and others wanting to get away from it all—lush and peaceful, it's the perfect escape from the modern world.

Moloka'i. North of Lāna'i and Maui, and east of O'ahu, Moloka'i is Hawai'i's fifth largest island, encompassing 380 square mi. On a clear night, the lights of Honolulu are visible from Moloka'i's western shore. Moloka'i is sparsely populated, with just under 7,000 residents, the majority of whom are native Hawaiians. Most of Moloka'i's 450,000 annual visitors travel from Maui or O'ahu to spend the day exploring its beaches, cliffs, and former leper colony on Kalaupapa Peninsula.

Lāna'i. Lying just off Maui's western coast, Lāna'i looks nothing like its sister islands, with pine trees and deserts in place of palm trees and beaches. Still, the tiny 140-square-mi island is home to nearly 2,500 residents and draws an average of 70,000 visitors each year to two resorts (one in the mountains and one at the shore), both operated by Four Seasons.

Geology

The Hawaiian Islands comprise more than just the islands inhabited and visited by humans. A total of 19 islands and atolls constitutes the State of Hawai'i, with a total landmass of 6,423.4 square mi. The islands are actually exposed peaks of a submerged mountain range called the Hawaiian-Emperor seamount chain. The range was formed as the Pacific plate moved very slowly (around 32 miles every

million years) over a "hotspot" in the Earth's mantle. Because the plate moved northwestwardly, the islands in the northwest portion of the archipelago (chain) are older, which is also why they're smaller—they have been eroding longer.

The Big Island is the youngest, and thus the largest, island in the chain. It is built from seven different volcanoes, including Mauna Loa which is the largest shield volcano on the planet. Mauna Loa and Kīlauea are the only Hawaiian volcanoes still in the phase of development where explosions occur with any sort of frequency. Mauna Loa last erupted in 1984, and Kīlauea is currently erupting and has been since 1983. Mauna Kea (Big Island), Hualālai (Big Island), and Haleakalā (Maui) are all in what's called the Post Shield stage of volcanic development—eruptions decrease steadily for up to 250,000 years before ceasing entirely. Kohala (Big Island), Lāna'i (Lāna'i), and Wai'anae (O'ahu) are considered extinct volcanoes, in the erosional stage of development; Ko'olau (O'ahu) and West Maui (Maui) volcanoes are extinct volcanoes in the rejuvenation stage—after lying dormant for hundreds of thousands of years, they began erupting again, but only once every several thousand years. There is currently an active undersea volcano called Lo'ihi that has been erupting regularly. If it continues its current pattern, it should breach the ocean's surface in tens of thousands of years.

Flora & Fauna

Though much of the plantlife associated with Hawai'i today (pineapple, hibiscus, orchid, plumeria) was brought there by Tahitian, Samoan, or European visitors, Hawai'i is also home to several endemic species, like the koa tree and the yellow hibiscus. Long-dormant volcanic craters are the perfect hiding place for rare plants (like the silversword, a rare cousin of the sunflower, which grows in Maui's Haleakalā crater and few other places on earth). Many of these endemic species are now threatened by the encroachment of introduced plants and animals. Hawai'i is also home to a handful of plants that have evolved into uniquely Hawaiian versions of their original selves. Mint, for example, develops its unique taste to keep wouldbe predators from eating its leaves. As there were no such predators in Hawai'i for hundreds of years, a mintless mint evolved; similar stories exist for the islands' nettle-less nettles, thorn-less briars.

Hawai'i's climate is well suited to growing several types of flowers, most of which are introduced species. Plumeria creeps over all of the islands; orchids run rampant on the Big Island; bright orange 'ilima light up the mountains of O'ahu. These flowers give the Hawaiian leis their color and fragrance.

As with the plantlife, the majority of the animals in Hawai'i today were brought here by visitors. Axis deer from India roam the mountains of Lāna'i. The Islands are home to dozens of rat species, all stowaways on long boat rides over from Tahiti, England, and Samoa; the mongoose was brought to keep the rats out of the sugar plantations. Most of Hawai'i's birds, like the nēnē (Hawai'i's state bird) and the Po'ouli owl are endemic; unfortunately about 80% are also endangered.

The ocean surrounding the Islands teems with animal life. Once scarce manta rays have made their way back to the Big Island; spinner dolphins and sea turtles can be found off the coast of all the Islands; and

every year from December to May, the humpback whales migrate past Hawai'i in droves.

History

Anthropologists believe that the Hawaiian Islands were initially settled by Polynesians from the Marquesas and Society Islands in approximately 300 AD. They were followed not long after by Tahitian settlers who quickly booted the Polynesians from the Islands. For whatever reason, exploration in this part of the world ceased for hundreds of years, and there are very few documented stories of any visitors to Hawai'i from the arrival of the Tahitians in the 300s to the arrival of British explorer Captain James Cook in 1778.

Frequent battles between warring chiefs dominated Hawaiian life throughout its first few centuries. In 1810, the chief Kamehameha from the Big Island united all of the Islands and tribes into one kingdom, just in time to protect the land and the culture from European explorers and Catholic missionaries. Though Cook and his compatriots are vilified now in Hawaiian history, they were welcomed as gods upon their initial arrival, and the natives bought guns and ammunition from the newcomers.

Under Kamehameha (from 1810 to 1872), the kingdom was relatively peaceful, despite the arrival of settlers from both Europe and America. Foreigners were accepted into the society, and they even participated in high levels of government. After the last of King Kamehameha's family had died without an heir, Kalakaua was appointed ruler (a great lover of hula, King Kalakaua was also known as the Merrie Monarch, which is where Hawai'i's yearly hula festival gets its name). Unfor-

tunately, Kalakaua was coerced into signing the Bayonet Constitution, which rendered the monarchy powerless. In 1893 Queen Lili'uokalani (Kalakaua's sister and heir to the throne) threatened to repeal the Bayonet Constitution and was subsequently overthrown by a group of American and European businessmen and government officials, aided by an armed militia. This led to the creation of the Republic of Hawai'i, which quickly became a Territory of the United States through resolutions passed by Congress (rather than through treaties). Hawai'i remained a territory for 60 years; Pearl Harbor was attacked as part of the United States in 1941 during World War II. It wasn't until 1959, however, that Hawai'i was officially admitted as the 50th State.

Legends & Mythology

Ancient deities play a huge role in Hawaiian life today—not just in daily rituals, but in the Hawaiians' reverence for their land. All of the gods and goddesses are associated with particular parts of the land, and most of them are connected with many parts thanks to the body of stories built up around each.

The goddess Pele lives in Kīlauea Volcano and rules over the Big Island. She is a feisty goddess known for turning enemies into trees or destroying the homes of adversaries with fire. She also has a penchant for gin, which is why you'll see gin bottles circling some of the craters at Volcanoes National Park. It's not the litter it appears to be, but rather an offering to placate the Volcano goddess. The Valley Isle's namesake, the demigod Maui, is a well-known Polynesian trickster. When his mother Hina complained that there were too few hours in the day, Maui promised to slow the sun. Upon hearing this, the god Moemoe teased

Maui for boasting, but undeterred, the demigod wove a strong cord and lassoed the sun. Angry, the sun scorched the fields until an agreement was reached: during summer, the sun would travel more slowly. In winter, it would return to its quick pace. For ridiculing Maui, Moemoe was turned into a large rock that still juts from the water near Kahakualoa.

One of the most important ways the ancient Hawaiians showed respect for their gods and goddesses was through the hula. Various forms of the hula were performed as prayers to the gods and as praise to the chiefs. Performances were taken very seriously, as a mistake was thought to invalidate the prayer, or even to offend the god or chief in question. Hula is still performed both as entertainment and as prayer; it is not uncommon for a hula performance to be included in an official government ceremony.

Hawai'i Today

After a long period of suppression, Hawaiian culture and traditions have experienced a renaissance over the last few decades. An unexpected result of rapid development fueled by mainland and Asian investments has been a resurgence of Hawaiian pride. There is a real effort to maintain traditions and to respect history as the Islands go through major changes and welcome more and more newcomers every day. New developments are required to have a Hawaiian cultural expert on staff to ensure cultural sensitivity and to educate newcomers.

Nonetheless, development remains a huge issue for all Islanders—land prices are skyrocketing, putting many areas out of reach for the native population. Traffic is becoming a problem on roads that were not designed to accommodate all the new drivers, and the Islands' limited natural resources are being seriously tapped. The government, though sluggish to respond at first, is trying to make development in Hawai'i as sustainable as possible. Rules for new developments protect natural as well as cultural resources, and local governments have set ambitious conservation goals (Honolulu's mayor wants to reduce energy usage by at least 20% by 2007). Despite all efforts to ease its effect on the land and its people, large-scale, rapid development is not anyone's ideal, and Islanders are understandably less than thrilled with the prospect of a million more tourists visiting every year or buying up property that residents themselves can't afford.

That said, the aloha spirit is alive and well. Though you may encounter the occasional "howlie" hater (howlie is pidgin for Mainlander or non-Hawaiian), the majority of Islanders are warm, a welcoming people who are proud that their home draws so many visitors and who are eager to share their culture with those who respect it.

Exploring Maui

WORD OF MOUTH

"There is no question in my mind—the Road to Hāna is a fantastic trip. We have taken the trip four times and loved it every time. Our best two trips were the ones where we spent the night."

—LGay

"Mākena State Park's cliffs were nice to photograph, and, if you're looking for rainbows, seems there is always one behind Lahaina in a light rain. (Just like in the postcards)."

—Peterman

www.fodors.com/forums

Updated by
Shannon
Wianecki

MAUI IS MORE THAN A SANDY BEACH with palm trees. The natural bounty of this place is impressive. Puʻu Kukui, the 5,788-foot interior of the West Maui Mountains, is one of the earth's wettest spots—annual rainfall of 400 inches has sculpted the land into impassable gorges and razor-sharp ridges. On the opposite side of the island, the blistering lava fields at ʻĀhihi-Kīnʻau receive scant rain. And just above this desert, *paniolo,* Hawaiian cowboys, herd cattle on rolling, fertile ranchlands reminiscent of Northern California.

But nature isn't all Maui has to offer—it's also home to a rich and vivid culture. In small towns like Pāʻia and Hāna you can see remnants of the past mingling with modern-day life. Ancient *heiau* (Hawaiian stone platforms once used as places of worship) line busy roadways. Old coral and brick missionary homes now house broadcasting networks. The antique smokestacks of sugar mills tower above communities where the children blend English, Hawaiian, Japanese, Chinese, Portugese, Filipino, and more into one colorful language. Hawaiʻi is a melting pot like no other. Visiting an eclectic mom-and-pop shop (like Komoda's Bakery) can feel like stepping into another country, or back in time. The more you look here, the more you will find.

WEST MAUI

Separated from the remainder of the island by steep *pali* (cliffs), West Maui has a reputation for attitude and action. Once upon a time, this was the haunt of whalers, missionaries, and the kings and queens of Hawaiʻi. Today, crowds stroll Front Street in Lahaina, beating the heat with ice cream or shave ice, while pleasure-seekers indulge in golf, shopping, and white-sand beaches in the Kāʻanapali and Kapalua resort areas.

Lahaina

Lahaina has been welcoming visitors for more than 200 years. In 1798, after waging a terrible war to unite the Hawaiian Islands, Kamehameha the Great chose Lahaina, then called *Lele,* as the seat of his monarchy. Warriors from Kamehameha's 800 war canoes that were stretched along the coast from Olowalu to Honokōwai, turned to the land and filled the lush valleys with networks of stream-fed *loi* or taro patches. For nearly 50 years, Lahaina remained the capital of the Hawaiian Kingdom. During this period, the scent of Hawaiian sandalwood brought Chinese traders to these waters. European whaling ships followed close behind, chasing the sperm whale from Japan to the Arctic. Lahaina became known around the world for its rough-and-tumble ways. Despite the efforts of several determined missionaries, small pox and venereal disease took a terrible toll on the native population.

Then, almost as quickly as it had come, the tide of foreign trade receded. The Hawaiian capital was moved to Honolulu in 1845 and by 1860, the sandalwood forests were empty and sperm whales nearly extinct. Luckily, Lahaina had already grown into an international, sophisticated (if sometimes rowdy) town, laying claim to the first printing press

2

and high school west of the Rockies. Sugar interests kept the town afloat until tourism stepped in. Keeping pace with the times, today's entrepreneurs lure visitors from around the world to Lahaina with interesting restaurants, shops, and galleries. Tourists can board sunset cruises or hum along to "Cheeseburger in Paradise" steps away from the battleground of ancient kings.

Top Sights

★ **Baldwin Home.** In 1836, missionary and doctor Dwight Baldwin moved his family into this attractive house of coral and stone. The home has been carefully restored to reflect the period; many of the original furnishings remain. You can view the family's grand piano, the carved four-poster bed, and most interestingly, Dr. Baldwin's dispensary. During a brief tour conducted by Lahaina Restoration Foundation volunteers, you'll be shown the "thunderpot" and told how the doctor single-handedly inoculated 10,000 Maui residents for small pox. ⊠ *696 Front St., Lahaina* ☎ *808/661–3262* ⊕ *www.lahainarestoration.org* ✉ *$3* ⊗ *Daily 10–4.*

Banyan Tree. This massive tree was planted in 1873. It's the largest of its kind in the state and provides a welcome retreat for the weary who come to sit under its awesome branches. The Banyan Tree is a popular and hard-to-miss meeting place if your party splits up for independent exploring. It's also a terrific spot to be when the sun sets—mynah birds settle in here for a screeching symphony, which can be an event in itself. ⊠ *E Front St., between Hotel and Canal Sts., Lahaina.*

Hale Pa'ahao (Old Prison). Lahaina's jailhouse dates to rowdy whaling days. Its name literally means "stuck-in-irons house," referring to the wall shackles and ball-and-chain restraints. The compound was built in the 1850s by convict laborers out of blocks of coral that had been salvaged from the demolished waterfront Fort. Most prisoners were sent here for desertion, drunkenness, or reckless horse riding. Today, a wax figure representing an imprisoned old sailor tells his recorded tale of woe. ⊠ *Waine'e and Prison Sts., Lahaina* ✉ *Free* ⊗ *Daily 8–5.*

> ### ART NIGHT
>
> If you arrange to spend a Friday afternoon exploring Front Street, you can dine in town and hang around for Art Night, when the galleries stay open into the evening and entertainment fills the streets.

Holy Innocents' Episcopal Church. Built in 1908, this beautiful open-air church is decorated with paintings depicting Hawaiian versions of Christian symbols, including a Hawaiian Madonna and child, rare or extinct birds, and native plants. The congregation is beautiful also, typically dressed in traditional clothing from Samoa and Tonga. Anyone is welcome to slip into one of the pews, carved from native woods. Queen Liliuokalani, Hawai'i's last reigning monarch, lived in a large grass house on this site as a child. ⊠ *South end of Front St. near Mokuhina St., Lahaina.*

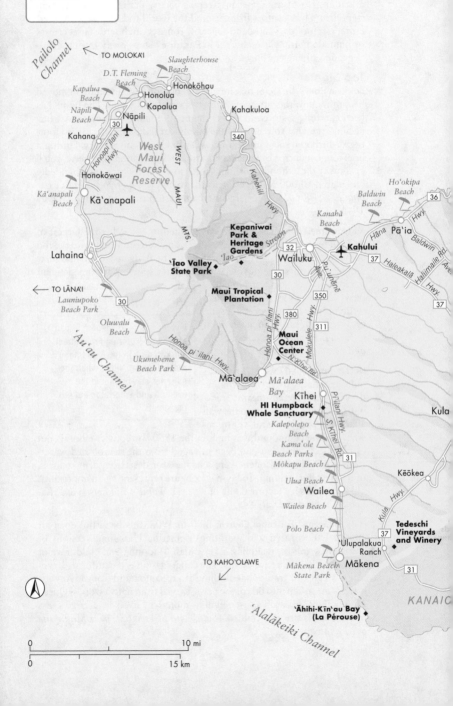

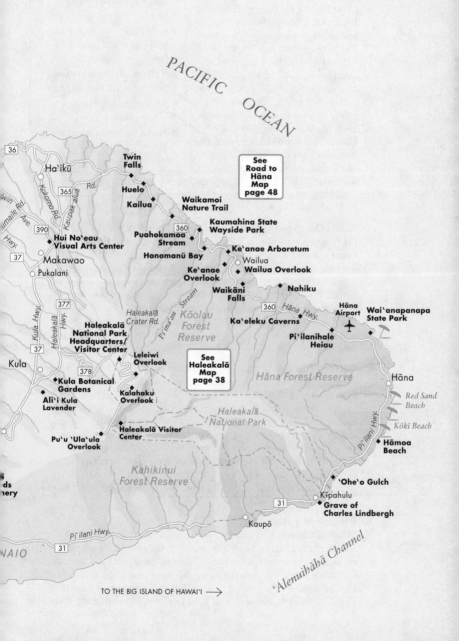

PACIFIC OCEAN

36

Ha'ikū

365 Kokomo Rd.

Kaupakalua Rd.

Twin
Falls

See
Road to
Hāna
Map
page 48

Huelo

Kailua

Waikamoi
Nature Trail

390 Hui No'eau
Visual Arts Center

Puahokamoa
Stream

360

Kaumahina State
Wayside Park

Makawao

37

Honomanū Bay

Ke'anae Arboretum

Wailua

Pukalani

Ke'anae
Overlook

Wailua Overlook

Haleakalā
Crater Rd.

Waikāni
Falls

Nahiku

377

Kula Hwy.

Haleakalā Hwy.

Haleakalā
National Park
Headquarters/
Visitor Center

Kōolau
Forest
Reserve

360

Hāna Hwy.

Hāna
Airport

Wai'anapanapa
State Park

Ka'eleku Caverns

37

Kula

378

Leleiwi
Overlook

See
Haleakalā
Map
page 38

Pi'ilanihale
Heiau

Hāna Forest Reserve

Hāna

Kula Botanical
Gardens

Kalahaku
Overlook

Red Sand
Beach

Ali'i Kula
Lavender

Haleakalā
National Park

Kōkī Beach

Haleakalā Visitor
Center

Pi'ilani Hwy.

Pu'u 'Ula'ula
Overlook

Hāmoa
Beach

ds
ery

Kahikinui
Forest Reserve

'Ohe'o Gulch

Kīpahulu

31

Grave of
Charles Lindbergh

Pi'ilani Hwy.

Kaupō

NAIO

31

'Alenuihāhā Channel

TO THE BIG ISLAND OF HAWAI'I →

Fodor'sChoice **Lahaina Court House.** The Lahaina
★ Restoration Foundation occupies
this charming old government building in the center of town. Pump the
knowledgeable staff for interesting
trivia and ask for their walking-tour
brochure, a comprehensive map to
historic Lahaina sites. Erected in
1859 and restored in 1999, the building has served as a customs and
court house, governor's office, post
office, vault and collector's office,
and police court. On August 12,
1898, its postmaster witnessed the
lowering of the Hawaiian flag when
Hawai'i became a U.S. territory. The
flag now hangs above the stairway.
You'll find terrific museum displays,

FUN THINGS TO DO IN WEST MAUI
■ Get into the Hawaiian swing of things at the Old Lahaina Lū'au.
■ Grab a bite to eat beside real boat captains at Lahaina Coolers.
■ Make an offering at the taoist altar in the Wo Hing Museum.
■ Sail into the sunset from Lahaina Harbor.
■ Attend the mynah symphony beneath the Banyan Tree.

the active Lahaina Arts Society, and an art gallery. ■ TIP➜ There's also
a public restroom. ✉ 649 Wharf St., Lahaina ☎ 808/661–0111 ✉ Free
☉ Daily 9–5.

Waiola Church and Cemetery. The Waiola Cemetery is actually older than
the neighboring church; it dates back to the death of Kamehameha the
Great's sacred wife, Queen Keōpūolani. She was one of the first Hawaiian monarchs to convert to Christianity and was buried here in 1823.
The church was erected in 1832 by Hawaiian chiefs and was originally
named Ebenezer by the queen's second husband and widower, Governor Hoapili. Aptly immortalized in James Michener's *Hawai'i* as the church
that wouldn't stand, it was burned down twice and demolished in two
windstorms. The present structure was put up in 1953 and named Waiola
(water of life). ✉ 535 Waine'e St., Lahaina ☎ 808/661–4349.

★ **Wo Hing Museum.** Smack-dab in the center of Front Street, this eye-
catching Chinese temple reflects the importance of early Chinese immigrants to Lahaina. Built by the Wo Hing Society in 1912, the
museum now contains beautiful artifacts, historic photos of old Lahaina, and a Taoist altar. Bon dances and moon festivals are held an-
nually on the grounds. Don't miss the films playing in the rustic
theater next door—some of Thomas Edison's first films, shot in
Hawai'i circa 1898, show Hawaiian wranglers herding steer onto
ships. Ask the docent for some starfruit from the tree outside, for the
altar or for yourself. ✉ 858 Front St., Lahaina ☎ 808/661–5553
✉ $1 ☉ Daily 10–4.

Places of Interest

505 Front Street. The quaint, New England–style mall on this quiet
stretch of Front Street has many treasures, notably a resident endangered
sea turtle. Year after year, turtle 5690 awes researchers and tourists alike
by laying a record eight nests in the sand just steps from the mall.
Catching sight of a nestling is rare, but 505's superb restaurants, galleries, surf shack, day spa, and local designer's boutique are accessible

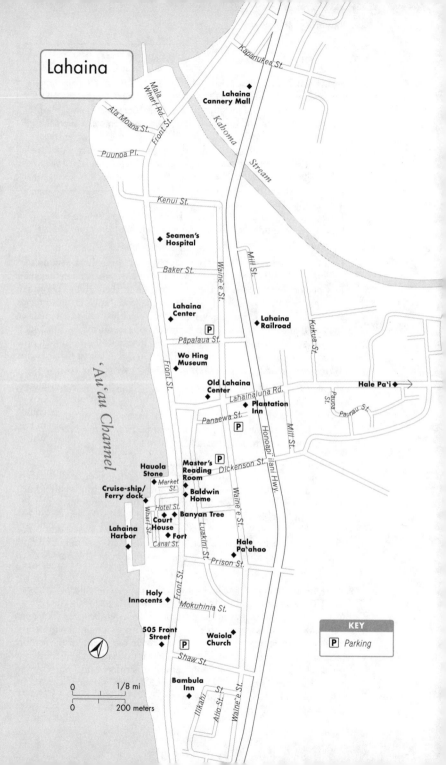

any day of the week. ⊠ *South end of Front St. near Shaw St., Lahaina.*

Fort. Used mostly as a prison, this fortress was positioned so that it could police the whaling ships that crowded the harbor. It was built from 1831 to 1832 after sailors, angered by a law forbidding local women from swimming out to ships, lobbed cannonballs at the town. Cannons raised from the wreck of a warship in Honolulu Harbor were brought to Lahaina and placed in front of the fort, where they still sit today. The building itself is an eloquent ruin. ⊠ *Canal and Wharf Sts., Lahaina.*

Hale Pa'i. Protestant missionaries established Lahainaluna Seminary as a center of learning and enlightenment in 1831. Six years later, they built this printing shop. Here at the press, they and their young Hawaiian scholars created a written Hawaiian language and used it to produce a Bible, history texts, and a newspaper. An exhibit displays a replica of the original Rampage press and facsimiles of early printing. The oldest U.S. educational institution west of the Rockies, the seminary now serves as Lahaina's public high school. ⊠ *980 Lahainaluna Rd., Lahaina* ☎ *808/661–3262* ✑ *Donations accepted* ☉ *Weekdays 10–3.*

Hauola Stone. Just visible above the tide is a gigantic stone perfectly molded into the shape of a low-backed chair. Used by ancient Hawaiians as a birthing stone, it sits in the Harbor at the intersection of salt and fresh water and was believed to promote health. ⊠ *In water behind public library on Front St., Lahaina* ✑ *Free.*

Lahaina Harbor. For centuries, Lahaina has drawn ships of all sizes to its calm harbor. King Kamehameha's conquering fleet of 800 carved *koa* canoes gave way to Chinese trading ships, Boston whalers, U.S. navy frigates, and finally, a slew of cruise ships, catamarans, and deep-sea fishing operators. During WWII, "a white tide" of navy seamen flooded the town. Stroll past the various tour boats, to see who's had the best luck fishing. If they're filleting their catch, you might glimpse eagle rays underwater snapping up the trimmings. ⊠ *Wharf St., Lahaina* ✑ *Free.*

☾ **Lahaina–Kā'anapali & Pacific Railroad.** Affectionately called the Sugarcane Train, this is Maui's only passenger train. It's an 1890s-vintage railway that once shuttled sugar but now moves sightseers between Kā'anapali and Lahaina. This quaint little attraction with its singing conductor is a big deal for Hawai'i but probably not much of a thrill for those more accustomed to trains (though children like it no matter where they grew up). A barbecue dinner with entertainment is offered on Thursday at 5 PM. ⊠ *1½ blocks north of Lahainaluna Rd. stoplight, at Hinau St., on Honoapi'ilani Hwy., Lahaina* ☎ *808/661–0080* ✑ *Round-trip $15.75, one-way $11.50, dinner train $65* ☉ *Daily 10:15–4.*

Waterfall on the Road to Hāna.

Windsurfer at Hoʻokipa Beach. (*opposite page, top*) Dancers at the Old Lahaina Lūʻau. (*opposite page, bottom*) Haleakalā National Park.

(*top*) Watching the sunrise at Haleakalā. (*bottom*) Green Sea Turtle. (*opposite*) Mākena Beach (popularly known as Big Beach).

(*top*) Humpback whale calf breaching. (*bottom left*) Fire knife dancer. (*bottom right*) Fruit stand.

(*top*) Kahakuloa, West Maui. (*bottom*) Horses on Maui's North Shore.

Wai'ānapanapa State Park on the Road to Hāna.

Master's Reading Room. This could be Maui's oldest residential building, constructed in 1834. In those days the ground floor was a mission's storeroom, and the reading room upstairs was for sailors. Today it houses local art and crafts for sale. ⊠ *Front and Dickenson Sts., Lahaina* ☎ *808/661–3262.*

North of Lahaina

As you drive north from Lahaina, the first resort community you come to is Kā'anapali, a cluster of high-rise hotels framing a beautiful white-sand beach. A little farther up the road lie the condo-filled beach towns of Nāpili, Kahana, and Honokōwai, followed by the stunning resort area, Kapalua. At the very end of the Honoapi'ilani Highway you'll find the remote village of Kahakuloa.

Kā'anapali

In ancient times, this area was known for its bountiful fishing (especially lobster) and its seaside cliffs. Pu'u Keka'a, known today as "Black Rock," was the site of many a heroic warrior's leap. But times change, the sleepy fishing village was washed away by the wave of Hawai'i's new economy: tourism. Clever marketers built this sunny shoreline into a playground for the world's vacationers. The theatrical look of Hawai'i tourism—planned resort communities where luxury homes mix with high-rise hotels, fantasy swimming pools, and a theme-park landscape—all began right here in the 1960s. Three miles of uninterrupted white beach and placid water form the front yard for this artificial utopia, with its 40 tennis courts and two championship golf courses. The six major hotels here are all worth visiting just for a look around, especially the Hyatt Regency Maui, which has a multimillion-dollar art collection and South African penguins in the lobby.

Whalers Village. While the kids hit Honolua Surf shop, mom can peruse Versace, Prada, Coach, and several fine jewelry stores at this casual, classy mall fronting Kā'anapali Beach. Pizza and Häagen-Dazs ice cream are available in the center courtyard. At the beach entrance, you'll find several good restaurants, including Leilani's and Hula Grill. ⊠ *2435 Kā'anapali Pkwy.* ☎ *808/661–4567* ⊕ *www.whalersvillage.com.*

Whalers Village Museum. A giant bony whale greets shoppers to Whalers Village. The massive skeleton is the herald of a small museum where you'll hear stories of the 19th-century *Moby-Dick* era. Baleen, ambergris, and other mysterious artifacts are on display. A short film features Hawaiian turtles and the folklore surrounding them. ⊠ *2435 Kā'anapali Pkwy., Suite H16* ☎ *808/ 661–5992* ⊡ *Free* ☉ *Daily 9:30 AM to 10 PM.*

WALKING TOURS
Lahaina's fascinating sidestreets are best explored on foot. Both the Baldwin House and the Lahaina Court House offer free self-guided walking tour brochures and maps. The Court House booklet is often recommended and includes more than 50 sites. The Baldwin House brochure is less-well-known but, in our opinion, easier to follow. It details a short but enjoyable loop tour of the town.

Kapalua

Beautiful and secluded, Kapalua is the West Side's northern-most resort community. The area got its first big boost in 1978, when the Maui Land & Pineapple Company (ML&P) built the luxurious Kapalua Bay Hotel. ML&P owns the entire area known as "Kapalua Resort," which includes the Ritz-Carlton, three golf courses, and the surrounding fields of Maui Gold pineapple. Plans are currently under way to demolish the Kapalua Bay Hotel and fashion an innovative coastal wellness retreat. The area's shopping and freestanding restaurants cater to dedicated golfers, celebrities who want to be left alone, and some of the world's richest folks. Mists regularly envelop Kapalua, which is cooler and quieter than its southern neighbors. The landscape of tall Cook pines and rolling fairways is reminiscent of Lāna'i, and the beaches and dining are among Maui's finest.

> ### CHEAP EATS
>
> In contrast to Kapalua's high-end glitz, the old **Honolua Store**, just above the Ritz-Carlton, still plies the groceries, fish nets, and household wares it did in plantation times. Hefty plate lunches, served at the deli until 2:30 PM, are popular with locals. ⊠ *504 Office Rd., Kapalua* ☎ *808/669-6128* ⊘ *Daily 6 AM–8 PM.*

Kahakuloa

Untouched by progress, this tiny village at the north end of Honoapi'ilani Highway is a relic of pre–jet travel Maui. Remote villages similar to Kahakuloa used to be tucked away in several valleys of this area. Many residents still grow taro and live in the old Hawaiian way. This is the wild side of West Maui. True adventurers will find terrific snorkeling and swimming along this coast, as well as some good hiking trails. *See* Water Sports & Activities *and* Golf, Hiking & Outdoor Activities *chapters.*

THE SOUTH SHORE

Blessed by more than its fair share of sun, the southern shore of Haleakalā was an undeveloped wilderness until the 1970s. Then the sun-worshippers found it; now restaurants, condos, and luxury resorts line the coast from the world-class aquarium at Mā'alaea Harbor, through working class Kīhei, to lovely Wailea, a resort community rivaling those on West Maui. Farther south, the road disappears and unspoiled wilderness still has its way.

Because the South Shore includes so many fine beach choices, a trip here (if you're staying elsewhere on the island) is an all-day excursion—especially if you include a visit to the aquarium. Get active in the morning with exploring and snorkeling, then shower in a beach park, dress up a little, and enjoy the cool luxury of the Wailea resorts. At sunset, settle in for dinner at one of the area's many fine restaurants.

Mā'alaea

Mā'alaea, pronounced Mah-*ah*-lye-*ah,* is not much more than a few condos, an aquarium, and a wind-blasted harbor—but that's more than enough for some visitors. Humpback whales seem to think Mā'alaea is tops for meeting mates. Green sea turtles treat it like their own personal spa, regularly seeking appointments with cleaner wrasses in the harbor. Surfers revere this spot for "freight train," reportedly the world's fastest wave.

A small Shinto shrine stands at the shore here, dedicated to the fishing god Ebisu Sama. Across the street, a giant hook often swings heavy with the sea's bounty, proving the worth of the shrine. Down Hau'oli Street (Hawaiian for *happy*) the Waterfront restaurant has benefited more than once from its close proximity to the harbor. At the end of Hau'oli Street (the town's single road), a small community garden is sometimes privy to traditional Hawaiian ceremonies. That's all, not much else. But the few residents here like it that way.

Mā'alaea Small Boat Harbor. With only 89 slips and so many good reasons to take people out on the water, this active little harbor needs to be expanded. The Army Corps of Engineers has a plan to do so, but harbor users are fighting it—particularly the surfers, who say the plan would destroy their surf breaks. In fact, the surf here is world renowned. The elusive spot to the left of the harbor called "freight train" rarely breaks, but when it does, it's said to be the fastest anywhere. ⊠ *Off Honoapi'ilani Hwy., Rte. 30.*

🅒 **Maui Ocean Center.** You'll feel as though you're walking from the seashore Fodor'sChoice down to the bottom of the reef, and then through an acrylic tunnel in ★ the middle of the sea at this aquarium, which focuses on Hawai'i and the Pacific. Special tanks get you close up with turtles, rays, sharks, and the unusual creatures of the tide pools. The center is part of a growing complex of retail shops and restaurants overlooking the harbor. ⊠ *Enter from Honoapi'ilani Hwy., Rte. 30, as it curves past Mā'alaea Harbor, Mā'alaea* ☎ *808/270–7000* ⊕ *www.mauioceancenter.com* ⊡ *$20* ⊙ *Daily 9–5.*

Kīhei

Twenty-five years ago a scant few adventurers lived in Kīhei. Now about one-third of the Maui population lives here in one of the fastest-growing towns in America. Development is still underway: a greenway for bikers and pedestrians is under construction, as is a multitude of new homes and properties.

Traffic lights and minimalls may not fit your notion of paradise, but Kīhei offers dependably warm sun, excellent beaches, and a front-row seat to marine life of all sorts. The county beach parks such as Kama'ole I, II, and III have lawns, showers, and picnic tables. ■ TIP➔ Remember: beach park or no beach park, the public has a right to the entire coastal strand. Besides all the sun and sand, the town's relatively

---

FUN THINGS TO DO ON THE SOUTH SHORE

- Swim with green sea turtles at Ulua beach.
- Spike a volleyball at Kalama Park.
- Witness the hammerheads feeding at the Maui Ocean Center.
- Follow the Hoapili Trail through an ancient Hawaiian village.
- Sink into Mākena State Beach Park's endlessly soft sand.
- Decipher whale song at the HI Humpback Whale Sanctuary.

inexpensive condos and excellent restaurants make this a home base for many Maui visitors.

★ ☾ **HI Humpback Whale Sanctuary.** The Sanctuary Education Center is beside a restored ancient Hawaiian fishpond, in prime humpback-viewing territory. Whether the whales are here or not, the center is a great stop for youngsters curious to know how things work underwater. Interactive displays and informative naturalists will explain it all. Throughout the year, the center hosts intriguing activities, ranging from moonlight tidal pool explorations to "Two-ton talks." ✉ *726 S. Kīhei Rd., Kīhei* ☎ *808/879–2818 or 800/831–4888* ⊕ *www.hawaiihumpbackwhale. noaa.gov* ▣ *Free* ☾ *Daily 10–3.*

★ ☾ **Kealia Pond National Wildlife Reserve.** Long-legged stilts casually dip their beaks in the shallow waters of this Wildlife Reserve as traffic shuttles by. If you take time to read the interpretive signs on the new boardwalk, you'll learn that endangered hawksbill turtles return to the sandy dunes here year after year. Sharp-eyed birders may catch sight of occasional migratory visitors, such as a falcon or osprey. ✉ *N. Kīhei Rd., Kīhei* ▣ *Free.*

Wailea & Farther South

Wailea, the South Shore's resort community, is slightly quieter and drier than its West Side sister, Kāʻanapali. Most visitors cannot pick a favorite and stay at both. The first two resorts were built here in the late 1970s. Soon a cluster of upscale properties sprung up, including the Four Seasons and the Fairmont Kea Lani. Check out the Grand Wailea Resort's chapel, which tells a Hawaiian love story in stained glass. The luxury of the resorts (edging on overindulgence) and the simple grandeur of the coastal views make the otherwise stark landscape an outstanding destination. A handful of perfect little beaches, all with public access, fronts the resorts.

ʻĀhihi-Kīnaʻu (La Pérouse Bay). Beyond Mākena Beach, the road fades away into a vast territory of black-lava flows, the result of Haleakalā's last eruption some 200 years ago. Also known as La Pérouse Bay, this is where Maui received its first official visit by a European explorer—the French admiral Jean-François de Galaup, Comte de La Pérouse, in 1786. Before it ends, the road passes through the ʻĀhihi-Kīnaʻu Marine Preserve, an excellent place for morning snorkel adventures (*see* Chapter 4, Water Activities & Tours). This is also the start of the Hoapili Trail, or "the King's Trail," where you can hike through the remains of one of Maui's ancient villages.

★ **Coastal Nature Trail.** A paved beach walk allows you to stroll among Wailea's prettiest properties, restaurants, and rocky coves. The trail teems with joggers in the morning hours. The *makai*, or ocean, side is landscaped with exceptionally rare native plants. Look for the silvery *hinahina*, named after the Hawaiian moon goddess because of its color. In winter this is a great place to watch whales. ✉ *Accessible from Polo or Wailea Beach parks.*

Shops at Wailea. Louis Vuitton, Tiffany, and the sumptuous Cos Bar lure shoppers to this elegant mall. Honolulu Coffee brews perfect shots of espresso to fuel those "shop 'til you drop" types. The kids can buy logo shirts in Pacific Sun while mom and dad ponder vacation ownership upstairs. Tommy Bahama's, Ruth's Chris, and Longhi's are all good dining options. ✉ *3750 Wailea Alanui* ☎ *808/891–6770* ⊕ *www.shopsatwailea.com.*

Fodor'sChoice ★ **Mākena Beach State Park.** "Big Beach" they call it—a huge stretch of heavenly golden sand without a house or hotel in sight. More than a decade ago, Maui citizens campaigned successfully to preserve this beloved beach from development. It's still wild, lacking in modern amenities (such as plumbing) but frequented by dolphins, turtles, and glorious sunsets. At the far left end of the beach, skimboarders catch air. On the right rises the beautiful hill called Pu'u Ōla'i, a perfect cinder cone. A climb over the steep rocks at this end leads to "Little Beach," where the (technically illegal) clothing-optional attitude prevails. On Sunday, Little Beach is a mecca for drummers and island gypsies. On any day of the week watch out for the mean shore break—those crisp, aquamarine waves are responsible for more than one broken arm.

CENTRAL MAUI

Kahului, where you most likely landed when you arrived on Maui, is the industrial and commercial center of the island. The area was developed in the early '50s to meet the housing needs of the large sugarcane interests here, specifically those of Alexander & Baldwin. The company was tired of playing landlord to its many plantation workers and sold land to a developer who promised to create affordable housing. The scheme worked, and "Dream City," the first planned city in Hawai'i, was born.

> **TIMING**
>
> You can explore Central Maui comfortably in little more than a half day. These are good sights to squeeze in on the way to the airport, or if you want to combine sightseeing with shopping. Hikers may want to expand their outing to a full day to explore 'Īao Valley State Park.

West of Kahului, Wailuku, the county seat since 1950, is the most charming town in Central Maui—though it wasn't always so. Its name means "Water of Destruction," after the fateful battle in 'Īao Valley that pitted King Kamehameha I against Maui warriors. Wailuku was a politically important town until the sugar industry began to decline in the 1960s and tourism took hold. Businesses left the cradle of the West Maui Mountains and followed the new market to the shore, where tourists arrived by the boatload. Wailuku still houses the county government, but has the feel of a town that's been asleep for several decades. The interesting shops and offices now inhabiting Main Street's plantation-style buildings serve as reminders of a bygone era.

Kahului & Wailuku

Top Sights

★ **Bailey House.** This was the home of Edward and Caroline Bailey, two prominent missionaries who came to Wailuku to run the first Hawai-

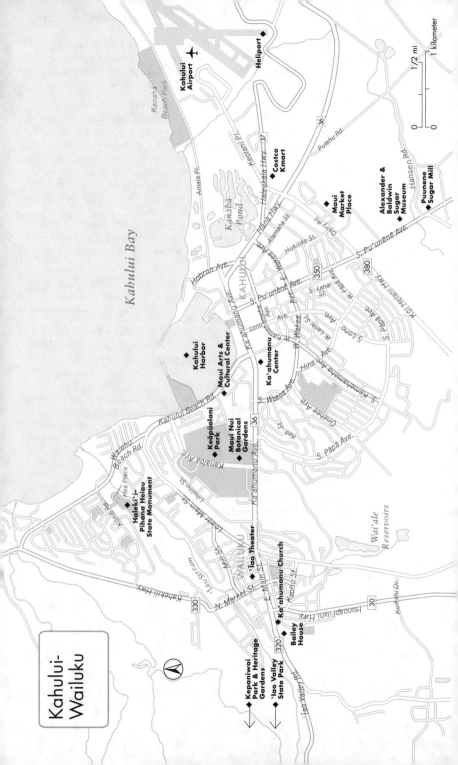

Kahului-Wailuku

Kahului Bay

Kanahā Beach Park

Kanahā Pond

Kahului Airport ✈

Heliport ◆

Costco ◆
Kmart

Maui Market ◆
Place

Alexander & ◆
Baldwin
Sugar
Museum

Puunene ◆
Sugar Mill

Amala Pl.

Keōlani Pl.

Haleakala Hwy.

37

36

Puleho Rd.

Hansen Rd.

Hana Hwy.

Dairy Rd.

Alamaha St.

Hukilike St.

S. Pu'unene Ave.

Hobron Ave.

Ka'ahumanu Ave.

KAHULUI

Kea St.

Wakea Ave.

W. Ka'ahumanu Ave.

350

380

Pu'unene Ave.

Lono Ave.

Lono Ave.

W. Papa Ave.

S. Lanai St.

S. Lanai St.

S. Lono Ave.

S. Pâpa Ave.

Kahului Harbor ◆

Maui Arts & ◆
Cultural Center

Ka'ahumanu ◆
Center

W. Market St.

Hina Ave.

Onehee Ave.

S. Kamehameha Ave.

Ko'i Helani Hwy.

Kahului Beach Rd.

Keōpūolani ◆
Park

Maui Nui ◆
Botanical
Gardens

S. Wakea Ave.

36

Kanaloa Ave.

Ka'ahumanu Ave.

Kea St.

S. Papa Ave.

Wai'ale Reservoirs

Waiehu Beach Rd.

Hea Place

Kahekili Hwy.

Haleki'i- ◆
Pihana Heiau
State Monument

Liholani St.

WAILUKU

'Iao Theater ◆

Ka'ahumanu Church ◆

Kaohu St.

Honoapi'ilani Hwy.

30

Kuikahi Dr.

'Iao Stream

Lower Main St.

Mill St.

E. Main St.

N. Market St.

330

Bailey ◆
House

320

Kepaniwai ◆
Park & Heritage
Gardens

'Iao Valley ◆
State Park

'Iao Valley Rd.

0   1 kilometer

0   1/2 mi

ian girls' school on the island, the Wailuku Female Seminary. The school's main function was to train girls in the "feminine arts." It once stood next door to the Baileys' home, which they called Halehō'ike'ike (House of Display), but locals always called it the Bailey House, and the sign painters eventually gave in. Construction of the house, between 1833 and 1850, was supervised by Edward Bailey himself. The Maui Historical Society runs a museum in the plastered stone house, with a small collection of artifacts from before and after the missionaries' arrival and with Mr. Bailey's paintings of Wailuku. Some rooms have missionary-period furniture. The Hawaiian Room has exhibits on the making of tapa cloth, as well as samples of pre-Captain Cook weaponry. ✉ *2375A Main St., Wailuku* ☎ *808/244–3326* ⊕ *www.mauimuseum. org* ✉ *$5* ☉ *Mon.–Sat. 10–4.*

> ## FUN THINGS TO DO IN CENTRAL MAUI
>
> ■ Unwind to slack key guitar at a Maui Arts & Cultural Center concert.
>
> ■ Pound tapa cloth at the Maui Nui Botanical Gardens.
>
> ■ Pick your way through 'Īao Valley's guava and ginger forest.
>
> ■ Imagine mastering the ancient weapons at the Bailey House.
>
> ■ Boost your fortune with a pair of Foo dogs bought on Market Street.

Fodor's Choice ★ **'Īao Valley State Park.** When Mark Twain saw this park, he dubbed it the Yosemite of the Pacific. Yosemite it's not, but it's a lovely deep valley with the curious **'Īao Needle,** a spire that rises more than 2,000 feet from the valley floor. You can take one of several easy hikes from the parking lot across 'Īao Stream and explore the junglelike area. This park has a beautiful network of well-maintained walks, where you can stop and meditate by the edge of a stream or marvel at the native plants and flowers (*see* Chapter 5, Golf, Hiking & Outdoor Activities). Locals come to jump from the rocks or bridge into the stream. Mist occasionally rises if there has been a rain, which makes being here even more magical. ✉ *Western end of Rte. 32* ✉ *Free* ☉ *Daily 7–7.*

☾ **Kepaniwai Park & Heritage Gardens.** This county park is a memorial to Maui's cultural roots, with picnic facilities and ethnic displays dotting the landscape. Among the displays are an early-Hawaiian shack, a New England–style saltbox, a Portuguese-style villa with gardens, and dwellings from such other cultures as China and the Philippines. Next door, the Hawai'i Nature Center has an interactive exhibit and hikes good for children.

The peacefulness here belies the history of the area. During his quest for domination, King Kamehameha I brought his troops from the Big Island of Hawai'i to the Valley Isle in 1790 and waged a successful and particularly bloody battle against the son of Maui's chief, Kahekili, near Kepaniwai Park. An earlier battle at the site had pitted Kahekili himself against an older Big Island chief, Kalani'ōpu'u. Kahekili prevailed, but the carnage was so great that the nearby stream became known as Wailuku (water of destruction) and the place where fallen warriors choked the stream's flow was called Kepaniwai (the water dam). ✉ *'Īao Valley Rd., Wailuku* ✉ *Free* ☉ *Daily 7–7.*

Market Street. An idiosyncratic assortment of shops makes Wailuku's Market Street a delightful place for a stroll. The Good Fortune Trading Company and Brown-Kobayashi carry interesting antiques and furnishings, whereas Gallerie Ha and the Sig Zane are sophisticated studio gift shops. Cafe Marc Aurel brews excellent espresso, which you can enjoy while sampling the selection of new and used CDs at the corner music shop. ✉ *Wailuku.*

Places of Interest

★ **Alexander & Baldwin Sugar Museum.** "A&B," Maui's largest landowner, was one of the "Big Five" companies that spearheaded the planting, harvesting, and processing of sugarcane. Although Hawaiian cane sugar is now being supplanted by cheaper foreign versions—as well as by sugar derived from inexpensive sugar beets—the crop was for many years the mainstay of the Hawaiian economy. You can find the museum in a small, restored plantation manager's house next to the post office and the still-operating sugar refinery (black smoke billows up when cane is burning). Historic photos, artifacts, and documents explain the introduction of sugarcane to Hawai'i and how plantation managers brought in laborers from other countries, thereby changing the Islands' ethnic mix. Exhibits also describe the sugar-making process. ✉ *3957 Hansen Rd., Pu'unēnē* ☎ *808/871–8058* ✑ *$5* ◷ *Mon.–Sat. 9:30–4:30; last admission at 4.*

> ### WHILE YOU'RE HERE
>
> You may want to combine sightseeing in Central Maui with some shopping. There are three large shopping centers here–Ka'ahumanu Center, Maui Mall, and Maui Marketplace (*see* Chapter 8, Shops & Spas). This is also one of the best areas on the island to stock up on groceries and basic supplies thanks to major big-box retailers, including Wal-Mart, Kmart, Costco, and Home Depot. Prepare yourself for a bit of a shock when you get your grocery bill–grocery prices, particularly for packaged goods, on Maui are much higher than on the mainland.

Haleki'i-Pihana Heiau State Monument. Stand here at either of the two *heiau* (ancient Hawaiian stone platforms once used as places of worship) and imagine the king of Maui surveying his domain. That's what Kahekili, Maui's last fierce king, did, and so did Kamehameha the Great after he defeated Kahekili's soldiers. Today the view is most instructive. Below, the once-powerful 'Iao Stream has been sucked dry and boxed in by concrete. Before you is the urban heart of the island. The suburban community behind you is all Hawaiian Homelands—property owned solely by native Hawaiians. ✉ *End of Hea Pl., off Kuhio Pl. from Waiehu Beach Rd., Rte. 340, Kahului* ✑ *Free* ◷ *Daily 7–7.*

☾ **Keōpūolani Park.** Covering 101 acres in Central Maui, this park reflects island residents' traditional love of sports. It was originally named "Maui Central Park," but school children argued before the County Council that it be named for Hawai'i's most sacred queen who was born near here, and forced to flee across the mountains when Kamehameha the Great's army arrived. The park includes seven playing fields, a running path, skate ramp, and grass ampitheater. ✉ *Kanaloa Ave. next to YMCA.*

The Boy Who Raised an Island

2

ACCORDING TO LEGEND, the island of Maui was named after a demigod whose father, Akalana, kept the heavens aloft and whose mother, Hina, guarded the path to the netherworld. Of their children, Maui was the only one who possessed magic powers, though he wasn't a good fisherman and was teased mercilessly by his brothers for it. Eventually, the cunning young Maui devised a way to catch his own fish: he distracted his brothers and pulled his line across theirs, switching the hooks and stealing the fish they had caught.

When Maui's brothers caught on to his deception, they refused to take him fishing. To console Maui, his father gave him a magic hook, the Manai'akalani. Akalana said that the hook was fastened to the heavens and

when it caught land a new continent would be born. Maui was able to convince his brothers to take him out one more time. As they paddled deep into the ocean, he chanted a powerful spell, commanding the hook to catch "the Great Fish." The hook caught more than a fish–as they paddled along, mountain peaks were lifted out of the water's depths.

As the mountains began to rise, Maui told his brothers to paddle quickly without looking back. They did so for two days, at which point their curiosity proved too much. One of the brothers looked back, and as he stopped paddling, Maui's magic line snapped. Maui had intended to raise an entire continent, but had only an island to show for his efforts.

★ **Maui Arts & Cultural Center.** An epic fund drive by the citizens of Maui led to the creation of this $32 million facility. The top-of-the-line Castle Theater seats 1,200 people on orchestra, mezzanine, and balcony levels; rock stars play the A&B Amphitheater. The MACC (as it's called) also includes a small black box theater, an art gallery with interesting exhibits, and classrooms. The building itself is worth a visit: it incorporates work by Maui artists, and its signature lava-rock wall pays tribute to the skills of the Hawaiians. But the real draw is the Schaeffer International Gallery, which houses superb rotating exhibits. ⊠ *Above harbor on Kahului Beach Rd.* ☎ *808/242–2787, 808/242–7469 box office* ⊕ *www.mauiarts.org* ☉ *Weekdays 9–5.*

★ ☾ **Maui Nui Botanical Gardens.** The fascinating plants grown here are representative of pre-contact Hawai'i. Both native and Polynesian-introduced species are cultivated—including ice-cream bananas, varieties of sweet potatoes and sugarcane, native poppies, hibiscus, and *anapanapa,* a plant that makes a natural shampoo when rubbed between your hands. Ethnobotany tours and presentations are offered on occasion. ⊠ *150 Kanaloa Ave.* ☎ *808/249–2798* ☉ *Daily 8–4* ☉ *Closed Sun.*

☾ **Maui Tropical Plantation & Country Store.** When Maui's once-paramount crop declined in importance, a group of visionaries decided to open an agricultural theme park on the site of this former sugarcane field. The

60-acre preserve, on Route 30 just outside Wailuku, offers a 30-minute tram ride through its fields with an informative narration covering growing processes and plant types. Children will probably enjoy the historical-characters exhibit as well as fruit-tasting, coconut-husking, and lei-making demonstrations, not to mention some entertaining spider monkeys. There's a restaurant on the property and a "country store" specializing in Made in Maui products. ⊠ *Honoapi'ilani Hwy., Rte. 30, Waikapu* ☎ *808/244–7643* ⊠ *Free; tram ride with narrated tour $9.50* ⊙ *Daily 9–5.*

Haleakalā National Park   See Page 37

UPCOUNTRY MAUI

The west-facing upper slopes of Haleakalā are locally called "Upcountry." This region is responsible for much of Hawai'i's produce—lettuce, tomatoes, strawberries, and sweet Maui onions for starters. As you drive along you'll notice cactus thickets mingled with purple jacaranda, wild hibiscus, and towering eucalyptus trees. Upcountry is also fertile ranch land; cowboys still work the fields of the historic 20,000-acre 'Ulupalakua Ranch and the 32,000-acre Haleakalā Ranch. Keep an eye out for *pueo*, Hawai'i's native owl, which hunts these fields during daylight hours.

The Kula Highway

Kula . . . most Mauians say it with a hint of a sigh. Why? It's just that much closer to heaven. On the broad shoulder of Haleakalā, this is blessed country. From the Kula Highway most of Central Maui is visible—from the lava-scarred plains of Kenaio to the cruise-ship-lighted waters of Kahului Harbor. Beyond the central valley's sugarcane fields, the plunging profile of the West Maui mountains can be seen in its entirety, wreathed in ethereal mist. If this sounds too prosaic a description, you haven't been here yet. These views, coveted by many, continue to drive real estate prices further skyward. Luckily, you can still have them for free—just pull over on the roadside and drink them in.

★ **Ali'i Kula Lavender.** Reserve a spot for tea or lunch at this lavender farm with a falcon's view. It's *the* relaxing remedy for those suffering from too much sun, shopping, or golf. Owners Ali'i and Lani lead tours through winding paths of therapeutic lavender varieties, proteas, succulents, and rare Maui worm-

> **FUN THINGS TO DO UPCOUNTRY**
>
> - Swig a cup of joe with a Hawaiian *paniolo* at Grandma's Coffee Shop in Kēōkea.
> - Nibble lavender scones with a view of the Valley Isle at Ali'i Kula Lavender Farm.
> - Gawk at the scenery along Kula Highway.
> - Taste pineapple wine at Tedeschi Vineyards.
> - Stumble across a plein air painter at the Hui.

Continued on page 43

HALEAKALĀ NATIONAL PARK

HALEAKALA CRATER

From Tropics to the Moon! Two hours, 38 mi, 10,023 feet—those are the unlikely numbers involved in reaching Maui's highest point, the summit of Haleakalā. Nowhere else on earth can you drive from sea level (Kahului) to 10,023 feet (the summit) in only 38 mi. And what's more shocking—in that short vertical ascent, you'll journey from lush, tropical-island landscape to the stark, moonlike basin of the volcano's enormous, otherworldly crater.

Established in 1916, Haleakalā National Park covers an astonishing 27,284 acres. Haleakalā Crater is the centerpiece of the park though it's not actually a crater. Technically, it's an erosional valley, flushed out by water pouring from the summit through two enormous gaps. The mountain has terrific camping and hiking, including a trail that loops through the crater, but the chance to witness this unearthly landscape is reason enough for a visit.

THE CLIMB TO THE SUMMIT

To reach Haleakalā National Park and the mountain's breathtaking summit, take Route 36 east of Kahului to the Haleakalā Highway (Route 37). Head east, up the mountain to the unlikely intersection of Haleakalā Highway and Haleakalā Highway. If you continue straight the road's name changes to Kula Highway (still Route 37). Instead, turn left onto Haleakalā Highway—this is now Route 377. After about 6 mi, make a left onto

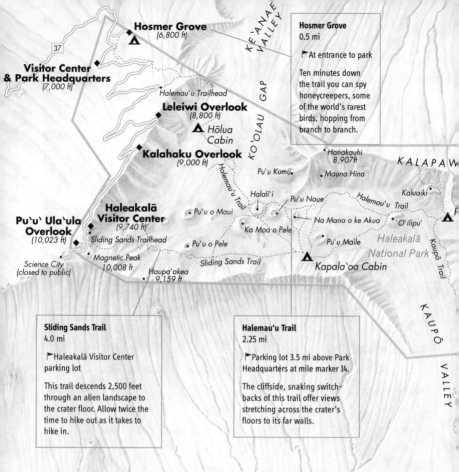

Hosmer Grove (6,800 ft)

Visitor Center & Park Headquarters (7,000 ft)

37

Halemau'u Trailhead

Leleiwi Overlook (8,800 ft)

Hōlua Cabin

Kalahaku Overlook (9,000 ft)

Haleakalā Visitor Center (9,740 ft)

Sliding Sands Trailhead

Pu'u' Ula'ula Overlook (10,023 ft)

Science City (closed to public)

Magnetic Peak 10,008 ft

Haupa'akea 9,159 ft

Sliding Sands Trail

KE'ANAE VALLEY

KO'OLAU GAP

KO'OLAU

Pu'u Kumu

Halali'i

Pu'u o Maui

Ka Moa o Pele

Pu'u o Pele

Pu'u Naue

Hanakauhi 8,907 ft

Mauna Hina

KALAPAW

Na Mana o ke Akua

Kaluaiki

O'ilipu

Haleakalā National Park

Pu'u Maile

Kapala'oa Cabin

Halemau'u Trail

Halemau'u Trail

KAUPO Trail

KAUPŌ VALLEY

Hosmer Grove
0.5 mi

➤ At entrance to park

Ten minutes down the trail you can spy honeycreepers, some of the world's rarest birds, hopping from branch to branch.

Sliding Sands Trail
4.0 mi

➤ Haleakalā Visitor Center parking lot

This trail descends 2,500 feet through an alien landscape to the crater floor. Allow twice the time to hike out as it takes to hike in.

Halemau'u Trail
2.25 mi

➤ Parking lot 3.5 mi above Park Headquarters at mile marker 14.

The cliffside, snaking switchbacks of this trail offer views stretching across the crater's floors to its far walls.

Crater Road (Route 378). After several long switchbacks (look out for downhill bikers!) you'll come to the park entrance.

■ **TIP→** Before you head up Haleakalā, call for the latest **park weather conditions** (☎ 808/877–5111). Extreme gusty winds, heavy rain, and even snow in winter are not uncommon. Because of the high altitude, the mountaintop temperature is often as much as 30 degrees cooler than that at sea level. Be sure to bring a jacket. Also make sure you have a full tank of gas. No service stations exist beyond Kula.■

There's a $10 parking fee to enter the park; but it's good for one week and can

be used at 'Ohe'o Gulch (Seven Sacred Pools), so save your receipt.

6,800 feet, Hosmer Grove. Just as you enter the park, Hosmer Grove has campsites and interpretive trails (*see* Hiking & Camping *on page 40*). Park rangers maintain a changing schedule of talks and hikes both here and at the top of the mountain. Call the park for current schedules.

7,000 feet, Park Headquarters/Visitor Center. Not far from Hosmer Grove, the Park Headquarters/Visitor Center (open daily from 8 to 4) has trail maps

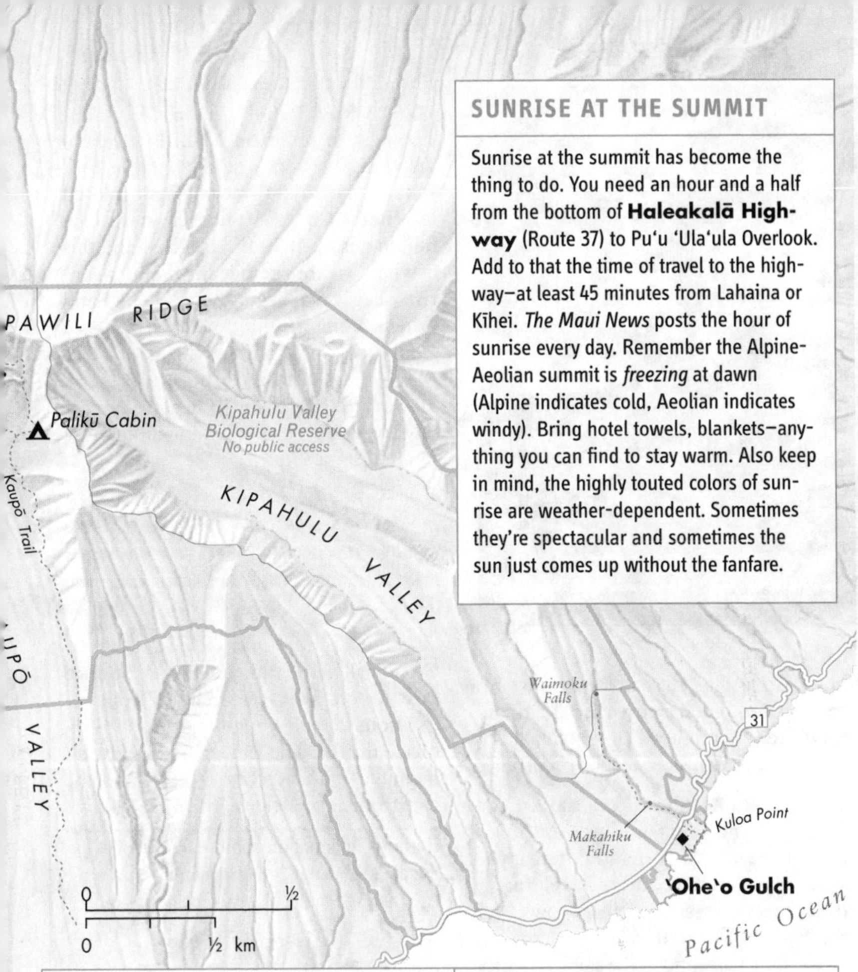

PAWILI   RIDGE

△ Palikū Cabin

Kipahulu Valley
Biological Reserve
No public access

Kaupō Trail

KIPAHULU   VALLEY

ŪPŌ VALLEY

Waimoku
Falls

31

Kuloa Point

Makahiku
Falls

◆ 'Ohe'o Gulch

Pacific Ocean

0   ½

0   ½ km

SUNRISE AT THE SUMMIT

Sunrise at the summit has become the thing to do. You need an hour and a half from the bottom of **Haleakalā Highway** (Route 37) to Pu'u 'Ula'ula Overlook. Add to that the time of travel to the highway—at least 45 minutes from Lahaina or Kīhei. *The Maui News* posts the hour of sunrise every day. Remember the Alpine-Aeolian summit is *freezing* at dawn (Alpine indicates cold, Aeolian indicates windy). Bring hotel towels, blankets—anything you can find to stay warm. Also keep in mind, the highly touted colors of sunrise are weather-dependent. Sometimes they're spectacular and sometimes the sun just comes up without the fanfare.

and displays about the volcano's origins and eruption history. Hikers and campers should check-in here before heading up the mountain. Maps, posters, and other memorabilia are available at the gift shop.

8,800 feet, Leleiwi Overlook. Continuing up the mountain, you come to Leleiwi Overlook. A short walk to the end of the parking lot reveals your first awe-inspiring view of the crater. The small hills in the basin are volcanic cinder cones (called *pu'u* in Hawaiian), each with a small crater at its top, and each the site of a former eruption.

WHERE TO EAT

KULA LODGE (✉ Haleakalā Hwy., Kula ☎ 808/878-2517) serves hearty breakfasts from 7 to 11 AM, a favorite with hikers coming down from a sunrise visit to Haleakalā's summit, as well as those on their way up for a late-morning tramp in the crater. Spectacular ocean views fill the windows of this mountainside lodge.

If you're here in the late afternoon, it's possible you'll experience a phenomenon called the Brocken Specter. Named after a similar occurrence in East Germany's

Silversword

10,023 feet, Pu'u 'Ula'ula Overlook.
The highest point on Maui is the Pu'u 'Ula'ula Overlook, at the 10,023-foot summit. Here you find a glass-enclosed lookout with a 360-degree view. The building is open 24 hours a day, and this is where visitors gather for the best sunrise view. Dawn begins between 5:45 and 7, depending on the time of year. On a clear day you can see the islands of Moloka'i, Lāna'i, Kaho'olawe, and Hawai'i (the Big Island). On a *really* clear day you can even spot O'ahu glimmering in the distance.

■ TIP➔ The air is very thin at 10,000 feet. Don't be surprised if you feel a little breathless while walking around the summit. Take it easy and drink lots of water. Anyone who has been scuba diving within the last 24 hours should not make the trip up Haleakalā.■

On a small hill nearby, you can see **Science City**, an off-limits research and communications center straight out of an espionage thriller. The University of Hawai'i maintains an observatory here, and the Department of Defense tracks satellites.

For more information about Haleakalā National Park, contact the **National Park Service** (☎ 808/572–4400, ⊕ www.nps.gov/hale).

HIKING & CAMPING

Exploring Haleakalā Crater is one of the best hiking experiences on Maui. The volcanic terrain offers an impressive diversity of colors, textures, and shapes—almost as if the lava has been artfully sculpted. The barren landscape is home to many plants, insects, and birds that exist nowhere else on earth and have developed intriguing survival mechanisms, such as the sun-reflecting, hairy leaves of the silversword, which allow it to survive the intense climate.

Stop at park headquarters to register and pick up trail maps on your way into the park.

Harz Mountains, the specter allows you to see yourself reflected on the clouds and encircled by a rainbow. Don't wait all day for this because it's not a daily occurrence.

9,000 feet, Kalahaku Overlook. The next stopping point is Kalahaku Overlook. The view here offers a different perspective of the crater and at this elevation, the famous silversword plant grows amid the cinders. This odd, endangered beauty grows only here, and at the same elevation on the Big Island's two peaks. It begins life as a silver, spiny-leaf rosette and is the sole home of a variety of native insects (it's the only shelter around). The silversword reaches maturity between 7 and 17 years, when it sends forth a 3- to 8-foot-tall stalk with several hundred tiny sunflowers. It blooms once, then dies.

9,740 feet, Haleakalā Visitor Center. Another mile up is the Haleakalā Visitor Center (open daily from sunrise to 3 PM). There are exhibits inside, and a trail from here leads to White Hill—a short easy walk that will give you an even better view of the valley.

2

HALEAKALĀ NATIONAL PARK

1-Hour Hike. Just as you enter Haleakalā National Park, **Hosmer Grove** offers a short 10-minute hike, and an hour-long, ${}^{1}/_{2}$-mi loop trail into the Waikamoi Cloud Forest that will give you insight into Hawai'i's fragile ecology. Anyone can go on the short hike, whereas the longer trail through the cloud forest is accessible only with park ranger-guided hikes. Call park headquarters for the schedule. Facilities here include six campsites (no permit needed, available on a first-come first-served basis), pit toilets, drinking water, and cooking shelters.

4-Hour Hikes. Two half-day hikes involve descending into the crater and returning the way you came. The first, **Halemau'u Trail** (trailhead is between mile markers 14 and 15), is 2 mi round-trip. The cliffside, snaking switchbacks of this trail offer views stretching across the crater's pu'u-speckled floor to its far walls. On clear days you can peer through the Ko'olau Gap to Hāna. Native flowers and shrubs grow along the trail, which is typically misty and cool (though still exposed to the sun). When you reach the gate at the bottom, head back up.

The other hike, which is 5 mi round-trip, descends down **Sliding Sands Trail** (trailhead is at the Haleakalā Visitor Center) into an alien landscape of reddish black cinders, lava bombs, and silverswords. It's easy to imagine life before humans in the solitude and silence of this place. Turn back when you hit the crater floor.

■ **TIP➜** Bring water, sunscreen, and a reliable jacket. These can be demanding hikes if you're unused to the altitude. Take it slowly to acclimate, and give yourself additional time for the uphill return trip.■

8-Hour Hike. The recommended way to explore the crater in a single, but full day is to go in two cars and ferry yourselves back and forth between the head of **Halemau'u Trail** and the summit. This way, you can hike from the summit down **Sliding Sands Trail**, cross the crater's floor, investigate the **Bottomless Pit** and **Pele's Paint Pot**, then climb out on the **switchback trail** (**Halemau'u**). When you emerge, the shelter of your waiting car will be very welcome (this is an 11.2-mi hike). If you don't have two cars, hitching a ride from Halemau'u back to the summit should be relatively safe and easy.

■ **TIP→** Take a backpack with lunch, water, sunscreen, and a reliable jacket for the beginning and end of the 8-hour hike. This is a demanding trip, but you will never regret or forget it.■

Overnight Hike. Staying overnight in one of Haleakalā's three cabins or two wilderness campgrounds is an experience like no other. You'll feel like the only person on earth when you wake up inside this enchanted, strange landscape. Nēnē and 'u'au (endangered storm petrels) make charming neighbors. The cabins, each tucked in a different corner of the crater's floor, are equipped with 12 bunk beds, wood-burning stoves, fake logs, and kitchen gear.

Hōlua cabin is the shortest hike, less than 4 hours (3.7 mi) from Halemau'u Trail. **Kapala'oa** is about 5 hours (5.5 mi) down Sliding Sands Trail. The most cherished cabin is **Palikū**, a solid eight-hour (9.3-mi) hike starting from either trail. It's nestled against the rain-forested cliffs above the Kaupō Gap. To reserve a cabin you have to apply to the National Park Service at least 90 days in advance and hope the lottery system is kind to you. Tent campsites at Hōlua and Palikū are free and easy to reserve on a first-come, first-served basis.

■ **TIP→** Toilets and nonpotable water are available—bring iodine tablets to purify the water. Open fires are not allowed and packing out your trash is mandatory.■

For more information on hiking or camping, or to reserve a cabin, contact the National Park Service (⊠ Box 369, Makawao 96768 ☎ 808/572-9306 ⊕ www.nps.gov/hale).

OPTIONS FOR EXPLORING

If you're short on time you can drive to the summit, take a peek inside, and drive back down. But the "House of the Sun" is really worth a day of your vacation time. There are lots of ways to experience the crater: by foot, bicycle, horseback, or helicopter.

BIKING
You cannot bike within the crater, but you can cruise the 38 mi from the summit down the outside of the mountain all the way to Pā'ia at sea level. The views along the way are exquisite, but dodging traffic can be a headache. If you rent bikes on your own, you'll need someone to ferry you up. Tours provide shuttle service and equipment.

HELICOPTER TOURS
Viewing Haleakalā from above can be a mind-altering experience, if you don't mind dropping $200 per person for a few blissful moments above the crater. Most tours buzz Haleakalā, where airspace is regulated, then head over to Hānā in search of waterfalls.

HORSEBACK RIDING
Several companies offer half-day, full-day, and even overnight rides into the crater. Advanced or at least confident riders can travel up the stunning Kaupō Gap with Charley's Trail Rides and stay overnight at Palikū.

For complete information on any of these activities, see Chapter 5, Golf, Hiking & Outdoor Activities wood. Their logo, a larger-than-life dragonfly, darts above chefs who are cooking up lavender-infused shrimp appetizers out on the lānai. The gift shop abounds with the farm's own innovative lavender products. ✉ *1100 Waipoli Rd., Kula* ☎ *808/878–3004* ⊕ *www.mauikulalavender. com* 🖃 *$25* ⚶ *Reservations essential* ☉ *Daily 9–4, tours at 11* AM.

Keōkea. More of a friendly gesture than a town, this tiny outpost is the last bit of civilization before Kula Highway becomes the winding backside road, heading east around to Hāna. A coffee tree pushes through the sunny deck at Grandma's Coffee Shop, the morning watering hole for Maui's cowboys who work at 'Ulupalakua or Kaupō ranch. Keōkea Gallery next door sells some of the most original artwork on the island. ■ TIP➔ The only restroom for miles is across the street at the public park, and the view makes stretching your legs worth it.

Kula Botanical Gardens. This well-kept garden has assimilated itself naturally into its craggy 6-acre habitat. There are beautiful trees here, including native koa (prized by woodworkers) and *kukui* (the state tree, a symbol of enlightenment). There's also a good selection of proteas, the flowering shrubs that have become a signature flower crop of Upcountry Maui. A natural stream feeds into a koi pond, which is also home to a pair of African cranes. ✉ *638 Kekaulike Hwy., Kula* ☎ *808/878–1715* 🖃 *$5* ☉ *Daily 9–4.*

Tedeschi Vineyards and Winery. You can tour the winery and its historic grounds, the former Rose Ranch, and sample the island's only wines: a pleasant Maui Blush, Maui Champagne, and Tedeschi's annual Maui Nouveau. The top-seller, naturally, is the pineapple wine. The tasting room is a cottage built in the late 1800s for the frequent visits of King Kalākaua. The cottage also contains the **'Ulupalakua Ranch History Room,** which tells colorful stories of the ranch's owners, the paniolo tradition that developed here, and Maui's polo teams. The old General Store may look like a museum, but in fact it's an excellent pit stop. ✉ *Kula Hwy., 'Ulupalakua Ranch* ☎ *808/878–6058* ⊕ *www.mauiwine.com* 🖃 *Free* ☉ *Daily 9–5, tours at 10:30 and 1:30.*

Makawao

This once-tiny town, at the intersection of Baldwin and Makawao avenues, has managed to hang on to its country charm (and eccentricity) as it has grown in popularity. The district was originally settled by Portuguese and Japanese immigrants who came to Maui to work the sugar plantations and then moved Upcountry to establish small farms, ranches, and stores. Descendants now work the neighboring Haleakalā and 'Ulupalakua ranches. Every July 4 the *paniolo* (Hawaiian cowboy) set comes out in force for the Makawao Rodeo. The cross-

HAWAIIAN CREAM PUFFS, YUM!

One of Makawao's most famous landmarks is **Komoda Store & Bakery** (3674 Baldwin Ave.; 808/572-7261), a classic mom-and-pop store that has changed little in three-quarters of a century, where you can get a delicious cream puff if you arrive early enough. They make hundreds but sell out each day.

roads of town—lined with chic shops and down-home eateries—reflects a growing population of people who came here just because they liked it. For those seeking lush greenery rather than beach-side accommodations, there are great, secluded little B&Bs in and around the town.

Hui No'eau Visual Arts Center. The main house of this nonprofit cultural center on the old Baldwin estate, just outside the town of Makawao, is an elegant two-story Mediterranean-style villa designed in the 1920s by the defining Hawai'i architect C. W. Dickey. "The Hui" is the grande dame of Maui's well-known arts scene. The exhibits are always satisfying, and the grounds might as well be a botanical garden. The Hui also offers classes and maintains working artists' studios. ⊠ *2841 Baldwin Ave., Makawao* ☎ *808/572–6560* 🖅 *Free* ☉ *Daily 10–4.*

THE NORTH SHORE

Blasted by winter swells and wind, Maui's North Shore draws water-sports thrill-seekers from around the world. But there's much more to this area of Maui than coastline. Inland, a lush, waterfall-fed garden of Eden beckons. In forested pockets, wealthy hermits have carved out a little piece of paradise for themselves. A few of them are even willing to invite you in, as guests at their vacation rentals.

North Shore action centers around the colorful town of Pā'ia and the windsurfing mecca, Ho'okipa Beach.

★ **Pā'ia**

This little town on Maui's north shore (at the intersection of Hāna Highway [Highway 36] and Baldwin Avenue) was once a sugarcane enclave, with a mill, plantation camps, and shops to serve the workers. The town boomed during World War II when the marines set up camp in nearby Ha'ikū. The old HC&S sugar mill finally closed and no sign of the military remains, but the town continues to thrive. In the '70s, Pā'ia became a hippie town as dropouts headed for Maui to open boutiques, galleries, and unusual eateries. In the '80s windsurfers discovered nearby Ho'okipa Beach and brought an international flavor to Pā'ia (to the benefit of the unusual eateries).

At the intersection of Hāna Highway and Baldwin Avenue, eclectic boutiques supply everything from high fashion to hemp oil candles. Some of Maui's best shops for surf trunks, Brazilian bikinis, and other beachware are here. The restaurants provide excellent people-watching and an array of dining options. A French-Caribbean bistro with a sushi bar in back, a French-Indian creperie, a neo-Mexican gourmet restaurant, and a fish market all compete for

FUN THINGS TO DO ON THE NORTH SHORE

- Buy a teeny-weenie Maui Girl bikini.
- Watch windsurfers somersault over waves at Ho'okipa.
- Get lost and find yourself in the Ha'ikū forest.
- Rub elbows with yogis and tow-in surfers at Anthony's Coffee Shop.
- Dig into a fish sandwich and fries at the Pā'ia Fishmarket.

MAUI SIGHTSEEING TOURS

THIS IS A BIG ISLAND TO SEE IN ONE DAY, so tour companies tend to offer specialized tours, visiting either Haleakalā or Hāna and its environs. A tour of Haleakalā and Upcountry is usually a half-day excursion and is offered in several versions by different companies for about $60 and up. The trip often includes stops at a protea farm and at Tedeschi Vineyards, the only place in Maui where wine is made. A Haleakalā sunrise tour starts before dawn so that you can get to the top of the dormant volcano before the sun peeks over the horizon. Because they offer island-wide hotel pickup, many sunrise trips leave around 2:30 AM.

A tour of Hāna is almost always done in a van, since the winding road to Hāna just doesn't provide a comfortable ride in bigger buses. Of late, Hāna has so many of these one-day tours that it seems as if there are more vans than cars on the road. Still, to many it's a more relaxing way to do the drive than behind the wheel of a car. Guides decide where you stop for photos. Tours run from $80 to $120.

When booking a tour, remember that some tour companies use air-conditioned buses, whereas others prefer small vans. Then you've got your minivans, your microbuses, and your minicoaches. The key is to ask how many stops you get and how many other passengers will be onboard—otherwise you could end up on a packed bus, sightseeing through a window.

Most of the tour guides have been in the business for years. Some were born in the Islands and have taken special classes to learn more about their culture and lore. They expect a tip ($1 per person at least), but they're just as cordial without one.

Maui Pineapple Plantation Tour. Explore one of Maui's pineapple plantations on this tour that takes you right into the fields in a company van. The 2½-hour, $26 trip gives you first-hand experience of the operation and its history, some incredible views of the island, and the chance to pick a fresh pineapple for yourself. Tours depart weekday mornings and afternoons from the Kapalua Logo Shop. ✉ *Kapalua Resort Activity Desk, 500 Office Rd., Kapalua* ☎ *808/669-8088.*

Polynesian Adventure Tours. This company uses large buses with floor-to-ceiling windows. The drivers are fun and really know the island. ☎ *808/877-4242 or 800/ 622-3011* ⊕ *www.polyad.com.*

Roberts Hawai'i Tours. This is one of the state's largest tour companies, and its staff can arrange tours with bilingual guides if asked ahead of time. Eleven-hour trips venture out to Kaupō, the wild area past Hāna. ☎ *808/871-6226 or 800/767-7551* ⊕ *www.roberts-hawaii.com.*

Temptation Tours. Temptation Tours has targeted members of the affluent older crowd (though almost anyone would enjoy these tours) who don't want to be herded onto a crowded bus. Tours in plush six-passenger limovans explore Haleakalā and Hāna, and range from $110 to $249 per person. The "Hāna Sky-Trek" includes a return trip via helicopter—perfect for those leery of spending the entire day in a van. ☎ *808/877-8888* ⊕ *www. mauitours.us.*

your patronage. This abundance is helpful because Pā'ia is the last place to snack before the pilgrimage to Hāna and the first stop for the famished on the return trip.

NEED A BREAK? **Anthony's Coffee** (⊠ 90 Hāna Hwy. ☎ 808/579–8340) roasts its own beans, sells ice cream and picnic lunches, and is a great place to eavesdrop on the local windsurfing crowd. **Charley's Restaurant** (⊠ 142 Hāna Hwy. ☎ 808/579–9453) is an easygoing saloon-type hangout with pool tables. **Mana Foods** (⊠ 49 Baldwin Ave. ☎ 808/579–8078), the North Shore's natural-foods store, has an inspired deli with wholesome hot-and-cold items. The long line at **Pā'ia Fishmarket Restaurant** (⊠ 2A Baldwin Ave, ☎ 808/579–8030) attests to the popularity of the tasty mahi sandwiches. Fresh fish can also be bought by the pound. Pā'ia has an excellent wine store, the **Wine Corner** (⊠ 113 Hāna Hwy. ☎ 808/579–8904), helpful because two good eateries nearby are BYOB.

Fodor'sChoice ★ **Ho'okipa Beach.** There's no better place on this or any other island to watch the world's finest windsurfers in action. The surfers know five different surf breaks here by name. Unless it's a rare day without wind or waves, you're sure to get a show. ■ TIP→ It's not safe to park on the shoulder. Use the ample parking lot at the county park entrance. ⊠ *2 mi past Pā'ia on Rte. 36.*

Ha'ikū

At one time this area vibrated around a couple of enormous pineapple canneries. Both have been transformed into rustic warehouse malls. Because of the post office next door, old Ha'ikū cannery earned the title of town center. Here you can snack on pizza at Colleen's or get massaged by the students at Spa Luna. Follow windy Ha'ikū Road to Pauwela Cannery, the other defunct factory-turned-hangout. Don't fret if you get lost. This jungle hillside is a maze of flower-decked roads that seem to double back upon themselves. Up Kokomo Road is a large pu'u capped with a grove of columnar pines, and the **4th Marine Division Memorial Park.** During World War II American GIs trained here for battles on Iwo Jima and Saipan. Locals nicknamed the cinder cone Giggle Hill because it was a popular hangout for Maui women and their favorite servicemen.

ROAD TO HĀNA

As you round the impossibly tight turn, a one-lane bridge comes into view. Beneath its worn surface, a lush forested gulch plummets toward the coast. The sound of rushing water fills the air, compelling you to search the overgrown hillside for waterfalls. This is the Road to Hāna, a 55-mi journey into the unspoiled heart of Maui. Tracing a centuries-old path, the road begins as a well-paved highway in Kahului and ends in the tiny town of Hāna on the islands' rain-gouged windward side.

Fodor's Choice Despite the twists and turns, the road to Hāna is not as frightening as it may sound. You're bound to be a little nervous approaching it the first time; but afterwards you'll wonder if somebody out there is making it sound tough just to keep out the hordes. The challenging part of the road takes only an hour and a half, but you'll want to stop often and let the driver enjoy the view, too. Don't expect a booming city when you get to Hāna. Its lure is its quiet timelessness. Like the adage says, the journey *is* the destination.

During high season, the road to Hāna tends to clog—well, not clog exactly, but develop little choo-choo trains of cars, with everyone in a line of six or a dozen driving as slowly as the first car. The solution: leave early (dawn) and return late (dusk). And if you find yourself playing the role of locomotive, pull over and let the other drivers pass. You can also let someone else take the turns for you—several companies offer van tours, which make stops all along the way (*see* Sightseeing Tours *earlier in this chapter*).

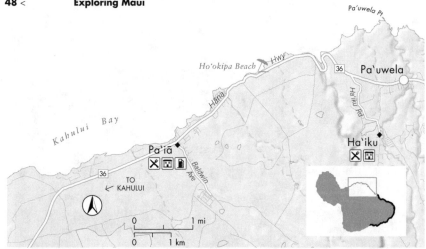

DRIVING THE ROAD TO HĀNA

Begin your journey in Pāʻia, the little town on Mauiʻs North Shore. Be sure to fill up your gas tank here. There are no gas stations along Hāna Highway, and the station in Hāna closes by 6 PM. You should also pick up a picnic lunch. Lunch and snack choices along the way are limited to rustic fruit stands.

About 10 mi past Pāʻia, at the bottom of Kaupakalua Road, the roadside mileposts begin measuring the 36 mi to Hāna town. The road's trademark noodling starts about 3 mi after that. Once the road gets twisty, remember that many residents make this trip frequently. You'll recognize them because they're the ones zipping around every curve. They've seen this so many times before they don't care to linger. Pull over to let them pass.

All along this stretch of road, waterfalls are abundant. Roll down your windows. Breathe in the scent of guava and ginger. You can almost hear the bamboo growing. There are plenty of places to pull completely off the road and park safely. Do this often, since the road's curves make driving without a break difficult.

❶ **Twin Falls.** Keep an eye out for the fruit stand just after mile marker 2. Stop here

and treat yourself to some fresh sugarcane juice. If you're feeling adventurous, follow the path beyond the stand to the paradisiacal waterfalls known as Twin Falls. Once a rough trail plastered with no trespassing signs, this treasured spot is now easily accessible. In fact, there's usually a mass of cars surrounding the fruit stand at the trail head. Several deep, emerald pools sparkle beneath waterfalls and offer excellent swimming and photo opportunities.

While it's still private property, the no trespassing signs have been replaced by colorfully painted arrows pointing away from residences and toward the falls. ■ TIP→ Bring water shoes for crossing streams along the way. Swim at your own risk and beware: flash floods here and in all East Maui stream areas can be sudden and deadly. Check the weather before you go.

❷ **Huelo & Kailua.** Dry off and drive on past the sleepy country villages of Huelo (near mile marker 5) and Kailua (near mile marker 6). The little farm town of Huelo has two quaint churches and several lovely B&Bs. It's a good place to stay if you value privacy, but it also provides an opportunity to meet local residents and learn about a rural lifestyle you might not expect to find on the Islands. The same can

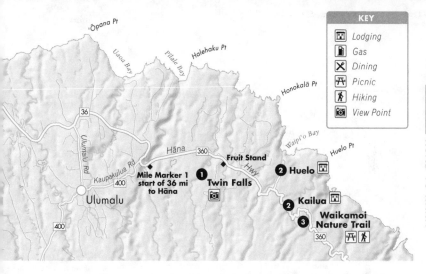

KEY

🏨 Lodging
⛽ Gas
✕ Dining
🏞 Picnic
🚶 Hiking
📷 View Point

be said for nearby Kailua, home to Alexander & Baldwin's irrigation employees.

❸ **Waikamoi Nature Trail.** Between mile markers 9 and 10, the Waikamoi Nature Trail sign beckons you to stretch your car-weary limbs. A short (if muddy) trail leads through tall eucalyptus trees to a coastal vantage point with a picnic table and barbecue. Signage reminds visitors QUIET, TREES AT WORK and BAMBOO PICKING PERMIT REQUIRED. Awapuhi, or Hawaiian shampoo ginger, sends up fragrant shoots along the trail.

❹ **Puahokamoa Stream.** About a mile farther, near mile marker 11, you can stop at the bridge over Puahokamoa Stream. This is one of many bridges you cross en route from Pā'ia to Hāna. It spans pools and waterfalls. Picnic tables are available, but there are no restrooms.

❺ **Kaumahina State Wayside Park.** If you'd rather stretch your legs and use a flush toilet, continue another mile to Kaumahina State Wayside Park (at mile marker 12). The park has a picnic area, restrooms, and a lovely overlook to the Ke'anae Peninsula. Hardier souls can camp here, with a permit. The park is open from 8 AM to 4 PM and admission is free. ☎ 808/984–8109

🕐 **TIMING TIPS**

With short stops, the drive from Pā'ia to Hāna should take you between two and three hours one-way. Lunching in Hāna, hiking, and swimming can easily turn the round-trip into a full-day outing. Since there's so much scenery to take in, we recommend staying overnight in Hāna. It's worth taking time to enjoy the waterfalls and beaches without being in a hurry. Try to plan your trip for a day that promises fair, sunny weather— though the drive can be even more beautiful when it's raining. ■ TIP→ If you decide to spend a night or two in Hāna, you may want to check any valuable luggage with the valet at your previous hotel. That way, you won't have to leave it in your car unattended when you stop to see the sights on your way to Hāna.

Ke'anae Peninsula

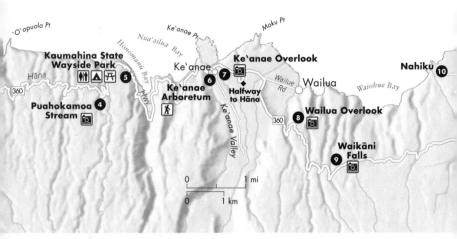

Near mile marker 14, before Ke'anae, you find yourself driving along a cliff side down into deep, lush Honomanū Bay, an enormous valley, with a rocky black-sand beach.

The Honomanū Valley was carved by erosion during Haleakalā's first dormant period. At the canyon's head there are 3,000-foot cliffs and a 1,000-foot waterfall, but don't try to reach them. There's not much of a trail, and what does exist is practically impassable.

6 Ke'anae Arboretum. Another 4 mi brings you to mile marker 17 and the Ke'anae Arboretum where you can add to your botanical education or enjoy a challenging hike into a forest. Signs help you learn the names of the many plants and trees now considered native to Hawai'i. The meandering Pi'ina'au Stream adds a graceful touch to the arbor-etum and provides a swimming pond.

You can take a fairly rigorous hike from the arboretum if you can find the trail at one side of the large taro patch. Be careful not to lose the trail once you're on it. A lovely forest waits at the end of the 25-minute hike. Access to the arboretum is free.

7 Ke'anae Overlook. A half mile farther down Hāna Highway you can stop at the Ke'anae Overlook. From this obser-

vation point, you can take in the patch-work-quilt effect the taro farms create below. The people of Ke'anae are working hard to revive this Hawaiian agricultural art and the traditional cultural values that the crop represents. The ocean provides a dramatic backdrop for the farms. In the other direction there are awesome views of Haleakalā through the foliage. This is a great spot for photos.

■ TIP→ Coming up is the halfway mark to Hāna. If you've had enough scenery, this is as good a time as any to turn around and head back to civilization.

8 Wailua Overlook. Between mile markers 20 and 21 you find Wailua Overlook. From the parking lot you can see Wailua Canyon, but you have to walk up steps to get a view

Taro Farm viewed from Hāna Highway

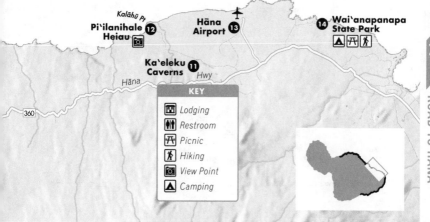

of Wailua Village. The landmark in Wailua Village is a church made of coral, built in 1860. Once called St. Gabriel's Catholic Church, the current Our Lady of Fatima Shrine has an interesting legend surrounding it. As the story goes, a storm washed enough coral up onto shore to build the church and then took any extra coral back to sea.

9 Waikāni Falls. After another ½ mi, past mile marker 21, you hit the best falls on the entire drive to Hāna, Waikāni Falls. Though not necessarily bigger or taller than the other falls, these are the most dramatic falls you'll find in East Maui. That's partly because the water is not diverted for sugar irrigation; the taro farmers in Wailua need all the runoff. This is a particularly good spot for photos.

10 Nahiku. At about mile marker 25 you see a road that heads down toward the ocean and the village of Nahiku. In ancient times this was a busy settlement with hundreds of residents. Now only about 80 people live in Nahiku, mostly native Hawaiians and some back-to-the-land types. A rubber grower planted trees here in the early 1900s, but the experiment didn't work out, and Nahiku was essentially abandoned. The road ends at the sea in a pretty landing. This is the rainiest, densest part of the East Maui rain forest.

Coffee Break. Back on the Hāna Highway, about 10 minutes before Hāna town, you can stop for—of all things—espresso. The tiny, colorful **Nahiku Ti Gallery and Coffee Shop** (between mile markers 27 and 28) sells local coffee, dried fruits and candies, and delicious (if pricey) banana bread. Sometimes the barbecue is fired up and you can try fish skewers or baked breadfruit (an island favorite nearly impossible to find elsewhere). The Ti Gallery sells Hawaiian crafts.

11 Ka'eleku Caverns. If you're interested in exploring underground, turn left onto 'Ula'ino Road, just after mile marker 31, and follow the signs to Ka'eleku Caverns. **Maui Cave Adventures** leads amateur spelunkers into a system of gigantic lava tubes, accentuated by colorful underworld formations.

Monday through Thursday, from 10:30 to 3:30, you can take a self-guided, 30- to 45-minute tour for $11.95 per person. Friday and Saturday, choose either the 75-minute walking tour (at 11:15 AM; $29 per person) or the two-and-a-half-hour adventure tour (at 1:15 PM; $79 per person). Gear—gloves, flashlight, and hard hat—is provided, and visitors must be at least six years of age (15 years of age for the adventure tour). Call ahead to reserve a spot on the guided tours. ☎ 808/248–7308 ⊕ www.mauicave.com

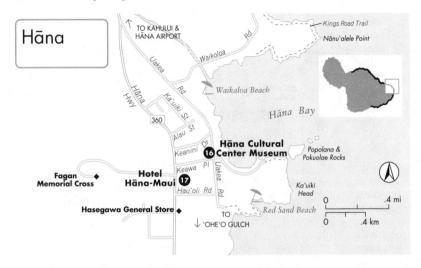

★ **⑫ Piʻilanihale Heiau.** Continue on ʻUlaʻino Road, which doubles back for a mile, loses its pavement, and even crosses a stream before reaching Kahanu Garden and Piʻilanihale Heiau, the largest prehistoric monument in Hawaiʻi. This temple platform was built for a great 16th-century Maui king named Piʻilani and his heirs. This king also supervised the construction of a 10-foot-wide road that completely encircled the island. (That's why his name is part of most of Maui's highway titles.)

Hawaiian families continue to maintain and protect this sacred site as they have for centuries, and they have not been eager to turn it into a tourist attraction. However, they now offer a brochure so you can tour the property yourself for $5 per person. Parties of four or more can reserve a guided tour, for $10 per person, by calling 48 hours in advance. Tours include the 122-acre **Kahanu Garden**, a federally funded research center focusing on the ethno botany of the Pacific. The heiau and garden are open weekdays from 10 AM to 2 PM. ☎ 808/248–8912

⑬ Hāna Airport. Back on the Hāna Highway, and less than ¹/₂ mi farther, is the turnoff for the Hāna Airport. Think of Amelia Earhart. Think of Waldo Pepper. If these picket-fence runways don't turn your thoughts to the derring-do of barnstorming pilots, you haven't seen enough old movies. Only the smallest planes can land and depart here, and when none of them happens to be around, the lonely wind sock is the only evidence that this is a working airfield. ☎ 808/248–8208

★ **⑭ Waiʻanapanapa State Park.** Just beyond mile marker 32 you reach Waiʻanapanapa State Park, home to one of Maui's only volcanic-sand beaches and some freshwater caves for adventurous swimmers to explore. The park is right on the ocean, and it's a lovely spot to picnic, camp, hike, or swim. To the left you'll find the black-sand beach, picnic tables, and cave pools. To the right you'll find cabins and an ancient trail which snakes along the ocean past blowholes, sea arches, and archaeological sites.

The tide pools here turn red several times a year. Scientists say it's explained by the arrival of small shrimp, but legend claims the color represents the blood of Popoalaea, a princess said to have been murdered in one of the caves by her husband, Chief Kaakea. Whichever you choose to believe, the drama of the landscape itself—black sand, green beach vines, azure water—is bound to leave a lasting impression.

With a permit you can stay in state-run cabins here for less than $45 a night—the price varies depending on the number of people—but reserve early. They often book up a year in advance. ☎ 808/984–8109

⓯ Hāna. By now the relaxed pace of life that Hāna residents enjoy should have you in its grasp, so you won't be discouraged to learn that "town" is little more than a gas station, a post office, and a ramshackle grocery.

Hāna, in many ways, is the heart of Maui. It's one of the few places where the slow pulse of island life is still strong. The town centers on its lovely circular bay, dominated on the right-hand shore by a pu'u called Ka'uiki. A short trail here leads to a cave, the birthplace of Queen Kā'ahumanu. This area is rich in Hawaiian history and legend. Two miles beyond town another pu'u presides over a loop road that passes two of Hāna's best beaches—Koki and Hāmoa. The hill is called Ka Iwi O Pele (Pele's Bone). Offshore here, at tiny 'Ālau Island, the demigod Maui supposedly fished up the Hawaiian islands.

Sugar was once the mainstay of Hāna's economy; the last plantation shut down in the '40s. In 1946 rancher Paul Fagan built the **Hotel Hāna-Maui** and stocked the surrounding pastureland with cattle. The cross you see on the hill above the hotel was put

there in memory of Fagan. Now it's the ranch and hotel that put food on most tables, though many families still farm, fish, and hunt as in the old days. Houses around town are decorated with glass balls and nets, which indicate a fisherman's lodging.

⓰ Hāna Cultural Center Museum. If you're determined to spend some time and money in Hāna after the long drive, a single turn off the highway onto Ukea Street, in the center of town, will take you to the Hāna Cultural Center Museum. Besides operating a well-stocked gift shop, it displays artifacts, quilts, a replica of an authentic *kauhale* (an ancient Hawaiian living complex, with thatch huts and food gardens), and other Hawaiiana. The knowledgeable staff can explain it all to you. ☎808/248–8622

⓱ Hotel Hāna-Maui. With its surrounding ranch, the upscale hotel is the mainstay of Hāna's economy. It's pleasant to stroll around this beautifully rustic property. The library houses interesting, authentic Hawaiian artifacts. In the evening, while local musicians play in the casual lobby bar, their friends jump up to dance hula. The Sea Ranch cottages across the road, built to look like authentic plantation housing from the outside, are also part of the hotel. *See Chapter 7, Where to Stay.*

Hala Trees, Wai'anapanapa State Park

Hāna

Don't be suprised if the mile markers suddenly start descending as you head past Hāna. Technically, Hāna Highway (Route 360) ends at the Hāna Bay. The road that continues south is Piʻilani Highway (Route 31)—though everyone still refers to it as the Hāna Highway.

⓲ Hāmoa Beach. Just outside Hāna, take a left on Haneoʻo Loop to explore lovely Hāmoa. Indulge in swimming or bodysurfing at this beautiful salt-and-pepper beach. Picnic tables, restrooms, and showers beneath the idyllic shade of coconut trees offer a more than comfortable rest stop.

The road leading to Hāmoa also takes you to **Kōkī Beach,** where you can watch the Hāna surfers mastering the swells and strong currents, and the seabirds darting over **Ālau,** the palm-fringed islet off the coast. The swimming is safer at Hāmoa.

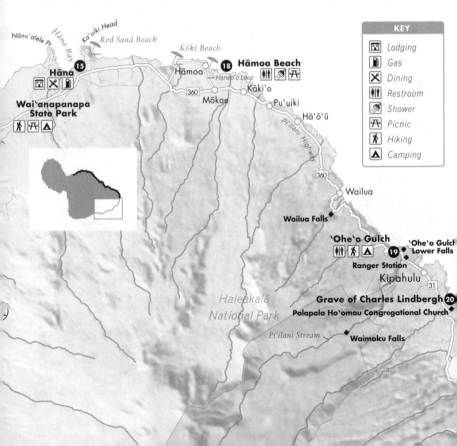

★ **⑲ 'Ohe'o Gulch.** Ten miles past town, at mile marker 42, you'll find the pools at 'Ohe'o Gulch. One branch of Haleakalā National Park runs down the mountain from the crater and reaches the sea here, where a basalt-lined stream cascades from one pool to the next. Some tour guides still call this area Seven Sacred Pools, but in truth there are more than seven, and they've never been considered sacred. You can park here—for a $10 fee—and walk to the lowest pools for a cool swim. The place gets crowded, since most people who drive the Hāna Highway make this their last stop.

If you enjoy hiking, go up the stream on the 2-mi hike to **Waimoku Falls.** The trail crosses a spectacular gorge, then turns into a boardwalk that takes you through an amazing bamboo forest. You can pitch a tent in the grassy campground down by the sea. *See Chapter 5, Golf, Hiking & Outdoor Activities.*

⑳ Grave of Charles Lindbergh. Many people travel the mile past 'Ohe'o Gulch to see the Grave of Charles Lindbergh. You see a ruined sugar mill with a big chimney on the right side of the road and then, on the left, a rutted track leading to Palapala Ho'omau Congregational Church. The simple one-room church sits on a bluff over the sea, with the small graveyard on the ocean side. The world-renowned aviator chose to be buried here because he and his wife, writer Anne Morrow Lindbergh, spent a lot of time living in the area. He was buried here in 1974. Since this is a churchyard, be considerate and leave everything exactly as you found it. Next to the churchyard on the ocean side is a small county park, a good place for a peaceful picnic.

Kaupō Road. The road to Hāna continues all the way around Haleakalā's "back side" through 'Ulupalakua Ranch and into Kula. The desertlike area, with its grand vistas, is unlike anything else on the island, but the road itself is bad, some-

TROPICAL DELIGHTS

The drive to Hāna wouldn't be as enchanting without a stop or two at one of the countless fruit and flower stands alongside the highway. Every 1/2 mi or so a thatched hut tempts passersby with apple bananas, liliko'i (passion fruit), avocados, or starfruit just plucked from the tree. Leave 50¢ or $1 in the can for the folks who live off the land. Huge bouquets of tropical flowers are available for a handful of change, and some farms will ship.

times impassable in winter. Car-rental agencies call it off-limits to their passenger cars and there is no emergency assistance available. The danger and dust from increasing numbers of speeding jeep drivers are making life tough for the residents, especially in Kaupō, with its 4 mi of unpaved road. The small communities around East Maui cling tenuously to the old ways. Please keep them in mind if you do pass this way. If you can't resist the adventure, try to make the drive just before sunset. The light slanting across the mountain is incredible. At night, giant potholes, owls, and loose cattle can make for some difficult driving.

Beaches

3

WORD OF MOUTH

"[Ho'okipa Beach] is world famous for wind surfing. This is where the Big Dogs go. Unless you are an expert, just go and watch. It's unbelievable . . . and free!"

—issy

"We drove ourselves to Hamoa beach, what a spectacular beach this was. The sand is gray; I had never seen sand like that—it was baby soft!"

—lasjas

Updated by
Elaine Gast

OF ALL THE HAWAIIAN ISLANDS, Maui's beaches are some of the most diverse. You'll find the pristine, palm-lined shores you expect with waters as clear and inviting as sea-green glass, but you'll also discover rich red- and black-sand beaches, craggy cliffs with surging whitecaps, and year-round sunsets that quiet the soul. As on the other isles, all Maui's beaches are public—but that doesn't mean it's not possible to find a secluded cove where you can truly get away from the world.

The island's leeward shores (the South Shore and West Side) have the calmest, sunniest beaches. Hit the beach early, when the aquamarine waters are as accommodating as bathwater. In summer, afternoon winds can be a sandblasting force, which can chase even the most dedicated sun worshippers away. From November through March, the South and West beaches are also great spots to watch the parade of whales that spend the winter in Maui's waters.

Windward shores (the North Shore and East Maui) offer more adventurous beachgoing. Beaches face the open ocean (rather than other islands) and tend to be rockier and more prone to powerful swells. This is particularly true in winter, when the legendary North Shore becomes a playground for experienced big-wave riders. Don't let this keep you away completely, however, some of the island's best beaches are those remote slivers of volcanic sand found on the wild windward shore.

WEST MAUI

West Maui beaches are legendary for their glittering aquamarine waters banked by long stretches of golden sand. Reef fronts much of the western shore, making the underwater panorama something to behold. The beaches listed here start in the north at Kapalua and head south past Kāʻanapali and Lahaina. Note that there are a dozen roadside beaches to choose from on Route 30; those listed here are the ones we like best.

Keep in Mind

The ocean is an amazing but formidable playground. Conditions can change quickly throughout the day. **Pay attention to any signs or flags** warning of high surf, rough currents, or jellyfish. It's best to watch the surf for a while before entering. Notice where other people are swimming and how often swells come in. Swells arrive in sets of five or six. If you should get caught in a largish swell, **don't panic.** Take a deep breath and dive beneath each oncoming wave. When you feel comfortable, you can swim back to shore with the swell.

Remember the ocean is also home to an array of fragile marine life. **Never stand on or touch coral reefs.** Hefty fines apply to anyone who chases or grabs at turtles, dolphins, and other federally protected animals. It's wise to avoid swimming at dawn, dusk, or in murky waters.

"Slaughterhouse" (Mokuleia) Beach. The island's northernmost beach is part of the Honolua-Mokuleia Marine Life Conservation District. "Slaughterhouse" is the surfers' nickname for what is officially Mokuleia. When the weather permits, this is a great place for bodysurfing and sunbathing. Concrete steps and a green railing help you get down the sheer cliff to the sand. The next bay over, Honolua, has no beach but offers one of the best surf breaks in Hawai'i. Often you can see competitions happening there; look for cars pulled off the road and parked in the pineapple field. ⊠ *Mile marker 32 on Rte. 30 past Kapalua* ⑁ *No facilities.*

D.T. Fleming Beach. Because the current can be quite strong, this charming, mile-long sandy cove is better for sunbathing than for swimming or water sports. Still it's one of the island's most popular beaches. Part of the beach runs along the front of the Ritz-Carlton's Beachhouse Bar & Grill—a good place to grab a cocktail and enjoy the view. ⊠ *Rte. 30, 1 mi north of Kapalua* ⑁ *Toilets, showers, picnic tables, grills/firepits, parking lot.*

Kapalua Beach. Kapalua was once named the "world's nicest beach." Walk through the tunnel at the end of Kapalua Place and you'll see why—the beach fronts a pristine bay good for snorkeling, swimming, and general lazing. Located just north of Nāpili Bay, this lovely, sheltered shore often remains calm late into the afternoon, although there may be strong currents offshore. This area is quite popular and is bordered by the Kapalua Resort so don't expect to have the beach to yourself. ⊠ *From Rte. 30, turn onto Kapalua Pl., walk through tunnel* ⑁ *Toilets, showers, parking lot.*

Ⓒ **Nāpili Beach.** Surrounded by sleepy condos, this round bay is a turtle-filled pool lined with a sparkling white crescent of sand. Sunbathers love this beach. The shorebreak is steep but gentle and it's easy to keep an eye on kids here as the entire bay is visible from any point in the water. The beach is right outside the Nāpili Kai Beach Club, a popular little resort for honeymooners, only a few miles south of Kapalua. It's also a terrific sunset spot. ⊠ *5900 Lower Honoapi'ilani Hwy., look for Nāpili Pl. or Hui Dr.* ⑁ *Showers, parking lot.*

FodorśChoice
★

★ Ⓒ **Kā'anapali Beach.** Stretching from the Sheraton Maui at its northernmost end to the Hyatt Regency Maui at its southern tip, Kā'anapali Beach

> **Don't Forget**
>
> All of the island's beaches are free and open to the public—even those that grace the front yards of fancy hotels—so you can make yourself at home on any one of them. Some of the prettiest beaches are often hidden by buildings; look for the blue, beach-access signs that indicate rights-of-way through condominiums, resorts, and other private properties.

is lined with resorts, condominiums, restaurants, and shops. If you're looking for quiet and seclusion, this is not the beach for you. But if you want lots of action, lay out your towel here. Also called "Dig Me Beach," this is one of Maui's best people-watching spots: catamarans, windsurfers, and parasailers head out from here while the beautiful people take in the scenery. A cement pathway weaves along the length of this 3-mi-long beach, leading from one astounding resort to the next.

The drop-off from Kā'anapali's soft, sugary sand is steep, but waves hit the shore with barely a rippling slap. The area at the northernmost end (in front of the Sheraton Maui), known as Black Rock, has prime snorkeling. The fish and eels here are tame from hand-feeding, but be aware—they can still bite! ✉ *Follow any of 3 Kā'anapali exits from Honoapi'ilani Hwy. and park at any hotel* ♿ *Toilets, showers, parking lot.*

Puamana Beach Park. Puamana is both a friendly beach park and a surf spot for mellow, longboard rides. With a narrow, sandy beach and grassy area providing plenty of shade, Puamana offers mostly calm swimming conditions and a good view of neighboring Lāna'i. Smaller than Launiupoko, this beach park tends to attract locals looking to surf and BBQ. ✉ *On Rte. 30, ¼ mi south of Lahaina* ♿ *Toilets, showers, picnic tables, grills/firepits.*

Launiupoko State Wayside Park. Launiupoko is the beach park of all beach parks. Both a surf break and a beach, it offers a little something for everyone with its inviting stretch of lawn, soft white sand, and gentle waves. The shoreline reef creates a protected wading pool, perfect for small children. Outside the reef, beginner surfers will find good longboard rides. From the long sliver of beach (good for walking), you'll enjoy superb views of neighbor islands, and landside, of deep valleys jetting through the West Maui mountains. Because of its endless sunshine and serenity—not to mention its many amenities—Launiupoko draws a crowd on the weekends, but there's space for everyone (and overflow parking across the street). ✉ *On Rte. 30, just south of Lahaina at mile marker 18* ♿ *Toilets, showers, picnic tables, grills/firepits.*

Oluwalu. Oluwalu is more an offshore snorkel spot than a beach, but it's a great place to watch for turtles and whales in-season. The beach is literally a pullover from the road, which can make for some unwelcome noise if you're looking for quiet. The entrance can be rocky (reef shoes help) but if you've got your snorkel gear, it's just a swim away to an extensive and diverse reef (200 yards). Shoreline visibility can vary, depending on the swell and time of day (late morning is best). Except for during a south swell, the waters are usually calm. A half mile north of mile marker 14 you'll find the rocky surf break, also called Oluwalu, which is a local (and at times, unfriendly) hangout, so it's better to stick to the beach. ⊠ *South of Oluwalu General Store, on Rte. 30 at mile marker 14* ⚐ *No facilities.*

Ukumeheme Beach Park. This popular park is also known as "Thousand Peaks," because the waves just keep coming. Beginning to intermediate wave riders will enjoy this as a good spot to longboard or boogie board. The beach itself leaves something to be desired, as it's more dead grass than sand, but there are plenty of BBQs, picnic tables, and some shade. Portable toilets are also available. ⊠ *On Rte. 30, near mile marker 12* ⚐ *Toilets, picnic tables, grills/firepits.*

THE SOUTH SHORE

Sandy beach fronts nearly the entire southern coastline of Maui, from Kīhei at the northern end to Mākena at the southern tip. The farther south you go, the better the beaches get. Kīhei has excellent beach parks right in town, with white sand, showers, restrooms, picnic tables, and BBQs. Good snorkeling can be found along the beaches' rocky borders. As good as Kīhei is, Wailea is even better. Wailea's beaches are cleaner, facilities tidier, and views even more impressive. ⚠ Note that break-ins have been reported at many of these beach parking lots. As you head out to Mākena, the terrain gets wilder. Bring lunch, water, and sunscreen with you. The following South Shore beaches are listed from north Kīhei southeast to Mākena.

Kalepolepo Beach Park. This tiny spit of beach and rock is the site of the ancient Kalepolepo Village, a large settlement and the prized property of Maui's King Kamehameha in the 1850s. Here the *maka 'ānana* (commoners) tended the man-made pond, farmed, fished, and raised taro. Today the park has lots of shady trees and stays pretty quiet, making it a good getaway from the crowd and sun. However, the beach (if you can call it that) is only a small sprinkling of sand, and swimming in the often-murky waters isn't recommended. Toilets are portable. ⊠ *726 S. Kīhei Rd., just south of Hawaiian Islands Humpback Whale National Marine Sanctuary* ⚐ *Toilets, picnic tables, grills/firepits, parking lot.*

Waipuliani Park. Fronting the Maui Sunset Resort, Waipuliani Park is a spectacular place to lay out or picnic on golf-course-quality grass. A small beach hides behind the dunes, although it's usually speckled with seaweed and shells; swimming isn't recommended as the park is not far

> **THE SUN**
>
> By far the biggest danger on the island is **sunburn**. The tropical sun is strong. Even at 9 AM, high SPF sunscreen–30 SPF or higher–is a must. Rash guards, those clingy-looking lycra swim shirts, offer the best protection. Before seeking shade under a coconut palm, be aware that winds can be strong enough to knock fruit off the trees and onto your head (go ahead and giggle but this really can and does happen).

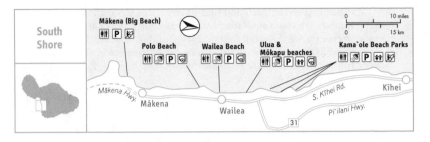

from a water-treatment plant. This park often hosts local activities, such as volleyball and croquet, and it attracts many dog lovers. Although it has a resort feel and can be crowded, it's still a perfect place to watch the sunset. ⊠ *From S. Kīhei Rd., turn at Star Market onto W. Waipuliani Rd.* ⚭ *Toilets, grills/firepits.*

Kalama Park. This 36-acre beach park is great for families and sports-lovers. With its extensive lawns and sports fields, the park has volleyball, baseball, tennis, and even a skateboard park. Stocked with grills, picnic pavilions, and plenty of shade, it's a recreational mecca. The beach itself is all but nonexistent, and swimming is fair—though you must brave the rocky steps down to the water. If you aren't completely comfortable with the rocky entrance, better to stick to the burgers and Bocci Ball here than venture into the ocean. ⊠ *On S. Kīhei Rd. across from Kīhei Kalama Village* ⚭ *Toilets, showers, picnic tables, grills/firepits, playground.*

The Cove Beach Park. Go to the Cove if you want to learn to surf. All of the surf schools are here in the morning, pushing longboard beginners onto the bunny-slope waves. For spectators there's a grassy area with some shade, and a tiny blink of a beach. If you aren't here to learn to surf, don't bother swimming. The water is sketchy at best, and there are plenty of better beaches. ⊠ *On S. Kīhei Rd., turn onto ʻIli ʻIli Rd.* ⚭ *No facilities.*

Charley Young Beach. This secluded 3-acre park at the north end of Kam I sits off the main drag in a residential area. The sand is soft and smooth, with a gentle slope into the ocean. A cloister of lava rocks shelters the beach from heavy afternoon winds, making this a mellow spot to laze around. The usually gentle waves make for good swimming, and you'll find good snorkeling along the rocks on the north end. Portable toilets are on-site. ⊠ *From S. Kīhei Rd., turn onto Kaiauʻ St., just north of Kamaʻole I* ⚭ *Toilets, shower.*

☾ **Kamaʻole I, II, and III.** Three steps from South Kīhei Road, you can find three golden stretches of sand separated by outcroppings of dark, jagged lava rocks. You can walk the length of all three beaches if you're willing to get your feet wet. The northernmost of the trio, Kamaʻole I (across from the ABC Store, in case you forgot your sunscreen), offers perfect swimming with a sandy bottom a long way out and an active volleyball court. If you're one of those people who likes your beach sans the sand, there's also a great lawn for you to spread out on at the south end of the beach. Kamaʻole II is nearly identical minus the lawn. The last beach, the one with all the people on it, is Kama'ole III, perfect for throwing disk or throwing down a blanket. This is a great family beach, complete with a playground, volleyball net, BBQs, kite flying, and frequently, rented inflatable castles—a birthday-party must for every cool kid living on the island.

Locally known as "Kam" I, II, and III, all three beaches have great swimming and lifeguards. In the morning the water can be as still as a lap pool. Kam III offers terrific breaks for beginning bodysurfers. ■ TIP➡ The public restrooms have seen better days; decent facilities are found at convenience stores and eateries across the street. ✉ *S. Kīhei Rd., between Ke Ali'i Alanui Rd. and Keonekai Rd.* ⚐ *Lifeguard, toilets, showers, picnic tables, grills/firepits, playground, parking lot.*

Keawakapu Beach. Who wouldn't love Keawakapu with its long stretch of golden sand, near-perfect swimming, and stunning views of the crater? It's great fun to walk or jog this beach south into Wailea (you can go all the way to the Renaissance), as the path is lined with remarkable residences—can you guess which one belongs to Stephen King? The winds pick up in the afternoon, so beware of irritating sand storms. Keawakapu has two entrances: one at the Mana Kai Maui Resort (look for the blue SHORELINE ACCESS sign and the parking at Kilohana Street), and the second at the dead end of Kīhei Road. Toilets are portable. ✉ *S. Kīhei Rd., at Kilohana St.* ⚐ *Toilets, showers, parking lot.*

☺ **Mōkapu & Ulua.** Look for a little road and public parking lot wedged between the first two big Wailea resorts—the Renaissance and the Marriott. This gets you to Mōkapu and Ulua beaches. Though there are no lifeguards, families love this place. Reef formations create tons of tide pools for kids to explore and the beaches are protected from major swells. Snorkeling is excellent at Ulua, the beach to the left of the entrance. Mōkapu, to the right, tends to be less crowded. ✉ *Wailea Alanui Dr., south of Renaissance resort entrance* ⚐ *Toilets, showers, parking lot.*

Wailea Beach. A road just after the Grand Wailea resort takes you to Wailea Beach, a wide, sandy stretch with snorkeling, swimming, and, if you're a guest of the Four Seasons resort, Evian spritzes! If you're not a guest at the Grand Wailea or Four Seasons, the private cabanas and chaise-lounges can be a little annoying, but any complaint is more than made up for by the calm, unclouded waters and soft, white sand. ✉ *Wailea Alanui Dr., south of Grand Wailea resort entrance* ⚐ *Toilets, showers, parking lot.*

Polo Beach. From Wailea Beach you can walk to this small, uncrowded crescent fronting the Fairmont Kea Lani resort. Swimming and snorkeling are great here and it's a good place to whale-watch. As at Wailea Beach, private cabanas occupy prime sandy real estate, but there's plenty of room for you and your towel, and even a nice grass picnic area. The pathway connecting the two beaches is a great spot to jog or leisurely take in awesome views of nearby Molokini and Kaho'olawe. Rare native plants grow along the ocean, or *makai,* side of the path; the honey-sweet smelling one is *naio,* or false sandalwood. ✉ *Wailea Alanui Dr.,* *south of Fairmont Kea Lani resort entrance* ⟳ *Toilets, showers, picnic tables, grills/firepits, parking lot.*

FodorśChoice ★ **Mākena (Big Beach).** Locals successfully fought to give Mākena—one of Hawai'i's most breathtaking beaches—state park protection. Also known as "Big Beach," this stretch of deep-golden sand abutting sparkling aqua water is 3,000-feet-long and 100-feet-wide. It's never crowded, no matter how many cars cram into the lots. The water is fine for swimming, but use caution. ⚠ The shore dropoff is steep and swells can get deceptively big. Despite the infamous "Makena cloud," a blanket that rolls in during the early afternoon and obscures the sun, it rarely rains here. For a dramatic view of Big Beach, climb Pu'u Ōla'i,

Forget your beach gear? No need to fear, Maui is the land-of-plenty when it comes to convenient stores just waiting to pawn off their boogie boards and beach mats. Look for Long's Drugs (in Kīhei and Kahului) or the ABC Stores (in Kā'napali, Lahaina, Kīhei, and more) for extra sunscreen, shades, towels, and umbrellas. If you want better deals and don't mind the drive into town, look for Kmart (424 Dairy Road) or Wal-Mart (101 Pakaula Street) in Kahului. For more extensive gear, check out Sports Authority (270 Dairy Road) in Kahului.

the steep cinder cone near the first entrance. Continue over the cinder cone's side to discover "Little Beach"—clothing-optional by popular practice. (Officially, nude sunbathing is illegal in Hawai'i.) On Sunday, free spirits of all kinds crowd Little Beach's tiny shoreline for a drumming circle and bonfire. Little Beach has the island's best bodysurfing (no pun intended). Skimboarders catch air at Big Beach's third entrance. Each of the three paved entrances has portable toilets. ⊠ *Off Wailea Alanui Dr.* ⟳ *Toilets, parking lot.*

THE NORTH SHORE

Many of the folks you see jaywalking in Pā'ia sold everything they owned to come to Maui and live a beach bum's life. Beach culture abounds on the North Shore. But these folks aren't sunbathers, they're big-wave riders, windsurfers, or kiteboarders. The North Shore is their challenging sports arena. Beaches here face the open ocean and tend to be rougher and windier than beaches elsewhere on Maui—but don't let that scare you off. On calm days, the reef-speckled waters are truly beautiful and offer a quieter and less commercial beach-going experience than the leeward shore. Beaches below are listed from Kahului (near the airport) eastward to Ho'okipa.

Kanahā Beach. Windsurfers, kiteboarders, joggers, and picnicking families like this long, golden strip of sand bordered by a wide grassy area with lots of shade. The winds pick up in the early afternoon, making for the best kiteboarding and windsurfing conditions—if you know what you're doing, that is. The best spot for watching kiteboarders is at the far left end of the beach. ⊠ *Drive through airport and make right*

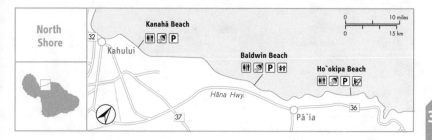

onto car-rental road (Koeheke); turn right onto Amala Pl. and take any left (there are 3 entrances) into Kanahā ⓑ Toilets, showers, picnic tables, grills/firepits, parking lot.

★ ⓒ **Baldwin Beach.** A local favorite, just west of Pā'ia town, Baldwin beach is a big body of comfortable white sand. This is a good place to stretch out, jog, or swim, though the waves can sometimes be choppy and the undertow strong. Don't be afraid of those big brown blobs floating beneath the surface, they're just pieces of alien seaweed awash in the surf. You can find shade along the beach beneath the ironwood trees, or in the large pavilion, a spot regularly overtaken by local parties and community events.

The long, shallow pool at the Kahului end of the beach is known as "Baby Beach." Separated from the surf by a flat reef wall, this is where ocean-loving families bring their kids (and sometimes puppies) to practice a few laps. The view of the West Maui Mountains is hauntingly beautiful from here. ⊠ Hāna Hwy., 1 mi west of Baldwin Ave. ⓑ Lifeguard, toilets, showers, picnic tables, grills/firepits, parking lot.

★ **Ho'okipa Beach.** If you want to see some of the world's finest windsurfers in action, hit this beach along Hāna Highway. The sport was largely developed right at Ho'okipa and has become an art and a career to some. This beach is also one of Maui's hottest surfing spots, with waves as high as 20 feet. This is not a good swimming beach, nor the place to learn windsurfing unless you're an expert, but plenty of picnic tables and BBQs are available for hanging out and watching the pros. Bust out your telephoto lens at the cliffside lookout. ⊠ 2 mi past Pā'ia on Rte. 36 ⓑ Toilets, showers, picnic tables, grills/firepits, parking lot.

EAST MAUI

Hāna's beaches will literally stop you in your tracks, they're that beautiful. Black-and-red sands stand out against pewter skies and lush tropical foliage creating picture-perfect scenes, which seem too breathtaking to be real. Rough conditions often preclude swimming, but that doesn't mean you can't explore the shoreline. Beaches below are listed in order from the west end of Hāna town eastward.

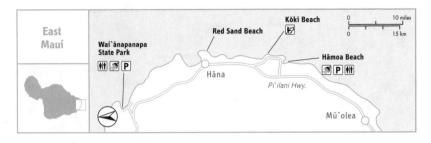

FodorsChoice **Wai'ānapanapa State Park.** Small but rarely crowded, this beach will re-
★ main in your memory long after visiting. Fingers of white foam rush onto
a black volcanic pebble beach fringed with green beach vines and palms.
Swimming here is both relaxing and invigorating: strong currents bump
smooth stones up against your ankles while seabirds flit above a black,
jagged sea arch draped with vines. At the edge of the parking lot, a sign
tells you the sad story of a doomed Hawaiian princess. Stairs lead
through a tunnel of interlocking Polynesian *hau* branches to an icy cave
pool—the secret hiding place of the ancient princess. ⚠ You can swim
in this pool, but be wary of mosquitoes! In the other direction, a 3-mi, dramatic coastal path continues beyond the campground, past sea arches,
blowholes, and cultural sites all the way to Hāna town. ✉ *Hāna Hwy.
near mile marker 32* ♿ *Toilets, showers, picnic tables, grills/firepits, parking lot.*

★ **Red Sand Beach (Kaihalulu Beach).** Kaihalulu Beach, better known as
Red Sand Beach, is unmatched in its raw and remote beauty. It's not
simple to find but when you round the last corner of the trail and are
confronted with the sight of it, your jaw is bound to drop. Earthy red
cliffs tower above the deep maroon sand beach and swimmers bob
about in a turquoise blue lagoon formed by volcanic boulders just offshore (it's like floating around in a
giant natural bath tub). It's worth
spending a night in Hāna just to
make sure you can get here early
and have some time to enjoy it before anyone else shows up.

Keep in mind, getting here is not
easy and you have to pass through
private property along the way—do
so at your own risk. You need to
tread carefully up and around
Ka'uiki (the red cinder hill); the
cliff-side cinder path is slippery and
constantly eroding. Hiking is not
recommended in shoes without
traction, or in bad weather. By popular practice, clothing on the beach
is optional. ✉ *At end of Uákea Rd.
past baseball field. Park near com-*

> ## BEACH SAFETY
>
> Some general rules of thumb
> when beach-going:
>
> ■ Check with lifeguards on beach
>   and surf conditions.
>
> ■ Always swim or snorkel with a
>   buddy.
>
> ■ Never turn your back on the
>   ocean.
>
> ■ Don't swim in murky water.
>
> ■ If the big lava-rock boulders
>   you're about to go exploring are
>   wet, that means a wave may
>   wash in and knock you down.
>
> ■ When in doubt, don't go out.

munity center, walk through grass lot to trail below cemetery ⚴ *No facilities.*

Kōkī Beach. You can tell from the trucks parked every which way alongside the road that this is a favorite local surf spot. ⚠ Watch conditions before swimming or bodysurfing, because the riptides here can be mean. Look for awesome views of the rugged coastline and a sea arch on the left end. *Iwa,* or white-throated frigate birds, dart like pterodactyls over Alau islet offshore. ⊠ *Haneoʻo Loop Rd., 2 mi east of Hāna town* ⚴ *No facilities.*

Hāmoa Beach. Why did James Michener describe this stretch of salt-and-pepper sand as the most "South Pacific" beach he'd come across, even though it's located in the North Pacific? Maybe it was the perfect half-moon shape, speckled with the shade of palm trees. Perhaps he was intrigued by the jutting black coastline, often outlined by rain showers out at sea, or the pervasive lack of hurry he felt once settled in here. Whatever it was, many still feel the lure. The beach can be crowded but nonetheless relaxing. Expect to see a few chaise longues and a guest-only picnic area set up by the Hotel Hāna-Maui. At times, the churning surf might intimidate beginning swimmers, but bodysurfing can be great here. ⊠ *½ mi past Kōki Beach on Haneoʻo Loop Rd., 2 mi east of Hāna town* ⚴ *Toilets, showers, picnic tables, parking lot.*

Water Activities & Tours

WORD OF MOUTH

"Have some kids teach you how to really catch the waves on a boogie board . . . we had so much fun, and it was even more fun surrounded by little kids who got a kick out of *us*."

—turn_it_on

"Molokini snorkeling can be wonderful (scuba diving is even better) and what's the worst that happens if it isn't? Several hours on a catamaran enjoying beautiful views—what's wrong with that?"

—bobludlow

Updated by
Elaine Gast

GETTING INTO (OR ONTO) THE WATER will be the highlight of your Maui trip. At Lahaina and Māʻalaea harbors you can board boats for snorkeling, scuba diving, deep-sea fishing, whale-watching, parasailing, and sunset cocktail adventures. You can learn to surf, catch a ferry to Lānaʻi, or grab a seat on a fast inflatable. Along the leeward coastline, from Kāʻanapali on the West Shore all the way down to the tip of ʻĀhihi-Kīnaʻu on the South Shore, you can discover great snorkeling and swimming. If you're a thrill-seeker, head out to the North Shore and Hoʻokipa, where surfers, kiteboarders, and windsurfers catch big waves and big air.

Boogie Boarding & Bodysurfing

Bodysurfing and "sponging" (as boogie boarding is called by the regulars) are great ways to catch some waves without having to master surfing—and there's no balance or coordination required. A boogie board (or "sponge") is softer than a hard, fiberglass surfboard, which means you can ride safely in the rough-and-tumble surf zone. If you get tossed around (which is half the fun), you don't have a heavy surfboard nearby to bang your head on, but you do have something to hang onto. Serious spongers invest in a single short-clipped fin to help propel them into the wave.

How to Catch a Wave

The technique for catching waves is the same with or without a board. Swim out to where the swell is just beginning to break, and position yourself toward shore. When the next wave comes, lie on your board (if you have one), kick like crazy, and catch it! You'll feel the push of the wave as you glide in front of the gurgling, foamy surf. When bodysurfing, put your arms over your head, bring your index fingers together (so you look like the letter 'A'), and stiffen your body like a board to achieve the same effect. If you don't like to swim too far out, stick with boogie boarding and bodysurfing close to shore. Shorebreak (if it isn't too steep) can be exhilarating to ride. You'll know it's too steep if you hear the sound of slapping when the waves hit the sand. You're looking for waves that curl over and break farther out, then roll, not slap onto the sand. Always watch first to make sure the conditions aren't too strong.

Best Spots

If you don't mind nudity (officially illegal, but practiced nonetheless), **Little Beach** (⊠ On Mākena Rd., first entrance to Mākena State Beach Park; climb rock wall at north end of beach) is the best break on the island for boogie boarding and bodysurfing. The shape of the sandy shoreline creates waves that break a ways out and tumble on into shore. Because it's sandy, you only risk stubbing a toe on the few submerged rocks, not a reef floor. Don't even think about boogie boarding at neighboring Big Beach—you'll be slapped like a flapjack onto the steep shore.

Kamaʻole III (⊠ S. Kīhei Rd.) is another good spot for bodysurfing and boogie boarding. It has a sandy floor, with 1- to 3-foot waves breaking not too far out. It's often crowded late into the day, especially on weekends when local kids are out of school. Don't let that chase you away, the waves are wide enough for everyone.

On the North Shore, **Pā'ia Bay** (⊠ Just before Pā'ia town, beyond large community building and grass field) has waves suitable for spongers and bodysurfers. ■ TIP→ Park in the public lot across the street and leave your valuables at home, as this beach is known for break-ins.

Equipment Rentals

Most condos and hotels have boogie boards available to guests—some in better condition than others (but beat-up boogies work just as well for beginners). You can also pick up a boogie board from any discount shop, such as Kmart or Long's Drugs, for upward of $30.

Auntie Snorkel. You can rent decent boogie boards here for $5 a day, or $15 a week. ⊠ 2439 S. Kīhei Rd. Kīhei ☎ 808/879–6263.

Honolua Surf. "Waverider" boogie boards with smooth undersides (better than the bumpy kind) can be rented from this surf shop for $8 a day, or $35 a week (with a $100 deposit). ⊠ 2411 S. Kīhei Rd., Kīhei ☎ 808/874–0999 ✉ 845 Front St., Lahaina ☎ 808/661–8848.

Deep-Sea Fishing

If fishing is your sport, Maui is your island. In these waters you'll find 'ahi, *aku* (skipjack tuna), barracuda, bonefish, *kawakawa* (bonito), mahimahi, Pacific blue marlin, ono, and *ulua* (jack crevalle). You can fish year-round and you don't need a license. ■ TIP→ Because boats fill up fast during busy seasons (Christmas, spring break, tournament weeks), consider making reservations before coming to Maui.

Plenty of fishing boats run out of Lahaina and Mā'alaea harbors. If you charter a private boat, expect to spend in the neighborhood of $600 to $800 for a thrilling half-day in the swivel seat. You can share a boat for much less if you don't mind close quarters with a stranger who may get seasick, drunk, or worse . . . lucky! Before you sign up, you should know that some boats keep the catch. They will, however, fillet a nice piece for you to take home. And if you catch a real beauty, you might even be able to have it professionally mounted.

■ TIP→ Don't go out with a boater who charges for the fish you catch—that's harbor robbery. You're expected to bring your own lunch and nonglass beverages. (Shop the night before, it's hard to find snacks at 6 AM.) Boats supply coolers, ice, and bait. 10%–20% tips are suggested.

Boats & Charters

★ **Finest Kind Inc.** A record 1,118-pound Blue Marlin was reeled in by the crew aboard *Finest Kind*, a lovely 37-foot Merritt kept so clean you'd never guess the action it's seen. Ask Captain Dave about his pet frigate bird—he's been around these waters long enough to befriend other expert fishers. This family-run company operates four boats and specializes in live bait. ⊠ *Lahaina Harbor, Slip 7* ☎ *808/661–0338* ⊕ *www. finestkindsportfishing.com.*

Hinatea Sportfishing. The active crew aboard this first-class, 41-foot Hatteras has the motto, "No boat rides here—we go to catch fish!" For those conservation-minded folks, Hinatea has tagged and released more marlin than any charter boat on Maui. ⊠ *Lahaina Harbor, Slip 27* ☎ *808/ 667–7548* ⊕ *www.fishmaui.com/hinatea.*

Iwa Lele Extreme Sportfishing. If you're serious about catching fish, and don't mind the 4:30 AM check-in time, this trip's for you. On a 39-foot custom Force, Captain Fuzzy will get you to the best fishing spots before the masses. You'll troll with lures and live bait—and hopefully, catch the big one. Check out their Web site for good fishing FAQs. ⊠ *Lahaina Harbor* ☎ *808/661–1118* ⊕ *www.fishmaui.com.*

Start Me Up Sportfishing. These 42-foot Bertram Sportfishers will give you one of the most comfortable fishing trips around. With 20 years in business, Start Me Up has a fleet of five boats, all relatively new, complete with all the amenities: air-conditioning, TV, VCR, refrigerator, microwave, and ice chest. They provide the tackle and equipment. Six-person max. ⊠ *Lahaina Harbor, Slip 12* ☎ *808/667–7879* ⊕ *www. startmeupsportfishing.com.*

Strikezone. This is the only charter that offers morning bottom-fishing trips (for smaller fish such as snapper), as well as deep-sea trips (for the big ones—ono, ahi, mahimahi, and marlin). *Strikezone* is a 43-foot Delta that offers plenty of room (16-person max). Lunch and softdrinks are included, and on bottom-fishing trips you can keep your catch. The cost is $150 per person for a pole; spectators can ride for $75. The six-hour bottom-fishing trip runs Monday, Wednesday, Friday, and Saturday; the six-hour deep-sea trips run Tuesday, Thursday, and Sunday. All trips leave at 6:30 AM. ⊠ *Māʻalaea Harbor, Slip 64, Māʻalaea* ☎ *808/ 879–4485.*

Kayaking

Kayaking is a fantastic way to experience Maui's coast up close. Floating aboard a plastic popsicle stick is easier than you might think, and allows you to cruise out to vibrant, living coral reefs and waters where dolphins and even whales roam. Kayaking can be a leisurely paddle or a challenge of heroic proportion,

> **TAKE NOTE**
>
> The ʻĀhihi-Kīnaʻu Natural Area Reserve at the southernmost point of South Maui is closed to commercial traffic and you may not take rented kayaks into the reserve.

depending on your ability, the location, and the weather. ■ TIP→ Though you can rent kayaks independently, we recommend taking a guide. An apparently calm surface can hide extremely strong ocean currents—and you don't *really* want to take an unplanned trip to Tahiti! Most guides are naturalists who will steer you away from surging surf, lead you to pristine reefs, and point out camouflaged fish, like the stalking hawkfish. Not having to schlep your gear on top of your rental car is a bonus. A half-day tour runs around $75. Custom tours can be arranged.

If you decide to strike out on your own, tour companies will rent kayaks for the day with paddles, life vests, and roof racks, and many will meet you near your chosen location. Ask for a map of good entries and plan to avoid paddling back to shore against the wind (schedule extra time for the return trip regardless). When you're ready to snorkel, secure your belongings in a dry pack on-board and drag your boat by its bowline behind you. (This isn't as bad as it sounds).

Best Spots

On the West Side, past the steep cliffs on the Honoapi'ilani Highway and before you hit Lahaina, there's a long stretch of inviting coastline, including **Ukumehame** and **Olowalu** beaches (⊠ Between mile markers 12 and 14 on Rte. 30). This is a good spot for beginners; entry is easy and there's much to see in every direc-tion. If you want to snorkel, the best visibility is farther out at Olowalu, at about 25 feet depth. ⚠ Watch for sharp *kiawe* thorns buried in the sand on the way into the water.

> ## OUTRIGGER-CANOE RACES
>
> Polynesians first traveled to Hawai'i by outrigger canoe, and racing the traditional craft is a fa-vorite pastime on the Islands. Ca-noes were revered in old Hawai'i, and no voyage could begin with-out a blessing, ceremonial chant-ing, and a hula performance to ensure a safe journey. In Lahaina in mid-May, the two-week **Festival of Canoes** (☎ 808/667–9193 ⊕ www.visitlahaina.com) includes a torch-lighting and awa-drinking ceremony, arts-and-crafts demon-strations, a chance for interna-tional canoe enthusiasts to mingle and observe how Polynesian ves-sels are rigged, and the launching of a "Parade of Canoes."

Mākena Landing (⊠ Off Mākena Rd.) is an excellent taking-off point for a South Maui adventure. Enter from the paved parking lot or the small sandy beach a little south. The bay itself is virtually empty, but the right edge is flanked with brilliant coral heads and juvenile turtles. If you round the point on the right, you come across **Five Caves,** a system of entic-ing underwater arches. In the morning you may see dolphins, and the arches are havens for lobsters, eels, and spectacularly hued butterfly fish. Check out the million-dollar mansions lining the shoreline and guess which celebrity lives where.

Equipment Rentals & Tours

Maui Sea Kayaking. Since 1988, this company has been guiding small groups (four-person trips) to secret spots along Maui's coast. They take great care in customizing their outings. For example, the guides ac-commodate kayakers with disabilities as well as senior kayakers, and they also offer kid-size gear. Among their more unusual programs are kayak surfing and wedding-vow renewal. Trips leave from various lo-cations, depending upon the weather. ☎ *808/572–6299* ⊕ *www.maui. net/~kayaking.*

Fodor'sChoice ★ **South Pacific Kayaks.** These guys pioneered recreational kayaking on Maui— they know their stuff. Guides are friendly, informative, and eager to help you get the most out of your experience; we're talking true, fun-loving, kayak geeks. Some activity companies show a strange lack of care for the marine environment; South Pacific stands out as adventurous *and* responsible. They offer a variety of trips leaving from both West Side and South Shore locations, including an advanced four-hour "Molokini Challenge." ☎ *800/776–2326 or 808/875–4848* ⊕ *www.southpacifickayaks.com.*

Kiteboarding

Catapulting up to 40 feet in the air above the breaking surf, kiteboarders hardly seem of this world. Silken kites hold the athletes aloft for precious seconds—long enough for the execution of mind-boggling tricks—then deposit them back in the sea. This new sport is not for the weak-kneed. No matter what people might tell you, it's harder to learn than windsurfing. The unskilled (or unlucky) can be caught in an upwind and carried far out in the ocean, or worse—dropped smack on the shore. Because of insurance (or the lack thereof), companies are not allowed to rent equipment. Beginners must take lessons, and then purchase their own gear. Devotees swear after your first few lessons, committing to buying your kite is easy.

> **ON THE SIDELINES**
>
> If you're not inclined to take to the air yourself, live vicariously by attending **Red Bull's King of the Air** (⊠ Ho'okipa Beach Park ☎ 808/573-3222 ⊕ www.redbullkingoftheair.com) showcase contest each fall. Contenders travel from as far as Poland and Norway to compete in this world-class big air and freestyle kiteboarding contest.

Aqua Sports Maui. "To air is human," or so they say at Aqua Sports, which calls itself the local favorite of kiteboarding schools. They've got a great location right near Kite Beach, at the west (left) end of Kanaha Beach, and offer basic through advanced kiteboarding lessons. Rates start at $210 for a three-hour basics course taught by certified instructors. ⊠ *90 Amala Pl., near Kite Beach, Kahului* ☎ *808/242–8015* ⊕ *www.mauikiteboardinglessons.com.*

Hawaiian Sailboarding Techniques. Pro kiteboarder Alan Cadiz will have you safely ripping in no time over at Naish Beach, (a ¼ mi past the bridge on Amala Place, just past Ka'a Point). A "Learn to Kitesurf" package starts at $225 for a three-hour private, all equipment included. HST is in the highly regarded Hi Tech Surf & Sports store, located in the Triangle Square shopping center. ⊠ *425 Koloa St., Kahului* ☎ *808/871–5423* ⊕ *www.hstwindsurfing.com.*

Kiteboarding School Maui. Call KSM, one of the first kiteboarding schools in the United States and the first on Maui, for one-on-one "flight lessons." Pro kiteboarders will induct you at Kite Beach, at the west (left) end of Kanaha Beach, providing instruction, equipment, snacks, and FAA guidelines. (Seriously, there are rules about avoiding airplanes at nearby Kahului Airport). Rates start at $290 for four hours or $490 for two-day private lessons. KSM is the only school that offers retail gear as well as instruction. ⊠ *22 Hāna Hwy., Kahului* ☎ *808/873–0015* ⊕ *www.ksmaui.com.*

Parasailing

Parasailing is an easy, exhilarating way to earn your wings: just strap on a harness attached to a parachute, and a powerboat pulls you up and over the ocean from a launching dock or a boat's platform. ■ TIP→ Keep in mind, parasailing is limited to Maui's West Side, and "thrill craft"—including parasails—are prohibited in Maui waters during Humpback whale calving season, December 15 to April 15.

Parasail Kaʻanapali. Rides here are shorter (six minutes), but they're also cheaper ($40 for a solo flight), and you get to fly as high as 900 feet. Early-bird (9 AM) flights are cheapest. Located at Mala Wharf in Lahaina; trips run daily in-season, except Saturday. ☎ 808/669–6555.

West Maui Parasail. Launch 400 feet above the ocean for a bird's-eye view of Lahaina, or be daring at 800 feet for smoother rides and better views. The captain will be glad to let you experience a "toe dip" or "freefall" if you request it. For safety reasons, passengers weighing less than 100 pounds must be strapped together in tandem. Hour-long trips departing from Lahaina Harbor, Slip #15, include 10-minute flights and run from $53 to $60. Early-bird (8–9 AM) flights are cheapest. ☎ 808/661–4060 ⊕ www.maui.net/~parasail.

UFO Parasail. UFO is the only parasail company in Kaʻanapali. They offer the standard 7-minute ride at 400 feet ($45), or 10-minute ride at 800 feet ($55). Observers are welcome aboard. Be prepared for lots of jokes about alien abduction. ☎ 808/661–7836 ⊕ www.ufoparasailing.com.

Sailing

With the islands of Molokaʻi, Lānaʻi, Kahoʻolawe, and Molokini a stone's throw away, Maui waters offer visually arresting backdrops for sailing adventures. Sailing conditions can be fickle, so some operations throw in snorkeling or whale-watching, and others offer sunset cruises. Winds are consistent in summer, but variable in winter, and afternoons are generally windier all throughout the year. Prices range from around $35 for two-hour trips to $75 for half-day excursions. ■ TIP→ You won't be sheltered from the elements on the trim racing boats, so be sure to bring a hat (one that won't blow away), a light jacket or cover-up, sunglasses, and extra sunscreen.

Boats & Charters

America II. This one-time America's Cup contender offers an exciting,

---

PRIVATE CHARTERS

If you want to steer clear of the crowds, and you don't mind paying the extra bucks, you might hire a private charter. It's like having your own sailboat on Maui. Although almost all sailing vessels (including those in this section) offer private charters, there are a few that cater to them specifically. Among the top three: *ShangriLa* is the largest and most luxurious 65-foot catamaran (☎ 888/855–9977 ⊕ www.sailingmaui.com); *Island Star* is a 57-foot Columbia offering customized trips out of Lahaina (☎ 800/669-7827 ⊕ www.islandstarsailing.com); and *Cinderella* is a swift and elegant 50-foot Columbia (☎ 808/244-0009 ⊕ www.maui.net/~sailmaui).

intimate alternative to crowded catamarans. For fast action, try a tradewind sail. Sunset sails are generally calmer—a good choice if you don't want to spend two hours fully exposed to the sun. Plan to bring a change of clothes, because you will get wet. ⊠ *Harbor Slip #5, Lahaina* ☎ *808/667–2195.*

Paragon. If you want to snorkel and sail, this is your boat. Many snorkel cruises claim to sail but actually motor most of the way; Paragon is an exception. Both Paragon vessels (one catamaran in Lahaina, the other in Māʻalaea) are ship-shape, and crews are competent and friendly. Their mooring in Molokini Crater is particularly good, and they often stay after the masses have left. The Lānaʻi trip includes a picnic lunch on the beach, snorkeling, and an afternoon blue water swim. Extras on their trips to Lānaʻi include mai tais and sodas, hot and cold pūpūs, and champagne. ⊠ *Lahaina and Māʻalaea Harbors* ☎ *808/244–2087* ⊕ *www.sailmaui.com.*

***Scotch Mist* Charters.** Follow the wind aboard this 50-foot Santa Cruz sailing yacht. Two-hour snorkeling, sunset, or whale-watching trips focus on the sail, and usually carry less than 25 passengers. ⊠ *Lahaina Harbor Slip #2* ☎ *877/464–6284 or 808/661–0386* ⊕ *www.scotchmistsailingcharters.com.*

Rafting

The high-speed, inflatable rafts you find on Maui are nothing like the raft that Huck Finn used to drift down the Mississippi. While passengers grip straps, these rafts fly, skimming and bouncing across the sea. Because they're so maneuverable, they go where the big boats can't—secret coves, sea caves, and remote beaches. Two-hour trips run around $50, half-day trips upward of $100. ⚠ Although safe, these trips are not for the faint of heart. If you have back or neck problems or are pregnant, you should reconsider this activity.

Blue Water Rafting. One of the only ways to get to the stunning Kenaio coast (the roadless southern coastline beyond ʻĀhihi-Kīnaʻu), this rafting tour begins trips conveniently at the Kīhei Boat ramp. Dolphins, turtles, and other marine life are the highlight of this adventure, along with sea caves, lava arches, and views of Haleakalā. Two-hour trips start at $45; longer trips cost $90 to $115 and include a deli lunch. ⊠ *7777 South Kīhei Rd., Kīhei* ☎ *808/879–7238* ⊕ *www.bluewaterrafting. com.*

Ocean Riders. This West Side tour crosses the ʻAuʻAu channel to Lānaʻi's Shipwreck Beach, then circles the island for 70 minutes of remote coast. For snorkeling, the "back side" of Lānaʻi is one of Hawaiʻi's unsung marvels. Tours depart from Mala Wharf, at the northern end of Front Street and include snorkle gear, a fruit breakfast, and a deli lunch. ⊠ *Lahaina* ☎ *808/661–3586* ⊕ *www.mauioceanriders.com.*

Scuba Diving

Maui is just as scenic underwater as it is on dry land. In fact, Maui has been rated one of the top 10 dive spots in North America. A big advantage on Maui is that divers see more large animals than they would in areas such as the Caribbean. It's common on any dive to see huge sea turtles, eagle rays, and small reef sharks, not to mention many varieties of angelfish, parrotfish, eels, and octopi. Unlike other popular dive destinations, most of the species are unique to this area. For example, of Maui's 450 species of reef fish, 25% are endemic to the island. In addition, the terrain itself is different from other dive spots. Here you'll find ancient and intricate lava flows, full of nooks where marine life hide and breed. Although the water tends to be a bit rougher—not to mention colder—here, divers are given a great thrill during Humpback Whale season, when you can actually hear whales singing underwater.

Some of the finest diving spots in all of Hawai'i lie along the Valley Isle's western and southwestern shores. Dives are best in the morning, when visibility can hold a steady 100 feet. If you're a certified diver, you can rent gear at any Maui dive shop simply by showing your PADI or NAUI card. Unless you're familiar with the area, however, it's probably best to hook up with a dive shop for an underwater tour. Tours include tanks and weights and start around $120. Wetsuits and BCs are rented separately, for an additional $15 to $30. Shops also offer introductory dives ($100–$160) for those who aren't certified. ■ TIP➔ Before signing on with any of these outfitters, it's a good idea to ask a few pointed questions about your guide's experience, the weather outlook, and the condition of the equipment.

Before you head out on your dive, be sure to check conditions. If you have access to the Internet, check the Glen James weather site, ⊕ www. hawaiiweathertoday.com, for a breakdown on the weather, wind, and visibility conditions.

Best Spots

Honolua Bay (✉ Between mile markers 32 and 33 on Rte. 30, look for narrow dirt road to left) has beach entry. This West Maui marine preserve is alive with many varieties of coral and tame tropical fish, including large *ulua, kāhala,* barracuda, and manta rays. With depths of 20 to 50 feet, this is a popular summer dive spot, good for all levels. ⚠ High surf often prohibits winter dives.

Only 3 mi offshore, **Molokini Crater** is world renowned for its deep, crystal-clear, fish-filled waters. A crescent-shape islet formed by the eroding top of a volcano, the crater is a marine preserve ranging 10 to 80 feet in depth. The numerous tame fish and brilliant coral dwelling within the crater make it a popular introductory dive site. On calm days, exploring the back side of Molokini (called Back Wall) can be a dramatic sight for advanced divers—giving them visibility of up to 150 feet. The enormous dropoff into the 'Alalākeiki Channel (to 350 feet) offers awesome seascapes, black coral, and chance sightings of larger pelagic fish and sharks.

On the South Shore, a popular dive spot is **Mākena Landing,** also called **Five Graves** or **Five Caves.** About ⅓ mi down Mākena Road, you'll feast on underwater delights—caves, ledges, coral heads, and an outer reef home to a large green sea turtle colony (called "Turtle Town"). ⚠ Entry is rocky lava, so be careful where you step. This area is for the more experienced diver. Rookies can enter farther down Mākena Road at Mākena Landing, and dive to the right.

South of Mākena Landing, the best diving by far is at 'Āhihi Bay and La Pérouse Bay, both South Maui marine preserves. In **'Āhihi Bay,** you'll find an area the locals call **Fishbowl,** which is a small cove right beside the road, next to a hexagon-shape house. Here you'll find excellent underwater scenery, with many types of fish and coral. △ Be careful of the rocky bottom entry (wear reef shoes if you have them). This area can get crowded, especially in high season. If you want to steer clear of the crowds, look for a second entry ½ mi farther down the road—a gravel parking lot at the surf spot called **Dumps.** Entry into the Bay here is more tricky, as the coastline is all lava.

La Pérouse Bay, formed from the last lava flow 20 years ago, brings you the best variety of fish—more than any other site. The lava rock provides a protective habitat, and all four types of Hawai'i's angelfish can be found here. To dive the spot called **Pinnacles,** enter anywhere along the shore, just past the private entrance to the beach. Again, wear your reef shoes, as entry is sharp. To the right, you'll be in the marine reserve; to the left, you're outside. Look for the white, sandy bottom with massive coral heads. Pinnacles is for experienced divers only.

Equipment Rental & Dive Tours

★ **Ed Robinson's Diving Adventures.** Ed wrote the book, literally, on Molokini. Because he knows so much, he includes a "Biology 101" talk with every dive. An expert marine photographer, he offers diving instruction and boat charters to South Maui, the backside of Molokini, and Lāna'i. Weekly night dives are available, and there's a 10% discount if you book three or more days. Check out the Web site for good info and links on scuba sites, weather, and sea conditions. ✉ *50 Koki St., Kīhei* ☎ *808/879–3584 or 800/635–1273* ⊕ *www.mauiscuba.com.*

Lahaina Divers. With more than 25 years of diving experience, this West Side shop offers tours of Maui, Molokini, and Lāna'i. Big charter boats (which can be crowded, with up to 30 passengers per boat) leave daily for Molokini crater, Back Wall, Lāna'i, Turtle Reef, and more. A Continental breakfast and deli lunch are included. Rates range from $99 to $180. For less experienced divers, they offer a "Discover Scuba" lesson daily. ✉ *143 Dickenson St., Lahaina* ☎ *808/667–7496 or 800/998–3483* ⊕ *www.lahainadivers.com.*

Maui Dive Shop. With six locations island-wide, Maui Dive Shop offers scuba charters, diving instruction, and equipment rental. Excursions, offering awe-inspiring beach and boat dives, go to Molokini Back Wall (most advanced dive), Shipwreck Beach on Lāna'i, and more. Night dives and customized trips are available, as are full SSI and PADI certificate programs. ✉ *1455 S. Kīhei Rd., Kīhei* ☎ *808/879–3388 or 800/542–3483* ⊕ *www.mauidiveshop.com.*

Mike Severns Diving. Mike takes small groups of certified divers to both popular and off-the-beaten-path dive sites. Boat trips leave from Kīhei Boat Ramp, and go wherever conditions are best: the Marine Life Conservation District, Molokini's Backwall, St. Anthony shipwreck, Mākena,

Diving 101

IF YOU'VE ALWAYS WANTED GILLS, Hawai'i is a good place to get them. Although the bulky, heavy equipment seems freakish on shore, underwater it allows you to move about freely, almost weightlessly. As you descend into another world, you slowly grow used to the sound of your own breathing and the strangeness of being able to do so 30-plus feet down.

Most resorts offer introductory dive lessons in their pools, which allow you to acclimate to the awkward breathing apparatus before venturing out into the great blue. If you aren't starting from a resort pool, no worries. Most intro dives take off from calm, sandy beaches, such as Ulua or Kā'anapali. If you're bitten by the deep-sea bug and want to continue diving, you should get certified. Only certified divers can rent equipment or go on more adventurous dives, such as night dives, open-ocean dives, and cave dives.

There are several certification companies, including PADI, NAUI, and SSI. PADI, the largest, is the most comprehensive. Once you begin your certification process, stick with the same company. The dives you log will not apply to another company's certification. (Dives with a PADI instructor, for instance, will not count toward SSI certification). Remember that you will not be able to fly or go to the airy summit of Haleakalā within eight hours of diving. An Open Water certification will take three to four days and cost around $300. From that point on, the sky . . . or rather, the sea's the limit!

La Pérouse, or the Kenaio Coast. You're free to have a guide during your dive, or go into the depths alone. ⊠ *Box 627, Kīhei* ☎ *808/879–6596* ⊕ *www.mikesevernsdiving.com.*

Shaka Divers. Shaka provides personalized dives including a great four-hour intro dive ($79), a refresher course ($79), scuba certification ($350), and shore dives ($49) to Mākena, Ulua, Five Graves (at Mākena Landing), Turtle Town, Bubble Cave, Black Sand Beach, and more. Typical dives last about an hour, with 30 to 45 feet visibility. Dives can be booked on short notice, with afternoon tours available (hard to find on Maui). Shaka also offers night dives, torpedo scooter dives, and "bug hunt" expeditions (lobster hunts). Look for the Scuba Bus, blowing bubbles as it drives down the road. ⊠ *24 Hakoi Pl., Kīhei* ☎ *808/250–1234* ⊕ *www.shakadivers.com.*

Snorkeling

No one should leave Maui without ducking underwater to meet a sea turtle, moray eel, or Humuhumunukunukuāpua'a—the state fish. Visibility is best in the morning, before the wind picks up.

There are two ways to approach snorkeling—by land or by sea. Daily around 7 AM, a parade of boats heads out to Lāna'i or Molokini Crater, that ancient cone of volanic cinder off the coast of Wailea. Boat trips offer some advantages—deeper water, seasonal whale-watching, crew assistance, lunch, and gear. But you don't need a boat; much of Maui's best snorkeling is found just steps from the road. Nearly the entire leeward coastline from Kapalua south to ʻĀhihi-Kīnaʻu offers prime opportunities to ogle fish and turtles. If you're patient and sharp-eyed, you may glimpse eels, octopi, lobsters, eagle rays, and even a rare shark or monk seal.

> **OCEAN ETIQUETTE**
>
> "Look, don't touch," is a good motto in the ocean where many creatures don't mind company, but may reveal hidden stingers if threatened. One more warning: Never stand or bump against coral. Touching it—even briefly—can kill the delicate creatures residing within the hard shell.

Best Spots

Snorkel sites here are listed from north to south, starting at the northwest corner of the island.

On the west side of the island, just north of Kapalua, **Honolua Bay** Marine Life Conservation District (✉ Between mile markers 32 and 33 on Rte. 30, dirt road to left) has a superb reef for snorkeling. When conditions are calm, it's one of the island's best spots with tons of fish and colorful corals to observe. ■ TIP→ Make sure to bring a fish key with you, as you're sure to see many species of triggerfish, filefish, and wrasses. The coral formations on the right side of the bay are particularly dramatic and feature pink, aqua, and orange varieties. Take care entering the water, there's no beach and the rocks and concrete ramp can be slippery.

The northeast corner of this windward-facing bay periodically gets hammered by big waves in winter and high-profile surf contests are held here. Avoid the bay then, and after a heavy rain (you'll know because Honolua stream will be running across the access path).

Just minutes south of Honolua, dependable **Kapalua Bay** (✉ From Rte. 30, turn onto Kapalua Pl., and walk through tunnel) beckons. As beautiful above the water as it is below, Kapalua is exceptionally calm, even when other spots get testy. Needle and butterfly fish dart just past the sandy beach, which is why it's sometimes crowded. ⚠ Sand can be particularly hot here, watch your toes!

Fodor'sChoice
★
We think **Black Rock** (✉ In front of Kāʻanapali Sheraton Maui, Kāʻanapali Pkwy.), at the northernmost tip of Kāʻanapali Beach, is tops for snorkelers of any skill. The entry couldn't be easier—dump your towel on the sand in front of the Sheraton Maui resort and in you go. Beginners can stick close to shore and still see lots of action. Advanced snorkelers can swim beyond the sand to the tip of Black Rock, or Kekaʻa Point, to see larger fish and eagle rays. One of the underwater residents, a turtle named "Volkswagen" for its hefty size, can be found here. He sits very still; you must look closely. Equipment can be rented on-site. Parking, in a small lot adjoining the hotel, is the only hassle.

Along Honoapiʻilani Highway (Route 30) there are several favorite snorkel sites including the area just out from the cemetery at **Hanakaoʻo Beach Park** (✉ Near mile marker 23 on Rte. 30). At depths of 5 and 10 feet, you can see a variety of corals, especially as you head [toward] Waihikuli Wayside Park. Farther down the highway, the sha[llow] reef at **Olowalu** (⊠ South of Olowalu General Store on Rte. 30[, mile] marker 14) is good for a quick underwater tour, though the bes[t part] is a ways out, at depths of 25 feet or more. Closer to shore, the visib[il]ity can be hit or miss, but if you're willing to venture out about 50 yard[s], you'll have easy access to an expansive coral reef with abundant fish life—no boat required. Swim offshore toward the pole sticking out of the reef. Except for during a South swell, this area is calm and good for families with small children; turtles are plentiful. Boats sometimes stop nearby (they refer to this site as "Coral Gardens") on their return trip from Molokini.

Excellent snorkeling is found down the coastline between Kīhei and Mākena. The best spots are along the rocky fringes of Wailea's **Mōkapu, Ulua, Wailea,** and **Polo** beaches (⊠ Off Wailea Alanui Rd.). Find one of the public parking lots sandwiched between Wailea's luxury resorts, and enjoy these beaches' sandy entries, calm waters with relatively good visibility, and variety of fish species. Of the four beaches, Ulua has the best reef. You can glimpse a box-shape pufferfish here, and listen to snapping shrimp and parrot fish nibbling on coral.

At the very southernmost tip of paved road in South Maui lies **'Āhihi-Kīna'u** Natural Area Reserve (⊠ Just before end of Mākena Alanui Rd., follow marked trails through trees), also referred to as La Pérouse Bay. Despite its barren, lava-scorched landscape, the area recently gained such popularity with adventurers and activity purveyors that it had to be closed to commercial traffic. A ranger is stationed at the parking lot to assist visitors. It's difficult terrain and sometimes crowded, but if you make use of the rangers' suggestions (stay on marked paths, wear sturdy shoes to hike in and out), you can experience some of the reserve's outstanding treasures, such as the sheltered cove known as the "fishpond." ■ TIP→ Be sure to bring water, this is a hot and unforgiving wilderness.

Snorkel Cruises

The same boats that offer whale-watching, sailing, and diving also offer snorkeling excurions. Trips usually include visits to two locales, lunch, gear, instruction, and possible whale or dolphin sightings. Some captains troll for fish along the way, and, if they're lucky, will occasionally catch big game fish such as a marlin or mahimahi.

Molokini Crater, a moon-shape crescent about 3 mi off the shore of Wailea, is the most popular snorkel cruise destination. You can spend half a day floating above the fish-filled crater for about $80. Some say it's not as good as it's made out to be, and that it's too crowded, but others consider it to be one of the best spots in Hawai'i. Visibility is generally outstanding and fish are incredibly tame. Your second stop will be somewhere along the leeward coast, either "Turtle Town" near Mākena or "Coral Gardens" toward Lahaina. ⚠ Be aware that on blustery mornings, there's a good chance the waters will be too rough to moor in Molokini and you'll end up snorkeling some place off the shore, which you could have driven to for free. For the safety of everyone on the boat, it's the captain's prerogative to choose the best spot for the day.

Continued on page 84

ities & Tours

Snorkeling > 81

outh toward
llow coral
at mile
spot
ii-

NG IN HAWAI'I

The waters surrounding the Hawaiian Islands are filled with life—from giant manta rays cruising off the Big Island's Kona Coast to humpback whales giving birth in Maui's Māʻalaea Bay. Dip your head beneath the surface to experience a spectacularly colorful world: pairs of milletseed butterflyfish dart back and forth, red-lipped parrotfish snack on coral algae, and spotted eagle rays flap past like silent spaceships. Sea turtles bask at the surface while tiny wrasses give them the equivalent of a shave and a haircut. The water quality is typically outstanding; many sites afford 30-foot-plus visibility. On snorkel cruises, you can often stare from the boat rail right down to the bottom.

Certainly few destinations are as accommodating to every level of snorkeler as Hawaiʻi. Beginners can tromp in from sandy beaches while more advanced divers descend to shipwrecks, reefs, craters, and sea arches just offshore. Because of Hawaiʻi's extreme isolation, the island chain has fewer fish species than Fiji or the Caribbean—but many of the fish that are here exist nowhere else. The Hawaiian waters are home to the highest percentage of endemic fish in the world.

The key to enjoying the underwater world is slowing down. Look carefully. Listen. You might hear the strange crackling sound of shrimp tunneling through coral, or you may hear whales singing to one another during winter. A shy octopus may drift along the ocean's floor beneath you. If you're hooked, pick up a waterproof fishkey from Long's Drugs. You can brag later that you've looked the Hawaiian turkeyfish in the eye.

Picasso Triggerfish

Milletseed Butterflyfish*

Yellow Tang

Moorish Idol

Hawaiian Whitespotted Toby*

Saddleback Wrasse*

Red-lipped Parrotfish

Hawaiian Turkeyfish*

Zebra Moray Eel

Stocky Hawkfish

Green Sea Turtle

Spotted Eagle Ray

*endemic to Hawai'i

4

SNORKELING IN HAWAI'I

POLYNESIA'S FIRST CELESTIAL NAVIGATORS: HONU

Honu is the Hawaiian name for two native sea turtles, the hawksbill and the green sea turtle. Little is known about these dinosaur-age marine reptiles, though snorkelers regularly see them foraging for *limu* (seaweed) and the occasional jellyfish in Hawaiian waters. Most female honu nest in the uninhabited Northwestern Hawaiian Islands, but a few sociable ladies nest on Maui beaches. Scientists suspect that they navigate the seas via magnetism—sensing the earth's poles. Amazingly, they will journey up to 800 miles to nest—it's believed that they return to their own birth sites. After about 60 days of incubation, nestlings emerge from the sand at night and find their way back to the sea by the light of the stars.

If you've tried snorkeling and are tentatively thinking about scuba, you may want to try *snuba,* a cross between the two. With snuba, you dive down 20 feet below the surface, only you're attached to an air hose from the boat. Many of the boats now offer snuba as well as snorkeling; expect to pay between $45 and $65.

Snorkel cruises vary slightly—some serve mai tais and steaks whereas others offer beer and cold cuts. You might prefer a large ferry boat to a smaller sailboat, or vice versa. Whatever trip you choose, be sure you know where to go to board your vessel; getting lost in the harbor at 6 AM is a lousy start to a good day. ■ TIP→ Bring sunscreen, an underwater camera (they're double the price onboard), a towel, and a cover-up for the windy return trip. Even tropical waters get chilly after hours of swimming, so consider wearing a rash guard. Wetsuits can usually be rented for a fee. Hats without straps will blow away, and valuables should be left at home.

★ **Ann Fielding's Snorkel Maui.** For a personal introduction to Maui's undersea universe, this guided tour is the undisputable authority. A marine biologist, Fielding—formerly with the University of Hawai'i, Waikīkī Aquarium, and the Bishop Museum, and the author of several guides to island sea life—is the Carl Sagan of Hawai'i's reef cosmos. She'll not only show you fish, but she'll also introduce you to *individual* fish. This is a good first experience for dry-behind-the-ears types. Snorkel trips include lunch and equipment. ☎ *808/572-8437* ⊕ *www.maui.net/~annf.*

Mahana Na'ia. This comfortable catamaran offers a value snorkel trip to Molokini. Although marketed as a sailboat, it rarely hoists its sails. The crew works hard to make up for a lackluster boat, providing good service and food on the cruise. Coffee and continental breakfast greet you at the dock, and beer and wine are served with barbecue chicken and salad for lunch. ✉ *Māʻalaea Harbor Slip #47* ☎ *808/871–8636* ⊕ *www.maui-snorkeling-adventures.com.*

Maui Classic Charters. This company offers two top-rate snorkel trips at a good value. Hop aboard the *Four Winds II,* a 55-foot, glass-bottom catamaran, for one of the most dependable snorkel trips around. You'll spend more time than the other charter boats do at Molokini and enjoy

---

TIPS ON SAFE SNORKELING

■ Snorkel with a buddy and stay together.

■ Choose a location where lifeguards are present.

■ Ask the lifeguard about conditions, especially currents, before getting in the water.

■ Plan your entry and exit points prior to getting in the water.

■ Swim into the current on entering and then ride the current back to your exit point.

■ Pop your head above the water periodically to ensure you aren't drifting too far out, or too close to rocks.

■ Think of the ocean as someone else's home—don't take anything that doesn't belong to you, or leave any trash behind.

■ Wear a rash guard, it will keep you from being fried by the sun.

■ When in doubt, don't go without a snorkeling professional; try a guided tour.

turtle-watching on the way home. The trip includes optional snuba ($45 extra), and a deluxe BBQ lunch, beer, wine, and soda. For a faster ride, try the *Maui Magic*, Mā'alaea's fastest power cat. This boat takes fewer people (45 max) than some of the larger vessels, and as an added bonus, they offer snuba and play Hawaiian music on the ride. This one's good for kids. ⊠ *Mā'alaea Harbor Slips #55 and #80* ☎ *808/879–8188 or 800/736–5740* ⊕ *www.mauicharters.com.*

Maui–Moloka'i Sea Cruises. If you're a landlubber who'd still like to see the sea, book a passage on the 92-foot *Prince Kuhio,* one of the largest air-conditioned cruise vessels in Maui waters. In addition to a deli-style lunch and open bar, they offer complimentary transportation to the harbor, which relieves you from parking and searching for the boat's slip at 7 AM. ⊠ *Mā'alaea Harbor* ☎ *808/242–8777 or 800/468–1287* ⊕ *www.mvprince.com.*

★ ☺ **Pacific Whale Foundation.** The knowledgeable folks here will treat you to a Molokini adventure like the others, only with a more ecological bent. Accordingly, they serve gardenburgers alongside the requisite barbecue chicken, and their fleet runs on bona-fide biodiesel fuel. This is an A-plus trip for kids, the crew assists with an onboard junior naturalist program and throws in a free wildlife guide and poster. The multihulled boats are smooth and some have swim on–off platforms. Best of all, a portion of the profits goes to protecting the very treasures you're paying to enjoy. ⊠ *Mā'alaea Harbor Slip* ☎ *800/942–5311 or 808/249–8811* ⊕ *www.pacificwhale.org.*

Paragon. With this company, you get to snorkel and sail—they have some of the fastest vessels in the state. As long as conditions are good, you'll hit prime snorkel spots in Molokini, Lāna'i, and occasionally, Coral Gardens. The Lāna'i trip includes a Continental breakfast, a picnic lunch on the beach, snacks, open bar, a snorkel lesson, and plenty of time in the water. The friendly crew takes good care of you, making sure you get the most value and enjoyment from your trip. ⊠ *Lahaina and Mā'alaea Harbors* ☎ *808/244–2087* ⊕ *www.sailmaui.com.*

Trilogy Excursions. The longest-running operation on Maui is the Coon family's Trilogy Excursions. In terms of comprehensive offerings, this company's got it: they have six beautiful multihulled sailing vessels (though they usually only sail for a brief portion of the trip) at three departure sites. All excursions are manned by energetic crews who will keep you entertained with stories of the islands and plenty of corny jokes. A full-day catamaran cruise to Lāna'i includes Continental breakfast and a deli lunch onboard; a guided van tour of the island; a "Snorkeling 101" class; and time to snorkel in the waters of Lāna'i's Hulopo'e Marine Preserve (Trilogy has exclusive commercial access). There are a barbecue dinner on Lāna'i and an optional dolphin safari. The company also offers a Molokini and Honolua Bay snorkel cruise. Many people consider a Trilogy excursion the highlight of their trip—but if you're not a good "group activity" person, or if you are looking to really sail, there may be better options for you. ⊠ *Mā'alaea Harbor Slip #99, or Lahaina Harbor* ☎ *808/661–4743 or 800/874–2666* ⊕ *www.sailtrilogy.com.*

Snorkel-Equipment Rental

Most hotels and vacation rentals offer free use of snorkel gear. Beachside stands fronting the major resort areas rent equipment by the hour or day. ■ TIP→ Don't shy away from asking for instructions, a snug fit makes all the difference in the world. A mask fits if it sticks to your face when you inhale deeply through your nose. Fins should cover your entire foot (unlike diving fins, which strap around your heel). If you're squeamish about using someone else's gear (or need a prescription lens), pick up your own at any discount shop. Costco and Longs have better prices than ABC stores; dive shops have superior equipment.

Maui Dive Shop. You can rent pro gear (including optical masks, boogie boards, and wet suits) from six locations island-wide. Pump these guys for weather info before heading out, they'll know better than last night's news forecaster, and they'll give you the real deal on conditions. ⊠ 1455 S. Kīhei Rd., Kīhei ☎ 808/873–3388 ⊕ www.mauidiveshop.com.

Snorkel Bob's. If you need gear, Snorkel Bob's will rent you a mask, fins, and a snorkel, and throw in a carrying bag, map, and snorkel tips for as little as $9 per week. Avoid the circle masks and go for the split-level, it's worth the extra cash. ⊠ Nāpili Village Hotel, 5425 Lower Honoapi'ilani Hwy., Nāpili ☎ 808/669–9603 ⊠ 1217 Front St., Lahaina ☎ 808/661–4421 ⊠ 1279 S. Kīhei Rd., Kīhei ☎ 808/875–6188 ⊠ 2411 S. Kīhei Rd., Kīhei ☎ 808/879–7449 ⊕ www.snorkelbob.com.

Surfing

Maui's diverse coastline has surf for every level of waterman or woman. Waves on leeward-facing shores (West and South Maui) tend to break in gentle sets all summer long. Surf instructors in Kīhei and Lahaina can rent you boards, give you onshore instruction, and then lead you out through the channel, where it's safe to enter the surf. They'll shout encouragement while you paddle like mad for the thrill of standing on water—some will even give you a helpful shove. These areas are great for beginners, the only danger is whacking a stranger with your board or stubbing your toe against the reef.

The North Shore is another story. Winter waves pound the windward coast, attracting water champions from every corner of the world. Adrenaline addicts are towed in by Jet Ski to a legendary, deep-sea break called *Jaws*. Waves here periodically tower upward of 40 feet, dwarfing the helicopters seeking to capture unbelievable photos. The only spot for viewing this phenomenon (which happens just a few times a year) is on private property. So, if you hear the surfers next to you crowing about Jaws "going off," cozy up and get them to take you with them.

Whatever your skill, there's a board, a break, and even a surf guru to accommodate you. A two-hour lesson is a good intro to surf culture. Surf camps are becoming increasingly popular, especially with women. One- or two-week camps offer a terrific way to build muscle and self-esteem simultaneously. **Maui Surfer Girls** (⊕ www.mauisurfergirls.com) immerses adventurous young ladies in wave-riding wisdom during two-week camps. Coed camps are sponsored by **Action Sports Maui** (⊕ www. actionsportsmaui.com).

Best Spots

Beginners can hang 10 at Kīhei's **Cove Park** (⊠ S. Kīhei Rd., Kīhei), a sometimes crowded but reliable 1- to 2-foot break. Boards can easily be rented across the street, or in neighboring Kalama Park parking lot. The only bummer is having to balance the 9-plus-foot board on your head while crossing busy South Kīhei Road. But hey, that wouldn't stop world-famous longboarder Eddie Aikau, now would it?

Long- or shortboarders can paddle out anywhere along Lahaina's coastline. One option is at **Launiupoko State Wayside** (⊠ Honoapiʻilani Hwy. near mile marker 18). The east end of the park has an easy break, good for beginners. Even better is **Ukumehame** (⊠ Honoapiʻilani Hwy. near mile marker 12), also called "Thousand Peaks." You'll soon see how the spot got it's name, the waves here break again and again in wide and consistent rows, giving lots of room for beginning and intermediate surfers.

Other good surf spots along the West Side include "Grandma's" at **Papalaua Park,** just after the pali (cliff)—where waves are so easy a grandma could ride 'em; **Puamana Beach Park** for a mellow longboard day; and **Lahaina Harbor,** which offers an excellent inside wave for beginners (called "Breakwall"), as well as the more advanced outside (a great left if there's a big South swell).

For advanced wave riders, **Hoʻokipa Beach Park** (⊠ 2 mi past Pāʻia on Haʻna Hwy.) boasts several well-loved breaks, including "Pavilions," "Lanes," "the Point," and "Middles." Surfers have priority until 11 AM, when windsurfers move in on the action. ⚠ Competition is stiff here, and the attitudes can be "aggro." If you don't know what you're doing, consider watching from the shore.

You can find out the wave report each day by checking page 2 of the *Maui News,* logging onto the Glen James weather site at ⊕ www. hawaiiweathertoday.com, or calling ☎ 808/871–5054 (for the weather forecast) or ☎ 808/877–3611 (for the surf report).

Surf Shops & Lessons

Big Kahuna. Rent surfboards (soft-top longboards) here for $15 for two hours, or $20 for the day. The shop also offers surf lessons, and rents kayaks and snorkel gear. Located across from Cove Park. ⊠ *Island Surf Bldg., 1993 S. Kīhei Rd. #2, Kīhei* ☎ *808/875–6395.*

★ **Goofy Foot.** Surfing "goofy foot" means putting your right foot forward. They might be goofy, but we like the right-footed gurus here. Their safari shop is just plain cool and only steps away from "Breakwall," a great beginner's spot in Lahaina. Two-hour classes with five or fewer students are $55, and six-hour classes with lunch and an ocean-safety course are $250. They promise you'll be standing within a two-hour lesson—or it's free. ⊠ *505 Front St., Lahaina* ☎ *808/244–9283* ⊕ *www. goofyfootsurfschool.com.*

Hāna Highway Surf. If you're heading out to the North Shore surf, you can pick up boards ranging from beginner's soft-tops to high-performance shortboards here for $20 per day. ⊠ *65 Hāna Hwy., Pā'ia* ☎ *808/ 579-8999.*

Hi Tech Surf & Sports. Locals hold Hi Tech with the utmost respect. They have some of the best boards, advice, and attitudes around. Rent surf boards for $20 per day (or soft boards for $14); $112 for the week. They rent even their best models— choose from longboards, short-boards, and hybrids. All rentals come with board bags, roof rags, and oh yeah, wax. ⊠ *425 Koloa St., Kahului* ☎ *808/877-2111* ⊕ *www. htmaui.com.*

Nancy Emerson School of Surfing. Nancy's motto is "If my dog can surf, so can you." Instructors here will get even the most shaky novice riding with their "Learn to Surf in One Lesson" program. A private lesson with Nancy herself—a pro surf champion and occasional Hollywood stunt double—costs $215 for one hour or $325 for two; lessons with her equally qualified instructors are $100 for one hour and $165 for two. They provide the boards and rash guards. ⊠ *505 Front St., Lahaina* ☎ *808/244-7873* ⊕ *www.mauisurfclinics.com.*

Second Wind. Surfboard rentals at this centrally located shop are a deal—good boards go for $18 per day or $90 per week. They also rent and sell their own *Elua Makani* boards (which means second wind in Hawaiian). Although they don't offer lessons themselves, they will book you with the best surfing, windsurfing, and kiteboarding lessons on the island. ⊠ *111 Hāna Hwy., Kahului* ☎ *808/877-7467 or 800/936-7787* ⊕ *www.secondwindmaui.com.*

Windsurfing

Something about Maui's wind and water stirs the spirit of innovation. Windsurfing, invented in the 1950s, found its true home at Ho'okipa in 1980. Seemingly overnight, windsurfing pros from around the world flooded Maui's north shore. Equipment evolved, amazing film footage was captured, and a new sport was born.

If you're new to the action, you can get lessons from the experts island-wide. For a beginner, the best thing about windsurfing is (unlike surfing) you don't have to paddle. Instead, you have to hold on like heck to a flapping sail, as it whisks you into the wind. Needless to say, you're going to need a little coordination and balance to carry this off. Instructors start you on a beach at Kanahā, where the big boys go. Lessons range from two-hour introductory classes to five-day advanced "flight school." If you're an old salt, pick up tips and equipment from the companies below.

Best Spots

After **Hoʻokipa Bay** (⊠ 2 mi past Pāʻia on Hāna Hwy.) was discovered by windsurfers three decades ago, this windy beach 10 mi east of Kahului gained an international reputation. The spot is blessed with optimal wave-sailing wind and sea conditions, and can offer the ultimate aerial experience.

In summer the windsurfing crowd heads south to **Kalepolepo Beach** (⊠ S. Kīhei Rd. near Ohukai St.). Trade winds build in strength and by afternoon a swarm of dragonfly sails can be seen skimming the whitecaps, with the West Maui mountains as a backdrop.

A great site for speed, **Kanahā Beach Park** (⊠ Behind Kahului Airport) is dedicated to beginners in the morning hours, before the waves and wind really get roaring. After 11 AM, the professionals choose from their quiver of sails the size and shape best suited for the day's demands. This beach tends to have smaller waves and forceful winds—sometimes sending sailors flying at 40 knots. ■ TIP→ If you aren't ready to go pro, this is a great place for a picnic while you watch from the beach.

Equipment Rental & Lessons

Action Sports Maui. The quirky, friendly professionals here will meet you at Kanahā, outfit you with your sail and board, and guide you through your first "jibe" or turn. They promise your learning time will be cut in half. Don't be afraid to ask lots of questions. Lessons are held at 9 AM every morning except Sunday at Kanahā, and start at $79 for a 2½-hour class. ⊠ 415 Dairy Rd., Kahului ☎ 808/871–5857 ⊕ www.actionsportsmaui.com.

Hi Tech Surf & Sports. Known locally as Maui's finest windsurfing school, Hawaiian Sailboarding Techniques (HST) (located in Hi Tech) brings you quality instruction by skilled sailors. Founded by Alan Cadiz, an accomplished World Cup Pro, the school sets high standards for a safe, quality windsurfing experience. Hi Tech itself offers excellent equipment rentals; $45 gets you a board, two sails, a mast, and roof racks for 24 hours. ⊠ 425 Koloa, Kahului ☎ 808/877–2111 ⊕ www.htmaui.com.

Second Wind. Located in Kahului, this company rents boards with two sails for $43 per day. Boards with three sails go for $48 per day. ⊠ 11 Hāna Hwy., Kahului ☎ 808/877–7467.

Whale-Watching

From November through April, whale-watching becomes one of the most popular activities on Maui. Boats leave the wharves at Lahaina and Māʻalaea in search of Humpbacks, allowing you to enjoy the awe-inspiring size of these creatures in closer proximity. As it's almost impossible *not* to see whales in winter on Maui, you'll want to prioritize: is adventure or comfort your aim? If close encounters with the giants of the deep are your desire, pick a smaller boat that promises sightings. If an impromptu marine-biology lesson sounds fun, go with the Pacific Whale Foundation. Two-hour forays into the whales' world start at $20. For those wanting to sip mai tais as whales cruise calmly by, stick with a sunset cruise on a boat with an open bar and pūpūs ($40 and up). ■ TIP→ Afternoon trips are generally rougher because the wind picks up, but some say this is when the most surface action occurs.

Every captain aims to please during whale season, getting as close as legally possible (100 yards). Crew members know when a whale is about to dive (after several waves of its heart-shape tail) but rarely can predict breaches (when the whale hurls itself up and almost entirely out of the water). Prime viewing space (on the upper and lower decks, around the railings) is limited, so boats can feel crowded even when half-full. If you don't want to squeeze in beside strangers, opt for a smaller boat with less bookings. Don't forget to bring sunscreen, sunglasses, light long sleeves, and a hat you can secure. Winter weather is less predictable, and at times, can be extreme, especially as the wind picks up. Arrive early to find parking.

Best Spots

From December 15 to May 1 the Pacific Whale Foundation has naturalists stationed in two places—on the rooftop of their headquarters and at the scenic viewpoint at **Mc-Gregor Point Lookout** (⊠ Between mile markers 7 and 8 on Honoapiʻilani Hwy., Rte. 30). Just like the commuting traffic, whales cruise along the *pali*, or cliff-side, of West Maui's Honoapiʻilani highway all day long. ⚠ Make sure to park safely before craning your neck out to see them.

The northern end of **Keawakapu Beach** (⊠ S. Kīhei Rd. near Kilohana Dr.) seems to be a whale magnet. Situate yourself on the sand or at the nearby restaurant, and you're bound to see a mama whale patiently teaching her calf the exact technique of flipper-waving.

HOW BIG IS BIG?

Before heading out for any water activity, be sure to get a weather and wave report, and make sure the surf report you get is the *full face value* of the wave. "Hawaiian style" cuts the wave size in half. For instance, a Hawaiian might say a wave is 5 feet high, which means 10 feet if you're from New Jersey or Florida. For years, scientists and surfers were using different measurements, as Hawaiʻi locals measured waves from median sea level to the crest. These days, most surf reports are careful to distinguish between the two—but it can still get confusing if you ask a local surfer, "how big da waves today, brah?"

CLOSE UP

The Humpback's Winter Home

THE HUMPBACK WHALES'
attraction to Maui is legendary. More
than half the Pacific's humpback
population winters in Hawai'i,
especially in the waters around the
Valley Isle, where mothers can be
seen just a few hundred feet offshore
training their young calves in the fine
points of whale etiquette. Watching
from shore it's easy to catch sight of
whales spouting, or even breaching—
when they leap almost entirely out of
the sea, slapping back onto the water
with a huge splash.

At one time there were thousands of
the huge mammals, but a history of
overhunting and marine pollution
dwindled the world population to
about 1,500. In 1966 humpbacks were
put on the endangered species list.
Hunting or harassing whales is illegal
in the waters of most nations, and in
the United States, boats and airplanes
are restricted from getting too close.
The word is still out, however, on the
effects military sonar testing has on
the marine mammals.

Marine biologists believe the
humpbacks (much like the humans)
keep returning to Hawai'i because of
its warmth. Having fattened
themselves in subarctic waters all
summer, the whales migrate south in
the winter to breed, and a rebounding
population of thousands cruise Maui
waters. Winter is calving time, and the
young whales, born with little
blubber, probably couldn't survive in
the frigid Alaskan waters. No one has
ever seen a whale give birth here, but
experts know that calving is their
main winter activity, since the 1- and
2-ton youngsters suddenly appear
while the whales are in residence.

The first sighting of a humpback
whale spout each season is exciting
and reassuring for locals on Maui. A
collective sigh of relief can be heard,
"Ah, they've returned." In the not-so-
far distance, flukes and flippers can be
seen rising above the ocean's surface.
It's hard not to anthropomorphize the
tail-waving, it looks like such an
amiable, human gesture. Each fluke is
uniquely patterned, like a human's
fingerprint, and used to identify the
giants as they travel halfway around
the globe and back.

4

Boats & Charters

America II. Want to see sails with your whales? In season, this America's
Cup contender offers early-morning whale-watching. Make no mistake:
these trips are for sailing die-hards. Don't expect many frills; this one's all
about the ride. ⊠ *Harbor Slip #5, Lahaina* ☎ *808/667–2195.*

Kiele V. The Hyatt Regency Maui's *Kiele V,* a 55-foot luxury catamaran,
does seasonal whale-watching excursions as well as daily snorkel trips, and
afternoon cocktail sails. A comfortable ride, the cat leaves from Kā'anapali Beach, which is more fun than the harbor. The trip costs $55 per adult
and includes pūpūs and an open bar. ⊠ *200 Nohea Kai Dr., Lahaina* ☎ *808/
667–4727.*

★ ☾ **Pacific Whale Foundation.** This nonprofit organization pioneered whale-watching back in 1979 and now runs four boats, with 15 trips daily. As the most

recognizable name in whale watching, the crew (with a certified marine biologist on-board) offers insights into whale behavior (do they *really* know what those tail flicks mean?) and suggests ways for you to help save marine life worldwide. The best part about these trips is the underwater hydrophone that allows you to actually listen to the whales sing. Trips meet at the Foundation's store, where you can buy whale paraphernalia, snacks, and coffee—a real bonus for 8 AM trips. Passengers are then herded much like migrating whales down to the harbor. These trips are more affordable than others, but you'll be sharing the boat with about 100 people in stadium seating. Once you catch sight of the wildlife up-close, however, you can't help but be thrilled. ⊠ *Māʻalaea Harbor* ☎ *800/942–5311 or 808/249–8811* ⊕ *www. pacificwhale.org.*

Pride Charters. Two-hour cruises narrated by a naturalist are offered aboard *Leilani,* a small, maneuverable boat with good viewing opportunities (39 passengers max). There's a main cabin, upper sundeck, and swim platform—and you can listen to the whales sing. Trips start at $26 per adult, and include pūpūs and an open bar. ⊠ *Māʻalaea Harbor, Slip #70 Māʻalaea* ☎ *877/867–7433* ⊕ *www.prideofmaui.com.*

PADDLE SURFING

Stand up paddle surfing, where you stand on a longboard and paddle out with a canoe oar, is the new "comeback kid" of surf sports. Traced back to some of the first surfers on Waikīkī, paddle surfing made its revival in recent years thanks to feats by Archie Kalepa, who crossed between Molokaʻi and Oʻahu; and Laird Hamilton, who conquered Jaws on a stand-up paddle board. Paddle boarding requires even more balance and coordination than regular surfing, and the learning curve is steep. But these days you can almost always see at least one lone paddler amid the pack—watch for them.

Golf, Hiking &
Outdoor Activities

WORD OF MOUTH

"Hike in the 'Īao Valley. It's quiet, green, lush and a totally different experience than the west side of Maui."

—Erin74

"Kapalua Plantation is the one course to play when you can only play one. It's a pretty special place; it's so unique. Where else could I have reached a 585-yard hole (#18) with a driver and a 3-iron? (The trades were sure blowing that day.)"

—kanunu

Updated by
Elaine Gast

YOU MAY COME TO MAUI to sprawl out on the sand, but it won't take long before you realize there's much more to Maui than the beach. The island's interior is vast and varied—a mecca of rain forest, valley, waterfalls, and mountains that provide a whirlwind of options for action and adventure. Whether you're riding horseback or backroading it on an ATV, there's plenty to keep you busy. This chapter will get your toes out of the sand, and into your hiking boots or golf shoes. For easy reference, activities are listed with golf and hiking first, followed by other activities in alphabetical order.

GOLF

Maui's natural beauty and surroundings offer some of the most jaw-dropping vistas imaginable on a golf course. Holes run across small bays, past craggy lava outcrops, and up into cool, forested mountains. Most courses feature mesmerizing ocean views, some close enough to feel the salt in the air. And although many of the courses are affiliated with resorts (and therefore a little pricier), the general public courses are no less impressive. You might even consider a ferry ride to the neighbor island of Lāna'i for a round on either of its two championship courses (*see* Chapter 11, Lāna'i).

Green Fees: Green fees listed here are the highest course rates per round on weekdays and weekends for U.S. residents. (Some courses charge non-U.S. residents higher prices.) Discounts are often available for resort guests and for those who book tee times on the Web. Rental clubs may or may not be included with green fees. Twilight fees are usually offered; call individual courses for information.

West Maui

★ **Kā'anapali Resort.** The Kā'anapali North Course (1962) is one of three in Hawai'i designed by Robert Trent Jones Sr., the godfather of modern golf architecture. The greens average a whopping 10,000 square feet, necessary because of the often-severe undulation. The par-4 18th hole (into the prevailing trade breezes, with out-of-bounds on the left, and a lake on the right) is notoriously tough. The South Course (Arthur Jack Snyder, 1976) shares similar seaside-into-the-hills terrain, but is rated a couple of strokes easier, mostly because putts are less treacherous. ✉ *2290 Kā'anapali Pkwy., Lahaina* ☎ *808/661–3691* ⊕ *www.kaanapaligolf.com* ⚐ *North Course: 18 holes. 6,136 yds. Par 71. Slope 126. Green Fee: $160. South Course: 18 holes. 6,067 yds. Par 71. Slope 122. Green Fee: $130* ☞ *Facilities: Driving range, putting green, rental clubs, golf carts, lessons, restaurant, bar.*

Fodor'sChoice **Kapalua Resort.** Perhaps Hawai'i's best known golf resort and the crown ★ jewel of golf on Maui, Kapalua hosts the PGA Tour's first event each January: the Mercedes Championships at the Plantation Course at Kapalua. Ben Crenshaw and Bill Coore (1991) tried to incorporate traditional shot values in a very nontraditional site, taking into account slope, gravity, and the prevailing trade winds. The par-5 18th, for instance, plays 663 yards from the back tees (600 yards from the resort tees). The hole drops 170 feet in elevation, narrowing as it goes to a partially guarded green, and plays downwind and down-grain. Despite the longer-than-usual distance, the slope is great enough and the wind at your back usually brisk enough to reach the green with two well-struck shots—a truly unbelievable finish to a course that will challenge, frustrate, and reward the patient golfer.

The Bay Course (Arnold Palmer and Francis Duane, 1975) is the most traditional of Kapalua's triad, with gentle rolling fairways and generous greens. The most memorable hole is the par-3 fifth, with a tee shot that must carry a turquoise finger of Onelua Bay. The Village Course at Kapalua (Palmer and Ed Seay, 1980) winds high into the West Maui Mountains through historic stands of Cook pines and eucalyptus, then out through pineapple fields and tall native grasses. The sixth hole is particularly dramatic: the tee is 100 feet above the fairway, with a dense stand of pines to the left and a lake to the right. **The Kapalua Golf Academy** (⊠ 1000 Office Rd. ☎ 808/669–6500) offers 23 acres of practice turf and 11 teeing areas, a special golf fitness gym, and an instructional bay with video analysis. Each of the three courses has a separate clubhouse. **The Bay Course:** ⊠ *300 Kapalua Dr., Kapalua* ☎ *808/ 669–8820* ⊕ *www.kapaluamaui.com/golf* ⅄ *18 holes. 6,051 yds. Par 72. Slope 133. Green Fee: $200* ☞ *Facilities: Driving range, putting green, rental clubs, pro shop, lessons, restaurant, bar.* **The Plantation Course:** ⊠ *2000 Plantation Club Dr., Kapalua* ☎ *808/669–8877* ⊕ *www. kapaluamaui.com/golf* ⅄ *18 holes. 6,547 yds. Par 73. Slope 135. Green Fee: $250* ☞ *Facilities: Driving range, putting green, golf carts, pull carts, rental clubs, pro shop, golf academy/lessons, restaurant, bar.* **The Village Course:** ⊠ *2000 Village Rd., Kapalua* ☎ *808/669–8835* ⊕ *www. kapaluamaui.com/golf* ⅄ *18 holes. 5,753 yds. Par 70. Slope 129. Green Fee: $185* ☞ *Facilities: Driving range, putting green, golf carts, pull carts, rental clubs, pro shop, golf academy/lessons, restaurant, bar.*

The South Shore

Elleair Golf Course. Formerly known as Silversword (1987), Elleair is an exacting test. Fairways tend to be narrow, especially in landing areas, and can be quite a challenge when the trade winds come up in the afternoon. The course is lined with enough coconut trees to make them a collective hazard, not just a nutty nuisance. ⊠ *1345 Pi'ilani Hwy., Kīhei* ☎ *808/874–0777* ⅄ *18 holes. 6,404 yds. Par 71. Slope 117. Green Fee: $100* ☞ *Facilities: Driving range, putting green, rental clubs, golf carts, lessons, restaurant.*

Fodor'sChoice **Mākena Resort.** Robert Trent Jones Jr. and Don Knotts (not the Barney
★ Fife actor) built the first course at Mākena in 1981. A decade later Jones was asked to create 18 totally new holes and blend them with the existing course to form the North and South courses, which opened in 1994. Both courses—sculpted from the lava flows on the western flank of Haleakalā—offer quick greens with lots of breaks, and plenty of scenic distractions. On the North Course, the fourth is one of the most picturesque inland par-3s in Hawai'i, with the green guarded on the right by a pond. The sixth is an excellent example of option golf: the fairway

Before You Hit the 1st Tee . . .

Golf is golf, and Hawai'i is part of the United States, but Island golf nevertheless has its own quirks. Here are a few tips to make your golf experience in the Islands more pleasant.

- Sunscreen. Buy it, apply it (minimum 30 SPF). The subtropical rays of the sun are intense, even in December. Good advice is to apply sunscreen, at a minimum, on the first and 10th tees.

- Stay hydrated. Spending four-plus hours in the sun and heat means you'll perspire away considerable fluids and energy.

- All resort courses and many daily fee courses provide rental clubs. In many cases, they're the latest lines from top manufacturers. This is true for both men and women, as well as lefthanders, which means you don't have to schlepp clubs across the Pacific.

- Pro shops at most courses are well-stocked with balls, tees, and other accoutrements, so even if you bring your own bag, it needn't weigh a ton.

- Come spikeless—very few Hawai'i courses still permit metal spikes. And most of the resort courses require a collared shirt.

- Maui is notorious for its trade winds. Consider playing early if you want to avoid the wind, and remember that while it'll frustrate you at times and make club selection difficult, you may very well see some of your longest drives ever.

- In theory you can play golf in Hawai'i 365 days a year, but there's a reason the Hawaiian Islands are so green. An umbrella and light jacket can come in handy.

- Unless you play a muni or certain daily fee courses, plan on taking a cart. Riding carts are mandatory at most courses and are included in the green fees.

is sliced up the middle by a gaping ravine, which must sooner or later be crossed to reach the green. Although trees frame most holes on the North Course, the South Course is more open. This means it plays somewhat easier off the tee, but the greens are trickier. The view from the elevated tee of the par-5 10th is lovely with the lake in the foreground mirroring the ocean in the distance. The par-4 16th is another sight to see, with the Pacific running along the left side. ⊠ 5415 Mākena Alanui, Mākena ☎ 808/879–3344 ⊕ www.princeresortshawaii.com ⏨. North Course: 18 holes. 6,567 yds. Par 72. Slope 139. Green Fee: $180. South Course: 18 holes. 6,630 yds. Par 72. Slope 138. Green Fee: $180 ☞ Facilities: Driving range, putting green, golf carts, rental clubs, pro shop, golf academy/lessons, restaurant, bar.

Fodor'sChoice **Wailea.** Wailea is one of just two Hawai'i resorts to offer three differ-
★ ent courses: Gold, Emerald, and Blue. Designed by Robert Trent Jones Jr., these courses share similar terrain, carved into the leeward slopes of Haleakalā. Although the ocean does not come into play, its beauty is visible on almost every hole. ■ TIP→ Remember, putts break dramatically toward the ocean.

Jones refers to the Gold Course at Wailea (1993) as the "masculine" course. Host to the Championship Senior Skins Game in February, it's

On the Sidelines

Maui has a number of golf tournaments, most of which are of professional caliber and worth watching. Many are also televised nationally. One attention-getter is the **Mercedes Championships** (☎ 808/669–2440) held in January. This is the first official PGA tour event, held on Kapalua's Plantation Course. The Aloha Section of the Professional Golfers Association of America hosts the **Verizon Hall of Fame** (☎ 808/669–8877) championship at the Plantation Course in May. A clambake feast on the beach tops off the **Kapalua Clambake Pro-Am** (☎ 808/669–8812) in July.

Over in Wailea, in June, on the longest day of the year, self-proclaimed "lunatic" golfers start out at first light to play 100 holes of golf in the annual **Ka Lima O Maui** (☎ 808/875–5111), a fund-raiser for local charities. The nationally televised **Championship Senior Skins** (☎ 808/875–5111) in January pits four of the most respected Senior PGA players against one another.

all trees and lava and regarded as the hardest of the three courses. The trick here is to note even subtle changes in elevation. The par-3 eighth, for example, plays from an elevated tee across a lava ravine to a large, well-bunkered green framed by palm trees, the blue sea, and tiny Molokini. The course has been labeled a "thinking player's" course because it demands strategy and careful club selection. The Emerald Course at Wailea (1994) is the "feminine" layout with lots of flowers and bunkering away from greens. This by no means suggests that it plays easy. Although this may seem to render the bunker benign, the opposite is true. A bunker well in front of a green disguises the distance to the hole. Likewise, the Emerald's extensive flower beds are designed to be dangerous distractions because of their beauty. The Gold and Emerald share a clubhouse, practice facility, and 19th hole. Judging elevation change is also key at Wailea's first course, the Blue Course (Arthur Jack Snyder, 1971). Fairways and greens tend to be wider and more forgiving than on the Gold or Emerald, and run through colorful flora that includes hibiscus, wiliwili, bougainvillea, and plumeria. **Blue Course:** ✉ *120 Kaukahi St., Wailea* ☎ *808/875–5155* ⊕ *www.waileagolf.com* ⛳ *18 holes. 6,765 yds. Par 72. Slope 129. Green Fee: $175.* ☞ *Facilities: Driving range, putting green, golf carts, rental clubs, pro shop, golf academy/lessons, restaurant, bar.* **Gold and Emerald Courses:** ✉ *100 Wailea Golf Club Dr., Wailea* ☎ *808/875–7450* ⊕ *www.waileagolf.com* ⛳ *Gold Course: 18 holes. 6,653 yds. Par 72. Slope 132. Green Fee: $185. Emerald Course: 18 holes. 6,407 yds. Par 72. Slope 130. Green Fee: $185* ☞ *Facilities: Driving range, putting green, golf carts, rental clubs, pro shop, golf academy/lessons, restaurant, bar.*

Central Maui

FodorsChoice   **The Dunes at Maui Lani.** This is Robin Nelson (1999) at his minimalist
★   best, a bit of British links in the middle of the Pacific. Holes run through ancient, lightly wooded sand dunes, 5 mi inland from Kahului Harbor.

Thanks to the natural humps and slopes of the dunes, Nelson had to move very little dirt and created a natural beauty. During the design phase he visited Ireland, and not so coincidentally the par-3 third looks a lot like the Dell at Lahinch: a white dune on the right sloping down into a deep bunker and partially obscuring the right side of the green—just one of several blind to semi-blind shots here. Popular with residents,

> **TIP!**
>
> Resort courses, in particular, offer more than the usual three sets of tees, sometimes four or five. So bite off as much or little challenge as you like. Tee it up from the tips and you'll end up playing a few 600-yard par-5s and see a few 250-yard forced carries.

this course has won several awards including "Best 35 New Courses in America" by *Golf Magazine* and "Five Best Kept Secret Golf Courses in America" by *Golf Digest*. ☒ *1333 Maui Lani Pkwy., Kahului* ☎ *808/ 873–0422* ⊕ *www.dunesatmauilani.com* ⅄. *18 holes. 6,841 yds. Par 72. Slope 121. Green Fee: $100* ☞ *Facilities: Driving range, putting green, golf carts, rental clubs, pro shop, golf academy/lessons, restaurant, bar.*

King Kamehameha Golf Club. The former Sandalwood Course (Robin Nelson, 1991) is back as the Kahili Course. After four years of lying fallow due to financial problems, Kahili now boasts two 18-hole courses—one private and one public—completely redone in 2005 by Nelson himself. Holes run along the slopes of the West Maui Mountains, overlooking Maui's central plain, and feature panoramic ocean views of both the north and south shores. Consistent winds negate the courses shorter length. ☒ *2500 Honoapi'ilani Hwy., Wailuku* ☎ *808/242– 7090* ⅄. *18 holes. 6,200 yds. Par 72. Slope 124. Green Fee: $95* ☞ *Facilities: Driving range, putting green, rental clubs, golf carts, pro shop, lessons, restaurant, bar.*

Waiehu Golf Course. Maui's lone municipal course, Waiehu is really two courses in one. The front nine opened in 1930 and features authentic seaside links that run along Kahului Bay. The back nine, which climbs up into the lower reaches of the West Maui Mountains through macadamia orchards, opened in 1963 (Arthur Jack Snyder). ☒ *200A Halewaiu Rd., Wailuku* ☎ *808/270–7400* ⅄. *18 holes. 6,330 yds. Par 72. Slope 120. Green Fee: $45, plus $16 per cart* ☞ *Facilities: Driving range, putting green, golf carts, pull carts, rental clubs, pro shop, restaurant, bar.*

Upcountry

Pukalani Golf Course. Located 1,110 feet above sea level, Pukalani (Bob E. and Robert L. Baldock, 1979) provides one of the finest vistas in all Hawai'i. Holes run up, down, and across the slopes of Haleakalā. The trade wind tends to come up in the late morning and afternoon. This— combined with frequent elevation change—makes club selection a test. The fairways tend to be wide, but greens are undulous and quick. ☒ *360 Pukalani St., Pukalani* ☎ *808/572–1314* ⊕ *www.pukalanigolf.com* ⅄. *18 holes. 6,945 yds. Par 72. Slope 127. Green Fee: $60* ☞ *Facilities: Driving range, putting green, rental clubs, golf carts, restaurant, bar.*

Saving the Best for Last

Among golf's great traditions is the 19th Hole. No matter how the first 18 go, the 19th is sure to offer comfort and cheer, not to mention a chilled beverage. Here's a look at some of the best.

O'Reilly's sits above the Kāʻanapali North Course's 18th green, and the food is so good it attracts nongolfers for breakfast, lunch, and dinner. Kapalua boasts three 19th holes with great fare and views—the **Plantation House** has a commanding view of the Plantation Course's 18th hole, the Pailolo Channel, and the island of Molokaʻi beyond; the **Pineapple Grill** overlooks the Bay Course's 18th; and **Vino's**

is the Village Course's popular watering-hole restaurant with a spectacular wine selection.

At Wailea's Gold and Emerald Courses, the **Sea Watch** restaurant overlooks the sea in a garden setting and serves excellent food, with a choice of single malt scotches and cigars. The **plantation-style clubhouse** at the King Kamehameha Golf Club's Kahili Course offers commanding views of the ocean on both sides of the island and of 10,000-foot Haleakalā. And though not affiliated with Elleair, golfers from this course frequent **Lulu's** and **Henry's** in the heart of Kīhei.

Lānaʻi

The Island of Lānaʻi features two championship caliber golf courses—the Challenge at Manele and the Experience at Koʻele—that are rarely crowded due to the exclusivity of the island. Both courses require a ferry ride from Lahaina harbor on Maui, but the extra effort is worth it. Transportation–golf packages are available through **Expeditions Ferry** (☎ 808/661-3756 ⊕ www.go-lanai.com). For reviews of the two courses, *see* Chapter 11, Lānaʻi.

HIKING

Hikes on Maui range from coastal seashore to verdant rain forest to alpine desert. Orchids, hibiscus, ginger, heliconia, and anthuriums grow wild on many trails, and exotic fruits like mountain apple, lilikoi, thimbleberry, and strawberry guava provide refreshing snacks for hikers. Ironically, much of what you see in lower altitude forests is alien, brought to Hawaiʻi at one time or another by someone hoping to improve upon nature. Plants like strawberry guava and ginger may be tasty, but they outcompete native forest plants and have become serious, problematic weeds.

The best hikes get you out of the imported landscaping and into the truly exotic wilderness. Hawaiʻi possesses some of the world's rarest plants, insects, and birds. Pocket field guides are available at most grocery or drug stores and can really illuminate your walk. Before you know it you'll be nudging your companion and pointing out trees that look like something out of a Dr. Suess book. If you watch the right branches quietly you can spot the same Honeycreepers or Happy-faced Spiders scientists have spent their lives studying.

Haleakalā National Park

Fodor'sChoice **Haleakalā Crater**

★ Hiking Haleakalā Crater is undoubtedly the best hiking on the island. There are 30 mi of trails, two camping areas, and three cabins. If you're in shape, you can do a day hike descending from the summit (along Sliding Sands Trail) to the crater floor. If you're in shape and have time, consider spending several days here amid the cinder cones, lava flows, and all that loud silence.

Going into the crater is like going to a different planet. In the early 1960s NASA actually brought moon-suited astronauts here to practice what it would be like to "walk on the moon." Today, on one of the many hikes—most moderate to strenuous—you'll traverse black sand and wild lava formations, follow the trail of blooming 'ahinahina (silverswords), watch for nēnē (Hawaiian geese) as they fly above you, and witness tremendous views of big sky and burnt-red cliffs. If you're lucky enough to camp or stay in one of the cabins, you'll fall asleep under a wide screen of shooting stars, while the 'alauahio birds murmur around you like a litter of pups.

The best time to go into the crater is in the summer months, when the conditions are generally more predictable. Be sure to bring layered clothing—and plenty of warm clothes if you're staying overnight. It may be scorching hot during the day, but it gets mighty chilly after dark. Ask a ranger about water availability before starting your hike. Note that overnight visitors must get a permit at park headquarters before entering the crater; day-use visitors do not need a permit. Cabins are $70 per night, and fit 12 people. They book months in advance by lottery, though it's possible to get lucky due to last-minute cancellations. To reserve a cabin, write at least two months in advance to Haleakalā National Park. ✉ Box 369, Makawao HI, 96768 ☎ 808/572–4459.

⇨ For detailed information on hikes in the crater, see Haleakalā National Park in Chapter 2, Exploring Maui.

'Ohe'o Gulch

A branch of Haleakalā National Park, 'Ohe'o Gulch is famous for its "sacred" pools (the area is sometimes called the "Seven Sacred Pools"). Truth is, there are more than seven pools, and there's nothing

> **KEEP IN MIND**
>
> Wear sturdy shoes while hiking; you'll want to spare your ankles from a crash course in loose lava rock. When hiking near streams or waterfalls, be extremely cautious, flash floods can occur at any time. Do not drink stream water or swim in streams if you have open cuts; bacteria and parasites are not the souvenir you want to take home with you. As with most outdoor activities, exposure poses the main danger. Wear sunscreen, a hat, and layered clothing, and be sure to drink plenty of water (even if you don't feel thirsty). At upper elevations, the weather is guaranteed to be extreme—alternately chilly or blazing.

sacred about them. The owner of the Hotel Hāna started calling the area "Seven Sacred Pools" to attract the masses to sleepy old Hāna. His plan worked and the name stuck, much to the chagrin of most Mauians.

The best time to visit the pools is in the morning, before the crowds and tour buses arrive. Start your day with a vigorous hike. 'Ohe'o has some fantastic trails to choose from, including our favorite, the Pipiwai Trail (see below). When you're done, nothing could be better than going to the pools, lounging on the rocks, and cooling off in the fresh-water reserves.

> ### MOSQUITOES
>
> Mosquitoes can be particularly pesky around pools and waterfalls—especially when the sun doesn't shine (dawn, dusk, and on overcast days). There's an easy solution: pack bug spray. It's a simple step that saves you lots of scratching later on. If you forget, ask to borrow some from a fellow hiker on the trail. People are pretty friendly on Maui and will be glad to help you out.

You'll find 'Ohe'o Gulch, on Route 31, 10 mi past Hāna town. All visitors must pay a $10 national park fee (per car not per person), which is valid for one week and can be used at Haleakalā's summit as well.

Pipiwai Trail. This moderate 2-mi trek upstream leads to the 400-foot Waimoku Falls, pounding down in all its power and glory. Follow signs from the parking lot up the road, past the bridge overlook, and uphill into the forest. Along the way you can take side trips and swim in the stream's basalt-lined pools. The trail bridges a sensational gorge and passes onto a boardwalk through a mystifying forest of giant bamboo. This stomp through muddy and rocky terrain takes around three hours to fully enjoy. It's best done early in the morning, before the touring crowds arrive (though it can never truly be called crowded). ✛ *Trailhead: On highway toward 'Ohe'o bridge, near mile marker 42 ☉ 3 hours, 4 mi round-trip.*

Kahakai Trail. This easy ¼-mi hike (more like a walk) stretches between Kuloa Point and the Kipahulu campground. You'll see rugged shoreline views and can stop to gaze at the surging waves below. ✛ *Trailhead: Kuloa Point ☉ 15 minutes, ½ mi round-trip.*

Kuloa Point Trail. An easy ½-mi walk, this trail takes you from the Kipahulu Visitor Center down to the Seven Sacred Pools at Kuloa Point. On the trail you pass native trees and precontact Hawai'ian sites. Don't forget to wear your suit and bring your towel if you plan to take a dip in the pools. Keep in mind: no lifeguards are on duty and you'll want to stick to the pools—don't even think about swimming in the ocean. ✛ *Trailhead: Kipahulu Visitor Center ☉ 30 minutes, 1 mi round-trip.*

Campsites. Down at the grassy sea cliffs at the Seven Sacred Pools, you can camp, no permit required, although you can stay only three nights. Toilets, grills, and tables are available, but there's no water and open fires are prohibited. For more information, call the Kipahulu Visitor Center. ☞ *Visitor Center:* ☎ *808/248–7375* ⊕ *www.nps.gov/hale.*

Continued on page 104

HAWAI'I'S PLANTS 101

Hawai'i is a bounty of rainbow-colored flowers and plants. The evening air is scented with their fragrance. Just look at the front yard of almost any home, travel any road, or visit any local park and you'll see a spectacular array of colored blossoms and leaves. What most visitors don't know is that the plants they are seeing are not native to Hawai'i; rather, they were introduced during the last two centuries as ornamental plants, or for timber, shade, or fruit.

Hawai'i boasts every climate on the planet, excluding the two most extreme: arctic tundra and arid desert. The Islands have wine-growing regions, cactus-speckled ranchlands, icy mountaintops, and the rainiest forests on earth.

Plants introduced from around the world, thrive here. The lush lowland valleys along the windward coasts are predominantly populated by non-native trees including yellow- and red-fruited **guava**, silvery leafed **kukui**, and orange flowered **tulip trees**.

The colorful **plumeria flower**, very fragrant and commonly used in lei making, and the giant multicolored **hibiscus flower** are both used by many women as hair adornments, and are two of the most common plants found around homes and hotels. The umbrella-like **monkeypod tree** from Central America provides shade in many of Hawai'i's parks including Kapiolani Park in Honolulu. Hawai'i's largest tree, found in Lahaina, Maui, is a giant **banyan tree**. It's canopy and massive support roots cover several acres. The native **o'hia tree**, with it's brilliant red brush like flowers, and the **hapu'u**, a giant tree fern, are common in Hawai'i's forests and are also used ornamentally in gardens and around homes.

Bougainvillea

Guava

Monkeypod Tree

Banyan Tree

O'hia Lehua

Tulip Tree

Plumeria

Pandanus

Hibiscus

Anthurium

Kukui Tree

Hapu'u Okina

5

HAWAI'I'S PLANTS 101

DID YOU KNOW?

Over 2,200 plant species are found in the Hawaiian Islands, but only about 1,000 are native. Of these, 282 are so rare, they are endangered. Hawai'i's endemic plants evolved from ancestral seeds arriving on the islands over thousands of years as baggage on birds, floating on ocean currents, or drifting on winds from continents thousands of miles away. Once here, these plants evolved in isolation creating many new species known nowhere else in the world.

Polipoli Forest

A good hiking area—and something totally unexpected on a tropical island—is Polipoli Forest (6,500 feet). During the Great Depression the government began a program to reforest the mountain, and soon cedar, pine, cypress, and even redwood took hold. Today, the area feels more like Vermont than Hawai'i. It's cold and foggy here, and often wet, but don't let that stop you from going. There's something about the enormity of the trees, the quiet mist and mysterious caves that will make you feel you've discovered an unspoken secret, and one you'll want to keep to yourself.

To reach the forest, take Route 37 all the way out to the far end of Kula. Then turn left at Route 377. After about a half mile, turn right at Waipoli Road. First you'll encounter switchbacks; after that the road is just plain bad, but passable. Signs say that four-wheel-drive vehicles are required, though standard cars have been known to make it. Use your best judgment. There are great trails here for all levels, along with a small campground, and a cabin that you can rent from the Division of State Parks.

Write far in advance for the **cabin** (✉ Box 1049, Wailuku 96793 ☎ 808/244–4354); for the campground, you can wait until you arrive in Wailuku and visit the **Division of State Parks** (✉ 54 High St. ☎ 808/984–8109).

Boundary Trail. This 4-mi moderate trail begins just past the Kula Forest Reserve boundary cattle guard on Polipoli Road, and descends into the lower boundary southward, all the way to the Ranger's cabin at the junction of the Redwood and Plum Trails. Link it with these trails, and you've got a hearty 5-mi day hike. The trail crosses many scenic gulches, with an overhead of tall eucalyptus, pine, cedar, and plum trees. Peep through the trees for wide views of Kula and Central Maui. ✛ *Trailhead: Polipoli Forest Campground* ⊙ *3–4 hrs, 5-mi loop.*

Redwood Trail. This easy and colorful hike winds through redwoods and conifers past the short Tie Trail down to the old ranger's cabin. Although the views are limited, groves of trees and flowering bushes abound. At the end of the trail is an old cabin site and three-way junction with the Plum Trail and the Boundary Trail. ✛ *Trailhead: From parking area at Polipoli campground, walk back up road ¼ mi and look to your left* ⊙ *1–2 hrs, 3.4 mi round-trip.*

Upper Waiakoa Trail. This scenic albeit rugged trail starts at the Polipoli Access Road (look for trailheads) and proceeds up Haleakalā through mixed pine and past caves and thick shrubs. It crosses the land of Kaonoulu to the land of Waiakoa,

KALAUPAPA TRAIL, MOLOKA'I

You can take an overnight trip to the island of Moloka'i for a day of hiking down to Kalaupapa Peninsula and back, by means of a 3-mi, 26-switchback trail. The trail is nearly vertical, traversing the face of some of the highest sea cliffs in the world. *See* A Tale of Tragedy & Triumph in Chapter 10, Moloka'i *for more information.*

In the Footsteps of Kings

A much neglected hike is the coastal **Hoapili Trail** (✉ Follow Mākena Alanui to end of paved road, walk through parking lot along dirt road, follow signs) beyond the 'Āhihi-Kīn'au Natural Area Reserve. Named after a bygone Hawaiian king, it follows the shoreline, threading through the remains of ancient Hawaiian villages. The once-thriving community was displaced by one of Maui's last lava flows. Later, King Hoapili was responsible for overseeing the creation of an island-wide highway. This remaining section, a wide path of stacked lava rocks, is a marvel to look at and walk on, though it's not the easiest surface for the ankles. (It's rumored to have once been covered in grass.) You can wander over to the Hanamanioa lighthouse, or quietly ponder the rough life of the ancients. Wear sturdy shoes and bring extra water. This is brutal territory with little shade and no facilities. Beautiful, yes. Accommodating, no.

5

where it reaches its highest point—7,800 feet. Here you'll find yourself in barren, raw terrain with fantastic views. At this point, you can either turn around, or continue on to the 3-mi Waiakoa Loop. Other than a cave shelter, there's no water or other facilities on either of these trails, so come prepared. ⚜ *Trailhead: Look for signs on Polipoli Access Rd.* ⊗ *5–6 hrs, 14 mi round-trip.*

★ 'Īao Valley State Park

In Hawaiian, 'Īao means "supreme cloud." When you enter this mystical valley in the middle of an unexpected rain forest, you'll know why. At 750 feet above sea level, the 10-mi valley clings to the clouds as if it's trying to cover its naked beauty. If you've been spending too many days in the sun, the cool shade and moist air may be just the welcome change you need.

One of Maui's great wonders, the valley is the site of a famous battle to unite the Hawaiian islands. Out of the clouds, the **'Īao Needle,** a tall chunk of volcanic rock, stands as a monument to the long-ago lookout for Maui warriors. Today, there's nothing warlike about it: the valley is a peaceful land of lush, tropical plants, clear pools and a running stream, and easy, enjoyable walks.

To get to 'Īao Valley State Park, go through Wailuku and continue to the west end of Route 32. The road dead ends into the parking lot. The park is open daily 7–7. Facilities are available. (For park information call ☎ 808/984–8109.)

'Īao Valley Trail. Anyone (including your grandparents) can take this easy hike from the parking lot at 'Īao Valley State Park. On your choice of two paved walkways, you can cross the 'Īao Stream and explore the junglelike area. Ascend the stairs up to the **'Īao Needle** for spectacular views of Central Maui, or pause in the garden of Hawaiian heritage plants and marvel at the local youngsters hurling themselves from the bridge

Hawai'i's Flora & Fauna

CLOSE UP

HAWAI'I BOASTS EVERY CLIMATE ON THE PLANET, excluding the two most extreme: arctic tundra and arid desert. The Islands have wine-growing regions, cactus-speckled ranchlands, icy mountaintops, and the rainiest forests on earth. The Galapagos has *nothing* on Hawai'i's biodiversity—more than 90% of Hawaiian plants and animals are endemic, meaning they exist nowhere else on earth. Most of the plants you see while walking around, however, aren't Hawaiian at all. Tropical flowers such as plumeria, orchids, red ginger, heliconia, and anthuriums are Asian or South American imports now growing wild on all the Islands.

Native Hawaiian plants are weird-looking, in the best sense. Take the silversword, for example. A giant, furry firework of a plant, it grows in one of the world's harshest climates: the summits of Haleakalā and Mauna Kea. Its 7-foot stalk, brimming with red or pale yellow flowers, blooms once and then dies. 'Ōhi'a trees—thought to be the favorite of Pele, the volcano goddess—bury their roots in fields of once-molten lava and sprout ruby pom-pom-like lehua blossoms. The deep yellow petals of 'ilima (once reserved for royalty) are tiny discs, which make the most elegant leis.

To match Hawai'i's unique flora, fantastic birds and insects evolved. Honeycreepers, distant relatives of the finch, have fabulously long, curved bills perfect for sipping nectar from lehua blossoms. The world's only carnivorous caterpillar can snatch a Hawaiian picture-wing fly from the air in less than a second. Hawai'i's state bird, the nēnē goose, is making a comeback from its former endangered status. It roams freely in parts of Maui, Kaua'i, and the Big Island. Pairs who mate for life are often spotted ambling across roads in Haleakalā or Hawai'i Volcanoes national park.

At the Kīlauea Point National Wildlife Refuge on Kaua'i, hundreds of Laysan albatross, wedge-tail shearwaters, red-footed boobies, and other marine birds glide and soar within photo-op distance of visitors to Kīlauea Lighthouse. Boobie chicks hatch in the fall and emerge from nests burrowed into cliff-side dirt banks and even under stairs—any launching pad from which the fledgling flyer can catch the nearest air current.

Hawai'i's two native mammals are rare sights. Doe-eyed Hawaiian monk seals breed in the northwestern Islands. With only 1,500 left in the wild, you probably won't catch many lounging on the beaches of Hawai'i's populated islands, though they have been spotted on the shores of Kaua'i in recent years. You can see rescued pups and adults along with Hawaiian green sea turtles at Sea Life Park and the Waikīkī Aquarium on O'ahu. The shy Hawaiian bat hangs out primarily at Kealakekua Bay on the Big Island.

into the chilly pools below. ✤ *Trailhead: 'Iao Valley parking lot* ⊙ *30 minutes, ½ mi round-trip.*

Guided Hikes

Hawai'i Nature Center. In 'Iao Valley, the Hawai'i Nature Center leads easy, interpretive hikes for children and their families. ⊠ *875 'Iao Valley Rd., Wailuku 96793* ☎ *808/ 244–6500.*

★ **Hike Maui.** Hike Maui is the oldest hiking company on the Islands, its rain forest, mountain ridge, crater, coastline, and archaeological-snorkel hikes are led by such knowledgeable folk as ethnobotanists and marine biologists. Prices range from $65 to $150 for hikes of 3 to 10 hours, including lunch. They also offer a private Heli Hike and Waterfalls for upward of $2,000, giving you everything you came to Maui to see. Hike Maui supplies waterproof day packs, rain ponchos, first-aid gear, water bottles, and transportation to the site. ☎ *808/879–5270* ⊕ *www.hikemaui.com.*

> ### DAY HIKE CHECKLIST
>
> - Water (at least 2 quarts per person)
> - Food—fruit and trail mix
> - Rain gear—especially if going into the crater
> - Hiking shoes with good ankle support
> - Layered clothing
> - Wide-brimmed hat and sunglasses
> - Sunscreen (SPF 30 or higher recommended)
> - Mosquito repellent

★ **Friends of Haleakalā National Park.** This nonprofit offers day and overnight service trips into the crater, and in the Kipahulu region. The purpose of your trip, the service work itself, isn't too much—mostly removing invasive plants and light cabin maintenance. Chances are you'll make good friends and have more fun than on a hike you'd do on your own. Trip leader Farley, or one of his equally knowledgable cohorts, will take you to places you'd never otherwise see, and teach you about the native flora and birds along the way. Bring your own water; share food in group dinners. ⊠ Free ☎ *808/248–7660* ⊕ *www.fhnp.org.*

Maui Eco Adventures. For excursions into remote areas, Maui Eco Adventures is your choice. The ecologically minded company leads hikes into private or otherwise inaccessible areas. Hikes, which can be combined with kayaking, mountain biking, or sailing trips, explore botanically rich valleys in Kahakuloa and East Maui, as well as Hāna, Haleakalā, and more. Guides are botanists, mountaineers, boat captains, and backcountry chefs. Most excursions are $120–$150. ⊠ *180 Dickenson St., Suite 101, Lahaina* ☎ *808/661–7720 or 877/661–7720* ⊕ *www.ecomaui.com.*

Maui Hiking Safaris. Hikes with Maui Hiking Safaries are limited to groups of eight or less. Excursions include hikes to waterfalls, Haleakalā, rain forests, and more. You can choose any two hikes to customize your own full-day tour. Hikes range from $60 to $129. ⊠ *273 Le-*

olani Pl., Pukalani ☎ *808/573–0168 or 888/445–3963* ⊕ *www.mauihikingsafaris.com.*

Paths in Paradise. Paths in Paradise is a small company offering specialized hikes into wetlands, rain-forest areas, and the crater. The owner, Renate Gassman-Duvall, is an expert birder and biologist. She helps hikers spot native honeycreepers feeding on lehua blossoms and supplies them with bird and plant check cards. Half-day hikes run $110, and full-day hikes are $135, with lunch and gear provided. ☎ *808/579–9294.*

★ **Sierra Club.** A great avenue into the island's untrammeled wilderness is Maui's chapter of the Sierra Club. Rather than venturing out on your own, join one of the club's hikes into pristine forests and valley isle watersheds, or along ancient coastal paths. Several hikes a month are led by informative naturalists who carry first aid kits and arrange waivers to access private land. Some outings include volunteer service, but most are just for fun. Bring your own food and water, sturdy shoes, and a suggested donation of $5—a true bargain. ⊠ *Box 791180, Pā'ia* ☎ *808/573–4147* ⊕ *www.hi.sierraclub.org/maui.*

OTHER OUTDOOR ACTIVITIES

Hawai'i, and Maui in particular, is world famous for its ocean activities and beaches. But if you look beyond the sandbox, you'll see that the entire island is one big playground. Tour operators make good use of the benefits of Maui's natural topography, perfect year-round climate, and sheer beauty. In the following pages you'll find some of the more worthwhile activities that Maui's interior has to offer.

ATV Tours

Haleakalā ATV Tours. Haleakalā ATV Tours explore the mountainside in their own way: propelled through the forest on 350 cc, four-wheel-drive, Honda Rancher all-terrain vehicles. The adventures begin at Haleakalā Ranch and rev right up to the pristine Waikamoi rain-forest preserve. Kids under 15 ride alongside in the exciting Argo Conquest, an eight-wheel amphibious vehicle. Two-hour trips go for $90, and 3½-hour trips are $135. Haleakalā ATV Tours is now offering combination ATV and Zipline tours with Skyline Eco Adventures on Monday and Thursday for $177. ☎ *808/661–0288* ⊕ *www.atvmaui.com.*

Bicycling

Maui County biking is safer and more convenient than in the past, but long distances and mountainous terrain keep it from being a practical mode of travel. Still, painted bike lanes enable riders to travel all the way from Mākena to Kapalua, and you'll see hardy souls battling the trade winds under the hot Maui sun.

Several companies offer guided downhill bike tours from the top of Haleakalā all the way to the coast. From peak to sea level it's 38 mi total with only about 400 yards of actual pedaling required. This activity is a great way to see the summit of the world's largest dormant volcano and enjoy an easy, gravity-induced bike ride, but isn't for those not confident in their ability to handle a bike. The ride is inherently dangerous due to the slope, sharp turns, and the fact that you're riding down an actual road with cars on it. That said, the guided bike companies do take every safety precaution. A few companies are now offering unguided (or as they like to say "self-guided") tours where they provide you with the bike and transportation to the top and then you're free to descend at your own pace. Sunrise is downright brisk at the summit, so dress in layers.

Best Spots

Though it's changing, at present there are few truly good spots to ride on Maui. Street bikers will want to head out to scenic **Thompson Road** (✉ Off Rte. 37, Kula Hwy., Keokea). It's quiet, gently curvy, and flanked by gorgeous views on both sides. Plus, because it's at a higher elevation, the air temperature is cooler and the wind lighter. The coast back down toward Kahului is worth the ride up. Mountain bikers can head up to **Polipoli Forest** (✉ Off Rte. 377, end of Waipoli Rd.). A bumpy trail leads through an unlikely forest of conifers. You'll likely forget you're in Hawaii, and the downhill run will give you a ride you won't soon forget.

Bike Rentals & Guided Trips

Haleakalā Bike Company. If you're thinking about an unguided Haleakalā bike trip, consider one of the trips offered by this company. Meet at the Old Haiku Cannery and take their van shuttle to the top. Along the way you'll learn about the history of the island, the volcano, and other Hawai'iana. Unlike the guided trips, food is not included although there are several spots along the way down to stop, rest, and eat. The simple, mostly downhill route takes you right back to the cannery where you started. HBC offers bike sales, rentals, and services as well. ✉ *810 Ha'ikū Rd., Suite 120, Ha'ikū* ☎ *808/575–9575, 888/922–2453* ⊕ *www.bikemaui.com.*

Island Biker. This is the premiere bike shop on Maui when it comes to rental, sales, and service. They offer 2005 Specialized standard front-shock bikes, road bikes, and full suspension mountain bikes. Daily or weekly rates range $35–$140, and include a helmet, pump, water bottle, and flat-repair kit. They can suggest various routes appropriate for mountain or road biking, or you can join them in a bi-weekly group ride. ✉ *415 Dairy Rd., Kahului* ☎ *808/877–7744* ⊕ *www.islandbikermaui.com.*

Maui Downhill. If biking down the side of Haleakalā sounds like fun, several companies are ready to book you a tour. Maui Downhill vans will pick you up at your resort, shuttle you to the mountaintop, help you onto a bike, and follow you as you coast down through clouds and gorgeous scenery into the town of Pā'ia. Haleakalā summit trips are available for sunrise or midday, sunset half trips from the crater to Kula are also offered. Lunch or breakfast is included, depending on your trip's start time; treks cost $150, discounts available for Internet bookings. ✉ *199 Dairy Rd., Kahului 96732* ☎ *808/871–2155 or 800/535–2453* ⊕ *www.mauidownhill.net.*

Maui Mountain Cruisers. Guided sunrise and midday bike trips "cruise" down Haleakalā for $139 (discounts available if booked in advance). Continental breakfast is provided and lunch is available for purchase. Nonbikers can ride down in a van for $55. ⊠ *Box 1356, Makawao* ☎ *808/871–6014 or 800/232–6284* ⊕ *www.mauimountaincruisers.com.*

West Maui Cycles. Servicing the west side of the island, WMC offers an assortment of cycles including front-suspension Giant bikes for $40 per day ($160 per week) and Cannondale road bikes for $50 per day ($200 per week). Sales and service available. ⊠ *1087 Limahana St., Lahaina* ☎ *808/661–9005.*

Hang Gliding & Paragliding

Hang Gliding Maui. Armin Engert will take you on an instructional powered hang-gliding trip out of Hāna Airport in east Maui. With more than 7,500 hours in flight and a perfect safety record, Armin flies you 1,000 feet over Maui's most beautiful coast. A 30-minute flight lesson costs $115, and a 60-minute lesson is $190. This is easily one of the coolest things you can do in Hāna. Snapshots of your flight from a wing-mounted camera cost an additional $25. ⊠ *Hāna Airport, Hāna* ☎ *808/572–6557* ⊕ *www.hanggglidingmaui.com.*

Maluhialani. The name means "beautiful serenity" in Hawaiian, which is appropriate for an airborne trip taking off from Kula, and soaring as far as the West Maui Mountains. Dwight Mounts, your pilot, built a grass runway on his scenic Upcountry property. ☎ *808/280–3307* ⊕ *www.maluhialani.com.*

Proflyght Paragliding. Proflyght is the only paragliding outfit on Maui to offer solo, tandem, and instruction at Polipoli State Park. The leeward slope of Haleakalā lends itself perfectly to paragliding with breathtaking scenery and upcountry air currents that increase and rise throughout the day. Polipoli creates tremendous thermals that allow one to peacefully descend 3,000 feet to the landing zone. Owner–pilot Dexter Clearwater boasts a perfect safety record with tandems and student pilots since taking over the company in 2002. Ask and Dexter will bring along his flying duck Chuckie or his paragliding pound puppie Daisy. Prices start at $175, with full certification available. ⊠ *Polipoli State Park, Kula* ☎ *808/874–5433* ⊕ *www.paraglidehawaii.com.*

Helicopter Tours

Helicopter flight-seeing excursions can take you over the West Maui Mountains, Hāna, Haleakalā Crater, even the Big Island lava flow, or Moloka'i. This is a beautiful, exciting way to see the island, and the *only* way to see some of its most dramatic areas and waterfalls. Tour prices usually include a videotape of your trip so you can relive the experience at home. Prices run from about $125 for a half-hour rain-forest tour to almost $400 for a two-hour mega-experience that includes a champagne toast on landing. Generally the 45–50 minute flights are the best value, and if you're willing to chance it, considerable discounts may be available if you call last minute.

It takes about 90 minutes to travel inside the volcano, then down to the village of Hāna. Some companies stop in secluded areas for refreshments. Helicopter-tour operators throughout the state come under sharp scrutiny for passenger safety and equipment maintenance. Don't be afraid to ask about a company's safety record, flight paths, age of equipment, and level of operator experience. Generally, though, if they're still in business they're doing something right.

Air Maui Helicopters. Air Maui prides itself on a perfect safety record, and provides 45–65 minutes flights covering the waterfalls of the West Maui mountains, Haleakalā Crater, Hāna, even the spectacular sea-cliffs of Moloka'i. Prices range $214–$276 with considerable discounts available on the Web site. ☒ *Kahului Heliport, Hangar 110, Kahului* ☎ *877/238–4942* ⊕ *www.airmaui.com.*

Blue Hawaiian Helicopters. Blue Hawaiian has provided aerial adventures in Hawai'i since 1985, and has been integral in some of the filming Hollywood has done on Maui. Its AStar helicopters are air-conditioned and have noise-blocking headsets for all passengers. Flights are 30–65 minutes and cost $125–$280. They also offer a fly–drive special to Hāna with Temptation Tours limo vans. ☒ *Kahului Heliport, Hangar 105, Kahului* ☎ *808/871–8844* ⊕ *www.bluehawaiian.com.*

Sunshine Helicopters. Sunshine offers tours of Maui and Moloka'i, as well as the Big Island, in its *Black Beauty* AStar or WhisperStar aircraft. A pilot-narrated video tape of your actual flight is available for purchase. Prices are $150–$370 for 30–65 minutes. First-class seating is available for a fee. ☒ *Kahului Heliport, Hangar 107, Kahului* ☎ *808/871–0722 or 800/544–2520* ⊕ *www.sunshinehelicopters.com.*

Horseback Riding

Several companies on Maui offer horseback riding that's far more appealing than the typical hour-long trudge over a dull trail with 50 other horses.

Charley's Trail Rides & Pack Trips. Rides with this company require a stout physical nature (but not a stout physique: riders must weigh less than 200 pounds). Overnight trips go from Kaupō, a *tiny* village nearly 20 mi past Hāna, up the slopes of Haleakalā, where you spend the night in the crater. Charley is a bona fide *paniolo* (Hawaiian cowboy), and tours with him include meals, park fees, and camping supplies for $250 per person. Book several weeks in advance if you'd prefer a cabin instead of a tent. ☎ *808/248–8209.*

Fodor'sChoice ★ **Maui Stables.** Hawaiian-owned and run, this company provides a trip back in time, to an era when life moved more slowly and reverently—though galloping is allowed, if you're able to handle your horse! Educational tours begin at the stable in remote Kipahulu (near Hāna), and pass through several historic Hawaiian sites. Before heading up into the forest, your guides intone the words to a traditional *oli*, or chant, asking for permission to enter. By the time you reach the mountain pasture overlooking Waimoku Falls, you'll feel lucky to have been a part of the tradition. Both morning and afternoon rides are available at $150 per rider. ⊠ *Between mile markers 40 and 41 on Hwy. 37, Hāna* 🕾 *808/ 248–7799* ⊕ *www.mauistables.com.*

FodorśChoice **Mendes Ranch.** Family-owned and run, Mendes operates out of the beau-
★ tiful ranchland of Kahakuloa on the windward slopes of the West Maui Mountains. Two-hour morning and afternoon trail rides ($110) are available with an optional barbecue lunch ($20). Cowboys will take you cantering up rolling pastures into the lush rain forest to view some of Maui's biggest waterfalls. Mendes caters to weddings and parties and offers private trail rides on request. Should you need accommodations they have a home and bunk for rent right on the property. ⊠ *Hwy. 340, Wailuku* 🕾 *808/244–7320 or 808/871–8222* ⊕ *www.mendesranch.com.*

Pi'iholo Ranch. The local wranglers here will lead you on a rousing ride through family ranchlands—up hillside pastures, beneath a eucalyptus canopy, and past many native trees. Morning picnic rides are 3½ hours and include lunch. Afternoon rides are two hours. Their well-kept horses navigate the challenging terrain easily, but hold on when deer pass by! Prices are $120–$160. Private rides and lessons are available. ⊠ *End of Waiahiwi Rd., Makawao* 🕾 *808/357–5544 or 866/572–5544* ⊕ *www. piiholo.com.*

Pony Express Tours. Pony Express Tours offers trips on horseback into Haleakalā Crater. The half-day ride goes down to the crater floor for a picnic lunch; the full-day excursion covers 12 mi of terrain and visits some of the crater's unusual formations. Both are a great way to see the top of the dormant volcano. The company also offers one- and two-hour rides on the slopes of the Haleakalā Ranch. Prices range from $65 to $195. 🕾 *808/667–2200 or 808/878–6698* ⊕ *www.ponyexpresstours.com.*

Polo

Polo is popular with the Upcountry paniolos on Maui. From April through June Haleakalā Ranch hosts "indoor" or arena contests on a field flanked by side boards. The field is on Route 377, 1 mi from Route 37. During the "outdoor" polo season, mid-August to the end of October, matches are held at Olinda Field, 1 mi above Makawao on Olinda Road. There's a $5 admission for most games, which start at 1:30 PM on Sunday. The **Manduke Baldwin Memorial Tournament** occurs on Memorial Day and is a popular two-day event. The Maui Polo Club draws challengers from Argentina, England, South Africa, New Zealand, and Australia. For information, call 🕾 *808/877–7744* or visit ⊕ www. mauipoloclub.com.

Rodeos

With dozens of working cattle ranches throughout the Islands, many youngsters learn to ride a horse before they can drive a car. Mauians love their rodeos and put on several for students at local high schools. Paniolos get in on the action, too, at three major annual events: the **Oskie Rice Memorial Rodeo,** usually staged the weekend after Labor Day; the **Cancer Benefit Rodeo** in April; and Maui's biggest event, drawing competitors from all the Islands as well as the U.S. mainland, the **4th of July Rodeo,** which comes with a full parade in Makawao town and other festivities that last for days. Cowboys are a tough bunch to tie down to a phone, but you can try calling the **Maui Roping Club** (☎ 808/572–2076) for information.

Tennis

Most courts charge by the hour but will let players continue after their initial hour for free, provided no one is waiting. In addition to the facilities listed below, many hotels and condos have courts open to nonguests for a fee. The best free courts are the five at the **Lahaina Civic Center** (✉ 1840 Honoapi'ilani Hwy., Lahaina ☎ 808/661–4685), near Wahikuli State Park. They're available on a first-come, first-served basis.

Kapalua Tennis Garden. This complex, home to the Kapalua Tennis Club, serves the Kapalua Resort with 10 courts, four lighted for night play, and a pro shop. You'll pay $12 an hour if you're a guest, $15 if you're not. ✉ *100 Kapalua Dr., Kapalua* ☎ *808/669–5677.*

Makena Tennis Club. Makena features six Plexipave courts, two of which are lighted for night play. Private lessons, rentals, ball machines, racquet stringing, and weekly clinics available. ✉ *Wailea Alanui, Mākena* ☎ *808/879–8777.*

Wailea Tennis Club. The club has 11 Plexipave courts (its famed grass courts are, sadly, a thing of the past), lessons, rentals, and ball machines. On weekday mornings clinics are given to help you improve ground strokes, serve, volley, or doubles strategy. Rates are $12 per hour, per person, with three lighted courts available for night play. ✉ *131 Wailea Ike Pl., Kīhei* ☎ *808/879–1958 or 800/332–1614.*

ON THE SIDELINES

At the **Kapalua Jr. Vet/Sr. Tennis Championships** in May, players compete in singles and doubles events. On Labor Day, the **Wilson Kapalua Open Tennis Tournament** calls Hawai'i's hottest hitters to Kapalua's Tennis Garden and Village Tennis Center. Also at the Tennis Center, Women's International Tennis Association professionals rally with amateurs in a week of pro-am and pro-doubles competition during the **Kapalua Betsy Nagelsen Tennis Invitational** in December. All events are put on by the **Kapalua Tennis Club** (☎ 808/669-5677). The Wailea Open Tennis Championship is held in spring or summer at the **Wailea Tennis Club** (☎ 808/879-1958).

5

Where to Eat

WORD OF MOUTH

"[Our best lunch was at] Mama's Fish House. Get the opakapaka. . . .
We had it upcountry style, and it was superb."

—beanweb24

"Sure, it's not the crazy, so-special-it's-stupid kind of place you'd
associate with gastronomic meccas, but Tastings blew me away
with impeccable flavor and fantastic service . . . too bad it's not
next door, because I'd be there every weekend."

—Ian M

www.fodors.com/forums

DINING PLANNER

Keep in Mind

Unless a resort is noted for its culinary department (such as the Ritz-Carlton or Four Seasons), you may find hotel restaurants somewhat overpriced and underwhelming. Head out to a free-standing restaurant with a menu more varied and less astronomically priced.

A Tip

Here on "survivor island," most residents depend on tipped wages. 18%–20% is standard for quality service. But beware of hotels: adding an automatic gratuity is standard practice for room service. Check your check.

Got Reservations?

Don't gamble. If you're dying to go to Mama's or the Old Lahaina Lū'au, make your reservations before leaving home. Everywhere else can be squeezed into, at least at the bar, at the last minute.

Early to Table

Most restaurants are packed from 6 to 8 PM—the sunset hours. By 8:30 many dining rooms have quieted down, and by 9:30 most are closed. If the place has a rowdy bar (or karaoke machine), you may be able to get food until 10 or 11.

What It Costs

If you want to dine well on the cheap, skip the touristy magazines and go for coupons advertised in the *Maui News*. Even upscale restaurants go half-price during the slow months (September–November). Ka'amaina discounts require a Hawai'i driver's license. Rather than feel left out, consider treating a local to dinner—you'll get their discount and directions to their secret surf spot.

Fast Facts

Dress: Maui's last jacket-required dining room closed years ago. This is paradise, after all. Wear what you like, but don't forget to bring a sweater or cover-up—many restaurants are open-air.

Tater tots: Even the fancy joints have a *keiki*, or kids' menu, and box of crayons hidden somewhere.

No butts about it: Smoking is prohibited in Hawai'i restaurants, though some bars that serve food will turn a blind eye.

WHAT IT COSTS				
$$$$	**$$$**	**$$**	**$**	**¢**
over $30	$20–$30	$12–$20	$7–$12	under $7

Restaurant prices are for a main course at dinner.

By Shannon
Wianecki

IN THE EARLY 1990S A FEW REBEL HAWAI'I CHEFS stopped ordering the standard expensive produce from the mainland and started sourcing local ingredients. Mixing the fruits and vegetables of Polynesia with classic European or Asian preparations, they spawned such dishes as 'ahi (yellowfin tuna) carpaccio, breadfruit soufflé, and lilikoʻi (passion fruit) cheesecake. Hawaiʻi Regional Cuisine was born and many of its innovators—Bev Gannon of Haliʻimaile General Store, Roy Yamaguchi of Roy's, and Peter Merriman of Hula Grill, to name a few—continue to raise the culinary bar around the island. Savvy restaurateurs have followed the lead, many offer tasting menus with excellent wine lists. Because of Maui's outstanding natural resources—prime agricultural land and the adjoining Pacific Ocean—most menus are filled with healthy options so you can feel free to indulge. Fresh fish selections, bursting ripe produce, and simple, stylized presentations characterize the very best. Expect to eat well at any price.

If you're hankering for ethnic or local-style cooking try wandering into the less-touristy areas such as Wailuku or Kahului. A good Hawaiian "plate lunch" will fulfill your daily requirement of carbohydrates: macaroni salad, two scoops of rice, and an entrée of, say, curry stew, teriyaki beef, or kālua (roasted in an underground oven) pig and cabbage.

6

WEST MAUI

Lahaina

American

★ **$–$$$** ✕ **Lahaina Coolers.** This breezy little café with a surfboard hanging from its ceiling serves such tantalizing fare as Evil Jungle Pasta (pasta with grilled chicken in spicy Thai peanut sauce) and linguine with prawns, basil, garlic, and cream. It also has pizzas, steaks, burgers, and desserts such as a chocolate taco filled with tropical fruit and berry salsa. Pastas are made fresh in-house. Don't be surprised to see a local fisherman walk through or a harbor captain reeling in a hearty breakfast. ✉ *180 Dickenson St., Lahaina* ☎ *808/661–7082* ▤ *AE, MC, V. $11–$26.*

Eclectic

$$–$$$ ✕ **Café Sauvage.** This eclectic little restaurant is in a courtyard on Front Street. The atmosphere is not as intimate or elegant as some of its neighboring, oceanfront restaurants, but the food is excellent and the prices are surprisingly low. Specialties include peppered 'ahi tuna, cajun seared scallops, and a petite filet mignon wrapped in bacon and served with truffle butter and red-wine sauce. The Seafood Sampler, which includes the fish of the day, tempura prawns, lobster ravioli, soup or salad, dessert and coffee, is a great deal. ✉ *844 Front St., Lahaina* ☎ *808/ 661–7600* ▤ *AE, MC, V. $16–$27.*

★ **$–$$** ✕ **Mala Ocean Tavern.** Perched above the tide-tossed rocks, this breezy "ocean tavern" is wholly satisfying. The menu, divided between *mala* (garden) and *moana* (ocean), is composed of small plates. The flatbread is crisp and flavorful, the hefty Kobe burger drips with Maytag blue cheese. Best of all is the calamari, lightly battered and fried with lemon slices, dipped in a spicy pesto. In the evening, the small bar is a coveted hang-

out. ✉ *1307 Front St., Lahaina* ☎ *808/661–9394* ▭ *AE, MC, V.*
$9–$15.

French

★ $$$–$$$$ ✕ **Chez Paul.** Since 1975 this tiny roadside restaurant between Lahaina
and Māʻalaea in Olowalu has been serving excellent French cuisine to
a packed house of repeat customers. Such dishes as fresh local fish
poached in white wine with shallots, cream, and capers typify the clas-
sical menu. If you can't resist foie gras, this is the place to have it. The
restaurant's offbeat exterior belies the fine art, linen-draped tables, and
wine cellar. Don't blink or you'll miss this small group of buildings hud-
dled in the middle of nowhere. ✉ *Honoapiʻilani Hwy., 4 mi south of*
Lahaina, Olowalu ☎ *808/661–3843* ⌕ *Reservations essential* ▭ *AE,*
D, MC, V ☾ *No lunch. $29–$45.*

$$$–$$$$ ✕ **Gerard's.** Owner and celebrated chef Gerard Reversade started
FodorsChoice cooking at the age of 10, and at 12 he was baking croissants. He hon-
★ ors the French tradition with such exquisitely prepared dishes as rack
of lamb in mint crust with thyme jus, and venison cutlets in a port
sauce with confit of chestnuts, walnuts, fennel, and pearl onions. The
menu changes once a year, but many favorites—such as the sinfully
good crème brûlée—remain. A first-class wine list, a lovely room, and
celebrity-spotting round out the experience. ✉ *Plantation Inn, 174*
Lahainaluna Rd., Lahaina ☎ *808/661–8939* ▭ *AE, D, DC, MC, V*
☾ *No lunch. $28–$47.*

Hawaiian–Pacific Rim

$$$–$$$$ ✕ **David Paul's Lahaina Grill.** Though the restaurant's namesake is only
FodorsChoice a consultant now, David Paul's is still a favorite. Beautifully designed,
★ it's adjacent to the elegant Lahaina Inn in a historic building on La-
hainaluna Road. The restaurant has an extensive wine cellar, an in-house
bakery, and splashy artwork decorating the walls. The house somme-
lier's suggestions keep up with the celebrated menu. Try the signature
tequila shrimp and firecracker rice along with the scrumptious triple-
berry pie. Demi portions are available at the bar. ✉ *127 Lahainaluna*
Rd., Lahaina ☎ *808/667–5117* ▭ *AE, DC, MC, V. $26–$42.*

$$$–$$$$ ✕ **Iʻo.** From its opening, this restaurant established itself as cutting edge
in Lahaina, both for its theatrical interior designed by the artist Dado
and for its contemporary Pacific Rim menu. A prized appetizer is the
Silken Purse—steamed wontons stuffed with roasted peppers, mushrooms,
macadamia nuts, and tofu. Favorite dinners include lemongrass-
coconut fish and nori-wrapped rare tuna, served with green-papaya salad.
Desserts to savor are the Hawaiian Vintage Chocolate Mousse and the
chocolate pâté with Kula strawberries. ✉ *505 Front St., Lahaina* ☎ *808/*
661–8422 ▭ *AE, D, DC, MC, V* ☾ *No lunch. $28–$32.*

¢–$$ ✕ **Aloha Mixed Plate.** Set right on the ocean, this funky open-air bar and
restaurant is a great place for *ono grinds*—good food in Hawaiian
slang. Crispy coconut prawns, taro burgers, shoyu chicken, and kahlua
pork are favorite island comfort foods (these are the things local kids
daydream about when they're sent away to college). You too can indulge
in these Hawaiian treats at this awesome outdoor location. ✉ *1286 Front*
St., Lahaina ☎ *808/661–3322* ▭ *AE, D, DC, MC, V. $5–$13.*

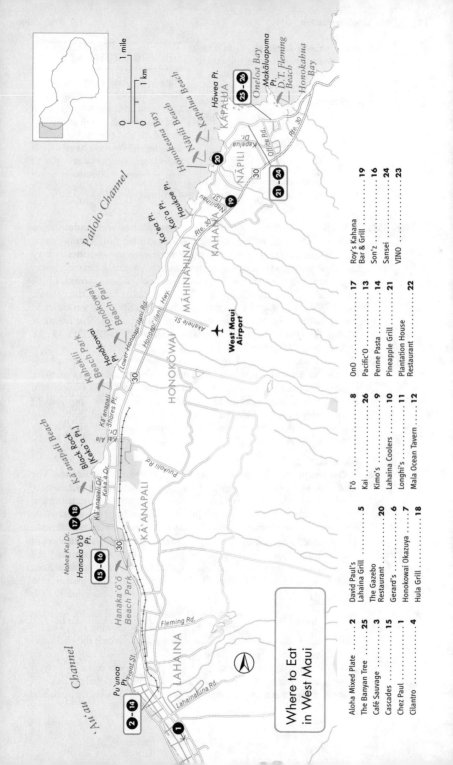

Where to Eat in West Maui

Aloha Mixed Plate **2**	David Paul's	I'ō **8**	OnO **17**	Roy's Kahana
The Banyan Tree **25**	Lahaina Grill **5**	Kai **26**	Pacific'O **13**	Bar & Grill **19**
Café Sauvage **3**	The Gazebo	Kimo's **9**	Penne Pasta **14**	Son'z **16**
Cascades **15**	Restaurant **20**	Lahaina Coolers **10**	Pineapple Grill **21**	Sansei **24**
Chez Paul **1**	Gerard's **6**	Longhi's **11**	Plantation House	VINO **23**
Cilantro **4**	Honokowai Okazuya **7**	Mala Ocean Tavern **12**	Restaurant **22**	
	Hula Grill **18**			

¢–$ ✕ **Honokowai Okazuya.** Don't expect to sit down at this miniature restaurant sandwiched between a dive shop and a salon—this is strictly a take-out joint. You can order local plate lunches, Chinese, vegetarian, or sandwiches. The spicy eggplant is delicious, and the fresh chow fun noodles are bought up quickly. ✉ *3600-D Lower Honoapi'ilani Hwy., Lahaina* ☎ *808/665–0512*

> **DID YOU KNOW?**
>
> Mark Ellman, one of the original Hawai'i Regional Cuisine gang, likes to zip up to his latest restaurant, Mala Ocean Tavern, on his moped. He's also the culinary brain behind Penne Pasta and Maui Tacos.

▭ *No credit cards* ✆ *Closed Sun. and daily 2:30–4:30. $7–$11.*

Italian

$$$–$$$$ ✕ **Longhi's.** A Lahaina establishment, Longhi's has been around since 1976, serving great Italian pasta as well as sandwiches, seafood, beef, and chicken dishes. The pasta is homemade, and the in-house bakery turns out breakfast pastries, desserts, and fresh bread. Even on a warm day, you won't need air-conditioning with two spacious, breezy, open-air levels to choose from. The black-and-white tile floors are a classic touch. There's a second restaurant on the South Shore, at the Shops at Wailea. ✉ *888 Front St., Lahaina* ☎ *808/667–2288* ✉ *The Shops at Wailea, 3750 Wailea Alanui Dr., Wailea* ☎ *808/891–8883* ▭ *AE, D, DC, MC, V. $25–$35.*

$–$$ ✕ **Penne Pasta.** Heaping plates of flavorful pasta and low-key, unintrusive service make this restaurant the perfect alternative to an expensive night out in Lahaina. The osso buco (Thursday's special) is sumptuous, and the traditional salad niçoise overflows with generous portions of olives, peppers, garlic 'ahi, and potatoes. Couples should split a salad and entrée, as portions are large. ✉ *180 Dickenson St., Lahaina* ☎ *808/661–6633* ▭ *AE, D, DC, MC, V* ✆ *No lunch weekends. $7–$15.*

Mexican

★ ¢–$ ✕ **Cilantro.** At last! Mexican food to brag about on the West Side! The flavors of Old Mexico are given new life here, where the tortillas are hand-pressed and no fewer than nine chiles are used to create the salsas. Rotisserie chicken tacos with jicama slaw are both mouthwatering and healthy. The Mother Clucker flautas with crema fresca and jalepeño jelly are not to be missed. Look for owner Paris Nabavi's collection of dead soldiers—tortilla presses worn from duty, now hand-painted and displayed up on the wall. ✉ *In Old Lahaina Center, 170 Papalaua Ave., Lahaina* ☎ *808/667–5444* ▭ *AE, MC, V. $7–$15.*

Seafood

★ $$$–$$$$ ✕ **Pacific'O.** You can sit outdoors at umbrella-shaded tables near the water's edge, or find a spot in the breezy, marble-floor interior. The exciting menu features fresh 'ahi-and-ono tempura, in which the two kinds of fish are wrapped around *tobiko* (flying-fish roe), then wrapped in nori, and wok-fried. There's a great lamb dish, too—a whole rack of sweet New Zealand lamb, sesame-crusted and served with roasted macadamia sauce and Hawaiian chutney. Live jazz is played Thursday through Sat-

Continued on page 124

AUTHENTIC TASTE OF HAWAI'I: LŪ'AU OR LAULAU?

The best place to sample Hawaiian food is at a backyard lū'au. Aunts and uncles are cooking, the pig is from a cousin's farm, and the fish is from a brother's boat.

But even locals have to angle for invitations to those rare occasions. So your choice is most likely between a commercial lū'au and a Hawaiian restaurant.

Most commercial lū'au will offer you little of the authentic diet; they're more about umbrella drinks, laughs, spectacle, and fun. Expect to spend some time and no small amount of cash.

For greater authenticity, folksy experiences, and rock-bottom prices, visit a Hawaiian restaurant (most are in anonymous storefronts in residential neighborhoods). Expect rough edges and some effort negotiating the menu.

In either case, much of what is known today as Hawaiian food would be as foreign to a 16th-century Hawaiian as risotto or chow mien. The pre-contact diet was simple and healthy–mainly raw and steamed seafood and vegetables. Early Hawaiians used earth ovens and heated stones to cook seafood, taro, sweet potatoes, and breadfruit and seasoned their food with sea salt and ground kukui nuts. Seaweed, fern shoots, sweet potato vines, coconut, banana, sugar cane, and select greens and roots rounded out the diet.

Successive waves of immigrants added their favorites to the ti leaf–lined table. So it is that foods as disparate as salt salmon and chicken long rice are now Hawaiian—even though there is no salmon in Hawaiian waters and long rice (cellophane noodles) is Chinese.

AT THE LŪʻAU: KĀLUA PORK

The heart of any lūʻau is the *imu*, the earth oven in which a whole pig is roasted. The preparation of an imu is an arduous affair for most families, who tackle it only once a year or so, for a baby's first birthday or at Thanksgiving, when many Islanders prefer to imu their turkeys. Commercial lūʻau operations have it down to a science, however.

THE ART OF THE STONE

The key to a proper imu is the *pohaku*, the stones. Imu cook by means of long, slow, moist heat released by special stones which can withstand a hot fire without exploding. Many Hawaiian families treasure their imu stones, keeping them in a pile in the back yard and passing them on through generations.

PIT COOKING

The imu makers first dig a pit about the size of a refrigerator, then lay down *kiawe* (mesquite) wood and stones, and build a white-hot fire that is allowed to burn itself out. The ashes are raked away, and the hot stones covered with banana and ti leaves. Well-wrapped in ti or banana leaves and a net of chicken wire, the pig is lowered onto the leaf-covered stones. *Laulau* (leaf-wrapped bundles of meats, fish, and taro leaves) may also be placed inside. Leaves—ti, banana, even ginger—cover the pig followed by wet burlap sacks (to create steam). The whole is topped with a canvas tarp and left to steam for the better part of a day.

OPENING THE IMU

This is the moment everyone waits for: The imu is unwrapped like a giant present and the imu keepers gingerly wrestle out the steaming pig. When it's unwrapped, the meat falls moist and smoky-flavored from the bone, looking and tasting just like Southern-style pulled pork, but without the barbecue sauce.

WHICH LŪʻAU?

The Feast at Lele. Top notch value and price, great wine list.

Old Lahaina Lūʻau. Intimate and the most traditional; a perennial sell-out.

Renaissance Wailea Sunset Beach Lūʻau. Festive and flashy, great spread

Outrigger Marriott Lūʻau. Imu ceremony and buffet.

MEA ʻAI ʻONO.
GOOD THINGS TO EAT.

LAULAU
Steamed meats, fish, and taro leaf in ti-leaf bundles: fork-tender, a medley of flavors; the taro resembles spinach.

LOMI LOMI SALMON
Salt salmon in a piquant salad or relish with onions, tomatoes.

POI (DON'T CALL IT LIBRARY PASTE.)
Islanders are beyond tired of jokes about poi, a paste made of pounded taro root.

Consider: The Hawaiian Adam is descended from *kalo* (taro). Young taro plants are called "keiki"–children. Poi is the first food after mother's milk for many Islanders. ʻAi, the word for food, is synonymous with poi in many contexts.

Not only that. We like it. "There is no meat that doesn't taste good with poi," the old Hawaiians said.

But you have to know how to eat it: with something rich or powerfully flavored. "It is salt that makes the poi go in," is another adage. When you're served poi, try it with a mouthful of smoky kālua pork or salty lomi lomi salmon. Its slightly sour blandness cleanses the palate. And if you don't like it, smile and say something polite. (And slide that bowl over to a local.)

Laulau

Lomi Lomi Salmon

Poi

6

E HELE MAI ʻAI! COME AND EAT!

Hawaiian restaurants tend to be inconveniently located in well-worn storefronts with little or no parking, outfitted with battered tables and clattering Melmac dishes, open odd (and usually limited) hours and days, and often so crowded you have to wait. But they personify aloha, invariably run by local families who welcome tourists who take the trouble to find them.

Many are cash-only operations and combination plates are a standard feature: one or two entrées, a side such as chicken long rice, choice of poi or steamed rice and–if the place is really old-style–a tiny portion of coarse Hawaiian salt and some raw onions for relish.

Most serve some foods that aren't, strictly speaking, Hawaiian, but are beloved of

kamaʻāina, such as salt meat with watercress (preserved meat in a tasty broth), or *akubone* (skipjack tuna fried in a vinegar sauce).

Our two favorites: **Aloha Mixed Plate** and **A.K.'s Café**.

AUTHENTIC TASTE OF HAWAIʻI: LŪʻAU OR LAULAU?

urday from 9 to midnight. ⊠ *505 Front St., Lahaina* ☎ *808/667–4341* ▭ *AE, D, DC, MC, V.*

$$–$$$$ ✕ **Kimo's.** On a warm Lahaina day, it's a treat to relax at an umbrella-shaded table on this restaurant's lānai, sip a mai tai, and watch sailboats glide in and out of the harbor. Outstanding seafood is just one of the options here; also good are Hawaiian-style chicken and pork dishes, and burgers. Try the signature dessert, Hula Pie: vanilla-macadamia nut ice cream topped with chocolate fudge and whipped cream in an Oreo-cookie crust. ⊠ *845 Front St., Lahaina* ☎ *808/661–4811* ▭ *AE, DC, MC, V.* *$17–$37.*

Kā'anapali

Continental

$$$–$$$$ ✕ **Son'z.** Chef Aaron Placourakis, formerly of Sarento's, Nick's, and Aaron's atop Ala Moana (on O'ahu), has taken over the Hyatt's beloved Swan Court. Now you can sample one of 3,000 bottles of wine (from the largest cellar in the state) while shielding your sourdough roll from the staring eyes of the swans. Steaks and seafood are featured. ⊠ *Hyatt Regency Maui, Kā'anapali Beach Resort, 200 Nohea Kai Dr., Kā'anapali* ☎ *808/661–1234* ▭ *AE, D, DC, MC, V. $28–$45.*

Hawaiian–Pacific Rim

$$–$$$$ ✕ **Cascades.** Above the Hyatt's wonderland swimming pools and beneath a canopy of interlocking *hau* trees, you can enjoy a sampler of island treats—pot stickers, teriyaki beef skewers, and *poke*. Toast to your good fortune with a kitschy tropical cocktail. If you've been out shopping late, you can order sushi until 10 PM, and light fare until 11 PM. ⊠ *Hyatt Regency Maui, Kā'anapali Beach Resort, 200 Nohea Kai Dr., Kā'anapali* ☎ *808/661–1234* ▭ *AE, D, DC, MC, V. $15–$29.*

$$–$$$$ ✕ **Hula Grill.** Genial chef-restaurateur Peter Merriman's bustling, family-oriented restaurant is in a re-created 1930s Hawaiian beach house, and every table has an ocean view. You can also dine on the beach, toes in the sand, at the Barefoot Bar, where Hawaiian entertainment is presented every evening. South Pacific snapper is baked with tomato, chili, and cumin aioli and served with a black bean, Maui onion, and avocado relish. Spareribs are steamed in banana leaves, then grilled with mango barbecue sauce over mesquitelike *kiawe* wood. ⊠ *Whalers Village, 2435 Kā'anapali Pkwy., Kā'anapali* ☎ *808/667–6636* ▭ *AE, DC, MC, V. $17–$32.*

$$–$$$$ ✕ **OnO.** This casual, fun restaurant features *pupu* (known elsewhere in the world as *tapas*). This is a good place to bring the kids. They can munch away on the beef tenderloin kebabs while you sample the Manila clams, Hokkaido scallops, and asparagus doused in a not-too-spicy Kim Chee cream. ⊠ *Westin, Kā'anapali Pkwy., Kā'anapali* ☎ *808/667–2525* ▭ *AE, DC, MC, V. $13–$32.*

North of Kā'anapali

American

¢–$ ✕ **The Gazebo Restaurant.** Even locals will stand in line up to half-an-hour for a table overlooking the beach at this restaurant, an actual open-air gazebo. The food is standard diner fare, but it's thoughtfully prepared. Breakfast choices include macadamia-nut pancakes and Portuguese-sausage omelets. There are satisfying burgers and salads at lunch. The friendly hotel staff puts out coffee for those waiting in line. ⊠ *Nāpili Shores Resort, 5315 Lower Honoapi'ilani Hwy., Nāpili* ☎ *808/669–5621* ▭ *No credit cards* ⊘ *No dinner. $3–$9.*

Hawaiian–Pacific Rim

★ **$$$$** ✕ **The Banyan Tree.** If you've never tried foie gras ice cream, don't be shy. The menu is daring but delectable. Nothing is prepared as it should be: the priciest dish, lobster and scallops, is a salad, and the fish of Hawai'ian royalty, *moi,* is served atop Indian-spice lentils with a yogurt sauce. We recommend placing your evening's fate in the care of the chef. The tasting menus and wine pairings provide an epicurean experience to be savored long afterward in memory. The open-beam restaurant's subdued atmosphere is charged with the sounds of live world music. ⊠ *Ritz-Carlton, Kapalua, 1 Ritz-Carlton Dr., Kapalua* ☎ *808/669–6200* ▭ *AE, D, DC, MC, V. $32–$48.*

★ **$$$–$$$$** ✕ **Roy's Kahana Bar & Grill.** Roy Yamaguchi's own sake brand ("Y") and Hawaiian fusion specialties, such as shrimp with sweet-and-spicy chili sauce and miso yaki butterfish, keep regulars returning for more. Locals know to order the incomparable chocolate soufflé immediately after being seated. Both restaurants, in Kahana and Kīhei, are in supermarket parking lots—it's not the view that excites, it's the food. ⊠ *Kahana Gateway Shopping Center, 4405 Honoapi'ilani Hwy., Kahana* ☎ *808/669–6999* ⊠ *Safeway Shopping Center, 303 Pi'ikea Ave., Kīhei* ☎ *808/891–1120* ▭ *AE, D, DC, MC, V. $25–$31.*

$$–$$$$ ✕ **Pineapple Grill.** Chef Joey Macadangdang heads the kitchen of Kapalua's newest restaurant. Hawai'i regional cuisine finds superb expression here, in dishes like the porcini-dusted opakapaka with yuzu veloutte. The braised short ribs are garnished with just enough Maui pineapple relish to heighten hidden lemongrass and anise flavors. But don't get attached to anything on the

> **DID YOU KNOW?**
>
> Roy Yamaguchi, one of the innovators of Hawai'i Regional Cuisine, has mentored many a young ambitious chef—including Chef Joey Macadangdang, now at his own restaurant, Pineapple Grill.

menu—Chef Joey likes to reinvent it regularly. If the weather isn't too cold, the outdoor tables facing the West Maui mountains can be even nicer than those with an ocean view. ⊠ *200 Kapalua Dr. Kapalua* ☎ *808/669–9600* ▭ *AE, MC, V. $17–$32.*

$$–$$$$ ✕ **Plantation House Restaurant.** It's hard to decide which is better here, the food or the view. Misty hills, grassy volcanic ridges lined with pine trees, and fairways that appear to drop off into the ocean provide an idyllic setting. The specialty is fresh island fish prepared according to different "tastes"—Upcountry Maui, Asian-Pacific, Provence, and others. The breeze through the large shuttered windows can be cool, so you may want to bring a sweater or sit by the fireplace. Breakfast here is a luxurious way to start your day. ⊠ *Plantation Course Clubhouse, 2000*

Plantation Club Dr., past Kapalua
☎ *808/669–6299* 🖃 *AE, MC, V.*
$18–$32.

Italian

$–$$$$ ✕ **VINO.** D. K. Kodama, the culinary mastermind behind Sansei, teamed up with Master Sommelier Chuck Furuya to create a strange child—an Italian tapas restaurant with a Japanese twist. The results have been hailed as, well, masterful. Set on the Kapalua golf course, the restaurant's active, somewhat noisy atmosphere encourages experimentation. Small plates of lamb chops, osso buco, or plump shrimp atop

Asian noodles with truffle butter are sure to tempt. Wines are served in Riedel stemware; flights can be sampled at the bar. ⊠ *2000 Village Rd., Kapalua* ☎ *808/661–8466* 🖃 *AE, D, DC, MC, V. $10–$50.*

Japanese

★ **$–$$$$** ✕ **Kai.** Master sushi chef Tadashi Yoshino sits at the helm of this intimate, ocean-view sushi bar, hidden behind the Lobby bar at the Ritz-Carlton, Kapalua. The menu includes sushi and hot Japanese entrées, but your best bet is to let Chef Yoshino design the meal. He might have yellowtail cheeks, fresh sea urchin, and raw lobster. He also makes lobster-head soup, a Japanese comfort food. ⊠ *Ritz-Carlton, Kapalua, 1 Ritz-Carlton Dr., Kapalua* ☎ *808/669–6200* 🖃 *AE, D, DC, MC, V. $10–$50.*

$–$$$
Fodor's Choice
★ ✕ **Sansei.** One of the best-loved restaurants on the island, Sansei is Japanese with a Hawaiian twist. Inspired dishes include *panko*-crusted 'ahi (panko are Japanese bread crumbs), spicy fried calamari, mango-and-crab-salad roll, and a decadent foie gras *nigiri* (served on rice without seaweed) sushi. Desserts often use local fruit; the Kula-persimmon crème brûlée is stunning. Both locations are now popular karaoke hangouts, serving late-night sushi at half price. ⊠ *Kapalua Shops, 115 Bay Dr., Kapalua* ☎ *808/666–6286* ⊠ *Kīhei Town Center, 1881 S. Kīhei Rd., Kīhei* ☎ *808/879–0004* 🖃 *AE, D, MC, V* ☺ *No lunch. $8–$30.*

THE SOUTH SHORE

Kīhei & North

American

★ **$–$$$** ✕ **Tastings Wine Bar & Grill.** A wedge of a restaurant, this tiny epicurean mecca is tucked in behind a number of rowdy bars on South Kīhei Road. The owner-chef hails from Healdsburg, California, and he brought his highly regarded restaurant with him. The menu features "tastings" of oysters, risotto, lamb chops, and seared *opakapaka* (Hawaiian pink snapper) with a number of well-chosen wines by the bottle or glass. At the

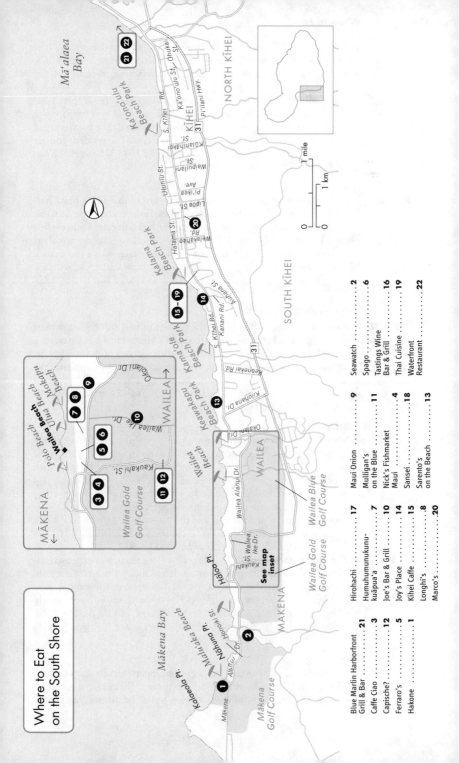

Where to Eat on the South Shore

Blue Martin Harborfront	Hirohachi **17**	Maui Onion **9**	Seawatch **2**
Grill & Bar **21**	Humuhumunukunu-	Mulligan's	Spago **6**
Caffe Ciao **3**	kuāpua'a **7**	on the Blue **11**	Tastings Wine
Capische? **12**	Joe's Bar & Grill **10**	Nick's Fishmarket	Bar & Grill **16**
Ferraro's **5**	Joy's Place **14**	Maui **4**	Thai Cuisine **19**
Hakone **1**	Kihei Caffe **15**	Sansei **18**	Waterfront
	Longhi's **8**	Sarento's	Restaurant **22**
	Marco's **20**	on the Beach **13**	

bar you can rub elbows with chefs and waiters from the island's best restaurants who come to spend their hard-earned tips here. ⊠ *1913 S. Kīhei Rd., Kīhei* ☎ *808/879–8711* ⊕ *www.tastingsrestaurant.com* ▭ *AE, D, DC, MC, V. $8–$27.*

¢–$ ✕ **Kihei Caffe.** People-watching is fun over a cup of coffee at this casual breakfast and lunch joint. Hearty, affordable portions will prepare you for a day of surfing across the street at Kalama Park. The bowl-shaped egg scramble is tasty and almost enough for two. The resident rooster may come a-beggin' for some of your muffin. ⊠ *1945 S. Kīhei Rd., Kīhei* ☎ *808/879–2230* ▭ *MC, V. $6–$10.*

Italian

$$$–$$$$ ✕ **Sarento's on the Beach.** The beachfront setting at this South Maui Italian setting is irresistible. Chef George Gomes, formerly of A Pacific Café, heads the kitchen. The menu features both traditional dishes—like penne Calabrese and seafood *fra diavolo*—as well as inventions such as swordfish saltimbocca, a strangely successful entrée with a prosciutto, Bel Paese cheese, radicchio, and porcini-mushroom sauce. The wine list includes some affordable finds. ⊠ *2980 S. Kīhei Rd., Kīhei* ☎ *808/875–7555* ▭ *AE, D, DC, MC, V* ☉ *No lunch. $27–$41.*

Japanese

★ ¢–$$ ✕ **Hirohachi.** A stone's throw from the flashier Sansei, Hirohachi has been serving authentic Japanese fare for years. Owner Hiro has discerning taste, he buys only the best from local fishermen and imports many ingredients from Japan. Order with confidence even if you can't read the Japanese specials posted on the wall, everything on the menu is high quality. ⊠ *1881 S. Kīhei Rd., Kīhei* ☎ *808/875-7474* ▭ *AE, MC, V* ☉ *Closed Mon. $6–$18.*

Seafood

$$–$$$$ ✕ **Waterfront Restaurant.** At this harborside establishment, fresh fish is prepared in a host of sumptuous ways: baked in buttered parchment paper; imprisoned in ribbons of angel-hair potato; or topped with tomato salsa, smoked chili pepper, and avocado. The varied menu also lists an outstanding rack of lamb and veal scallopini. Visitors like to come early to dine at sunset on the outdoor patio. Enter Māʻalaea at the Maui Ocean Center and then follow the blue WATERFRONT RESTAURANT signs to the third condominium. ⊠ *50 Hauʻoli St., Māʻalaea* ☎ *808/244–9028* ▭ *AE, D, DC, MC, V* ☉ *No lunch. $19–$53.*

$–$$$ ✕ **Blue Marlin Harborfront Grill & Bar.** This is a casual, less expensive alternative to the Waterfront Restaurant. It's as much a bar as it is a grill, but the kitchen nonetheless sends out well-prepared, substantial servings of fresh fish, burgers, and salads. The sidewalk tables have a lovely view of the harbor. ⊠ *Māʻalaea Harbor Village, at Old Māʻalaea Rd. and Honoapiʻilani Hwy., next to Maui Ocean Center, Māʻalaea* ☎ *808/244–8844* ▭ *AE, MC, V. $10–$28.*

Thai

★ $–$$ ✕ **Thai Cuisine.** Fragrant tea and coconut-ginger chicken soup begin a satisfying meal at this excellent Thai restaurant. The care that goes into the decor here (reflected in the glittering Buddhist shrines, fancy napkin folds, and matching blue china) also applies to the cuisine. The lean and moist meat of the red-curry duck rivals similar dishes at resort restaurants, and the fried bananas with ice cream are wonderful. ⊠ *In Kukui Mall, 1819 S. Kīhei Rd., Kīhei* ☎ *808/875–0839* ☰ *AE, D, DC, MC, V. $8–$17.*

Vegetarian

$–$$ ✕ **Joy's Place.** You may see Joy in the back, whipping up one of her fantastic, vitamin-packed soups. Her glowing skin and smile are testaments to her healthful, culinary wizardry. Try a sandwich or green leaf wrap filled with veggies and a creamy spread. If you have a hint of a cold, a spicy potion is available to ward it off. ⊠ *In Island Surf Bldg., 1993 S. Kīhei Rd., Suite 17, Kīhei* ☎ *808/879–9258* ☰ *MC, V. $4–$14.*

Wailea & South

American

$$$–$$$$ ✕ **Joe's Bar & Grill.** Owners Joe and Bev Gannon, who run the immensely popular Hāli'imaile General Store, have brought their flair for food home to roost in this comfortable treetop-level restaurant at the Wailea Tennis Club, where you can dine while watching court action from a balcony seat. With friendly service and such dishes as New York strip steak with caramelized onions, wild mushrooms, and Gorgonzola cheese crumble, there are lots of reasons to stop in at this hidden spot. ⊠ *131 Wailea Ike Pl., Wailea* ☎ *808/875–7767* ☰ *AE, MC, V. $20–$38.*

$$–$$$ ✕ **Seawatch.** The Plantation House's South Shore sister restaurant has an equally good view, and almost as delicious a menu. Breakfast is especially nice here—the outdoor seating is cool in the morning, overlooking the parade of boats heading out to Molokini. The crab-cake Benedicts are a well-loved standard. Avoid seats above their private catering section, which can be noisy. ⊠ *100 Golf Club Dr., Wailea* ☎ *808/875–8080* ☰ *AE, D, DC, MC, V. $16–$28.*

★ $–$$$ ✕ **Maui Onion.** Forget the overrated Cheeseburger in Paradise in Lahaina—Maui Onion has the best burgers on the island, hands down, and phenomenal onion rings as well. They coat the onions in pancake batter, dip them in panko, then fry them until they're golden brown. ⊠ *Renaissance Wailea, 3550 Wailea Alanui Dr., Wailea* ☎ *808/879–4900* ☰ *AE, D, DC, MC, V. $10–$24.*

Hawaiian–Pacific Rim

$$$–$$$$ ✕ **Humuhumunukunukuāpua'a.** Wrestle with the restaurant's formidable name—the name of the state fish—or simply watch the fish swim by in the 2,100-gallon tank at the bar. The thatch-roof building actually floats on a lagoon, creating an atmosphere that tends to outshine the food. We recommend skipping the dining room and enjoying *pūpū* at the bar. Try their signature 'ahi traps (delectable chunks of seared fish on lemongrass stalks) with an over-the-top cocktail. If you do try the dining room, you can fetch your own spiny lobster (which is best simply grilled) from a cage below the water's surface or try *laulau*, a traditional Hawaiian preparation of fish or meat steamed in leaves. ⊠ *Grand Wailea Re-*

6

sort, 3850 Wailea Alanui Dr., Wailea ☏ *808/875–1234* ▭ *AE, D, DC, MC, V. $28–$38.*

★ $$$–$$$$ ✕ **Spago.** Celebrity chef and owner Wolfgang Puck wisely brought his fame to this gorgeous locale. Giant sea-anemone prints, modern-art-inspired lamps, and views of the shoreline give diners something to look at while waiting. The solid menu delivers with dishes like seared scallops with asparagus and *pohole* (fiddlehead fern) shoots, and "chinois" lamb chops with Hunan eggplant. The beef dish, with braised celery, Armagnac, and horseradish potatoes, may be the island's priciest—but devotees swear it's worth every cent. ⊠ *Four Seasons Resort, 3900 Wailea Alanui Dr., Wailea* ☏ *808/879–2999* ▭ *AE, D, DC, MC, V* ☾ *No lunch. $29–$57.*

Irish

¢–$$ ✕ **Mulligan's on the Blue.** If you're hankering for bangers and mash or shepherd's pie, stop in at this pub on Wailea's Blue golf course. You'll be greeted by a nearly all-Irish staff, and before you know it, you'll be sipping a heady pint of Guinness. The Wailea Nights dinner show is outstanding—and a terrific deal to boot. Breakfast is a good value for the area, and the view is one of the best. ⊠ *100 Kaukahi St., Wailea* ☏ *808/ 874–1131* ▭ *AE, D, DC, MC, V. $6–$18.*

Italian

$$$–$$$$ ✕ **Capische?** Hidden up at the quiet Blue Diamond Resort, this restau-
Fodor'sChoice rant is one local patrons would like kept secret. A circular stone atrium
★ gives way to a small piano lounge, where you can find the best sunset view on the island. You can count on the freshness of the ingredients in superb dishes like the quail saltimbocca, and the saffron *vongole*—a colorful affair of squid-ink pasta and spicy saffron broth. Tables nestled in the downstairs garden have a peek at the "chef's cave" where a different region of Italy is explored each month. Intimate and well conceived, Capische, with its seductive flavors and ambience, ensures a romantic night out. ⊠ *Blue Diamond Resort, 555 Kaukahi St., Wailea* ☏ *808/879–2224* ▭ *AE, D, DC, MC, V* ☾ *No lunch. $26–$45.*

★ $$$–$$$$ ✕ **Ferraro's.** Overlooking Wailea Beach, this outdoor restaurant is beautiful both day and night. For lunch, indulge in a lobster and grapefruit sandwich—we haven't found its superior yet. At dinner begin your feast with the crab lumpmeat gazpacho and make use of the wine list's excellent Italian offerings. The service here is unparalleled. Occasionally you can catch celebrities gossiping at the bar. ⊠ *Four Seasons Resort Maui, Wailea Alanui Dr., Wailea* ☏ *808/874–8000* ▭ *AE, D, DC, MC, V. $26–$40.*

$$–$$$$ ✕ **Caffe Ciao.** Caffe Ciao brings Italy to the Fairmont Kea Lani. Authentic, fresh gnocchi and lobster risotto taste especially delicious in the open-air café, which overlooks the swimming pool. For casual European fare, try the poached-tuna salad, grilled panini, or pizza from the wood-burning oven. Locals have long known Caffe Ciao's sister deli as the sole source for discerning palates: delectable pastries, tapenades, mustards, and even $50 bottles of truffle oil. ⊠ *Fairmont Kea Lani, 4100 Wailea Alanui Dr., Wailea* ☏ *808/875–4100* ▭ *AE, D, DC, MC, V. $13–$32.*

Japanese

$$$–$$$$ ✕ **Hakone.** The Japanese food served at this restaurant in the Maui Prince hotel has a great reputation. Each night, a different "Special Attraction Buffet" is served: Crazy Crab, Sake Sampler, or the Japanese buffet with numerous dishes of raw, cooked, hot, cold, sweet, and savory items. At $44, it's a good value for the quality of food presented. Impeccably fresh sushi, traditional cooked dishes, and an impressive sake list round out the menu. ⊠ *Maui Prince, 5400 Mākena Alanui Rd., Mākena* ☎ *808/874–1111* ▭ *AE, MC, V* ⊘ *No lunch. $20–$44.*

Seafood

$$$–$$$$ ✕ **Nick's Fishmarket Maui.** This romantic spot serves fresh seafood using the simplest preparations: mahimahi with Kula-corn relish, 'ahi pepper fillet, and *opakapaka* (Hawaiian pink snapper) with rock shrimp in a lemon-butter-caper sauce, to name a few. Everyone seems to love the Greek Maui Wowie salad made with local onions, tomatoes, avocado, feta cheese, and bay shrimp. Service is somewhat formal, but it befits the beautiful food presentations and extensive wine list. ⊠ *Fairmont Kea Lani, 4100 Wailea Alanui Dr., Wailea* ☎ *808/879–7224* ▭ *AE, D, DC, MC, V* ⊘ *No lunch. $27–$49.*

CENTRAL MAUI

American

¢–$ ✕ **Maui Bake Shop.** Wonderful breads baked in old brick ovens (dating to 1935), hearty lunch fare, and irresistible desserts make this a popular spot in Central Maui. Baker José Krall was trained in France, and his wife, Claire, is a Maui native whose friendly face you often see when you walk in. Standouts include the focaccia and homemade soups. ⊠ *2092 Vineyard St., Wailuku* ☎ *808/242–0064* ▭ *AE, D, MC, V* ⊘ *Closed Sun. No dinner. $4–$8.*

Chinese

¢–$$ ✕ **Dragon Dragon.** Whether you're a party of 10 or 2, this is the place to share seafood-tofu soup, spareribs with garlic sauce, or fresh Dungeness crab with four sauces. Tasteful, simple decor complements the solid menu. The restaurant shares parking with the Maui Megaplex and makes a great pre- or post-movie stop. ⊠ *In Maui Mall, 70 E. Kaahumanu Ave., Kahului* ☎ *808/893–1628* ▭ *AE, D, MC, V. $6–$17.*

Hawaiian

¢–$$ ✕ **A.K.'s Café.** Nearly hidden between auto-body shops and karaoke bars is this wonderful, bright café. Affordable, tasty entrées such as grilled tenderloin with wild mushrooms or garlic-crusted ono with ginger relish come with a choice of two sides. The flavorful dishes are healthy, too—Chef Elaine Rothermal previously instructed island nutritionists on how to prepare health-conscious versions of local favorites. Try the Hawaiian french-fried sweet potatoes, the steamed *ulu* (breadfruit), or the poi. ⊠ *1237 Lower Main, Wailuku* ☎ *808/244–8774* ▭ *D, MC, V* ⊘ *Closed Sun. $4–$14.*

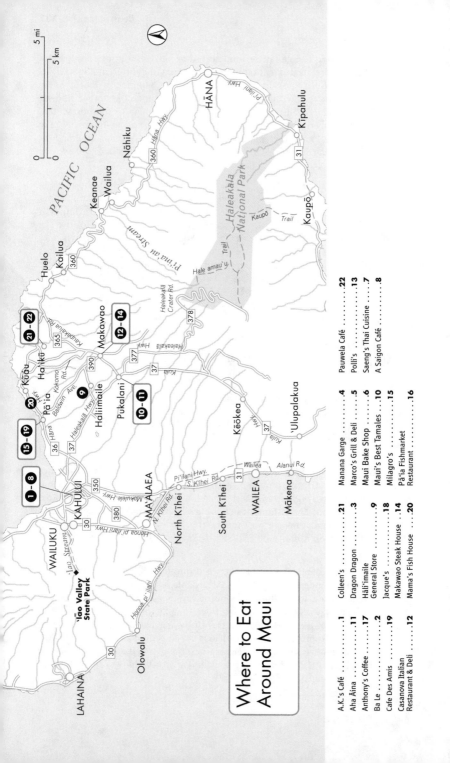

Where to Eat Around Maui

A.K.'s Café **1**
Aha 'Āina **11**
Anthony's Coffee **17**
Ba Le **2**
Cafe Des Amis **19**
Casanova Italian
Restaurant & Deli **12**

Colleen's **21**
Dragon Dragon **3**
Hāli'imaile
General Store **9**
Jacque's **18**
Makawao Steak House . . **14**
Mama's Fish House **20**

Manana Garge **4**
Marco's Grill & Deli **5**
Maui Bake Shop **6**
Maui's Best Tamales . . . **10**
Milagro's **15**
Pā'ia Fishmarket
Restaurant **16**

Pauwela Café **22**
Polli's **13**
Saeng's Thai Cuisine **7**
A Saigon Café **8**

WHERE TO WINE

DON'T LET THE PINEAPPLE WINE FOOL YOU, Maui residents can sip syrah with the best of them. At **Tastings** (✉ 1913 S. Kīhei Rd. ☎ 808/879–8711) on the South Shore, you can sample oysters, risotto, and steak with a number of wines by the bottle or glass. Small and smartly designed, this epicurean mecca is tucked in between a number of rowdy bars in Kīhei. **Marc Aurel's Espresso & Wine Bar** (✉ 28 Market St., Wailuku ☎ 808/244–0852) has an even wider selection of wines by the glass. The impressive five-page wine menu reads like a novel and is complemented by Marc's own *tzatziki* (fresh cucumber dip) and a terrific assortment of cheeses. This favorite Wailuku watering hole is popular for *pau hanas*, or after-work drinks, so be sure to stop by before 9 PM.

On the West Side, try **Vino** (✉ 2000 Village Rd., Kapalua ☎ 808/661–8466). Beloved island chef–restaurateur, D. K. Kodama (the force behind Sansei), opened this eclectic dining experience on the golf course, tweaking some of his favorite recipes and creating new ones to match his Master Sommelier's recommendations.

True connoisseurs might wrap their vacation around the **Kapalua Wine & Food Festival** (☎ 800/527–2782 ⊕ www.kapaluamaui.com). Well into its 25th year, this extravaganza sponsored by Kapalua Resort pairs many of the island's top chefs with great wines from around the world. It kicks off in mid-July and events are spread out over four days.

Italian

$–$$$ ✗ **Marco's Grill & Deli.** This convenient eatery outside Kahului Airport (look for the green awning) serves reliable Italian food that's slightly overpriced. Homemade pastas appear on the extensive menu, along with an unforgettably good Reuben sandwich and the best tiramisu on the island. The local business crowd fills the place for breakfast, lunch, and dinner. The Kīhei branch is in a gorgeous new building with a grand piano. ✉ *444 Hāna Hwy., Kahului* ☎ *808/877–4446* ✉ *1445 S. Kīhei Rd., Kīhei* ☎ *808/874–4041* ⊟ *AE, D, DC, MC, V. $7–$27.*

Latin

$$–$$$ ✗ **Mañana Garage.** Parked in downtown Kahului is this restaurant, which makes the most of its automobile theme—it's probably the only place you can have your wine served out of buckets with crankshaft stems. Chef Tom Lelli's cuisine ranges from Cuban to Brazilian to Mexican, with a few Hawaiian touches thrown in for good measure. The best dishes include ceviche marinated in coconut milk and lime, 'ahi sashimi, and quesadillas made with homemade corn tortillas. For dessert, the pound-cake ice-cream sandwich with sweet potato and praline is a must. There's lively music on the weekends. ✉ *33 Lono Ave., Kahului* ☎ *808/873–0220* ⊟ *AE, D, MC, V* ☉ *No lunch weekends. $16–$29.*

Thai

$–$$ ✗ **Saeng's Thai Cuisine.** Choosing a dish from the six-page menu here requires determination, but the food is worth the effort, and most dishes

Menu Guide

Much of the Hawaiian language encountered during a stay in the Islands will appear on restaurant menus and lists of lū'au fare. Here's a quick primer.

'ahi: *yellowfin tuna.*

aku: *skipjack, bonito tuna.*

'ama'ama: *mullet; it's hard to get but tasty.*

bento: *a box lunch.*

haupia: *a light, gelatinlike dessert made from coconut.*

imu: *the underground ovens in which pigs are roasted for lū'au.*

kālua: *to bake underground.*

kaukau: *food. The word comes from Chinese but is used in the Islands.*

kimchee: *Korean dish of pickled cabbage made with garlic and hot peppers.*

Kona coffee: *coffee grown in the Kona district of the Big Island.*

laulau: *literally, a bundle. Laulau are morsels of pork, chicken, butterfish, or other ingredients wrapped with young taro shoots in ti leaves for steaming.*

liliko'i: *passion fruit, a tart, seedy yellow fruit that makes delicious desserts and jellies.*

limu: *edible seaweed, often used in poke or even massage treatments.*

lomilomi: *to rub or massage; also a massage. Lomilomi salmon is fish that has been rubbed with onions and herbs, commonly served with minced onions and tomatoes.*

lū'au: *a Hawaiian feast, also the leaf of the taro plant used in preparing such a feast.*

lū'au leaves: *cooked taro tops with a taste similar to spinach.*

mahimahi: *mild-flavored dolphinfish, not the marine mammal.*

mai tai: *potent rum drink with orange and lime juice, from the Tahitian word for "good."*

malasada: *a Portuguese deep-fried doughnut without a hole, dipped in sugar.*

manapua: *dough wrapped around diced pork.*

manō: *shark.*

moi: *fish once farmed and served only to Hawaiian royalty.*

niu: *coconut.*

onaga: *pink or red snapper.*

ono: *a long, slender mackerel-like fish; also called wahoo.*

'ono: *delicious; also hungry.*

'opihi: *a tiny shellfish, or mollusk, found on rocks; also called limpets.*

pāpio: *a young ulua or jack fish.*

pohā: *Cape gooseberry. Tasting a bit like honey, the pohā berry is often used in jams and desserts.*

poi: *a paste made from pounded taro root, a staple of the Hawaiian diet.*

poke: *chopped, pickled raw tuna, tossed with herbs and seasonings.*

pūpū: *Hawaiian hors d'oeuvre.*

saimin: *long thin noodles and vegetables in broth, often garnished with small pieces of fish cake, scrambled egg, luncheon meat, and green onion.*

sashimi: *raw fish thinly sliced and usually eaten with soy sauce.*

ti: *a member of the agave family. The fragrant leaves are used to wrap food while cooking and removed before eating.*

uku: *deep-sea snapper.*

ulua: *a member of the jack family that also includes pompano and amberjack. Also called crevalle, jack fish, and jack crevalle.*

can be tailored to your taste buds: hot, medium, or mild. Begin with spring rolls and a dipping sauce, move on to such entrées as Evil Prince Chicken (cooked in coconut sauce with Thai herbs), or red-curry shrimp, and finish up with tea and tapioca pudding. Asian artifacts, flowers, and a waterfall decorate the dining room, and tables on a veranda satisfy lovers of the outdoors. ⊠ *2119 Vineyard St., Wailuku* ☎ *808/244–1567* ▭ *AE, MC, V. $8–$13.*

Vietnamese

★ **$–$$** ✕ **A Saigon Café.** The only store-front sign announcing this small, delightful hideaway is one reading OPEN. Once you find it, treat your-self to *banh hoi chao tom*, more commonly known as "shrimp pops burritos" (ground marinated shrimp,

> **DID YOU KNOW?**
>
> A Saigon Café is famous for more than its food—regulars love the theatrical waiter known as "Elvis."

steamed and grilled on a stick of sugarcane). Fresh island fish is always available and vegetarian fare is well represented—try the green-papaya salad. The white interior serves as a backdrop for Vietnamese carvings in this otherwise unadorned space. Background music includes one-hit wonders from the early '70s. ⊠ *1792 Main St., Wailuku* ☎ *808/243–9560* ▭ *D, MC, V. $9–$19.*

¢–$ ✕ **Ba Le.** Tucked into the mall's food court is the best, cheapest fast food on the island. The famous soups, or *pho*, come laden with seafood or rare beef, fresh basil, bean sprouts, and lime. Tasty sandwiches are served on crisp French rolls—lemongrass chicken is a favorite. The word is out, so the place gets busy at lunchtime, though the wait is never long. ⊠ *Kau Kau Corner food court, Maui Marketplace, 270 Dairy Rd., Kahului* ☎ *808/877–2400* ▭ *AE, D, DC, MC, V. $4–$8.*

UPCOUNTRY

American

¢–$ ✕ **Aha Āina.** If you're staying Upcountry, this cozy home-style restau-rant is a cheap and good breakfast spot. Locals pack the tables on the weekends, enjoying the huevos rancheros with kālua pork, pancakes, and specialty omelets. ⊠ *7 Aewa St., Pukalani* ☎ *808/572–2395* ▭ *No credit cards* ☺ *No dinner. $3–$10.*

Hawaiian–Pacific Rim

★ **$$–$$$$** ✕ **Hāli'imaile General Store.** What do you do with a lofty wooden build-ing surrounded by sugarcane and pineapple fields that was a tiny town's camp store in the 1920s? If you're Bev and Joe Gannon, you invent a legendary restaurant. The Szechuan barbecued salmon and Hunan-style rack of lamb are classics, as is the sashimi napoleon appetizer: a tower of crispy wontons layered with 'ahi and salmon. Pastry chef Teresa Gannon makes an unbelievable pineapple upside-down cake. The restau-rant even has its own cookbook. ⊠ *900 Hāli'imaile Rd., take left exit halfway up Haleakalā Hwy., Hāli'imaile* ☎ *808/572–2666* ▭ *MC, V. $15–$35.*

Italian

$$–$$$$ ✕ **Casanova Italian Restaurant & Deli.**
This family-owned Italian dinner
house is an Upcountry institution.
The pizzas, baked in a brick wood-
burning oven imported from Italy,
are the best on the island, especially
the *tartufo*, or truffle oil pizza. The
daytime deli serves outstanding sand-
wiches and espresso. After dining
hours, local and visiting entertain-
ers heat up the dance floor. ✉ *1188
Makawao Ave., Makawao* ☎ *808/
572–0220* 🖃 *D, DC, MC, V.*
$13–$33.

Mexican

$–$$ ✕ **Polli's.** This Mexican restaurant
not only offers standards such as
enchiladas, chimichangas, and faji-
tas but will also prepare any item on
the menu with seasoned tofu or vegetarian taco mix—and the meatless
dishes are just as good as the real
thing. A special treat are the *bunue-
los*—light pastries topped with cinnamon, maple syrup, and ice cream.
The intimate interior is plastered
with colorful sombreros and other
cantina knickknacks. ✉ *1202 Makawao Ave., Makawao* ☎ *808/572–
7808* 🖃 *AE, D, DC, MC, V. $8–$18.*

★ **¢** ✕ **Maui's Best Tamales.** The owner of this tiny tamale haven can sometimes be seen surrounded by towers of fresh Kula corn. From these she
makes indisputably "Maui's best tamales." Her daily specials—chipo-
tle pork or chicken mole—are divine. This is a great spot to grab a bite
to eat while touring Upcountry. ✉ *In Pukalani Sq., 81 Makawao Ave.,
Pukalani* ☎ *808/573–2998* 🕙 *Closes at 6 PM. $3–$7.*

Steak

$$–$$$ ✕ **Makawao Steak House.** A restored 1927 house on the slopes of
Haleakalā is the setting for this *paniolo* restaurant, which serves consistently good prime rib, rack of lamb, and fresh fish. Three fireplaces,
friendly service, and an intimate lounge create a cozy, welcoming atmosphere. ✉ *3612 Baldwin Ave., Makawao* ☎ *808/572–8711* 🖃 *D, DC,
MC, V* 🕙 *No lunch. $18–$28.*

THE NORTH SHORE

American

$–$$ ✕ **Colleen's.** Hidden up a jungly road in Hāʻiku, this is the neighbor-
hood hangout for windsurfers, yoga teachers, and just plain beautiful

---

**BEST BETS FOR
BREAKFAST**

Colleen's (Upcountry). Eavesdrop
on surfers here, while munching
on a scone or breakfast burrito
packed with cheese, egg, and
potatoes.

Gazebo Restaurant (West Maui).
If you're a sucker for coconut
syrup, "nēnē" eggs, and a view
of the Pacific, this place is worth
the wait.

Plantation House (West Maui).
Good luck deciding which is more
delicious, the crab cake Benedict
or the view of Molokaʻi.

Kihei Caffe (South Shore). Hearty,
affordable portions will prepare
you for a day of surfing across the
street at Kalama Park.

Seawatch (South Shore). Your debate can grow even more finicky at
the Plantation House's sister
restaurant—are the Benedicts better here, with this view?

NEW ON THE BLOCK

Not yet open by this writing, these new restaurants promise to be worth trying. If they're not—let us know! On the rooftoop of the **Lahaina Store Grille & Oyster Bar** (⊠ 744 Front St., Lahaina ☎ 808/661–9090) overlooking Front Street in Lahaina, you will be able to sample oysters and other delights beneath the stars—and perhaps beside some, as it's sure to be a late-night spot for visiting celebs.

In one of the few oceanfront locations on Front Street, **Blu** (⊠ 839 Front St., Lahaina) will plate up high-quality Mediterranean fare. Open for lunch and dinner, this latest project by award-winning chef Aaron Placourakis and the Tri-Star team is a sure hit.

Adam Condon and Ted Woody (the former executive chef and bar manager of Spago, respectively) hit the road to open **Ted & Adam: The Place**

(⊠ 300 Mā'alaea Rd., Mā'alaea ☎ 808/243–2206) in wind-tossed Mā'alaea. Their version of "eclectic" cuisine influenced by Mediterranean and European flavors will be served, along with rotisserie items and pizza. Is it an excellent adventure? You tell us.

On the South Side, try **Cafe O Lei** (⊠ 1280 S. Kīhei Rd., Kīhei ☎ 808/891–1368). Once again Chef Dana Pastula works her kitchen magic. Expect the same affordable, tasty dishes served at the former location: spicy chicken wraps and satisfying Asian salads.

At last, pizza in Wailea! Mike O' Dwyer, the owner of Mulligan's On the Blue will open the **Wailea Pizza Company** (⊠ Wailea Ike Pl., Wailea ☎ 808/874–1234) in the new neighborhood shopping plaza.

people. For breakfast, the pastries tend to be jam-packed with berries and nuts, rather than butter and flakiness. Sandwiches are especially good, served on giant slices of homemade bread. For dinner you can't go wrong with the beef tenderloin salad or a piping hot pizza. ⊠ *In Hā'iku Cannery, 810 Kokomo Rd., Hā'iku* ☎ *808/575–9211* ▭ *AE, DC, MC, V. $7–$19.*

★ **$–$$** ✕ **Pā'ia Fishmarket Restaurant.** The line leading up to the counter of this tiny corner fishmarket attests to the popularity of the tasty fish sandwiches. Bench seating is somewhat grimy (you aren't the only one to have enjoyed fries here), but you really won't find a better fish sandwich. Don't bother with the other menu items—go for your choice of fillet served on a soft bun with a dollop of slaw and some grated cheese. As we say in Hawai'i, 'ono! ⊠ *2A Baldwin Ave., Pā'ia* ☎ *808/579–8030* ▭ *AE, DC, MC, V. $7–$19.*

¢–$ ✕ **Anthony's Coffee.** This is a great place to eavesdrop on the local windsurfing crowd. The coffee is excellent—they roast their own beans. For breakfast, try the veggie benedict. Picnic lunches are available and there's an ice-cream counter. Bonus: free Wi-Fi. ⊠ *90 Hāna Hwy., Pā'ia* ☎ *808/579–8340* ▭ *AE, DC, MC, V* ☉ *No dinner. $3–$7.*

¢–$ ✕ **Pauwela Café.** Ultracasual and ultrafriendly, this spot just off Hāna Highway is worth the detour. Order a kālua-pork sandwich and a piece of coffee cake and pass the afternoon. The large breakfast burritos and homemade soups are also good. ⊠ *375 W. Kuiaha Rd., off Hāna Hwy. past Haʻikū Rd., Haʻikū* ☎ *808/575-9242* ☉ *No dinner. $3–$7.*

Eclectic

$–$$$ ✕ **Jacque's.** Jacque, an amiable French chef, won the hearts of the wind-surfing crowd when he opened this hip, ramshackle bar and restaurant. French-Caribbean dishes like *Jacque's Crispy Little Poulet* (chicken) reveal the owner's expertise. The outdoor seating can be a little chilly at times; coveted spots at the sushi bar inside are snatched up quickly. ⊠ *120 Hāna Hwy., Pāʻia* ☎ *808/579-8844* ⊟ *AE, D, MC, V. $11–$22.*

¢–$ ✕ **Cafe Des Amis.** Papier-mâché wrestlers pop out from the walls at this small creperie. French crêpes with Gruyère, and Indian wraps with lentil curry are among the choices, all served with wild greens and sour cream or chutney on the side. The giant curry bowls are mild but tasty, served with delicious chutney. For dessert there are crêpes, of course, filled with chocolate, Nutella, cane sugar, or banana. ⊠ *42 Baldwin Ave., Pāʻia* ☎ *808/579-6323* ⊟ *AE, D, MC, V. $6–$11.*

Mexican

$–$$$ ✕ **Milagro's.** Delicious fish tacos are found at this corner hangout, along with a selection of fine tequilas. Latin fusion recipes ignite fresh fish and vegetables. The location at the junction of Baldwin Avenue and Hāna Highway makes people-watching under the awning shade a lot of fun. Lunch and happy hour (3–5) are the best values; the prices jump at dinnertime. ⊠ *3 Baldwin Ave., Pāʻia* ☎ *808/579-8755* ⊟ *AE, D, DC, MC, V. $8–$29.*

Seafood

★ $$$$ ✕ **Mama's Fish House.** For years Mama's has been *the* destination for special occasions. A stone- and shell-engraved path leads you up to what would be, in an ideal world, a good friend's house. The Hawaiian nautical theme is hospitable and fun—the menu even names which boat reeled in your fish. But, sadly, fame has gone to this restaurant's head. Prices bulged while portions shrank and dinner reservations start at 4:30 PM. If you're willing to fork over the cash, the daily catch baked in a creamy caper sauce or steamed in traditional lūʻau leaves is still worth trying. Mama's is marked by a tiny fishing boat perched above the entrance about 1½ mi east of Pāʻia on Hāna Highway. ⊠ *799 Poho Pl., Kūʻau* ☎ *808/579-8488* ⌂ *Reservations essential* ⊟ *AE, D, DC, MC, V. $32–$48.*

Where to Stay

WORD OF MOUTH

"[Peace of Maui] is my favorite place to stay in Maui. Owners are friendly! I really enjoyed talking to others who were staying there. . . . Convenient to Haleakalā for hiking. I felt at home."

–Brian

"The stress melts off you the minute you walk through the door. The breakfast is fabulous. You feel like you have the run of the place. The Ho'oilo House doesn't miss a beat."

–Debbie

www.fodors.com/forums

LODGING PLANNER

Resorts

The resorts are clustered along the leeward (west and south) shores, meaning they are hot and sunny in summer and in winter (with periodic downpours). Kā'anapali (in West Maui), the original resort community, has the most action, feeding off the old whaler's haunt, Lahaina town. Kapalua, farther north, is more private and serene, and catches a bit more wind and rain. On the South Shore, posh Wailea has excellent beaches and designer golf courses.

Apartment Rentals

Along with the condos listed in this chapter, Maui has condos you can rent through central booking agents. Most agents represent more than one condo complex (some handle single-family homes as well), so be specific about what kind of price, space, facilities, and amenities you want. The following are multiproperty agents: **Destination Resorts** (✉ 3750 Wailea Alanui Dr., Wailea 96753 ☎ 800/367–5246 ⊕ www.drhmaui.com); **Maui Windsurfari** (✉ 425 Koloa St., Kahului 96732 ☎ 808/871–7766 or 800/736–6284 ⊕ www.windsurfari. com).

What It Costs

The prices listed in this guide are the rack rates given by the hotels at this writing. Always ask about special packages and discounts when making your reservations. The Web is also a great resource for discount rooms. In Hawai'i, room prices can vary dramatically depending on whether or not a room has an ocean view. To save money, ask for a garden or mountain view.

Keep in Mind

Most resorts now charge parking and facility fees. What once was complimentary is now tacked on as a "resort fee." Thankfully, condos haven't followed suit just yet—sometimes local calls are still free.

Condos

If you're willing to compromise on luxury, you can find convenient condos on the West Side (in Nāpili or Kahana) or on the South Shore (in Kīhei). Many are oceanfront and offer the amenities of a hotel suite without the cost. Furnishings can be a little scruffy, however, and rarely do condos have central air-conditioning—something to consider if you aren't used to sleeping in humidity.

B&Bs & Rentals

Most of the accommodations Upcountry and in Hāna are B&Bs or vacation rentals. Few offer breakfast, but most deliver ample seclusion and a countryside experience. If you're booking off the Internet, it pays to fact-check. Questions to ask before making the deposit: how far from the airport/beach/ shops is it? Will I have a private bathroom and kitchen? Are there a phone and TV in the room?

WHAT IT COSTS				
$$$$	**$$$**	**$$**	**$**	**¢**
over $200	$150–$200	$100–$150	$60–$100	under $60

Hotel prices are for two people in a double room in high season, including tax and service.

By Shannon
Wianecki

MAUI'S ACCOMMODATIONS COME IN THREE SIZES: small, medium, and gargantuan. Small B&Bs are personal and charming—often a few rooms or a cottage beside the owner's own home. They open a window into authentic island life. Medium-size condominiums are less personal (you won't see the owner out trimming the bougainvillea) but highly functional—great for longer stays or families who want no-fuss digs. The resorts are out of this world. They do their best to improve on nature, trying to re-create what is beautiful about Maui. And their best is pretty amazing. Opulent gardens, fantasy swimming pools with slides (some with swim-up bars), waterfalls, spas, and championship golf courses make it hard to work up the willpower to leave the resort and go see the real thing.

WEST MAUI

West Maui is a long string of small communities, beginning with Lahaina at the south end and meandering into Kāʻanapali, Honokowai, Kahana, Nāpili, and Kapalua. Here's the breakdown on what's where: Lahaina is the business district with all the shops, shows, restaurants, historic buildings, churches, and rowdy side streets. Kāʻanapali is all glitz: fancy resorts set on Kāʻanapali Beach. Honokowai, Kahana, and Nāpili are quiet little nooks characterized by comfortable condos built in the late 1960s. All face the same direction, and get the same consistently hot, humid weather. Kapalua, at the northern tip, faces windward, and has a cooler climate and slightly more rain.

7

Lahaina

Lahaina doesn't have a huge range of accommodations, but it does make a great headquarters for active families, or those not looking to spend a bundle on resorts. One major advantage is the proximity of restaurants, shops, and activities—everything is within walking distance. It's a business district, however, and won't provide the same peace and quiet afforded by resorts or secluded vacation rentals. Still, Lahaina has a nostalgic charm, especially early in the morning before the streets have filled with visitors and vendors.

Hotels & Resorts

★ $$$–$$$$ 🏨 **Plantation Inn.** Charm sets this inn apart, tucked into a corner of a busy street in the heart of Lahaina. Filled with Victorian and Asian furnishings, it's reminiscent of a southern plantation home. Secluded lānai draped with hanging plants face a central courtyard, pool, and a garden pavilion perfect for morning coffee. Each guest room or suite is decorated differently, with hardwood floors, French doors, slightly dowdy antiques, and four-poster beds. (We think number 10 is nicest.) Suites have kitchenettes and whirlpool baths. A generous breakfast is included in the room rate, and one of Hawaiʻi's best French restaurants, Gerard's, is on-site. Breakfast, coupled with free parking in downtown Lahaina, makes this a truly great value, even if it's 10 minutes from the beach. ✉ *174 Lahainaluna Rd., Lahaina 96761* ☎ *808/667–9225 or 800/ 433–6815* 🖷 *808/667–9293* ⊕ *www.theplantationinn.com* 🛏 *18 rooms* ♻ *A/C, restaurant, fans, refrigerators, cable TV, pool, hot tub* ➡ *AE, MC, V. $170–$265.*

Honeymooner Hideaways

After a barefoot wedding on the beach, honeymooners can slip away in style to Suite 301, a luxurious oceanfront room at the Four Seasons Resort Maui (✉ 3900 Wailea Alanui Dr., Wailea ☎ 808/874-8000 or 800/334-6284 ⊕ www.fshr.com). Equipped with a butler's kitchen, concierge service, formal dining for 10, and a large private lawn, this suite is perfect for entertaining your wedding party. But forget them, the real draw is the hedonistic marble bathroom with its deep-soaking tub and eucalyptus rain shower. Room service will trail flower petals from your door to the tub, ending at a bottle of champagne. The haunt of celebrities, this suite must be booked far in advance.

Most locals, if asked, will say they'd like to retire in Keokea. They might even mention The Star Lookout (✉ 622 Thompson Rd., Keokea ☎ 907/346-8028 ⊕ www.starlookout.com) with a dreamy look in their eyes. Why? Hidden away halfway up Haleakalā, this charming 100-year-old perch is an ideal getaway. It's chilly enough in the evening to snuggle up, and in the morning it's brisk enough to enjoy jogging on the sleepy one-lane road. You can imagine typing out the first chapter of the "Great American Novel" while your partner sips coffee and the French doors let in a dizzying view of Maui from your bed. If you decide you never want to leave, the Star does offer monthly discounts.

For those who don't want to disappear entirely, the Plantation Inn (✉ 174 Lahainaluna Rd., Lahaina ☎ 808/667-9225 or 800/433-6815 ⊕ www.theplantationinn.com) is a good choice. Embedded in the action of Front Street, the charming old-world inn is an oasis of hospitality. We think the Southeast Asian decor in the deluxe room is the most romantic, with its dramatic four-poster bed. Next door, acclaimed restaurant Gerard's is a perfect destination for an anniversary dinner.

★ **$$-$$$** 🏨 **Lahaina Inn.** This antique jewel right in the heart of town is classic Lahaina—a two-story wooden building that will transport you back to the turn of the 20th century. The nine small rooms and three suites shine with authentic period furnishings, including quilted bedcovers, antique lamps, and Oriental carpets. You can while away the hours in a wicker chair on your balcony, sipping coffee and watching Old Lahaina town come to life. An excellent Continental breakfast is served in the parlor and the renowned restaurant, David Paul's, is downstairs. ✉ *127 Lahainaluna Rd., Lahaina 96761* ☎ *808/661-0577 or 800/669-3444* 🖷 *808/667-9480* ⊕ *www.lahainainn.com* ⌨ *9 rooms, 3 suites* ♿ *A/C, Internet room; no room TVs, no smoking* ⊟ *AE, D, MC, V. $125-$175.*

B&Bs & Vacation Rentals

$$$$ 🏨 **Ho'oilo House.** If you really want to treat yourself to a luxurious getaway, spend a few nights at this Bali-inspired B&B. In the foothills of
FodorśChoice the West Maui Mountains, just south of Lahaina town, this stunning
★ property brings the words "quiet perfection" to mind. As you enter the

house your eye is immediately drawn to the immense glass doors that open onto a small but sparkling pool and a breathtaking view of the Pacific. Almost all of the furnishings and the materials used to build the house were imported from Bali. Two "conversation tables" in the common area are filled with Balinese cushions, providing great spots to snack, chat, or just relax. Each room is uniquely decorated and features traditional Balinese doors with Mother of Pearl inlay, a custom bed, a private lānai, a huge bathroom with a giant bathtub, and best of all—a private outdoor shower. ⊠ *138 Awaiku St., Lahaina 96961* ☎ *808/667–6669* 🖷 *808/661–7857* ⊕ *www.hooilohouse.com* 🗗 *5 rooms* ♨ *A/C, fans, Wi-Fi, in-room safes, cable TV, pool, massage; no kids, no smoking* ▤ *AE, MC, V. $245, 3-night minimum.*

$–$$$ 🖫 **The Makai Inn.** Of the 18 rooms here, the Orchid is the nicest, facing Lahaina Harbor and benefiting from the ocean breeze. There's a sliding door separating the bedroom from the living area—the other units achieve the same effect with beaded curtains. The furnishings aren't terribly attractive and you might find a smudge of red Lahaina dirt here and there, but the lānai are perfect for daydreaming. Suzie, the landlord, lives on property, and keeps a flock of cheerful Java sparrows well-fed in the garden courtyard. ⊠ *1415 Front St., Lahaina 96761* ☎ *808/662–3200 or 800/870–9004* 🖷 *808/661–9027* ⊕ *www.makaiinn.net* 🗗 *18 rooms* ♨ *Fans, kitchens, some Internet, BBQ, laundry facilities; no A/C, no TV* ▤ *AE, MC, V. $89–$151.*

$–$$ 🖫 **Bambula Inn.** This casual sprawling house in a quiet Lahaina residential area has two studio apartments, one attached to the house and one freestanding. No breakfast is served; this is a move-in-and-hang-out beach house. Just across the street is a small beach, and moored just offshore is a sailboat hand-built by the owner. He likes to take his guests out for whale-watching and sunset sails, no charge. He also provides snorkel equipment. This is a friendly, easygoing way to visit Lahaina. ⊠ *518 Ilikahi St., Lahaina 96761* ☎ *808/667–6753 or 800/544–5524* 🖷 *808/667–0979* ⊕ *www.bambula.com* 🗗 *2 studios* ♨ *A/C in some rooms, fans, kitchens, kitchenettes, cable TV* ▤ *AE, D, MC, V. $85–$125.*

Kā'anapali

Kā'anapali is a playground—a long stretch of beach lined with over-the-top resorts, shopping, and restaurants. Expect top-class service here. Everything you could want is just a few steps from your room—including the calm waters of sun-kissed Kā'anapali Beach. Wandering along the beach path between resorts is a recreational activity unto itself. Weather is dependably warm, and for that reason as well as all the others, Kā'anapali is a popular—at times downright crowded—destination.

Hotels & Resorts

$$$$ 🖫 **Hyatt Regency Maui.** Fantasy landscaping with splashing waterfalls, swim-through grottoes, a lagoonlike swimming pool, and a 130-foot waterslide wows guests of all ages at this active Kā'anapali resort. Stroll through the lobby past museum-quality art, brilliant parrots, and . . . South African penguins (like we said, fantasy). It's not necessarily Hawaiian, but it is photogenic. At the southern end of Kā'anapali Beach, this resort is in the midst of the action. Also on the premises is Spa Moana,

WHERE TO STAY IN WEST MAUI

HOTEL NAME	Worth Noting	Cost $	Pools	Beach	Golf Course	Tennis Courts	Gym	Spa	Children's Programs	Rooms	Restaurants	Other	Location
Hotels & Resorts													
❻ Hyatt Regency Maui	130-ft water slide	400–660	1	yes	yes	6	yes	yes	3–12	815	4		Kā'anapali
❾ Kā'anapali Beach Hotel	Hula & lei-making classes	185–610	1	yes	priv.					430	3		Kā'anapali
★ ❹ Lahaina Inn	Historic property	125–175								12		no TVs	Lahaina
❽ Mauian Hotel	On Napili Bay	145–195	1	yes						44		no TVs	Napili
★ ❸ Plantation Inn	Gerard's restaurant	170–265	1							18	1		Lahaina
★ ❷⓪ Ritz-Carlton, Kapalua	Banyan Tree restaurant	395–705	1	yes	priv.	10	yes	yes	5–12	548	3	shops	Kapalua
⑪ Royal Lahaina Resort	Cottage units available	130–2,000	3	yes	priv.	11			5–12	516	3		Kā'anapali
★ ⑩ Sheraton Maui	Nightly torch-lighting ritual	360–640	1	yes	priv.	3	yes	yes	5–12	510	2		Kā'anapali
❽ The Westin Maui Resort	The Heavenly Spa	360–700	5	yes	priv.	3	yes	yes	0–12	761	3		Kā'anapali
Condos													
⑭ Aston at Papakea Resort	Cultural classes	200–550	2	yes	yes	4			5–12	364		kitchens	Honokowai
⑫ El Dorado	On golf course	165–375	3	yes						258		kitchens	Kā'anapali
❼ Kā'anapali Ali'i	Great location	360–760	2	yes	yes	6				264		kitchens	Kā'anapali
⑬ Mahana at Kā'anapali	Spacious rooms	260–675	1	yes						145		kitchens	Honokowai
⑯ Mahina Surf	Free parking and phone	130–240	1							50		kitchens	Mahinahina
⑮ Makani Sands	Small private beach	140–345	1	yes						20		kitchens	Honokowai
★ ⑲ Napili Kai Beach Club	Outstanding beach	200–700	4	yes					6–12	162		kitchens	Napili
⑰ Sands of Kahana	Kid's putting green	150–435	2	yes		3				162		kitchens	Kahana
B&Bs & Vacation Rentals													
❷ Bambula Inn	Studio apartments	85–125								2		kitchens	Lahaina
★ ❶ Ho'oilo House	Private outdoor showers	245	1							5		no kids	Lahaina
❺ The Makai Inn	Nice views	89–150								18		no A/C	Lahaina

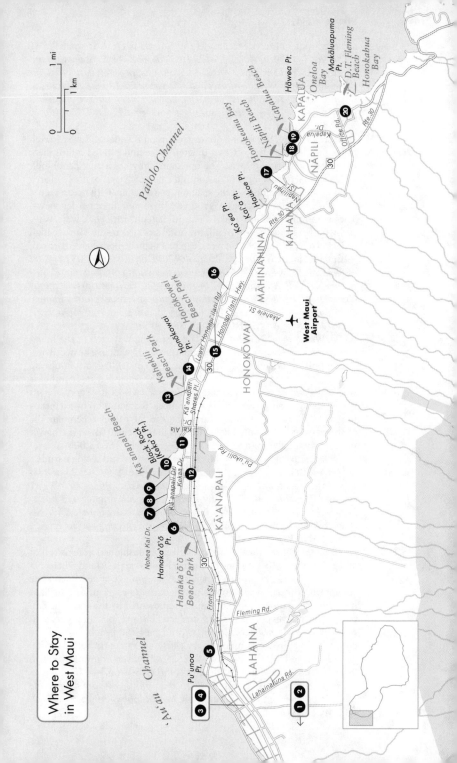

an oceanfront, full-service facility. ✉ *200 Nohea Kai Dr., Kā'anapali 96761* ☎ *808/661–1234 or 800/233–1234* 🖷 *808/667–4499* ⊕ *www.maui. hyatt.com* ↩ *815 rooms* ⚴ *A/C, 4 restaurants, in-room data ports, in-room safes, cable TV with movies and video games, 2 18-hole golf courses, 6 tennis courts, pool, health club, spa, beach, 6 bars, library, children's programs (ages 3–12), no-smoking floors* 🖃 *AE, D, DC, MC, V.* $275–$660.

$$$$ 🏨 **Sheraton Maui.** Set among dense gardens on Kā'anapali's best stretch
Fodor'sChoice of beach, the Sheraton offers a quieter, more understated atmosphere
★ than its neighboring resorts. The open-air lobby has a crisp, cool look with minimal furnishings and decor, and sweeping views of the pool area and beach. The majority of the spacious rooms come with ocean views; only one of the six buildings has rooms with mountain or garden views. The swimming pool looks like a natural lagoon, with rock waterways and wooden bridges. Best of all, the hotel sits next to the 80-foot-high "Black Rock," from which divers leap in a nightly torch-lighting ritual. ✉ *2605 Kā'anapali Pkwy., Kā'anapali 97671* ☎ *808/661–0031 or 888/ 488–3535* 🖷 *808/661–0458* ⊕ *www.starwood.com/hawaii* ↩ *510 rooms* ⚴ *A/C, 2 restaurants, in-room safes, refrigerators, 3 tennis courts, pool, health club, hair salon, hot tub, spa, beach, lobby lounge, children's programs (ages 5–12), laundry facilities, Internet room, business services* 🖃 *AE, D, DC, MC, V.* $360–$640.

$$$$ 🏨 **The Westin Maui Resort & Spa.** The cascading waterfall in the lobby of this hotel gives way to an "aquatic playground" with five heated swimming pools, abundant waterfalls (15 at last count), lagoons complete with pink flamingos, and a premier beach. The water features combined with a spa and fitness center, and privileges at two 18-hole golf courses make this an active resort—great for families. Relaxation is by no means forgotten. Elegant dark-wood furnishings in the rooms accentuate the crisp linens of "Heavenly Beds." Rooms in the Beach Tower are newer but slightly smaller than those in the Ocean Tower. The 13,000-square-foot Heavenly Spa features 11 treatment rooms and a yoga studio. ✉ *2365 Kā'anapali Pkwy., Kā'anapali 96761* ☎ *808/667–2525 or 888/ 488–3535* 🖷 *808/661–5831* ⊕ *www.starwood.com/hawaii* ↩ *761 rooms* ⚴ *3 restaurants, cable TV with movies, golf privileges, 5 pools, health club, hair salon, 3 hot tubs, spa, beach, lobby lounge, babysitting, children's programs (infant–12), Internet, meeting rooms* 🖃 *AE, D, DC, MC, V.* $360–$700.

$$$–$$$$ 🏨 **Kā'anapali Beach Hotel.** This attractive, old-fashioned hotel is full of aloha. Locals say that it's one of the few resorts on the island where visitors can get a true Hawaiian experience. The vintage-style Mixed Plate restaurant, known locally for its native cuisine program, has displays honoring the many cultural traditions represented by the staff: the employees themselves contributed the artifacts. The spacious rooms are simply decorated in wicker and rattan and face the beach beyond the courtyard. There are complimentary classes in authentic hula dancing, lei-making, and 'ukulele playing. ✉ *2525 Kā'anapali Pkwy., Kā'anapali 96761* ☎ *808/661–0011 or 800/262–8450* 🖷 *808/667–5978* ⊕ *www. kbhmaui.com* ↩ *430 rooms* ⚴ *A/C, 3 restaurants, in-room safes, cable TV with movies, golf privileges, pool, beach, lobby lounge* 🖃 *AE, D, DC, MC, V.* $185–$610.

$$–$$$$ 🏨 **Royal Lahaina Resort.** Two-story cottages, each divided into four units, distinguish the Royal Lahaina from other mega-resorts. The first buildings built in Kā'anapali, the gracious cottages open to the trade winds on two sides and have a nostalgic, old Hawaiian feel. The "deluxe" units in the 12-story tower aren't really deluxe—the property as a whole is slated for a revamp, but it's one of the less-expensive options on Kā'anapali Beach. The Oceanside Beach House is a two-bedroom cottage with its own pool, perfect for entertaining guests in truly royal fashion. The walkway to the wedding gazebo is lined with stepping-stones engraved with the names of past brides and grooms and their wedding dates. ✉ *2780 Keka'a Dr., Kā'anapali 96761* 🕾 *808/661–3611 or 800/447–6925* 🖷 *808/661–3538* ⊕ *www.hawaiianhotels.com* ➾ *516 rooms* ✆ *A/C, 3 restaurants, cable TV, golf privileges, 11 tennis courts, 3 pools, beach, Internet café* ▭ *AE, D, DC, MC, V. $130–$2,000.*

Condos

$$$–$$$$ 🏨 **El Dorado.** This fine condo complex, which wraps around the Kā'anapali golf course's sixth fairway, offers several perks, most notably air-conditioning in the units and access to a fully outfitted beach cabana on a semi-private beach. The complex itself isn't exactly on the beach—it's a quick golf-cart–trip away. While resort guests get scolded for dragging lounge chairs onto neighboring resort beaches, you can relax in luxury. Not only will you have beach chairs at your disposal, but a full kitchen and lounge area, too. The privately managed units are tastefully decorated with modern appliances and spacious bathrooms. Those overseen by the Outrigger aren't as up-to-date, but are still a good value for pricey Kā'anapali. ✉ *2661 Keka'a Dr., Kā'anapali 96761* 🕾 *808/283–8219* 🖷 *808/661–5478* ⊕ *www.lahainagrill.com/eldorado.htm* ➾ *258 units* ✆ *A/C, kitchens, cable TV, some units with Internet, 18-hole golf course, 3 pools, beach, laundry facilities, concierge* ▭ *AE, D, DC, MC, V. $165 studio, $210 1-bedroom, $375 2-bedroom.*

$$$$ 🏨 **Kā'anapali Ali'i.** Four 11-story buildings are laid-out so well that the feeling of seclusion you'll enjoy may make you forget you're in a condo complex. Instead of tiny units, you'll be installed in an ample one- or two-bedroom apartment. All units have great amenities: a chaise in an alcove, a sunken living room, a whirlpool, and a separate dining room, though some of the furnishings are dated. The Kā'anapali Ali'i is maintained like a hotel, with daily maid service, an activities desk, and 24-hour front-desk service. ✉ *50 Nohea Kai Dr., Kā'anapali 96761* 🕾 *808/667–1400 or 800/642–6284* 🖷 *808/661–1025* ⊕ *www.classicresorts.com* ➾ *264 units* ✆ *A/C, in-room safes, kitchens, 18-hole golf course, 6 tennis courts, 2 pools, sauna, beach, laundry facilities* ▭ *AE, D, DC, MC, V. 1-bedroom $360–$540, 2-bedroom $490–$760.*

Upper West Side

The Upper West Side is how locals refer to the neighborhoods north of Kā'anapali: Honokowai, Mahinahina, Kahana, Nāpili, and finally, Kapalua. They seamlessly blend into one another along Lower Honoapi'ilani Highway. Each has a few shops and restaurants and a secluded bay or two to call its own. Many visitors have found a second home here, at one of the condominiums nestled between beach access roads and groves of mango trees. You won't get the stellar service of a resort, but you'll be among the locals here, in a relatively quiet part of the island. Be prepared for a long commute, if you're planning to do much exploring elsewhere on the island. Kapalua is the farthest town of them all, but well worth all the driving to say at the elegant Ritz-Carlton, which is surrounded by misty greenery and overlooks beautiful D. T. Fleming beach.

Hotels & Resorts

★ **$$$$** ▣ **Ritz-Carlton, Kapalua.** If butler-drawn baths and brocade drapery are your cup of tea, book a room at this elegant hillside property. Although not set directly on the sand, the resort does command views of D. T. Fleming Beach, and Honolua Bay—and the multilevel pool and two hot tubs are open 24 hours. The grounds are private and secluded, despite being in the midst of Kapalua's collection of hotels, shops, restaurants, and golf courses. A full-time cultural adviser, Clifford Nae'ole, educates employees and guests alike in Hawaiian traditions. Tuesday night Slack Key guitar performances are not to be missed. This is a great jumping-off point for golfers—privileges are available at three championship courses, and the island of Lāna'i, with its two renowned courses is a quick ferry ride away. The dining is outstanding here; the decor needs some attention. ⊠ *1 Ritz-Carlton Dr., Kapalua 96761* 🕾 *808/669–6200 or 800/262–8440* 🖷 *808/665–0026* ⊕ *www.ritzcarlton.com/resorts/kapalua* ⇨ *548 rooms* ⟁ *A/C, 3 restaurants, in-room data ports, in-room safes, cable TV with movies, golf privileges, 10 tennis courts, pool, health club, hair salon, massage, beach, lobby lounge, shops, spa, children's programs (ages 5–12), laundry service, business services* ▤ *AE, D, DC, MC, V. $395–$705.*

$$–$$$ ▣ **Mauian Hotel.** If you're looking for a quiet place to stay, this nostalgic hotel way out in Napīli may be for you. The rooms have neither TVs nor phones—such noisy devices are relegated to the 'Ohana Room, where a Continental breakfast is served daily. The simple two-story buildings date from 1959, but have been renovated with bright islander furnishings. Rooms include well-equipped kitchens. Best of all, the 2-acre property opens out onto lovely Napīli Bay. ⊠ *5441 Lower Honoapi'ilani Hwy., Napīli 96761* 🕾 *808/669–6205 or 800/367–5034* 🖷 *808/669–0129* ⊕ *www.mauian.com* ⇨ *44 rooms* ⟁ *A/C, kitchens, pool, beach, hair salon, shuffleboard, laundry facilities, Internet; no room phones, no room TVs* ▤ *AE, D, MC, V. $145–$195.*

Condos

$$$$ ▣ **Mahana at Kā'anapali.** Though the address claims Kā'anapali, this 12-story condominium complex is really in quiet, neighboring Honokowai. Spacious rooms and living areas can accommodate families easily. Built in 1974, the property has been regularly updated since, but the decor in individually owned units may vary. An elegant pool faces a sandy beach, which isn't, unfortunately, recommended for swimming because of the shallow reef. ⊠ *110 Kā'anapali Shores Pl., Honokowai 96761* 🕾 *808/ 661–8751* 🖷 *808/661–5510* ⊕ *www.astonhotels.com* ⇨ *45 studios, 72 1-bedroom units, 28 2-bedroom units* ⟁ *A/C, BBQs, in-room data ports, in-room safes, fans, kitchens, cable TV, tennis courts, pool, beach, shuffleboard, concierge* ▤ *AE, MC, V. Studios $260–$345, 1-bedroom $325–$465, 2-bedroom $520–$675.*

$$$-$$$$ ☷ **Aston at Papakea Resort.** Although this oceanfront condominium has no beach, there are several close by. And with classes on swimming, snorkeling, pineapple cutting, and more, you'll have plenty to keep you busy. Papakea has built-in privacy because its units are spread out among 11 low-rise buildings on some 13 acres of land; bamboo-lined walkways between buildings and fish-stocked ponds add to the serenity. Fully equipped kitchens and laundry facilities make longer stays easy here. ⊠ *3543 Lower Honoapi'ilani Hwy., Honokowai 96761* ☎ *808/669–4848 or 800/ 922–7866* 🖷 *808/922–8785* ⊕ *www.aston-hotels.com* ☞ *364 units △ A/C, kitchens, putting green, 4 tennis courts, 2 pools, hot tub, sauna, children's programs (ages 5–12), laundry facilities* ▤ *AE, MC, V. Studios $200–$225, 1-bedroom $245–$290, 2-bedroom $450–$550.*

GROCERIES & TAKEOUT

Foodland. This large grocery store should have everything you need, including video rentals and a Starbucks. ⊠ *Old Lahaina Center, 845 Waine'e St., Lahaina* ☎ *808/661– 0975.*

Gaby's Pizzeria and Deli. The friendly folks here will toss a pie for takeout. ⊠ *505 Front St., Lahaina* ☎ *808/661–8112.*

The Maui Fish Market. It's worth stopping by this little fish market for an oyster or a cup of fresh-fish chowder. You can also get live lobsters and fillets marinated for your barbecue. ⊠ *4405 Lower Honoapi'ilani Hwy., Honokowai* ☎ *808/665–9895.*

7

★ **$$$-$$$$** ☷ **Nāpili Kai Beach Club.** On 10 beautiful beachfront acres—the beach here is one of the best on the West Side for swimming and snorkeling— the Nāpili Kai draws a loyal following. Hawaiian-style rooms are done in seafoam and mauve, with rattan furniture; shoji doors open onto the lānai. The rooms closest to the beach have no air-conditioning, but ceiling fans usually suffice. "Hotel" rooms have only mini-refrigerators and coffeemakers, while studios and suites have fully equipped kitchenettes. This is a family-friendly place, with children's programs and free classes in hula and lei-making. Packages that include a car, breakfast, and other extras are available if you stay five nights or longer. ⊠ *5900 Lower Honoapi'ilani Hwy., Nāpili 96761* ☎ *808/669–6271 or 800/367–5030* 🖷 *808/669–5740* ⊕ *www.napilikai.com* ☞ *162 units △ A/C in some rooms, in-room data ports, fans, kitchenettes, cable TV, 2 putting greens, 4 pools, exercise equipment, hot tub, beach, shuffleboard, children's programs (ages 6–12), dry cleaning, concierge* ▤ *AE, MC, V. Hotel Room $200–$290, Studios $250–$325, 1-bedroom $385–$450, 2-bedroom $555–$700.*

$$$-$$$$ ☷ **Sands of Kahana.** Meandering gardens, spacious rooms, and an on-site restaurant distinguish this large condominium complex. Primarily a time-share property, a few units are available as vacation rentals. The upper floors benefit from their height—matchless ocean views stretch away from private lanai. The oceanfront penthouse, which accommodates up to eight, is a bargain at $435 during peak season. Kids can enjoy their own pool area near a putting green and ponds filled with giant koi. Raul Bermudez, the restaurant's chef took first place in the 2004 "Taste of Lahaina" festival. ⊠ *4299 Lower Honoapi'ilani Hwy., Kahana*

96761 ☎ *808/669–0423 or 800/669–0400* 🖷 *808/669–8409* ⊕ *www. sands-of-kahana.com* ➾ *162 units* ⚴ *A/C in some rooms, restaurant, BBQs, in-room data ports, fans, kitchens, cable TV, putting green, 3 tennis courts, 2 pools, hot tub, beach, volleyball, concierge* ▤ *AE, MC, V. 1-bedroom $225–$265, 2-bedroom $325–$375, 3-bedroom $435.*

$$–$$$$ 🖾 **Mahina Surf.** Mahina Surf stands out from the many condo complexes lining the oceanside stretch of Honoapiʻilani Highway by being both well-managed and affordable. You won't be charged fees for parking, check-out, or local phone use, and discount car rentals are available. The individually owned units are typically overdecorated, but each one has a well-equipped kitchen and an excellent ocean view. The quiet complex is a short amble away from Honokowai's grocery shopping, beaches, and restaurants. ⊠ *4057 Lower Honoapiʻilani Hwy., Mahinahina 96761* ☎ *808/669–6068 or 800/367–6086* 🖷 *808/669–4534* ⊕ *www. mahinasurf.com* ➾ *25 1-bedroom, 25 2-bedroom units* ⚴ *BBQs, fans, kitchens, cable TV, some units with broadband Internet, in-room safes, pool, concierge, laundry facilities* ▤ *AE, MC, V. 1-bedroom $130–$210, 2-bedroom $160–$240.*

$$–$$$$ 🖾 **Makani Sands.** This centrally located, slightly older complex offers an economical way to see the West Side. Rooms have wide lanai, which hang over a small sandy beach below. The corner rooms (ending in 01) are best, with wraparound views. A small freshwater pool is available for cooling off. The back bedrooms may be noisy at night, as they're close to the road. ⊠ *3765 Lower Honoapiʻilani Hwy., Honokowai 96761* ☎ *808/669–8223 or 800/227–8223* 🖷 *808/665–0756* ⊕ *www. makanisands.com* ➾ *20 units* ⚴ *BBQs, fans, kitchens, in-room data ports, cable TV, in-room VCRs, in-room data ports, pool, beach, laundry facilities* ▤ *AE, MC, V. 1-bedroom $145–$155, 2-bedroom $205, 3-bedroom $245–$345; 3-night minimum.*

THE SOUTH SHORE

The South Shore is composed of two main communities: resort-filled Wailea and down-to-earth Kīhei. In general, the farther south you go, the fancier the accommodations get. ■ TIP➔ North Kīhei tends to have great prices but windy beaches scattered with seaweed. (Not a problem if you don't mind driving 5–10 minutes to save a few bucks.) As you travel down South Kīhei Road, you can find condos both on and off inviting beach parks, and close to shops and restaurants. Once you hit Wailea, the opulence quotient takes a giant leap—perfectly groomed resorts gather around Wailea and Polo beaches. This resort wonderland mimics (some say improves upon) Kāʻanapali. The two communities continuously compete over which is more exclusive and which has better weather—in our opinion it's a definite draw.

Kīhei

If you're a beach lover, you won't find many disadvantages to staying in Kīhei. A string of welcoming beaches stretches from tip to tip. Snorkeling, boogie boarding, and barbequeing find their ultimate expression here. Affordable condos line South Kīhei Road; however, some find the busy traffic and the strip-mall shopping distinctly un-Maui and prefer quieter hideaways.

Hotels & Resorts

$$–$$$$ ▦ **Maui Coast Hotel.** You might never notice this elegant hotel because it's set back off the street. The standard rooms are fine—very clean and modern—but the best deal is to pay a little more for one of the suites. In these you'll get an enjoyable amount of space and jet nozzles in the bathtub. You can sample nightly entertainment by the large, heated pool or work out in the new fitness center until 10 PM. The 6-mi-long stretch of Kamaʻole Beach I, II, and III is across the street. ⊠ *2259 S. Kīhei Rd., Kīhei 96753* ☎ *808/874–6284, 800/895–6284, or 800/426–0670* 🖷 *808/875–4731* ⊕ *www.westcoasthotels.com* 🖙 *265 rooms, 114 suites* ⚲ *A/C, 2 restaurants, in-room safes, refrigerators, cable TV with movies, 2 tennis courts, pool, exercise equipment, 2 hot tubs, dry cleaning, laundry service* ▤ *AE, D, DC, MC, V. $145–$235.*

$–$$$$
FodorśChoice
★
▦ **Mana Kai Maui.** This unsung hero of South Maui hotels may be older than its competitors, but that only means it's closer to the beach—beautiful Keawakapu. Hotel rooms with air-conditioning are remarkably affordable for the location. Two-room condos with private lānai benefit from the hotel amenities, such as daily maid service and discounts at the oceanfront restaurant downstairs. Shoji screens and bamboo furniture complement the marvelous ocean views, which in winter are punctuated by the visiting humpback whales. ⊠ *2960 S. Kīhei Rd., Kīhei 96753* ☎ *808/879–2778 or 800/367–5242* 🖷 *808/879–7825* ⊕ *www.crhmaui.com* 🖙 *49 hotel rooms, 49 1-bedroom condos* ⚲ *A/C, restaurant, in-room safes, refrigerators, cable TV, pool, hair salon, hot tub, beach, meeting rooms* ▤ *AE, D, DC, MC, V. Hotel rooms $100–$135, condos $180–$310.*

Condos

$$$–$$$$ ▦ **Kamaʻole Sands.** "Kam" Sands is a good choice for the active traveler; there are tennis and volleyball courts to keep you in shape, and the ideal family beach (Kamaʻole III) waits across the street. Eleven four-story buildings wrap around 15 acres of grassy slopes with swimming pools, a small waterfall, and BBQs. Condos are equipped with modern conveniences, but there's a relaxed, almost retro feel to the place. All units have kitchens, laundry facilities, and private lānai. The property has a 24-hour front desk and an activities desk. ■ TIP→ (Attention home owners: privately owned house-trade options are available at www.kamaole-sands.com.) ⊠ *2695 S. Kīhei Rd., Kīhei 96753* ☎ *808/874–8700 or 800/367–5004* 🖷 *808/879–3273* ⊕ *www.castleresorts.com/KSM* 🖙 *309 units* ⚲ *A/C in some rooms, restaurant, fans, in-room data ports, kitchens, some cable TV, some in-room VCRs, 4 tennis courts, pool, 2 hot tubs, wading pool, volleyball* ▤ *AE, D, DC, MC, V. 1-bedroom $195–$275, 2-bedroom $275–$375, 3-bedroom $485.*

★ $$–$$$$ ▦ **Hale Hui Kai.** Bargain hunters who stumble across this small three-story condo complex will think they've died and gone to heaven. The beachfront units are older, but many of them have been renovated. Some have marble countertops in the kitchens and all have outstanding views. But never mind the interior, you'll want to spend all of your

WHERE TO STAY ON THE SOUTH SHORE

HOTEL NAME	Worth Noting	Cost $	Pools	Beach	Golf Course	Tennis Courts	Gym	Spa	Children's Programs	Rooms	Restaurants	Other	Location
Hotels & Resorts													
★ 4 Fairmont Kea Lani	Villas available	385–2,800	3	yes	priv.			yes	yes	5–12	450	3	shops	Wailea
★ 5 Four Seasons Resort	Luxurious	365–890	1	yes	priv.	2	yes	yes	5–12	380	3		Wailea
6 Grand Wailea	Spa Grande	485	3	yes	priv.		yes	yes	5–12	779	5	shops	Wailea
15 Mana Kai Maui	Great prices	100–310	1	yes						98	3		Kihei
7 Marriott Wailea Resort	Package deals avail.	319–379	3	yes	priv.	2		yes	5–12	516	3		Wailea
17 Maui Coast Hotel	Beach across the street	145–235	1	yes						379	2		Kihei
★ 1 Maui Prince	Secluded beach	335–525	2	yes	yes	6	yes		5–12	310	4		Mākena
9 Renaissance Wailea	VIP club available	309–419	2	yes					5–12	345	3		Wailea
Condos													
★ 14 Hale Hui Kai	Oceanfront lounge	120–365	1	yes						40		kitchens	Kihei
16 Kama'ole Sands	Beach across the street	195–485	1			4				309	1	kitchens	Kihei
18 Luana Kai	Poolside BBQs	99–269	1			4				113		no A/C	Kihei
★ 2 Mākena Surf	Secluded gated community	465–765	2	yes	priv.					71		kitchens	Wailea
19 Maui Sunseeker Resort	Beach across the street	115–165								4		kitchens	Kihei
★ 3 Polo Beach Club	Location, location, location	360–570	1	yes	priv.					71		kitchens	Wailea
10 Wailea 'Ekahi	Studios available	210–510	4	yes	priv.					300		kitchens	Wailea
8 Wailea 'Elua	Gated Community	270–925	2	yes	priv.					150		kitchens	Wailea
★ 12 Wailea 'Ekolu	Good prices	180–260	2	no	priv.					160		kitchens	Wailea
B&Bs & Vacation Rentals													
11 Amanda and George's	1-BR suite	120	2			4				1		kitchens	Wailea
13 Eva Villa	360° views from rooftop	130–150	1							3		kitchens	Wailea

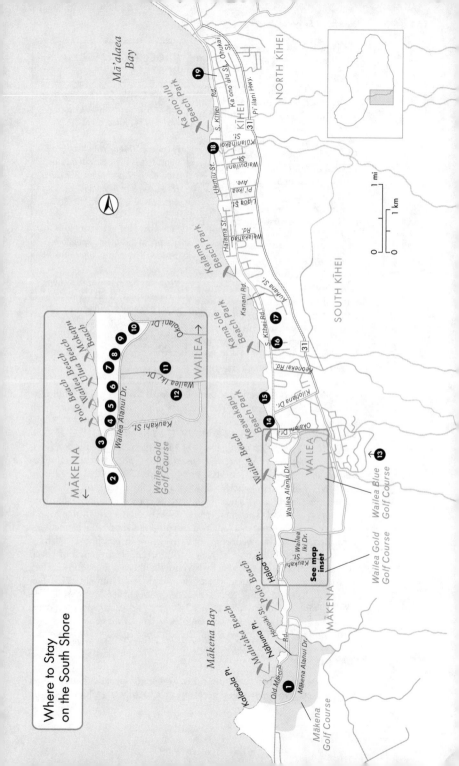

Where to Stay
on the South Shore

time outdoors—in the shady lava-rock lobby that overlooks a small pool perfect for kids, or on gorgeous Keawakapu beach just steps away. Light sleepers should avoid the rooms just above the neighboring restaurant, Sarento's, but definitely stop in there for dinner. ⊠ *115 S. Kīhei Rd., Kīhei 96753* 🕾 *808/879–1219 or 800/809–6284* 🖷 *808/879–0600* ⊕ *www.beachbreeze.com* ⊅ *40 units* ♤ *Fans, kitchens, cable TV, in-room VCRs, in-room safes, pool, beach, laundry facilities* ⊟ *AE, D, DC, MC, V. 1-bedroom $275, 2-bedroom $275–$375.*

$–$$$$ 🏨 **Luana Kai.** Set up house at this North Kīhei condominium-by-the-sea. Units are older with slightly dated furnishings, but each one comes with everything you need to make yourself at home: a fully equipped kitchen with dishwasher, laundry facilities, TV, VCR, and stereo equipment. There are three different room plans, suited for couples, families, or friends traveling together. The pool area is a social place, with five gas grills, a full outdoor kitchen, and Jacuzzis. The property adjoins a grassy county park with tennis courts, and the beach is a short way down the road. ⊠ *940 S. Kīhei Rd., Kīhei 96753* 🕾 *808/879–1268 or 800/669–1127* 🖷 *808/879–1455* ⊕ *www.luanakai.com* ⊅ *113 units* ♤ *BBQs, fans, kitchens, in-room VCRs, putting green, 4 tennis courts, pool, hot tub, shuffleboard; no A/C* ⊟ *AE, DC, MC, V. 1-bedroom $99–$129, 2-bedroom $119–$169, 3-bedroom $219–$269; 4-night minimum.*

$$–$$$ 🏨 **Maui Sunseeker Resort.** The care put into this property is noticeable from the sign on the road. This small North Kīhei hotel is a great value for the area and is private and relaxed. You can opt for a simple but attractively furnished studio, one-bedroom, or two-bedroom penthouse; all have kitchenettes and full baths, as well as BBQs. The 4-mi stretch of beach across the street isn't the best for swimming, but it's great for strolling and watching windsurfers, whales (in winter), and sunsets. ⊠ *551 S. Kīhei Rd., Kīhei 96753* 🕾 *808/879–1261 or 800/532–6284* 🖷 *808/874–3877* ⊕ *www.mauisunseeker.com* ⊅ *4 units* ♤ *A/C, kitchenettes, cable TV, some in-room VCRs, hot tub, laundry facilities, Internet room* ⊟ *MC, V. Studios $115, 1-bedroom $135, 2-bedroom $165; 3-night minimum.*

Wailea & Mākena

Wailea is warm, serene, and luxurious. Less action-packed than the West Side resorts, the properties here tend to focus on ambience—little

---

GROCERIES & VIDEO RENTALS

Eskimo Candy. Stop here for fresh fish or fish-and-chips. ⊠ *2665 Wai Wai Pl., Kīhei* 🕾 *808/879–5686.*

Premiere Video. With two locations, this is the best video store around. ⊠ *North Kīhei, 357 Huku Li'i Pl.* 🕾 *808/875-0500* ⊠ *South Kīhei, 2439 S. Kīhei Rd.* 🕾 *808/875-1113.*

Safeway. Find every variety of grocery at this giant superstore. ⊠ *277 Pi'ikea Ave., Kīhei* 🕾 *808/891-9120.*

Who Cut the Cheese. This shop has great party foods: *fromage*, fancy balsamics, and wines. ⊠ *Azeka Marketplace, 1279 S. Kīhei Rd., Suite 309* 🕾 *808/874-3930.*

thoughtful details and big scenery. Nightlife is pretty much nil, save for a few swank bars and a boisterous Irish pub. But you'll have your choice of sandy beaches with good snorkeling. Farther south, Mākena is a little less developed, a little more wild; more stars can be seen here at night. Expect everything—even bottled water—to double in price when you cross the line from Kīhei to Wailea.

Hotels & Resorts

$$$$ 🏨 **Fairmont Kea Lani Hotel Suites & Villas.** Gleaming white spires and tiled
Fodor'sChoice   archways are the hallmark of this stunning resort. Spacious suites have
★   microwaves, stereos, and marble bathrooms. But the villas are the real lure. Each is two-story and has a private plunge pool, two (or three) large bedrooms, a laundry room, and a fully equipped kitchen—BBQ and margarita blender included. Best of all, maid service does the dishes. A fantastic haven for families, the villas are side by side in a sort of miniature neighborhood. Request one on the end, with an upstairs sundeck. The resort offers good dining choices, a gourmet deli, and a small, almost private beach. ✉ *4100 Wailea Alanui Dr., Wailea 96753* ☎ *808/875–4100 or 800/882–4100* 🖷 *808/875–1200* 🌐 *www.kealani.com* 🛏 *413 suites, 37 villas* ☖ *A/C, 3 restaurants, in-room data ports, microwaves, refrigerators, in-room VCRs, golf privileges, 3 pools, health club, hair salon, 2 hot tubs, spa, beach, lobby lounge, shops, children's programs (ages 5–12)* ➟ *AE, D, DC, MC, V. Suites $385–$665, villas $1,600–$2,800.*

$$$$ 🏨 **Four Seasons Resort.** Impeccably stylish, subdued, and relaxing describe
Fodor'sChoice   most Four Seasons properties; this one fronting award-winning Wailea
★   beach is no exception. Thoughtful luxuries—like Evian spritzers poolside and room-service attendants who toast your bread in-room—earned this Maui favorite its reputation. The property has an understated elegance, with beautiful floral arrangements, courtyards, and private cabanas. Most rooms have an ocean view (avoid those over the parking lot in the North Tower), and you can find terry robes and whole-bean coffee grinders in each. Choose between three excellent restaurants, including Wolfgang Puck's Spago. The recently renovated spa is small but expertly staffed. Honeymooners: request Suite 301, with its round tub and private lawn. ✉ *3900 Wailea Alanui Dr., Wailea 96753* ☎ *808/874–8000 or 800/334–6284* 🖷 *808/874–6449* 🌐 *www.fourseasons.com/maui* 🛏 *380 rooms* ☖ *A/C, 3 restaurants, in-room data ports, in-room safes, refrigerators, cable TV with movies and video games, golf privileges, 2 tennis courts, pool, health club, spa, beach, bicycles, badminton, croquet, volleyball, 3 bars, recreation room, children's programs (ages 5–12)* ➟ *AE, D, DC, MC, V. $365–$890.*

$$$$ 🏨 **Grand Wailea.** "Grand" is no exaggeration for this opulent sunny, 40-acre resort. Elaborate water features include a "canyon riverpool" with slides, caves, a tarzan swing, and a water elevator. Tropical garden paths meander past artwork by Léger, Warhol, Picasso, Botero, and noted Hawaiian artists—sculptures even hide in waterfalls. Spacious ocean-view rooms are outfitted with stuffed chaises, comfortable desks, and oversize marble bathrooms. Spa Grande, the island's most comprehensive spa facility, offers you everything from mineral baths to massage. For kids, Camp Grande has a full-size soda fountain, game room, and movie theater. Although not the place to go for quiet or for especially attentive service, the property is astounding. ⊠ *3850 Wailea Alanui Dr., Wailea 96753* ☎ *808/875–1234 or 800/888–6100* 🖷 *808/874–2442* ⊕ *www.grandwailea.com* ⟿ *779 rooms* ⚬ *A/C, 5 restaurants, in-room data ports, in-room safes, cable TV with movies, golf privileges, 3 pools, health club, hair salon, indoor and outdoor hot tubs, spa, beach, racquetball, 6 bars, nightclub, recreation room, shops, children's programs (ages 5–12)* ⊟ *AE, D, DC, MC, V. $485.*

$$$$ 🏨 **Marriott Wailea Resort.** The Marriott (formerly the Outrigger) was built before current construction laws were put in place, so rooms sit much closer to the crashing surf than at most resorts. Wailea Beach is a few steps away, as are the Shops at Wailea. The tropical lobby and interior spaces showcase a remarkable collection of Hawaiian and Pacific Rim artifacts. All of the spacious rooms have private lānai and are styled with a tropical theme. There are golf privileges at three nearby courses, as well as tennis privileges at the Wailea Tennis Club. The Mandara Spa provides beauty and relaxation treatments as well as massage. Although not as fancy as its neighbors, this resort is a solid deal for Wailea—especially if you take advantage of package deals. ⊠ *3700 Wailea Alanui Dr., Wailea 96753* ☎ *808/879–1922 or 800/922–7866* 🖷 *808/874–8331* ⊕ *www.marriotthawaii.com* ⟿ *516 rooms* ⚬ *A/C, 3 restaurants, in-room data ports, in-room safes, cable TV with video games, golf privileges, 3 pools, hair salon, 2 hot tubs, spa, beach, children's programs (ages 5–12), dry cleaning, laundry service, business services* ⊟ *AE, D, DC, MC, V. $319–$379.*

★ **$$$$** 🏨 **Maui Prince.** This isn't the most luxurious resort on the South Shore—it could actually use a face-lift—but it has many pluses that more than

---

Family Reunion Headquarters

For adventurous families, the lovely cottage at **Peace of Maui** (⊠ 1290 Hali`imaile Rd., Hali`imaile ☎ 808/572–5045 or 888/475–5045 ⊕ www.peaceofmaui.com) makes a great headquarters. The casual digs are affordable and less than 15 minutes from most everything (on the North Shore, that is). We can't say enough about the friendliness of the owners here—you'll want to adopt them into your family. Call far in advance to make sure you can rent the whole shebang.

Kama`ole Sands (⊠ 2695 S. Kīhei Rd., Kīhei 96753 ☎ 808/874–8700 or 800/367–5004 ⊕ www.castleresorts.com/KSM) is an easy spot for launching family activities.

Two-bedroom units have everything a family needs: kitchens, laundry facilities, and pool access. The complex is across the street from Kam III beach park to boot—a great place for family barbecues, Frisbee championships, or kite-flying contests.

On the other end of the spectrum there are the villas at the **Fairmont Kea Lani** (⊠ 4100 Wailea Alanui Dr., Wailea ☎ 808/875–4100 or 800/882–4100 ⊕ www.kealani.com). Twice as luxurious (and about six times more costly), a two-story villa is a posh hangout zone for the family. In-laws and cousins can book suites, while activities focus around the villa with its fully equipped kitchen, plunge pool, and BBQ.

make up for the somewhat dated decor. The location is superb. Just south of Mākena, the hotel is on a secluded piece of land surrounded by two magnificent golf courses and abutting a beautiful, near-private beach. The pool area is simple (two round pools), but surrounded by beautiful gardens that are quiet and understated compared to the other big resorts. The attention given to service is apparent from the minute you walk into the open-air lobby—the staff is excellent. Rooms on five levels all have ocean views (in varying degrees) and surround the courtyard, which has a Japanese garden with a bubbling stream. ⊠ *5400 Mākena Alanui Rd., Mākena 96753* ☎ *808/874–1111 or 800/321–6284* ⊟ *808/879–8763* ⊕ *www.princeresortshawaii.com* ⟿ *310 rooms ᗢ A/C, 4 restaurants, in-room safes, some in-room VCRs, 2 18-hole golf courses, 6 tennis courts, 2 pools, exercise equipment, hot tub, beach, badminton, croquet, shuffleboard, children's programs (ages 5–12), business services, meeting rooms* ⊟ *AE, DC, MC, V. $335–$525.*

$$$$ ⊞ **Renaissance Wailea Beach Resort.** Most of the rooms here are positioned on fantastic Mōkapu Beach. A giant ceremonial canoe enhances the lobby area. Outside you can find exotic gardens, waterfalls, and reflecting ponds. A decent value package offers discounts at the restaurants and the hotel's own lūʻau, performed on-site three nights a week. The VIP Mōkapu Beach Club building has 26 luxury accommodations closest to the beach, and its own concierge, pool, and beach cabanas. Mōkapu Beach Club guests also have access to nearby golf and tennis facilities. ⊠ *3550 Wailea Alanui Dr., Wailea 96753* ☎ *808/879–4900 or 800/992–4532* ⊟ *808/874–6128* ⊕ *www.renaissancehotels.com* ⟿ *345 rooms ᗢ A/C, 3 restaurants, in-room data ports, refrigerators, cable TV with movies and video games, 2 pools, health club, hot tub, beach, basketball, Ping-Pong, shuffleboard, lobby lounge, children's programs (ages 5–12)* ⊟ *AE, D, DC, MC, V. $309–$419.*

Condos

★ **$$$$** ⊞ **Polo Beach Club.** This wonderful, old eight-story property lording over a hidden section of Polo beach somehow manages to stay under the radar. From your giant corner window, you can look down at the famed Kea Lani villas, and know you've scored the same great locale at a fraction of the price. Individually owned apartments are well-cared for and feature top-of-the-line amenities, such as stainless-steel kitchens, marble floors, and valuable artwork. The property is no-smoking and an underground parking garage keeps vehicles out of the blazing Kīhei sun. ⊠ *3750 Wailea Alanui Dr., Wailea 96753* ☎ *808/879–1595 or 800/367–5246* ⊟ *808/874–3554* ⊕ *www.drhmaui.com* ⟿ *71 units ᗢ A/C, fans, Wi-Fi, kitchens, cable TV, in-room VCRs, pool, hot tub, tennis privileges, beach, golf privileges, laundry facilities; no smoking* ⊟ *AE, MC, V. 1-bedroom $360–$385, 2-bedroom $430–$570.*

★ **$$$–$$$$** ⊞ **Mākena Surf.** For travelers who've done all there is to do on Maui and just want simple, luxurious relaxation, this is the spot. The security gate entrance gives way to manicured landscaping dotted with palm trees. The secluded complex is designed so that it's hard to tell they're actually three-story buildings. Water aerobics and tennis clinics are regularly offered. "B" building is oceanfront; "A," "C," and "G" are the best value, just a bit farther from the shore. Privacy envelops the grounds—which makes the place a favorite with visiting celebrities. ⊠ *3750 Wailea Alanui Dr., Wailea 96753* ☎ *808/879–1595 or 800/367– 5246* 🖷 *808/874–3554* ⊕ *www.drhmaui.com* 🖛 *100 units* ⚲ *A/C, BBQs, fans, Wi-Fi, kitchens, cable TV, in-room VCRs, in-room safes, 2 pools, 2 hot tubs, 4 tennis courts, beach, golf privileges, laundry fa- cilities* ▤ *AE, MC, V. 1-bedroom $465–$635, 2-bedroom $600–$765, 3-bedroom $825–$880, 4-bedroom $1,390.*

$$$–$$$$
Fodor'sChoice
★

🏨 **Wailea 'Ekahi, 'Elua, and 'Ekolu.** The Wailea Resort started out with three upscale condominium complexes named, appropriately, 'Ekahi, 'Elua, and 'Ekolu (One, Two, and Three). The individually owned units, managed by Destination Resorts Hawai'i, represent some of the best val- ues in this high-class neighborhood. All benefit from daily house-keep- ing, air-conditioning, high-speed Internet, free long distance, lush landscaping, and preferential play at the neighboring world-class golf courses and tennis courts. You're likely to find custom appliances and sleek furnishings befitting the million-dollar locale. ■ TIP→ The concierges here will stock your fridge with groceries—even hard-to-find dietary items—for a nominal fee. 'Ekolu, farthest from the water, is the most affordable, and benefits from a hill-side view; 'Ekahi is a large V-shape property focus- ing on Keawakapu beach; 'Elua has 24-security security and overlooks Ulua beach. ⊠ *3750 Wailea Alanui Dr., Wailea 96753* ☎ *808/879–1595 or 800/367–5246* 🖷 *808/874–3554* ⊕ *www.drhmaui.com* 🖛 *594 units* ⚲ *A/C, fans, Wi-Fi, kitchens, cable TV, in-room VCRs, 8 pools, 2 hot tubs, tennis privileges, 2 beaches, golf privileges, laundry facilities* ▤ *AE, MC, V. Studios $210, 1-bedroom $180–$550, 2-bedroom $215–$725, 3-bedroom $655–$925.*

B&Bs & Vacation Rentals

$$
🏨 **Amanda and George's Wonderful Wailea Condominium.** Exceptionally tasteful decor (a king-size bed, a leather couch, lovely artwork) makes this one-bedroom suite live up to its name. The views are nice, and the location is outstanding—on the Blue golf course, it's a quick drive (or seven-minute jog) to South Maui's best beaches, restaurants, and shops. The kitchen and bathroom are well-appointed and spotless. Amenities include use of the two pools and Jacuzzis on the grounds and access to the famed Wailea Tennis Club. ⊠ *At Grand Champions, Wailea Ike Pl. #25, Wailea 96753* ☎ *808/891–2214* ⊕ *www.travelmaui.com/condo rental/wailea* 🖛 *1 suite* ⚲ *A/C, BBQ, fans, kitchen, cable TV, 2 pools, 2 hot tubs, 4 tennis courts, laundry facilities; no smoking* ▤ *No credit cards. $120, 5-night minimum.*

$$
🏨 **Eva Villa.** A waterfall and lilies provide an elegant welcome at this B&B in the residential neighborhood above Wailea. Three modern, 600-square-foot suites come furnished with queen-size beds and sleeper sofas, kitchens stocked with Continental breakfasts, and access to the pool and Jacuzzi. Rick and Dale Pounds, the congenial owners who live on-property, even provide guests with a farewell CD of island photos and music. The real treasure, however, is the 360-degree ocean and moun- tain view from the rooftop patio, accompanied by a telescope. ⊠ *815 Kumulani Dr., Wailea 96753* ☎ *808/874–6407* ⊕ *www.mauibnb.com* 🖛 *3 suites* ⚲ *BBQ, fans, kitchens, cable TV, pool, hot tub, laundry fa- cilities, Internet room. $130–$150.*

CENTRAL MAUI

Kahului and Wailuku, the industrial centers that make up Central Maui, are not known for their lavish accommodations. The exceptions, of course, make the rule, and the few listed below meet some travelers' needs perfectly.

B&Bs & Vacation Rentals

$$–$$$
Fodor'sChoice
★

🏠 **Old Wailuku Inn.** This historic home, built in 1924, may be the ultimate Hawaiian B&B. Each room is decorated with the theme of a Hawaiian flower, and the flower motif is worked into the heirloom Hawaiian quilt on each bed. Other features include 10-foot ceilings, floors of native hardwoods, and (depending on the room) delightful bathtubs and Swiss jet showers. The first-floor rooms have private gardens. A hearty breakfast is included. ⊠ *2199 Kaho'okele St., Wailuku 96793* 🕾 *808/ 244–5897 or 800/305–4899* ⊕ *www.mauiinn.com* ⇌ *7 rooms* ⚅ *A/C, in-room data ports, some cable TV, in-room VCRs, library, business services* 🖃 *AE, D, DC, MC, V. $120–$180.*

¢–$
🏠 **Banana Bungalow Maui Hostel.** A typical lively and cosmopolitan hostel, Banana Bungalow offers the cheapest accommodations on the island. Private rooms have one queen or two single beds; bathrooms are down the hall. Dorm rooms are available for $22 per night. Free daily tours to waterfalls, beaches, and Haleakalā Crater make this a stellar deal. (Yes, the tours are *free.*) The property's amenities include free high-speed Internet access in the common room, kitchen privileges, a Jacuzzi, and banana trees ripe for the picking. Though it's tucked in a slightly rough-around-the-edges corner of Wailuku, the old building has splendid mountain views. ⊠ *310 N. Market St., Wailuku 96793* 🕾 *808/244– 5090 or 800/846–7835* ⊕ *www.mauihostel.com* ⇌ *38 rooms* ⚅ *BBQ, kitchen, laundry facilities, Internet; no A/C* 🖃 *MC, V. Dorm rooms $22, private rooms $44–$66.*

UPCOUNTRY

Upcountry accommodations (those in Kula, Makawao, and Hali'imaile) are on country estates and are generally small, privately owned vacation rentals, or B&Bs. At high elevation, these lodgings offer splendid views of the island, temperate weather, and a "getting away from it all" feeling—which is actually the case, as most shops and restaurants are a fair drive away, and beaches even farther. You'll definitely need a car here.

Hotels & Resorts

$$–$$$
🏠 **Kula Lodge.** This hotel isn't typical for Hawai'i: the lodge inexplicably resembles a chalet in the Swiss Alps, and two units even have gas fireplaces. Charming and cozy in spite of the nontropical ambience, it's a good spot for a romantic stay. Units are in two wooden cabins; four have lofts in addition to the ample bed space downstairs. On 3 acres, the lodge has startling views of Haleakalā and two coasts, enhanced by the surrounding tropical gardens. The property has an art gallery and a protea store that will pack flowers for you to take home. ⊠ *Haleakalā Hwy., Rte. 377* ⌂ *R.R. 1, Box 475, Kula 96790* 🕾 *808/878–2517 or*

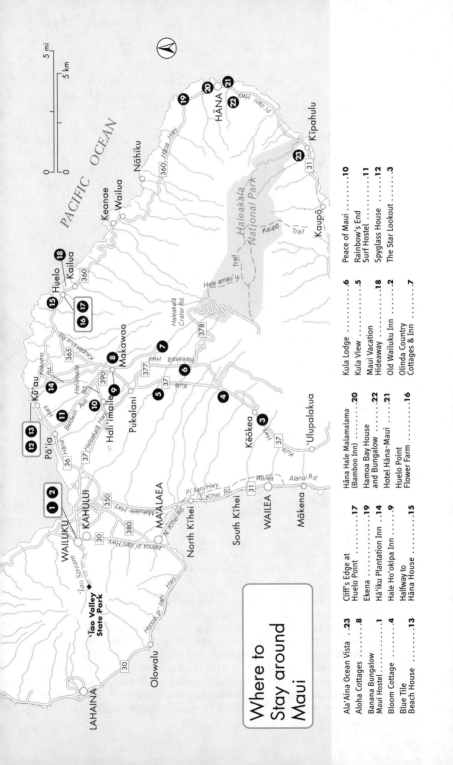

Where to Stay around Maui

PACIFIC OCEAN

Haleakalā National Park

‘Īao Valley State Park

800/233–1535 ⊞ *808/878–2518* ⊕ *www.kulalodge.com* ⟳ *5 units* ♿ *Restaurant, shop; no A/C, no room phones, no room TVs* ▭ *AE, MC, V. $110–$165.*

B&Bs & Vacation Rentals

★ **$$$$** ▦ **Aloha Cottages.** The two secluded cottages on this property, the Bali Bungalow and the Thai Treehouse, are perfect for honeymooners or anyone else seeking a romantic getaway. The property abounds with tropical plants allowing each cottage complete privacy. Intricate woodwork and furnishings, all imported from Bali, add a touch of exoticism to the interiors. Each cottage has a large comfortable bed, fully equipped kitchen, and outdoor hot tub on a private lānai. Ranjana, your hostess, is happy to assist you with planning activities and booking restaurants. She can also arrange for a private massage, yoga lessons, or even a candlelight dinner in the "Lotus House" on the property. The restaurants and shops of Makawao are a short drive away. ✉ *1879 Olinda Rd., Makawao 96768* ☎ *808/573–8500* ⊕ *www.alohacottage.com* ⟳ *2 rooms* ♿ *Fans, kitchens, in-room data ports, cable TV, in-room VCRs, outdoor hot tubs; no A/C, no kids, no smoking* ▭ *MC, V. $245–$275, 3-night minimum.*

$$–$$$$ ▦ **Olinda Country Cottages & Inn.** This restored Tudor home and adjacent cottages are so far up Olinda Road above Makawao you'll keep thinking you must have passed them. The Inn, which sits amid an 8½-acre protea farm surrounded by forest and some wonderful hiking trails, has five accommodations: two upstairs bedrooms with private baths; the downstairs Pineapple Sweet; a romantic cottage, which looks like a dollhouse from the outside; and best of all, Hidden Cottage, which has a private hot tub. Bring warm clothes—the mountain air can be chilly. Breakfast is served in the common living room. ✉ *2660 Olinda Rd., Olinda 96768* ⊞⊞ *808/ 572–1453* ☎ *800/932–3435* ⊕ *www.mauibnbcottages.com* ⟳ *3 rooms, 2 cottages* ♿ *Some cable TV; no A/C, no smoking* ▭ *No credit cards. $140–$245, 2- to 3-night minimum.*

$$$ ▦ **The Star Lookout.** Hidden away halfway up Haleakalā, this charming 100-year-old perch is an ideal getaway. With a view of most of the Valley Isle, this retreat is remote, serene, and deliciously temperate—you'll want to snuggle up, rather than blast the A/C. Up to six people can be accommodated in this inventively designed house, but four is more comfortable, and two is downright romantic. Snipping a few fresh herbs from the garden will make cooking while on vacation all the more fun. ✉ *622 Thompson Rd., Keokea* ☎ *907/346–8028* ⊕ *www.starlookout. com* ⟳ *1 house* ♿ *Kitchen, cable TV, in-room VCR, hot tub; no A/C* ▭ *No credit cards. $200.*

$$–$$$ ▦ **Bloom Cottage.** The name comes from the abundance of roses and other flowers that surround this well-run, classic B&B. The property consists of a main house and separate cottage. This is life in the slow lane, with quiet, privacy, and a living room fireplace for when the evenings are nippy. The furnishings are very Ralph Lauren, with a cowhide flourish suited to this ranch-country locale. The 1906 house has three rooms and is good for four to six people willing to share a single bathroom. The cottage is ideal for a couple. ✉ *229 Kula Hwy., Kula 96790* ☎ *808/579–8282* ⊞ *661/ 393–5015* ⊕ *www.hookipa.com/bloom_cottage.html* ⟳ *1 house, 1 cot-*

tage ⚬ *Kitchens, cable TV, in-room VCRs, laundry facilities; no A/C, no smoking* ⊟ *AE, D, MC, V. $125–$165, 3-night minimum.*

$–$$ 🖻 **Hale Ho'okipa Inn.** This handsome 1924 Craftsman-style house in the heart of Makawao town is a good base for excursions to the crater or to Hāna. The owner has furnished it with antiques and fine art, and allows guests to peruse her voluminous library of Hawai'i-related books. The house is divided into three single rooms, each prettier than the next, and the South Wing, which

GROCERIES & VIDEO RENTALS

Head to **Pukalani Terrace Center** (⊠ 55 Pukalani St., Pukalani) for pizza, a bank, post office, hardware store, and Starbucks. There's also a **Foodland** (📞 808/572–0674), which has fresh sushi and a good seafood section in addition to the usual grocery store fare, and **Paradise Video** (📞 808/572–6200).

sleeps four and includes the kitchen. There's also a separate cottage on the property, which sleeps two to four. All rooms have private claw-foot baths. This inn has a distinct plantation-era feel with squeaky wooden floors and period furnishings to boot. ⊠ *32 Pakani Pl., Makawao 96768* 📞 *808/572–6698* 📠 *808/572–2580* ⊕ *www.maui-bed-and-breakfast.com* 🛏 *3 rooms, 1 2-bedroom suite, 1 cottage* ⚬ *A/C in some rooms, cable TV, library* ⊟ *No credit cards. $95–$145.*

$ 🖻 **Kula View.** This affordable home-away-from-home sits in peaceful, rural Kula. At an elevation of 2,000 feet, the climate is pleasantly temperate. Guests stay in the entire upper floor of a tastefully decorated house with a private entrance, deck, and gardens. A commanding view of Haleakalā stretches beyond the French doors. The hostess provides an "amenity basket," a very popular Continental breakfast, advice on touring, and even beach towels or warm clothes for your crater trip. ⊠ *600 Holopuni Rd., Kula 96790* 📞 *808/878–6736* ⊕ *www.kulaview.com* 🛏 *1 room* ⚬ *Kitchenette; no A/C* ⊟ *No credit cards. $95.*

¢–$ 🖻 **Peace of Maui.** This Upcountry getaway is ideal for budget-minded travelers who want to be out and active all day. Well situated for accessing the rest of the island, it's only 15 minutes from Kahului and less than 10 from Pā'ia, Ha'ikū, and Makawao. Six modest double rooms in a "lodge" have pantries and mini-refrigerators. The kitchen, two bathrooms, and living room are shared. An amply equipped separate cottage (including fresh-cut flowers) sleeps four to six and overlooks the North Shore and the West Maui Mountains. You'll have sweeping views of rainbow-washed pineapple fields here. If you're lucky, the family dog will sit near the Jacuzzi while you relax after a hard day's adventuring. ⊠ *1290 Hali'imaile Rd., Hali'imaile 96768* 📞 *808/572–5045 or 888/475–5045* ⊕ *www.peaceofmaui.com* 🛏 *6 rooms with shared bath, 1 cottage* ⚬ *Refrigerators, cable TV, hot tub, Internet room; no A/C* ⊟ *No credit cards. $55–$100.*

THE NORTH SHORE

A string of unique accommodations starts in the North Shore surf town of Pā'ia, passes through tiny Kū'au, then winds along the rain-forested

Hāna Highway through Hā'iku and Huelo. Many are oceanfront—not necessarily beachfront—with tropical gardens overflowing with ginger, bananas, and papayas. Some have heart-stopping views or the type of solitude that seeps in, easing your tension before you know it. Several have muddy driveways and nightly bug symphonies. This is a rain forest, after all. Brief, powerful downpours let loose frequently here, especially in Hā'iku and Huelo. You'll need a car to enjoy staying on the North Shore.

B&Bs & Vacation Rentals

$$$$ ☒ **Huelo Point Flower Farm.** Amid verdant foliage, this cluster of architecturally impressive houses face dramatic Waipio Bay. Three of the four rentals have cathedral ceilings, all have amazing views. The **Main House,** with a sunken tub in the master bath and a large patio with a private hot tub, accommodates up to eight. The two-bedroom **Guesthouse** has floor-to-ceiling glass windows, a spacious patio, and a private hot tub facing the ocean. The small **Gazebo Cottage** has a half bath, kitchenette, and an outdoor shower. Set back from the cliff, the **Carriage House** has a loft bedroom with a queen-size bed, a den with a double bed, and two spacious decks. An organic orchard and Olympic-size ozonized pool are special treats. Don't try to find this secluded rental at night—it's next door to the Cliff's Edge at the end of a long, partly paved road. ☒ *Door of Faith Rd. off Hāna Hwy., Huelo* ☎ *Box 1195, Pā'ia 96779* ☎ *808/ 572–1850* ⊕ *www.maui.net/~huelopt* ➥ *4 units* ᗢ *In-room VCRs, pool, hot tub; no A/C* ⊟ *AE, MC, V. $225–$495.*

$$$–$$$$ ☒ **Cliff's Edge at Huelo Point.** Perched on a 300-foot cliff overlooking Waipio Bay, you can sometimes spot turtles swimming below this 2-acre multimillion-dollar estate. The guest houses are resplendent, with well-equipped kitchens, entertainment systems, and large bathtubs. But it's the heart-stopping views from the private hot tubs that keep regulars coming back. The brand new Bali cottage is wildly popular, decked out entirely in elegant Balinese imports. In the main house, the Penthouse and King suite each have breathtaking views, private entrances, lanai, and kitchenettes. You're free to pick fruit and flowers from the lush grounds. You'll be far from it all out here, in a remote paradise. ☒ *Door of Faith Rd., Huelo* ☎ *Box 1095, Hā'iku 96708* ☎ *808/572–4530* ⊕ *www.cliffsedge. com* ➥ *2 rooms, 2 houses* ᗢ *Wi-Fi, kitchens, cable TV, BBQ, pool, 3 hot tubs; no kids under 13* ⊟ *AE, MC, V. Rooms $165–$195, guest houses $300–$325; 3-night minimum.*

$–$$$$ ☒ **Blue Tile Beach House.** This large house is reminiscent of a Mediterranean villa with fountains, arched doorways, and yes, lots of blue tile. It sits on Tavares Bay, a tiny, semi-private surfing beach. The two suites have plenty of extras: spacious living areas, carved wood, granite countertops, multijet showers, Jacuzzis—one even has a sauna. The individual rooms are small, tasteful, and privy to the immensely relaxing grounds. A large, two-story lobby in the center of the house can be booked for special functions. ☒ *367 Hāna Hwy., Kū'au* ☎ *808/579–8608 or 800/ 475–6695* ⊕ *www.beachvacationmaui.com* ➥ *2 suites, 4 rooms* ᗢ *Fans, kitchenettes, cable TV, hot tub, sauna, beach, surfing; no A/C* ⊟ *MC, V. Suites $250, rooms $90–$150; 3-night minimum.*

7

★ **$–$$** Hāʻiku Plantation Inn. Water lilies and a shade tree bedecked in orchids greet you at this forested bend in the road. A remnant of Hāʻiku's plantation history, this gracious estate was built in 1870 for the company doctor. A feeling of wellness persists—revered Hawaiian healer Kahu Lyons Naʻone teaches traditional medicine and *hoʻoponopono,* literally "making right," on-site. A small massage *hale* stands beside a thatched roof gazebo in a lush garden of *ulu* (breadfruit), *lilikoi* (passion fruit), sugarcane, bananas, and pineapple. Rooms are uncluttered

GROCERIES & VIDEO RENTALS

The **Hāʻiku Cannery** (✉ 810 Hāʻiku Rd., Hāʻiku) is home to **Hāʻiku Grocery** (☎ 808/575–9291), a somewhat limited grocery store where you can find the basics: veggies, meats, wine, snacks, and ice cream. **88-Cent Video** (☎ 808/575–2723) is also here, along with a laundromat, bakery, and hardware store. The post office is across the street.

and charming with private baths; the Plumeria room has a claw-foot tub. ✉ *555 Hāʻiku Rd., Hāʻiku* ☎ *808/575–7500* ⊕ *www.haikuplantation.com* ⤳ *5 rooms* ⌂ *Cable TV, kitchen, library, hot tub, fitness classes, massage; no A/C* ⊟ *AE, MC, V. $99–$129.*

$–$$ Halfway to Hāna House. A private studio on Maui's lush rural north coast, this serene retreat includes a two-person hammock, surrounding organic gardens, and great ocean views. It's a short walk from here to natural pools, waterfalls, and hiking areas. The room comes with optional Continental breakfast and a well-supplied kitchenette—all the equipment you need to do your own thing. ✉ *Hāna Hwy., Huelo* ✆ *Box 675, Haʻikū 96708* ☎ *808/572–1176* ⊟ *808/572–3609* ⊕ *www.halfwaytohana.com/paradise.html* ⤳ *1 room* ⌂ *Kitchenette; no A/C* ⊟ *No credit cards. $85–$105, 3-night minimum.*

$–$$ Maui Vacation Hideaway. The warm ocean breeze rolls through these pretty rentals, shooing the mosquitoes away. The decor is both whimsical and calming—expect colorfully painted walls and sheer curtains. The saltwater pool is fed by a waterfall. Fully equipped kitchens and Wi-Fi make these studios an ideal home away from home. Allergy-prone travelers can relax here—no chemicals or pesticides are used on the property. This is a perfect spot if you want quiet, gorgeous scenery, and don't mind being a fair drive from civilization. ✉ *240 N. Holokai Rd., Hāʻiku* ☎ *808/572–2775* ⊟ *808/573–2775* ⊕ *www.mauivacationhideaway.com* ⤳ *3 rooms* ⌂ *Fans, Wi-Fi, kitchens, cable TV, in-room VCRs, pool, laundry facilities; no A/C. $85–$105, 3-night minimum.*

$–$$ Spyglass House. This eccentric old beach property is somewhere Pippi Longstocking might have lived after cashing in her pirate father's gold: splendid views of the Pacific, stained-glass windows, wood floors, even a room called the "Crow's Nest." Rooms in the main house are a tad classier and larger, with better views than those in the Dolphin house, but all are nice. The two houses can be rented together, accommodating up to 20 for special occasions. Your hostess, Poni, is a singer-songwriter and avid surfer who may fill you in on the weekly surf report. ✉ *367 Hāna Hwy., Kūʻau* ☎ *808/579–8608 or 800/475–6695* ⊕ *www.*

spyglassmaui.com 🛏 *6 rooms* ⚒ *Kitchen, hot tub; no A/C* ▤ *MC, V* 🌐 *Rooms $85–$150.*

¢ 🏠 **Rainbow's End Surf Hostel.** "Rainbow" is right: the kitchen in this colorful hostel is painted a cheery fuschia with lime trim. A quick stroll from Pā'ia's shops, beaches, and restaurants, this active place is a cheap headquarters for surfers and adventurers. A giant wooden longboard decorates the hallway and surfboards can be stored out back. Free Internet access is available in the cozy (if sometimes hot) common area. Built in the 1940s, the home's shared bathrooms and kitchen areas are humble, but never dirty. Make sure to get a room with a good cross-breeze; the midday heat can be stifling. ✉ *221 Baldwin Ave., Pā'ia* ☎ *808/ 579–9057* 🌐 *www.mauigateway.com/~riki* 🛏 *3 four-person dorm rooms, 3 private rooms* ⚒ *Kitchen, cable TV with VCR, Internet room; no A/C. $25 dorm rooms, $55 private rooms.*

HĀNA

Why stay in Hāna when it's so far from everything? In a world where everything moves at high speed, Hāna still travels on horseback, ambling along slowly enough to smell the fragrant vines hanging from the trees. But old-fashioned and remote do not mean tame—this is a wild coast, known for heart-stopping scenery and passionate downpours. Leave city expectations behind, the single grocery may run out of milk, and the only videos to rent may be several years old. The dining options are slim. ■ TIP➔ If you're staying for several days, or at a vacation rental, stock up on groceries before you head out to Hāna. Even with these inconveniences, Hāna is a place you won't want to miss.

Hotels & Resorts

$$$$ 🏠 **Hotel Hāna-Maui.** Tranquility envelops Hotel Hāna's ranch setting, with Fodor$Choice its unobstructed views of the Pacific. Small, secluded, and quietly luxu-
★ rious, this property is a departure from the usual resort destinations. Spacious rooms (680 to 830 square feet) have bleached-wood floors, authentic kapa-print fabric furnishings, and sumptuously stocked minibars at no extra cost. Spa suites and a heated *watsu* (massage performed in warm water) pool complement a state-of-the-art spa-and-fitness center. The Sea Ranch Cottages with individual hot tubs are the best value. Horses nibble wild grass on the sea-cliff nearby. A shuttle takes you to beautiful Hāmoa Beach. ✉ *Hāna Hwy.* ✉ *Box 9, Hāna 96713* ☎ *808/248–8211 or 800/ 321–4262* 📠 *808/248–7264* 🌐 *www.hotelhanamaui.com* 🛏 *19 rooms, 47 cottages, 1 house* ⚒ *A/C, 2 restaurants, 2 tennis courts, 2 pools, gym, hot tub, spa, beach, horseback riding, bar, library, Internet room; no room TVs* ▤ *AE, D, DC, MC, V. $295–$725.*

B&Bs & Vacation Rentals

$$$–$$$$ 🏠 **Ekena.** "Ekena" means Garden of Eden, and the grounds here are full of tropical fruit trees and exotic

---

BED-AND-BREAKFASTS

Additional B&Bs on Maui can be found by contacting **Bed & Breakfast Hawai'i** (☎ 808/733-1632 🌐 www.bandb-hawaii.com), or **Bed and Breakfast Honolulu** (☎ 808/595-7533 or 800/288-4666 🌐 www.hawaiibnb.com).

flowers. A hillside location makes for commanding views of the ocean. There are two houses, each with a fully equipped kitchen. Jasmine, the smaller of the two, is suited to parties of two. The main house, Sea Breeze, is huge (2,600 square feet), with two large suites, but occupancy is restricted to a maximum of four people. ⊠ *Off Hāna Hwy.* ⬡ *Box 728, Hāna 96713* ☎🖶 *808/248–7047* ⊕ *www.maui.net/~ekena* ➥ *2 houses* ⚴ *Fans, kitchens, cable TV, in-room VCRs, laundry facilities; no A/C, no kids under 14* ⊟ *No credit cards. $150–$275, 3-night minimum.*

SHOPPING IN HĀNA

Hasegawa General Store. The one-stop shopping option in Hāna is charming, old, ramshackle Hasegawa's. Buy fishing tackle, hot dogs, ice cream, and eggs here. You can rent videos and buy the newspaper, which isn't always delivered on time. Check out the bulletin board for local events. Be sure to take a Hasegawa T-shirt home with you as proof of your stay out in heavenly Hāna. ⊠ *5165 Hāna Hwy.* ☎ *808/248-8231.*

★ **$$$–$$$$** 🏨 **Hamoa Bay House & Bungalow.** This Balinese-inspired property is sensuous and secluded—a private sanctuary in a fragrant jungle. There are two buildings: the main house is 1,300 square feet and contains two bedrooms; one of them is a suite set apart by a breezeway. There are a screened veranda with an ocean view and an outdoor lava-rock shower accessible to all guests. The 600-square-foot bungalow is a treetop perch with a giant bamboo bed and a hot tub on the veranda. Hamoa Beach is a short walk away. ⊠ *Hāna Hwy.* ⬡ *Box 773, Hāna 96713* ☎ *808/248–7884* 🖶 *808/248–7047* ⊕ *www.hamoabay.com* ➥ *1 house, 1 bungalow* ⚴ *Kitchen, in-room VCRs, laundry facilities; no kids under 14, no smoking* ⊟ *No credit cards. $195–$250, 3-night minimum.*

★ **$$–$$$$** 🏨 **Hāna Hale Malamalama (Bamboo Inn).** If you're looking for the amenities and activities of a resort, you won't be happy here. But if you want lots of nature and little distraction, this place is perfect. The two duplexes and three cottages overlook a natural spring-fed fish pond and the remains of a *heiau* (an ancient Hawaiian stone platform once used as a place of worship). A black sand beach, surrounded by lush tropical forest is steps away. Accommodations are simple but clean with rustic bamboo furniture, full kitchens, large bathrooms, and private lānai. Don't be surprised to find a few ants, they come with all the scenery. A Continental breakfast is served in the "lobby," a Polynesian-style, open-air hut. The roar of the ocean and the rustling of palm trees adds a soothing backdrop to the stunning setting. This is paradise as nature meant it to be. ⬡ *Box 374, Hana 96713* ☎ *808/248–8211* ⊕ *www.hanahale. com* ➥ *4 rooms, 3 cottages* ⚴ *BBQs, fans, in-room data ports, kitchens, cable TV, in-room DVDs, Internet, no-smoking rooms; no A/C* ⊟ *MC, V. $135–$250.*

$$$ 🏨 **Ala'Aina Ocean Vista.** This B&B is on the grounds of an old banana plantation past 'Ohe'o Gulch (about a 40-minute drive from Hāna). Banana trees still populate the property alongside mango, papaya, and avocado trees. There's also a Balinese garden, complete with a lotus-shape pond. The single room has a private lānai with an outdoor kitchenette, outdoor shower (there's a regular shower in the room as well), and astonishing views of the coastline. Sam and Mercury, a mother-daughter team, live in the main house on-site and are available to give tips and advice about exploring the area. This is a simple, back-to-nature kind of spot, perfect for a couple who wants some time alone away from everything. ✉ *Off Hwy. 31, 10 mi past Hāna* ⌖*SR 184-A, Hāna 96713* ☎*808/ 248–7824 or 877/216–1733* ⊕*www.hanabedandbreakfast.com* ⇲*1 room* ⚒ *BBQ, kitchenette, in-room TV/VCR with movies; no A/C* ⊟*No credit cards. $165, 2-night minimum.*

7

Shops & Spas

WORD OF MOUTH

"Don't miss the Maui swap meet, held every Saturday from 7 AM until noon. The local artists and local farmers bring all of their goods, and you can buy things for a fraction of the price you will find in the shops."

–Nancy1013

"The spa at the Grande Wailea is out of this world if you want to splurge."

–KimF

SHOPS

By Shannon Wianecki

Whether you're searching for a dashboard hula dancer or an original Curtis Wilson Cost painting, you can find it on Front Street in Lahaina or at the Shops at Wailea. Art sales are huge in the resort areas, where artists regularly show up to promote their work. Alongside the flashy galleries are standards like Quicksilver and ABC store, where you can stock up on swim trunks, sunscreen, and flip-flops.

Don't miss the great boutiques lining the streets of small towns like Pā'ia and Makawao. You can purchase boutique fashions and art while strolling through these charming, quieter communities. Notably, several local designers—Tamara Catz, Sig Zane, and Maui Girl—all produce top-quality island fashions. In the neighboring galleries, local artisans turn out gorgeous work in a range of prices. Special souvenirs include rare hardwood bowls and boxes, prints of sea life, Hawaiian quilts, and blown glass.

Specialty food products—pineapples, coconuts, or Maui onions—and Made in Maui jams and jellies make great, less-expensive souvenirs. Cook Kwee's Maui Cookies have gained a following, as have Maui Potato Chips. Coffee sellers now offer Maui-grown-and-roasted beans alongside the better-known Kona varieties. Remember that fresh fruit must be inspected by the U.S. Department of Agriculture before it can leave the state, so it's safest to buy a box that has already passed inspection.

Business hours for individual shops on the island are usually 9 to 5, seven days a week. Shops on Front Street and shopping centers tend to stay open later (until 9 or 10 on weekends).

West Maui

Shopping Centers

Lahaina Cannery Mall. In a building reminiscent of an old pineapple cannery are 50 shops and an active stage. The mall hosts fabulous free events year-round (like the International Jazz Festival). Recommended stops include Na Hoku, purveyor of striking Hawaiian heirloom jewelry and pearls; Totally Hawaiian Gift Gallery; and Kite Fantasy, one of the best kite shops on Maui. An events schedule is on the Web site. ⊠ *1221 Honoapi'ilani Hwy., Lahaina* ☎ *808/661–5304* ⊕ *www.lahainacannery.com.*

Lahaina Center. Island department store Hilo Hattie Fashion Center anchors the complex and puts on a free hula show at 2 PM every Wednesday and Friday. In addition to Hard Rock Cafe, Banana Republic, and a

> ### MAUI'S BEST OMIYAGE
>
> *Omiyage* is the Japanese term for food souvenirs.
>
> - Lavender salt rub from **Ali'i Kula Lavender.**
> - Aloha Taro pancake mix from any grocery store.
> - Pickled mango from **Camellia Seed Shop.**
> - Maui Gold Pineapple from **Take Home Maui.**
> - NickyBeans from **Maui Coffee Roasters.**

four-screen cinema, you can find a replica of an ancient Hawaiian village complete with three full-size thatch huts built with 10,000 feet of Big Island 'ōhi'a wood, 20 tons of *pili* grass, and more than 4 mi of handwoven coconut *senit* (twine). There's all that *and* validated parking. ⊠ *900 Front St., Lahaina* ☎ *808/667–9216.*

Whalers Village. Chic Whalers Village has a whaling museum and more than 50 restaurants and shops. Upscale haunts include Louis Vuitton, Ferragamo, Versace, and Chanel Boutique. The complex also offers some interesting diversions: Hawaiian artisans display their crafts daily; hula dancers perform on an outdoor stage weeknights from 7 to 8;

> ### BEST MADE-ON-MAUI GIFTS
>
> - *Koa* jewelry boxes from **Maui Hands.**
> - Fish-shape sushi platters and bamboo chopsticks from the **Maui Crafts Guild.**
> - Black pearl pendant from **Maui Divers.**
> - Handmade Hawaiian quilt from **Hāna Coast Gallery.**
> - Jellyfish paperweight from **Hot Island Glassblowing Studio & Gallery.**
> - Fresh plumeria lei, made by you!

and three films spotlighting whales and marine history are shown daily for free at the Whale Center of the Pacific. ⊠ *2435 Kā'anapali Pkwy., Kā'anapali* ☎ *808/661–4567.*

Clothing

Hilo Hattie Fashion Center. Hawai'i's largest manufacturer of aloha shirts and mu'umu'u also carries brightly colored blouses, skirts, and children's clothing. ⊠ *Lahaina Center, 900 Front St., Lahaina* ☎ *808/661–8457.*

Honolua Surf Company. If you're not in the mood for a matching aloha shirt and mu'umu'u ensemble, check out this surf shop—popular with young men and women for surf trunks, casual clothing, and accessories. ⊠ *845 Front St., Lahaina* ☎ *808/661–8848.*

Maggie Coulombe. Maggie Coulombe's cutting-edge fashions have the style of SoHo and the heat of the Islands. The svelte, body-clinging designs are unique and definitely worth a look. ⊠ *505 Front St., Lahaina* ☎ *808/662–0696.*

Galleries

Lahaina Galleries. Works of both national and international artists are displayed at the gallery's two locations in West Maui. ⊠ *828 Front St., Lahaina* ☎ *808/667–2152* ⊠ *Kapalua Resort, Bay Dr., Kapalua* ☎ *808/669–0202.*

Lahaina Printsellers Ltd. Hawai'i's largest selection of original antique maps and prints pertaining to Hawai'i and the Pacific is available here. You can also buy museum-quality reproductions and original oil paintings from the Pacific Artists Guild. A second, smaller shop is at 505 Front Street. ⊠ *Whalers Village, 2435 Kā'anapali Pkwy., Kā'anapali* ☎ *808/667–7617.*

Martin Lawrence Galleries. Martin Lawrence displays the works of noted mainland artists, including Andy Warhol and Keith Haring, in a bright

8

Continued on page 174

ALL ABOUT LEIS

Leis brighten every occasion in Hawai'i, from birthdays to bar mitzvahs to baptisms. Creative artisans weave nature's bounty—flowers, ferns, vines, and seeds—into gorgeous creations that convey an array of heartfelt messages: "Welcome," "Congratulations," "Good luck," "Farewell," "Thank you," "I love you." When it's difficult to find the right words, a lei expresses exactly the right sentiments.

WHERE TO BUY THE BEST LEIS

These florists carry a nice variety of leis: **A Special Touch** (Emerald Plaza, 142 Kupuohi St., Ste. F-1, Lahaina, 808/661–3455); **Kahului Florist** (Maui Mall, 70 E. Ka'ahumanu Ave., Kahului, 808/877–3951 or 800/711–8881); and **Wailea Flowers by Cora** (1280 S. Kīhei Rd., Ste. 126, Kīhei, 808/879–7249 or 800/339–0419). **Costco, Kmart, Wal-Mart,** and **Safeway** also sell leis, but their choices are usually limited to "basics" such as orchid, plumeria, and tuberose.

LEI ETIQUETTE

■ To wear a closed lei, drape it over your shoulders, half in front and half in back. Open leis are worn around the neck, with the ends draped over the front in equal lengths.

■ Pīkake, ginger, and other sweet, delicate blossoms are "feminine" leis. Men opt for cigar, crown flower, and carnation, which are sturdier and don't emit as much fragrance.

■ Leis are always presented with a kiss, a custom that supposedly dates back to World War II when a hula dancer fancied an officer at a U.S.O. show. Taking a dare from members of her troupe, she took off her lei, placed it around his neck, and kissed him on the cheek.

■ You shouldn't wear a lei before you give it to someone else. Hawaiians believe the lei absorbs your *mana* (spirit); if you give your lei away, you'll be giving away part of your essence.

ORCHID

Growing wild on every continent except Antarctica, orchids—which range in color from yellow to green to purple—comprise the largest family of plants in the world. There are more than 20,000 species of orchids, but only three are native to Hawai'i—and they are very rare. The pretty lavender vanda you see hanging by the dozens at local lei stands has probably been imported from Thailand.

MAILE

Maile, an endemic twining vine with a heady aroma, is sacred to Laka, goddess of the hula. In ancient times, dancers wore maile and decorated hula altars with it to honor Laka. Today, "open" maile leis usually are given to men. Instead of ribbon, interwoven lengths of maile are used at dedications of new businesses. The maile is untied, never snipped, for doing so would symbolically "cut" the company's success.

'ILIMA

Designated by Hawai'i's Territorial Legislature in 1923 as the official flower of the island of O'ahu, the golden 'ilima is so delicate it lasts for just a day. Five to seven hundred blossoms are needed to make one garland. Queen Emma, wife of King Kamehameha IV, preferred 'ilima over all other leis, which may have led to the incorrect belief that they were reserved only for royalty.

PLUMERIA

This ubiquitous flower is named after Charles Plumier, the noted French botanist who discovered it in Central America in the late 1600s. Plumeria ranks among the most popular leis in Hawai'i because it's fragrant, hardy, plentiful, inexpensive, and requires very little care. Although yellow is the most common color, you'll also find plumeria leis in shades of pink, red, orange, and "rainbow" blends.

PĪKAKE

Favored for its fragile beauty and sweet scent, pīkake, was introduced from India. In lieu of pearls, many brides in Hawai'i adorn themselves with long, multiple strands of white pīkake. Princess Kaiulani enjoyed showing guests her beloved pīkake and peacocks at Āinahau, her Waikīkī home. Interestingly, pīkake is the Hawaiian word for both the bird and the blossom.

KUKUI

The kukui (candlenut) is Hawai'i's state tree. Early Hawaiians strung kukui nuts (which are quite oily) together and burned them for light; mixed burned nuts with oil to make an indelible dye; and mashed roasted nuts to consume as a laxative. Kukui nut leis may not have been made until after Western contact, when the Hawaiians saw black beads from Europe and wanted to imitate them.

and friendly gallery. ✉ *Lahaina Market Pl., Front St. and Lahainaluna Rd., Lahaina* ☎ *808/661–1788.*

Village Gallery. This gallery, with two locations on the island, showcases the works of such popular local artists as Betty Hay Freeland, Wailehua Gray, Margaret Bedell, George Allen, Joyce Clark, Pamela Andelin, Stephen Burr, and Macario Pascual. ✉ *120 Dickenson St., Lahaina* ☎ *808/661–4402* ✉ *Ritz-Carlton, 1 Ritz-Carlton Dr., Kapalua* ☎ *808/669–1800.*

Jewelry

Haimoff & Haimoff Creations in Gold. This shop carries the original work of several jewelry designers, including the renowned Harry Haimoff. ✉ *Kapalua Resort* ☎ *808/669–5213.*

Jessica's Gems. Jessica's has a good selection of Hawaiian heirloom jewelry, and its Lahaina store specializes in black pearls. ✉ *Whalers Village, 2435 Kā'anapali Pkwy., Kā'anapali* ☎ *808/661–4223* ✉ *858 Front St., Lahaina* ☎ *808/661–9200.*

Lahaina Scrimshaw. Here you can buy brooches, rings, pendants, cuff links, tie tacks, and collector's items adorned with intricately carved sailors' art. ✉ *845A Front St., Lahaina* ☎ *808/661–8820* ✉ *Whalers Village, 2435 Kā'anapali Pkwy., Kā'anapali* ☎ *808/661–4034.*

Maui Divers. This company has been crafting gold and coral into jewelry for more than 20 years. ✉ *640 Front St., Lahaina* ☎ *808/661–0988.*

Central Maui

Shopping Centers

Ka'ahumanu Center. This is Maui's largest mall with 75 stores, a movie theater, an active stage, and a food court. The mall's interesting rooftop, composed of a series of manta ray–like umbrella shades, is easily spotted. Stop at Camellia Seed Shop for what the locals call "crack seed," a delicacy made from dried fruits, nuts, and lots of sugar. Other stops here include mall standards such as Macy's, Gap, and American Eagle Outfitters. ✉ *275 Ka'ahumanu Ave., Kahului* ☎ *808/877–3369.*

Maui Mall. The anchor stores here are Longs Drugs and Star Market, and there's a good Chinese restaurant, Dragon Dragon. The Tasaka Guri Guri Shop is an oddity—it's been around for nearly a hundred years, selling an ice-cream–like confection called "guri guri." The mall also has a whimsically designed 12-screen megaplex. ✉ *70 Ka'ahumanu Ave., Kahului* ☎ *808/877–7559.*

Maui Marketplace. On the busy stretch of Dairy Road, just outside the Kahului Airport, this behemoth marketplace couldn't be more conveniently located. The 20-acre complex houses several outlet stores and big retailers, such as Pier One Imports, Sports Authority, and Borders Books & Music. Sample local food at the Kau Kau Corner food court. ✉ *270 Dairy Rd., Kahului* ☎ *808/873–0400.*

Clothing

Bohemia. Tucked in a tiny mall next to Kahului Harbor, this consignment shop overflows with vintage Hawaiiana, as well as top-quality designer resale. ☒ *101 Ka'ahumanu Ave., Kahului* ☎ *808/893–2500.*

Hi-Tech. Stop here immediately after deplaning to stock up on surf trunks, windsurfing gear, bikinis, and sundresses. ☒ *425 Koloa Rd., Kahului* ☎ *808/877–2111.*

176 ∨

Sig Zane. Local clothing designer Sig Zane draws inspiration from island botanical treasures—literally. His sketches of Hawaiian flowers such as *puakenikeni* and *maile* decorate the brightly colored fabrics featured in his shop. The aloha shirts and dresses here are works of art—original and not too flashy. ☒ *53 Market St., Wailuku* ☎ *808/249–8997.*

Food Specialties

Maui Coffee Roasters. This café and roasting house near Kahului Airport is the best stop for Kona and Island coffees. The salespeople give good advice and will ship items. You even get a free cup of joe in a signature to-go cup when you buy a pound of coffee. ☒ *444 Hāna Hwy., Unit B, Kahului* ☎ *808/877–2877* ⊕ *www.hawaiiancoffee.com.*

The South Shore

Shopping Centers

Azeka Place Shopping Center. Azeka II, on the *mauka* (toward the mountains) side of S. Kīhei Road, has Longs Drugs (the place for slippers), the Coffee Store (the place for iced mochas), Who Cut the Cheese (the place for aged gouda), and the Nail Shop (the place for shaping, waxing, and tweezing). Azeka I, the older half on the makai side of the street, has a decent Vietnamese restaurant and Kīhei's post office. ☒ *1280 S. Kīhei Rd., Kīhei.*

Kīhei Kalama Village Marketplace. This is a fun place to investigate. Shaded outdoor stalls sell everything from printed and hand-painted T-shirts and sundresses to jewelry, pottery, wood carvings, fruit, and gaudily painted coconut husks—some, but not all, made by local craftspeople. ☒ *1941 S. Kīhei Rd., Kīhei* ☎ *808/879–6610.*

Rainbow Mall. This mall is one-stop shopping for condo guests—it offers video rentals, Hawaiian gifts, plate lunches, and a liquor store. ☒ *2439 S. Kīhei Rd., Kīhei.*

The Shops at Wailea. Stylish, upscale, and close to most of the resorts, this mall brings high fashion to Wailea. Luxury boutiques such as Gucci, Fendi, Cos Bar, and Tiffany & Co. have shops, as do less-expensive chains like Gap, Guess, and Tommy Bahama's. Several good restaurants face the ocean, and regular Wednesday-night events include live entertainment, art exhibits, and fashion shows. ☒ *3750 Wailea Alanui Dr., Wailea* ☎ *808/891–6770.*

...hing

...ilo Hattie Fashion Center. Hawai'i's largest manufacturer of aloha shirts and mu'umu'u also carries brightly colored blouses, skirts, and children's clothing. ✉ *297 Pi'ikea Ave., Kīhei* ☎ *808/875–4545.*

Honolua Surf Company. If you're in the mood for colorful print tees and sundresses, check out this surf shop. It's popular with young men and women for surf trunks, casual clothing, and accessories. ✉ *2411 S. Kīhei Rd., Kīhei* ☎ *808/874–0999.*

Nell. Far better than typical resort boutiques, this expansive shop at the Fairmont Kea Lani carries truly stylish resort clothing for women. If you've recently spied a pretty bracelet on a celebrity in a magazine, there's a good chance you can find it here. ✉ *Fairmont Kea Lani, 4100 Wailea Alanui Dr., Wailea* ☎ *808/875–4100.*

Sisters & Company. Opened by four sisters, this little shop has a lot to offer—current brand-name clothing such as Tamara Catz and ener-chi, locally made jewelry, beach sandals, and gifts. Sister No. 3, Rhonda, runs a tiny, ultrahip hair salon in back. ✉ *1913 S. Kīhei Rd., Kīhei* ☎ *808/875–9888.*

Tommy Bahama's. It's hard to find a man on Maui who *isn't* wearing a TB-logo aloha shirt. For better or worse, here's where you can get yours. Make sure to grab a Barbados Brownie on the way out at the restaurant, which is attached to the shop. ✉ *The Shops at Wailea, 3750 Wailea Alanui Dr., Wailea* ☎ *808/879–7828.*

Upcountry, the North Shore & Hāna

Clothing

Biasa Rose. This boutique offers hip island styles for the whole family. The owners have also created unique gifts—pillows, napkins, photo albums—with batik fabrics they've acquired while traveling through Indonesia. ✉ *104 Hāna Hwy., Pā'ia* ☎ *808/579–8602.*

Collections. This eclectic boutique is brimming with pretty jewelry, humorous gift cards, Italian bags and sandals, yoga wear, and Asian print silks. ✉ *3677 Baldwin Ave., Makawao* ☎ *808/572–0781.*

Moonbow Tropics. If you're looking for an aloha shirt that won't look out of place on the mainland, make a stop at this little store, which sells the best-quality shirts on the island. ✉ *36 Baldwin Rd., Pā'ia* ☎ *808/ 579–8592.*

Fodor's Choice ★ **Tamara Catz.** This Maui designer already has a world-wide following, and her sarongs and super-stylish beachwear have been featured in many fashion magazines. If you're looking for a sequined bikini or a delicately embroidered sundress, this is the place to check out. ✉ *83 Hāna Hwy., Pā'ia* ☎ *808/579–9184.*

SWIMWEAR **Hāna Hwy. Surf.** You can grab trunks and bikinis, and a board, if needed, at this surf shack on the North Shore. ✉ *65 Hāna Hwy, Pā'ia* ☎ *808/ 579–8980.*

Fodor's Choice ★ **Maui Girl.** This is *the* place for swimwear, cover-ups, beach hats, and sandals. Maui Girl designs its own suits and imports teenier versions from Brazil as well. Tops and bottoms can be purchased separately, greatly increasing your chances of finding a suit that actually fits. ✉ *13 Baldwin Ave., Pā'ia* ☎ *808/579–9266.*

Galleries

★ **Hāna Coast Gallery.** One of the best places to shop on the island, this 3,000-square-foot gallery has fine art and jewelry on consignment from local artists. ✉ *Hotel Hāna-Maui, Hāna Hwy., Hāna* ☎ *808/248–8636 or 800/637–0188.*

Hāna Cultural Center. The center sells distinctive island quilts and other Hawaiian crafts. ✉ *4974 Uakea St., Hāna* ☎ *808/248–8622.*

Hot Island Glassblowing Studio & Gallery. With furnaces glowing bright orange and loads of mesmerizing sculptures on display, this is an exciting place to visit. The working studio, set back from Makawao's main street in a little courtyard is owned by a family of glassblowers. ✉ *3620 Baldwin Ave., Makawao* ☎ *808/572–4527.*

Fodor'sChoice **Maui Crafts Guild.** This is one of the more interesting galleries on Maui.
★ Set in a two-story wooden building alongside the highway, the Guild is crammed with treasures. Resident artists craft everything in the store—from Norfolk-pine bowls to *raku* (Japanese lead-glazed) pottery to original sculpture. The prices are surprisingly low. Upstairs, gorgeous pieces of handcrafted hardwood furniture are on display. ✉ *43 Hāna Hwy., Pā'ia* ☎ *808/579–9697.*

★ **Maui Hands.** This gallery shows work by dozens of local artists, including *paniolo*-theme lithographs by Sharon Shigekawa, who knows whereof she paints: she rides each year in the Kaupō Roundup. ✉ *3620 Baldwin Ave., Makawao* ☎ *808/572–5194.*

Jewelry

Master Touch Gallery. The exterior of this shop is as rustic as all the old buildings of Makawao, so there's no way to prepare yourself for the elegance of the handcrafted jewelry displayed within. Owner David Sacco truly has the "master touch." ✉ *3655 Baldwin Ave., Makawao* ☎ *808/572–6000.*

BEST BETS FOR SWIMWEAR

- **Hi-Tech.** ✉ *425 Koloa Rd., Kahului* ☎ *808/877-2111.*
- **Honolua Surf Company.** ✉ *845 Front St., Lahaina* ☎ *808/661-8848* ✉ *2411 S. Kīhei Rd., Kīhei* ☎ *808/874-0999.*
- **Maui Girl.** ✉ *13 Baldwin Ave., Pā'ia* ☎ *808/579-9266.*
- **Hāna Hwy. Surf.** ✉ *65 Hāna Hwy., Pā'ia* ☎ *808/579-8980.*

Grocery Stores on Maui

Foodland. In Kīhei town center, this is the most convenient supermarket for those staying in Wailea. It's open round-the-clock. ✉ *1881 S. Kīhei Rd., Kīhei* ☎ *808/879–9350.*

Lahaina Square Shopping Center Foodland. This Foodland serves West Maui and is open daily from 6 AM to midnight. ✉ *840 Waine'e St., Lahaina* ☎ *808/661–0975.*

Mana Foods. Stock up on local fish and grass-fed beef for your barbecue here. You can find the best selection of organic produce on the island, as well as a great bakery and deli at this typically crowded health-food store. ✉ *49 Baldwin Ave., Pā'ia* ☎ *808/579–8078.*

Safeway. Safeway has three stores on the island open 24 hours daily. ✉ *Lahaina Cannery Mall, 1221 Honoapiʻilani Hwy., Lahaina* ☎ *808/667–4392* ✉ *170 E. Kamehameha Ave., Kahului* ☎ *808/877–3377* ✉ *277 Piikea Ave., Kīhei* ☎ *808/891–9120.*

SPAS

Traditional Swedish massage and European facials anchor most spa menus, though you'll also find shiatsu, ayurveda, aromatherapy, and other body treatments drawn from cultures across the globe. *Lomi Lomi,* traditional Hawaiian massage involving powerful strokes down the length of the body, is a regional specialty passed down through generations. Many treatments incorporate local plants and flowers. *Awapuhi,* or Hawaiian ginger, and *noni,* a pungent-smelling fruit, are regularly used for their therapeutic benefits. *Limu,* or seaweed, and even coffee is employed in rousing salt scrubs and soaks. And this is just the beginning.

★ **The Spa at Four Seasons Resort.** The Four Seasons' hawklike attention to detail is reflected here. Thoughtful gestures like fresh flowers beneath the massage table (to give you something to stare at) and a choice of music relax you before your treatment even begins. The spa is genuinely stylish and serene, and the therapists are among the best. If you're looking to lounge all day here though, it's a bit small. For a private, outdoor experience, the oceanfront massage *hales* (structures) are particularly charming and well worth the extra $25. ✉ *3900 Wailea Alanui Dr., Wailea* ☎ *808/874–8000 or 800/334–6284* ⊕ *www.fourseasons.com* ☞ *$125 50-minute massage, $370 3-treatment packages* ♿ *Hair salon, steam room. Gym with: cardiovascular machines, free weights, weight-training equipment. Services: aromatherapy, body wraps, facials, hydrotherapy, massage. Classes and programs: aquaerobics, meditation, personal training, Pilates, Spinning, tai chi, yoga.*

Fodor'sChoice **Spa Grande, Grand Wailea.** Built to satisfy an indulgent Japanese billio-
★ niare, this 50,000-square-foot spa makes others seem like well-appointed closets. Slathered in honey and wrapped up in the steam room (if you go for the Aliʻi honey steam wrap), you'll feel like royalty. All treatments include a loofah scrub and a trip to the *termé,* a hydrotherapy circuit including a Roman Jacuzzi, furo bath, plunge pool, powerful waterfall and Swiss jet showers, and five therapeutic baths. (Soak for 10 minutes in the moor mud to relieve sunburn or jellyfish stings.) Plan to arrive an hour before your treatment to fully enjoy the baths. The termé is available separately for $55 ($80 for nonhotel guests). At times—especially during the holidays—this wonderland can be crowded. ✉ *3850 Wailea Alanui Dr., Wailea* ☎ *808/875–1234 or 800/888–6100* ⊕ *www.grandwailea.com* ☞ *$145 50-minute massage, $325 half-day spa packages* ♿ *Hair salon, hot tub, sauna, steam room. Gym with: cardiovascular machines, free weights, racquetball, weight-training equipment. Services: aromatherapy, body wraps, facials, hydrotherapy, massage, Vichy shower. Classes and programs: aquaerobics, cycling, Pilates, qigong, yoga.*

SPA TIPS

- Arrive early for your treatment so you can enjoy the steam room and other amenities.
- Bring a comfortable change of clothing and remove your jewelry.
- Most spas are clothing-optional. If a swimsuit is required for a hydrotherapy treatment, you will be notified.

- If you're pregnant, or have allergies, inform the receptionist before booking a treatment.
- Your therapist should be able to explain the ingredients of all products being used in your treatment. If anything stings or burns, say so immediately.
- Gratuities of 15%–20% are suggested.

Fodor'sChoice ★ **The Spa at Hotel Hāna Maui.** A bamboo gate opens into an outdoor sanctuary with a lava-rock pool and hot tub; at first glimpse this spa seems to have been organically grown, not built. The decor here can hardly be called decor—it's an abundant, living garden. Taro varieties, orchids, and ferns still wet from Hāna's frequent downpours nourish the spirit as you rest with a cup of jasmine tea, or take an invigorating dip in the plunge pool. Signature aromatherapy treatments utilize *Honua*, the spa's own sumptuous blend of sandalwood, coconut, ginger, and vanilla orchid essences. Daily yoga classes round out a perfectly relaxing experience. ⊠ *3850 Wailea Alanui Dr., Wailea* ☎ *808/875–1234 or 800/888–6100* ⊕ *www.hotelhanamaui.com* ☞ *$125 60-minute massage, $250 spa packages* ♨ *Hair salon, hot tubs (indoor and outdoor), sauna, steam room. Gym with: cardiovascular machines, free weights, weight-training equipment. Services: aromatherapy, body wraps, facials, hydrotherapy, massage. Classes and programs: meditation, Pilates, yoga.*

Spa Kea Lani, Fairmont Kea Lani Hotel Suites & Villas. Once one of the island's nicest, this tiny spa is scheduled for a major renovation. We anticipate great things. Until then, opt for a poolside massage—treatments by the divinely serene adult pool can be reserved on the spot. If the pool feels too exposed, we recommend the spa's Citrus Glow treatment: a private hydrotherapy treatment followed by an exfoliating massage. ⊠ *4100 Wailea Alanui Dr., Wailea* ☎ *808/875–4100 or 800/659–4100* ⊕ *www.kealani.com* ☞ *$120 55-minute massage, $295 spa packages* ♨ *Hair salon, steam room. Gym with: cardiovascular machines, free weights, weight-training equipment. Services: aromatherapy, body wraps, facials, hydrotherapy, massage, Vichy shower. Classes and programs: aquaerobics, yoga.*

Spa Moana, Hyatt Regency Maui. Spa Moana's oceanfront salon has a million-dollar view; it's a perfect place to beautify before your wedding or special anniversary. An older facility, it's still spacious and well-appointed, offering numerous innovative treatments such as the Kā'anapali Coffee Scrub or the Maui Sugar Scrub, in addition to traditional Swedish and Thai massage, reiki, and shiatsu. For body treatments, the oceanfront rooms

8

are a tad too warm—request one in back. In conjunction with Spa Moana, the Maui Wellness Institute offers two-day programs including workshops on kinesiology, feng shui, sex, and chocolate. Er . . . yum. ✉ *200 Nohea Kai Dr., Lahaina* ☎ *808/661–1234 or 800/233–1234* ⊕ *www.hyatt.com* ☞ *$150 50-minute massage, $420 all-day spa packages* ⚲ *Hair salon, hot tub, sauna, steam room. Gym with: cardiovascular machines, free weights, weight-training equipment. Services: aromatherapy, body wraps, facials, hydrotherapy, massage, Vichy shower. Classes and programs: aquaerobics, Pilates, tai chi, yoga.*

> ## BUDGET-FRIENDLY SPAS
>
> If hotel spa prices are a little intimidating, try **Spa Luna** (✉ 810 Hā'iku Rd., Hā'iku ☎ 808/575–2440), a day spa, which is also an aesthetician's school. In the former Hā'iku Cannery, it offers services ranging from massage to microdermabrasion. You can opt for professional services, but the student clinics are the real story here. The students are subject to rigorous training, and their services are offered at a fraction of the regular cost ($25 for a 50-minute massage).

★ **The Spa at the Westin Maui.** An exquisite 80-minute Lavender Body Butter treatment is the star of this spa's menu, thanks to a partnership with a local lavender farm. Other options include cabana massage (for couples, too) and water lily sunburn relief with green tea. The brand-new facility is flawless, and it's worth getting a treatment just to sip lavender lemonade in the posh oceanview waiting room (it's coed, so keep your robe tightly tied). The open-air yoga studio and the gym offer energizing workouts. Bridal parties can request a private area within the salon. ✉ *Westin Kā'anapali, 2365 Kā'anapali Pkwy., Kā'anapali* ☎ *808/667–2525* ⊕ *www.westinmaui.com* ☞ *$115 50-minute massage, $137–$411 day spa packages* ⚲ *Hair salon, hot tub, sauna, steam room. Gym with: cardiovascular machines, free weights, weight-training equipment. Services: aromatherapy, body wraps, facials, hydrotherapy, massage, Vichy shower. Classes and programs: aquaerobics, yoga.*

Waihua, Ritz-Carlton, Kapalua. If the stress of traveling has fried your nerves (or even if it hasn't), book a Waihua signature treatment such as "Harmony" or "Family Relations," which employs aromatherapy, hot stones, and massage. High-quality, handcrafted products enhance treatments inspired by Hawaiian culture, such as the *lomi lomi* massage with healing plant essences followed by a salt foot scrub. The newly refurbished facility lacks some of the other spas' amenities but does offer superb services and a well-stocked boutique. Attention fitness junkies: personal DVD players are attached to the state-of-the-art cardiovascular machines. ✉ *1 Ritz-Carlton Dr., Kapalua* ☎ *808/669–6200 or 800/262–8440* ⊕ *www.ritzcarlton.com* ☞ *$120 60-minute massage, $320 half-day spa packages* ⚲ *Hair salon, sauna, steam room. Gym with: cardiovascular machines, free weights, weight-training equipment. Services: aromatherapy, body wraps, facials, massage. Classes and programs: aquaerobics, nutrition, yoga.*

Entertainment & Nightlife

WORD OF MOUTH

"We also went to the Feast at Lele and would give it thumbs up! We decided on the Feast because we wanted a table to ourselves and no buffet. The food was very good and the show was excellent. You will not be disappointed with this lū'au."

–Spikeit

"Mulligan's is an Irish pub, notable for its live entertainment, which we enjoyed immensely."

–Iregeo

By Elaine Gast   **LOOKING FOR WILD ISLAND NIGHTLIFE?** We can't promise you'll always find it here. This quiet island has little of Waikīkī's after-hours decadence, and the club scene (if you want to call it that) can be quirky, depending on the season and the day of the week. But sometimes Maui will surprise you with a big-name concert, outdoor festival, or special event, and it seems the whole island usually shows up for the party.

Before 10 PM, there's a lot to offer by way of lūʻau shows, dinner cruises, and tiki-lighted cocktail hours. Aside from that, you should at least be able to find some down-home DJ-spinning or the strum of acoustic guitars at your nearest watering hole. Lahaina and Kīhei are your best bets for action. Lahaina tries to uphold its reputation as a party town, and succeeds every Halloween when thousands of masqueraders converge for a Mardi Gras–style party on Front Street. Kīhei is a bit more local, and in parts, can be something of a rough and rowdy crowd. On the right night, both towns stir with activity, and if you don't like one scene, there's always next door.

Outside of Lahaina and Kīhei, you might be able to hit an "on" night in Pāʻia (North Shore) or Makawao (Upcountry), mostly on weekend nights. Your best bet? Pick up the free *Maui Time Weekly*, or Thursday's edition of the *Maui News*, where you'll find a listing of all your after-dark options, island-wide.

★ The **Maui Arts & Cultural Center** (✉ 1 Cameron Way, near harbor on Kahului Beach Rd. ☎ 808/242–2787) is the hub of all high-brow arts and quality performances. Their events calendar features everything from rock to reggae to Hawaiian slack key, international dance and circus troupes, political and literary lectures, art films, cult classics—you name it. Each Wednesday (and occasionally Friday) evenings, the MACC (as it's locally known) hosts movie selections from the Maui Film Festival. The complex includes the 1,200-seat Castle Theater, a 4,000-seat amphitheater for large outdoor concerts, the 350-seat McCoy Theater for plays and recitals, and a courtyard café offering preshow dining and drinks. For information on current events, check the **Events Box Office** (☎ 808/242–7469) or the *Maui News*.

ENTERTAINMENT

Lūʻau

A trip to Hawaiʻi isn't complete without a good lūʻau. With the beat of drums and the sway of hula, lūʻau give you a snippet of Hawaiian culture left over from a long-standing tradition. Early Hawaiians celebrated many occasions with lūʻau—weddings, births, battles, and more. The feasts originally brought people together as an offering to the gods, and to practice *hoʻokipa*, the act of welcoming guests. The word *lūʻau* itself refers to the taro root, a staple of the Hawaiian diet, which, when pounded, makes a grey, puddinglike substance called poi. You'll find poi at all the best feasts, along with platters of salty fish, fresh fruit, and kālua pork.

Lū'au are still held by locals today to mark milestones or as informal, family-style gatherings. For tourists, they are a major attraction, and for that reason, have become big business. Keep in mind—some are watered-down tourist traps just trying to make a buck, others offer a night you'll never forget. As the saying goes, you get what you pay for. ■ TIP→ Many of the best lū'au book weeks, sometimes months, in advance, so reserve early. Plan your lū'au night early on in your trip to help you get into the Hawaiian spirit.

★ **The Feast at Lele.** "Lele" is an older, more traditional name for Lahaina. This feast redefines the lū'au by crossing it with island-style fine dining in an intimate beach setting. Each course of this succulent sit-down meal expresses the spirit of specific island culture—Hawaiian, Samoan, Tongan, Tahitian—and don't forget dessert. Dramatic Polynesian entertainment accompanies the dinner, along with excellent wine and liquor selections. This is the most expensive lū'au on the island for a reason: Lele is top-notch. ⊠ *505 Front St., Lahaina* ☎ *808/667–5353* ⚑ *Reservations essential* ⊕ *www.feastatlele.com* ⚐ *$99 adult, $69 child* ☉ *Nightly at sunset; 5:30 PM in winter, 6:00 PM in summer.*

Fodor'sChoice **Old Lahaina Lū'au.** Many consider this the best lū'au on Maui; it's certainly the most traditional. Located right on the water, at the northern end of town, the Old Lahaina Lū'au is small, personal, and as authentic as it gets. Sitting either at a table or on a *lauhala* mat, you'll dine on all-you-can-eat Hawaiian cuisine: pork *lau lau*, 'ahi poke, *lomi lomi* salmon, Maui-style mahimahi, *haupia* (coconut pudding), and more. At sunset the show begins a historical journey that relays key periods in Hawai'i's history, from the arrival of the Polynesians to the influence of the missionaries and, later, tourism. The tanned, talented performers will charm you with their music, chanting, and variety of hula styles (modern and *kahiko*, the ancient way of communicating with the gods). But if it's fire dancers you want to see, you won't find them here, as they aren't considered traditional. Although it's performed nightly, this lū'au sells out regularly. Make your reservations when planning your trip to Maui. You can cancel up until 10 AM the day of the scheduled show. ⊠ *1251 Front St., makai of Lahaina Cannery Mall, Lahaina* ☎ *808/667–1998* ⚑ *Reservations essential* ⊕ *www.oldlahainaluau.com* ⚐ *$85 adult, $55 child* ☉ *Nightly at 5:15 PM in winter, 5:45 PM in summer.*

Outrigger Marriott Lū'au. Right next door to the Renaissance, you'll find the Outrigger lū'au—a show of similar quality. Like its neighbor, it offers an open bar, a tasty buffet, and a sunset backdrop that can't be beat. The show features an *imu* (oven) ceremony to start, and Polynesian dancers representing Tonga, Samoa, and more. If you're lucky, the tanned, grass-skirted beauties might hand-pick you for a hula lesson on stage. ⊠ *3700 Wailea Alanui Dr.* ☎ *808/879–1922* ⚑ *Reservations essential* ⚐ *$75 adult, $35 child* ☉ *Mon., Tues., Thurs., and Fri. 4:30 PM.*

Renaissance Wailea Sunset Beach Lū'au. Held on the manicured greens of Wailea, the Renaissance offers a good show and an even better spread. You'll find an open bar and standard lū'au fare, plus some extras—kālua pork, teriyaki steak, grilled fish, and an outstanding dessert tray (try the chocolate macadamia tarts). As long as you don't mind the corny jokes, the show is festive and flashy, especially the Samoan fire-

continued on page 187

MORE THAN A FOLK DANCE

Hula has been called "the heartbeat of the Hawaiian people." Also, "the world's best-known, most misunderstood dance." Both true. Hula isn't just dance. It is storytelling. No words, no hula.

Chanter Edith McKinzie calls it "an extension of a piece of poetry." In its adornments, implements, and customs, hula integrates every important Hawaiian cultural practice: poetry, history, genealogy, craft, plant cultivation, martial arts, religion, protocol. So when 19th-century Christian missionaries sought to eradicate a practice they considered depraved, they threatened more than just a folk dance.

With public performance outlawed and private hula practice discouraged, hula went underground for a generation, to rural villages. The fragile verbal link by which culture was transmitted from teacher to student hung by a thread. Even increasing literacy did not help because hula's practitioners were—and, to a degree, still are—a secretive and protected circle.

As if that weren't bad enough, vaudeville, Broadway, and Hollywood got hold of the hula, giving it the glitz treatment in an unbroken line from "Oh, How She Could Wicky Wacky Woo" to "Rock-A-Hula Baby." Hula became shorthand for paradise: fragrant flowers, lazy hours. Ironically, this development assured that hundreds of Hawaiians could make a living performing and teaching hula. Many danced 'auana (modern form) in performance; but taught kahiko (traditional), quietly, at home or in hula schools.

Today, 30 years after the cultural revival known as the Hawaiian Renaissance, language immersion programs have assured a new generation of proficient–and even eloquent–chanters, song-writers, and translators. Visitors can see more, and more authentic, hula than anytime in the last 200 years.

Like the culture of which it is the beating heart, hula has survived.

Lei *po'o*. Head lei. In kahiko, greenery only. In 'auana, flowers.

Face emotes appropriate expression. Dancer should not be a smiling automaton.

Shoulders remain relaxed and still, never hunched, even with arms raised. No bouncing.

Eyes always follow leading hand.

Lei. Hula is rarely performed without a shoulder lei.

Arms and hands remain loose, relaxed, below shoulder level—except as required by interpretive movements.

Traditional hula skirt is loose fabric, smocked and gathered at the waist.

Hip is canted over weight-bearing foot.

Knees are always slightly bent, accentuating hip sway.

In kahiko, feet are flat. In 'auana, may be more arched, but not tiptoes or bouncing.

Kupe'e. Ankle bracelet of flowers, shells, or—traditionally—noise-making dog teeth.

MORE THAN A FOLK DANCE

9

BASIC MOTIONS

Speak or Sing

Moon or Sun

Grass Shack or House

Mountains or Heights

Love or Caress

At backyard parties, hula is performed in bare feet and street clothes, but in performance, adornments play a key role, as do rhythm-keeping implements.

In hula kahiko (traditional style), the usual dress is multiple layers of stiff fabric (often with a pellon lining, which most closely resembles *kapa*, the paper-like bark cloth of the Hawaiians). These wrap tightly around the bosom but flare below the waist to form a skirt. In pre-contact times, dancers wore only kapa skirts. Monarchy-period hula is performed in voluminous Mother Hubbard mu'umu'u or high-necked muslin blouses and gathered skirts. Men wear loincloths or, for monarchy period, white or gingham shirts and black pants—sometimes with red sashes.

In hula 'auana (modern), dress for women can range from grass skirts and strapless tops to contemporary tea-length dresses. Men generally wear aloha shirts, but sometimes grass skirts over pants or even everyday gear. (One group at a recent competition wore wetsuits to do a surfing song!)

SURPRISING HULA FACTS

■ Grass skirts are not traditional; workers from Kiribati (the Gilbert Islands) brought this custom to Hawai'i.

■ In olden-day Hawai'i, *mele* (songs) for hula were composed for every occasion—name songs for babies, dirges for funerals, welcome songs for visitors, celebrations of favorite pursuits.

■ Hula *ma'i* is a traditional hula form in praise of a noble's genitals; the power of the *'ali* (royalty) to procreate gave *mana* (spiritual power) to the entire culture.

■ Hula students in old Hawai'i adhered to high standards: scrupulous cleanliness, no sex, daily cleansing rituals, certain food prohibitions, and no contact with the dead. They were fined if they broke the rules.

WHERE TO WATCH

■ Kā'anapali Beach Hotel: Employees break into song at any excuse, teach daily hula lessons, and staff a free nightly hour-long hula show and torchlighting ceremony. ☎ 808/661-0011.

■ Feast of Lele: Nightly beachside lū'au includes show that strives for authenticity. ☎ 866/244-5353.

■ Whalers Village: Twice-weekly free evening hula shows (usually Wednesday and Saturday, but check schedule). ☎ 808/661-4567.

■ Hula festivals: Festival of Hula, January, Lahaina Cannery Mall; Na Mele O Maui/Emma Farden Sharpe Hula Festival, December, Kā'anapali Resort.

knife dance finale. ⊠ *3350 Wailea Alanui Dr.* ☎ *888/349–7888* ⊕ *www.renaissancewaileabeachluau.com* ⚓ *Reservations essential* ✉ *$65 adult, $30 child* ☉ *Wed. and Fri. 5:30 PM.*

Dinner & Sunset Cruises

There's no better place to see the sun set on the Pacific than from one of Maui's many boat tours. You can find a tour to fit your mood, as you can choose anything from a quiet, sit-down dinner, to a festive, beer-swigging booze cruise.

Tours leave from Māʻalaea or Lahaina harbors. Be sure to arrive at least 15 minutes early (count in the time it will take to park). The dinner cruises typically feature music and are generally packed—which is great if you're feeling social, but you might have to fight for a good seat. You can usually get a much better meal at one of the local restaurants, and opt instead for a different type of tour. Most nondinner cruises offer *pūpūs* (appetizers) and an open bar, and sometimes a chocolate and champagne toast.

Winds are consistent in summer, but variable in winter—sometimes making for a rocky ride. If you're worried about sea sickness, you might consider a catamaran, which is much more stable than a monohaul. Keep in mind, the boat crews are experienced in dealing with such matters. The best advice? Take Dramamine before the trip, and if you feel sick, sit in the shade (but not inside the cabin), place a cold rag or ice on the back of your neck, and *breathe* as you look at the horizon. In the worst-case scenario, aim downwind—and shoot for distance.

America II **Sunset Sail.** The star of this two-hour cruise is the craft itself—a 1987 America's Cup 12-meter class contender that will take you on a wild ride. This trip is all about the sail, so you can count out any cocktails or fancy food. But if it's adventure you're looking for, you will go fast, you will get wet . . . and you will have fun. Private charters available. ⊠ *Slip 6, Lahaina Harbor, Lahaina* ☎ *808/667–2195* ✉ *$38* ☉ *Daily 4–6 PM.*

Kaulana **Cocktail Cruise.** This two-hour sunset cruise prides itself on its live music and festive atmosphere. Accommodating up to 100 people, the cruise generally attracts a younger, more boisterous crowd. *Pūpūs,* such as meatballs, smoked salmon, and teriyaki pineapple, are served, and the open bar includes frozen drinks. ⊠ *Lahaina Harbor, Lahaina* ☎ *808/667–9595* ⊕ *www.kaulana-of-maui.com* ✉ *$49* ☉ *Weekdays 5–7:30 PM.*

> ### STARGAZING
>
> For nightlife of a different sort, children and astronomy buffs should try stargazing at **Tour of the Stars**, a one-hour program held nightly on the roof or patio of the Hyatt Regency Maui. **Romance of the Stars,** with champagne and chocolate-covered strawberries, is held on Friday and Saturday nights at 11. Check in at the hotel lobby 15 minutes prior to starting time. ⊠ *Lahaina Tower, Hyatt Regency Maui, 200 Nohea Kai Dr., Kāʻanapali* ☎ *808/661-1234 Ext. 4727* ✉ *$20–$25* ☉ *Nightly at 8, 9, and 10; Fri. and Sat. romantic program at 11.*

9

Pacific Whale Foundation Dinner or Cocktail Cruise. All aboard the sleek double-deck power catamaran *Ocean Quest* for a dinner of grilled steak and chicken, mahimahi, and Island Rum Macadamia Nut pie. This cruise holds up to 147 people, so it can be crowded. You might opt for the 50-foot catamaran sail on *Manute'a*, a relaxing "booze cruise," with hot and cold appetizers, live entertainment, and an open bar. ⊠ *Ocean Discovery Store, 612 Front St., Lahaina* ☎ *808/249–8811* ⊕ *www.pacificwhale.org* 🖃 *$79 dinner cruise, $49 cocktail cruise* ☉ *Daily, call for seasonal check-in times. No cocktail cruise Fri.*

Paragon Champagne Sunset Sail. This 47-foot catamaran brings you a performance sail within a personal setting. Limited to groups of 24 (with private charters available), you can spread out on deck and enjoy the gentle trade winds. An easygoing, attentive crew will serve you hot and cold pūpūs, such as grilled chicken skewers, spring rolls, and a veggie platter, along with beer, wine, mai tais, and champagne at sunset. This is one of the best trips around. ⊠ *Loading Dock, Lahaina Harbor* ☎ *808/244–2087* ⊕ *www.sailmaui.com* 🖃 *$44* ☉ *Mon., Wed., Fri. evenings only; call for check-in times.*

Pride Charters. A 65-foot catamaran built specifically for Maui's waters, the *Pride of Maui* has a spacious cabin, dance floor, and large upper deck for unobstructed viewing. Evening cruises include cocktails and a buffet of *pūpūs* such as grilled chicken, beef and veggie kebabs, and warm Asian wontons. ⊠ *Mā'alaea Harbor, Mā'alaea* ☎ *877/867–7433* ⊕ *www. prideofmaui.com* 🖃 *$47* ☉ *Tues. and Sat. 5–7:30 PM.*

Scotch Mist Charters. Sailing is at its best on this two-hour "champagne and chocolate" cruise. The 25-passenger Santa Cruz 50 sloop *Scotch Mist II* will give you an intimate and exhilarating ride. Private charters are available. ⊠ *Slip 2, Lahaina Harbor, Lahaina* ☎ *808/661–0386* ⊕ *www.scotchmistsailingcharters.com* 🖃 *$45* ☉ *Daily, call for seasonal check-in times.*

Spirit of Lahaina Cocktail or Dinner Cruise. This double-deck, 65-foot catamaran offers you a choice of a full-dinner cruise, featuring freshly grilled steak, mahimahi, and shrimp, or a cocktail cruise with appetizers, drinks, and dessert. Both cruises feature contemporary Hawaiian music and hula show. ⊠ *Slip 4, Lahaina Harbor* ☎ *808/662–4477* ⊕ *www.spiritoflahaina. com* 🖃 *$69 dinner cruise, $49 cocktail cruise* ☉ *Daily 5–7:15 PM.*

Film & Theater

In the heat of the afternoon, a theater may feel like paradise. There are megaplexes showing first-run movies in Kukui Mall (Kīhei), Lahaina Center, and Maui Mall and Ka'ahumanu Shopping Center (Kahului). For live theater, check local papers for events and showtimes.

Maui Academy of Performing Arts. For a quarter-century, this nonprofit performing arts group has offered fine productions, as well as dance and drama classes for children and adults. Recent shows have included *Peter Pan*, the *Complete Works of William Shakespeare*, and the *Wizard of Oz*. Call ahead for performance venue. ⊠ *2027 Main St., Wailuku* ☎ *808/244–8760* ⊕ *www.mauiacademy.org* 🖃 *$10–$12.*

★ **Maui Film Festival.** In this ongoing celebration, the Maui Arts & Cultural Center features art-quality films every Wednesday (and sometimes Friday) evening at 5 and 7:30 PM, accompanied by live music, dining, and poetry in the Candlelight Café. In summer an international weeklong festival attracts big-name celebrities to Maui for cinema under the stars. ☎ 808/ 572–3456 recorded program information ⊕ www.mauifilmfestival.com.

Maui OnStage. Located at the Historic 'Iao Theater, this nonprofit theater group stages four to six shows per season. Look for upcoming productions such as *Seussical* and *Go-Go Beach*. Each October, they hold an "Evening of Stars" Masquerade Ball, which can be a hoot of the costumed kind. ⊠ 'Iao Theatre, 68 N. Market St., Wailuku ☎ 808/242– 6969 🎫 Musicals $10–$15, nonmusicals $8–$13.

★☾ **"Ulalena" at Maui Theater.** One of Maui's hottest tickets, "'Ulalena" is a 75-minute musical extravaganza that is well received by audiences and Hawaiian-culture experts alike. Cirque de Soleil–inspired, the ensemble cast (20 singer-dancers and a five-musician orchestra) mixes native rhythms and stories with acrobatic performance. High-tech stage wizardry gives an inspiring introduction to island culture. It has auditorium seating, and beer and wine are for sale at the concession stand. There are dinner-theater packages in conjunction with top Lahaina restaurants. ⊠ 878 Front St., Lahaina ☎ 808/661–9913 or 877/688–4800 ⚓ Reservations essential 🎫 $48–$68 ☉ Tues.–Sat. at 6:30 PM.

Warren & Annabelle's. This is one show not to miss—it's serious comedy with an amazing sleight-of-hand. Magician Warren Gibson entices his guests into his swank nightclub with red carpets and a gleaming mahogany bar, and plies them with à la carte appetizers (coconut shrimp, crab cakes), desserts (rum cake, crème brûlée), and "smoking cocktails." Then, he performs tableside magic while his ghostly assistant, Annabelle, tickles the ivories. This is a nightclub, so no one under 21 is allowed. ⊠ Lahaina Center, 900 Front St. ☎ 808/667–6244 ⚓ Reservations essential 🎫 $45 or $75, including food and drinks ☉ Mon.–Sat. at 5.

BARS & CLUBS

Your best bet when it comes to bars on Maui? If you walk by and it sounds like it's happening, go in. If you want to scope out your options in advance, be sure to check the free *Maui Time Weekly,* found at most stores and restaurants, to find out who's playing where. The *Maui News* also publishes an entertainment schedule in its Thursday edition of the "Maui Scene." With an open mind (and a little luck), you can usually find a good scene for fun.

> **MAUI MIDNIGHT**
>
> If you want to see any action on Maui, head out early. Otherwise, you might be out past what locals call "Maui Midnight," where as early as 9 PM the restaurants close and the streets empty. What can you expect, though, when most people wake up with the sun? After a long, salty day of sea and surf, you might be ready for some shut-eye yourself.

West Maui

Cheeseburger in Paradise. This Front Street joint is known for—what else?—big beefy cheeseburgers (not to mention a great spinach-nut burger). This is a casual place to start your evening, as they usually have live music and big, fruity cocktails for happy hour. There's no dance floor, but the second-floor balcony gives you a bird's-eye view of Lahaina's Front Street action. ⊠ *811 Front St., Lahaina* ☎ *808/ 661–4855.*

Hard Rock Cafe. You've seen one Hard Rock Cafe, you've seen them all. However, Maui's Hard Rock brings you Reggae Monday, featuring our beloved local reggae star Marty Dread. $5 cover, 10 PM. ⊠ *Lahaina Center, 900 Front St., Lahaina* ☎ *808/667–7400.*

> ### MAI TAI
>
> Don't let your sweet tooth fool you. Maui's favorite drink—the mai tai—can be as lethal as it is sweet. The Original Trader Vic's recipe calls for 2 ounces of aged dark rum, mixed with almond syrup, orange curaçao, the juice of one lime, and (wouldn't you know it) rock candy syrup. Mama's Fish House on the North Shore, makes the best-tasting mai tai in town. Of course, in its lush, old-Hawai'i setting, Mama's could make just about any drink taste good.

Longhi's. This upscale, open-air restaurant is the spot on Friday nights, when there's usually live music and a bumping dance floor. Here you'll mingle with what locals call Maui's beautiful people, so be sure to dress your casual best. $5 cover, 10 PM. ⊠ *Lahaina Center, 888 Front St., next to Hard Rock Cafe, Lahaina* ☎ *808/667–2288.*

Moose McGillycuddy's. The Moose offers no-cover live or DJ music on most nights, drawing a young, mostly single crowd who come for the burgers, beer, and dance floor beats. ⊠ *844 Front St., Lahaina* ☎ *808/ 667–7758.*

Pacific'O. Looking to stare longingly into your beloved's eyes? This is your place. This exclusive restaurant and martini bar brings you live jazz, right on the beach, from 9 to midnight on weekend nights. Guest musicians—George Benson, for example—sometimes sit in. ⊠ *505 Front St., Lahaina* ☎ *808/667–4341.*

★ **Paradice Bluz.** Live local bands and comedians frequent the stage at this popular, underground West Side hangout. This place is as close to a real night club as you'll find in Lahaina. It's dark and smoky, with a swanky lounge area, pool tables, and a decent lineup of bands and DJs. Expect to pay a hefty cover ($12–$20). ⊠ *744 Front St., Lahaina* ☎ *808/667– 5299.*

The Sly Mongoose. Off the beaten tourist path, the Sly Mongoose is the seediest dive bar in town, and one of the friendliest. The bartender will know your name and half your life history inside of 10 minutes, and she makes the strongest mai tai on the island. ⊠ *1036 Limahana Pl., Lahaina* ☎ *808/661–8097.*

The South Shore

Hāpa's Brewhaus & Restaurant. You can almost never go wrong with Hāpa's. Famed local performer Willi K. owns Monday nights at this club, which has a large stage, a roomy dance floor, good sound, and a wild array of spinning disco lights. The place gets packed on other nights as well, offering a constant influx of hip-hop, reggae, sometimes even punk and metal. Tuesday is Ultra Fab techno night (gay-friendly), and Wednesday is half-price ladies night. When it's not crowded, there's always televised sports and tasty brews. ⊠ *Lipoa Center, 41 E. Lipoa St., Kīhei* ☎ *808/879-9001.*

Kahale's Beach Club. A friendly, casual dive bar, Kahale's offers live music (usually Hawaiian), drinks, and burgers every day from 10 AM until 2 in the morning. If the place is empty, try the Tiki Bar or Lulu's next door. ⊠ *36 Keala Pl., Kīhei* ☎ *808/875-7711.*

> ## WHAT'S A LAVA FLOW?
>
> Can't decide between a pina colada or strawberry daiquiri? Go with a Lava Flow—a mix of light rum, coconut and pineapple juice, and a banana, with a swirl of strawberry puree. Add a wedge of fresh pineapple and a paper umbrella, and mmm . . . good. Try one at Lulu's in Kīhei.

Life's a Beach. This place brings in a young, rambunctious bunch looking to par-tay (read: meat market). But hey, if you dig lingerie contests and half-price Jagermeister shots, who are we to judge? Friday and Saturday is live music, Sunday is karaoke. ⊠ *1913 S. Kīhei Rd., Kīhei* ☎ *808/891-8010.*

Lulu's. Lulu's could be your favorite bar in any beach town. It's a second-story, open-air tiki and sports bar, with a pool table, small stage, and dance floor to boot. The most popular night is Salsa Thursday, with dancing and lessons until 11. Friday is country night; Saturday is house. ⊠ *1945 S. Kīhei Rd., Kīhei* ☎ *808/879-9944.*

★ **Mulligan's on the Blue.** Frothy pints of Guinness and late-night fish-and-chips—who could ask for more? Sunday nights feature foot-stomping Irish jams that will have you dancing a jig, and singing something about "a whiskey for me-johnny." Twice weekly, Mulligan's also brings you the more mellow *Wailea Nights,* an inspired dinner show performed by members of the band "Hapa." ⊠ *Blue Golf Course, 100 Kaukahi St., Wailea* ☎ *808/874-1131.*

Tsunami's. Located in one of Maui's most elite resorts, Tsunami's scene feels chic and electric. You can dance to DJ hip-hop, house, techno, and Top 40—or occasional live music. The place packs in a sophisticated crowd that spins on the dance floor under laser beam lights. Weekend nights are the best, from 9:30 to 1. The dress code is strictly enforced—no jeans or shirts without a collar. $10 cover. ⊠ *Grand Wailea, 3850 Wailea Alanui Dr., Wailea* ☎ *808/875-1234.*

Upcountry & the North Shore

Casanova Italian Restaurant & Deli. Casanova can bring in some big acts, which in the past have included Kool and the Gang, Los Lobos, and Taj Majal. Most Friday and Saturday nights, though, it attracts a hip, local scene with live bands and eclectic DJs spinning house, funk, and world music. Don't miss the costume theme nights. Wednesday is for Wild Wahines (code for ladies drink half price), which can be more on the smarmy side. Cover $5–$15. ⊠ *1188 Makawao Ave., Makawao* ☎ *808/572-0220.*

Charley's. The closest thing to country Maui has to offer, Charley's is a down-home, divey bar in the heart of Pā'ia. It recently expanded its offerings to include disco, house, industry, and lounge nights. If you're lucky, you might even see Willy Nelson hanging here. ✉ *142 Hāna Hwy., Pāʻia* ☎ *808/579–9453.*

Jacques. Jacques was once voted by locals as the "best place to see suspiciously beautiful people from around the world." On Friday nights, the crowd spills onto the cozy streets of Pāʻia, as funky DJs spin latino, world lounge, salsa, and live jazz. ✉ *120 Hāna Hwy., Pāʻia* ☎ *808/ 579–8844.*

Moloka'i

WORD OF MOUTH

"It was a beautiful experience, and we really didn't do anything. Beautifully boring. We walked to the beach twice a day . . . read our books a lot, walked a lot, played golf once, looked for whales, talked to a few people . . . and just hung out. I'd go again in a heartbeat."

—pdx

WELCOME TO MOLOKA'I

TOP 5
Reasons to Go

1. **Kalaupapa Peninsula:** Hike or take a mule ride down the world's tallest sea cliffs to a fascinating, historic community.

2. **Biking Single-Track Trails at Moloka'i Ranch:** A complex network of trails offers some of the best mountain-bike experiences in the world.

3. **Deep-Sea Fishing:** Big sport fish are plentiful in these waters, as are gorgeous views of several islands.

4. **Nature:** Deep valleys, sheer cliffs, and the untamed ocean are the main attractions on Moloka'i.

5. **Pāpōhaku Beach:** This 3-mi stretch of sand is one of the most sensational beaches in all of Hawai'i.

■ **TIP→→** Directions on the island are often given as *mauka* (toward the mountains) and *makai* (toward the ocean).

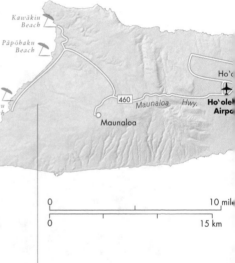

Kawākiu Beach

Pāpōhaku Beach

Kapukahehu Beach

460   Maunaloa   Hwy.

Maunaloa

Ho'ole

Ho'ole
Airpo

| 0 | | 10 mile |
| 0 | | 15 km |

The most arid part of the island, the West End has two inhabited areas: the coastal stretch includes a few condos and luxury homes, and the largest beaches on the island. Nearby, the hilltop hamlet of Maunaloa boasts the finest accommodation on the island, the Lodge at Moloka'i Ranch.

Getting Oriented

Shaped like a long bone, Moloka'i is only about 10 mi wide on average, and four times that long. The North Shore thrusts up from the sea to form the tallest sea-cliffs on Earth, while the South Shore slides almost flat into the water, then fans out to form the largest shallow-water reef system in the United States. Surprisingly, the highest point on Moloka'i rises only to about 4,000 feet.

The island's only true town, Kaunakakai, with its mile-long wharf, lies in Central Moloka'i. Nearly all the island's eateries and stores are in or close to Kaunakakai. Highway 470 crosses the center of the island, rising to the top of the sea-cliffs and the Kalaupapa overlook.

The scenic drive around the East End passes through the green pastures of Pu'u O Hoku Ranch and climaxes with a descent into Hālawa Valley. The farther east you go, the lusher the island gets.

MOLOKA'I PLANNER

What You Won't Find on Moloka'i

Moloka'i is a great place to be outdoors. And that's a good thing, because with only about 7,000 residents Moloka'i has very little of what you would call "indoors." There are no tall buildings, no traffic lights, no street lights, no stores bearing the names of national chains, and almost nothing at all like a resort. Among the Hawaiian Islands, Moloka'i has distinguished itself as the one least interested in attracting tourists. At night the whole island grows dark, creating a velvety blackness and a wonderful, rare thing called silence.

Where to Stay

Moloka'i appeals most to travelers who appreciate genuine Hawaiian hospitality rather than swanky digs. Aside from the upscale Lodge at Moloka'i Ranch, most hotel and condominium properties range from adequate to funky. Visitors who want to lollygag on the beach should choose one of the condos or home rentals at the West End. Locals tend to choose Hotel Moloka'i, located seaside just 2 mi from Kaunakakai, with its on-site restaurant, bar, and live music. Travelers who want to immerse themselves in the spirit of the island should seek out a bed-and-breakfast or cottage, the closer to the East End the better.

Additional planning details are listed in Moloka'i Essentials at the end of this chapter.

Timing Is Everything

If you're keen to explore Moloka'i's beaches, coral beds, or fishponds, summer is your best bet for non-stop calm seas and sunny skies. For a real taste of Hawaiian culture, plan your visit around a festival. In January, islanders and visitors compete in ancient Hawaiian games at the Ka Moloka'i Makahiki Festival. The Moloka'i Ka Hula Piko, an annual daylong event in May, draws the state's premiere hula troupes, musicians, and storytellers to perform. The Festival of Lights includes an Electric Light Parade down the main street of Kaunakakai in December. While never crowded, the island is busier during these events—book accommodations and transportation six months in advance.

Will It Rain?

Moloka'i's weather mimics that of the other islands: mid- to low 80s year-round, slightly rainier during winter. Because the island's accommodations are clustered at low elevation or along the leeward coast, warm weather is a dependable constant for visitors (only 15 to 20 inches of rain fall each year on the coastal plain). As you travel up the mountainside, the weather changes with bursts of forest-building downpours.

Cell Phones and the Internet

Communication with the outside world is a real challenge on Moloka'i. Most of the island lies outside the range of cell-phone service. Even regular telephone service, at Hotel Moloka'i for example, can be unreliable. Travelers who absolutely need to stay in touch with home or the office should get a room at the Lodge at Moloka'i Ranch.

EXPLORING MOLOKA'I

By Paul Wood
Updated by
Joana Varawa

The first thing to do on Moloka'i is to drive everywhere. It's a feat you can accomplish in less than a day. Basically you have one 40-mi west-to-east highway (two lanes, no stop lights) with three side trips: the little West End town of Maunaloa; the Highway 470 drive (just a few miles) to the top of the North Shore and the overlook of Kalaupapa Peninsula; and the short stretch of shops in Kaunakakai town. After you learn the general lay of the land, you can return for in-depth experiences on foot.

West Moloka'i

The region is largely made up of the 53,000-acre Moloka'i Ranch. The rolling pastures and farmlands are presided over by Maunaloa, a sleepy little plantation town with a dormant volcano of the same name. West Moloka'i has another claim to fame: Pāpōhaku, the island's best beach.

▌ A GOOD
DRIVE

This driving tour focuses on two of Moloka'i's tourist areas. If you're approaching the west end from Kaunakakai on Route 460 (also called Maunaloa Highway), turn right at mile marker 15 down Kaluako'i Road and right again at the sign for **Kaluako'i Hotel and Golf Club ❶** ▶. Take time to enjoy the grounds and the beach.

Back behind the wheel, turn right out of Kaluako'i Hotel and Golf Club and follow Kaluako'i Road 2 mi west until it dead-ends. This shoreline drive takes you past a number of lovely parks, including **Pāpōhaku Beach ❷**, the largest white-sand beach on the island. Look for a big sign on the side of the road.

Turn around and follow Kaluako'i Road back past the resort entrance, and continue uphill to the intersection with Route 460. Turn right and drive 2 mi on Route 460 (Maunaloa Highway) to **Maunaloa ❸**, a former plantation town that was torn down and replaced with—guess what—buildings resembling a plantation town. This hamlet is headquarters for Moloka'i Ranch, site of the island's one movie theater and its one resortlike accommodation, the rustic-elegant Lodge at Moloka'i Ranch. The Lodge is home to a colorful kite factory; it's the starting point for some of Hawaii's best mountain-bike trails; and it's the portal to luxurious Kaupoa Campground and beautifully derelict Hale O Lono Harbor. Food and gas are available here, too.

10

TIMING

If you follow this excursion at a leisurely Moloka'i pace, it will take you the better part of a day, particularly if your accommodations are not on the West End. A walk around Kaluako'i Hotel and Golf Club can take an hour or more.

Another hour can fly by at Pāpōhaku Beach as you dig your toes in its sands and picnic on its shady grassy area. Allow one hour for exploring Maunaloa's main street to shop for souvenirs and chat with local shop owners. Don't try to do your shopping on Sunday, or you may find many CLOSED signs on the doors.

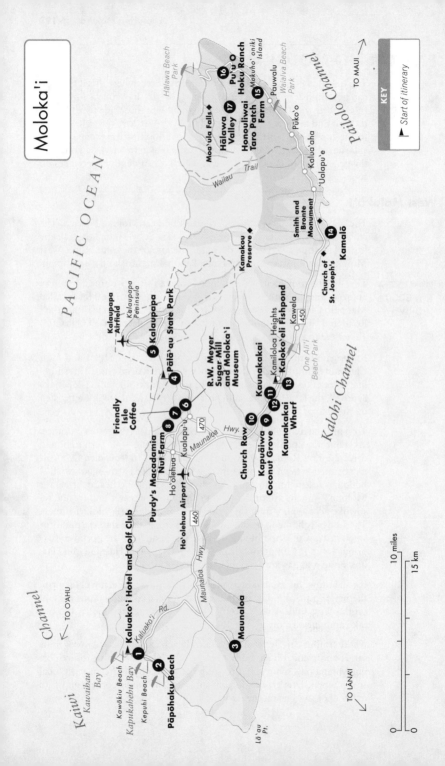

Moloka'i

PACIFIC OCEAN

Kaiwi Channel

TO OAHU

Kawākiu Bay
Kawākiu Beach
Kapukahehu Bay
Kepuhi Beach

1 Kaluako'i Hotel and Golf Club

Kaluako'i Rd.

2 Pāpōhaku Beach

Lā'au Pt.

TO LĀNA'I

3 Maunaloa

Maunaloa Hwy.

Maunaloa Hwy.

460

Ho'olehua Airport

Ho'olehua

Purdy's Macadamia Nut Farm

470

Kualapu'u

Friendly Isle Coffee

8 **7** **1**
6

Kalaupapa Airfield

Kalaupapa Peninsula

5 Kalaupapa

4 Pālā'au State Park

R.W. Meyer Sugar Mill and Moloka'i Museum

Kamakou Preserve

Wailau Trail

Moa'ula Falls ◆

17 Hālawa Valley

Hālawa Beach Park

16 Pu'u O Hoku Ranch

15 Honouliwai Taro Patch Farm

Mokuho'oniki Island

Pāwalu

Waialua Beach Park

Pūko'o

Kalua'aha

'Uolapu'e

Smith and Bronte Monument ◆

14 Kamalō
Church of St. Joseph's ◆

Kamiloloa Heights

10 Church Row

9 Kapuāiwa Coconut Grove

11 Kaunakakai

12
13 Kaloko'eli Fishpond

Kaunakakai Wharf

Kawela

450

One Ali'i Beach Park

Kalohi Channel

Pailolo Channel

TO MAUI

KEY

▲ Start of itinerary

0 — 10 miles

0 — 15 km

What to See

► ❶ **Kaluako'i Hotel and Golf Club.** This late-1960s resort passed through several owners, and the hotel itself is now closed, awaiting its next incarnation. Some very nice condos are still operating here, however. Stroll the grounds—an impressive 6,700 acres of beachfront property, including the newly revived golf course and 5 mi of coastline. ⊠ *Kaluako'i Rd., Maunaloa* ☎ *808/552–2555 or 888/552–2550.*

★ ❸ **Maunaloa.** This sleepy town was developed in 1923 to support the island's pineapple plantation. Although the fields of golden fruit have gone fallow, some of the workers' dwellings still stand, anchoring the west end of Moloka'i. Colorful local characters run the half-dozen businesses (including a kite shop and an eclectic old market) along the town's short main street. This is also the headquarters for Moloka'i Ranch. ⊠ *Western end of Maunaloa Hwy., Rte. 460.*

❷ **Pāpōhaku Beach.** The most splendid stretch of white sand on Moloka'i, Pāpōhaku is also the island's largest beach—it stretches 3 mi along the western shore. Even on busier days you're likely to see only a handful of other people. If the waves are up, swimming is dangerous. ⊠ *Kaluako'i Rd.; 2 mi beyond Kaluako'i Hotel and Golf Club.*

GUIDED TOURS

Moloka'i Off-Road Tours and Taxi. Visit Hālawa Valley, Kalaupapa Lookout, Maunaloa town, and other points of interest in the comfort of an air-conditioned van on four- or six-hour tours. Pat and Alex Pua'a, your personal guides, will even help you mail a coconut back home. Tours start at $85 per person and usually begin at 9 AM. Charters are also available. ☎ *808/553-3369.*

Central Moloka'i

Most residents live central, near the island's one and only true town, Kaunakakai. It's just about the only place on the island to get food and supplies. It *is* Moloka'i. Go into the shops along and around Ala Mālama Street. Buy stuff. Talk with people. You'll learn the difference between being a tourist and being a visitor.

A GOOD DRIVE

Drive north on Route 470 until it ends at **Pālā'au State Park** ❹ ►, where you can admire knockout views of **Kalaupapa** ❺ and the Kalaupapa Peninsula. Bring along a light jacket for cooler upland weather in fall and winter.

On the way back down the hill on Route 470, stop at the **R. W. Meyer Sugar Mill and Moloka'i Museum** ❻ to see photos and machinery from earlier times. Then turn right on Farrington Highway to visit the little town of Kualapu'u, where **Friendly Isle Coffee** ❼ has a plantation store and espresso bar and offers tours of its coffee fields and processing plant. A five-minute drive west takes you to **Purdy's Macadamia Nut Farm** ❽ in Ho'olehua.

Head back on Farrington Highway, and then take a right onto Route 470; go down the rest of the hill and turn left on Route 460. Near the

10

ocean on Route 460 are two stops of note that are practically right across the road from each other: **Kapuāiwa Coconut Grove** ❾ and **Church Row** ❿. Follow Route 460 east to reach **Kaunakakai** ⓫, Moloka'i's "big city." **Kaunakakai Wharf** ⓬ is the home base for deep-sea fishing excursions and other aqua adventures.

TIMING Get into the Moloka'i rhythm and take a full day to explore the highlands and the town. Drive up to the top of the road and walk the easy forest trails to the Kalaupapa Lookout and the phallic stone. On the way down the hill stop for an hour each at the historic sugar mill, the macadamia farm, and the coffee plantation. Then hit Kaunakakai and indulge yourself. ■ TIP➔ Don't forget that Central Moloka'i (except for a few restaurants) closes at sunset and all day Sunday.

If you take the mule ride to Kalaupapa, you should still have the time (if not the grit) to stop at some interesting sites listed in the tour after you dismount.

What to See

❿ **Church Row.** Standing together along the highway are several houses of worship with primarily native Hawaiian congregations. Notice the unadorned, boxlike style of architecture so similar to missionary homes. ⊠ *Mauka (toward the mountains) side of Rte. 460, 5½ mi southwest of airport.*

❼ **Friendly Isle Coffee.** Visit the headquarters of a 500-acre plantation of Moloka'i coffee. The espresso bar serves java in artful ways, sandwiches, and *liliko'i* (passion fruit) cheesecake. The gift shop offers a wide range of Moloka'i handicrafts and memorabilia, and, of course, coffee. ⊠ *Farrington Hwy., off Rte. 470, Kualapu'u* ☎ *800/709–2326 or 808/567–9023* ⊕ *www.molokaicoffee.com.*

❺ Kalaupapa, "A Tale of Tragedy & Triumph **See Page 201**

❾ **Kapuāiwa Coconut Grove.** At first glance this looks like a sea of coconut trees. Close-up you can see that the tall, stately palms are planted in long rows leading down to the sea. This is one of the last surviving royal groves planted by Prince Lot, who ruled Hawai'i as King Kamehameha V from 1863 until his death in 1872. Watch for falling coconuts; protect your head and your car. ⊠ *Makai side of Rte. 460, 5½ mi south of airport.*

FodorśChoice ★

★ ⓫ **Kaunakakai.** Kaunakakai looks like an Old West movie set. Along the one-block main drag is a cultural grab bag of restaurants and shops. People are friendly and willing to supply directions. The preferred dress is shorts and a tank top, and no one wears anything fancier than a mu'umu'u or aloha shirt. ⊠ *Rte. 460, about 3 blocks north of Kaunakakai Wharf.*

Continued on page 205

Father Damien's Church, St. Philomena

A TALE OF TRAGEDY & TRIUMPH

For those who crave drama, there is no better destination than Mokoka'i's Kalaupapa Peninsula—but it wasn't always so. For 100 years this remote strip of land was "the loneliest place on earth," a feared place of exile for those suffering from leprosy (now known as Hansen's Disease).

The world's tallest sea cliffs, rain-chiseled valleys, and tiny islets dropped like exclamation points along the coast emphasize the passionate history of the Kalaupapa Peninsula. Today, it's impossible to visit this stunning National Historic Park and view the evidence of human ignorance and heroism without responding. You'll be tugged by emotions—awe and disbelief for starters. But you'll also glimpse humorous facets of every day life in a small town. Whatever your experience here may be, chances are you'll return home feeling that the journey to present-day Kalaupapa is one you'll never forget.

THE SETTLEMENT'S EARLY DAYS

Father Damien with patients outside St. Philomena church.

IN 1865, PRESSURED BY FOREIGN RESIDENTS, the Hawaiian Kingdom passed "An Act to Prevent the Spread of Leprosy." Anyone showing symptoms of the disease was to be permanently exiled to Kalawao, the north end of Kalaupapa Peninsula—a spot walled in on three sides by nearly impassable cliffs. The peninsula had been home to a fishing community for 900 years, but those inhabitants were evicted and the entire peninsula declared settlement land.

The first 12 patients were arrested and sent to Kalawao in 1866. People of all ages and many nationalities followed, taken from their homes and unceremoniously dumped on the isolated shore. Officials thought the patients could become self-sufficient, fishing and farming sweet potatoes in the stream-fed valleys. That was not the case. Settlement conditions were deplorable.

Father Damien, a Belgian missionary, was one of four priests who volunteered to serve the leprosy settlement at Kalawao on a rotating basis. His turn came first; when it was up, he refused to leave. He is credited with turning the settlement from a merciless exile to a place where hope could be heard in the voices of his recruited choir. He organized the building of the St. Philomena church, nearly 300 houses, and a home for boys. A vocal advocate for his adopted community, he pestered the church for supplies, administered medicine, and oversaw the nearly daily funerals. Sixteen years after his arrival, in 1889, he died from the effects of leprosy, having contracted the disease during his service. Known around the world for his sacrifice, Father Damien was beatified by the Catholic Church in 1995, achieving the first step toward Sainthood.

Mother Marianne heard of the mission while working at a hospital in Syracuse, New York. Along with six other Franciscan Sisters, she volunteered to work with those with leprosy in the Islands. They sailed to the desolate Kalaupapa Peninsula in November of 1888. Like the Father, the Sisters were considered saints for their tireless work. Mother Marianne stayed at Kalaupapa until her death in 1918; she was beatified by the Catholic Church in 2005.

VISITING KALAUPAPA TODAY

Kalaupapa Peninsula

FROZEN IN TIME, Kalaupapa's one-horse town has unbeatable charm. Signs posted here and there remind residents when the bank will be open (once monthly), where to pick up lost sunglasses, and what's happening at the tiny town bar. The town has the nostalgic, almost naive ambience expected from a place almost wholly segregated from modern life.

About 30 former patients remain at Kalaupapa (by choice, as the disease is controlled by drugs and the patients are no longer carriers), but many travel frequently to other parts of the world and all are over the age of 60. Richard Marks, the town sheriff and owner of Damien Tours, will likely retire soon, as will the elderly postmistress. They haven't, however, lost their chutzpah. Having survived a lifetime of prejudice and misunderstanding, Kalaupapa's residents aren't willing to be pushed around any longer—several recently made the journey to Honolulu to ask for the removal of a "rude and insensitive" superintendent.

To get a feel for what their lives were like, visit the National Park Service Web site (⊕ www.nps.gov/kala/docs/start.htm) or buy one of several heartbreaking memoirs at the park's library-turned-bookstore.

THE TRUTH ABOUT HANSEN'S DISEASE

■ A cure for leprosy has been available since 1941. Multi-drug therapy, a rapid cure, has been available since 1981.

■ With treatment, none of the disabilities traditionally associated with leprosy need occur.

■ Most people have a natural immunity to leprosy. Only 5% of the world's population is even susceptible to the disease.

■ There are still about 500,000 new cases of leprosy each year, at least two-thirds are in India.

■ All new cases of leprosy are treated on an outpatient basis.

■ The term "leper" is offensive and should not be used. It is appropriate to say "a person is affected by leprosy" or "by Hansen's Disease."

A TALE OF TRAGEDY & TRIUMPH

10

GETTING HERE

The Kalaupapa Trail and Peninsula are all part of Kalaupapa National Historic Park (☎ 808/567–6802 ⊕ www.nps.gov/kala/), which is open every day but Sunday. Keep in mind, there are no public facilities (except an occasional restroom) anywhere in the park. Pack your own food and water, as well as light rain gear, sunscreen, and bug repellent.

Hiking: Hiking allows you to travel at your own pace and stop frequently for photos—not an option on the mule ride. The hike takes about 1 hour down and 1½ hours up. You'll want to hit the trail by 8 AM to avoid a trail hazard—fresh mule poop.

Mule-Skinning: You'll be amazed as your mule trots up to the edge of the switchback, swivels on two legs, and com-

Kalaupapa Beach & Peninsula

THE KALAUPAPA TRAIL

Unless you fly, the only way into Kalaupapa National Historic Park is on a dizzying switchback trail. The switchbacks are numbered—26 in all—and descend 1,700 feet to sea level in just under 3 mi. The steep trail is really more of a staircase, and most of the trail is shaded. Keep in mind, however, footing is uneven and little exists to keep you from pitching over the side. If you don't mind heights, you can stare straight down to the ocean for most of the way. *Access Kalaupapa Trail off Hwy. 470 near the Kalaupapa Overlook. There is ample parking near end of Hwy. 470.*

TO HIKE OR TO RIDE?

There are two ways to get down the Kalaupapa Trail: in your hiking boots, or on a mule.

pletes a sharp-angled turn—26 times. The guides tell you the mules can do this in their sleep, but that doesn't take the fear out of the first few switchbacks. Make reservations well in advance. *Moloka'i Mule Ride,* ☎*808/567–6088* ⊕ *www.muleride.com.*

IMPORTANT PERMIT INFORMATION

The only way to visit Kalaupapa settlement is on a tour. Book through Damien Tours (☎ 808/567–6171) if you're hiking or flying in; Moloka'i Mule Ride (☎ 808/567–6088) if you're riding. Daily tours are offered Monday through Saturday. Be sure to reserve in advance. Visitors ages 16 and under are not allowed at Kalaupapa, and photographing patients without their explicit permission is forbidden.

⑫ Kaunakakai Wharf. Docks, once bustling with watercraft exporting pineapples, now host boats shipping out potatoes, tomatoes, baby corn, herbs, and other produce. The wharf is also the starting point for excursions, including deep-sea fishing, sailing, snorkeling, whale-watching, and scuba diving. ⊠ *Rte. 450 and Ala Mālama St.; drive makai on Kaunakakai Pl., which dead-ends at wharf.*

Fodor'sChoice **Moloka'i Mule Ride.** Mount a friendly mule and wind along a 3-mi, 26-
★ switchback trail to reach the town of Kalaupapa. The path was built in 1886 as a supply route for the settlement below. Once in Kalaupapa, you can take a guided tour of the town and have a picnic lunch. The trail is very steep, down some of the highest sea cliffs in the world. Only those in good shape should attempt the ride, as two hours each way on a mule can take its toll. The entire event takes seven hours. It's wise to make reservations ahead of time, as spots are limited. The same outfit can also arrange for you to hike down or fly in, or some combination of a hike in and fly out. *See A Tale of Tragedy & Triumph special feature, above, for more information.* ⊠ *100 Kala'e Hwy., Rte. 470, Kualapu'u* ☎ *808/567–6088* ⊕ *www.muleride.com* ☑ *$165* ☺ *Mon.–Sat. 8–3:30.*

★ ▶ **❹ Pālā'au State Park.** One of the island's few formal recreation areas, this cool retreat covers 233 acres at a 1,000-foot elevation. A short path through a heady pine forest leads to **Kalaupapa Lookout,** a magnificent overlook with views of the town of Kalaupapa and the 1,664-foot-high sea cliffs protecting it. Informative plaques have facts about leprosy, Father Damien, and the colony itself. The park is also the site of **Phallic Rock,** known as Kauleonānāhoa to the ancient Hawaiians. It's said that if women sit by this large rock formation they will become more fertile. The park is well maintained, with camping facilities, restrooms, and picnic tables. ⊠ *Take Rte. 460 west from Kaunakakai and then head mauka on Rte. 470, which ends at park* ☎ *No phone* ☑ *Free* ☺ *Daily dawn–dusk.*

❽ Purdy's Macadamia Nut Farm. Moloka'i's only working macadamia-nut farm is open for educational tours hosted by the knowledgeable and entertaining owner. A family business on Hawaiian homestead land in Ho'olehua, the farm takes up 1½ acres with a flourishing grove of some 50 trees more than 70 years old. Taste a delicious nut right out of its shell, or fresh macadamia-blossom honey; then buy some at the shop on the way out. Look for Purdy's sign behind Moloka'i High School. ⊠ *Lihipali Ave., Ho'olehua* ☎ *808/567–6601* ☑ *Free* ☺ *Weekdays 9:30–3:30, Sat. 10–2.*

❻ R. W. Meyer Sugar Mill and Moloka'i Museum. Built in 1877, this old mill has been reconstructed as a testament to Moloka'i's agricultural history. The equipment is still in working order, including a mule-driven cane crusher, redwood evaporating pans, some copper clarifiers, and a steam engine. A museum with changing exhibits on the island's early history and a gift shop are on-site as well. The facility serves as a campus for Elderhostel programs. ⊠ *Rte. 470, 2 mi southwest of Pālā'au State Park, Kala'e* ☎ *808/567–6436* ☑ *$2.50* ☺ *Mon.–Sat. 10–2.*

10

East Moloka'i

On the beautifully undeveloped East End of Moloka'i, you can find ancient fishponds, a magnificent coastline, splendid ocean views, and a gaping valley that's been inhabited for centuries. The east is flanked by Mt. Kamakou, the island's highest point at 4,961 feet, and home to the Nature Conservancy's Kamakou Preserve. Mist hangs over waterfall-filled valleys, and ancient lava cliffs jut out from the sea.

▌ A GOOD
DRIVE

On Route 450, the farther east you drive, the wilder the coastline, changing from white sandy beaches to rocky shores. Much of the road hugs the shore as it twists and turns. Be forewarned: it's fraught with bumps, blind curves, and potholes. There are, however, several turnouts along the way next to coves and small stretches of sand. There's very little traffic out here, so no need to hurry. Keep your eyes open for mile markers: at times, they're the only references for locating sights.

Six miles east of Kaunakakai, look offshore to see **Kaloko'eli Fishpond** ⑬ ▶, surrounded by the most picturesque of Moloka'i's historic rock walls. After another 5 mi you reach the natural harbor of **Kamalō** ⑭. En route is the stark white Church of St. Joseph's, built in 1876. It's one of four houses of worship built by Father Damien. The statue of him here is frequently adorned with flower lei. Close to mile marker 20 at a small but deeply curved bay, an unpaved road leads a short distance off the highway to **Honouliwai Taro Patch Farm** ⑮. After that the road climbs and winds through **Pu'u O Hoku Ranch** ⑯, a vast Upcountry expanse with sparkling ocean panoramas. Route 450 dead-ends at the beach in the lush **Hālawa Valley** ⑰, the site of a courageous new effort to restore an ancient Hawaiian way of life.

TIMING

If you include the tour of Hālawa Valley (which you should) plan on spending a full day in this meandering expedition. If you take it as a scenic drive with occasional stops, half a day is plenty.

What to See

⑰ **Hālawa Valley.** As far back as AD 650 a busy community lived in this valley, one of the oldest recorded habitations in Hawai'i. Hawaiians lived in a perfectly sustainable relationship with the valley's resources, growing taro and fishing, until the 1960s, when pressures of the modern economy forced the old-timers to abandon their traditional lifestyle. Now a new generation of Hawaiians has returned to the valley and begun the challenging work of clearing trees and restoring the taro fields. Much of this work involves rerouting stream water to flow through carefully engineered level ponds called lo'i. The taro plants with their big dancing leaves grow in the submerged mud of the lo'i, where the water is always cool and flowing. The Hālawa Valley Cooperative gives tours of this restoration project and leads hikes through the valley, which is home to many historic sites and the 3-mi trail to Moa'ula Falls, a 250-foot cascade. The $75 fee ($45 for children) goes to support the restoration work. ⊠ *Eastern end of Rte. 450* ☏ *800/274–9303 or 808/553–9803* ⊕ *www.gomolokai.com.*

⑮ Honouliwai Taro Patch Farm. Although they are not reviving an entire valley and lifestyle, like the folks in Hālawa, Jim and Lee Callahan are reviving taro cultivation on their small East End farm watered by a year-round spring. The owners provide 1½-hour educational tours so visitors can experience all phases of taro farming, from planting to eating. Lee was born and raised in Thailand, so she uses a traditional southeast Asian farm device—a docile, plow-pulling water buffalo named Bigfoot. Tours are available every day, but you must call for an appointment. ⊠ *East of mile marker 20, mauka side, where sign says "Honouliwai Is a Beautiful Place to Be"* ☎ *808/558–8922* ⊕ *www.angelfire.com/film/chiangmai/index.html* ☞ *$20.*

★ ⌐ **⑬ Kaloko'eli Fishpond.** With its narrow rock walls connecting two points of the shore, Kaloko'eli is typical of the numerous fishponds that define southern Moloka'i. Many of them were built around the 13th century. This early type of aquaculture, particular to Hawai'i, exemplifies the ingenuity of precontact Hawaiians. One or more openings were left in the wall, where gates called *makaha* were installed. These gates allowed seawater and tiny fish to enter the enclosed pond but kept larger predators out. The tiny fish would then grow too big to get out. At one time there were 62 fishponds around Moloka'i's coast. ⊠ *Rte. 450, about 6 mi east of Kaunakakai.*

OFF THE
BEATEN
PATH

★

KAMAKOU PRESERVE Tucked away on the slopes of Mt. Kamakou, Moloka'i's highest peak, the 2,774-acre preserve is a dazzling wonderland full of wet 'ōhi'a (hardwood trees of the myrtle family, with red blossoms called lehua flowers) forests, rare bogs, and native trees and wildlife. Guided hikes, limited to eight people, are held on the first Saturday of each month. Reservations are required well in advance. You can visit the park without a tour, but you need a good four-wheel-drive vehicle, and the Nature Conservancy requests that you sign in at the office and get directions first. ⊠ *The Nature Conservancy, 23 Pueo Pl., Kualapu'u* ☎ *808/553–5236* ⊕ *www.nature.org* ☞ *Free; donation suggested for guided hike, $10 members, $25 nonmembers, includes 1-yr membership.*

⑭ Kamalō. A natural harbor used by small cargo ships during the 19th century, this is also the site of the **Church of St. Joseph's,** a tiny white church built by Father Damien in the 1880s. The door is always unlocked. Slip inside and sign the guestbook. The congregation keeps this church in beautiful condition. ⊠ *Rte. 450, about 11 mi east of Kaunakakai, on makai side.*

NEED A
BREAK?

The best place to grab a snack or stock up on picnic supplies is the **Neighborhood Store 'N Counter** (⊠ *Rte. 450, 16 mi east of Kaunakakai, Puko'o* ☎ *808/558–8498*). It's the only place on the East End where you can find essentials such as ice and bread, and not-so-essentials such as burgers and shakes.

⑯ Pu'u O Hoku Ranch. A 14,000-acre private spread in the highlands of East Moloka'i, Pu'u O Hoku was developed in the '30s by wealthy industrialist Paul Fagan. Route 450 cuts right through this rural gem with its

10

green pastures and grazing horses and cattle. As you drive along, enjoy the splendid views of Maui and Lāna'i. The small island off the coast is Mokuho'oniki, a humpback-whale nursery where the military practiced bombing techniques during World War II. The ranch offers horseback trail rides, two large guest cottages, and a retreat facility for groups. ⊠ *Rte. 450 about 20 mi east of Kaunakakai* ☎ *808/558–8109* ⊕ *www.puuohoku.com.*

BEACHES

Moloka'i's strange geography gives the island plenty of drama and spectacle along the shorelines but not so many places for seaside basking and bathing. The long North Shore consists mostly of towering cliffs that plunge directly into the sea. Much of the South Shore is enclosed by a huge reef that stands as far as a mile offshore and blunts the action of the waves. Within this reef you will find a thin strip of sand, but the water here is flat, shallow, and clouded with silt. This reef area is best suited to kayaking or learning how to windsurf.

The big, fat, sandy beaches lie along the West End. The largest of these— one of the largest in the Islands—is Pāpōhaku Beach, which adjoins a

> **KEEP IN MIND!**
>
> Unlike protected shorelines such as Kā'anapali on Maui, the coasts of Moloka'i are exposed to rough sea channels and dangerous rip currents. The ocean tends to be calmer in the morning and in summer. No matter what the time, however, always study the sea before entering. Unless the water is placid and the wave action minimal, it's best to simply stay on shore or keep within touch of solid ground. And don't forget to protect yourself with sunblock. Cool breezes make it easy to underestimate the power of the sun.

grassy park shaded by a grove of *kiawe* (mesquite) trees. These stretches of West-End sand are generally unpopulated. ⚠ The solitude can be a delight, but it should also be a caution; the sea here can be treacherous. At the East End, where the road hugs the sinuous shoreline, you encounter a number of pocket-size beaches in rocky coves, good for snorkeling. The road ends at Hālawa Valley with its unique double bay.

If you need beach gear, head to Moloka'i Fish & Dive at the west end of Kaunakakai's one commercial strip. You can rent equipment (snorkels, boogie boards, kayaks) from Moloka'i Outdoors, in the lobby of Hotel Moloka'i.

All of Hawai'i's beaches are free and open to the public. None of the beaches on Moloka'i have telephones or lifeguards and they're all under the jurisdiction of the **Department of Parks, Land and Natural Resources** (✑ Box 153, Kaunakakai 96746 ☎ 808/553–1745).

West Moloka'i

Moloka'i's West End looks across a channel to the island of O'ahu. Crescent-shaped, this cup of coastline holds the island's best sandy beaches as well as the most arid and sunny weather. Developers have envisioned resorts here and a few signs of this development dream mark the coast—good-looking condos, the Kaluakoʻi Resort (now closed), and some expensive ocean-view homes. Remember: all beaches are public property, even those that front these developments. Beaches below are listed from north to south.

Kawākiu Beach. Seclusion is the reason to come to this remote beach, accessible only by four-wheel drive or a 45-minute walk. The white-sand beach is beautiful. ⚠ Rocks and undertow can make swimming extremely dangerous at times, so use caution. ⊠ *Past Ke Nani Kai condos on Kaluakoʻi Rd., look for dirt road off to right. Park here and hike in or, with 4WD, drive along dirt road to beach* ☞ *No facilities.*

Kepuhi Beach. Kaluakoʻi Hotel is closed but nine holes of its golf course are open, and so is this half-mile of ivory white sand. The beach shines beautifully against the turquoise sea, black outcroppings of lava, and magenta bougainvillea flowers of the resort's landscaping. When the water is perfectly calm, lava ridges in the water make good snorkeling spots. With any surf at all, however, the water around these rocky places churns and foams, wiping out visibility and making it difficult to avoid being slammed into the jagged rocks. ⊠ *Kaluakoʻi Hotel and Golf Club, Kaluakoʻi Rd.* ☞ *Toilets, showers.*

FodorśChoice ★ **Pāpōhaku Beach.** One of the most sensational beaches in Hawaiʻi, Pāpōhaku is a 3-mi-long strip of light golden sand, the longest of its kind on the island. ⚠ Some places are too rocky for swimming, so look carefully before entering the water and go in only when the waves are small (generally in summer). There's so much sand here that Honolulu once purchased barge-loads in order to replenish Waikiki Beach. Molokaʻi people laugh about the fact that gradually, year by year, the sea is returning all that sand to the place it's meant to be. A shady beach park just inland is the site of the Ka Hula Piko Festival of Hawaiian Music and Dance, held each year in May. The park is also a great sunset-facing spot for a rustic afternoon barbecue. ⊠ *Kaluakoʻi Rd.; 2 mi south of Kaluakoʻi Hotel and Golf Club* ☞ *Toilets, showers, picnic tables, grills/firepits.*

Kapukahehu Bay. Locals like to surf just out from this bay in a break called Dixie's or Dixie Maru. The sandy protected cove is usually completely deserted during the weekdays but can fill up when the surf is up. The water in the cove is clear and shallow with plenty of well-worn rocky areas. These conditions make for excellent snorkeling, swimming, and boogie-boarding on calm days. ⊠ *Drive about 3½ mi south of Pāpōhaku Beach to end of Kaluakoʻi Rd.; beach-access sign points to parking lot* ☞ *No facilities.*

Central Molokaʻi

The South Shore is mostly a huge, reef-walled pool of flat saltwater edged with a thin strip of gritty sand and stones, mangrove swamps, and the amazing system of fishponds constructed by the residents of ancient Molokaʻi. From this shore you can look out across glassy water to see people standing on top of the sea—actually, way out on top of the reef—casting fishing lines into the distant waves. This is not a great area for beaches, but is interesting in its own right.

10

One Ali'i Beach Park. Clear, close views of Maui and Lāna'i across the Pailolo Channel dominate One Ali'i Beach Park (*One* is pronounced *o-nay*, not *won*), the only decent beach park on the island's south-central shore. Moloka'i folks gather here for family reunions and community celebrations; the park's tightly trimmed expanse of lawn could accommodate the entire island population. Swimming within the reef is perfectly safe, but don't expect to catch any waves. ⊠ *Rte. 450, east of Hotel Moloka'i* ⚲ *Toilets, showers, picnic tables.*

East Moloka'i

The East End unfolds as a coastal drive with turnouts for tiny cove beaches—good places for snorkeling, shore-fishing, or scuba exploring. Rocky little Mokuho'oniki Island marks the eastern point of the island and serves as a nursery for humpback whales in the winter. The road loops around the East End, then descends and ends at Hālawa Valley.

Waialua Beach Park. This arched strip of golden sand, a roadside pull-off near mile marker 20, also goes by the name Twenty Mile Beach. The water here, protected by the flanks of the little bay, is often so clear and shallow (sometimes too shallow) that even from land you can watch fish swimming among the coral heads. ■ TIP→ This is the most popular snorkeling spot on the island, a pleasant place to stop on the drive around the East End. ⊠ *Drive east on Rte. 450 to mile marker 20* ⚲ *No facilities.*

Hālawa Beach Park. The vigorous water that gouged the steep, spectacular Hālawa Valley, also carved out two bays side by side. Coarse sand and river rock has built up against the sea along the wide valley mouth, creating some protected pool areas that are good for wading or floating around. Most people come here just to hang out and absorb the beauty of this remote valley. Sometimes you'll see people surfing, but it's not wise to entrust your safety to the turbulent open sea along this coast, except on the calmest summer days. ⊠ *Drive east on Rte. 450 to dead-end* ⚲ *Toilets.*

WATER ACTIVITIES & TOURS

Moloka'i's unique shoreline topography limits opportunities for water sports. The North Shore is all seacliffs; the South Shore is largely encased by a huge, taming reef. ⚠ Open-sea access at West End and East End beaches should be used with caution because seas are rough, especially in winter. Generally speaking, there's no one around—certainly not lifeguards—if you get into trouble. For this reason alone, guided excursions are recommended. At least be sure to ask for advice from outfitters or residents. Two kinds of water activities predominate: kayaking within the reef area, and open-sea excursions on charter boats, most of which tie up at Kaunakakai Wharf.

Boogie Boarding, Bodysurfing & Surfing

You rarely see people boogie boarding or bodysurfing on Moloka'i and the only surfing is for advanced wave riders only. One outfitter, **Moloka'i Outdoors** (⊠ Hotel Moloka'i Lobby ☎ 808/553–4227) rents boogie boards for $5 a day, $20 a week. The best spots for boogie boarding, when conditions are safe (occasional summer mornings), are the West End beaches, especially Kepuhi Beach at the old Kaluako'i Hotel. Or seek out waves at the East End around mile marker 20.

Two companies offer good surf–snorkel excursions—for advanced surfers only—with guides. One is **Moloka'i Fish and Dive** (⊠ Hotel Moloka'i Activities Desk ☎ 808/553–5926), the island's main resource for all outdoor activities. The other is **Fun Hogs Hawai'i** (⊠ Kaunakakai Wharf ☎ 808/567–6789), which takes people to good wave action on its charter boat *Ahi*.

Fishing

For Moloka'i people, as in days of yore, the ocean is more of a larder than a playground. It's common most any day to see residents fishing along the shoreline or atop the South-Shore reef, using poles or lines. If you'd like to try your hand at this form of local industry, go to **Moloka'i Fish and Dive** (⊠ Hotel Moloka'i Activities Desk ☎ 808/553–5926) for gear and advice. You can also rent poles from **Moloka'i Outdoors** (⊠ Hotel Moloka'i Lobby ☎ 808/553–4227) for $5 a day.

Deep-sea fishing by charter boat is a great Moloka'i adventure. The sea channels here, though often rough and windy, provide gorgeous views of several islands. The big sport fish are plentiful in these waters, especially mahimahi, small marlin, and various kinds of tuna. Generally speaking, boat captains will customize the outing to your interests, share a lot of information about the island, and let you keep some or all of your catch. That's Moloka'i style—personal and friendly.

Boats & Charters

Alyce C. The six-passenger, 31-foot cruiser runs excellent sportfishing excursions. The cost is $400 for a nine-hour trip, $300 for five to six hours. Shared charters are available. Gear is provided. It's a rare day when you don't snag at least one mahimahi. ⊠ *Kaunakakai Wharf* ☎ *808/ 558–8377* ⊕ *www.alycecsportfishing.com.*

Fun Hogs Hawai'i. Trim and speedy, the 27-foot flybridge sport-fishing boat named *Ahi* takes people out for half-day ($400), six-hour ($500), and full-day ($600) sportfishing excursions. Skipper Mike Holmes also provides one-way or round-trip journeys to Lāna'i, as well as (in winter only) sunset cruises. ⊠ *Kaunakakai Wharf* ☎ 808/567–6789.

Moloka'i Action Adventures. Walter Naki's Moloka'i roots go back forever, and he knows the island intimately. What's more, he has traveled (and fished) all over the globe, and he's a great talker. He will create customized fishing and hunting expeditions and gladly share his wealth of experience. His 21-foot Boston Whaler is usually to be seen at the mouth of Hālawa Valley, in the East End. ☎ *808/558–8184.*

Kayaking

Moloka'i's South Shore is enclosed and tamed by the largest reef system in the United States—an area of shallow, protected sea that stretches over 30 mi. This reef gives inexperienced kayakers an unusually safe,

10

calm environment for shoreline exploring. ⚠ Outside the reef, Molokaʻi waters are often rough and treacherous. Kayakers out here should be strong, experienced, and cautious.

Best Spots

The **South Shore Reef** area is superb for flat-water kayaking any day of the year. It's best to rent a kayak at Hotel Molokaʻi and slide into the water right there, though another easy entry spot is Kaunakakai Wharf, either side. Get out in the morning before the wind picks up and paddle east, exploring the ancient Hawaiian fishponds. When you turn around to return, you'll usually get a push home by the wind, which blows strong and westerly along this shore in the afternoon.

Independent kayakers who are confident about testing their skills in rougher seas can launch at the West End of the island from **Hale O Lono Harbor** (at the end of a long dirt road from Maunaloa town). At the East End of the island, enter the water near mile marker 20 or beyond and explore in the direction of Mokuhoʻoniki Island. ⚠ Kayaking anywhere outside the South Shore Reef is safe only on calm days in summer.

Lessons & Equipment Rentals

Molokaʻi Fish and Dive. At the west end of Kaunakakai's commercial strip, this all-around outfitter provides guided kayak excursions inside the South Shore Reef. One excursion paddles through a dense mangrove forest and explores a huge, hidden ancient fishpond. One bonus of going with guides: if the wind starts blowing hard, they can tow you back with their boat. The fee is $85 for the half-day trip. Check at the store (on Ala Mālama Street) for numerous other outdoor activities. ⊠ *61 Ala Mālama St., Kaunakakai* ☎ *808/553–5926.*

Molokaʻi Outdoors. This is the place—right on the shoreline in Central Molokaʻi, 2 mi east of Kaunakai—to rent a kayak for exploring on your own. Kayaks rent for $12 to $15 an hour. Car racks and extra paddles are also available. ⊠ *Hotel Molokaʻi lobby* ☎ *808/553–4477.*

Sailing

Molokaʻi is a place of strong predictable winds that make for good and sometimes rowdy sailing. The island views in every direction are stunning. Kaunakakai Wharf is the home base for all of the island's charter sailboats.

Gypsy Sailing Adventures. The 33-plus-foot ocean-going catamaran *Star Gypsy* has a large salon, three staterooms, and a fully equipped galley. They do any kind of sailing you want—"any kind of adventure that's prudent and safe"—from two-hour explorations of Molokaʻi's huge reef (stopping at otherwise inaccessible coves and beaches) to interisland cruising (Maui and Lānaʻi). In summer, this company does two-day trips that explore the island's North Shore. Full days cost $500 to $750, depending on the amount of catering involved. Half days are $300. ⊠ *Kaunakakai Wharf* ☎ *808/553–5852.*

Molokaʻi Charters. The 42-foot Cascade sloop *Satan's Doll* is your craft with Molokaʻi Charters. The company arranges two-hour sails for $40 per person. Half-day sailing trips cost $50 per person, including soft drinks and snacks. One commendable trip is the sail to Lāna‘i with stops for snorkeling. A minimum of four people is required, but shared charters can be arranged. ⊠ *Kaunakakai Wharf* ☎ *808/553–5852.*

Scuba Diving

Moloka‘i Fish and Dive is the only PADI-certified purveyor of scuba gear, training, and dive trips on Moloka‘i. Shoreline access for divers is extremely limited, even nonexistent in winter. Boat diving is the way to go. Without guidance, visiting divers can easily find themselves in risky situations with wicked currents. Proper guidance, though, opens an undersea world rarely seen.

Moloka‘i Fish and Dive. Tim and Susan Forsberg, owners, can fill you in on how to find dive sites, rent you the gear, or hook you up with one of their PADI-certified dive guides to take you to the island's best underwater spots. (They work with Fun Hogs Hawai‘i's 27-foot power boat called *Ahi.*) They know the island's best blue holes and underwater cave systems, and they can take you swimming with hammerhead sharks. ⊠ *61 Ala Mālama St., Kaunakakai* ☎ *808/553–5926.*

Snorkeling

During the times when swimming is safe—mainly in summer—just about every beach on Moloka‘i offers good snorkeling along the lava outcroppings in the island's clean and pristine waters.

Best Spots

Kepuhi Beach. In winter, the sea here is deadly. But in summer, this half-mile-long beach offers plenty of rocky nooks that swirl with sea life. The presence of outdoor showers is a bonus. Take Kaluako‘i Road all the way to the West End. Park at Kaluako‘i Resort (it's presently closed) and walk through the lobby area to the beach.

Waialua Beach Park. A thin curve of sand rims a sheltered little bay loaded with coral heads and aquatic life. The water here is shallow—sometimes so shallow that you bump into the underwater landscape—and it's crystal clear. To find this spot, head to the East End on Route 450, and pull off near mile marker 20. When the sea is calm, you'll find several other good snorkeling spots along this stretch of road.

Dive Tours & Equipment Rental

Rent snorkel sets from either of the two outfitters previously mentioned—Moloka‘i Outdoors in the lobby of Hotel Moloka‘i, or Moloka‘i Fish and Dive in Kaunakakai. Rental fees are nominal—$6 a day. All the charter boats carry snorkel gear and include dive stops.

Fun Hogs Hawai‘i. Mike Holmes, captain of the 27-foot power boat *Ahi,* knows the island waters intimately, likes to have fun, and is willing to arrange any type of excursion—for example, one dedicated entirely to snorkeling. His 2½-hour snorkel trips leave early in the morning and explore rarely seen fish and turtle posts outside the reef west of the wharf. Bring your own food and drinks; the trips cost $65 per person. ⊠ *Kaunakakai Wharf* ☎ *808/567–6789.*

10

Moloka'i Charters. The 42-foot sloop *Satan's Doll* harnesses the power of wind to seek the island's best snorkel spots. The full-day snorkeling excursion to the island of Lāna'i costs $100 per person. Four passengers are the minimum they will carry. Soft drinks and a picnic lunch are included. ⚠ You can generally count on rough seas for the afternoon return channel crossing. ⊠ *Kaunakakai Wharf* ☎ *808/658–0559.*

Whale-Watching

Maui gets all the credit for the local wintering humpback-whale population. Most people don't realize that the beautiful big cetaceans also come to Moloka'i. Mokuho'oniki Island at the East End serves as a whale nursery and playground, and the whales pass back and forth along the South Shore. This being Moloka'i, whale-watching here will never involve floating amid a group of boats all ogling the same whale.

Alyce C. Although this six-passenger sportfishing boat is usually busy hooking mahimahi and marlin, the captain gladly takes three-hour excursions to admire the humpback whales. The price is about $65 per person, depending on the number of passengers in the group. ⊠ *Kaunakakai Wharf* ☎ *808/558–8377* ⊕ *www.alycecsportfishing.com.*

Fun Hogs Hawai'i. The *Ahi*, a flybridge sportfishing boat, takes 2½-hour whale-watching trips in the morning from December to April. The cost is $65 per person. Bring your own snacks and drinks. ⊠ *Kaunakakai Wharf* ☎ *808/567–6789.*

Gypsy Sailing Adventures. Being a catamaran, the *Star Gypsy* can drift silently under sail and follow the whales without disturbing them. Captain Richard Messina and crew share a lot of knowledge about the whales and pride themselves on being ecologically-minded. The 2½-hour trip costs $75 and includes soft drinks and water. ⊠ *Kaunakakai Wharf* ☎ *808/658–0559.*

GOLF, HIKING & OUTDOOR ACTIVITIES

Biking

Street biking on this island is a dream for peddlers who like to eat up the miles. Moloka'i's few roads are long, straight, and extremely rural. You can really stretch out and go for it—no traffic lights and most of the time no traffic.

Rentals & Tours

If you don't happen to be one of those athletes who always travels with your own customized cycling tool, you can rent something from **Moloka'i Bicycle** (☎ 808/553–3931) in Kaunakakai. Another place to rent bikes is **Moloka'i Outdoors** (☎ 808/553–4227), based in the lobby of Hotel Moloka'i.

East End Trails. Moloka'i Bicycle will take mountain-bikers out to two-wheel the expansive East End spread of Pu'u O Hoku Ranch. You might ride along an eastern ridge rimming Hālawa Valley to four waterfalls and a remote pool for swimming, or pedal on sea cliffs to a secluded beach. ☎ *808/553–3931 Moloka'i Bicycle.*

Na'iwa Mountain Trails. Guides from Moloka'i Fish and Dive take biking extremists on a gorgeous but challenging adventure in Na'iwa—the remote central mountains—for convoluted forest courses, daredevil verticals (if you want), and exhilarating miles at the brink of the world's tallest sea cliffs. ✉ *61 Ala Mālama St., Kaunakakai* ☎ *808/553–5926.*

★ **Single-Track Trails at Moloka'i Ranch.** Moloka'i Ranch, headquartered in the small town of Maunaloa, has developed some of the best mountainbike experiences in the world, compared favorably by enthusiasts to Moab and Hood River. Moloka'i Fish and Dive runs the activity desk at the Ranch, and has a well-stocked rental shop for mountain bikes and related two-wheel gear. With or without guides, you can head out from here to a complex network of trails that are rated like ski slopes according to their difficulty. Excursions can be super-challenging or as easy as a mild gravity ride over miles of twisty terrain down to the coast, with van transport back. ✉ *61 Ala Mālama St., Kaunakakai* ☎ *808/553–5926.*

Golf

While the golf is good on Moloka'i, there isn't much of it—just two courses and a total of 27 holes.

Ironwood Hills Golf Course. Like the other 9-hole plantation era courses with which it shares lineage, Ironwood Hills is not for everyone. It helps if you like a bit of rugged history with your golf, and can handle the occasionally rugged conditions. On the plus side, most holes here offer lovely views of the ocean and the island of Lāna'i. Fairways are kukuya grass and run through pine, ironwood, and eucalyptus trees. Carts are rented, but there's not always someone there to rent you a cart—in which case, there's a wooden box for your green fee (honor system), and happy walking. ✉ *Kala'e Hwy., Kualapu'u* ⛳ *9 holes. 3,088 yds. Par 35. Green Fee: $20* ☞ *Facilities: Putting green, golf carts, pull carts.*

★ **Kaluakoi Golf Course.** Kaluakoi Golf Course, associated with the Lodge at Moloka'i Ranch, has more ocean frontage than any other Hawai'i course. Ted Robinson (1976) was given a fantastic site and created some excellent holes, starting with the par-5 first, with the beach on the right from tee to green. The course, closed by former owners for financial reasons, reopened in 2002 after substantial refurbishing. The front nine is generally flat, never running far from the sea, and providing dramatic views of the island of O'ahu. The back nine winds through rolling hills and dense forest. ✉ *Moloka'i Ranch, Maunaloa* ☎ *808/552–0255* ⊕ *www.molokairanch.com* ⛳ *18 holes. 6,200 yds. Par 72. Green Fee: $70* ☞ *Facilities: Driving range, putting green, golf carts, rental clubs.*

10

Hiking

Rural and rugged, Moloka'i is an excellent place for hiking. Roads and developments are few, so the outdoors is always beckoning. The island is steep, so hikes often combine spectacular views with hearty physical exertion. Because the island is small, you can traverse quite a bit of it on foot and come away with the feeling of really knowing the place.

And you won't see many other people around. Most of the time, it's just you and the *'aina* (the land).

Kalaupapa Trail. You can make a day of hiking down to Kalaupapa Peninsula and back by means of a 3-mi, 26-switchback trail. The trail is nearly vertical, traversing the face of some of the highest sea cliffs in the world. *See* A Tale of Tragedy & Triumph *special feature earlier in this chapter for more information.*

Kamakou Preserve. Four-wheel drive is essential for this half-day (minimum) journey into the Moloka'i highlands. The Nature Conservancy of Hawai'i manages the 2,774-acre Kamakou Preserve, one of the last stands of Hawai'i's native plants and birds. A long, rough dirt road, that begins not far from Kaunakakai town, leads to the preserve. The road is not marked, so you must check in with the **Nature Conservancy's Moloka'i office** (⊠ At Moloka'i Industrial Park about 3 mi west of Kaunkakai, 23 Pueo Pl. ☎ 808/553–5236 ⊕ www.nature.org), for directions. Let them know that you plan to visit the preserve, and pick up the informative 24-page brochure with trail maps.

On your way up to the preserve, be sure to stop at Waikolu Overlook, which gives a head-spinning view into a precipitous North-Shore canyon. Once inside the preserve, various trails are clearly marked. The trail of choice—and you can drive right to it—is the 1½-mi boardwalk trail through Pēpē'ōpae Bog, an ecological treasure-trove. Organic deposits here date back at least 10,000 years, and the plants are undisturbed natives. This is the true landscape of prediscovery Hawai'i. It's a mean trek; you have to be tough, nimble, and reverential all at the same time.

■ TIP➔ Wear long pants and bring rain gear. Your shoes ought to provide good traction on a slippery, narrow boardwalk.

Kawela Cul-de-Sacs. Just east of Kaunakakai, three streets—Kawela One, Two, and Three—jut up the mountainside from the Kamehameha V Highway. These roads end in cul-de-sacs that are also informal trailheads. Rough dirt roads work their way from here to the top of the mountain. The lower slopes are dry, rocky, steep, and austere. (It's good to start in the cool of the early morning.) A hiker in good condition can get all the way up into the high forest in two or three hours. There's no park ranger and no water fountain—these are not for the casual stroller. But if you're prepared for the challenge, you will be well rewarded.

Guided Hikes

Historical Hikes of West Moloka'i. This company has six guided hikes, ranging from two to six hours. The outings focus on Moloka'i's cultural past taking you to sites such as an ancient quarry, an early fishing village, or high sea cliffs where Hawaiian chiefs played games during the traditional *Makahiki* (harvest festival) season. Backpacks are provided, as is lunch on intermediate and advanced hikes. Guides Lawrence and Catherine Aki also run A Hawaiian Getaway vacation rental. ⊠ *The Lodge at Moloka'i Ranch Activity Desk, Maunaloa Hwy., Maunaloa* ☎ *808/552–2797, 808/553–9803, or 800/274–9303* ⊕ *www.gomolokai.com* ⊡ *$45–$125.*

Hālawa Valley Cultural Waterfall Hike. Hālawa is a gorgeous, steep-walled valley carved by two rivers and rich in history. Site of what could be the earliest Polynesian settlement in Hawai'i, Hālawa sustained island culture with its ingeniously designed *lo'i,* or taro fields. In the 1960s the valley became derelict and increasingly mysterious. Now Hawaiian families are restoring the lo'i and walking people through the valley, which includes two-thirds of Moloka'i's *luakini heiau* (sacred temples). Half-day visits, morning or afternoon, cost $75 (less for children) and support the work of restoration. Call ahead to visit any day at 9:30 AM or 2 PM. Bring water, food, and insect repellent. ☎ *808/553–9803 or 808/274–9303* ⊕ *www.gomolokai.com* 🖃 *$75.*

Horseback Riding

Pu'u O Hoku Ranch. Set on the prow of the island's Maui-facing East End, this ranch keeps a stable of magnificent, amiable horses that are available for trail rides starting at $55 an hour. The peak experience is a four-hour beach ride ($120) that culminates at a secluded cove where the horses are happy to swim, rider and all. Bring your own lunch. This is a good experience for people with little or no horse skills. They match skill-levels with appropriate steeds. ⊠ *Rte. 450, 20 mi east of Kaunakakai* ☎ *808/558–8109* ⊕ *www.puuohoku.com.*

WHERE TO EAT

During a week's stay, you might easily hit all the dining spots worth a visit, then return to your favorites for a second round. The dining scene is fun because it's a microcosm of Hawai'i's diverse cultures. You can find locally grown vegetarian foods, spicy Filipino cuisine, and Hawaiian fish with a Japanese influence—such as *'ahi* or *aku* (types of tuna), mullet, and moonfish grilled, sautéed, or mixed with seaweed and eaten raw as *poke* (marinated raw fish). Most eating establishments are on Ala Mālama Street in Kaunakakai, with pizza, pasta, and ribs only a block away. What's more, the price is right.

WHAT IT COSTS				
$$$$	**$$$**	**$$**	**$**	**¢**
RESTAURANTS over $30	$20–$30	$12–$20	$7–$12	under $7

Restaurant prices are for a main course at dinner.

West Moloka'i

★ **$$–$$$$** ✕ **Maunaloa Room.** Order-haute cuisine appetizers such as coconut-crusted shrimp, Moloka'i *'opihi* (a crunchy limpet), or *lumpia* (egg roll) stuffed with *kālua* duck (roasted in an underground oven). Entrées follow a steak-and-seafood theme, and the catch of the day can be prepared with *alae* (a pale-orange salt found in Moloka'i and Kaua'i). Inside, wagon-wheel chandeliers with electric candles typify the hotel restaurant's ranch fixtures. A dinner on the outside deck can't be beat. ⊠ *The Lodge at Moloka'i Ranch, 8 Maunaloa Hwy., Maunaloa* ☎ *808/660–2725* ▤ *AE, MC, V. $14–$31.*

10

Central Moloka'i

$$ ✕ **Oceanfront Dining Room.** This is *the* place to hang out on Moloka'i. Locals relax at the bar listening to live music on weekends, or they come in for theme-night dinners (posters around town tell you what's in store for the week). Prime-rib specials on Friday and Saturday nights draw a crowd. Try the broiled baby back ribs smothered in barbecue sauce. Every Friday from 4 to 6 PM Moloka'i's *kūpuna* (old-timers) bring their instruments here for a lively Hawaiian jam session, a wonderful experience of grassroots aloha spirit. ☒ *Hotel Moloka'i, Kamehameha V Hwy., Kaunakakai* ☎ 808/553–5347 ⊟ AE, DC, MC, V. *$12–$18.*

$–$$ ✕ **Kamuela's Cookhouse.** Kamuela's is the only eatery in rural Kualapu'u. From the outside, this laid-back diner looks like a little plantation house; inside, paintings of hula dancers and island scenes enhance the green-and-white furnishings. Typical fare is a plate of chicken or pork *katsu* served with rice. They shut down the grill by 2 PM, so unless you order takeout ahead of time, this is not a dinner option. It's across the street from the Kualapu'u Market. ☒ *Farrington Hwy., 1 block west of Rte. 470, Kulapūu* ☎ 808/567–9655 ⊟ No credit cards ☉ Closed Mon. No dinner. *$8–$20.*

$–$$ ✕ **Moloka'i Pizza Cafe.** A cheerful, busy restaurant, Moloka'i Pizza is a popular gathering spot for families. Pizza, sandwiches, salads, pasta, fresh fish, and homemade pies are simply prepared and tasty. Kids keep busy on a few little coin-operated rides. ☒ *Kaunakakai Pl. on Wharf Rd., Kaunakakai* ☎ 808/553–3288 ⊟ No credit cards. *$8–$19.*

$ ✕ **Oviedo's.** This modest lunch counter specializes in *adobos* (stews) with traditional Filipino spices and sauces. Try the tripe, pork, or beef adobo for a real taste of tradition. The locals say that Oviedo's makes the best roast pork in the state. You can eat in or take out. ☒ *145 Ala Mālama St., Kaunakakai* ☎ 808/553–5014 ⊟ No credit cards ☉ No dinner. *$8–$9.*

¢–$ ✕ **Kanemitsu Bakery and Restaurant.** Come here for a taste of *lavosh*, a
Fodor'sChoice pricey flatbread flavored with sesame, taro, Maui onion, Parmesan
★ cheese, or jalapeño. Or try the round Moloka'i bread—a sweet, pan-style white loaf that makes excellent cinnamon toast. ☒ *79 Ala Mālama St., Kaunakakai* ☎ 808/553–5855 ⊟ No credit cards ☉ Closed Tues. *$4–$8.*

¢–$ ✕ **Moloka'i Drive Inn.** Fast food Moloka'i-style is served at a walk-up counter. Hot dogs, fries, and sundaes are on the menu, but residents usually choose the foods they grew up on, such as saimin, plate lunches, shaved ice (snow cone), and the beloved *loco moco* (rice topped with a hamburger and a fried egg, covered in gravy). ☒ *857 Ala Mālama St., Kaunakakai* ☎ 808/553–5655 ⊟ No credit cards. *$3–$9.*

¢–$ ✕ **Paddler's Inn.** A roomy, comfortable restaurant with an extensive menu, Paddler's Inn is right in Kaunakakai town but on the ocean side of Kamehameha V Highway. There are three eating areas—standard restaurant seating, a shady cool bar, and an open-air courtyard where you can sit at a counter eating raw fish and drinking beer while getting cooled with spray from an overhead misting system. The food is a blend of island-style and standard American fare (fresh poke every day; a prime

rib special every Friday night). There's live entertainment every night.
⊠ *10 Mohala St., Kaunakakai* ☎ *808/553–5256* ☰ *AE, DC, MC, V.*
$5–$14.

¢–$ ✕ **Sundown Deli.** This clean little rose-color deli focuses on freshly made
takeout food. Sandwiches come on half a dozen types of bread, and the
Portuguese bean soup and chowders are rich and filling. Specials, such
as vegetarian quiche, change daily. ⊠ *145 Ala Mālama St., Kaunakakai*
☎ *808/553–3713* ☰ *No credit cards* ⊙ *Closed Sun. No dinner. $4–$8.*

¢ ✕ **Outpost Natural Foods.** A well-stocked store, Outpost is the heart of
Moloka'i's health-food community. At the counter you can get fresh juices
and delicious sandwiches geared toward the vegetarian palate. It's a great
place to pick up local produce and all the ingredients you need for a
picnic lunch. ⊠ *70 Makaena St., Kaunakakai* ☎ *808/553–3377* ☰ *AE,*
MC, V ⊙ *Closed Sat. No dinner. $3–$5.*

WHERE TO STAY

The coastline along the West End has ocean-view condominium units
and luxury homes available as vacation rentals. In the hills above, little Maunaloa town offers the superb Lodge at Moloka'i Ranch and the
oddly luxurious seaside tents at Kaupoa Beach Village. Central Moloka'i
has B&Bs with extremely helpful owners, two seaside condominiums,
and the icon of the island—Hotel Moloka'i. The only lodgings on the
East End are some guest cottages in magical settings.

	WHAT IT COSTS				
	$$$$	**$$$**	**$$**	**$**	**¢**
HOTELS	over $200	$150–$200	$100–$150	$60–$100	under $60

Hotel prices are for two people in a standard double room in high season, including tax and service.

West Moloka'i

Hotels & Resorts

$$$$ 🏨 **The Lodge at Moloka'i Ranch.** Moloka'i's plushest accommodation is
Fodor'sChoice this Old West–style lodge. Ranching memorabilia and local artwork adorn
★ guest-room walls, with each of the 22 suites individually decorated. All
rooms have private lānai and some have skylights. An impressive stone
fireplace warms up the central Great Room, and there's a games room
for pleasant socializing during cool Moloka'i evenings. Pathways and
a greenhouse delineate the grounds. Spa facilities include massage rooms,
a juice bar, and men's and women's saunas. ⊠ *Maunaloa Hwy., Box*
259, Maunaloa 96770 ☎ *888/627–8082* ⊕ *www.molokairanch.com*
↩ *22 rooms* � ⑂ *Restaurant, in-room safes, refrigerators, in-room data*
ports, pool, gym, massage, sauna, spa, beach, boating, fishing, moun-
tain bikes, billiards, hiking, horseback riding, horseshoes, bar, lounge,
library, recreation room, children's programs (ages 5–12) ☰ *AE, D, MC,*
V. $418–$508.

10

★ **$$$–$$$$**   ⌂ **Kaupoa Beach Village.** This dream-come-true campground consists of two-bedroom canvas bungalows, mounted on wooden platforms. Don't let the presence of ecotravelers fool you—the rooms are unexpectedly luxurious, with queen-size beds, self-composting flush toilets, and private outdoor showers. Breakfast, lunch, and dinner are served family-style in an open-air pavilion (price not included in room rate). Extensive activities, including snorkeling, kayaking, clay shooting, and mountain biking, are available. ⊠ *Maunaloa Hwy., Box 259, Maunaloa 96770* ☎ *888/627–8082* ⊕ *www.molokairanch.com* ⇆ *40 tents* ⚬ *Restaurant, fans, beach, snorkeling, boating, mountain bikes, hiking, horseback riding, airport shuttle; no A/C, no room phones, no room TVs* ⊟ *AE, D, MC, V. $280–$370.*

Condos & Vacation Rentals

$$$$ ⌂ **Hale Aloha.** This spacious four-bedroom, three-bath vacation rental is on 12 secluded acres, has ocean views, and is surrounded by woodlands and an orchard. Wood floors stretch the length of the house, connecting the two kitchens. A wraparound porch leads to a gazebo-covered hot tub. Rooms are open and simple, with wood-beam ceilings. The managers of this property, 1-800-Molokai, also handle a number of other West-End condos for as little as $100 a night. ⊠ *Kaluako'i Rd., Box 20, Maunaloa 96770* ☎ *800/665–6524 or 808/552–2222* ⊕ *www.1-800-molokai.com* ⇆ *1 house* ⚬ *Fans, kitchen, cable TV, in-room VCRs, pool, hot tub; no A/C* ⊟ *AE, MC, V. $214–$500.*

★ **$–$$$$**   ⌂ **Paniolo Hale.** Perched high on a ledge overlooking the beach, Paniolo Hale is one of Moloka'i's best condominium properties. Some units have spectacular ocean views. Studios and one- or two-bedroom units all have beautiful screened lānai and well-equipped kitchens. Rooms are tidy and simple. The property is adjacent to the Kaluako'i Golf Course and a stone's throw from the Kaluako'i Hotel and Golf Club. ⊠ *Lio Pl., Box 1979, Kaunakai 96748* ☎ *808/553–8334 or 800/367–2984* 🖷 *808/553–3783* ⊕ *www.molokai-vacation-rental.com* ⇆ *77 condos* ⚬ *Kitchens, microwaves, 18-hole golf course, golf privileges, pool, paddle tennis* ⊟ *AE, MC, V. $95–$275.*

$–$$$ ⌂ **Kaluako'i Villas.** Studios and one-bedroom ocean-view suites are decorated in blue and mauve, with island-style art, rattan furnishings, and private lānai. Units are spread out in 21 two-story buildings covering 29 acres, adjacent to the now defunct Kaluako'i Resort. The view toward the ocean looks across the newly revived golf course. The seclusion and sunsets make this a great find. ⊠ *1131 Kaluako'i Rd., Box 200, Maunaloa 96770* ☎ *808/552–2721 or 800/367–5004* 🖷 *808/552–2201* ⊕ *www.castleresorts.com*

> ### WHERE TO SPA
>
> **Moloka'i Lomi Massage** has herbal remedies, and the staff offers nutritional advice to keep you at the top of your form. Allana Noury has been studying natural medicine for more than 30 years and is a licensed massage therapist, herbalist, and naturopathic physician. Ask for a traditional Hawaiian *lomi lomi* treatment. A 30-minute massage is $35; one hour is $55. It's just across the street from the Friendly Market in Kaunakakai. ⊠ *107 Ala Mālama, Kaunakakai* ☎ *808/553-8034.*

🛏 *47 units, 2 cottages ☖ Fans, kitchens, in-room VCRs, 18-hole golf course, pool, beach, shops; no A/C* ▤ *AE, MC, V. $75–$200.*

$-$$ 🏨 **Ke Nani Kai.** These pleasant one- and two-bedroom condo units have ocean views and use of the facilities at the former Kaluako'i Hotel and Golf Club. Furnished lānai have flower-laden trellises, and the spacious interiors are decorated with rattans and pastels. Each unit has a washer-dryer unit and a fully equipped kitchen. The beach is a five-minute walk away. ✉ *Kaluako'i Rd., Box 289, Maunaloa 96770* ☏ *808/553–8334 or 800/367–2984* 🖷 *808/553–3784* ⊕ *www.molokai-vacation-rental. com* 🛏 *120 units (22 rentals) ☖ Fans, kitchens, cable TV, 18-hole golf course, 2 tennis courts, pool, laundry facilities; no A/C* ▤ *AE, D, DC, MC, V. $95–$150.*

Central Moloka'i

Hotels & Resorts

$-$$$ 🏨 **Hotel Moloka'i.** Friendly staff members here embody the aloha spirit.
Fodor'sChoice Low-slung Polynesian-style buildings with wood roof shingles are set
★ waterside. Simple, tropical furnishings with white rattan accents fill the rooms, and a basket swing awaits on the lānai. The Oceanfront Dining Room serves breakfast, lunch, dinner, and libations—with entertainment on weekend nights. Ask about deals in conjunction with airlines and rental-car companies when you make your reservation. ✉ *Kamehameha V Hwy., Box 1020, Kaunakakai 96748* ☏ *808/553–5347* 🖷 *808/553–5047* ⊕ *www.hotelmolokai.com* 🛏 *45 rooms ☖ Restaurant, fans, some kitchenettes, cable TV, pool, lounge, laundry facilities; no A/C* ▤ *AE, D, DC, MC, V. $100–$160.*

Condos & B&Bs

$$ 🏨 **Moloka'i Shores.** Every room in this oceanfront, three-story condominium complex has a view of the water. One-bedroom, one-bath units or two-bedroom, two-bath units all have full kitchens and furnished lānai, which look out on 4 acres of manicured lawns with picnic tables. There's a great view of Lāna'i in the distance. ✉ *1000 Kamehameha V Hwy., Box 1887, Kaunakakai 96748* ☏ *808/553–5954 or 800/535–0085* ⊕ *www.marcresorts.com* 🖷 *800/633–5085* 🛏 *100 units ☖ Fans, kitchens, cable TV, pool, shuffleboard; no A/C* ▤ *AE, D, MC, V. $129.*

$-$$ 🏨 **Wavecrest.** This oceanfront condominium complex is convenient if you want to explore the east side of the island—it's 3 mi east of Kaunakakai. Individually decorated one- and two-bedroom units have full kitchens. Each has a furnished lānai, some with views of Maui and Lāna'i. Be sure to ask for an updated unit

---

GROCERY STORES

Friendly Market Center (✉ 93 Ala Mālama St., Kaunakakai ☏ 808/553–5595) is the best-stocked supermarket on the island. **Misaki's Inc.** (✉ 78 Ala Mālama St., Kaunakakai ☏ 808/553–5505) is a good spot for housewares, beverages, and food staples. **Moloka'i Wines 'n' Spirits** (✉ 77 Ala Mālama St., Kaunakakai ☏ 808/553–5009) carries a good selection of fine wines and liquors, as well as gourmet cheese and snacks.

10

when you make your reservation. The shallow water here is bad for swimming but good for fishing. ✉ *Rte. 450 near mile marker 13* 🏠 *Friendly Isle Realty, 75 Ala Mālama, Kaunakakai 96748* ☎ *808/553–3666 or 800/600–4158* 🖷 *808/553–3867* ⊕ *www.molokairesorts.com* 🖥 *126 units* ⚲ *Fans, kitchens, 2 tennis courts, pool, beach, shuffleboard; no A/C* ▭ *V. $85–$125.*

¢–$ 🏨 **A Hawaiian Get.** If you want to learn about Moloka'i's history and culture, consider staying here: gracious hosts Lawrence and Catherine Aki have an extensive library and also conduct cultural hikes through their company, Historical Hikes of West Moloka'i (*see* Hiking *earlier in this chapter*). Two rooms in the home are available. Small and simply decorated, both have double beds and one has a TV and VCR. Guests use the same entrance, bathroom, and living room as the proprietors. It's within walking distance of Kaunakakai town. ✉ *270 Kaiwi St., Kaunakakai 96748* ☎ *808/553–9803 or 800/274–9303* ✉ *mcai@aloha.net* 🖥 *2 rooms* ⚲ *Fans, some cable TV, some in-room VCRs, hair salon, library, laundry facilities; no A/C* ▭ *No credit cards. $50–$75.*

East Moloka'i

B&Bs & Vacation Rentals

$$$ 🏨 **Dunbar Beachfront Cottages.** These two spotlessly clean two-bedroom, one-bath cottages with complete kitchens—each with its own secluded beach—are set about ¼ mi apart. The beach is good for swimming and snorkeling during the summer months and great for whale-watching in winter. Covered lānai have panoramic vistas of Maui, Lāna'i, and Kaho'olawe across the ocean. ✉ *King Kamehameha V Hwy., mile marker 18, HC01, Box 901, Kaunakakai 96748* ☎ *808/558–8153 or 800/673–0520* 🖷 *808/558–8153* ⊕ *www.molokai-beachfront-cottages.com* 🖥 *2 cottages* ⚲ *BBQ, fans, kitchens, in-room VCRs, beach; no A/C, no smoking* ▭ *No credit cards. $170, 3-night min.*

$$ 🏨 **Pu'u O Hoku Ranch.** At the east end of Moloka'i, near mile marker 25, lie these three ocean-view accommodations, on 14,000 isolated acres of pastures and forest. One country cottage has two bedrooms, basic wicker furnishings, and *lau hala* (natural fiber) woven matting on the floors. An airy four-bedroom cottage has a small deck and a somewhat Balinese air. For large groups—family reunions, for example—the Ranch has a lodge with 11 rooms, nine bathrooms, and a large kitchen. The full lodge goes for $1,250 nightly (rooms are not available on an individual basis). Inquire about horseback riding on the property. ✉ *Rte. 450, Box 1889, Kaunakakai 96748* ☎ *808/558–8109* 🖷 *808/558–8100* ⊕ *www.puuohoku.com* 🖥 *1 2-bedroom cottage, 1 4-bedroom cottage, 11 rooms in lodge* ⚲ *Kitchens, pool, hiking, horseback riding; no A/C* ▭ *MC, V. $140.*

$–$$ 🏨 **Kamalō Plantation Cottage and Moanui Beach House.** Both of these Polynesian-style cottages have a fully equipped kitchen, living room, dining room, and deck. Kamalō is at the base of a mountain and sleeps two. Moanui sleeps four and has a TV and VCR. It's on a good snorkeling beach and has great views from its huge deck. Homegrown fruit and fresh-baked bread are provided for breakfast at both cottages. ✉ *East*

of Kaunakakai off Rte. 450 ⌕ *HC 01, Box 300, Kaunakakai 96748*
📠 *808/558–8236* ⊕ *www.molokai.com/kamalo* ⇌ *2 cottages* ⚬ *Fans, kitchens; no A/C* ▭ *No credit cards. $95–$150.*

$ ▢ **Honomuni House.** This cottage sits on an acre of tropical gardens that are complemented by waterfalls and a freshwater stream. The rental can sleep up to four and includes one bedroom, one bath, a large living-dining room with pullout couch, and a kitchen. An outdoor shower with hot water is an added bonus. It's 17 mi east of Kaunakakai on Route 450. ⊠ *Rte. 450, HC 1, Box 700, Kaunakakai 96748* ☎ *808/558–8383* ⇌ *1 house* ⚬ *Kitchen; no A/C, no room TVs* ▭ *No credit cards. $85 per night; $550 per week.*

SHOPPING

Moloka'i has one main commercial area: Ala Mālama Street in Kaunakakai. There are no department stores or shopping malls, and the clothing available is typical island wear. A handful of family-run businesses line the main drag of Maunaloa, a rural plantation town.

Most stores in Kaunakakai are open Monday through Saturday between 9 and 6. In Maunaloa most shops close by 4 in the afternoon and all day Sunday.

Arts & Crafts
The **Big Wind Kite Factory and Plantation Gallery** (⊠ 120 Maunaloa Hwy., Maunaloa ☎ 808/552–2364) has custom-made appliquéd kites you can fly or display. Designs range from hula girls to tropical fish. Also in stock are kite-making kits, paper kites, minikites, and wind socks. Ask to go on the factory tour, or take a free kite-flying lesson. The gallery is intermingled with the kite shop and carries everything from locally made crafts to Hawaiian books and CDs, sunglasses, and incense.

Kamakana Fine Arts Gallery (⊠ 110 Ala Mālama St., Kaunakakai ☎ 808/553–8520) only represents artists who live on the island, including world-class talent in photography, wood carving, ceramics, and Hawaiian musical instruments. This business actively supports the local community by showcasing talents that might otherwise go undiscovered. It's above American Savings Bank.

Clothing
Casual, knockabout island wear is sold at **Imports Gift Shop** (⊠ 82 Ala Mālama St., Kaunakakai ☎ 808/553–5734), across from Kanemitsu Bakery. **Moloka'i Island Creations** (⊠ 62 Ala Mālama St., Kaunakakai ☎ 808/553–5926) carries exclusive swimwear, beach cover-ups, sun hats, and tank tops. **Moloka'i Surf** (⊠ 130 Kamehameha V Hwy., Kaunakakai ☎ 808/553–5093) is known for its wide selection of Moloka'i T-shirts, swimwear, and sports clothing.

Grocery Stores
Friendly Market Center (⊠ 90 Ala Mālama St., Kaunakakai ☎ 808/553–5595) is the best-stocked supermarket on the island. Its slogan—"Your family store on Moloka'i"—is truly credible: hats, T-shirts, and sun-and-surf essentials keep company with fresh produce, groceries, liquor, and

10

sundries. Locals say the food is fresher here than at the other major supermarket. It's open weekdays 8:30–8:30 and Saturday 8:30–6:30.

Victuals and travel essentials are available at the **Maunaloa General Store** (⊠ 200 Maunaloa Hwy., Maunaloa ☎ 808/552–2346). Open Monday–Saturday 8 to 6, it's convenient for guests staying at the nearby condos of the Kaluako'i Resort area. The store sells meat, produce, dry goods, drinks, and all the little things you find in a general store.

Misaki's Inc. (⊠ 78 Ala Mālama St., Kaunakakai ☎ 808/553–5505) is a grocery with authentic island allure. It has been in business since 1922. Pick up housewares and beverages here, as well as your food staples, Monday through Saturday 8:30 to 8:30, and Sunday 9 to noon.

Don't let the name **Moloka'i Wines 'n' Spirits** (⊠ 77 Ala Mālama St., Kaunakakai ☎ 808/553–5009) fool you. Along with a surprisingly good selection of fine wines and liquors, the store also carries gourmet cheeses and snacks. It's open Sunday through Thursday 9 AM to 10 PM, Friday and Saturday until 10:30.

Island Goods & Jewelry

Imports Gift Shop (⊠ 82 Ala Mālama St., Kaunakakai ☎ 808/553–5734) sells a decent collection of 14-karat-gold chains, rings, earrings, and bracelets, plus a jumble of Hawaiian quilts, pillows, books, and postcards. It also carries Hawaiian heirloom jewelry, a unique style of jewelry, inspired by popular Victorian pieces, that has been crafted in Hawai'i since the late 1800s. These stunning gold pieces are made to order with your Hawaiian name inscribed on them.

Moloka'i Island Creations (⊠ 62 Ala Mālama St., Kaunakakai ☎ 808/553–5926) carries its own unique line of jewelry, including sea opal, coral, and sterling silver, as well as other gifts and resort wear.

Sporting Goods

Moloka'i Bicycle (⊠ 80 Mohala St., Kaunakakai ☎ 808/553–3931 or 800/709–2453 ⊕ www.bikehawaii.com/molokaibicycle) rents and sells mountain and road bikes as well as jogging strollers, kids' trailers, helmets, and racks. It supplies maps and information on biking and hiking and will drop off and pick up equipment for a fee nearly anywhere on the island. Call or stop by after 4 PM to arrange what you need.

Moloka'i Fish and Dive (⊠ 61 Ala Mālama St., Kaunakakai ☎ 808/553–5926) is *the* source for sporting needs, from snorkel rentals to free advice. These folks handle all activities for the Lodge at Moloka'i Ranch.

NIGHTLIFE

Local nightlife consists mainly of gathering with friends and family, sipping a few cold ones, strumming 'ukuleles and guitars, singing old songs, and talking story. Still, there are a few ways to kick up your heels for a festive night out. Pick up a copy of the weekly *Moloka'i Dispatch*—and see if there's a church supper or square dance. The bar at the Hotel Moloka'i is always a good place to drink by the tiki torches. Most nights they have some kind of live music by island performers. The "Aloha Friday" weekly gathering here, 4 to 6 PM, always attracts a couple dozen old-timers with guitars and 'ukuleles. This impromptu, feel-good event is a peak experience for any Moloka'i trip. The Paddler's Inn in Kaunakakai has live music every night. It's open until 2 AM on weekends.

MOLOKA'I ESSENTIALS

Transportation

BY AIR

If you're flying in from the mainland United States, you must first make a stop in Honolulu. From there, it's a 25-minute trip to the Friendly Isle.

AIRPORTS: Moloka'i's transportation hub is Ho'olehua Airport, a tiny airstrip 8 mi west of Kaunakakai and about 18 mi east of Maunaloa. An even smaller airstrip serves the little community of Kalaupapa on the North Shore.

🚩 **Ho'olehua Airport** ☎ 808/567-6140. **Kalaupapa Airfield** ☎ 808/567-6331.

CARRIERS: Island Air, the puddle-jumper arm of Aloha Airlines, provides daily flights between Moloka'i and O'ahu or Maui on its 37-passenger de Haviland Dash-8 aircrafts. Pacific Wings operates chartered flights of its nine-passenger Cessna between O'ahu and Moloka'i.

If you fly into the airstrip at Kalaupapa, your arrival should coincide with one of the authorized ground tours. Otherwise you'll be asked to leave. Pacific Wings and Moloka'i Air Shuttle fly from Honolulu to Kalaupapa. Paragon Air runs charter flights from Maui to Kalaupapa.

🚩 **Island Air** ☎ 800/323-3345 ⊕ www.islandair.com. **Moloka'i Air Shuttle** ☎ 808/567-6847 in Honolulu. **Pacific Wings** ☎ 808/873-0877 or 888/575-4546 ⊕ www.pacificwings.com

TO & FROM THE AIRPORT: From Ho'olehua Airport, it takes about 10 minutes to reach Kaunakakai and 25 minutes to reach the West End of the island by car. There's no public bus.

Shuttle service for two passengers costs about $18 from Ho'olehua Airport to Kaunakakai. A trip to Moloka'i Ranch costs $28, divided by the number of passengers. For shuttle service, call Moloka'i Off-Road Tours and Taxi or Molokai Outdoors.

🚩 **Moloka'i Off-Road Tours and Taxi** ☎ 808/553-3369. **Moloka'i Outdoors** ☎ 808/553-4227 ⊕ www.molokai-outdoors.com.

BY CAR

If you want to explore Moloka'i from one end to the other, it's best to rent a car. With just a few main roads to choose from, it's a snap to drive around here.

The gas stations are in Kaunakakai and Maunaloa. When you park your car, be sure to lock it—thefts do occur. Drivers must wear seat belts or risk a $75 fine. Children under three must ride in a federally approved child passenger-restraint device, easily leased at the rental agency. Ask your rental agent for a free *Moloka'i Drive Guide*.

10

CAR RENTAL: Budget maintains a counter near the baggage-claim area at the airport. Dollar also has offices at Ho'olehua Airport, and your rental car can be picked up in the parking lot. Expect to pay $40–$50 per day for a standard compact and $50–$70 for a midsize car. Rates are seasonal and may run higher during the peak winter months. It's best to make arrangements in advance. If you're flying on Island Air or Hawaiian Airlines, see whether fly-drive package deals are available—you might luck out on a less-expensive rate. Hotels and outfitters might also offer packages.

Locally owned Island Kine Rent-a-Car offers airport or hotel pickup and sticks to one rate year-round for vehicles in a broad spectrum from two- and four-wheel drives to 15-passenger vans. The same is true for Moloka'i Rentacar, located right on the main street in Kaunakakai.

🚗 Major Agencies **Budget** ☎ 808/451-3600 or 800/527-7000 ⊕ www.budget.com. **Dollar** ☎ 808/567-6156 or 800/367-7006 ⊕ www.dollar.com.

🚗 Local Agencies **Island Kine Rent-a-Car** ☎ 808/553-5242 ⊕ www.molokai-car-rental.com. **Moloka'i Rentacar** ✉ 82 Ala Mālama, Kaunakakai ☎ 808/553-3929 🖶 808/553-9808.

BY FERRY

The Moloka'i Ferry crosses the channel every day between Lahaina (Maui) and Kaunakakai, making it easy for West Maui visitors to put Moloka'i on their itineraries. The 1½-hour trip takes passengers but not cars, so arrange ahead of time for a car rental or tour at the arrival point. The easiest way to do this is to contact Moloka'i Outdoors, who will arrange your transportation and lodgings. Tack this trek onto the end of a vacation in West Maui.

🚢 **Moloka'i Ferry** ☎ 808/667-2585 ⊕ www.molokaiferry.com.

Contacts & Resources

EMERGENCIES

Round-the-clock medical attention is available at Moloka'i General Hospital. Severe cases or emergencies are often airlifted to Honolulu.

🚑 Emergency Services **Ambulance and general emergencies** ☎ 911. **Coast Guard** ☎ 808/552-6458 on O'ahu. **Fire** ☎ 808/553-5601 in Kaunakakai, 808/567-6525 at Ho'olehua Airport. **Police** ☎ 808/553-5355.

🏥 Hospital **Moloka'i General Hospital** ✉ 280A Puali St., Kaunakakai ☎ 808/553-5331.

VISITOR INFORMATION

There's tourist information available in kiosks and stands at the airport in Ho'olehua or at the Moloka'i Visitors Association.

Molokaievents.com, Inc., has information on island events and can help you plan your own events on the island.

ℹ️ **Maui Visitors Bureau** 🏠 On Maui: Box 580, Wailuku 96793 ☎ 808/244-3530 ⊕ www.visitmaui.com. **Molokaievents.com, Inc.** ☎ 808/567-6789 ⊕ www.molokaievents.com. **Moloka'i Visitors Association** ✉ 10 Kamehameha V Hwy., Box 960, Kaunakakai ☎ 808/553-5221 or 800/800-6367 ⊕ molokai-hawaii.com.

Lāna'i

WORD OF MOUTH

"If you are going for golf or tennis or lazing around in the sun, it is wonderful. Other than that, it is very, very low key with minimal shopping and no evening activities."

—breckgal

"The day we went [to Polihua Beach] it was only us and three locals who were fishing. The sand is so soft, and the water is crystal clear."

—alex

WELCOME TO LĀNA'I

Polihua Beach

TOP 5
Reasons to Go

1. **Seclusion & Serenity:** Lāna'i is small: local motion is slow motion. Go home rested instead of exhausted.

2. **Garden of the Gods:** Walk amid the eerie red rock spires that ancient Hawaiians believed to be the home of the spirits.

3. **A Dive at Cathedrals:** Explore underwater pinnacle formations and mysterious caverns lit by shimmering rays of light.

4. **Dole Square:** Hang out in the shade of the Cook Pines and talk story with the locals.

5. **Lāna'i Pine Sporting Clays & Archery Range:** Play a Pacific William Tell, aiming your arrow at a pineapple.

■ TIP→→ Directions on the island are often given as *mauka* (toward the mountains) and *makai* (toward the ocean).

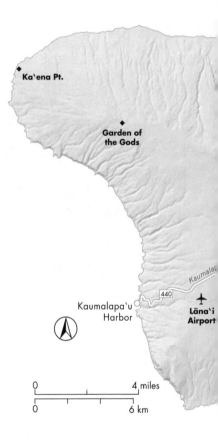

Ka'ena Pt.

Garden of the Gods

Kaumalar

440

Kaumalapa'u Harbor

Lāna'i Airport

```
0                    4 miles
0                    6 km
```

Hulopo'e Beach   *Garden of the Gods*

Getting Oriented

Unlike the other Hawaiian islands with their tropical splendors, Lāna'i looks like a desert: kiawe trees right out of Africa, red dirt roads that glow molten at sunset, and a deep blue sea that literally leads to Tahiti. Lāna'ihale (house of Lāna'i), the mountain that bisects the island, is carved into deep canyons by rain and wind on the windward side, and the dryer leeward side slopes gently to the sea, where waves pound against surf-carved cliffs.

Spinner Dolphins

Windward Lāna'i is the long white sand beach at the base of Lāna'ihale. Now uninhabited, it was once occupied by thriving Hawaiian fishing villages and a sugar cane plantation.

WINDWARD LĀNA'I

Keomuku Hwy

Lāna'i City

◆ Lodge at Kō'ele

UPCOUNTRY

▲ Mt. Lāna'ihale 3,370ft

Manele Rd

440

Four Seasons Resort Lāna'i at Mānele Bay ◆

Mānele Bay

Lāna'i City is really a tiny plantation village. Locals hold conversations in front of Dole Park shops and from their pickups on the road, and kids ride bikes in colorful impromptu parades while cars wait for them.

Cool and serene, **Upcountry** is graced by Lāna'i City, towering Cook Pine trees, and misty mountain vistas.

The more developed beach side of the island, **Mānele Bay** and harbor is where it's happening: swimming, picnicking, off-island excursions, and boating are all concentrated in this very accessible area.

Lāna'i Pine Archery

LĀNAʻI PLANNER

Sunsets and Moonrises

One of the best ways to tap into Lānaʻi's Pacific Island pace is to take the time not just to watch the sun set but also to watch the moon rise. The best sunset-viewing spots are the veranda at The Lodge, the grassy field past the Lodge's tennis courts, Hulopoʻe Beach, and the Challenge at Mānele clubhouse. For full moons, nothing beats the trail that leads to Puʻu Pehe or the many stopping places along Keōmoko Road.

Navigating Without Signs

Lānaʻi has no traffic, no traffic lights, and only three paved roads. Bring along a good topographical map, study it, and keep in mind your directions. Stop from time to time and re-find landmarks and gauge your progress. Distance is better measured in the condition of the road than in miles. Watch out for other jeep drivers who also don't know where they are. Never drive to the edge of lava cliffs, as rock can give way under you.

Timing Is Everything

Whales are seen off Lānaʻi's shores from December through April. A Pineapple Festival on the 4th of July Saturday in Dole Park features local food, Hawaiian entertainment, a pineapple eating and cooking contest and fireworks. Buddhists hold their annual outdoor Obon Festival honoring departed ancestors with joyous dancing, food booths, and taiko drumming in early July. Lānaʻi celebrates the statewide Aloha Festivals in mid-October with a hometown parade, car contests, more food, and more music. Beware hunting season weekends—from mid-February through mid-May, and mid-July through mid-October. Most of the private lodging properties are booked way in advance.

Car Rentals

Renting a four-wheel-drive vehicle is expensive but almost essential. There are only 30 mi of paved road on the island. The rest of your driving takes place on bumpy, muddy, secondary roads, which generally aren't marked. Be sure to make reservations far in advance of your trip, because Lānaʻi's fleet of vehicles is limited.

Additional planning details are listed in Lānaʻi Essentials at the end of this chapter.

Will It Rain?

As higher mountains on Maui capture the trade wind clouds, Lānaʻi receives little rainfall and has a desert ecology. It's always warmer at the beach and can get cool or even cold (by Hawaiian standards) upcountry. Consider the wind direction when planning your day. If it's blowing a gale on the windward beaches, head for the lee at Hulopoʻe or check out Garden of The Gods. Overcast days, when the wind stops or comes lightly from the southwest, are common in whale season. Try a whale watching trip or the windward beaches.

EXPLORING LĀNA'I

Updated by
Joana Varawa

Most of Lāna'i's sights are out of the way—rent a four-wheel-drive, ask for a road map, be sure you have a full tank, and bring a snack and plenty of water. Ask your hotel's concierge about road conditions and driving directions before you set out.

Lāna'i has an ideal climate year-round, hot and sunny at the sea and a few delicious degrees cooler Upcountry. In Lāna'i City, the nights and mornings can be almost chilly when a mystic fog or harsh trade winds settle in.

The main road in Lāna'i, Route 440, refers to both Kaumalapau Highway and Mānele Road. On the Islands, the directions *mauka* (toward the mountains) and *makai* (toward the ocean) are often used.

Lāna'i City & Mānele Bay

Pineapples once blanketed the Pālāwai, the great basin south of Lāna'i City. Before that it was a vast dryland forest; now most of it is fenced-in pasture or a game bird reserve, and can only be viewed from the Mānele Road. Although it looks like a volcanic crater, it isn't. Some say that the name Pālāwai is descriptive of the mist that sometimes fills the basin at dawn and looks like a huge shining lake.

A GOOD DRIVE

Start at the Lodge at Kō'ele to get a glimpse of early-ranching history. The lone **Norfolk Pine ❶** ➤ in front of the Lodge, planted in 1875, inspired the ranch manager to plant the pine forest that blankets the *hale* and serves as the island's watershed. On the left stands **Ka Lokahi o Ka Mālamalama Church ❷**.

Pause in **Lāna'i City ❸** for an espresso, and then drive south on Route 440 until you reach a major intersection. Turn left on Highway 440 East, and drive through the Pālāwai down a winding, steep hill. At the bottom awaits **Mānele Bay ❹** and the island's only true swimming area, Hulopo'e Beach. Backtrack up the hill. Just before the road goes up to the city is a large, carved boulder with an arrow pointing to the **Lu'ahiwa-Petroglyphs ❺**—take the dirt road on the right to reach them.

Return to the Highway 440 intersection. Follow Highway 440 past the airport to **Kaumalapau Harbor ❻**, the island's main seaport and a great sunset spot.

TIMING

You could explore this small area in half a day, but if you like water sports, you may indulge in a few hours at Hulopo'e Beach. The wind often picks up in the afternoon, so it's best to swim early. The south is sunny, clear, and warm, so wear sunscreen and find shade at midday.

What to See

Halulu Heiau. The well-preserved remains of an impressive *heiau* at Kaunolu village, which was actively used by Lāna'i's earliest residents, attest to this spot's sacred history. As late as 1810, this hilltop temple was considered a place of refuge, where those who had broken *kapu*

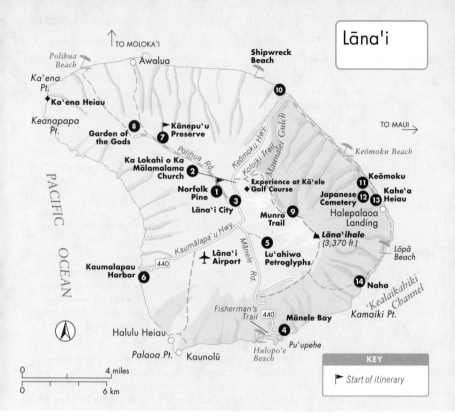

Lāna'i

TO MOLOKA'I

Polihua Beach

Ka'ena Pt.

♦ Ka'ena Heiau

Keanapapa Pt.

8 Garden of the Gods

7 ► Kānepu'u Preserve

Shipwreck Beach

10

TO MAUI →

Keōmoku Beach

Polihua Rd.

Keōmoku Hwy.

Koloiki Trail

Maunalei Gulch

PACIFIC OCEAN

2 Ka Lokahi o Ka Mālamalama Church

1 Norfolk Pine

3 Lāna'i City

♦ Experience at Kō'ele Golf Course

5 Munro Trail

9

Kaumālapa'u Hwy.

Mānele Rd.

Lāna'i Airport

Lu'ahiwa Petroglyphs

Japanese Cemetery **12** **13** Kahe'a Heiau

11 Keōmoku

Halepalaoa Landing

▲ Lāna'ihale (3,370 ft.)

Lōpā Beach

Kaumalapau Harbor **6** 440

Fisherman's Trail 440

Mānele Bay

4

Halulu Heiau ◇

Palaoa Pt. Kaunolū

Hulopo'e Beach

Pu'upehe

Kealaikahiki Channel

Kamaiki Pt.

14 Naha

0 — 4 miles
0 — 6 km

KEY

► Start of itinerary

(taboos) were forgiven and where women and children could find safety in times of war. If you explore the area, be very respectful, take nothing with you and leave nothing behind. This place is hard to find, so get someone to mark a map for you. The road down has recently been graded, but is quite sandy and soft at the bottom. ⊠ *From Lāna'i City follow Hwy. 440 west toward Kaumalapau Harbor. Pass airport, then look for carved boulder on hill on your left. Turn left on dirt road, follow it to another carved boulder, then head downhill.*

2 **Ka Lokahi o Ka Mālamalama Church.** This picturesque church was built in 1938 to provide services for Lāna'i's growing population—for many people, the only other Hawaiian church, in coastal Keōmuku, was too far away. A classic structure of preplantation days, the church had to be moved from its original Lāna'i Ranch location when the Lodge at Kō'ele was built. Sunday services are still held, in Hawaiian and English; visitors are welcome, but are requested to attend quietly. ⊠ *Left of entrance to Lodge at Kō'ele.*

6 **Kaumalapau Harbor.** Built in 1926 by the Hawaiian Pineapple Company, which later became Dole, this is Lāna'i's principal seaport. The cliffs that flank the western shore are as much as 1,000 feet tall. Water activities aren't allowed here, but it's a dramatic sunset spot. The harbor is closed to visitors on barge days: Wednesday, Thursday, and Friday. ⊠ *From Lāna'i City follow Hwy. 440 (Kaumalapau Hwy.) west as far as it goes.*

Kaunolū. Close to the island's highest cliffs, Kaunolū was once a prosperous fishing village. This important archaeological site includes a major heiau, terraces, stone floors, and house platforms. The impressive 90-foot drop to the ocean through a gap in the lava rock is called **Kahekili's Leap.** Warriors would make the dangerous jump into the shallow 12 feet of water below to show their courage. Hawai'i's King Kamehameha I is said to have visited the village to collect taxes and enjoy the excellent fishing found in the offshore waters. A newly graded road gets soft and sandy at the bottom. Get a marked map before you set out. ⊠ *From Lāna'i City follow Hwy. 440 (Kaumalapau Hwy.) west; at carved boulder on hill, turn left onto dirt road; go until you reach the second carved boulder and then head makai.*

❸ **Lāna'i City.** This tidy plantation town, built in 1924 by Jim Dole, is home to old-time residents and recently arrived resort workers, and is slowly changing from a quiet rural village to a busy little town. A simple grid of roads here is lined with stately Cook pines, and all the basic services a person might need. The pace is slow and the people are friendly. Visit the **Lāna'i Arts & Cultural Center** to get a glimpse of this island's creative abundance. ⊠ *339 7th Ave.*

❺ **Lu'ahiwa Petroglyphs.** On a steep slope overlooking the Pālāwai Basin are 34 boulders with carvings. Drawn in a mixture of ancient and historic styles dating to the late 1700s and early 1800s, the simple stick-figures depict animals, people, and mythic beings. A nearby heiau, or temple, no longer visible, was used to summon the rains and was dedicated to the god Kāne. Do not draw on or deface the carvings, and do not add to the collection. ⊠ *From Lāna'i City turn left on Hwy. 440 (Mānele Rd.) and continue to first dirt road on your left, marked by large carved boulder and sign. Follow road the road marked by the boulder through fields; do not go left uphill but continue going straight and when you see boulders on hillside, park and walk up to petroglyphs.*

❹ **Mānele Bay.** The site of a Hawaiian village dating from AD 900, Mānele Bay is flanked by lava cliffs hundreds of feet high. Though a Marine Life Conservation District, it's the island's only public boat harbor and was the location of most post-contact shipping until Kaumalapau Harbor was built in 1926. The ferry to and from Maui also pulls in here. Public restrooms, water, and picnic tables make it a nice pit-stop—you can watch the boating activity as you rest and refuel.

Just offshore you can catch a glimpse of **Pu'upehe.** Often called Sweetheart Rock, the isolated 80-foot-high islet carries a sad Hawaiian legend that is probably not true. The rock is said to be named after Pehe, a woman so beautiful that her husband, afraid that others would steal her away, kept her hidden in a sea cave. One day, while Pehe was alone, the surf surged into the cave and she drowned. Her grief-stricken husband buried her on the summit of this rock and then jumped to his own

FODOR'S FIRST PERSON

Joana Varawa
Writer

I first came to Lāna‘i in 1977 to study whales and dolphins. The Lāna‘i Company allowed me to set up an observation camp on the cliff above the entrance to Mānele Harbor. My research station comprised a tent, which I never slept in, and an outside pallet with a mattress, which I did sleep on. Everything I owned fit in a big basket.

And so I began the best year of my entire life. I called my cliff-top aerie my million-dollar condo (a million was worth more then), and each morning I would make my coffee, sit on the rocks overlooking the sea, and watch the dolphins in their early-morning resting ritual. They had a way of getting rid of whale-watching boats by sending out bow riders who would lead the boats away from the school, which would then resume its lazy circling in the deep water under the cliff. I would walk to the beach on a path unblemished by footprints, and enter the crystal water, pushing myself to go farther and longer until I was comfortable

in the ocean. One memorable time I swam out to the dolphins only to find a shark sculling peacefully beneath me. Panic was no option, so I followed him, thinking it better than turning my back and yelling, and he slowly melted into the distance. Admittedly, my return to shore was the best swim I ever made, in the shortest time.

One night I listened to the heart-stopping pounding of a whale smashing her tail against the water beneath me, a booming that seemed to rock the foundations of the land itself, and in the morning discovered the form of a creamy white-and-turquoise baby whale at her side, and understood I had heard a whale giving birth.

The island revealed itself to me in all its beauty. My companions were geckos, mice, and deer, and I knew the time by the moon's stately progress and the stars slowly turning above me. I was not an observer, but an equal participant in the great unfolding of life. I had come to learn about the whales and dolphins, but ultimately I learned the most about myself.

death. A more authentic, if less romantic, story is that the enclosure on the summit is a shrine to birds, built by bird-catchers. Archaeological investigation has revealed that the enclosure was not a burial place. ✉ *From Lāna‘i City follow Hwy. 440 (Mānele Rd.) south to bottom of hill and look for harbor on your left.*

▶ ❶ **Norfolk Pine.** More than 100 feet high, this majestic pine tree was planted here, at the former site of the manager's house, in 1875. Almost 30 years later, George Munro, then the ranch manager, would observe how, in foggy weather, water collected on its foliage, forming a natural rain. This fog drip led Munro to supervise the planting of Cook pines along the ridge of Lāna‘ihale and throughout the town in order to add to the island's water supply. ✉ *Entrance of Lodge at Kō‘ele.*

Garden of the Gods & Windward Lāna'i

The north and east sections of Lāna'i are wild and untouched. An inaccessible heiau is the only trace of human habitation, with the exception of stacks of rocks marking old shrines, and trails. Four-wheel drive is a must to explore this side of the isle, and be prepared for hot, rough conditions. Pack a picnic lunch and bring plenty of drinking water.

A GOOD DRIVE

Set out north of the Lodge at Kō'ele on Keōmoku Highway: turn left on the road between the Stables at Kō'ele and the tennis courts at the large carved boulder on the right of the road. Follow the dirt road a short distance and turn right at the fence line onto Polihua Road, which heads north through deserted pastures, old pineapple fields, past the dryland forest of **Kānepu'u Preserve** ⓐ ▶ and, 1½ mi beyond, the **Garden of the Gods** ⓑ.

Return to Keōmoku Highway and head east. After about 1 mi, make a right onto the only road in sight, Cemetery Road, and you're on your way to the **Munro Trail** ⓒ, a 9-mi route that runs over the top of Lāna'ihale, the mountain that rises above Lāna'i City. Unofficially the Munro trail is a one-way road, although you may meet someone coming toward you from the south side, so be careful.

Back on Keōmoku Highway, head makai—at an unofficial scenic point between mile markers 4 and 5 you'll find awesome views of Moloka'i on your left, and Maui, on your right, and a first glimpse of the abandoned World War II oiler at **Shipwreck Beach** ⓒ.

If you feel adventurous, head southeast at the fork in the road where the beach starts, and follow the dirt road along the coast. During the rainy season the shoreline road may be impassable at places crossed by stream beds. Note that many of the spur roads leading to the windward beaches from the coastal dirt road cross private property and are closed off by chains. Look for open spur roads with recent tire marks (a fairly good sign that they are safe to drive on). It's best to park on firm ground and walk in to avoid getting your car mired in the sand.

The landscape changes from coastal dunes to *kiawe* forest (kiawe is a mesquite-type wood; watch for thorns!). Dozens of tall coconut trees announce the site of the old village **Keōmoku** ⓒ, once a bustling sugar-mill town. Pause at the **Japanese Cemetery** ⓒ. Nearby are the buried ruins of a temple called **Kahe'a Heiau** ⓒ, but you will need an experienced guide to find it. The road passes deserted Lōpā Beach and ends 3 mi later at the remnants of an old Hawaiian fishpond at **Naha** ⓒ.

TIMING

Give yourself a full day to tour the island's northern and eastern reaches. Keep your eye on the sky: the highlands tend to attract heavy fog. If you're a hiker, you'll want a day just to enjoy the journey up to Lāna'ihale. Since many of the roads are bumpy, it takes more time to reach sights than it does to actually experience them. But getting there is half the fun.

What to See

⑧ Garden of the Gods. This preternatural plateau is scattered with boulders of different sizes, shapes, and colors, the products of a million years of wind erosion. Time your visit for sunset, when the rocks begin to glow—from rich red to purple—and the fiery globe sinks to the horizon. Magnificent views of the Pacific Ocean, Molokaʻi, and, on clear days, Oʻahu provide the perfect backdrop for photographs.

FodorsChoice
★

The ancient Hawaiians shunned Lānaʻi for hundreds of years, believing the island was the inviolable home of spirits. Standing beside the oxidered rock spires of this strange, raw landscape, you might be tempted to believe the same. This lunar savannah still has a decidedly eerie edge; but the shadows disappearing on the horizon are those of mouflon sheep and axis deer, not the fearsome spirits of lore. According to tradition, the spirits were vanquished by Kāʻululaʻau, a chief's son from Maui who was exiled here for destroying his father's prized breadfruit groves. The clever boy outwitted and exhausted the spirits, and announced their banishment with a giant bonfire. ⊠ *From Stables at Kōʻele, follow dirt road through pasture, turn right at crossroad marked by carved boulder, head through abandoned fields and ironwood forest to open red-dirt area marked by a carved boulder.*

⑫ Japanese Cemetery. In 1899 sugar came to this side of Lānaʻi. A plantation took up about 2,400 acres and seemed a profitable proposition, but that same year, disease wiped out the labor force. This authentic Buddhist shrine commemorates the Japanese workers who died. ⊠ *6½ mi southeast from where Keōmuku Hwy. dead-ends at Shipwreck Beach, on dirt road running along north shore.*

⑬ Kaheʻa Heiau. What was once an important place of worship for the people of Lānaʻi may be hard to find through the kiawe overgrowth. The wharf at **Halepaloa Landing** has been rebuilt however. The wharf was used by the Maunalei Sugar Company (1899) to ship cane, and some say the company failed because the sacred stones of the heiau were used for the construction of the cane railroad. Angry gods turned the drinking water salty, forcing the sugar company to close in 1901. There's good public beach access here and clear shallow water for swimming, but no other facilities. ⊠ *6½ mi southeast from where Keōmuku Hwy. dead-ends at Shipwreck Beach, on dirt road running along north shore.*

▶ **⑦ Kānepuʻu Preserve.** The 590 acres of this native dryland forest were under the stewardship of the Nature Conservancy of Hawaiʻi until recently and are now managed by Castle & Cooke Resorts. Kānepuʻu contains the largest remnant of this rare indigenous forest type. More than 45 native species of plants, including the endangered Hawaiian gardenia, grow in the shade of such rare trees as Hawaiian sandalwood, olive, and ebony. A short self-guided loop trail, with eight signs illustrated by local artist Wendell Kahoʻohalahala, reveals this ecosystem's beauty and the challenges it faces. ⊠ *Polihua Rd., 6 mi north of Lānaʻi City.*

⑪ Keōmoku. There's an eerie beauty about Keōmoku, with its faded memories and forgotten homesteads. During the late 19th century, this busy

Lāna'i community of some 900 to 2,000 residents served as the head-quarters of Maunalei Sugar Company. After the company failed, the land was used for ranching, but by 1954 the area lay abandoned. Its church, **Ka Lanakila O Ka Mālamalama,** was built in 1903. It has been partially restored by volunteers, and visitors often leave some small token, a shell or faded lei, as an offering. Among the overgrown kiawe trees you may find the remnants of a Portuguese beehive-shape communal bread oven, or the weathered boards of what was the last windmill. ⊠ *5 mi along unpaved road southeast of Shipwreck Beach.*

★ ❾ **Munro Trail.** This 9-mi jeep trail along a fern- and pine-clad narrow ridge was named after George Munro, manager of the Lāna'i Ranch Co., who began a reforestation program in the 1950s to restore the island's much-needed watershed. The trail climbs **Lāna'ihale** (House of Lāna'i), which, at 3,370 feet, is the island's highest point; on clear days you'll be treated to a panorama of canyons and almost all of the Hawaiian Islands. ⚠ The one-way road gets very muddy, and trade winds can be strong. A sheer drop-off in some sections requires an attentive driver. Keep an eye out for hikers along the way. You can also hike the MunroTrail (⇨ *See* Hiking *later in this chapter*), though it's a difficult trek: it's steep, the ground is un-even, and there's no water. ⊠ *From Lodge at Kō'ele head north on Keōmoku Hwy. for 1¼ mi, then turn right onto dirt road; trailhead is ½ mi past cemetery on right.*

❶❹ **Naha.** An ancient rock-walled fishpond—visible at low tide—lies here, where the sandy shorelines end and the cliffs begin their rise along the island's shores. The beach is a frequent resource for local fisherfolk. ⚠ Treacherous currents make this a dangerous place for swimming. ⊠ *East side of Lāna'i, at end of dirt road that runs from end of Keōmoku Hwy. along eastern shore.*

★ ❿ **Shipwreck Beach.** The rusting World War II tanker may be a clue that the waters off this 8-mi stretch of sand aren't friendly. Strong trade winds have propelled innocent vessels onto the reef since at least 1824, when the first shipwreck was recorded. Some believe that the unknown oiler you see stranded today, however, was merely abandoned. ⚠ The water is unsafe for swimming; stick to beachcombing. ⊠ *End of Keōmoku Hwy. heading north.*

BEACHES

Lāna'i offers miles of secluded white-sand beaches on its windward side, and the moderately developed Hulopo'e Beach, which is adjacent to the Four Seasons Resort Lāna'i at Mānele Bay. Hulopo'e is accessible by car or hotel shuttle bus; to reach the windward beaches you'll need a four-wheel-drive vehicle. An offshore reef, rocks, and coral make swimming on the windward side problematic, but it's fun to splash around in the shallow water. Driving on the beach itself is illegal and can be danger-ous. Beaches are listed alphabetically.

The Coastal Road

Road conditions can change overnight and become impassable due to rain in the uplands. Car-rental agencies should be able to give you updates before you hit the road. Many of the spur roads leading to the windward beaches from the coastal dirt road cross private property and are closed off by chains. Look for open spur roads with recent tire marks (a fairly good sign that they are safe to drive on). It's best to park on firm ground and walk in to avoid getting your car mired in the sand.

Hulopo'e Beach. A short stroll from the Four Seasons Resort Lāna'i at Mānele Bay, Hulopo'e is considered one of the best beaches in all of Hawai'i. The sparkling crescent of this Marine Life Conservation District beckons with calm waters safe for swimming almost year-round, great snorkeling reefs, tide pools, and, sometimes, spinner dolphins. A shady, grassy beach park is perfect for picnics. If the shore break is pounding, or if you see surfers riding big waves, stay out of the water. ⊠ *From Lāna'i City follow Hwy. 440 (Mānele Rd.) south to bottom of hill; turn right, road dead-ends at beach parking lot* ☞ *Toilets, showers, picnic tables, grills, parking lot.*

Lōpā Beach. A popular surfing spot for locals, Lōpā is also an ancient fishpond. With majestic views of West Maui and Kaho'olawe, this remote, white-sand beach is a great place for a picnic. ⚠ Don't let the sight of surfers fool you: the channel's currents are too strong for swimming. ⊠ *East side of Lāna'i, 7 mi south down a dirt road that runs from end of Keōmuku Hwy. along eastern shore* ☞ *No facilities.*

Polihua Beach. This often-deserted beach should get a star for beauty with its long, wide stretch of white sand and clear views of Moloka'i. The dirt road to get here can be bad with deep, sandy places (when it rains it's impassable), however, and frequent high winds whip up sand and waves. ⚠ Strong currents and a sudden drop in the ocean floor make swimming extremely dangerous. On the northern end, the beach ends at a rocky lava cliff with some interesting tide pools. Polihua is named after the sea turtles that lay their eggs in the sand. Do not drive on the beach and endanger their nests. Curiously, wild bees sometimes gather around your car for water at this beach. To get rid of them, put out water some place away from the car and wait a bit. ⊠ *Windward Lāna'i, 11 mi from Lāna'i City, past Garden of the Gods* ☞ *No facilities.*

Shipwreck Beach. Beachcombers come to this fairly accessible beach for shells and washed-up treasures; photographers for great shots of Moloka'i, just across the 9-mi wide Kalohi Channel; and walkers for the long stretch of sand. It may still be possible to find glass ball fishing floats but more common is waterborne debris from the Moloka'i channel. Kaiolohia, its Hawaiian name, is a favorite local diving spot. ⚠ An offshore reef and rocks in the water mean that it's not for swimmers, though you can play in the shallow water on the shoreline. ⊠ *North shore, 10 mi north of Lāna'i City at end of Keōmuku Hwy.* ☞ *No facilities.*

WATER ACTIVITIES & TOURS

Boat Tours & Charters

Trilogy Oceansports Lāna'i. If you're staying in Lāna'i and want to play on the ocean, Trilogy is your outfitter.

A 2½-hour blue-water snorkeling and adventure rafting trip includes lessons, equipment, and a hot barbecue lunch at the Trilogy Pavilion when you return to Mānele harbor. Tours are offered Monday, Tuesday, Thursday, and Friday; costs are $91 for adults and $46 for kids 15 and under.

On Wednesday you can opt for a Snorkel and Sail aboard one of their large catamarans, departing at 11:15 AM. This trip is perfect if you want to sleep in or spend your early morning over a leisurely breakfast. The three-hour sail includes the barbecue lunch and a cruise up the coast to a remote snorkel site. The tour costs $134 for adults, $67 for children.

Serious divers should go for Trilogy's two-tank dive; location depends on the weather. You must be certified, so don't forget your documentation. The $149 fee includes a light breakfast of cinnamon rolls and coffee. Beginners (minimum age 12) can try a one-tank introductory dive for $80. You'll wade into Hulopo'e Bay with an instructor at your side; actual dive time is 20 to 30 minutes. Certified divers can choose a 35- to 40-minute wade-in dive at Hulopo'e for $70.

If that's not enough, sign up for a blue-water dolphin watch, whale-watching sail, or a sunset cruise. You can book trips through your hotel concierge, but try online first, where discounts are often available. ☎ 888/628–4800 ⊕ www.sailtrilogy.com.

Deep-Sea Fishing

Some of the best sportfishing grounds in Maui County are off the southwest shoreline of Lāna'i. Pry your eyes open and go deep-sea fishing in the early morning, with departures at 6 or 6:30 AM from Mānele Harbor. Prime seasons are spring and summer, although good catches have been landed year-round. Mahimahi, ono, 'ahi, and marlin are prized catches, with mahi andono (which means delicious in Hawaiian) preferred eating.

Kila Kila. Jeff Menze, with 30 years' experience in Hawaiian waters, captains this elegant 53-foot Merritt, which has world records to its credit. If there are fish to find, Menze can find them. The sleek *Kila Kila* has a fly bridge, spacious cockpit, air-conditioned salon, showers, and two toilets. Menze and his crew clean

THE COUSTEAU FALLACY

Never turn your back on the ocean seems easy to remember, but many forget it. Much to the amusement of water-smart locals, hundreds of visitors get smashed trying to wade in backwards, wearing fins, mask, and snorkel. Wading in facing the waves is equally dangerous, so always swim in past the breakers, and in the comparative calm put on your fins, then mask and snorkel. It will save you, at the least, getting laughed at, or at the worst, getting seriously injured.

your catch, cut fillets, and send them up to the Mānele chefs to be cooked to order. Or you can take the fillets for a picnic barbeque or dinner elsewhere. A four-hour trip with up to six passengers costs $825; a full-day run is $1,200. Pastries and soft drinks are provided. A sunset sail and sightseeing along the coast are other options, but they do not allow snorkeling. Book with the concierge at the resort. ☎ 808/565–2387 or 808/565–4555.

Fish-N-Chips. This 32-foot Hatteras Sport Fisher with tuna tower will get you to the fishing grounds in comfort, and Captain Jason will do everything except reel in the big one for you. Plan on trolling along the south coast for ono and around the point at Kaunolu for mahi or marlin. A trip to the offshore buoy often yields skipjack tuna or big 'ahi, and the captain and crew are always open to a bit of bottom fishing for fun and relaxation. Fishing gear, sodas, and water are included. Let them know if you would also like breakfast or lunch for an additional charge. A four-hour charter (six-passenger maximum) will set you back $625; each additional hour costs $110. You can keep up to ⅓ of all fish caught. Shared charters on Sunday and Wednesday are $130 per person. Book with the concierge at your resort or give them a call directly. ☎ 808/565–7676.

Kayaking

Lāna'i's southeast coast offers leisurely paddling inside the windward reef. Curious sea turtles and friendly manta rays may tag along for company. There are miles of scenic coastline with deserted beaches on the inside reef to haul up on for an informal picnic. When the wind comes from the southwest, the windward coast is tranquil. Kayaking along the leeward cliffs is more demanding with rougher seas and strong currents. No kayaking is permitted in the Marine Conservation District at Hulopo'e Bay.

Early mornings tend to be calmer. The wind picks up as the day advances. ⚠ Expect strong currents along all of the coasts. Experience on the water is advised, and knowing how to swim is essential.

■ TIP➔ There's one major drawback to kayaking on Lāna'i: you'll have to travel with your own kayak or arrange for a Maui vendor to meet you on the island, as there are no kayak rentals or guides on Lāna'i.

Scuba Diving

When you have a dive site such as Cathedrals—with eerie pinnacle formations and luminous caverns—it's no wonder that scuba-diving buffs consider exploring the waters off Lāna'i akin to having a religious experience.

Just outside of Hulopo'e Bay, the boat dive site **Cathedrals** was named the best cavern dive site in the Pacific by *Skin Diver* magazine. Shimmering light makes the many openings in the caves look like stained-glass windows. A current generally keeps the water crystal clear, even if it's turbid outside. In these unearthly chambers, large ulua and small reef shark add to the adventure. **Sergeant Major Reef**, off Kamaiki Point, is named for big schools of yellow- and black-striped manini (Sergeant

Major fish) that turn the rocks silvery as they feed. The site is made up of three parallel lava ridges, a cave, and an archway, with rippled sand valleys between the ridges. Depths range 15–50 feet.

Trilogy (⇨ *See* Boat Tours & Charters, *above*) is the only company running boat dives from Lānaʻi.

Snorkeling

Snorkeling is the easiest ocean sport available on the island, requiring nothing but a snorkel, mask, fins, and good sense. Purchase equipment in Lānaʻi City if you don't bring your own. The basic rules of snorkeling are: never turn your back on the ocean; wait to enter the water until you are sure no big sets are coming; and observe the activity of locals on the beach. If little kids are playing in the shore break, it's usually safe to enter (although little local kids are expert wave riders). Put your mask and fins on once you have passed the shore break, rather than trying to wade in with fins through the waves.

Hulopoʻe Beach is an outstanding snorkeling destination. The bay is a State of Hawaiʻi Marine Conservation District and no spear-fishing or diving is allowed. Schools of manini feeding on the coral coat the rocks with flashing silver, and you can view kala, uhu, and papio in all their rainbow colors. Wade in from the sandy beach, the best snorkeling is toward the left. Beware of rocks and surging waves. When the resident spinner dolphins are in the bay, it's courteous to watch them from the shore. If swimmers and snorkelers go out, the dolphins may leave and be deprived of their necessary resting place. Another wade-in snorkel spot is just beyond the break wall at **Mānele Small Boat Harbor.** Enter over the rocks just past the boat ramp. ⚠ It's dangerous to enter if waves are breaking.

Book with Trilogy (⇨ *See* Boat Tours & Charters, *above*) for snorkel sails.

GOLF, HIKING & OUTDOOR ACTIVITIES

Biking

Many of the same red-dirt roads that invite hikers are excellent for biking, offering easy flat terrain and long clear views. There's only one hitch: you may have to bring your own bike, as there are no rentals or tours for nonresort guests available.

A favorite biking route is along the fairly flat red-dirt road northward from Lānaʻi City through the old pineapple fields to Garden of the Gods. Start your trip on Keōmuku Highway in town. Take a left just before the Lodge's tennis courts, and then a right where the road ends at the fenced pasture, and continue on to the north end and the start of Polihua and Awalua dirt roads. If you're really hardy you could bike down to Polihua Beach and back, but it would be a serious all-day trip. In wet weather these roads turn to slurry and are not advisable. Go in the early morning or late afternoon because the sun gets hot in the middle of the day. Take plenty of water, spare parts, and snacks.

For the exceptionally fit, it's possible to bike from town down the Keōmuku Highway to the windward beaches and back, or to bike the Munro Trail (⇨ See Hiking, below). Experienced bikers also bike up and down the Mānele Highway from Mānele Bay to town.

Camping

Camping isn't encouraged outside Lāna'i's one official campground at Hulopo'e: the island is privately owned; islanders are keen on privacy; and, unless you know about local conditions, camping on the beach can be hazardous.

Castle & Cooke Resorts Campground. The inviting, grassy campground at Hulopo'e Beach has shade trees, clean restrooms, BBQ grills, and beachside showers. Buy charcoal in Lāna'i City, as well as basic camping supplies and food. Cutting fire wood is not allowed and camping on the beach itself is reserved for residents only. Call in advance; it's $20 for a permit, plus a $5 fee per person per night (three-night limit). ☎ 808/565-2970 for permits and advance reservations.

Golf

Lāna'i has just three courses and a total of 45 holes (not counting an 18-hole putting course), but all three are good and offer very different environments and challenges. The two resort courses, especially, are so different, it's hard to believe that they're on the same island, let alone just 20 minutes apart by resort shuttle.

Cavendish Golf Course. At this unique 9-holer, there's no phone, no clubhouse, no starter, just a slotted wooden box on the first tee requesting a monetary donation—go ahead, be generous!—to help with maintenance costs. This is a legacy of the plantation era, designed in 1947 by E. B. Cavendish, superintendent of factory guards, and is used by locals for Sunday tournaments and popular skins games. Holes run through chutes of stately Norfolk pines, and most greens are elevated. ⊠ Call Lodge at Kō'ele for directions ⚐ 9 holes. 3,071 yds. Par 36. Green Fee: Donation ⌕ No facilities.

The Challenge at Mānele. Designed by Jack Nicklaus (1993), this course sits right over the water of Hulopo'e Bay. Built on lava outcroppings, the course features three holes on cliffs that use the Pacific Ocean as a water hazard. The five-tee concept challenges the best golfers—tee shots over natural gorges and ravines must be precise. This dramatic, unspoiled natural terrain is a stunning backdrop, and every hole offers majestic ocean views. ⊠ 1 Challenge Dr., Lāna'i City ☎ 808/565-2222 ⊕ www. go-lanai.com ⚐ 18 holes. 6,310 yds. Par 72, slope 126. Green Fee: $225 ⌕ Facilities: Driving range, putting green, golf carts, rental clubs, pro shop, lessons, restaurant, bar.

The Experience at Ko'ele. The Experience at Ko'ele is a challenging Greg Norman (1991) layout that begins at an elevation of 2,000 feet. The front nine moves dramatically through ravines wooded with pine, koa, and eucalyptus trees; seven lakes and streams with cascading waterfalls dot the course. No other course offers a more incredible combination of highland terrain, inspired landscape architecture, and range of play challenges. Quite different from the sea-level Challenge at Mānele, it's hard to believe that these two courses are separated by only a 20-minute resort shuttle ride. ✉ *Kaimuko Dr., Lāna'i City* ☎ *808/565–4653* ⊕ *www.go-lanai.com* ⅃. *18 holes. 6,310 yds. Par 72, slope 134. Green Fee: $225* ☞ *Facilities: Driving range, putting green, golf carts, rental clubs, pro shop, lessons, restaurant, bar.*

Hiking

Only 30 mi of Lāna'i's roads are paved. But red-dirt roads and trails, ideal for hiking, will take you to sweeping overlooks, isolated beaches, and shady forests. Don't be afraid to leave the road to follow deer trails, but make sure to keep your landmarks in clear sight so you can always retrace your steps, if necessary. Or take a self-guided walk through Kāne Pu'u, Hawai'i's largest native dryland forest. You can explore the Munro Trail over Lāna'ihale with views of plunging canyons, or hike along an old, coastal fisherman trail or across Koloiki Ridge. Wear hiking shoes, a hat, and sunscreen, and carry plenty of water.

BEST TRAILS **Koloiki Ridge** is a marked, moderate trail that starts behind the Lodge at Kō'ele takes you along the cool and shady Munro Trail to overlook the windward side, with impressive views of Maui, Moloka'i, Maunalei Valley, and Naio Gulch. The average time for the 5-mi round-trip is three hours. Bring snacks and water, and take your time.

Local fishermen still use the **Lāna'i Fisherman Trail** to get to their favorite fishing spots. The trail takes about 1½ hours to hike and follows the rocky shoreline below the Four Seasons Resort Lāna'i at Mānele Bay, along cliffs bordering the golf course. Caves and tide pools beckon beneath you, but be careful climbing down. The marked trail entrance begins at the west end of Hulopo'e Beach. Keep your eyes open for spinner dolphins cavorting off-shore and the silvery flash of fish feeding in the pools below you. The condition of the trail varies with weather and frequency of maintenance.

Pu'u Pehe Trail begins to the left (facing the ocean) of Hulopo'e Beach, travels a short distance around the coastline, and then climbs up a sharp, rocky rise. At the top, you're level with the offshore stack of Pu'u Pehe and can overlook miles of coastline in both directions. The trail is not difficult, but it's hot and steep. ⚠ *Never go next to the edge, as the cliff can easily give way.* The hiking is best in the early morning or late afternoon, and it's a perfect place to look for whales in season (December–April). Wear shoes, this is not a hike for sandals or slip-ons.

The **Munro Trail** is the real thing: a strenuous 9-mi trek that begins behind the Lodge and follows the ridge of Lāna'ihale through the rain forest. The island's most demanding hike, it has an elevation gain of 1,400 feet and leads to a lookout at the island's highest point, Lāna'ihale. It's also a narrow dirt road so watch out for careening jeeps that are as unfamiliar with the terrain as you are. The trail is named after George Munro, who supervised the planting of Cook pine trees and eucalyptus windbreaks. Mules used to wend their way up the mountain carrying the pine seedlings. Unless you arrange for someone to pick you up at the trail's end, you have a long boring hike back through the Palawai Basin to return to your starting point. The top is often cloud-shrouded and can be windy and muddy, so check conditions before you start.

Horseback Riding

Stables at Kō'ele. The subtle beauty of the high country slowly reveals itself to horseback riders. Sunset rides, private saunters, and two-hour adventures traverse leafy trails with scenic overlooks. There's a fancy horse-drawn carriage for romantic couples and well-trained horses for riders of all ages and skill levels. Prices start at $85 for one hour and climb to $150 for a two-hour private ride. Book rides at The Lodge at Kō'ele. ☎ 808/565–4555.

Sporting Clays & Archery

★ **Lāna'i Pine Sporting Clays and Archery Range.** Outstanding rustic terrain, challenging targets, and a well-stocked pro shop make this sporting-clays course top-flight in the expert's eyes. Sharpshooters can complete the meandering 14-station course, with the help of a golf cart, in 1½ hours. There are group tournaments, and even kids can enjoy skilled instruction at the archery range and compressed air rifle gallery. The $45 archery introduction includes an amusing "pineapple challenge"—contestants are given five arrows with which to hit a pineapple target. The winner takes home a crystal pineapple as a nostalgic souvenir of the old Dole Plantation days. Guns and ammunition are provided with the lessons. ✉ *Just past Cemetery Rd. on windward side of island, first left off Keōmuku Hwy.* ☎ 808/559–4600.

> **MYTHOLOGICAL MYTHS**
>
> When tour boats travel the coast, their captains give out the "fafa" about places they are passing. Some of the "fafa" gets pretty fanciful and departs wildly not only from the truth, but from myth as well. The more outlandish or romantic the better, but the real stories suffer in the telling. This is how a bird shrine on the top of Pu'u Pehe has become the grave of an imprisoned princess. Place names shift around with the whim of the story-teller. So, since there's plenty of salt in the sea, take your stories with a grain or two.

WHERE TO EAT

Lāna'i's own version of Hawai'i regional cuisine draws on the fresh bounty provided by local hunters and fishermen, combined with the skills of well-trained chefs. The upscale menus at the Lodge at Kō'ele and the Four Seasons Resort Lāna'i at Mānele Bay encompass European-inspired cuisine and innovative preparations of quail, 'ahi, wild deer, and boar. Lāna'i City's eclectic ethnic fare runs from construction-worker-size local plate lunches to Cajun ribs and pesto pasta.

WHAT IT COSTS				
$$$$	**$$$**	**$$**	**$**	**¢**
RESTAURANTS over $30	$20–$30	$12–$20	$7–$12	under $7

Prices are for one main course at dinner.

Mānele Bay

★ **$$$–$$$$** ✕ **'Ihilani.** The fine dining room at the Four Seasons Resort Lāna'i at Mānele Bay shimmers with crystal chandeliers and gleaming silver in a serene setting illuminated by floor-to-ceiling etched-glass doors. Executive chef Oliver Beckert offers an upscale version of Italian comfort food designed around fresh local fish. Puna goat cheese ravioli with pine nuts and baby vegetables, and *onaga* (red snapper) served alla Puttanesca, with artichoke puree, and a spicy tomato and caper sauce, are good choices. Service is nonintrusive but attentive. ⊠ *Four Seasons Resort Lāna'i at Mānele Bay* ☎ *808/565–2296* ⌂ *Reservations essential* ▭ *AE, DC, MC, V* ☽ *No lunch. $20–$44.*

$$–$$$$ ✕ **The Challenge At Mānele Clubhouse.** This terraced restaurant has a stunning view of the legendary Pu'u Pehe offshore island, which only enhances its imaginative fare. Tuck into a Hulopo'e Bay prawn BLT, pan-seared opakapaka, or pad thai noodles with shrimp and crab in a macadamia nut curry sauce. Specialty drinks add to the informal fun. ⊠ *Four Seasons Resort Lāna'i at Mānele Bay* ☎ *808/565–2290* ▭ *AE, DC, MC, V* ☽ *No dinner. $14–$36.*

$$–$$$$ ✕ **Four Seasons Hulopo'e Court.** The Hulopo'e overlooks the wide sweep of the bay and offers an extensive breakfast buffet, lunch, and dinner in airy comfort. Choose between indoor or outdoor tables, with comfortable chairs upholstered in beige and burgundy. Cream-colored walls provide a restful backdrop indoors, and pale pink umbrellas shade the terrace dining. Fresh baked pastries and made-to-order omelets ensure your day will start well. For lunch the 'ahi or mahimahi tacos is a good choice; at dinner the daily fish special, the baked Pacific prawns stuffed with Dungeness crab, or Kurobuta pork chops marinated in Hoisin sauce with Lāna'i pineapple relish are all local favorites. Their chocolate cake is perfect. ⊠ *Four Seasons Resort Lāna'i at Mānele Bay* ☎ *808/565–2290* ⌂ *Reservations essential* ▭ *AE, DC, MC, V. $19–$34.*

$$–$$$$ ✕ **The Ocean Grill Bar & Restaurant.** Poolside at the Four Seasons Resort Lāna'i at Mānele Bay, the Ocean Grill offers informal lunch and dinner in a splendid setting. The big yellow and white umbrellas are cool and cheerful, and bamboo-inspired upholstered chairs in yellow and green are deliciously comfortable. Favorite lunch items include the kālua (pit-roasted) pork and cheese quesadilla, or the rare 'ahi (tuna) salade niçoise with fresh island greens. The dinner menu includes seasonal fresh island fish—onaga (red snapper), opakapaka (white snapper), and hapu'upu'u (sea bass), or an herb crusted rack of lamb. The view of Hulopo'e Bay is stunning, the service is Four Season's brand of cool aloha, and the decor is impeccable. ⊠ *Four Seasons Resort Lāna'i at Mānele Bay* ☎ *808/565–2000* ▭ *AE, DC, MC, V "New for 2006." $12–$40.*

Upcountry & Lāna'i City

$$$$ ✕ **Formal Dining Room.** Reflecting the Lodge's country manor elegance,
Fodor'sChoice this romantic octagonal restaurant is one of the best in the state. Inti-
★ mate tables are clustered close to a roaring fireplace with room between
for private conversation. Expanding Hawai'i regional cuisine, the changing menu includes the signature crispy seared moi (a fish once reserved
for Hawaiian chiefs). Start with tiny roasted quail on baby greens and
finish with a warm pear soufflé (ordered in advance). Expect visiting
chefs as well as a master sommelier who provides exclusive wine pairings. Service is flawless. ⊠ *Lodge at Kō'ele* ☎ *808/565–7300* ⌁ *Reservations essential* 🛅 *Jacket required* ▤ *AE, DC, MC, V* ⊗ *No lunch.*
$42–$46.

$$–$$$$ ✕ **Henry Clay's Rotisserie.** With the only bar and comparatively fine din-
ing in Lāna'i City, this is a lively spot, right at the Hotel Lāna'i. Louisiana-
style ribs, Cajun-style shrimp, and gumbo add up to what chef Henry
Clay Richardson calls "American country," but he brings it back home
with island venison and locally caught fish. A fireplace and paintings
by local artists add to the upcountry feel. Large parties can be accom-
modated and are sometimes quite noisy. ⊠ *Hotel Lāna'i, 828 Lāna'i
Ave., Lāna'i City* ☎ *808/565–7211* ▤ *MC, V. $17–$35.*

$$–$$$$ ✕ **The Terrace.** Floor-to-ceiling glass doors open onto formal gardens and
lovely vistas of the mist-clad mountains. Breakfast, lunch, and dinner
are served in an informal atmosphere with attentive service. Try poached
eggs on crab cakes to start the day and a free-range strip loin with pesto
mashed potatoes to finish it. A complete wine list and the soothing sounds
of the grand piano in the Great Hall in the evening complete the ambience. ⊠ *Lodge at Kō'ele* ☎ *808/565–7300* ▤ *AE, DC, MC, V. $12–$35.*

$$–$$$ ✕ **Pele's Other Garden.** Mark and Barbara Zigmond's colorful little
eatery is a deli and bistro all in one. For lunch, deli sandwiches or daily
hot specials reward an arduous hike. At night the restaurant turns into
an intimate tablecloth-dining bistro, complete with soft jazz music. A
nice wine list enhances an Italian-inspired menu. Start with bruschetta,
then choose from a selection of pasta dishes or pizzas. ⊠ *811 Houston
St., Lāna'i City* ☎ *808/565–9628 or 888/764–3354* ▤ *AE, DC, MC,
V. $16–$22.*

$–$$ ✕ **The Experience at Ko'ele Clubhouse.** The clubhouse overlooks the emer-
ald greens of the golf course. Sit inside and watch sports on the TV or
on the terrace to enjoy the antics of lumbering wild turkey families. A
grilled fresh-catch sandwich is accompanied by fries, or try their succulent hamburgers, the best on the island. Salads and sandwiches, beer
and wine, soft drinks, and some not very inspiring deserts complete the
menu. ⊠ *Lodge at Kō'ele* ☎ *808/565–4605* ▤ *AE, DC, MC, V* ⊗ *No
dinner. $8–$15.*

¢–$$ ✕ **Blue Ginger Café.** This cheery eatery is a Lāna'i City institution. Own-
ers Joe and Georgia Abilay have made this place into one of the town's
most popular hangouts with consistent, albeit simple, food. Locally in-
spired paintings and photos line the walls inside, while the town passes
the outdoor tables in parade. For breakfast, try the Portuguese sausage
omelet with rice or fresh pastries. Lunchtime selections range from

burgers and pizza to Hawaiian staples such as saimin and *musubi* (fried Spam wrapped in rice and seaweed). Try a shrimp stir-fry for dinner. ✉ *409 7th Ave., Lāna'i City* ☎ *808/565–6363* ▭ *No credit cards. $7–$14.*

¢–$ ✕ **565 Café.** Named after the only telephone prefix on Lāna'i, this is a convenient stop for anything from pizza to a Pālāwai chicken breast-sandwich on fresh-baked foccacia. Make a quick stop for plate lunches or try a picnic pūpū platter of chicken katsu to take along for the ride. If you need a helium balloon for a party, you can find that here, too. The patio and outdoor tables are kid-friendly, and an outdoor Saturday afternoon flea market adds to the quirkiness. ✉ *408 8th St., Lāna'i City* ☎ *808/565–6622* ▭ *No credit cards. $7–$20.*

¢   ✕ **Lāna'i Coffee.** A block off Dole Park, you can sit outside on the large deck, sip cappuccinos, and watch the slow-pace life of the town slip by. Bagels with lox, deli sandwiches, and pastries add to the caloric content, while blended espresso shakes and gourmet ice cream complete the old-world illusion. Caffeine-inspired specialty items make good gifts and souvenirs. ✉ *604 'Ilima St., Lāna'i City* ☎ *808/565–6962* ☉ *Closed Sun. $4–$7.*

WHERE TO STAY

Though Lāna'i has few properties, it does have a range of price options. Four Seasons manages both the Lodge at Kō'ele and the Four Seasons Resort Lāna'i at Mānele Bay. Although the room rates are different, guests can partake of all the resort amenities at both properties. If you're on a budget, seek out a friendly bed-and-breakfast or consider the Hotel Lāna'i. Vacation house rentals, a great option for families, give you a feel for everyday life on the island. In hunting seasons, from mid-February through mid-May, and from mid-July through mid-October, most of the private properties are booked way in advance.

WHAT IT COSTS				
$$$$	**$$$**	**$$**	**$**	**¢**
HOTELS over $200	$150–$200	$100–$150	$60–$100	under $60

Prices are for two people in a standard double room in high season, including tax and service.

Hotels & Resorts

★ $$$$ 🏨 **Four Seasons Resort Lāna'i at Mānele Bay.** Reached by a sweeping circular driveway lined with red rose bushes, this refurbished and refurnished ornate property overlooking Hulopo'e Bay has spectacular views of Lāna'i's coastline and beyond. Courtyard gardens, breezeways, and bridges connect two-story guest-room buildings. The architecture combines Mediterranean and Asian elements; elaborate life-size paintings of Chinese court officials, gold brocade warrior robes, and antique vases, sculpture, and artifacts decorate the open-air lobbies. Hulopo'e Beach's white-sand crescent, with facilities for resort guests, is just below the pool terrace, and a *keiki* (children's) program focuses on the island's cultural and environmental heritage, with petroglyph walks, crab hunting, 'ukulele playing, and more. A state-of-the-art fitness center overlooks the sea, and an adjacent movement studio offers yoga, tai chi, and personal training. ✑ *Box 631380, Lāna'i City 96763* ☎ *808/565–2000 or 800/321–4666* 🖷 *808/565-2483* ⊕ *www.fourseasons.com* ◄ *215 rooms, 21 suites* ₺ *3 restaurants, room service, in-room broadband, in-room safes, minibars, cable TV with movies and video games, in-room DVD players, 18-hole golf course, 3 tennis courts, pool, health club, spa, billiards, 2 bars, recreation room, library, babysitting, children's programs (ages 5–13), laundry service, Internet room, no-smoking rooms* ▭ *AE, DC, MC, V. $400–$900.*

$$$$
Fodor'sChoice
★

Lodge at Kō'ele. In the highlands edging Lāna'i City, this grand country estate, managed by Four Seasons, exudes luxury and quiet romance. Secluded by old pines, 1½ mi of paths meander through formal gardens with a huge reflecting pond, a wedding gazebo, and an orchid greenhouse. Afternoon tea is served in front of the immense stone fireplaces beneath the high-beamed ceilings of the magnificent Great Hall. The music room lounge is a relaxing haven after a day on the Lodge's golf course or sporting clays range. A long veranda, furnished with wicker lounge chairs, looks out over rolling green pastures toward spectacular sunsets. ✑ *Box 360310, Lāna'i City 96763* ☎ *808/565–7300 or 800/321–4666* 🖷 *808/565–3868* ⊕ *www.lodgeatkoele.com* ◄ *84 rooms, 12 suites* ₺ *2 restaurants, room service, fans, in-room safes, minibars, cable TV with movies and video games, 18-hole golf course, shop, tennis courts, pool, gym, hot tub, massage, bicycles, archery, croquet, hiking, horseback riding, lawn bowling, bar, library, children's programs (ages 5–12), laundry service, no-smoking rooms, Internet room* ▭ *AE, DC, MC, V. $400–$575.*

$$–$$$
Hotel Lāna'i. Built in 1923 to house visiting pineapple executives, this 10-room inn was once the only accommodation on the island. The recently refurbished plantation-inspired rooms, with country quilts, light pinewoods, and local art, make it seem like you're staying in someone's home. Rooms with porches overlooking the pine trees and Lāna'i City are especially nice. The restaurant has a small bar. A self-serve Continental breakfast with fresh-baked breads is served on the veranda and is included in the rate. ✉ *828 Lāna'i Ave., Lāna'i City 96763* ☎ *808/565–7211 or 800/795–7211* 🖷 *808/565–6450* ⊕ *www.hotellanai.com* ◄ *10 rooms, 1 cottage* ₺ *Restaurant; no a/c, no room TVs, no smoking* ▭ *AE, MC, V. $115–$175.*

B&Bs & Vacation Rentals

All vacation rentals are in Lāna'i City, where altitude and prevailing-trade winds replace air-conditioning. During hunting seasons, rentals are booked months—possibly years—in advance.

$$–$$$
Sheila Black. A log cabin cottage next to the Black's residence on "Haole Hill" is available as a vacation rental. This simply furnished, family-friendly, two-bedroom, two-bath cottage offers a fully equipped kitchen

with all appliances, linens, pine trees, and country peace. It can accommodate up to seven, with extra beds in the living room ($15 extra per night per additional person over four). ✉ *656 Pu'ulani Pl., 96763* ☎ *808/565–6867* 🖷 *808/565–7695* ✎ *adblack@aloha.net* 🛏 *2-bedroom cottage* ♨ *Kitchen, cable TV; no a/c, no smoking* 🚫 *No credit cards. 2-bedroom cottage $150.*

$ 🏠 **Dreams Come True.** Michael and Susan Hunter rent out a four-bedroom, four-bathroom plantation home in the heart of Lāna'i City, available in its entirety or as individual guest rooms. Antiques gleaned from many trips through South Asia add to the atmosphere. Some rooms have canopy beds, and each has its own marble bath with whirlpool tub. The living room has a TV and VCR, and the kitchen is available for guest use. There's also a veranda and garden. Enjoy the Hunters' company and gather information about the island each morning, when a home-cooked full breakfast becomes a special occasion. They will arrange vehicle rental and book activities, too. ✉ *1168 Lāna'i St., Lāna'i City 96763* ☎ *808/565–6961 or 800/566–6961* 🖷 *808/565–7056* ⊕ *www.circumvista.com/dreamscometrue.html* 🛏 *3 rooms* ♨ *Laundry facilities; no a/c, no room phones, no room TVs, no smoking* 🚫 *AE, D, MC, V. $99.*

$ 🏠 **Hale Moe.** Momi Suzuki has turned her elegant esthetic into a peaceful Japanese-inspired retreat. This serenely furnished bed-and-breakfast has a well-tended garden with expansive views of the distant ocean. There's a TV in the living room and a kitchen available for guest use. Help yourself to coffee and continental breakfast on the sunny deck. Momi will advise you on where to go and what to do on the island. Sometimes her jeep is available for rent as well. You can also rent the three-bedroom, three-bath house for $300 a night with a limit of six people. 🖅 *Box 630196, 96763* ☎ *808/565–9520* ⊕ *staylanai.com* 🛏 *3 rooms* ♨ *No a/c, no phones in some rooms, no TV in some rooms, no smoking* 🚫 *No credit cards. $80–$90.*

¢ 🏠 **McOmber Enterprises.** Five different houses in Lāna'i City are available as short-term economy vacation rentals. They can accommodate from two to eight persons. Kitchens are fully furnished and equipped, and linens are supplied. 🖅 *Box 630646, 96763* ☎ *808/565–6071* ✎ *mcomber@aloha.net* 🛏 *5 houses* ♨ *Kitchen, laundry facilities; no a/c, no room phones, no TV in some rooms, no smoking* 🚫 *No credit cards. $35 per person per night.*

SHOPS & SPAS

Shopping at Dole Park

A miniforest of Cook Pine trees in the center of Lāna'i City surrounded by small shops and restaurants, Dole Park is the closest thing to a mall on Lāna'i. Except for the high-end resort boutiques and pro shops, it provides the island's only shopping. A morning or afternoon stroll around the park offers an eclectic selection of gifts and clothing, plus a chance to chat with residents. Friendly general stores are straight out of the '20s, and new galleries and a boutique have original art and fashions for men, women, and children. The shops close on Sunday and after 5 PM, except for the general stores, which are open a bit later.

General Stores

International Food and Clothing Center. You may not find everything the name implies, but this old-fashioned emporium does stock items for your everyday needs, from fishing gear to beer. It's a good place for last-minute camping supplies. ✉ 833 'Ilima Ave., Lāna'i City ☎ 808/565–6433.

Lāna'i City Service. In addition to being a gas station, auto parts store, and car-rental operation, this outfit sells Hawaiian gift items, sundries, T-shirts, beer, sodas, and bottled water in the **Plantation Store.** Open 7 to 7 daily for gas and sundries; auto parts store open weekdays 7–4. ✉ 1036 Lāna'i Ave., Lāna'i City ☎ 808/565–7227.

Pine Isle Market. This is one of Lāna'i City's two supermarkets, stocking everything from cosmetics to canned vegetables. It's a great place to buy fresh fish. Take a look at the photographs of famous local fish and fishermen over the beer case. ✉ 356 8th St., Lāna'i City ☎ 808/565–6488.

Richard's Shopping Center. Richard Tamashiro founded this store in 1946, and the Tamashiro clan continues to run the place. Along with groceries, the store has a fun selection of Lāna'i T-shirts. Richard's has a good selection of what they call "almost" fine wines, and a few gourmet food items. ✉ 434 8th St., Lāna'i City ☎ 808/565–6047.

Sergio's Oriental Store. Sergio's, the closest thing to a Costco on Lāna'i, has Filipino sweets and pastries, case loads of sodas, water, juices, family-size containers of condiments, and frozen fish and meat. Open 8 to 8 daily. ✉ 831-D Houston St., Lāna'i City ☎ 808/565–6900.

Specialty Stores

Dis 'n Dat. This tiny, jungle-green shop packs in thousands of art, gift, and jewelry items in a minuscule space enlivened by a glittering crystal ceiling. Fanciful garden ornaments, serene Buddhas, and Asian antiques add to the charm. Owners Barry and Suzie Osman are visitor-friendly and will help with almost anything you need. ✉ 418 8th St., Lāna'i City ☎ 808/565–9170.

Gifts with Aloha. Casual resort wear is sold alongside a great collection of Hawaiiana books and the work of local artists, including ceramic ware, *raku* (Japanese-style lead-glazed pottery), fine handblown glass, and watercolor prints. Look for a complete selection of Hawaiian music CDs and Lāna'i-designed Stone Shack shirts. ✉ 811-B Houston St., Lāna'i City ☎ 808/565–6589.

Heart of Lāna'i. The bright yellow house behind the Hotel Lāna'i shows watercolors by Denise Hennig, oil paintings by Macario Pascual, and bowls and 'ukulele by Cyrus Keanini. Afternoon tea is served at the gallery Tuesday through Saturday from 2:30 to 4:30. ✉ 758 Queens St., Lāna'i City ☎ 808/565–7815.

Lāna'i Arts and Cultural Center. Local artists practice and display their crafts at this dynamic center. Workshops in the pottery, photography, woodworking, and painting studios welcome visitors, and individual instruction may be arranged. The center's gift shop sells original art and unique Lānaʻi handicrafts. ✉ *337 7th Ave., Lānaʻi City* ☎ *808/565–7503.*

Local Gentry. This tiny, classy store has clothing for every need, from casual men's and women's beachwear to evening resort wear, shoes, jewelry, and hats. A small selection of fashionable children's apparel is also available. Proprietor Jenna Gentry will mail your purchases for the cost of the postage. ✉ *363 7th St., Lānaʻi City* ☎ *808/565–9130.*

Mike Carrol Gallery. The dreamy, soft-focus oil paintings of resident painter Mike Carroll are showcased along with wood bowls and koa ʻukulele by Warren Osako, and fish-print paper tapestries by Joana Varawa. Local photographer Ron Gingerich, island artist Cheryl McElfresh, and jeweler Susan Hunter are also featured. ✉ *443 7th St., Lānaʻi City* ☎ *808/565–7122.*

Spas

If you're looking for rejuvenation, the whole island could be considered a spa, though the only spa facilities are at the Four Seasons Resort Lānaʻi at Mānele Bay or the Health Center at the Lodge at Kōʻele. For a quick polish in town, try Neda at **Island Images** (☎ 808/565–7870) for haircuts, waxing, and eyebrow shaping with threads (an ancient technique); Kathy at **Highlights** (☎ 808/565–7207) for hair, nails, and makeup; or Nita at **Nita's In Style** (☎ 808/565–8082) for hair care.

Lodge at Kōʻele's Healing Arts Center. Adjacent to the Lodge's pool and Jacuzzis, this bright, modest center provides cardiovascular equipment and free weights. Pump iron and watch yourself in the floor-to-ceiling mirrors or look out at the formal gardens and majestic trees. A single massage room offers specialty treatments and massages. ✉ *Lodge at Kōʻele* ☎ *808/565–7300* ⊕ *www.fourseasons.com* ☞ *$105–$145 50-minute massage. Gym with: cardiovascular machines, free weights. Services: aromatherapy, body wraps, hot rock massage, facials, chemical peel, lash and brow tinting, herbal therapy consulting. Classes and programs: yoga.*

The Spa at Mānele. State-of-the-art pampering enlists a panoply of oils and unguents that would have pleased Cleopatra. The Spa After Hours Experience drenches you in private services including pineapple tea, a neck and shoulder massage, and a 50-minute treatment of your choice. Then melt down in the sauna or steam room, finish off with a scalp massage and light pūpū, and ooze out to your room. The *Aliʻi* banana coconut scrub and pineapple citrus polish treatments have inspired their own cosmetic line. Massages in private *hale* (houses) in the courtyard gardens are available for singles or couples. A tropical fantasy mural, granite stone floors, eucalyptus steam rooms, and private cabanas overlooking the sea set the scene for indulgence. ✉ *Four Seasons Resort Lānaʻi at Mānele Bay* ☎ *808/565–2000* ⊕ *www.fourseasons.com* ☞ *$135–$145 50-minute massage; $320 per person 2-hr Spa After Hours Experience (2-person minimum), $20 extra for use of facilities with a*

50-minute massage. Hair salon, sauna, steam room. Gym with: cardiovascular equipment, free weights. Services: aromatherapy, reflexology, body wraps, facials, pedicures, hair care, nails, waxing. Classes and programs: yoga, tai chi, aquaerobics, hula classes, guided hikes, personal training.

NIGHTLIFE

Lāna'i is certainly not known for its nightlife. Fewer than a handful of places stay open past 9 PM. At the resorts, excellent piano music or light live entertainment makes for a quiet, romantic evening. Another romantic alternative is star-watching from the beaches or watching the full moon rise in all its glory.

Hotel Lāna'i. A visit to the small, lively bar here is an opportunity to visit with locals. Last call is at 9. ☎ *808/565–7211.*

Lāna'i Theater and Playhouse. This 153-seat, '30s landmark presents first-run movies Friday through Tuesday, with showings at 6:30 and 8:30. This is also the venue that shows films from the Hawai'i Film Festival. ✉ *465 7th Ave., Lāna'i City* ☎ *808/565–7500.*

Lodge at Kō'ele. The cozy cocktail bar stays open until 11 PM. The Lodge also features quiet piano music in its Great Hall every evening from 7 to 10, as well as special performances by well-known Hawaiian entertainers and local hula dancers. The Saturday afternoon keiki hula show is at 12:30. ☎ *808/565–7300.*

Four Seasons Resort Lāna'i at Mānele Bay. Hale Aheahe (House of Gentle Breezes), the classy open-air lounge, with upscale pūpū and complete bar, offers musical entertainment Tuesday through Saturday evenings from 5:30 to 9:30. There's a Saturday keiki hula show in the grand lobby at 2:30. ☎ *808/565–7700.*

LĀNA'I ESSENTIALS

Transportation

BY AIR
You can reach Lāna'i from O'ahu's Honolulu International Airport via Island Air. Island Air offers several flights daily on 18-passenger Dash-6s and 37-seat Dash-8s; round-trip tickets start at $150 depending on the season. Royal Hawaiian Air Service has two daily flights to and from Honolulu. Traveling from other islands requires a stop in Honolulu and a transfer to Island Air and is booked through Aloha Airlines.

AIRPORT The airport has a federal agricultural inspection station so that guests departing to the mainland can check luggage directly.
🛈 Lāna'i Airport ☎ 808/565-6757.

TO & FROM THE AIRPORT
Lāna'i Airport is a 10-minute drive from Lāna'i City. If you're staying at the Hotel Lāna'i, the Lodge at Kō'ele, or the Four Seasons Resort Lāna'i

at Mānele Bay, you'll be met by a shuttle for a $25 fee, which includes all transportation for the length of your stay. Day rates are $5 round-trip to town, and $10 round-trip to Mānele. See the resort receptionist at the airport. Dollar will pick you up if you're renting a car or jeep. Call from the red courtesy phone at the airport.

BY CAR

There are only 30 mi of paved road on the island. Keōmuku Highway starts just past the Lodge at Kō'ele and runs north to Shipwreck Beach. Mānele Road (Highway 440) runs south down to Mānele Bay and Hulopo'e Beach. Kaumalapau Highway (also Highway 440) heads west to Kaumalapau Harbor. The rest of your driving takes place on bumpy, muddy, secondary roads, which generally aren't marked.

You'll never find yourself in a traffic jam, but it's easy to get lost on the unmarked dirt roads. Before heading out, ask for a map at your hotel desk and verify that you're headed in the right direction. Always remember mauka (toward the mountain) and makai (toward the sea) for basic directions. If you're traveling on dirt roads, take water. People still drive slowly here, wave, and pull over to give each other lots of room. The only gas station on the island is in Lāna'i City, at Lāna'i City Service (open 7–7 daily).

CAR RENTAL Renting a four-wheel-drive vehicle is expensive but almost essential. Make reservations far in advance of your trip, because Lāna'i's fleet of vehicles is limited. Lāna'i City Service, a subsidiary of Dollar Rent A Car, is open daily 7–7. Jeep Wranglers and minivans go for $139 a day, full-size cars are $80, and compact cars are about $60.
🚗 **Lāna'i City Service** ⊠ Lāna'i Ave. at 11th St. ☎ 808/565-7227 or 800/533-7808

BY FERRY

Expeditions' ferries cross the channel five times daily, departing from Lahaina on Maui and Mānele Bay Harbor on Lāna'i. The crossing takes 45 minutes and costs $25 each way.
🚗 **Expeditions** ☎ 808/661-3756 or 800/695-2624 ⊕ www.go-lanai.com.

TO & FROM THE Lāna'i City Service will shuttle you from the harbor to downtown for
HARBOR $10 one-way. However, the service is only available if they're already making the trip. The resort shuttle will bring you from the harbor to the Four Seasons Resort Lāna'i at Mānele Bay for a day fee of $5 round-trip or to town for a day-fee of $10 round-trip. See the shuttle driver.
🚗 **Lāna'i City Service** ⊠ Lāna'i Ave. at 11th St. ☎ 808/565-7227 or 800/533-7808.

BY SHUTTLE

A shuttle transports hotel guests among the Hotel Lāna'i, the Lodge at Kō'ele, the Four Seasons Resort Lāna'i at Mānele Bay, and the airport. A $25 fee covers all transportation during the length of stay.

Contacts & Resources

EMERGENCIES

In an emergency, dial **911** to reach an ambulance, the police, or the fire department.

The Lāna'i Family Clinic, part of the Straub Clinic & Hospital, is the island's health-care center. It's open daily from 8 to 5 and closed on weekends. There's a limited pharmacy. In emergencies, call 911 or go to the emergency room of the hospital next door.

🔃 **Straub Clinic & Hospital** ⊠ 628 7th St., Lāna'i City ☎ 808/565-6423 clinic, 808/565-6411 hospital.

VISITOR INFORMATION

Lāna'i Visitor's Bureau is your best bet for general information and maps. Feel free to stop in between 8 AM and 4 PM. The Maui Visitors Bureau also has some information on the island.

🔃 **Lāna'i Visitor's Bureau** ⊠ 431 7th St., Suite A, Lāna'i City 96763 ☎ 808/565-7600. **Maui Visitors Bureau** ☎ 808/244-3530 ⊕ www.visitlanai.com

UNDERSTANDING
MAUI

HAWAI'I AT A GLANCE

Fast Facts

Nickname: Aloha State
Capital: Honolulu
State song: "Hawai'i Pono'i"
State bird: The nēnē, an endangered land bird and variety of goose
State flower: Yellow Hibiscus Brackenridgii
State tree: Kukui (or candlenut), a Polynesian-introduced tree
Administrative divisions: There are four counties with mayors and councils: City and County of Honolulu (island of O'ahu), Hawai'i County (Hawai'i Island), Maui County (islands of Maui, Moloka'i, Lāna'i, and Kahoolawe), and Kaua'i County (islands of Kaua'i and Ni'ihau)
Entered the Union: August 21, 1959, as the 50th state
Population: 1,334,023
Life expectancy: Female 82, male 76
Literacy: 81%

Ethnic groups: Hawaiian/part Hawaiian 22.1%; Caucasian 20.5%; Japanese 18.3%; Filipino 12.3%; Chinese 4.1%
Religion: Roman Catholic 22%; Buddhist, Shinto, and other East Asian religions 15%; Mormon 10%; Church of Christ 8%; Assembly of God and Baptist 6% each; Episcopal, Jehovah's Witness, and Methodist 5% each
Language: English is the first language of the majority of residents; Hawaiian is the native language of the indigenous Hawaiian people and an official language of the state; other languages spoken include Samoan, Chinese, Japanese, Korean, Spanish, Portuguese, Filipino, and Vietnamese

The loveliest fleet of islands that lies anchored in any ocean.
—Mark Twain

Geography & Environment

Land area: An archipelago of 137 islands encompassing a land area of 6,422.6 square mi in the north-central Pacific Ocean (about 2,400 mi from the West Coast of the continental U.S.)
Coastline: 750 mi
Terrain: Volcanic mountains, tropical rain forests, verdant valleys, sea cliffs, canyons, deserts, coral reefs, sand dunes, sandy beaches
Natural resources: Dimension limestone, crushed stone, sand and gravel, gemstones
Natural hazards: Hurricanes, earthquakes, tsunamis
Flora: More than 2,500 species of native and introduced plants throughout the islands
Fauna: Native mammals include the hoary bat, Hawaiian monk seal, and

Polynesian rat. The humpback whale migrates to Hawaiian waters every winter to mate and calve. More than 650 fish and 40 different species of shark live in Hawaiian waters. Freshwater streams are home to hundreds of native and alien species. The humuhumunukunukuāpua'a (Hawaiian triggerfish) is the unofficial state fish.
Environmental issues: Plant and animal species threatened and endangered due to hunting, overfishing, overgrazing by wild and introduced animals, and invasive alien plants

Hawai'i is not a state of mind, but a state of grace.
—Paul Theroux

Economy

Tourism and federal defense spending continue to drive the state's economy. Efforts to diversify in the areas of science and technology, film and television production, sports, ocean research and development, health and education, tourism, agriculture, and floral and specialty food products are ongoing.

GSP: $40.1 billion
Per-capita income: $30,000
Inflation: 1%
Unemployment: 4.3%
Work force: 595,450
Debt: $7.3 billion
Major industries: Tourism, federal government (defense and other agencies)
Agricultural products: Sugar, pineapple, papayas, guavas, flower and nursery products, asparagus, alfalfa hay, macadamia nuts, coffee, milk, cattle, eggs, shellfish, algae
Exports: $616 million
Major export products: Aircraft and parts, naphthas, medical equipment and supplies, fruit, steel scrap, electronic components, unleaded gasoline, artwork, cocoa, coffee, flowers, macadamia nuts
Imports: $2.6 billion
Major import products: Crude oil, electronic and digital equipment, coal, passenger motor vehicles

In what other land save this one is the commonest form of greeting not "Good day," or "How d'ye do," but "Love?" That greeting is "Aloha"–love, I love, my love to you . . . It is a positive affirmation of the warmth of one's own heart, giving.
—Jack London

Debate has waxed and waned for more than a century over how and when to return to native Hawaiians more than 1 million acres of land and other assets seized when American business interests overthrew the island monarchy in 1893. Certain native factions still advocate a return to independent nationhood. Sovereignty gained new momentum in the 1990s with the passage of a federal law formally apologizing for the overthrow and urging reconciliation. Momentum has since fizzled. Hawaii's current governor has renewed efforts to have Congress recognize Hawaiians as an indigenous people, much like Native Americans and Alaskans. The governor also has pledged to support continued funding of health care, language, and other cultural programs, and to achieve state and federal obligations to distribute homestead lands to qualified Hawaiians.

Did You Know?

- Hawai'i is home to the world's most active volcano: Kīlauea, on the Big Island.

- 'Iolani Palace had electricity and telephones installed several years before the White House, and is the only palace on U.S. soil.

- Hawai'i has about 12% of all endangered plants and animals in the U.S.; 75% of the country's extinct plants and birds were Hawaiian.

- The Royal Hawaiian Band is the only intact organization from the time of Hawaiian monarchy that is fully functional and still preserves Hawai'i's musical history.

THE ALOHA SHIRT: A COLORFUL SWATCH OF ISLAND HISTORY

ELVIS PRESLEY had an entire wardrobe of them in the '60s films *Blue Hawaii* and *Paradise, Hawaiian Style*. During the '50s, entertainer Arthur Godfrey and bandleader Harry Owens often sported them on television shows. John Wayne loved to lounge around in them. Mick Jagger felt compelled to buy one on a visit to Hawai'i in the 1970s. Dustin Hoffman, Steven Spielberg, and Bill Cosby avidly collect them.

The roots of the aloha shirt go back to the early 1930s, when Hawai'i's garment industry was just beginning to develop its own unique style. Although locally made clothes did exist, they were almost exclusively for plantation workers and were constructed of durable palaka or plain cotton material.

Out of this came the first stirrings of fashion: Beachboys and schoolchildren started having sport shirts made from colorful Japanese kimono fabric. The favored type of cloth was the kind used for children's kimonos—bright pink and orange floral prints for girls; masculine motifs in browns and blues for boys. In Japan, such flamboyant patterns were considered unsuitable for adult clothing, but in the Islands such rules didn't apply, and it seemed the flashier the shirt, the better—for either sex. Thus, the aloha shirt was born.

It was easy and inexpensive in those days to have garments tailored to order; the next step was moving to mass production and marketing. In June 1935 Honolulu's best-known tailoring establishment, Musa-Shiya, advertised the availability of "Aloha shirts—well tailored, beautiful designs and radiant colors. Ready-made or made to order . . . 95¢ and up." This is the first known printed use of the term that would soon refer to an entire industry. By the following year, several local manufacturers had begun full-scale production of "aloha wear." One of them, Ellery Chun of King-Smith, registered as local trademarks the terms "Aloha Sportswear" and "Aloha Shirt" in 1936 and 1937, respectively.

These early entrepreneurs were the first to create uniquely Hawaiian designs for fabric as well—splashy patterns that would forever symbolize the Islands. A 1939 *Honolulu Advertiser* story described them as a "delightful confusion [of] tropical fish and palm trees, Diamond Head and the Aloha Tower, surfboards and leis, 'ukuleles and Waikīkī beach scenes."

The aloha wear of the late 1930s was intended for—and mostly worn by—tourists, and interestingly, a great deal of it was exported to the mainland and even Europe and Australia. By the end of the decade, for example, only 5% of the output of one local firm, the Kamehameha Garment Company, was sold in Hawai'i.

World War II brought this trend to a halt, and during the postwar period aloha wear really came into its own in Hawai'i itself. A strong push to support local industry gradually nudged island garb into the workplace, and kama'āina began to wear the clothing that previously had been seen as attire for visitors.

In 1947, for example, male employees of the City and County of Honolulu were first allowed to wear aloha shirts "in plain shades" during the summer months. Later that year, the first observance of Aloha Week started the tradition of "bankers and bellhops . . . mix[ing] colorfully in multihued and tapa-designed Aloha shirts every day," as a local newspaper's Sunday magazine supplement noted in 1948. By the 1960s, "Aloha Friday," set aside specifically for the wearing of aloha attire, had become a tradition. In the following decade the suit and tie practically disappeared as work attire in Hawai'i, even for executives.

Most of the Hawaiian-theme fabric used in manufacturing aloha wear was designed in the Islands, then printed on the mainland or in Japan. The glowingly vibrant rayons of the late '40s and early '50s (a period now seen as aloha wear's heyday) were at first printed on the East Coast, but manufacturers there usually required such large orders that local firms eventually found it impossible to continue using them. By 1964, 90% of Hawaiian fabric was being manufactured in Japan—a situation that still exists today.

Fashion trends usually move in cycles, and aloha wear is no exception. By the 1960s the "chop suey print" with its "tired clichés of Diamond Head, Aloha Tower, outrigger canoes [and] stereotyped leis" was seen as corny and garish, according to an article published in the *Honolulu Star-Bulletin*. But it was just that outdated aspect that began to appeal to the younger crowd, who began searching out old-fashioned aloha shirts at the Salvation Army and Goodwill thrift stores. These shirts were dubbed "silkies," a name by which they're still known, even though most of them were actually made of rayon.

Before long, what had been 50¢ shirts began escalating in price, and a customer who had balked at paying $5 for a shirt that someone had already worn soon found the same item selling for $10—and more. By the late 1970s, aloha-wear designers were copying the prints of yesteryear for their new creations.

The days of bargain silkies are now gone. The few choice aloha shirts from decades past that still remain are offered today by specialized dealers for hundreds of dollars apiece, causing many to look back to the time when such treasures were foolishly worn to the beach until they fell apart. The best examples of vintage aloha shirts are now rightly seen as art objects, worthy of preservation for the lovely depictions they offer of Hawai'i's colorful and unique scene.

— DeSoto Brown

HAWAIIAN VOCABULARY

Although an understanding of Hawaiian is by no means required on a trip to the Aloha State, a *malihini*, or newcomer, will find plenty of opportunities to pick up a few of the local words and phrases. Traditional names and expressions are widely used in the Islands, thanks in part to legislation enacted in the early '90s to encourage the use of the Hawaiian language. You're likely to read or hear at least a few words each day of your stay. Such exposure enriches a trip to Hawai'i.

With a basic understanding and some uninhibited practice, anyone can have enough command of the local tongue to ask for directions and to order from a restaurant menu. One visitor announced she would not leave until she could pronounce the name of the state fish, the *humuhumunukunukuāpua'a*. Luckily, she had scheduled a nine-day stay.

Simplifying the learning process is the fact that the Hawaiian language contains only eight consonants—*H, K, L, M, N, P, W,* and the silent *'okina*, or glottal stop, written '—plus one or more of the five vowels. All syllables, and therefore all words, end in a vowel. Each vowel, with the exception of a few diphthongized double vowels such as *au* (pronounced "ow") or *ai* (pronounced "eye"), is pronounced separately. Thus *'Iolani* is four syllables (ee-oh-la-nee), not three (yo-la-nee). Although some Hawaiian words have only vowels, most also contain some consonants, but consonants are never doubled.

Pronunciation is simple. Pronounce *A* "ah" as father; *E* "ay" as in weigh; *I* "ee" as in marine; *O* "oh" as in no; *U* "oo" as in true.

Consonants mirror their English equivalents, with the exception of *W*. When the letter begins any syllable other than the first one in a word, it is usually pronounced as a *V*. *'Awa*, the Polynesian drink, is pronounced "ava," *'ewa* is pronounced "eva."

Nearly all long Hawaiian words are combinations of shorter words; they are not difficult to pronounce if you segment them into shorter words. *Kalaniana'ole*, the highway running east from Honolulu, is easily understood as *Kalani ana 'ole*. Apply the standard pronunciation rules—the stress falls on the next-to-last syllable of most two- or three-syllable Hawaiian words—and Kalaniana'ole Highway is as easy to say as Main Street.

Now about that fish. Try *humu-humu nuku-nuku āpu a'a*.

The other unusual element in Hawaiian language is the *kahakō*, or macron, written as a short line (ˉ) placed over a vowel. Like the accent (´) in Spanish, the kahakō puts emphasis on a syllable that would normally not be stressed. The most familiar example is probably *Waikīkī*. With no macrons, the stress would fall on the middle syllable; with only one macron, on the last syllable, the stress would fall on the first and last syllables. Some words become plural with the addition of a macron, often on a syllable that would have been stressed anyway. No Hawaiian word becomes plural with the addition of an *S,* since that letter does not exist in the *'ōlelo Hawai'i* (which is Hawaiian for "Hawaiian language").

What follows is a glossary of some of the most commonly used Hawaiian words. Don't be afraid to give them a try. Hawaiian residents appreciate visitors who at least try to pick up the local language.

'a'ā: rough, crumbling lava, contrasting with *pāhoehoe*, which is smooth.

'ae: yes.

aikane: friend.

āina: land.

akamai: smart, clever, possessing savoir faire.

akua: god.

ala: a road, path, or trail.

ali'i: a Hawaiian chief, a member of the chiefly class.

aloha: love, affection, kindness; also a salutation meaning both greetings and farewell.

ʻānuenue: rainbow.

ʻaʻole: no.

ʻapōpō: tomorrow.

ʻauwai: a ditch.

auwē: alas, woe is me!

ʻehu: a red-haired Hawaiian.

ʻewa: in the direction of ʻEwa plantation, west of Honolulu.

hala: the pandanus tree, whose leaves (*lau hala*) are used to make baskets and plaited mats.

hālau: school.

hale: a house.

hale pule: church, house of worship.

ha mea iki or **ha mea ʻole:** you're welcome.

hana: to work.

haole: ghost. Since the first foreigners were Caucasian, *haole* now means a Caucasian person.

hapa: a part, sometimes a half; often used as a short form of *hapa haole*, to mean a person who is part-Caucasian; thus, the name of a popular local band, whose members represent a variety of ethnicities.

hauʻoli: to rejoice. *Hauʻoli Makahiki Hou* means Happy New Year. *Hauʻoli lā hānau* means Happy Birthday.

heiau: an outdoor stone platform; an ancient Hawaiian place of worship.

holo: to run.

holoholo: to go for a walk, ride, or sail.

holokū: a long Hawaiian dress, somewhat fitted, with a yoke and a train. Influenced by European fashion, it was worn at court, and at least one local translates the word as "expensive muʻumuʻu."

holomū: a post–World War II cross between a *holokū* and a muʻumuʻu, less fitted than the former but less voluminous than the latter, and having no train.

honi: to kiss; a kiss. A phrase that some tourists may find useful, quoted from a popular hula, is *Honi Kaʻua Wikiwiki:* Kiss me quick!

honu: turtle.

hoʻomalimali: flattery, a deceptive "line," bunk, baloney, hooey.

huhū: angry.

hui: a group, club, or assembly. A church may refer to its congregation as a *hui* and a social club may be called a *hui*.

hukilau: a seine; a communal fishing party in which everyone helps to drive the fish into a huge net, pull it in, and divide the catch.

hula: the dance of Hawaiʻi.

iki: little.

ipo: sweetheart.

ka: the. This is the definite article for most singular words; for plural nouns, the definite article is usually *nā.* Since there is no S in Hawaiian, the article may be your only clue that a noun is plural.

kahuna: a priest, doctor, or other trained person of old Hawaiʻi, endowed with special professional skills that often included the gift of prophecy or other supernatural powers; the plural form is kāhuna.

kai: the sea, saltwater.

kalo: the taro plant from whose root poi is made.

kamaʻāina: literally, a child of the soil; it refers to people who were born in the Islands or have lived there for a long time.

kanaka: originally a man or humanity in general, it is now used to denote a male Hawaiian or part-Hawaiian, but is occasionally taken as a slur when used by non-Hawaiians. *Kanaka maoli,* originally a full-blooded Hawaiian person, is used by some native Hawaiian rights activists to embrace part-Hawaiians as well.

kāne: a man, a husband. If you see this word on a door, it's the men's room. If you see *kane* on a door, it's probably a misspelling; that is the Hawaiian name for the skin fungus tinea.

kapa: also called by its Tahitian name, *tapa,* a cloth made of beaten bark and usually dyed and stamped with a repeat design.

kapakahi: crooked, cockeyed, uneven. You've got your hat on *kapakahi.*

kapu: keep out, prohibited. This is the Hawaiian version of the more widely known Tongan word *tabu* (taboo).

kapuna: grandparent; elder.

kēia lā: today.

keiki: a child; *keikikāne* is a boy, *keiki-wahine* a girl.

kona: the leeward side of the Islands, the direction (south) from which the *kona* wind and *kona* rain come.

kula: upland.

kuleana: a homestead or small plot of ground on which a family has been installed for some generations without necessarily owning it. By extension, *kuleana* is used to denote any area or department in which one has a special interest or prerogative. You'll hear it used this way: If you want to hire a surfboard, see Moki; that's his *kuleana*. And conversely: I can't help you with that; that's not my *kuleana*.

lā: sun.

lamalama: to fish with a torch.

lānai: a porch, a balcony, an outdoor living room. Almost every house in Hawai'i has one. Don't confuse this two-syllable word with the three-syllable name of the island, Lāna'i.

lani: heaven, the sky.

lau hala: the leaf of the *hala*, or pandanus tree, widely used in Hawaiian handicrafts.

lei: a garland of flowers.

limu: sun.

lolo: stupid.

luna: a plantation overseer or foreman.

mahalo: thank you.

makai: toward the ocean.

malihini: a newcomer to the Islands.

mana: the spiritual power that the Hawaiian believed inhabited all things and creatures.

manō: shark.

manuwahi: free, gratis.

mauka: toward the mountains.

mauna: mountain.

mele: a Hawaiian song or chant, often of epic proportions.

Mele Kalikimaka: Merry Christmas (a transliteration from the English phrase).

Menehune: a Hawaiian pixie. The *Menehune* were a legendary race of little people who accomplished prodigious work, such as building fishponds and temples in the course of a single night.

moana: the ocean.

mu'umu'u: the voluminous dress in which the missionaries enveloped Hawaiian women. Now made in bright printed cottons and silks, it is an indispensable garment in a Hawaiian woman's wardrobe. Culturally sensitive locals have embraced the Hawaiian spelling but often shorten the spoken word to "mu'u." Most English dictionaries include the spelling "muumuu," and that version is a part of many apparel companies' names.

nani: beautiful.

nui: big.

ohana: family.

'ono: delicious.

pāhoehoe: smooth, unbroken, satiny lava.

Pākē: Chinese. This *Pākē* carver makes beautiful things.

palapala: document, printed matter.

pali: a cliff, precipice.

pānini: prickly pear cactus.

paniolo: a Hawaiian cowboy, a rough transliteration of *español*, the language of the Islands' earliest cowboys.

pau: finished, done.

pilikia: trouble. The Hawaiian word is much more widely used here than its English equivalent.

puka: a hole.

pupule: crazy, like the celebrated Princess Pupule. This word has replaced its English equivalent in local usage.

pu'u: volcanic cinder cone.

waha: mouth.

wahine: a female, a woman, a wife, and a sign on the ladies' room door; the plural form is *wāhine*.

wai: freshwater, as opposed to saltwater, which is *kai*.

wailele: waterfall.

wikiwiki: to hurry, hurry up (since this is a reduplication of *wiki*, quick, neither W is pronounced as a V).

SMART TRAVEL TIPS

Finding out about your destination before you leave home means you won't spend time organizing everyday minutiae once you've arrived. You'll be more streetwise when you hit the ground as well, better prepared to explore the aspects of Maui, Lāna'i, and Moloka'i that drew you here in the first place. The organizations in this section can provide information to supplement this guide; contact them for up-to-the-minute details. Happy landings!

AIR TRAVEL

Hawai'i is a major destination for U.S., Asian, Australian, New Zealand, and South Pacific air carriers. Some of the major airlines fly direct to Maui, allowing you to bypass connecting flights out of Honolulu. For travelers arriving into O'ahu or the Big Island, short interisland flights to Maui depart frequently from early morning until mid-evening.

BOOKING

When you book, look for nonstop flights and remember that "direct" flights stop at least once. Try to avoid connecting flights, which require a change of plane. Two airlines may operate a connecting flight jointly, so ask whether your airline operates every segment of the trip; you may find that the carrier you prefer flies you only part of the way. To find more booking tips and to check prices and make online flight reservations, log on to www.fodors.com.

CARRIERS

From the U.S. mainland, American, ATA, Delta, Continental, and United serve Maui and Honolulu (American and United also serve the Big Island and Kaua'i). Northwest flies into Honolulu only.

Aloha Airlines flies from California—Oakland, Sacramento, San Diego, and Orange County—to Maui, Honolulu, and the Big Island. Aloha also flies from Las Vegas and Reno, Nevada. Hawaiian Airlines serves Maui and Honolulu from Las Vegas, Los Angeles, Phoenix, Portland, Sacramento, San Diego, San Francisco, San Jose, and Seattle. In addition to Aloha and Hawaiian, Island Air and Pacific

Wings also provide interisland service. Paragon Airlines offers private charter service to all the Islands.

🛪 Major Airlines **ATA** ☎ 800/435-9282 ⊕ www.ata.com. **American** ☎ 800/433-7300 ⊕ www.aa.com. **Continental** ☎ 800/523-3273 ⊕ www.continental.com. **Delta** ☎ 800/221-1212 ⊕ www.delta.com. **Northwest** ☎ 800/225-2525 ⊕ www.nwa.com. **United** ☎ 800/241-6522 ⊕ www.united.com.

🛪 Interisland Flights **Aloha Airlines** ☎ 800/367-5250 ⊕ www.alohaairlines.com. **Hawaiian Airlines** ☎ 800/367-5320 ⊕ www.hawaiianair.com. **Island Air** ☎ 800/323-3345 ⊕ www.islandair.com. **Pacific Wings** ☎ 888/575-4546 ⊕ www.pacificislandtravel.com. **Paragon Airlines** ☎ 808/244-3356 ⊕ www.paragon-air.com.

CHECK-IN & BOARDING

Always **find out your carrier's check-in policy.** Plan to arrive at the airport about two hours before your scheduled departure time for domestic flights and 2½ to 3 hours before international flights. You may need to arrive earlier if you're flying from one of the busier airports or during peak air-traffic times. Plan to **arrive at the airport 45 to 60 minutes before departure for interisland flights.**

Although Maui's Kahului Airport is smaller and more casual than Honolulu International, during peak times it can also be quite busy. Allot extra travel time to all airports during morning and afternoon rush-hour traffic periods.

To avoid delays at airport-security checkpoints, try not to wear any metal. Jewelry, belt and other buckles, steel-toe shoes, and barrettes are among the items that can set off detectors.

Assuming that not everyone with a ticket will show up, airlines routinely overbook planes. When everyone does, airlines ask for volunteers to give up their seats. In return, these volunteers usually get a several-hundred-dollar flight voucher, which can be used toward the purchase of another ticket, and are rebooked on the next available flight out. If there are not enough volunteers, the airline must choose who will be denied boarding. The first to get bumped are passengers who checked in late and those flying on discounted tickets, so get to the gate and check-in as early as possible, especially during peak periods.

Always **bring a government-issued photo ID** to the airport; even when it's not required, a passport is best.

AGRICULTURAL INSPECTION

Plants and plant products are subject to regulation by the Department of Agriculture, both on entering and leaving Hawai'i. **Upon leaving the Islands, you're required to have your bags X-rayed and tagged** at one of the airport's agricultural-inspection stations before you proceed to check-in. Pineapples and coconuts with the packer's agricultural-inspection stamp pass freely; papayas must be treated, inspected, and stamped. All other fruits are banned for export to the U.S. mainland. Flowers pass except for gardenia, rose leaves, jade vine, and mauna loa. Also banned are insects, snails, soil, cotton, cacti, sugarcane, and all berry plants.

You'll have to **leave dogs and other pets at home.** A 120-day quarantine is imposed to keep out rabies, which is nonexistent in Hawai'i. If specific pre- and post-arrival requirements are met, animals may qualify for a 30-day or 5-day-or-less quarantine.

🛪 U.S. Customs and Border Protection ✉ For inquiries and equipment registration, 1300 Pennsylvania Ave. NW, Washington, DC 20229 ⊕ www.cbp.gov ☎ 877/287-8667 or 202/354-1000 ✉ For complaints, Customer Satisfaction Unit, 1300 Pennsylvania Ave. NW, Room 5.2C, Washington, DC 20229.

CUTTING COSTS

Check local and community newspapers when you're on the Islands for deals and coupons on interisland flights. Both Hawaiian Airlines and Aloha Airlines have stopped offering the once-popular multi-island air passes, but there are other ways to save money on interisland fares. Sign up for either airline's free frequent-flyer programs, and you'll be eligible for excellent online specials that aren't available by phone or elsewhere.

The least expensive airfares to Hawai'i are usually priced for round-trip travel and usually must be purchased in advance. Airlines generally allow you to change your return date for a fee; most low-fare tickets, however, are nonrefundable. It's smart to call a number of airlines and check the Internet; when you are quoted a good price, book it on the spot—the same fare may not be available the next day, or even the next hour. Always check different routings and look into using alternate airports. Also, price off-peak flights and red-eye, which may be significantly less expensive than others. Travel agents, especially low-fare specialists (➪ Discounts & Deals), are helpful.

Consolidators are another good source. They buy tickets for scheduled flights at reduced rates from the airlines, then sell them at prices that beat the best fare available directly from the airlines. (Many also offer reduced car-rental and hotel rates.) Sometimes you can even get your money back if you need to return the ticket. Carefully read the fine print detailing penalties for changes and cancellations, purchase the ticket with a credit card, and confirm your consolidator reservation with the airline.

▮ Consolidators AirlineConsolidator.com ⊕ www.airlineconsolidator.com, for international tickets. **Best Fares** ⊕ www.bestfares.com; $59.90 annual membership. **Cheap Tickets** ⊕ www. cheaptickets.com. **Expedia** ⊕ www.expedia.com. **Hotwire** ⊕ www.hotwire.com. **Luxury Link** (⊕ www.luxurylink.com) has auctions (surprisingly good deals) as well as offers on the high-end side of travel. **Onetravel.com** ⊕ www.onetravel.com. **Orbitz** ⊕ www.orbitz.com. **Priceline.com** ⊕ www. priceline.com. **Travelocity** ⊕ www.travelocity.com.

ENJOYING THE FLIGHT

State your seat preference when purchasing your ticket, and then repeat it when you confirm and when you check in. For more legroom, you can request one of the few emergency-aisle seats at check-in, if you're capable of moving obstacles comparable in weight to an airplane exit door (usually between 35 pounds and 60 pounds)—a Federal Aviation Administration requirement of passengers in these seats. Seats behind a bulkhead also offer more legroom, but they don't have under-

seat storage. Don't sit in the row in front of the emergency aisle or in front of a bulkhead, where seats may not recline. **SeatGuru.com has more information about specific seat configurations, which vary by aircraft.**

Ask the airline whether a snack or meal is served on the flight. If you have dietary concerns, request special meals when booking. These can be vegetarian, low-cholesterol, or kosher, for example. It's a good idea to pack some healthful snacks and a small (plastic) bottle of water in your carry-on bag. On long flights, try to maintain a normal routine, to help fight jet lag. At night, get some sleep. By day, eat light meals, drink water (not alcohol), and move around the cabin to stretch your legs. For additional jet-lag tips consult *Fodor's FYI: Travel Fit & Healthy* (available at bookstores everywhere).

Smoking policies vary from carrier to carrier. Most airlines prohibit smoking on all of their flights; others allow smoking only on certain routes or certain departures. Ask your carrier about its policy.

FLYING TIMES

Flying time is about 10 hours from New York, 8 hours from Chicago, 5 hours from Los Angeles, and 15 hours from London, not including layovers.

HOW TO COMPLAIN

If your baggage goes astray or your flight goes awry, complain right away. Most carriers require that you **file a claim immediately.** The Aviation Consumer Protection Division of the Department of Transportation publishes *Fly-Rights,* which discusses airlines and consumer issues and is available online. You can also find articles and information on mytravelrights.com, the Web site of the nonprofit Consumer Travel Rights Center.

▮ Airline Complaints Aviation Consumer Protection Division ✉ U.S. Department of Transportation, Office of Aviation Enforcement and Proceedings, C-75, Room 4107, 400 7th St. SW, Washington, DC 20590 ☎ 202/366-2220 ⊕ airconsumer.ost.dot.gov. **Federal Aviation Administration Consumer Hotline** ✉ For inquiries: FAA, 800 Independence Ave.

SW, Washington, DC 20591 ☎ 800/835-5322 ⊕ www.faa.gov.

RECONFIRMING

Check the status of your flight before you leave for the airport. You can do this on your carrier's Web site, by linking to a flight-status checker (many Web booking services offer these), or by calling your carrier or travel agent.

AIRPORTS

All of Hawai'i's major islands have their own airports, but Honolulu's International Airport is the main stopover for most flights—both international and Mainland. From Honolulu, there are departing flights to Maui leaving almost every hour from early morning until evening. In addition, some carriers now offer nonstop service directly from the Mainland to Maui on a limited basis. Flights from Honolulu into Lāna'i and Moloka'i are offered several times a day. Hawai'i's airports are "open-air," meaning you can enjoy those tradewind breezes up until the moment you step on the plane.

HONOLULU/O'AHU AIRPORT

Hawai'i's major airport is Honolulu International, on O'ahu, 20 minutes (9 mi) west of Waikīkī. To travel interisland from Honolulu, you can depart from either the interisland terminal or the commuter-airline terminal, located in two separate structures adjacent to the main overseas terminal building. A free bus service, the Wiki Wiki Shuttle, operates between terminals.

🛪 **Honolulu International Airport (HNL)** ☎ 808/836-6413.

MAUI AIRPORTS

Maui has two major airports. Kahului Airport handles major airlines and interisland flights; it's the only airport on Maui that has direct service from the mainland. Kapalua–West Maui Airport is served by Aloha Airlines and Pacific Wings. If you're staying in West Maui and you're flying in from another island, you can avoid the hour drive from the Kahului Airport by flying into Kapalua–West Maui Airport. The tiny town of Hāna in East Maui also has an airstrip, served by commuter planes

from Honolulu and charter flights from Kahului and Kapalua. Flying here is a great option if you want to avoid the long and windy drive to Hāna from one of the other airports.

🛪 **Kahului Airport (OGG)** ☎ 808/872-3893. **Kapalua–West Maui Airport (JHM)** ☎ 808/669-0623. **Hāna Airport (HNM)** ☎ 808/248-8208.

MOLOKA'I & LĀNA'I

Moloka'i's Ho'olehua Airport is small and centrally located, as is Lāna'i Airport. Both rural airports handle a limited number of flights per day. Visitors coming from the mainland to these islands must first stop in O'ahu and change to an interisland flight.

🛪 **Lāna'i: Lāna'i Airport (LNY)** ☎ 808/565-6757. **Moloka'i: Ho'olehua Airport (MKK)** ☎ 808/567-6361.

BOAT & FERRY TRAVEL

There is daily ferry service between Lahaina, Maui, and Mānele Bay, Lāna'i, with Expeditions Lāna'i Ferry. The 9-mi crossing costs $50 cash (or $52 if you pay with a credit card) round-trip, per person and takes about 45 minutes or so, depending on ocean conditions (which can make this trip a rough one). Moloka'i Ferry offers twice daily ferry service between Lahaina, Maui and Kaunakakai, Moloka'i. Travel time is about 90 minutes each way and the roundtrip fare is $40 per person. Reservations are recommended for both ferries. A high-speed interisland ferry service that will run between Maui, Honolulu, the Big Island, and Kaua'i is scheduled to begin sometime in 2006.

🛪 Boat & Ferry Information **Expeditions Lāna'i Ferry** ☎ 800/695-2624 ⊕ www.go-lanai.com. **Molokai Ferry** ☎ 866/307-6524 ⊕ www.molokaiferry.com.

BUS TRAVEL

Getting around by bus on Maui is limited and car rental is recommended.

BUS TRAVEL ON MAUI

Maui Public Transit, operated by Roberts Hawai'i, offers seven routes in and between various central, south, and west Maui communities from Monday through Saturday. There's no service on Sunday. Passengers can travel among Wailuku,

Kāʻanapali, Kahului, Kapalua, Kīhei, Wailea, Māʻalaea, and Lahaina. Inexpensive one-way, round-trip, and all-day passes are available.

🚍 **Roberts Hawaiʻi** ☎ 808/871-4838 ⊕ www.co. maui.hi.us/bus.

BUSINESS HOURS

Even people in paradise have to work. Generally local business hours are weekdays 8–5. Banks are usually open Monday–Thursday 8:30–3 and until 6 on Friday. Some banks have Saturday-morning hours.

Many self-serve gas stations stay open around-the-clock, with full-service stations usually open from around 7 AM until 9 PM. U.S. post offices are generally open weekdays 8:30 AM–4:30 PM and Saturday 8:30–noon.

MUSEUMS & SIGHTS

Most museums generally open their doors between 9 AM and 10 AM and stay open until 5 PM Tuesday–Saturday. Many museums operate with afternoon hours only on Sunday and close on Monday. Visitor-attraction hours vary throughout the state, but most sights are open daily with the exception of major holidays such as Christmas. **Check local newspapers or visitor publications upon arrival for attraction hours and schedules if visiting over holiday periods.** The local dailies carry a listing of "What's Open/What's Not" for those time periods.

SHOPS

Stores in resort areas sometimes open as early as 8, with shopping-center opening hours varying from 9:30 to 10 on weekdays and Saturday, a bit later on Sunday. Bigger malls stay open until 9 weekdays and Saturday and close at 5 on Sunday. Boutiques in resort areas may stay open as late as 11.

CAR RENTAL

While on Maui, you can rent anything from an econobox to a Ferrari convertible. On Lānaʻi and Molokaʻi, four-wheel-drive vehicles are recommended for exploring off the beaten path. It's wise to make

reservations in advance, especially if visiting during peak seasons or for major conventions or sporting events.

Rates begin at $25 a day ($170 a week) for an economy car with air-conditioning, automatic transmission, and unlimited mileage. This does not include vehicle registration fee and weight tax, insurance, sales tax, and a $3-per-day Hawaiʻi state surcharge.

🚗 **Major Agencies Alamo** ☎ 800/327-9633 ⊕ www.alamo.com. **Avis** ☎ 800/331-1212 ⊕ www. avis.com. **Budget** ☎ 800/527-0700 ⊕ www. budget.com. **Hertz** ☎ 800/654-3131 ⊕ www.hertz. com. **National Car Rental** ☎ 800/227-7368 ⊕ www.nationalcar.com. **Thrifty** ☎ 800/847-4389 ⊕ www.thrifty.com.

CUTTING COSTS

Many rental companies in Hawaiʻi offer coupons for discounts at various attractions that could save you money later on in your trip.

For a good deal, book through a travel agent who will shop around. Also, price local car-rental companies—whose prices may be lower still, although their service and maintenance may not be as good as those of major rental agencies—and research rates on the Internet. Consolidators that specialize in air travel can offer good rates on cars as well (⇨ Air Travel). Remember to ask about required deposits, cancellation penalties, and drop-off charges if you're planning to pick up the car in one city and leave it in another. If you're traveling during a holiday period, also make sure that a confirmed reservation guarantees you a car.

Do look into wholesalers, companies that do not own fleets but rent in bulk from those that do and often offer better rates than traditional car-rental operations. Prices are best during off-peak periods. Rentals booked through wholesalers often must be paid for before you leave home.

🚗 **Local Agencies AA Aloha Cars-R-Us** ☎ 800/ 655-7989 ⊕ www.hawaiicarrental.com. **Aloha Rent A Car** ☎ 877/452-5642 ⊕ www.aloharentacar.com. **Hoʻokipa Haven** ☎ 808/579-8282 or 800/398-6284 ⊕ www.hookipa.com on Maui.

INSURANCE

When driving a rented car you are generally responsible for any damage to or loss of the vehicle. You also may be liable for any property damage or personal injury that you may cause while driving. Before you rent, see what coverage you already have under the terms of your personal auto-insurance policy and credit cards.

For about $9 to $25 a day, rental companies sell protection, known as a collision- or loss-damage waiver (CDW or LDW), that eliminates your liability for damage to the car; it's always optional and should never be automatically added to your bill. In most states you don't need a CDW if you have personal auto insurance or other liability insurance. However, **make sure you have enough coverage to pay for the car.** If you do not have auto insurance or an umbrella policy that covers damage to third parties, purchasing liability insurance and a CDW or LDW is highly recommended.

REQUIREMENTS & RESTRICTIONS

In Hawai'i you must be 21 years old to rent a car and you must have a valid driver's license and a major credit card. Those under 25 will pay a daily surcharge of $15–$25.

In Hawai'i your unexpired mainland driver's license is valid for rental for up to 90 days.

SURCHARGES

Before you pick up a car in one city and leave it in another, ask about drop-off charges or one-way service fees, which can be substantial. Also inquire about early-return policies; some rental agencies charge extra if you return the car before the time specified in your contract, whereas others give you a refund for the days not used. Most agencies note the tank's fuel level on your contract; to avoid a hefty re-fueling fee, return the car with the same tank level. If the tank was full, refill it just before you turn in the car, but be aware that gas stations near the rental outlet may overcharge. It's almost never a deal to buy a tank of gas with the car when you rent it; the understanding is that you'll return it empty, but some fuel usually remains.

Surcharges may apply if you're under 25 or if you take the car outside the area approved by the rental agency. You'll pay extra for child seats (about $8 a day), which are compulsory for children under five, and usually for additional drivers (up to $25 a day, depending on location).

CAR TRAVEL

Traffic on Maui can be very bad branching out from Kahului to and from Pā'ia, Kīhei, and Lahaina. Drive here during peak hours and you'll know why local residents are calling for restrictions on development. Parking along many streets is curtailed during these times, and towing is strictly practiced. Read curbside parking signs before leaving your vehicle, even at a meter.

GASOLINE

Regardless of today's fluctuating gas prices, you can pretty much count on having to pay more for gasoline on Maui than on the U.S. mainland.

ROAD CONDITIONS

Maui's roads and streets, although they may challenge the visitor's tongue, are generally well marked. **Keep an eye open for the Hawai'i Visitors and Convention Bureau's red-caped King Kamehameha signs,** which mark major attractions and scenic spots. Ask for a map at the car-rental counter. Free publications containing good-quality road maps can be found at the aiport, hotels, and resorts, and in shopping areas.

Maui has its share of impenetrable areas, although four-wheel-drive vehicles rarely run into problems on the island. Moloka'i and Lāna'i have fewer roadways, but car rental is still worthwhile and will allow plenty of interesting sightseeing. **Opt for a four-wheel-drive vehicle** if dirt-road exploration holds any appeal.

RULES OF THE ROAD

Be sure to **buckle up.** Hawai'i has a strictly enforced seat-belt law for front-seat passengers. Children under four must be in a car seat (available from car-rental agencies). Children 18 and under, riding in the backseat, are also required by state law to use seat belts. The highway speed limit is usually 55 mph. In-town traffic moves from 25 to 40 mph. Jaywalking is very common, so be particularly watchful for pedestrians, especially in congested areas. Unauthorized use of a parking space reserved for persons with disabilities can net you a $150 fine.

Asking for directions will almost always produce a helpful explanation from the locals, but you should be prepared for an island term or two. Instead of using compass directions, remember that Hawai'i residents refer to places as being either *mauka* (toward the mountains) or *makai* (toward the ocean) from one another.

CHILDREN IN HAWAI'I

Sunny beaches and many family-oriented cultural sites, activities, and attractions make Maui a very *keiki-* (child-) friendly place. Here kids can snorkel with a humuhumunukunukuāpua'a, surf with a boogie board, hike inside a dormant volcano, or ride a sugarcane train. Parents should **use caution on beaches and during water sports.** Even waters that appear calm can harbor powerful rip currents. Be sure to **read any beach-warning guides your hotel may provide. Stick to kid-friendly beaches** that have shallow tide pools or are protected by reefs (look for the ☺ symbol in this guide). And remember that the sun's rays are in operation full-force year-round here. Sunblock for children is essential.

Most major resort chains on the island offer activity programs for kids ages 5 to 12. These kid clubs provide opportunities to learn about local culture, make friends with children from around the world, and experience age-appropriate activities while giving moms and dads a "time-out." Upon arrival, check out the daily local newspapers for children's events. *The Maui News* features "Maui Scene" every Thursday, a listing of special events around the island, many ideal for children.

If you're renting a car, don't forget to arrange for a car seat when you reserve. For general advice about traveling with children, consult *Fodor's FYI: Travel with Your Baby* (available in bookstores everywhere).

FLYING

If your children are two or older, ask about children's airfares. As a general rule, infants under two not occupying a seat fly at greatly reduced fares or even for free. But if you want to guarantee a seat for an infant, you have to pay full fare. Consider flying during off-peak days and times; most airlines will grant an infant a seat without a ticket if there are available seats.

Experts agree that it's a good idea to use safety seats aloft for children weighing less than 40 pounds. Airlines set their own policies: if you use a safety seat, U.S. carriers usually require that the child be ticketed, even if he or she is young enough to ride free, because the seats must be strapped into regular seats. And even if you pay the full adult fare for the seat, it may be worth it, especially on longer trips. Do **check your airline's policy about using safety seats during takeoff and landing.** Safety seats are not allowed everywhere in the plane, so get your seat assignments as early as possible.

When reserving, request children's meals or a freestanding bassinet (not available at all airlines) if you need them. But note that bulkhead seats, where you must sit to use the bassinet, may lack an overhead bin or storage space on the floor.

LODGING

Families can't go wrong choosing resort locations that are part of larger hotel chains such as Hilton, Hyatt, Sheraton, Outrigger, and Westin. Many of these resorts are on the island's best beaches, have activities created for children, and are centrally located. Many condominium resorts now also offer children's activities and amenities during holiday periods.

Most hotels in Maui allow children under a certain age to stay in their parents' room at no extra charge, but others charge for them as extra adults; be sure to find out the cutoff age for children's discounts. Also **check for special seasonal programs,** such as "kids eat free" promotions.

🄵 Best Choices **Embassy Suites Hotels** ☎ 800/362-2779 ⊕ embassysuites.hilton.com. **Four Seasons Hotels and Resorts** ☎ 800/819-5053 ⊕ www.fourseasons.com. **Hyatt Hotels & Resorts**

☎ 888/591-1234 ⊕ www.hyatt.com. **Marriott** ☎ 888/236-2427 ⊕ www.marriott.com. **Molokai Ranch** ☎ 888/627-8082 ⊕ www.molokairanch. com. **Outrigger Hotels & Resorts** ☎ 800/688-7444 ⊕ www.outrigger.com. **ResortQuest Hawaii** ☎ 877/997-6667 ⊕ www.resortquesthawaii.com. **Starwood Hotels and Resorts** ☎ 888/625-5144 for Westin and Sheraton ⊕ www.starwood.com. **The Ritz-Carlton Hotels and Resorts** ☎ 800/241-3333 ⊕ www.ritzcarlton.com.

SIGHTS & ATTRACTIONS

Places that are especially appealing to children are indicated by a rubber-duckie icon (◔) in the margin. Top picks for children run the gamut from natural attractions kids can enjoy for free to some fairly expensive amusements. On Maui, kid favorites include the Sugarcane Train that runs between Lahaina and Kā'anapali, snorkel cruises to Molokini Crater, and whale-watching after a visit to the Maui Ocean Center.

At the Lodge & Beach Village at Moloka'i Ranch on Moloka'i, families can sleep in canvas bungalows and enjoy everything from star gazing and spear fishing to horseback riding with a *paniolo* (Hawaiian cowboy). On Lāna'i, four-wheel-drive off-road adventure tours take families to destinations such as Shipwreck Beach and Mānele Bay, where the dolphins sometimes come to play.

CONSUMER PROTECTION

Whether you're shopping for gifts or purchasing travel services, **pay with a major credit card** whenever possible, so you can cancel payment or get reimbursed if there's a problem (and you can provide documentation). If you're doing business with a particular company for the first time, contact your local Better Business Bureau and the attorney general's offices in your state and (for U.S. businesses) the company's home state as well. Have any complaints been filed? Finally, if you're buying a package or tour, always consider travel insurance that includes default coverage (⇨ Insurance).

🛈 BBBs **Council of Better Business Bureaus** ✉ 4200 Wilson Blvd., Suite 800, Arlington, VA 22203 ☎ 703/276-0100 ⎙ 703/525-8277 ⊕ www. bbb.org.

CRUISE TRAVEL

When Pan Am's amphibious *Hawai'i Clipper* touched down on Pearl Harbor's waters in 1936, it marked the beginning of the end of regular passenger-ship travel to the Islands. From that point on, the predominant means of transporting visitors would be by air, not by sea. Today, however, cruising to Hawai'i is making a comeback.

Norwegian Cruise Lines offers four "freestyle" cruises (no set meal times, less formal clothing, more nightlife choices) with seven-day Hawai'i itineraries on three U.S.-flagged ships, *Pride of Aloha, Pride of America,* and the newest, *Pride of Hawaii.* To get the best deal on a cruise, **consult a cruise-only travel agency.**

Carnival, Celebrity, Holland America, Princess, and Royal Caribbean cruise lines include Hawai'i in a number of itineraries that typically begin and end on the U.S. West Coast. Most of these itineraries include a port of call in Maui. To learn how to plan, choose, and book a cruise-ship voyage, consult *Fodor's FYI: Plan & Enjoy Your Cruise* (available in bookstores everywhere).

🛈 Cruise Lines **Carnival** ☎ 888/227-6482 ⊕ www.carnival.com. **Celebrity** ☎ 800/647-2251 ⊕ www.celebritycruises.com. **Holland America** ☎ 877/724-5425 ⊕ www.hollandamerica.com. **Norwegian Cruise Lines** ☎ 800/327-7030 ⊕ www. norwegiancruiselines.com. **Princess** ☎ 800/774-6237 ⊕ www.princess.com. **Royal Caribbean Cruise Line** ☎ 866/562-7625 ⊕ www. royalcaribbean.com.

CUSTOMS & DUTIES

IN AUSTRALIA

Australian residents who are 18 or older may bring home A$900 worth of souvenirs and gifts (including jewelry), 250 cigarettes or 250 grams of cigars or other tobacco products, and 2.25 liters of alcohol (including wine, beer, and spirits). Residents under 18 may bring back A$450 worth of goods. If any of these individual allowances are exceeded, you must pay duty for the entire amount (of the group of products in which the allowance was exceeded). Members of the same family traveling together may pool their allowances. Prohibited items include meat products. Seeds, plants, and fruits need to be declared upon arrival.

🖪 **Australian Customs Service** ✏ Locked Bag 3000, Sydney International Airport, Sydney, NSW 2020 ☎ 02/6275–6666 or 1300/363–263, 02/8334–7444 or 1800/020–504 quarantine-inquiry line 🖨 02/8339–6714 ⊕ www.customs.gov.au.

IN CANADA

Canadian residents who have been out of Canada for at least seven days may bring in C$750 worth of goods duty-free. If you've been away fewer than seven days but more than 48 hours, the duty-free allowance drops to C$200. If your trip lasts 24 to 48 hours, the allowance is C$50; if the goods are worth more than C$50, you must pay full duty on all of the goods. You may not pool allowances with family members. Goods claimed under the C$750 exemption may follow you by mail; those claimed under the lesser exemptions must accompany you. Alcohol and tobacco products may be included in the seven-day and 48-hour exemptions but not in the 24-hour exemption. If you meet the age requirements of the province or territory through which you reenter Canada, you may bring in, duty-free, 1.5 liters of wine or 1.14 liters (40 imperial ounces) of liquor or 24 12-ounce cans or bottles of beer or ale. Also, if you meet the local age requirement for tobacco products, you may bring in, duty-free, 200 cigarettes, 50 cigars or cigarillos, and 200 grams of tobacco. You may have to pay a minimum duty on tobacco products, regardless of whether or not you exceed your personal exemption. Check ahead of time with the Canada Border Services Agency or the Department of Agriculture for policies regarding meat products, seeds, plants, and fruits.

You may send an unlimited number of gifts (only one gift per recipient, however) worth up to C$60 each duty-free to Canada. Label the package UNSOLICITED GIFT—VALUE UNDER $60. Alcohol and tobacco are excluded.

🖪 **Canada Border Services Agency** ✉ Customs Information Services, 191 Laurier Ave. W, 15th fl., Ottawa, Ontario K1A 0L5 ☎ 800/461–9999 in Canada, 204/983–3500 or 506/636–5064 ⊕ www.cbsa.gc.ca.

IN NEW ZEALAND

All homeward-bound residents may bring back NZ$700 worth of souvenirs and gifts; passengers may not pool their allowances, and children can claim only the concession on goods intended for their own use. For those 17 or older, the duty-free allowance also includes 4.5 liters of wine or beer; one 1,125-ml bottle of spirits; and either 200 cigarettes, 250 grams of tobacco, 50 cigars, or a combination of the three up to 250 grams. Meat products, seeds, plants, and fruits must be declared upon arrival to the Agricultural Services Department.

🖪 **New Zealand Customs** ✉ Head office: The Customhouse, 17–21 Whitmore St., Box 2218, Wellington ☎ 04/473–6099 or 0800/428–786 ⊕ www.customs.govt.nz.

IN THE U.K.

If you're a U.K. resident and your journey was wholly within the European Union, you probably won't have to pass through customs when you return to the United Kingdom. If you plan to bring back large quantities of alcohol or tobacco, check EU limits beforehand. In most cases, if you bring back more than 200 cigars, 3,200 cigarettes, 400 cigarillos, 3 kilograms of tobacco, 10 liters of spirits, 110 liters of beer, 20 liters of fortified wine, and/or 90 liters of wine, you have to declare the goods upon return.

From countries outside the European Union, including the United States, you may bring home, duty-free, 200 cigarettes, 50 cigars, 100 cigarillos, or 250 grams of tobacco; 1 liter of spirits or 2 liters of fortified or sparkling wine or liqueurs; 2 liters of still table wine; 60 ml of perfume; 250 ml of toilet water; plus £145 worth of other goods, including gifts and souvenirs. Prohibited items include meat and dairy products, seeds, plants, and fruits.

🖪 **HM Customs and Excise** ✉ Portcullis House, 21 Cowbridge Rd. E, Cardiff CF11 9SS ☎ 0845/010–9000 or 0208/929–0152 advice service, 0208/929–6731 or 0208/910–3602 complaints ⊕ www.hmce.gov.uk.

DISABILITIES & ACCESSIBILITY

The Society for the Advancement of Travel for the Handicapped has named Hawai'i the most accessible vacation spot for people with disabilities. Ramped visitor areas and specially equipped lodgings are relatively common. Travelers with vision impairments who use a guide dog don't have to worry about quarantine restrictions. All you need to do is present documentation that the animal is a trained guide dog and has a current inoculation record for rabies. Access Aloha Travel is the state's only travel planner specializing in the needs of Hawai'i-bound travelers with disabilities. The company can arrange accessible accommodations, sightseeing, dining, activities, medical equipment rentals, and personal care attendants. Access Aloha and Accessible Vans of Hawaii rent wheelchairs and scooter vans on Maui.

🔳 Local Resources **Access Aloha Travel** ⊠ 414 Kuwili St., Suite 101, Honolulu 96817 ☎ 800/480–1143 or 808/545–1143 🖷 808/545–7657 ⊕ www.accessalohatravel.com. **Disability and Communication Access Board** ⊠ 919 Ala Moana Blvd., Room 101, Honolulu 96814 ☎ 808/586–8121.

LODGING

Despite the Americans with Disabilities Act, the definition of accessibility seems to differ from hotel to hotel. Some properties may be accessible by ADA standards for people with mobility problems but not for people with hearing or vision impairments, for example.

If you have mobility problems, ask for the lowest floor on which accessible services are offered. If you have a hearing impairment, check whether the hotel has devices to alert you visually to the ring of the telephone, a knock at the door, and a fire/emergency alarm. Some hotels provide these devices without charge. Discuss your needs with hotel personnel if this equipment isn't available, so that a staff member can personally alert you in the event of an emergency.

If you're bringing a guide dog, get authorization ahead of time and write down the name of the person with whom you spoke.

Travelers with disabilities and people using wheelchairs find it easy to get around Hawai'i's resorts and hotels, with indoor-outdoor layouts that are easily navigated. If choosing a smaller hotel or a condo or apartment rental, inquire about ground-floor accommodations and **check to see if rooms will accommodate wheelchairs and if bathrooms are accessible.** Many hotels now offer special-needs rooms featuring larger living spaces and bathrooms equipped for guests who require additional assistance.

RESERVATIONS

When discussing accessibility with an operator or reservations agent, ask hard questions. Are there any stairs, inside *or* out? Are there grab bars next to the toilet *and* in the shower/tub? How wide is the doorway to the room? To the bathroom? For the most extensive facilities meeting the latest legal specifications, opt for newer accommodations. If you reserve through a toll-free number, consider also calling the hotel's local number to confirm the information from the central reservations office. Get confirmation in writing when you can.

TRANSPORTATION

Kapalua Executive Transportation & Super Shuttle provides an accessible taxi and tour service on the island of Maui. Those who prefer to do their own driving may rent hand-controlled cars from Alamo, Avis, Budget, Hertz, and National. All require at least 48 hours' notice. You can use the windshield card from your own state to park in spaces reserved for people with disabilities.

The U.S. Department of Transportation Aviation Consumer Protection Division's online publication *New Horizons: Information for the Air Traveler with a Disability* offers advice for travelers with a disability, and outlines basic rights. Visit DisabilityInfo.gov for general information.

🔳 **Kapalua Executive Transportation & Super Shuttle** ☎ 800/833–2303 ⊕ www.mauishuttle.com. 🔳 Complaints **Aviation Consumer Protection Division** (⇨ Air Travel) for airline-related problems; for airline travel advice and rights ⊕ airconsumer.ost.dot.gov/publications/horizons.htm. **Departmen-**

tal Office of Civil Rights ✉ For general inquiries, U.S. Department of Transportation, S-30, 400 7th St. SW, Room 10215, Washington, DC 20590 ☎ 202/366-4648, 202/366-8538 TTY 🖷 202/366-9371 ⊕ www.dotcr.ost.dot.gov. **Disability Rights Section** ✉ NYAV, U.S. Department of Justice, Civil Rights Division, 950 Pennsylvania Ave. NW, Washington, DC 20530 ☎ ADA information line 202/514-0301, 800/514-0301, 202/514-0383 TTY, 800/514-0383 TTY ⊕ www.ada.gov. **U.S. Department of Transportation Hotline** ☎ For disability-related air-travel problems, 800/778-4838 or 800/455-9880 TTY.

TRAVEL AGENCIES

In the United States, the Americans with Disabilities Act requires that travel firms serve the needs of all travelers. Some agencies specialize in working with people with disabilities.

🎦 Travelers with Mobility Problems **Access Aloha Travel** ✉ 414 Kuwili St., Suite 101, Honolulu, HI 96817 ☎ 800/480-1143 or 808/545-1143 🖷 808/545-7657 ⊕ www.accessalohatravel.com. **Accessible Vans of Hawaii** ✉ 355 Hukilike St., Suite 121A, Kahului, HI 96732 ☎ 808/871-7785 or 800/303-3750 🖷 808/871-7536 ⊕ www.accessiblevanshawaii.com. **CareVacations** ✉ No. 5, 5110-50 Ave., Leduc, Alberta, Canada, T9E 6V4 ☎ 780/986-6404 or 877/478-7827 🖷 780/986-8332 ⊕ www.carevacations.com, for group tours and cruise vacations. **Flying Wheels Travel** ✉ 143 W. Bridge St., Box 382, Owatonna, MN 55060 ☎ 507/451-5005 🖷 507/451-1685 ⊕ www.flyingwheelstravel.com.

🎦 Travelers with Developmental Disabilities **New Directions** ✉ 5276 Hollister Ave., Suite 207, Santa Barbara, CA 93111 ☎ 805/967-2841 or 888/967-2841 🖷 805/964-7344 ⊕ www.newdirectionstravel.com. **Sprout** ✉ 893 Amsterdam Ave., New York, NY 10025 ☎ 212/222-9575 or 888/222-9575 🖷 212/222-9768 ⊕ www.gosprout.org.

DISCOUNTS & DEALS

Be a smart shopper and compare all your options before making decisions. A plane ticket bought with a promotional coupon from travel clubs, coupon books, and direct-mail offers or purchased on the Internet may not be cheaper than the least expensive fare from a discount ticket agency. And always keep in mind that what you get is just as important as what you save.

DISCOUNT RESERVATIONS

To save money, look into discount reservations services with Web sites and toll-free numbers, which use their buying power to get a better price on hotels, airline tickets (⇨ Air Travel), even car rentals. When booking a room, always **call the hotel's local toll-free number** (if one is available) rather than the central reservations number—you'll often get a better price. Always ask about special packages or corporate rates.

🎦 **Expedia** ☎ 800/397-3342 ⊕ www.expedia.com. **Hotels** ☎ 800/246-8557 ⊕ www.hotels.com. **Quickbook** ☎ 800/789-9887 ⊕ www.quickbook.com. **Travelocity** ☎ 888/872-8356 ⊕ www.travelocity.com. **Turbotrip.com** ☎ 800/473-7829 ⊕ www.turbotrip.com.

PACKAGE DEALS

Don't confuse packages and guided tours. When you buy a package, you travel on your own, just as though you had planned the trip yourself. Fly–drive packages, which combine airfare and car rental, are often a good deal. In cities, ask the local visitor's bureau about hotel and local transportation packages that include tickets to major museum exhibits or other special events.

EATING & DRINKING

Food in Hawai'i is a reflection of the state's diverse cultural makeup and tropical location. Fresh seafood is the hallmark of Hawai'i regional cuisine, and its preparations are drawn from across the Pacific Rim, including Japan, the Philippines, Korea, and Thailand. "Hawaiian food," however, is a cuisine in its own right. Meals in resort areas are costly but often excellent. The restaurants we list are the cream of the crop in each price category.

MEALTIMES

Unless otherwise noted, the restaurants listed in this guide are open daily for lunch and dinner.

RESERVATIONS & DRESS

Maui is decidedly casual. Aloha shirts and shorts or long pants for men and island-style dresses or casual resort wear for women are standard attire for evenings in most hotel restaurants and local eateries.

T-shirts and shorts will do the trick for breakfast and lunch.

Reservations are always a good idea; we mention them only when they're essential or not accepted. Book as far ahead as you can, and reconfirm as soon as you arrive. (Large parties should always call ahead to check the reservations policy.) We mention dress only when men are required to wear a jacket or a jacket and tie.

SPECIALTIES

Fish, fruit, and fresh island-grown produce are the base of Hawai'i regional cuisine. The "plate lunch" is the heart of most Hawaiians' days and usually consists of grilled teriyaki chicken, beef, or fish, served with two scoops of white rice and two side salads. *Poke*, marinated raw tuna, is a local hallmark. Take note, in general, when you order a regular coffee, you get coffee with milk and sugar.

WINE, BEER & SPIRITS

Hawai'i has a new generation of micro-breweries, including on-site microbreweries at many restaurants. The drinking age in Hawai'i is 21 years of age, and a photo ID must be presented to purchase alcoholic beverages. Bars are open until 2 AM; venues with a cabaret license can stay open until 4 AM. No matter what you might see in the local parks, drinking alcohol in public parks or on the beaches is illegal. It's also illegal to have open containers of alcohol in motor vehicles.

ECOTOURISM

Hawai'i's connection to its environment is spiritual, cultural, and essential to its survival. You'll find a rainbow of natural attractions to explore, from the ribbons of beaches to the summit of a dormant volcano. There are 13 climatic regions in the world, and Maui, Moloka'i, and Lāna'i offer ecotravelers a glimpse of most of them. Maui offers the exhilaration of a rain-forest hike in Hāna, the cool Upcountry climes of Kula, and the awe-inspiring Haleakalā Crater. Moloka'i and Lāna'i, two of the least-developed islands, hold adventures best experienced on foot and by four-wheel-drive vehicle, or even by mule. Ecotouring in Hawai'i gives you the opportunity to learn from local guides who are familiar with the *aina* (land) and Hawai'i's unique cultural heritage. Many of these tours take visitors to locations less traveled, so it helps to be in good physical shape. The views at the ends of these roads are an exceedingly rich reward.

Nature and all its ornaments are sacred to Hawaiians, so before taking pieces of lava rock home for souvenirs, listen to what residents (and some vacationers) will tell you: don't touch! Hapless travelers who take "souvenir" rocks speak of "bad-luck" consequences in the form of stalled cars, travel delays, and bouts of illness. Park rangers spin tales about lava rocks mailed from around the world with attached tales of woe and pleas for the rocks to be put back. If nothing else, with millions of visitors a year, there aren't enough cool rocks to go around.

During the winter months be sure to watch the beachfronts for endangered sea turtles, or recently laid nests. If you spot one, notify local authorities—they'll be thankful for your help in tracking these elusive creatures.

🚩 **Alternative-Hawai'i** ☎ 808/695-5113 ⊕ www. alternative-hawaii.com. **Hawai'i Ecotourism Association** ☎ 877/300-7058 ⊕ www. hawaiiecotourism.org.

ETIQUETTE & BEHAVIOR

Hawai'i was admitted to the Union in 1959, so residents can be pretty sensitive when visitors refer to their own hometowns as "back in the States." Remember, when in Hawai'i, refer to the contiguous 48 states as "the Mainland" and not as the United States. When you do, you won't appear to be such a *malahini* (newcomer).

GAY & LESBIAN TRAVEL

A few small hotels and some bed-and-breakfasts in Hawai'i are favored by gay and lesbian visitors; Purple Roofs is a listing agent for gay-friendly accommodations in Hawai'i. Pacific Ocean Holidays specializes in prearranging package tours for independent gay travelers. The organization also offers an online directory of gay-owned and gay-friendly businesses and community resources on Maui.

For details about the gay and lesbian scene, consult *Fodor's Gay Guide to the USA* (available in bookstores everywhere).

🔲 Local Resources **Pacific Ocean Holidays** 🏠 Box 88245, Honolulu 96830 🖀 808/923-2400 or 800/735-6600 🌐 www.gayHawaiivacations.com or www.gayHawaii.com. **Purple Roofs** 🌐 www.purpleroofs.com.

🔲 Gay- & Lesbian-Friendly Travel Agencies **Different Roads Travel** ✉ 155 Palm Colony, Palm Springs, CA 92264 🖀 310/289-6000 or 800/429-8747. **Skylink Travel and Tour/Flying Dutchman Travel** ✉ 1455 N. Dutton Ave., Suite A, Santa Rosa, CA 95401 🖀 707/546-9888 or 800/225-5759 🖷 707/636-0951 serving lesbian travelers.

HEALTH

Hawai'i is known as the Health State. The life expectancy here is 79 years, the longest in the nation. Balmy weather makes it easy to remain active year-round, and the low-stress aloha attitude certainly contributes to general well-being. When visiting the Islands, however, there are a few health issues to keep in mind.

The Hawai'i State Department of Health recommends that you drink 16 ounces of water per hour to avoid dehydration when hiking or spending time in the sun. **Use sunblock, wear UV-reflective sunglasses, and protect your head with a visor or hat for shade.** If you're not acclimated to warm, humid weather you should allow plenty of time for rest stops and refreshments. When visiting freshwater streams, be aware of the tropical disease leptospirosis, which is spread by animal urine and carried into streams and mud. Symptoms include fever, headache, nausea, and red eyes. If left untreated it can cause liver and kidney damage, respiratory failure, internal bleeding, and even death. To avoid this, don't swim or wade in freshwater streams or ponds if you have open sores and **don't drink from any freshwater streams or ponds.**

On the Islands, fog is a rare occurrence, but there can often be "vog," an airborne haze of gases released from volcanic vents on the Big Island. During certain weather conditions such as "Kona Winds," the vog can settle over the Islands and wreak havoc with respiratory and other health conditions, especially asthma or emphysema. If susceptible, stay indoors and get emergency assistance if needed.

PESTS & OTHER HAZARDS

The Islands have their share of bugs and insects that enjoy the tropical climate as much as visitors do. Most are harmless but annoying. When planning to spend time outdoors in hiking areas, **wear long-sleeved clothing and pants** and **use mosquito repellent containing deet.** In very damp places you may encounter the dreaded local centipede. On the Islands they usually come in two colors, brown and blue, and they range from the size of a worm to an 8-inch cigar. Their sting is very painful, and the reaction is similar to bee- and wasp-sting reactions. When camping, **shake out your sleeping bag before climbing in, and check your shoes in the morning,** as the centipedes like cozy places. If planning on hiking or traveling in remote areas, always carry a first-aid kit and appropriate medications for sting reactions.

INSURANCE

The most useful travel-insurance plan is a comprehensive policy that includes coverage for trip cancellation and interruption, default, trip delay, and medical expenses (with a waiver for preexisting conditions).

Without insurance you'll lose all or most of your money if you cancel your trip, regardless of the reason. Default insurance covers you if your tour operator, airline, or cruise line goes out of business—the chances of which have been increasing. Trip-delay covers expenses that arise because of bad weather or mechanical delays. Study the fine print when comparing policies.

U.K. residents can buy a travel-insurance policy valid for most vacations taken during the year in which it's purchased (but check preexisting-condition coverage).

Always **buy travel policies directly from the insurance company**; if you buy them from a cruise line, airline, or tour operator that goes out of business you probably won't be covered for the agency or operator's default, a major risk. Before making any purchase, review your existing health and home-owner's policies to find what they cover away from home.

🔁 Travel Insurers In the U.S.: **Access America** 📠 2805 N. Parham Rd., Richmond, VA 23294 ☎ 800/729-6021 🖷 800/346-9265 ⊕ www.accessamerica.com. **Travel Guard International** ✉ 1145 Clark St., Stevens Point, WI 54481 ☎ 800/826-4919 or 715/345-1041 🖷 715/345-1990 ⊕ www.travelguard.com.

FOR INTERNATIONAL TRAVELERS

For information on customs restrictions, *see* Customs & Duties.

CAR RENTAL

When picking up a rental car, non-U.S. residents need a reservation voucher for any prepaid reservations that were made in the traveler's home country, a passport, a driver's license, and a travel policy that covers each driver.

CAR TRAVEL

Driving in the United States is on the right. Obey speed limits posted along roads and highways. Bookstores, gas stations, and convenience stores sell maps.

CONSULATES & EMBASSIES

🔁 Australia **Australian Consulate** ✉ 1000 Bishop St., Honolulu 96813 ☎ 808/524-5050.
🔁 Canada **Canadian Consulate** ✉ 1000 Bishop St., Honolulu 96813 ☎ 808/524-5050.
🔁 New Zealand **New Zealand Consulate** ✉ 900 Richards St., Room 414, Honolulu 96813 ☎ 808/543-7900.
🔁 United Kingdom **British Consulate** ✉ 1000 Bishop St., Honolulu 96813 ☎ 808/524-5050.

CURRENCY

The dollar is the basic unit of U.S. currency. It has 100 cents. Coins are the copper penny (1¢); the silvery nickel (5¢), dime (10¢), quarter (25¢), and half-dollar (50¢); and the golden $1 coin, replacing a now-rare silver dollar. Bills are denominated $1, $5, $10, $20, $50, and $100, all mostly green and identical in size; designs and background tints vary. In addition, you may come across a $2 bill, but the chances are slim. The exchange rate at this writing is US$1.73 per British pound, 85¢ per Canadian dollar, 74¢ per Australian dollar, and 70¢ per New Zealand dollar.

ELECTRICITY

The U.S. standard is AC, 110 volts/60 cycles. Plugs have two flat pins set parallel to each other.

EMERGENCIES

For police, fire, or ambulance, **dial 911** (0 in rural areas).

INSURANCE

Britons and Australians need extra medical coverage when traveling overseas.

🔁 Insurance Information In the U.K.: **Association of British Insurers** ✉ 51 Gresham St., London EC2V 7HQ ☎ 020/7600-3333 🖷 020/7696-8999 ⊕ www.abi.org.uk. In Australia: **Insurance Council of Australia** ✉ Level 3, 56 Pitt St. Sydney, NSW 2000 ☎ 02/9253-5100 🖷 02/9253-5111 ⊕ www.ica.com.au. In Canada: **RBC Insurance** ✉ 6880 Financial Dr., Mississauga, Ontario L5N 7Y5 ☎ 800/387-4357 or 905/816-2559 🖷 888/298-6458 ⊕ www.rbcinsurance.com. In New Zealand: **Insurance Council of New Zealand** ✉ Level 7, 111-115 Customhouse Quay, Box 474, Wellington ☎ 04/472-5230 🖷 04/473-3011 ⊕ www.icnz.org.nz.

MAIL & SHIPPING

You can buy stamps and aerograms and send letters and parcels in post offices. Stamp-dispensing machines can occasionally be found in airports, office buildings, drugstores, and the like. You can also deposit mail in the stout, dark blue, steel bins at strategic locations everywhere and in the mail chutes of large buildings; pickup schedules are posted. You can deposit packages at public collection boxes as long as the parcels are affixed with proper postage and weigh less than one pound. Packages weighing one or more pounds must be taken to a post office or handed to a postal carrier.

For mail sent within the United States, you need a 39¢ stamp for first-class letters weighing up to 1 ounce (24¢ for each additional ounce) and 24¢ for postcards. You pay 84¢ for 1-ounce airmail letters and 75¢ for airmail postcards to most other countries; to Canada and Mexico, you need a 63¢ stamp for a 1-ounce letter and 55¢ for a postcard. An aerogram—a single sheet of lightweight blue paper that folds into its own envelope, stamped for overseas airmail—costs 75¢.

To receive mail on the road, have it sent c/o General Delivery at your destination's main post office (use the correct five-digit ZIP code). You must pick up mail in person within 30 days and show a driver's license or passport.

PASSPORTS & VISAS

When traveling internationally, carry your passport even if you don't need one (it's always the best form of ID) and **make two photocopies of the data page** (one for someone at home and another for you, carried separately from your passport). If you lose your passport, promptly call the nearest embassy or consulate and the local police.

Visitor visas aren't necessary for Canadian or European Union citizens, or for citizens of Australia who are staying fewer than 90 days.

☎ Australian Citizens **Passports Australia** ☎ 131-232 ⊕ www.passports.gov.au. **United States Consulate General** ✉ MLC Centre, Level 59, 19–29 Martin Pl., Sydney, NSW 2000 ☎ 02/9373-9200, 1902/941-641 fee-based visa-inquiry line ⊕ usembassy-australia.state.gov/sydney.

☎ Canadian Citizens **Passport Office** ✉ To mail in applications: Foreign Affairs Office, Gatineau, Québec K1A 0G3 ☎ 800/567-6868, 866/255-7655 TTY ⊕ www.ppt.gc.ca.

☎ New Zealand Citizens **New Zealand Passports Office** ✉ For applications and information, Level 3, Boulcott House, 47 Boulcott St., Wellington ☎ 0800/22-5050 or 04/474-8100 ⊕ www.passports.govt.nz. **Embassy of the United States** ✉ 29 Fitzherbert Terr., Thorndon, Wellington ☎ 04/462-6000 ⊕ usembassy.org.nz. **U.S. Consulate General** ✉ Citibank Bldg., 3rd fl., 23 Customs St. E, Auckland ☎ 09/303-2724 ⊕ usembassy.org.nz.

☎ U.K. Citizens **U.K. Passport Service** ☎ 0870/521-0410 ⊕ www.passport.gov.uk. **American Consulate General** ✉ Danesfort House, 223 Stranmillis Rd., Belfast, Northern Ireland BT9 5GR ☎ 028/9038-6100 🖶 028/9068-1301 ⊕ www.usembassy.org.uk. **American Embassy** ✉ For visa and immigration information or to submit a visa application via mail (enclose an SASE), Consular Information Unit, 24 Grosvenor Sq., London W1A 2LQ ☎ 090/5544-4546 or 090/6820-0290 for visa information (per-minute charges), 0207/499-9000 main switchboard ⊕ www.usembassy.org.uk.

TELEPHONES

All U.S. telephone numbers consist of a three-digit area code and a seven-digit local number. Within many local calling areas, you dial only the seven-digit number. Within some area codes, you must dial "1" first for calls outside the local area. To call between area-code regions, dial "1" then all 10 digits; the same goes for calls to numbers prefixed by "800," "888," "866," and "877"—all toll-free. For calls to numbers preceded by "900" you must pay—usually dearly.

For international calls, dial "011" followed by the country code and the local number. For help, dial "0" and ask for an overseas operator. The country code is 61 for Australia, 64 for New Zealand, 44 for the United Kingdom. Calling Canada is the same as calling within the United States, although you might not be able to get through on some toll-free numbers. Most local phone books list country codes and U.S. area codes. The country code for the United States is 1.

For operator assistance, dial "0." To obtain someone's phone number, call directory assistance at 555–1212 or occasionally 411 (free at many public phones). To have the person you're calling foot the bill, phone collect; dial "0" instead of "1" before the 10-digit number.

At pay phones, instructions often are posted. Usually you insert coins in a slot (usually 25¢–50¢ for local calls) and wait for a steady tone before dialing. When you call long-distance, the operator tells you how much to insert; prepaid phone cards, widely available in various denominations, are easier. Call the number on the back, punch in the card's personal identification number when prompted, then dial your number.

If you're taking your cell phone on vacation with you, make sure roaming is included, otherwise, your minutes and bill will quickly add up. Prepaid phone cards are convenient and cost-effective.

LANGUAGE

English is the primary language on the Islands. Making the effort to learn some Hawaiian words can be rewarding, however. Despite the length of many Hawaiian words, the Hawaiian alphabet is actually one of the world's shortest, with only 12 letters: the five vowels, *a, e, i, o, u,* and seven consonants, *h, k, l, m, n, p, w.* Hawaiian words you are most likely to encounter during your visit to the Islands are *aloha* (hello), *mahalo* (thank you), *keiki* (child), *haole* (Caucasian or foreigner), *mauka* (toward the mountains), *makai* (toward the ocean), and *pau* (finished, all done). Hawaiian history includes waves of immigrants, each bringing their own language. To communicate with each other, they developed a sort of slang known as "pidgin." If you listen closely, you will know what is being said by the inflections and by the extensive use of body language. For example, when you know what you want to say but don't know how to say it, just say "you know, da kine." For an informative and somewhat-hilarious view of things Hawaiian, check out Jerry Hopkins's series of books titled *Pidgin to the Max* and *Fax to the Max,* available at most local bookstores in the Hawaiiana sections.

LEI GREETINGS

When you walk off a long flight, perhaps a bit groggy and stiff, nothing quite compares with a Hawaiian lei greeting. The casual ceremony ranks as one of the fastest ways to make the transition from the worries of home to the joys of your vacation. Though the tradition has created an expectation that everyone receives this floral garland when they step off the plane, the state of Hawai'i cannot greet each of its nearly 7 million annual visitors.

Still, it's easy to **arrange for a lei ceremony for yourself or your companions before you arrive.** Contact Ali'i Leis if you have not signed up with a tour company that provides it. If you really want to be wowed by the experience, request a lei of tuberoses, some of the most divine-smelling blossoms on the planet. Ali'i Leis requires two days' notice and charges

$19.95 for a standard greeting on Maui.
🎫 **Ali'i Leis** ☎ 808/877-3521 🖷 808/877-0757.

LODGING

No matter what your budget, you'll find a great place to stay in Maui County. Whether you're seeking an oceanfront resort with loads of amenities or a quiet vacation rental where the only sounds you'll hear are the birds, Maui, Moloka'i, and Lāna'i have something for everyone. Maui also boasts dozens of family-style condominiums at reasonable prices. B&Bs are becoming increasingly popular as visitors look for a real slice of Hawai'i away from the crowds. Often tucked into nooks of the Islands you would normally never see, they are competitively priced, highly personalized, and great for relaxing.

The lodgings we list are the cream of the crop in each price category. We always list the facilities that are available, but we don't specify whether they cost extra. When pricing accommodations, always ask what's included and what costs extra.

APARTMENT & HOUSE RENTAL

If you want a home base that's roomy enough for a family and comes with cooking facilities, consider a furnished rental. These can save you money, especially if you're traveling with a group. Home-exchange directories sometimes list rentals as well as exchanges. In addition, many of the companies listed under hotels and condominiums offer vacation villas for daily, weekly, and monthly rentals.
🎫 International Agents **Hideaways International** ✉ 767 Islington St., Portsmouth, NH 03801 ☎ 603/430-4433 or 800/843-4433 🖷 603/430-4444 ⊕ www.hideaways.com, annual membership $185. **Vacation Home Rentals Worldwide** ✉ 235 Kensington Ave., Norwood, NJ 07648 ☎ 201/767-9393 or 800/633-3284 🖷 201/767-5510 ⊕ www.vhrww.com. 🎫 Exchange Clubs **HomeLink International** ✉ 2937 N.W. 9th Terr., Fort Lauderdale, FL 33311 ☎ 954/566-2687 or 800/638-3841 🖷 954/566-2783 ⊕ www.homelink.org; $80/year for Web-only membership; $125/year for Web access and two directories. **Intervac U.S.** ✉ 30 Corte San Fernando,

Tiburon, CA 94920 ☎ 800/756-4663 🖷 415/435-7440 ⊕ www.intervacus.com; $128.88 yearly for a listing, on-line access, and a catalog; $78.88 without catalog.

HOSTELS

No matter what your age, you can save on lodging by staying at hostels. The Banana Bungalow Maui Hostel, the only hostel in Maui County, is popular among windsurfers and backpackers. It offers free tours of Maui, airport/beach shuttles, and Internet service. Located in Wailuku, there are private rooms with garden and mountain views and four- and six-person dorm rooms.

🚺 **Banana Bungalow Maui Hostel** ☎ 800/846-7835 ⊕ www.mauihostel.com.

HOTELS & CONDOMINIUMS

All hotels and condominiums listed have private bath unless otherwise noted.

🚺 **Toll-Free Numbers Best Western** ☎ 800/780-7234 ⊕ www.bestwestern.com. **Castle Resorts & Hotels** ☎ 800/367-5004 ⊕ www.castleresorts.com. **Condominium Rentals Hawaii** ☎ 800/367-5242 ⊕ www.maui-vacations.com. **Destination Resorts Hawaii** ☎ 800/367-5246 ⊕ www.drhmaui.com. **Embassy Suites** ☎ 800/362-2779 ⊕ www.embassysuites.com. **Fairmont Hotels & Resorts** ☎ 800/257-7544 ⊕ www.fairmonthotels.com. **Four Seasons Hotels and Resorts** ☎ 800/332-3442 ⊕ www.fourseasons.com. **Grand Wailea Resort** ☎ 800/888-6100 ⊕ www.grandwailea.com. **Hotel Hāna Maui** ☎ 800/321-4262 ⊕ www.hotelhanamaui.com. **Hotel Lanai** ☎ 877/665-2624 ⊕ www.hotellanai.com. **Hotel Molokai** ☎ 800/535-0085 ⊕ www.hotelmolokai.com. **Hyatt Hotels & Resorts** ☎ 800/591-1234 ⊕ www.hyatt.com. **Kāʻanapali Aliʻi** ☎ 800/642-6284 ⊕ www.kaanapalialii.com. **Lahaina Inn** ☎ 800/669-3444 ⊕ www.lahainainn.com. **The Lodge & Beach Village at Molokai Ranch** ☎ 888/627-8082 ⊕ www.molokairanch.com. **Marc Resorts Hawaii** ☎ 800/535-0085 ⊕ www.marcresorts.com. **Marriott** ☎ 800/236-2427 ⊕ www.marriott.com. **Premier Resorts** ☎ 800/771-3533 ⊕ www.premier-resorts.com. **Prince Resorts Hawaii** ☎ 866/774-6236 ⊕ www.princeresortshawaii.com. **Renaissance Hotels & Resorts** ☎ 800/468-3571 ⊕ www.marriott.com. **The Ritz-Carlton Hotels and Resorts** ☎ 800/241-3333 ⊕ www.ritzcarlton.com. **Royal Lahaina Resort** ☎ 808/661-3611 ⊕ www.2maui.com. **Starwood Hotels & Resorts (Sheraton and Westin Hotels)** ☎ 800/625-5144 ⊕ www.starwood.com. **Sullivan Properties** ☎ 800/332-1137 ⊕ www.mauiresorts.com.

MEDIA

Hawaiʻi is wired to a variety of media, including network television, cable television, Web-based media, newspapers, magazines, and radio. Many of the resorts and hotels throughout Maui, Molokaʻi, and Lānaʻi include an additional visitor-information channel on your in-room television. Consult your in-room directory to get channel and scheduling information and to find out the special activities or events that might be happening during your visit.

NEWSPAPERS & MAGAZINES

Each of the Islands has its own daily newspaper, available through many hotel bell desks; in sundry stores, restaurants, and cafés; and at newsstands. Many hotels will deliver one to your room on request. On Maui and Lānaʻi, it's the *Maui News*. On Molokaʻi, it's the *Molokaʻi Island Times* and the *Dispatch*. *Pacific Business News* provides the latest in statewide business news.

RADIO & TELEVISION

Radio airwaves on the Islands are affected by natural terrain, so don't expect to hear one radio station islandwide. For Hawaiian music, tune your FM radio dial to 93.5 KPOA or 103.7 KNUQ for Jawaiian tunes. News junkies can get their fill of news and talk by tuning to 1110 KAOI on the AM radio dial. National Public Radio enthusiasts can tune to the FM dial for NPR programming on 90.7 KKUA.

Television channels on the Islands are plentiful between network and cable channels. Channel allocation varies by island and location. You can find the following network programming with its channel and local affiliate call sign: FOX (2) KHON, ABC (4) KITV, UPN/WB (5) KHVE, CBS (9) KGMB, PBS (10) KHET, and NBC (13) KHNL.

MONEY MATTERS

Prices throughout this guide are given for adults. Substantially reduced fees are almost always available for children, students, and senior citizens. For information on taxes, *see* Taxes.

ATMS

Automatic teller machines for easy access to cash are everywhere on the Islands. ATMs can be found in shopping centers, small convenience and grocery stores, inside hotels and resorts, as well as outside most bank branches. For a directory of locations, call 800/424–7787 for the Master-Card/Cirrus/Maestro network; or 800/843–7587 for the Visa/Plus network.

CREDIT CARDS

Throughout this guide, the following abbreviations are used: **AE**, American Express; **D**, Discover; **DC**, Diners Club; **MC**, MasterCard; and **V**, Visa.

🔢 Reporting Lost Cards **American Express** ☎ 800/992–3404. **Diners Club** ☎ 800/234–6377. **Discover** ☎ 800/347–2683. **MasterCard** ☎ 800/622–7747. **Visa** ☎ 800/847–2911.

NATIONAL PARKS & STATE PARKS

Maui County boasts one of the most spectacular national parks in the country. Stretching for nearly 30,000 acres from the summit at Haleakalā crater to the lush, verdant valleys of Kīpahulu, Haleakalā National Park affords dozens of opportunities for exploration. Moloka'i's Kalaupapa National Historical Park was once a leper colony where victims of Hansen's disease were sent into exile in the late 1800s and cared for by Father Damien, a Belgian missionary.

State parks throughout Maui, Moloka'i and Lāna'i encompass thousands of acres and include many beautiful beaches and coastal areas. The State Parks Division of the Hawai'i State Department of Land and Natural Resources can provide information on state parks and historic areas.

Look into discount passes to save money on park entrance fees. For $50, the National Parks Pass admits you (and any passengers in your private vehicle) to all national parks, monuments, and recreation areas, as well as other sites run by the National Park Service, for a year. (In parks that charge per person, the pass admits you, your spouse and children, and your parents, when you arrive together.) Camping and parking are extra. The $15 Golden Eagle Pass, a hologram you affix to your National Parks Pass, functions as an upgrade, granting entry to all sites run by the NPS, the U.S. Fish and Wildlife Service, the U.S. Forest Service, and the Bureau of Land Management. The upgrade, which expires with the parks pass, is sold by most national-park, Fish-and-Wildlife, and BLM fee stations. A major percentage of the proceeds from pass sales funds National Parks projects.

Both the Golden Age Passport ($10), for U.S. citizens or permanent residents who are 62 and older, and the Golden Access Passport (free), for persons with disabilities, entitle holders (and any passengers in their private vehicles) to lifetime free entry to all national parks, plus 50% off fees for the use of many park facilities and services. (The discount doesn't always apply to companions.) To obtain them, you must show proof of age and of U.S. citizenship or permanent residency—such as a U.S. passport, driver's license, or birth certificate—and, if requesting Golden Access, proof of disability. The Golden Age and Golden Access passes are available only at NPS-run sites that charge an entrance fee. The National Parks Pass is also available by mail and phone and via the Internet.

🔢 **National Park Foundation** ✉ 11 Dupont Circle NW, Suite 600, Washington, DC 20036 ☎ 202/238–4200 ⊕ www.nationalparks.org. **National Park Service** ✉ National Park Service/Department of Interior, 1849 C St. NW, Washington, DC 20240 ☎ 202/208–6843 ⊕ www.nps.gov. **National Parks Conservation Association** ✉ 1300 19th St. NW, Suite 300, Washington, DC 20036 ☎ 202/223–6722 or 800/628–7275 ⊕ www.npca.org.

🔢 Passes by Mail & Online **National Park Foundation** ⊕ www.nationalparks.org. **National Parks Pass** National Park Foundation 🗂 Box 34108, Washington, DC 20043 ☎ 888/467–2757 ⊕ www.nationalparks.org; include a check or money order payable to the National Park Service, plus $3.95 for shipping and handling (allow 8 to 13 business days from date of receipt for pass delivery), or call for passes.

State Parks **State Parks Division, Hawai'i State Department of Land and Natural Resources** ✉ 1151 Punchbowl St., Room 310, Honolulu 96813 ☎ 808/587-0300 ⊕ www.hawaii.gov.

PACKING

Hawai'i is casual: sandals, bathing suits, and comfortable, informal clothing are the norm. In summer, synthetic slacks and shirts, although easy to care for, can be uncomfortably warm.

Probably the most important thing to tuck into your suitcase is sunscreen. This is the tropics, and the ultraviolet rays are powerful, even on overcast days. Doctors advise putting on sunscreen when you get up in the morning, whether it's cloudy or sunny. Don't forget to **reapply sunscreen periodically during the day,** since perspiration can wash it away. Consider using sunscreens with a sun protection factor (SPF) of 15 or higher. There are many tanning oils on the market in Hawai'i, including coconut and *kukui* (the nut from a local tree) oils, but they can cause severe burns. Too many Hawaiian vacations have been spoiled by sunburn and even sun poisoning. Hats and sunglasses offer important sun protection, too. Both are easy to find in island shops, but if you already have a favorite packable hat or sun visor, bring it with you, and don't forget to wear it. All major hotels in Hawai'i provide beach towels.

As for clothing in the Hawaiian Islands, there's a saying that when a man wears a suit during the day, he's either going for a loan or he's a lawyer trying a case. Only a few upscale restaurants require a jacket for dinner. The aloha shirt is accepted dress in Hawai'i for business and most social occasions. Shorts are acceptable daytime attire, along with a T-shirt or polo shirt. There's no need to buy expensive sandals on the mainland—here you can get flip-flops for a couple of dollars and off-brand sandals for $20. Golfers should remember that many courses have dress codes requiring a collared shirt; call courses you're interested in for details. If you're not prepared, you can pick up appropriate clothing at resort pro shops. If you're visiting in winter or planning to visit a high-altitude area, **bring a sweater or light- to medium-weight jacket.** A polar fleece pullover is ideal, and makes a great impromptu pillow.

In your carry-on luggage, pack an extra pair of eyeglasses or contact lenses and enough of any medication you take to last a few days longer than the entire trip. You may also ask your doctor to write a spare prescription using the drug's generic name, as brand names may vary from country to country. In luggage to be checked, **never pack prescription drugs, valuables, or undeveloped film.** And don't forget to carry with you the addresses of offices that handle refunds of lost traveler's checks. Check *Fodor's How to Pack* (available at online retailers and bookstores everywhere) for more tips.

To avoid customs and security delays, carry medications in their original packaging. Don't pack any sharp objects in your carry-on luggage, including knives of any size or material, scissors, nail clippers, and corkscrews, or anything else that might arouse suspicion.

To avoid having your checked luggage chosen for hand inspection, don't cram bags full. The U.S. Transportation Security Administration suggests packing shoes on top and placing personal items you don't want touched in clear plastic bags.

CHECKING LUGGAGE

You're allowed to carry aboard one bag and one personal article, such as a purse or a laptop computer. Make sure what you carry on fits under your seat or in the overhead bin. Get to the gate early, so you can board as soon as possible, before the overhead bins fill up.

Baggage allowances vary by carrier, destination, and ticket class. On international flights, you're usually allowed to check two bags weighing up to 50 pounds (23 kilograms) each, although a few airlines allow checked bags of up to 88 pounds (40 kilograms) in first class. Some international carriers don't allow more than 66 pounds (30 kilograms) per bag in business class and 44 pounds (20 kilograms) in economy. If you're flying to or through the United Kingdom, your luggage cannot exceed 70 pounds (32 kilograms) per bag. On domestic flights, the limit is usually 50 to 70 pounds (23 to 32 kilograms) per bag. In general, carry-on bags shouldn't exceed 40 pounds (18 kilograms). Most airlines won't accept bags that weigh more than 100 pounds (45 kilograms) on domestic or international flights. Expect to pay a fee for baggage that exceeds weight limits. Check baggage restrictions with your carrier before you pack.

Airline liability for baggage is limited to $2,500 per person on flights within the United States. On international flights it amounts to $9.07 per pound or $20 per kilogram for checked baggage (roughly $540 per 50-pound bag), with a maximum of $634.90 per piece, and $400 per passenger for unchecked baggage. You can buy additional coverage at check-in for about $10 per $1,000 of coverage, but it often excludes a rather extensive list of items, shown on your airline ticket.

Before departure, itemize your bags' contents and their worth, and label the bags with your name, address, and phone number. (If you use your home address, cover it so potential thieves can't see it readily.) Include a label inside each bag and **pack a copy of your itinerary.** At check-in, make sure each bag is correctly tagged with the destination airport's three-letter code. Because some checked bags will be opened for hand inspection, the U.S. Transportation Security Administration recommends that you leave luggage unlocked or use the plastic locks offered at check-in. TSA screeners place an inspection notice inside searched bags, which are re-sealed with a special lock.

If your bag has been searched and contents are missing or damaged, file a claim with the TSA Consumer Response Center as soon as possible. If your bags arrive damaged or fail to arrive at all, file a written report with the airline before leaving the airport.

▐ Complaints **U.S. Transportation Security Administration Contact Center** ☎ 866/289-9673 ⊕ www.tsa.gov.

SAFETY

Hawai'i is generally a safe tourist destination, but it's still wise to follow the same common sense safety precautions you would normally follow in your own hometown. Hotel and visitor-center staff can provide information should you decide to head out on your own to more remote areas. **Rental cars are magnets for break-ins, so don't leave any valuables in the car, not even in a locked trunk.** Avoid poorly lighted areas, beach parks, and isolated areas after dark as a precaution. When hiking, **stay on marked trails,** no matter how alluring the temptation might be to stray. Weather conditions can cause landscapes to become muddy, slippery, and tenuous, so staying on marked trails will lessen the possibility of a fall or getting lost. Ocean safety is of the utmost importance when visiting an island destination. **Don't swim alone, and follow the international signage posted at beaches** that alerts swimmers to strong currents, man-of-war jellyfish, sharp coral, high surf, sharks, and dangerous shore breaks. At coastal lookouts along cliff tops, heed the signs indicating that waves can climb over the ledges. Check with lifeguards at each beach for current conditions, and **if the red flags are up, indicating swimming and surfing are not allowed, don't go in.** Waters that look calm on the surface can harbor strong currents and undertows, and many people who were just wading have been dragged out to sea.

LOCAL SCAMS

Be wary of those hawking "too good to be true" prices on everything from car rentals to attractions. Many of these offers are just a lure to get you in the door for time-share presentations. When handed a flyer, read the fine print before making the decision to participate.

WOMEN IN HAWAI'I

Women traveling alone are generally safe on the Islands, but always follow the safety precautions you would use in any major destination. When booking hotels, **request rooms closest to the elevator,** and always keep your hotel-room door and balcony doors locked. Stay away from isolated areas after dark; camping and hiking solo are not advised. If you stay out late visiting nightclubs and bars, **use caution when exiting night spots** and returning to your lodging.

SENIOR-CITIZEN TRAVEL

Hawai'i is steeped in a tradition that gives great respect to elders, or *kupuna,* and considers them "keepers of the wisdom." Visitors may not be so esteemed, but senior citizens traveling in Hawai'i will find discounts, special senior citizen–oriented activities, and buildings with easy access. Many lodging facilities have discounts for members of the American Association of Retired Persons (AARP).

To qualify for age-related discounts, mention your senior-citizen status up front when booking hotel reservations (not when checking out) and before you're seated in restaurants (not when paying the bill). Be sure to have identification on hand. When renting a car, ask about promotional car-rental discounts, which can be cheaper than senior-citizen rates.

🛈 Educational Programs **Elderhostel** ✉ 11 Ave. de Lafayette, Boston, MA 02111 ☎ 877/426–8056, 978/323–4141 international callers, 877/426–2167 TTY 🖶 877/426–2166 ⊕ www.elderhostel.org.

SHOPPING

KEY DESTINATIONS

Maui County offers a delightful array of shopping opportunities. For larger shopping malls, there are Ka'ahumanu Shopping Center and Maui Mall in Kahului, the Shops at Wailea, Kapalua Shops, and Whaler's Village in Kā'anapali. If you're driving to Hāna, you'll want to stop at the Ching Store to fill up on gas and groceries. You'll find the perfect island attire at Hilo Hatti, which offers the largest collection of Hawaiian fashions in the islands. On Lāna'i, Pine Isle Market can help you fill a picnic basket for a day at the beach. A must-do on Moloka'i is a visit to Moloka'i Plumerias where you can pick your own flowers in the orchard and make a traditional Hawaiian lei. The beautiful fragrance will make you want to stay in the

islands forever. Exclusive shops can often be found in the lobbies of luxury hotels.

SMART SOUVENIRS

Aloha shirts and resort wear, Hawaiian-music recordings, shell leis, coral jewelry, traditional quilts, island foods, Kona coffee, and koa-wood products are just a few of the gifts that visitors to Hawai'i treasure. For the more elegant gift items, check out the Hawaiian boutiques in major island shopping centers as well as those tucked away in smaller shopping areas in residential districts. Island crafts fairs and swap meets offer a bargain bazaar of standard items such as T-shirts and tiki statues as well as original works by local artisans.

WATCH OUT

Souvenirs made from coral or tortoise shell may not have been harvested legally, so in the interest of preserving Hawai'i's environment, it's best to avoid these.

STUDENTS IN HAWAI'I

Hawai'i is a popular destination for exchange students from around the world, who mainly attend the University of Hawai'i in Honolulu. Contact your hometown university about study and internship possibilities. Be sure to ask about discounts for students at all museums and major attractions and be prepared to show ID to qualify.

🛈 IDs & Services **STA Travel** ☎ 212/627–3111, 800/781–4040 24-hr service center in the U.S. ⊕ www.sta.com. **Travel CUTS** ✉ 187 College St., Toronto, Ontario M5T 1P7, Canada ☎ 800/592–2887 in U.S., 888/359–2887 in Canada 🖶 416/979–8167 ⊕ www.travelcuts.com.

TAXES

SALES TAX

There's a 4.16% state sales tax on all purchases, including food. A hotel room tax of 7.25%, combined with the sales tax of 4%, equals an 11.41% rate added onto your hotel bill. A $3-per-day road tax is also assessed on each rental vehicle.

TIME

Hawai'i is on Hawaiian Standard Time, 5 hours behind New York, 2 hours behind

Los Angeles, and 10 hours behind London. When the U.S. mainland is on daylight saving time, Hawai'i is not, so add an extra hour of time difference between the Islands and U.S. mainland destinations. You may find that things generally move more slowly here. That has nothing to do with your watch—it's just the laid-back way called Hawaiian time.

TIPPING

Tip cab drivers 15% of the fare. Standard tips for restaurants and bar tabs run from 15% to 20% of the bill, depending on the standard of service. Bellhops at hotels usually receive $1 per bag, more if you have bulky items such as bicycles and surfboards. Tip the hotel room maid $1 per night, paid daily. Tip doormen $1 for assistance with taxis; tips for concierge vary depending on the service. For example, tip more for "hard-to-get" event tickets or dining reservations.

TOURS & PACKAGES

Because everything is prearranged on a prepackaged tour or independent vacation, you spend less time planning—and often get it all at a good price.

BOOKING WITH AN AGENT

Travel agents are excellent resources. But it's a good idea to collect brochures from several agencies, as some agents' suggestions may be influenced by relationships with tour and package firms that reward them for volume sales. If you have a special interest, find an agent with expertise in that area. The American Society of Travel Agents (ASTA) has a database of specialists worldwide; you can log on to the group's Web site to find one near you.

Make sure your travel agent knows the accommodations and other services of the place being recommended. Ask about the hotel's location, room size, beds, and whether it has a pool, room service, or programs for children, if you care about these. Has your agent been there in person or sent others whom you can contact?

Do some homework on your own, too: local tourism boards can provide information about lesser-known and small-

niche operators, some of which may sell only direct.

BUYER BEWARE

Each year consumers are stranded or lose their money when tour operators—even large ones with excellent reputations—go out of business. So check on the operator. Ask several travel agents about its reputation, and try to **book with a company that has a consumer-protection program.** (Look for information in the company's brochure.) In the United States, members of the United States Tour Operators Association are required to set aside funds (up to $1 million) to help eligible customers cover payments and travel arrangements in the event that the company defaults. It's also a good idea to choose a company that participates in the American Society of Travel Agents' Tour Operator Program; ASTA will act as mediator in any disputes between you and your tour operator.

Remember that the more your package or tour includes, the better you can predict the ultimate cost of your vacation. Make sure you know exactly what is covered, and beware of hidden costs. Are taxes, tips, and transfers included? Entertainment and excursions? These can add up.

🎫 Tour-Operator Recommendations **American Society of Travel Agents** (⇨ Travel Agencies). **CrossSphere–The Global Association for Packaged Travel (also known as NTA)** ✉ 546 E. Main St., Lexington, KY 40508 ☎ 859/226–4444 or 800/ 682–8886 🖷 859/226–4414 ⊕ www.CrossSphere. com. **United States Tour Operators Association (USTOA)** ✉ 275 Madison Ave., Suite 2014, New York, NY 10016 ☎ 212/599–6599 🖷 212/599–6744 ⊕ www.ustoa.com.

TRANSPORTATION AROUND MAUI

Renting a car is definitely recommended for those who plan to move beyond their hotel lounge chair. **Reserve your vehicle in advance,** particularly during peak travel times and during major island events, when the car-rental fleets are limited. Most major companies have airport counters and complimentary transportation for pickup/drop-off back at the airport upon departure.

Taxis can also be found at island airports, through your hotel doorman, in the more popular resort areas, or by contacting local taxi companies by telephone. Flag-down fees are $2, and each additional mile is $1.70. Most companies will also provide a car and driver for half-day or daylong island tours if you absolutely don't want to rent a car, and a number of companies also offer personal guides. Remember, however, that rates are quite steep for these services, ranging from $100 to $200 or more per day.

TRAVEL AGENCIES

A good travel agent puts your needs first. Look for an agency that has been in business at least five years, emphasizes customer service, and has someone on staff who specializes in your destination. In addition, **make sure the agency belongs to a professional trade organization.** The American Society of Travel Agents (ASTA) has more than 10,000 members in some 140 countries, enforces a strict code of ethics, and will step in to mediate agent-client disputes involving ASTA members. ASTA also maintains a directory of agents on its Web site; ASTA's TravelSense.org, a trip planning and travel advice site, can also help to locate a travel agent who caters to your needs. (If a travel agency is also acting as your tour operator, *see* Buyer Beware *in* Tours & Packages.)

Local Agent Referrals **American Society of Travel Agents (ASTA)** ✉ 1101 King St., Suite 200, Alexandria, VA 22314 ☎ 703/739–2782, 800/965–2782 24-hr hotline 🖶 703/684–8319 ⊕ www. astanet.com and www.travelsense.org. **Association of British Travel Agents** ✉ 68–71 Newman St., London W1T 3AH ☎ 0901/201–5050 ⊕ www.abta. com. **Association of Canadian Travel Agencies** ✉ 350 Sparks St., Suite 510, Ottawa, Ontario K1R 7S8 ☎ 613/237–3657 🖶 613/237–7052 ⊕ www.acta. ca. **Australian Federation of Travel Agents** ✉ Level 3, 309 Pitt St., Sydney, NSW 2000 ☎ 02/9264–3299 or 1300/363–416 🖶 02/9264–1085 ⊕ www.afta.com.au. **Travel Agents' Association of New Zealand** ✉ Level 5, Tourism and Travel House, 79 Boulcott St., Box 1888, Wellington 6001 ☎ 04/499–0104 🖶 04/499–0786 ⊕ www.taanz.org.nz.

VISITOR INFORMATION

Before you go, contact the Hawai'i Visitors & Convention Bureau (HVCB) for general information on Maui, Lāna'i, or Moloka'i, free brochures that include an accommodations and car-rental guide, and an entertainment and dining guide containing one-line descriptions of bureau members. Take a virtual visit to the islands on the Web, which can be most helpful in planning many aspects of your vacation. The HVCB site has a calendar section that allows you to see what local events are in place during the time of your stay.

Tourist Information **Hawai'i Visitors & Convention Bureau** ✉ 2270 Kalakaua Ave., Suite 801, Honolulu 96815 ☎ 808/923–1811, 800/464–2924 for brochures ⊕ www.gohawaii.com. In the U.K. contact the **Hawai'i Visitors & Convention Bureau** ⌂ 36 Southwark Bridge Rd., London SE1 9EU ☎ 020/7202–6384 🖶 020/7928–0722 ⊕ www. gohawaii.com.

Government Advisories **Consular Affairs Bureau of Canada** ☎ 800/267–6788 or 613/944–6788 ⊕ www.voyage.gc.ca. **U.K. Foreign and Commonwealth Office** ☎ 020/7008–1500 ⊕ www.fco.gov. uk/travel. **Australian Department of Foreign Affairs and Trade** ☎ 300/139–281 travel advisories, 02/6261–3305 Consular Emergency Centre ⊕ www. smartraveller.gov.au. **New Zealand Ministry of Foreign Affairs and Trade** ☎ 04/439–8000 ⊕ www. mft.govt.nz.

WEB SITES

Do check out the World Wide Web when planning your trip. You'll find everything from weather forecasts to virtual tours of resorts. Be sure to visit Fodors.com (⊕ www.fodors.com), a complete travel-planning site. You can research prices and book plane tickets, hotel rooms, rental cars, vacation packages, and more. In addition, you can post your pressing questions in the Travel Talk section. Other planning tools include a currency converter and weather reports, and there are loads of links to travel resources.

For more information on Maui, Moloka'i, and Lāna'i, visit ⊕ www.visitmaui.com (Maui Visitors Bureau), ⊕ www.molokai-hawaii.com (Moloka'i Visitors Association), ⊕ www.visitlanai.net (Lāna'i

Visitors Bureau), and ⊕ www.gohawaii.com, the official Web site of the Hawai'i Visitors & Convention Bureau.

The Web site ⊕ www.search-hawaii.com has an engine that can search all linked Hawaiian Web pages by topic or word.

Also visit ⊕ www.hshawaii.com for the Hawai'i State Vacation Planner and ⊕ www.hawaii.gov, the state's official Web site, for all information on the destination, including camping.

INDEX

PHOTO CREDITS

Cover Photo (Adult Green Sea Turtle with snorkeler along West Coast of Maui): *Michael S. Nolan/age fotostock.* F5, *SUNNYphotography.com/Alamy.* **Chapter 1: Experience Maui:** 1, *David Fleetham/Alamy.* 2 (top), *S. Alden/PhotoLink/Photodisc.* 2 (bottom left), *Douglas Peebles/age fotostock.* 2 (bottom right), *Walter Bibikow/viestiphoto.com.* 3 (top), *Ron Dahlquist/Maui Visitors Bureau.* 3 (bottom left), *Walter Bibikow/viestiphoto.com.* 3 (lower right), *Chris Hammond/viestiphoto.com.* 5, *Maui Visitors Bureau.* 6 (left), *Danita Delimont/Alamy.* 6 (top center), *David Schrichre/Photo Resource Hawaii.* 6 (bottom center), *David Fleetham/Alamy.* 6 (right), *Andy Jackson/Alamy.* 7 (top left), *David Fleetham/Alamy.* 7 (bottom left), *Mitch Diamond/Alamy.* 7 (bottom right), *Jim Cazel/Photo Resource Hawaii/Alamy.* 7 (right), *Starwood Hotels and Resorts.* 8 (top left), *Jim Cazel/Photo Resource Hawaii/Alamy.* 8 (bottom left), *Robert Holmes/Alamy.* 8 (right), *SuperStock/age fotostock.* 9 (left), *Jim Cazel/Photo Resource Hawaii/Alamy.* 9 (top right), *Andre Jenny/Alamy.* 9 (bottom left), *Douglas Peebles Photography/Alamy.* 9 (bottom right), *Douglas Peebles Photography/Alamy.* 12-13, *Dana Edmunds/Starwood Hotels and Resorts.* 14, *Douglas Peebles/age fotostock.* 15 (left), *Joe Solem/HVCB.* 15 (right), *Danita Delimont/Alamy.* 16, *SuperStock/age fotostock.* 17 (left), *David Olsen/Photo Resource Hawaii/Alamy.* 17 (right), *SuperStock/age fotostock.* **Chapter 2: Exploring Maui:** 19, *Maui Visitors Bureau.* 37, *National Park Service.* 40, *Maui Visitors Bureau.* 41, *Karl Weatherly/Photodisc.* 42, *Maui Visitors Bureau.* 47, *Chris Hammond/viestiphoto. com.* 49, *Ron Dahlquist/Maui Visitors Bureau.* 50, *Chris Hammond/viestiphoto.com.* 53, *Richard Genova/viestiphoto.com.* 54, *SuperStock/age fotostock.* 55, *Chris Hammond/viestiphoto.com.* **Chapter 3: Beaches:** 57, *Brent Bergherm/age fotostock.* **Chapter 4: Water Activities & Tours:** 69, *Eric Sanford/ age fotostock.* 82, *Ron Dahlquist/HVCB.* **Chapter 5: Golf, Hiking & Outdoor Activities:** 93, *Superstock/ age fotostock.* 102, *Luca Tettoni/viestiphoto.com.* 103, *Jack Jeffrey.* **Chapter 6: Where to Eat:** 115, *Douglas Peebles Photography/Alamy.* 121, *Polynesian Cultural Center.* 122 (top), *Douglas Peebles Photography.* 122 (top center), *Douglas Peebles Photography/Alamy.* 122 (center), *Dana Edmunds/Polynesian Cultural Center.* 122 (bottom center), *Douglas Peebles Photography/Alamy.* 122 (bottom), *Purcell Team/ Alamy.* 123 (top, top center, and bottom center), *HTJ/HVCB.* 123 (bottom), *Oahu Visitors Bureau.* **Chapter 7: Where to Stay:** 139, *Renaissance Wailea Beach Resort.* **Chapter 8: Shops & Spas:** 169, *Douglas Peebles Photography/Alamy.* 172 (top), *Linda Ching/HVCB.* 172 (bottom), *Sri Maiava Rusden/HVCB.* 173 (top), *leisofhawaii.com.* 173 (2nd from top), *kellyalexanderphotography.com.* 173 (3rd, 4th, and 5th from top), *leisofhawaii.com.* 173 (bottom), *kellyalexanderphotography.com.* **Chapter 9: Entertainment & Nightlife:** 181, *Gaetano Images, Inc./Alamy.* 184, HVCB. 185, *Thinkstock LLC.* **Chapter 10: Molokai:** 193, *Greg Vaughn/Alamy.* 194 (top), *Walter Bibikow/viestiphoto.com.* 194 (bottom left and right), *Molokai Visitors Association.* 195 (top), *Molokai Ranch.* 195 (center), *Walter Bibikow/viestiphoto. com.* 195 (bottom left), *Douglas Peebles/age fotostock.* 195 (bottom right), *Walter Bibikow/viestiphoto. com.* 201, *Walter Bibikow/viestiphoto.com.* 202, *IDEA.* 203-04, *Walter Bibikow/viestiphoto.com.* **Chapter 11: Lanai:** 227, *Walter Bibikow/viestiphoto.com.* 228 (top), *Walter Bibikow/viestiphoto.com.* 228 (bottom left), *Lanai Visitors Bureau.* 228 (bottom right), *Walter Bibikow/viestiphoto.com.* 229 (top), *Michael S. Nolan/age fotostock.* 229 (bottom left and right), *Lanai Image Library.* 230, *Lanai Image Library.* **Color Section:** Waterfall on the Road to Hana: *Superstock/age fotostock.* Windsurfer at Hookipa Beach: *Superstock/age fotostock.* Dancers at the Old Lahaina Luau: *Chad Ehlers/Stock Connection Distribution/Alamy.* Haleakala National Park: *Phil Degginger/Alamy.* Watching the sunrise at Haleakala: *Ken Ross/viestiphoto.com.* Green Sea Turtle: *SUNNYphotography.com/Alamy.* Makena Beach (popularly known as Big Beach): *Tomas Del Amo/Alamy.* Humpback whale calf breaching: *Michael S. Nolan/age fotostock.* Fire knife dancer: *David Olsen/Photo Resource Hawaii/Alamy.* Fruit stand: *Ron Dahlquist/ Maui Visitors Bureau.* Kahakuloa, West Maui: *Walter Bibikow/age fotostock.* Horses on Maui's North Shore: *Superstock/Alamy.* Waianapanapa State Park on the Road to Hana: *Richard Genova/viestiphoto. com.*

NOTES

NOTES

NOTES

NOTES

ABOUT OUR WRITERS

Elaine Gast is a freelance writer and communications consultant for foundations, nonprofits, businesses, and individuals. A published author of six books, Elaine writes out of her home in Kula, Maui, and travels frequently to the mainland—sharing her writing services nationwide. Elaine has a Masters of Science in Professional Writing from Towson University in Baltimore, a certificate in nonfiction writing from Charles University in Prague, and is a certified yoga instructor. To learn more, visit Elaine's Web site at www.fourwindswriting.com.

Cathy Sharpe, our Smart Travel Tips updater, was born and reared on O'ahu. For 13 years she worked at a Honolulu public-relations agency representing major travel-industry clients. Now living in Maryland, she is a marketing consultant. She returns home once a year to visit family and friends, relax at her favorite beaches, and enjoy island cuisine.

Joana Varawa has lived on Lāna'i for 30 years and is editor of *The Lāna'i Times*. She writes for Hawaiian and Aloha airlines magazines, has authored three books, and—along with her beloved dog—could lead you around "her" island blindfolded, investigating deer trails and supervising sunsets.

Shannon Wianecki was raised on Maui and loves divulging its secrets. With over a decade of experience in the travel industry, she splits her time between writing and conservation. She is the food editor for *Maui nō ka 'oi* magazine and the outreach coordinator for a high-school science curriculum based on the ecosystems of Haleakalā.